Loving
Leah

JOAN CROMBIE

FIRST EDITION

ISBN: 978-1-953576-10-1

Library of Congress Control Number: 2021913657

Published by

3741 Linden Avenue SE | Grand Rapids, MI 49548

Printed in the United States

Dedication

This book is dedicated to the spiritual leaders who have watched over my life: Gary and Stella Gilbertson, Bill and Darlene Davis, Rod and Mary Aguillard, Mike and Michelle Frie, and Keith and Penny Tucci. Thank you for faithfully and sacrificially pursuing God, teaching His Word, modeling Christlikeness, and loving well.

Prologue

The toaster popped. Ava Jane Wilkes spread her perfectly darkened toast with peanut butter and returned to her drop-leaf table to resume journaling.

Ah—Saturday mornings. Rising early was worth the sacrifice for these quiet, solitary moments in the apartment while her hormonal minefield of a teenager slept in. Slowly Ava inhaled her coffee and took a sip, pondering her latest single-parenting woe as she eyed the open volume before her. A hectic week at the diner didn't hold a candle to offspring drama. She could only hope things would turn around soon.

Shifting in the hardback chair, Ava yawned into the back of her hand and then scrawled out another paragraph, marveling how ink on paper helped her mentally untangle and recharge. She paused, twirling the pen, wondering what she and Ed Davison would do on their day together. She had just crunched into her first bite of toast when she heard his pickup truck rumble into the parking lot below.

Already? Glancing at the clock, she calculated that he must have left before dawn for his ninety-minute jaunt from New Hampton. She strained for a visual confirmation through her second-floor patio window, then rushed to splash her face with water and snatch her chenille robe from behind the bathroom door, having just belted it when he gave his rhythmic taps. She opened to him standing in the dingy hallway looking smart in his Western-cut jacket and cowboy boots, the graying edges of his hair matching the yoke of his coat. She still pinched herself that she had a boyfriend, much less someone like him.

"You're early!"

Ed placed an affectionate peck on her cheek as he entered. "Good morning! Not *that* early."

"Yes, you are!" she countered. "You're two hours early! I'm not even dressed yet! What's going on?" Doubtless he had something up his sleeve.

He faced her in the compact living room. "I'd like to take you and Lenore out somewhere!"

"You're too late—I've already eaten. Well, I was just now." She gestured toward the table.

"Nope, not that."

"Then what?"

"You'll see when we get there." He flashed a mysterious smile. "Go get dressed!"

"Now?"

He nodded. "Yeah. Right now!"

He was winsome and charming, but she had barely even tasted her coffee. "Where are we going?"

He shook his head. "Trust me."

She let out a little breath. "Ed! This early? What's going on?"

"I told you! I'm taking you somewhere. And Lenore."

"Well, if you won't tell me where, at least tell me how long we'll be gone."

"Half the day."

"What?" She shook her head in protest. "No, Ed. I've been asked to cover someone's shift tonight!"

"That's why I'm here now!" He extended his wrist beyond his coat sleeve to check his watch. "We'll be back in plenty of time for you to get to work. I promise!"

"But I'll be going in tired!" She gathered a dirty plate and a cluster of cups from an end table, hauling them to her tiny kitchen to join the unwashed dishes in the sink. "I can't go-go-go all day and then work all evening on top of it. I didn't get off last night until 11:30. I was supposed to clock out at ten. They lost two servers this week, and the restaurant is already understaffed as it is! They need me!"

He followed her. "I won't wear you out—I promise."

She sighed, leaning back against the counter, tightening her belt. "You need to give me some warning! I didn't plan for this, Ed! I'm not dressed, and Lenore isn't even out of bed."

"It's okay—I'll wait." He looked almost giddy in his determined refusal to budge.

"But—"

"Okay, little Havi," he cut in, stepping forward to cup her elbow, leaning his forehead against hers. He'd started calling her that lately—her new "victory name," he called it. He said it had a special meaning about who she was becoming. She didn't really get it, but she liked that he used it and the way it sounded when he said it. He spoke softly: "I understand you don't like spontaneity, but I'm asking you to trust me on this. Please. You'll like it! I know you will!"

She could see a fixed intention in his eyes—those brown, smiling eyes. Kind eyes framed by the tiny crow's-feet on his temples. She thought him very handsome for a man in his upper forties, thirteen years her senior. He was freshly shaven and smelled good, and her heart skipped a beat with his nearness. There wasn't much use in resisting him. She knew there wasn't another option for her day. Plus, she did very much want to be with him. She was flattered and amazed that he still pursued her.

Her mouth twisted into a reluctant smile. "Well, all right. I'll go— wherever it is we're going."

"Good. And Lenore."

She nodded. "Yes, but I'm warning you—this is super early for Lenore, and she does *not* like to be rushed!"

"You won't be sorry. But if you can, try to hurry. Richard's waiting in the car."

"Well, have him come in, for heaven's sake! Goodness, Ed—what are we doing?"

"Go on now—get dressed!" He waved her on toward the little bedroom she shared with her daughter.

Quietly Ava pulled a sweater and her jeans out of a drawer, allowing Lenore as many extra minutes of sleep as possible. That Ed wanted both her daughter and his son to be there clearly communicated something special was going down. She caught her eye in the mirror, the butterflies twirling in her stomach. She'd known for some time it was moving in this direction. Why else would he have taken her for drives through new housing developments trolling for her opinion on preferred house styles? He was planning to sell his old family farmstead and move to Bridgewater to marry her—she knew it! She'd bet her entire life savings on that—had she any money in savings. Her best guess for today's adventure was house hunting as a family with a marriage proposal tucked in somewhere—whether before, during, or after. The thought of it both thrilled and terrified her!

She liked him. From the moment he had walked into Grady's Diner on that fine spring day, she knew there was something special about him, and the spark of interest had been mutual. He was the nicest, kindest man she had ever met, so the thought of moving forward in the relationship was a dream. But her excitement was also mixed with anxiety—*dread* almost—though for reasons completely unrelated to him. No, she had her mother, Marlena Corolla, to thank for that part.

Long ago her mother had married her dream man too, way back when, only to find herself pregnant and abandoned for another woman during her first year of marriage. Thus, Ava grew up without a dad, raised by her single-parent mom. Many years later, when it was Ava's turn to marry, her groom, Marcus Bender, decided at the last minute that he didn't want to be married to her, but rather than tell her so, he simply didn't show up at the church on their wedding day. Instead, he left a cowardly note with a lousy explanation on his apartment door before heading out of town with his car tightly packed with all his belongings. It had both shattered her heart and humiliated her. In anger, her mother, Marlena, pronounced that there must be some sort of hex on the women of the family, and she gave it a name—the Corolla Curse.

At the time Ava hadn't given her mother's decree much thought. Reeling from what Marcus had done, she was simply trying to hold it together and survive the pain of rejection. But down the road, when her heart had healed and she finally chanced to trust again, love came knocking in the form of handsome and magnetic Curt Wilkes, and once more the curse cruelly sprang to life when he—as Ava's new husband—did the same thing to her that her biological father had done to her mother. While she was pregnant with their child, Ava discovered that her husband had gotten a little too close to a coworker of his. So close, in fact, that he decided to leave and move in with her instead.

And here she was some fifteen years later with a teenage daughter. Ava glanced over at Lenore where she lay sound asleep on her stomach sprawled across the bed, breathing hard, her coarse blond hair fanned around her shoulders. Now her protective walls were again persistently challenged—this time by the remarkable Ed Davison, who was so unlike all the other boyfriends who had made their large promises of love and then left her. Ed loved God. Surely that meant something this time. Surely that would make a difference, wouldn't it? Yet Ava could not block the foreboding thought that any step forward in the relationship would surely jinx her again, and how many times could she put her heart through that? Or Lenore's, for that matter, for Grandma Marlena had ground in their Corolla fate hard.

Two weeks ago Mary McAllister, Ava's coworker-become-spiritual mentor, had confronted Ava's fears in the parking lot after work while they leaned against their cars, facing each other in their dirty aprons, smelling like french fries.

"If you don't want to be with him, you should break it off. You know where he wants this relationship to go, so if you think he's not for you, quit leading him on. You'll only hurt him and yourself."

"No, I *do* like him," Ava replied defensively. "I'm definitely in love with him."

"Then what's the problem? You seem so reluctant. Standoffish. What are you so nervous about? I'm not pushing you or anything, Ava, but he's a decent guy. I'd hate for him to get the wrong idea and back off."

"No, it's—it's nothing. I need to trust, I guess. I'm having a tough time moving forward with the past still hanging over my head."

Mary pulled her graying hair behind an ear, studying Ava's face. "What *about* your past?"

Ava shook her head. "It's nothing. I don't really want to talk about it."

The older woman folded her arms. "Listen, honey—I gotta tell you something true. Whatever you don't deal with in the past you'll carry with you into the future. Any leftover baggage will transfer right into a marriage with Ed. You're bound to repeat it. I'd advise you to deal with it."

"Well, don't worry. It wasn't me. Not that I was perfect, of course. I'm not saying that. It's just that I've had some really bad luck with guys."

"Uh-huh. Like what?"

Reluctantly Ava told Mary about the thing her mother suspected doomed all the women of the family.

Mary's forehead crinkled in concern. She opened her car door and gestured. "Hon, let's sit together for a bit. I'd like to talk about this a little more and maybe pray through it."

Ava shook her head, embarrassed. "No, I don't want to make a big deal out of it. A lot of it probably had to do with me anyway. And besides, Lenore's waiting for me at home. I told her I'd come straight home from work."

Her head swung side to side. "Ava, Ava. Believe me, this is the *best* thing you could ever do for Lenore. You don't want this repeated in her. Come on, girl. Get in the car. We're going to pray and do some business!"

The talk with Mary had taken a huge weight off her shoulders, but still it was hard work to keep her mind from reverting to fear—given her history of two failed marriages and a handful of other loser boyfriends. Well, technically *one* failed marriage, since she and Marcus hadn't actually gone through their ceremony.

All things are new, she told herself, pulling the sweater over her head and donning some matching earrings. She passed a hairbrush through her hair and made herself smile. *Have faith. Just believe.*

"Lenore," she said softly, gently patting her daughter's arm. "Lenore, you need to get up." Her daughter's body was quite developed for an almost-sixteen-year-old, her tempestuous hormones yielding an emotional roller coaster ride of hair-raising twists and dives. Ava regretted having to wake her.

Lenore stirred, murmuring sleepily, "I'm still tired."

"No, hon—you need to get up. Ed's here. He's taking us somewhere."

Lenore's eyes cracked open slightly. "I'm not going. I'll stay home."

"Sorry, but you have to come."

She lifted her head almost painfully from the mattress, her cheek creased by the sheet. "Where?"

"I don't know."

"I don't want to go."

"Not an option today, Lenore. You gotta get up. I let you sleep as long as I could, but you have to get dressed."

She groaned. "Why? Why do I have to do this? No one asked *me* if I wanted to go! You're always making plans for me!"

"I know. Come on now. You need to get up."

"Can't I stay with my friend Jody?"

"Nope. Sorry."

She gave an angry grunt, rolling onto her side. "So what are we doing?"

Ava retrieved her shoes from the closet. "Something special, I hear. Get dressed right away, please. Richard's here, too, and we're leaving soon." As she closed the door, Lenore spouted something about how much she hated everybody making plans for her life.

About five minutes later Lenore emerged from her room fully dressed.

"Good morning, hon," Ed said, rising from the arm of the couch where he had perched.

At her daughter's sullen expression, Ava spoke up. "Use the bathroom, Lenore—then get your coat. Richard's outside waiting for us."

As the bathroom door shut hard, Ava turned to see Ed pull a white cloth out of his coat pocket. She frowned, noting the embroidered corner of the fabric.

"Why do you have a dish towel?"

Ed smiled mischievously.

Ava made a sound. "*No*, Ed! Absolutely not! You are *not* putting that thing on my head! It'll wreck my hair!"

After riding blindfolded in Ed's Chevy pickup for well over an hour, Ava concluded that family house-hunting in Bridgewater was clearly *not* on their day's agenda. Her second-best guess—judging by the distance they had travelled—was that their destination was Wilkes State Park, and if so, she wouldn't be disappointed. If Ed were going to propose, he'd take her someplace special, and the state park on the bluffs overlooking the Mississippi was one of her favorite spots, not to mention that it shared her last name. And it was sweet of him to want both Lenore and his son Richard there too. *Then* they'd go house hunting—in the proper order, of course—and she knew just where to look. She'd always liked the quiet east side of Bridgewater, and hopefully they could find a place within walking distance of Bard Lewis High School, which would help her tremendously, for then she could work a long day at the restaurant without having to run out to pick up her daughter.

She shifted on the seat beside Ed, mentally planning out their future, struggling to stifle the annoyance she felt at the cotton dish towel still bound securely around her head. Over the muffle of the radio, Ed was sharing long, fascinating tales about exploratory business trips he'd made in his younger days to South Africa to visit copper mines.

"Ed, *please* tell me we're almost there!" she cut in, her words escaping more impatiently than she intended.

"Yep. Couple more minutes," he said, seamlessly continuing his story.

Proving his word, he slowed the truck and turned, and she heard the crunch of gravel under the tires as they proceeded more slowly down what felt like some sort of country lane. Ed's son Richard suddenly gripped the back of her seat.

"Whoa—Dad! Look how far they got on the—"

"Richard!" Ed's firm utterance silenced him. "Don't give it away!"

Ed's hand touched her arm. "We're here, Havi, but hold on a tiny bit longer." There was excitement in his voice too.

She waited as he got out and crossed the gravel to her side of the vehicle. Behind her Richard hopped out of the truck with a whoop of a laugh, and suddenly Ava wondered if her second guess was a bust too. Were

11

they—were they at the *farm*? Why would he take her there? What would be special about going to his old family farmstead, especially if he were going to propose? Yes, it'd be special to *him* since he grew up there, but they didn't even live there! Since they'd moved back from Indiana after Ed's mother's passing, he and Richard had been living in an apartment in New Hampton while they cleaned out her house. There was nothing that set the farm apart as special to Ava. Not for a proposal anyway. Unless she was way off on that idea too. It could be that she had entirely misjudged the whole day!

Her door opened, and Ed took her hand. "All right, Havi—out with you! Careful of your head."

"This better be worth it," she murmured, yielding to his guidance. The scent of wood and sawdust hung heavily in the air.

He led her forward a few steps, squared her shoulders in a specific direction, then reached up to loosen her dishtowel blindfold. The bright sun and chilly November air hit her face simultaneously, causing her eyes to water, but she saw in an instant what the trip was about. She was partially right—they were on the farm all right, but instead of the old box-style post-depression era farmhouse with its narrow white clapboard siding, she saw a sprawl of new construction before her, a skeleton of a rambler, newly framed with fresh lumber, the sides and roof above bare sheets of plywood. She was too stunned to speak.

"Surprise!" Ed said quietly, wrapping his arm around her shoulders for a side hug.

Now that the news was out, Richard, who had dutifully contained his excitement, burst forth with chatter. "Miss Ava, Lenore—we're building a *house*! Isn't it cool? This is the hardest secret I've ever kept in my life! I'm going in!" His tennis shoes flapped across the frozen ground as he took off to hoist his fourteen-year-old body up on a pile of boards to reach the front door.

He was staying in New Hampton. It felt like a punch in the gut, and beside her, Ed's words became a jumble of sounds that she had difficulty understanding. All along she'd had this idea he'd be moving to Bridgewater to be near her, and now a crazy panic gripped her. He hadn't let on. He'd acted as if everything were normal, but he'd been moving on with his life. He wanted to stay friends.

"You—never told me about this!" she said numbly. It was all she could think of to say. He was *staying* in New Hampton. She lost her bet. Her imaginary life savings were depleted.

She had not seen this coming. Did he think that the hour-and-a-half distance between Bridgewater and New Hampton was incidental? That she'd just pop down to see him on the weekends or vice versa? How long could that last? She worked a full five days a week and every other Saturday, and she was tired. One thing she had learned in life was that weekend-only relationships weren't realistic. Plus, he had done it all in secret. He had kept this from her for a reason, and that had happened to her too many times in life. Already her heart was retreating, running for cover from what was inevitably coming.

Ed peered into her face. "So what do you think?"

"You're building a house!" she replied lightly, keeping her eyes fixed on the raw construction lest he see her disappointment.

Drawing back his head, he let out a loud laugh. "Yes, I am! Come on—I'll show it to you! Come on, Lenore!" he called over his shoulder. "You come, too, sweetheart! It's time to do some exploring!"

Ava turned to see her daughter standing beside the oversized pickup with her hands in the pockets of her navy wool coat, staring expressionless at the house, her wiry hair frizzed out around her collar. Her heart turned over thinking of Lenore having to deal with another one of her boyfriends leaving them. Hadn't she had enough? Why had Ed insisted that she come? She knew he wasn't being cruel on purpose, but he most certainly was naive to what he was doing to them both.

"Over here," Ed said, leading her by the hand into the shell of the garage and across the dirt floor to the opening into the house. A plywood box served as a makeshift step. Ed climbed up ahead of her and reached back to help her up.

"This'll be the back foyer," he explained. "There'll be a deep coat closet here"—he waved to the right and then gestured left—"and stairs to the basement there. This hall behind the garage will lead to a back door. There's nothing here now, but I'll have a bathroom plumbed in on one side of the hall and a laundry room on the other. A main floor laundry is nice, right?" He looked at her.

"Yeah," Ava nodded. It felt colder out of the sun. She zipped her coat up more tightly around her neck.

He turned to the broader part of the house, his cowboy boots echoing across the bare plywood. "All this over here will be the kitchen, a large one, with plenty of cupboard space. And it's on the south side, with sunlight all year round. Maybe a small table could go here. Kitchen cabinets and a countertop will go there dividing the room, and on the other side is an area for a dining room." He gestured toward a bare hole where a window would be set in. "Those windows will overlook the yard in the back. Won't it be great?"

Ava looked out at the dilapidated farmhouse where it stood awkwardly too close to the new construction with its peeling paint. Beyond it stood the abandoned barn with the squatty grain shed adjacent to it. Surrounding them both were empty cattle corrals.

"What's going to happen with that?" she asked, gesturing to the house.

He made a wistful sound through his cheek. "Oh, eventually we'll demo the house. We'll have to. Can't have two. The old one's gotta go."

She remained facing the window. Maybe Mary McAllister had been right. Maybe her hesitancy had finally caught up to her. Maybe she'd given the impression she *wanted* to remain friends. Perhaps he thought she didn't care that much about him, and now he was giving up on her and moving on with his own life—thanks to her fear of the old family curse.

Ed had moved on to another part of the house. "These studs here will be a wall dividing the—" He stopped. "Ava?"

She turned.

He looked questioningly at her.

"I'm sorry—what?"

He indicated an area with his head. "The living room. This'll be the living room."

She lifted her chin in a nod, glancing at the empty space as she approached. "Okay."

He sighed, dropping his arms. "All right—what's wrong?"

Briefly she met his eyes and looked away.

"What's going on? You've barely spoken three words since we've been here. What—you aren't excited about this?" He spread his arm.

"No, I like it," she answered. "It's not that."

"Well, then, what?" He waited, watching her.

Ava fiddled nervously with her gloves. "You never told me you were building a house."

"Yeah, I know. I wanted to—"

"If you're planning on moving on with your life, I'm okay with that, but you need to tell me straight. I don't need any more surprises in my life, and neither does Lenore."

He blinked in surprise. "What?"

"I've invested a lot in this relationship, Ed. Lenore has too. It's just not going to work to have you here in New Hampton and us up there. I can't do it!"

"Now hold on! What are you saying? I'm not bailing on you, if that's what you think."

"Ed, I can't do it. It's just not going to work." Wearily she shook her head. "It's just too much for me to be driving back and forth, with work and Lenore and everything else—"

He cocked his head, a strange expression on his face. "Are you breaking up with me?"

She stopped, feeling that all-too-familiar knot in her stomach.

After a long silence he carefully spoke, "Ava, I'm not building this house for me. I'm building this house for *us*."

She met his eyes.

He opened his hands. "Are you *kidding* me? What else? I thought that would be obvious! I want to marry you, and I want you to come live here with me—with us. You and Lenore. But if that's not what you want—" His voice trailed off.

Her cheeks burned as suddenly she felt so foolish. "I—I thought maybe you were wanting to move on with your life. Without me."

He stared incredulously. "Why on earth would I bring you here if I was thinking that?"

She shook her head. "I don't know! My mind went down this really bad path. I guess—I guess I'm still—I don't know—*afraid*. You know what happened to me before—with Marc and Curt. I told you about all that. It's sort of my default to think that—"

"I'm not them."

"I know, but—"

"Ava, I *love* you! I want you with me the rest of my life. You're the only thing keeping me here. Otherwise, I'd move back east."

She wiped a tear from her eye with her glove. "I'm sorry, Ed. I got confused."

He took her hands in his. "Ava Jane Wilkes, listen to me. I'm not going anywhere unless you tell me flat out that you don't want me in your life anymore."

"Well, I won't be doing that." She closed her eyes, letting out her breath. "I'm sorry! Honestly, Ed, I feel so *stupid*. My friend Mary at work has been talking to me about not living out of fear, but I'm so new to following God that I'm still figuring out what that looks like. I was—caught off guard."

He sighed. "Well, I guess I'm sorry too. This—this all totally backfired!" He waved toward the plywood wall. "It might have been a bit overwhelming."

She nodded, offering a little smile. "It's kind of a big deal—building a house and everything!"

"I know," he voiced with a bit of shame. "I guess I've had my own battles with fear. I thought you'd balk at the idea of moving to New Hampton and say no to me altogether. I was hoping the house would convince you to say yes."

"Seriously? That's a pretty big bribe and a *terrible* reason to marry you!"

"I didn't want to lose you." Sheepishly, he added, "I hope it's at least tempting. You get to decide what it looks like inside!"

"You realize you're asking me to leave my job, which is a good job for me. I like working at Grady's!"

"Havi, darling, I have more than enough money to care for you and Lenore."

"And Lenore!" She flayed her hands. "She'd be moving away from her school and all her friends. She's not going to like this! Not one bit!"

He nodded grimly. "I've thought of that. But a fresh start might be good for her. Richard has had to change schools too, and he's doing fine. At least they'd be together."

She bit her lip. Ed did have a point. This school year with Lenore had been atrocious, and Ava was fearful for her. It wouldn't be the worst thing to get her away from the bad influences she'd been hanging with.

"Come here," he said, leading her through the skeleton frame. "The kids will each have their own rooms right here, with a huge bathroom across the hall for them to share. And back here"—he pulled her into the center of a large space—"this bedroom will be ours." He gave her a sportive smile, raising his eyebrows playfully.

She smiled. "I wrecked your proposal. How were you planning to ask me?"

He laughed. "Yeah, this isn't exactly how I envisioned it." He pointed through the window opening. "I *was* going to ask you in that tree beside the barn and give you this." From inside his coat he produced a wrapped gift the size of a paperback novel.

A book? In a tree? She frowned. "That's not terribly romantic, Ed."

"It's a nice tree!" he protested. "It's got a great little nook up there to sit on." He handed her the package. "But here—you can open this now."

She took it with a sigh. "Ed Davison, what do you even see in me?"

"I see a bright and fiery redhead who loves God and cares for people."

"You know I dye my hair, don't you? I could go blond next week."

"Then you'll be my bright and beautiful blond. I'll even love you gray."

Her mouth curled into a smile.

"That's more like it," he said, his eyes dancing.

"I'm not very spiritually mature," she warned. "I know that's important to you."

"It's a process, my dear, and you're on your way. See my parents' old house out there?" He jerked his head in its direction. "Right now there are two houses on this farm, the old one and the new. Each day my builder does a little more work on the new—first the foundation, then the shell, then the roof. It's taken some time, and there's a lot yet to be done, but eventually we'll be living in it, and the old will be dismantled. That's what a new life in Christ is like. You keep focusing on the new, not the old." He drew her hand up to kiss it. "Say you'll marry me, Havi. I'm not getting any younger."

She raised her chin. "You haven't officially asked me yet."

He pulled her close and brought his face near hers. "I've been waiting for you to trust me. Will you marry me, Ava Jane Wilkes?"

It occurred to her that it was more a matter of her trusting God, but at the moment she was lost in those eyes of his. "Yes, Ed Davison, I'd be happy to marry you."

"Good," he said softly. "I'm very glad about that. Now let me kiss you!"

They were interrupted by the sound of Richard calling to them across the house. "Dad, Ava, I think something's up with Lenore! She just left!"

Ava turned abruptly, peering through the sparse lumber walls to where Richard gazed out the front of the house. "What? What do you mean she *left*?"

"She just took off," he said, pointing outside.

"Took off?"

"Yeah, she's out walking along the road!"

Ava turned to Ed, but he had already started in long strides across the house. "Come on—let's go!"

Chapter One

L eah Ava Labanora licked the remaining peanut butter off her spoon and dropped it into the sink. It wasn't much of a lunch, but she had to keep moving.

"Brutus!" She nudged the foam bed on the floor to rouse her roommate's eight-pound piglet of a dog. In fifteen minutes she was leaving for her grocery stop before her hair appointment, and if that dog didn't go outside, he would surely make another mess on her carpet. She wasn't about to shampoo it for the third time this month!

"Brutus! Hey, buddy—wake up!" She bumped his bed again and reached down to scratch the elderly mutt, who promptly twisted onto his back, his furry stick legs shooting straight up.

Generally she liked dogs, but this one tested her patience, even if he was cute in his forlorn way. They weren't even allowed to have dogs in the apartment, but Celeste wouldn't be parted from her tawny Chihuahua-mix dog-child. "He's so small," she said, like somehow that waived the rule on the lease. Leah felt sorry for it. It lived a pathetic life, sleeping the day away when Celeste wasn't there and making perpetual laps around their apartment when she was, beating a path across the linoleum as he looped through their alley kitchen again and again. Plus, his short light hair showed up on every piece of fabric she owned. Every single one.

"Come on!" She jiggled his body, then made her way to the apartment door, urging him to follow. "Brutus, come!"

Reluctantly the old dog pulled himself up to give a lethargic stretch, then stood blinking daftly beside his bed, as if unable to figure out how to cross the room.

Indeed, the floor was a maze. Yesterday was Celeste's laundry day, and either she hadn't had enough change for the dryer again or it was out of order, for the carpet and the furniture were entirely covered with jeans, shirts, socks, and underwear all laid out to dry. The whole place smelled mountain fresh. Giving up, Leah went to get the dog, and since his squatty legs struggled to do stairs, she hauled him down the two flights to deposit him onto the grass outside their apartment.

Her morning was supposed to have been relaxing, but waking up to a pacing dog, a scattered mess of food-encrusted dishes in the kitchen, and damp clothes strewn everywhere hadn't been conducive to a quiet morning of chilling at home. She probably should have worked a half day instead. Now her hard-earned PTO had fizzled, and her afternoon appointments were about to start—first her hair, followed by a meeting with the family lawyer, and then a jaunt to the property management office to renew her lease, the latter of which she wished-to-God she didn't have to do, but she needed a place to live and couldn't afford the apartment alone. Nevertheless, having Celeste there was better than Carlos.

Sort of.

It was a toss-up.

Leah sighed, remembering the argument she'd had with her grandmother about him on this exact sidewalk. Grandma Havi thought it wasn't proper for her as a Christian to have Carlos living there and had urged her to have him move out. Good grief—like Leah cared about being "immoral"! At the time she didn't have the heart to tell her grandma she wasn't into the Jesus stuff anymore. What good had it done to live the straight and narrow when everyone else seemed free to sin and lightning wasn't striking them? And besides, Carlos had been good for her. If it hadn't been for him yanking her out of the gutter, who knew where she would be? He had rescued her from a dark, destructive road, and she was grateful for that.

Of course, all along she had known her grandmother was right. As nice as Carlos was, she knew they'd hit a dead end sooner or later, for he had been a weapon—no denying it. She had clearly dated him to spite ex-fiancé Jake DeSoto, plain and simple, and although she *had* cared for him, she mostly needed him—in her sick way. He had shown up right after her fiasco with Jake when she was hurting the most, his time and tenderness all it took to entangle herself in a web of codependence, where in return for comfort she gave him all the benefits of her body and an apartment to boot.

Despite its sting, the big talk with Grandma Havi *had* brought some clarity of mind. First, her conscience started bothering her, and second, she knew she didn't love Carlos enough to see herself with him the rest of her life. And she was pretty sure love wasn't the key component for why Carlos was there either!

Plus, they argued a lot about religion. Carlos had been notably assertive with his religious opinions, and Leah often butted heads with him, correcting his big, bold statements about things that weren't even in the Bible. Granted, she was light years away from living up to her own beliefs, but she had read enough of the Bible to know that what Carlos believed was what Reid Tanner, her old pastor at Anchor Church, called twisted truth and religious mumbo jumbo. It drove her crazy!

On top of that, Carlos' mother had begun to hint that the two of them should get married in their family's church, and Leah wanted to stay a million miles away from going through that again. Yes, Grandma Havi's cage rattling had helped Leah to see that the longer they stayed together, the harder it would be to split. Trying to be as nice as possible—it's-not-you-it's-me—she asked him to leave before Thanksgiving, afraid that if she waited any longer, she might get sentimental over the holidays. After he left, Leah immediately put an ad on the community college social media page for a female roommate, partly to ensure that she didn't make the same stupid mistake twice in a row by rebounding again.

That was how she found Celeste, the nineteen-year-old college student from France, a country where apparently elves, maids, or mothers did all household chores. Leah sighed. At least Carlos had picked up after himself. But what was she to do—give Celeste the boot because she was messy and quirky? She wouldn't do that to a foreigner. She hated being stuck, but her only solution—apart from winning the lottery—was moving back in with her mother, and there was no way *that* was going to happen. So here she was.

"Brutus, go potty!" Leah reminded the dog where it stood drowsily soaking in the sun on the lawn. She checked the time on her phone, then held it up to pose for a "before hair" selfie, saving it with the date.

This would be her first hair appointment in five months. Her last one, scheduled in January, had been cancelled out of necessity. Leah had been in the parking lot after work that day, hurrying to clear a couple of inches of snow off her car in order to get to the salon on time when she'd felt the vibration of her phone going off in her pocket. Leah recalled how aggravated she had been to take her mittens off and reach beneath the folds of her coat and sweater to get it. Who would have thought it would be her mother calling to tell her that her grandparents had been killed in a car accident?

Leah had sat alone in her car that cold, dark evening, sobbing with her head down on the steering wheel while the windows inside fogged over from the dampness of her tears and wet coat and mittens. She'd had to blow the fan on high for a good while to see to drive to her mom's house. Grandma Havi had been the most significant person in her life, and her heart still ached with the loss. Thank God the thing with Carlos hadn't been left hanging between them.

"Hey!" Leah snapped her fingers. "Go potty, you silly dog!"

Casting a look back at her, the mutt ambled slowly out of view around the building, as if needing his privacy.

Given the glum association to her grandparents, Leah had not rescheduled her hair appointment after the funeral but instead let her hair grow out and return to its natural dingy blond color. But now, a full five months later, she was eagerly looking forward to her cut and dye. In fact, she had purposely scheduled her appointment for this particular date—four years to the day of what would have been her wedding—in celebration that Jake DeSoto no longer controlled her mind or emotions. She had her counselor, Pam, to thank for that victory. And in honor of the occasion, she was doing something fun—she was going a fresh platinum blond with the barest lavender highlights, a well-researched decision about which she was thoroughly jazzed. Leah was breaking out!

Thinking of Pam made her smile.

"You should try to reinvent yourself," the woman had suggested in one of their sessions—oddly only days before her grandparents' terrible accident. Pam, a graying, minimal-makeup, sixty-something hippie had spoken her wisdom with unreserved confidence. "It'll give you something to focus on instead of the past. We could call this your 'Year of Freedom'— the relaunching of Leah Labanora!"

Leah thought her advice sounded suspiciously like a New Year's resolution in disguise, but she complied, grasping at anything in her desperation to move on from being stuck getting over Jake, around whom her life had been built for nearly eight years: four as a couple and four since their breakup, the latter of which was why she was seeing a counselor in the first place, but that was her little secret from the world. There was no sense in broadcasting how badly she was struggling—after all, she'd already won the Miss Naive America title with what had happened. One trophy was enough.

So at Pam's recommendation, Leah had made her bucket list of new things to try doing—small things, like eating more naturally, reading new authors, taking up tennis, and jogging in the morning, tame feats to most people, certainly, but significant for Leah, considering she hadn't been keen on tennis or running before. And so far she was enjoying stepping out of her box—except that the running thing wasn't turning out to be all that hot, but she was determined not to give up.

But not only small things. Her relaunching project had brought about a bigger change too. After her grandparents' funeral, Leah made the choice to start going by her middle name "Ava," instead of her first, in honor of her grandmother, whose name had been Ava Jane Davison. Leah greatly disliked her first name anyway, and her grandmother's passing gave her a natural reason and valid excuse to dump it and further disconnect herself from Jake.

Since their first date on the day she turned eighteen, the two of them had been linked together by the Anchor Church crowd—Jacob and Leah—and each person who'd brought it up to her thought they'd made the cleverest discovery: *Hey—like Jacob and Leah in the Bible!* So, when it dawned on Leah that tweaking her name was at least one thing in her life within her power to change, she did so quickly. Not only was the association to her grandmother a positive one, but her new name would be a constant reminder of her fresh start in life. Her Year of Freedom, as Pam had dubbed it. Besides, plenty of people went by their middle names.

Not wanting to be rash, Leah had slept on the idea for a full week before moving ahead with it. Then she printed out small announcement cards with a brief explanation of the change to hand out at the accounting office where she worked. Of course, she still used "Leah" for her legal signature, but to the rest of her acquaintances she requested to henceforth be known as "Ava Labanora."

Her mother, Lenore, had simply rolled her eyes. "Right," she said. "I'll give it a week."

Leah checked the time again on her cell phone. Why was that dumb dog taking so long? She had less than a five-minute margin if she was going to pick up Celeste's supper items before her appointment. She stretched her neck to peek beside the building.

"Brutus!" she hollered.

His little head rose from where he lay on his side in the sun.

She whistled sharply through her teeth. "Come!"

After no response Leah went to scoop up his plump body and put him in the apartment.

The grocery store was crowded, as it was the tail end of the lunch hour. Now slightly behind schedule, Leah debated skipping the jaunt in altogether, but since Celeste insisted on a specific type of olives for her dinner recipe and this was the most logical opportunity to get them, she decided to go for it, making a beeline for the pickled foods section.

Right off the bat Leah tensed as an old Anchor Church acquaintance approached down the aisle in her direction—one of the elderly ushers who had served there—but he merely nodded and kept on walking. Thank God he hadn't stopped to chat like all the other Anchor-ites lately. Since her wedding disaster, she'd hardly been able to go anywhere without having to psych herself up for the chance of bumping into people from her old church. Upon sighting them, she usually veered for the opposite side of the store or street or parking lot, wherever she happened to be, evading them before they could spot her. It was no wonder. That church had been the center of her life, and everybody had had a front-row seat to her humiliation.

Pam had helped her deal with that too.

"It's all about boundaries," she had instructed, her black erasable marker squeaking in illustration across the office whiteboard. "Let's draw a big imaginary circle around all of them. Now listen: You do not have to live in their circle"—tap, tap, tap—"and you don't have to let them into yours! You are *separate* from them! You have autonomy! You have the power of choice! And your happiness is not dependent on them *or* this Jesus fellow they push!"

The circle business seemed goofy at first, but her advice did help, and over time she ran into people less and less anyway. Until lately, that is, for things had changed. In fact, Leah had started a tally.

In the last two months Leah had counted *fourteen* separate personal encounters with people from her old Anchor crowd—fourteen! Heavens, had they all had a meeting and decided to target her or something? *Commence Project Leah!* She was starting to feel like a homing device for squirming-uncomfortable conversations, for each person she met seemed overly eager to talk. *Hey, Leah—it's you! Wow, Leah—you look great! We've missed you, Leah! We're all praying for you, Leah! We'd love to have you back, Leah.* It was one more reason she was glad to be going by "Ava" now!

Oh, she was nice to them. There was no reason for her to be a jerk even if they were painful reminders of her Day from Hell. She had a well-practiced smile for all, coupled with a demure well-maybe-sometime-I-will response, but internally she knew going back to Anchor Church was not an option for her. It would never be an option. She had stood alone on her darkest day.

"Hey, did you hear about Leah and Jake?"

Leah would never forget the awfulness of being in the third stall of the bathroom when two of her closest church friends had popped in.

"I was *there*! I was coming into the church when it happened! Oh, my word—you should have heard it—her mother came *unhinged*!"

"I feel sorry for her. I heard the very same thing happened to her grandma!"

"Yeah, it's so freaky! It's like a curse or something! Geez—whatever you do, don't let her near your brothers!" A burst of laughter as a paper towel was torn from the dispenser.

Those girls lived outside her circle now.

Let it go, Leah told herself as she scanned the grocery shelves for the prized olives. Manzanilla. Pimento stuffed. Garlic stuffed. Jumbo black. There—kalamata! Finding the proper brand, she snatched the requested jar and hustled back to the checkout counter that appeared to have the shortest line.

Tapping her heel impatiently, Leah eyed the impulse items as the line inched forward. Doritos. Nope, don't need those. Nutella sticks. Or those. Another yard forward. Pistachios. Pass. Then, in perfect harmony with her day thus far, her worst nightmare occurred. Stuck now in the middle of the line, she suddenly noticed Rachel Steinburg's whole family—minus Rachel—up ahead at the front of the line paying for their groceries, and she was unable to budge from her place in the train of carts. Leah felt a rush of dread. Crud—she was trapped! Immediately she turned to feign interest in the tabloids slightly behind her.

Itching with curiosity, Leah dared to peek back, observing Rachel's mother visiting pleasantly with the clerk as their items were beeped across the counter. The dark-haired girl beside her had to be Becky, Rachel's little sister. She looked just like Rachel at that same age, with the same long, thick, wavy hair. Becky had been only eleven four years ago when Leah had been preparing for her wedding, and she was much taller now and had a chest. Ben, her brother, stood off to the side, towering over his dad, Mark, who was now inserting his debit card to pay for their groceries. Ben was surely out of high school by now. Probably finishing his first year of college.

As Leah covertly watched, one of them must have said something funny, for Mark Steinburg suddenly laughed out loud, turning in her direction. Instantly Leah sank to her knees to examine the candy bars on the lower shelf of the narrow aisle. Yikes, the dead *last* thing she wanted was to be noticed by them! She wouldn't even know how to respond!

She had loved the Steinburgs like her own family. She and Rachel had practically lived at each other's houses during high school—well, between Rachel's and the DeSotos' houses, back-to-back on the same block. Rachel had been her bosom friend. Rachel and Leah—inseparable and like sisters since they'd met at Bible camp at the age of sixteen. When Leah had gotten engaged, she asked Rachel to be her maid of honor first thing. How was she to know that someone she trusted so completely had it in her to do something so devastating? And now she'd never speak to her or her family again. Right this moment she could hardly believe how close they were in proximity to her—well, not Rachel herself, but the rest of them, and this was way too close for comfort!

For half a minute or so Leah continued to squat, shuffling through chocolate bars, pretending to read labels until she heard them wish the checkout clerk a good day. She waited below a little bit longer, then slowly straightened, relieved to see them pushing their loaded cart toward an exit. Silently she let out a long breath.

Suddenly someone right behind her called out, "Say, Anne! Anne Steinburg! Over here!"

Before Leah could turn away, Rachel's mother glanced back over her shoulder, looking straight into Leah's face, starting as she recognized her. Unconsciously Leah sidled toward the candy display, but there was nowhere to escape. It was too late—their eyes had met!

Unaware, the woman behind her continued: "Hey, will you see Rachel today?"

Leah's cheeks burned as Anne Steinburg left her shopping cart and took a few steps closer. Her gaze rose to look beyond Leah as she answered.

"Hi, Josey. Yes, we're headed over there right now."

"Oh, good. I lost my phone. Can you let her know our group is cancelled tonight?"

"Sure. I'll tell her."

"Great—glad I ran into you! Thanks!"

"Yeah. Bye, Josey!"

Anne Steinburg's eyes flicked back to Leah. "Good to see you, sweetie," she said quietly. "You look great."

Leah stood frozen. She couldn't move, couldn't speak. Couldn't do anything but swallow and stare back at her. Anne Steinburg gave a sad smile, then turned to catch up to her family, who were rolling their groceries through the automatic doors to the parking lot.

"Leah?" the woman behind her inquired.

She already knew who it was. In a fog, she turned to face one of her would-have-been bridesmaids, who stared back in surprise.

"Oh, my stars—that *is* you! I haven't seen you in years!"

Josey Banks. Josey Banks—but now with long, platinum-blond hair. Long, full, and beautifully curled platinum-blond hair. Josey Banks, one of her former friends from Anchor, who four years ago when Leah's world crashed in, rushed to coddle Rachel Steinburg. Josey Banks, who now carried on amiably in conversation without pause, as if nothing life-shattering had ever happened in their past.

"How *are* you? I thought it looked like you, but your hair was darker, and I didn't recognize you! Seriously, how *are* you, Leah? We've missed you! We'd love to have you back at Anchor!"

Numbly Leah sputtered something about not recognizing her either because of *her* hair.

"Oh, I know! I just had it done!" she purred, running a manicured hand over it. "I'm getting married next weekend. In fact, tomorrow Nick and I move into our new apartment—at Brownstone! You still live somewhere over there, don't you? We're moving into 204."

Leah blinked. Apartment 204 was right across the hall. Right across the stinkin' hall!

Somehow—she was not sure how—but somehow Leah managed to finish the conversation and make it out of the store with both her sanity and her Greek olives, but she was so distracted she couldn't remember where she had parked. When she found her car, she restrained herself from kicking it and having a meltdown when she got inside. Eight minutes! She'd been in that store for a measly eight minutes, and her Anchor hounding total had jumped to an even sixteen, and that was counting only Anne, not the rest of the Steinburgs! Running into them was enough to wreck her day all by itself! Good grief—she wished she could disappear from this stupid town!

Hey, hey, now—no need for drama! Pam's sing-songy voice played in her head. *Set your boundaries! Draw your circles!*

Right! How the heck-in-the-world was she supposed to do that when *her* circle felt like the stage to a freak show for the entire church? The wedding-eve disaster. The gossip-worthy family curse. Her crazy mother and a drunk for a dad. Her moral nosedive. Carlos. Who knew what bizarre episode was next? So much for the pure youth group girl who had had everything going for her! *Gah*, her life was an utter humiliation!

The worst thing was that she had *liked* those people! The Anchor folks had been her family—her closest relationships! She missed them. She had *mourned* them. And she knew they weren't her primary offenders, but she couldn't face them. Plus, the Steinburgs and the DeSotos still went to church there, so end of story.

Anyway, Leah didn't want to go to church anywhere. In all honesty, she felt like God needed to be put in one of Pam's little circles too. The All-Seeing Almighty had stood by as one of the spectators on the most devastating day of her life and left her on her own. That felt equally as hurtful as what had actually happened. He *knew*, and he had let it all unfold! And so she had set some boundaries, all right. Bosom friends could no longer be trusted, and neither could God!

Breathe, girl. Leah loosened her white-knuckled grip on the steering wheel, pulling herself together. Haircut. Go to your haircut. Just do the next thing. Placing her keys in the ignition, she started her car and put it into drive, making it to her appointment with two minutes to spare.

They were running behind. As Leah waited on the hard plastic chair, a chorus of voices swirled through her head: *Reinvent yourself—you should try to reinvent yourself! Good to see you, sweetie—you look great! Boundaries, boundaries! Draw a little circle! I thought it looked like you— your hair. We're moving into 204. Good to see you, sweetie.* Leah stared at the outdated magazine in her lap. She called me "sweetie." Anne Steinburg had the nerve to call me "sweetie"! *Good to see you, sweetie—you look great. Leah? Oh, my stars—that* is *you! Your hair—*

"Ava Labanora? Come on back, dear, I'm ready for you!"

Leah dropped the magazine onto her chair and followed her stylist.

"So what are we doing today?" she asked after Leah was situated. "You mentioned on the phone that you're thinking platinum instead of your usual blond."

Leah met her eyes in the mirror. "Uh, I've changed my mind. I'd like to go dark instead."

"All right. So—reddish brown? Chestnut?"

"Darker."

"Okay, like a dark brown?"

"How about black? How about black—with maybe some blue highlights or something? And I want it cut short!"

You have autonomy! You have the power of choice! Yes, she did.

Nearly four hours later Leah slid into the driver's seat of her car. Tossing her purse aside, she pulled down the visor mirror and snorted in disbelief at her new look. Holy cow! Was it ever dark—dark as a crow! But classy, sort of. She turned her head, fingering the silky-smooth, chin-length strands. The bluish-purplish highlights layered delicately over the black were shimmery—iridescent almost, like starling feathers. It was pretty, she thought, *tasteful*, rather than high-schoolish, which was an enormous relief, for halfway through she'd nearly had a panic that the whole thing might bomb and look like it was scavenged from someone's leftover Halloween kit! She wiggled her head and let out a laugh. Hellloo—what a change! One thing was clear—her mother was going to *freak*!

Sitting there in her car with the sun shining through her open sunroof, Leah felt strangely empowered by her daring decision. For one thing, no one from Anchor would recognize her now—not unless they were right up in her face, an unlikely occurrence. Facetiously she imagined herself in a witness protection scenario or something. Now maybe she could *finally* slip under the radar in this claustrophobic hometown of hers! And as for Josey Banks across the hall—*pfft!* Leah guessed she'd probably be too occupied with her new husband and perfect life to notice her or care.

Rummaging through her handbag, she found her favorite lipstick and applied a fresh coat, loving how the splash of color popped. *Nice!* Tomorrow her coworkers were going to wonder who the new accountant was! She couldn't wait to see their faces! And Pam, too, would be surprised for sure but undoubtedly delighted by her deed. If this weren't reinventing herself, what was? Leah ran her hand up the nape of her neck—it felt so bare! No doubt such a change would take a bit of getting used to, but she liked the new look—she liked it a lot!

A glance at the dashboard clock indicated she still had some time before she needed to head over to the law office. Leah flapped the visor back up and pulled out her phone to check for the address. While on it, she checked her bank balance too, relieved to find she was still in the black after paying for her hair adventure. Good. Her rent was due, and things were tight, as new car tires had not been in her budget for May, but Grandpa Ed had always emphasized the importance of timely car maintenance.

Closing out of the app, she noticed two new texts from Celeste.

"Working late. No supper. Let Brutus out when you get home. Thx."

Dang! She had gotten those olives for nothing! She scrolled down.

"Did you get my text? Did you let him out?"

"Not going home," Leah texted back. "Appointments." She wasn't sure how long the family thing would take at the lawyer's office, and after that was the meeting with her landlord. The outlook for her carpet wasn't good.

Within seconds three emojis arrived: a surprised face, a sad face, and a poop pile. Leah groaned, wishing it were funny. She studied the text, debating her reply. After a minute she closed the app without responding. *Boundaries*, she reminded herself. *Her* dog, *her* problem! She didn't have to take on Celeste's responsibilities, didn't have to tell her what she needed to do. She would let Celeste deal with whatever was waiting for them at home. She hoped it would pan out as reasonably.

Her thumb moved to open her calendar, and her eyes lingered on the date. It had been four years now. Four years to the very day. Four years since her Horrific Friday Day from Hell, the day her dreams had turned into a nightmare. This year was the first year she had not approached the dreadful date with a countdown. In fact, she'd thought more about her hair appointment than Jake! That itself was a great sign that she was at least *starting* to move forward, thanks to Pam. And although she was thinking of him at this very moment, still it wasn't as bad as the previous years. Today he was mostly a passing thought and other things took more prominence.

Like her next appointment. And with the date on her calendar open, Leah noted the address of Duvall & Ross, Attorneys at Law, then popped her phone into the cup holder beside her. She had better be on her way. Backing away from the salon, however, she met her eyes in the rear-view mirror and wondered for a brief second what Jake would have thought of her new hair.

Leah found the law office easily and parked beside her mother's Buick on the street in front. She wasn't exactly sure what to expect at this meeting. All she knew from her mother was that some affairs of Grandpa Ed and Grandma Havi's estate were going to be discussed and she was requested to attend. She was glad it was far enough past the funeral for the intensity of her emotions to have faded. She had been a mess back in January. She didn't anticipate it being that difficult today—she hoped it wouldn't be, but she wasn't sure. She had an aversion to crying in general, but crying in front of people was something she absolutely despised. Lawyers were businesslike, she reassured herself.

Her grandparents' funeral hadn't been the first funeral Leah had ever been to, but it was the first of someone close, and a double funeral at that—two people she so dearly loved laid to rest at the same time. Her throat tightened thinking of them. Grandma Havi had been the warmest, most affectionate person she had ever known.

Grabbing her purse, Leah drew in a breath, steeling herself for the appointment. It was time to suck it up. Snatching a few tissues out of the console just in case, she stuffed them into the side pocket of her bag, then resolutely got out of the car.

As she reached the office door, it suddenly swung open, smacking into her.

"Oh, excuse me—I'm so sorry!" the man coming out exclaimed.

"No problem!" Leah said brusquely, backing a step and looking up from his chest into the face of—into the face of Reid Tanner! A burst of adrenaline zinged her. Pastor Reid himself—of all people! Pastor Reid, who had taken her and Jake through twelve weeks of premarital counseling. She skirted around him to duck inside, hoping he hadn't recognized her.

"Leah!"

Crud—he had.

Ding! Her tally flicked to seventeen. She looked back over her shoulder, wrinkling her forehead as if trying to remember who he was. "Oh, hi!" she said. It was a lame effort, she knew. After all, he had been her pastor since she'd been sixteen—up until she disappeared from Anchor four years ago.

"Hey—how are you doing?" He held the door.

She flashed her most winning smile. "Good—I'm good! How are you?" It was the polite thing to say that said absolutely nothing.

"I've been thinking about you lately! You still living here in Bridgewater?"

"Yep, still here!" She couldn't think of anything to ask him. *You still at the church?* No, she didn't want to ask that.

"What have you been up to?" His eyes searched her face.

"Oh, not much. Just working." His hair was grayer than when she'd seen him last. "Look—I'm sorry—" She gestured over her shoulder with her thumb. "I'm, um, running a little late for my appointment."

"Right. Hey—nice to see you, Leah!"

"Oh, thanks. Nice to see you too. Tell your wife hello."

Leah gave a wave as she turned away, and Reid Tanner let the door fall closed behind her. Alone in the small entry hallway, she paused with her hands on her cheeks. Of all people! Dismayed, she reached to feel her bare neck at the edge of the bob. She doubted Pastor Reid had even *noticed* her new hair!

Have a seat, Leah. She could still hear his voice on that awful day.

A spurt of giggling in the next room caught her attention. As she stepped into the main office foyer, she spotted a dark-haired young man in

31

a suit half-sitting on the edge of the receptionist's desk, leaning forward, obviously schmoozing the pretty girl behind it.

"Alex! Alex, knock it off! Not here!" the girl chided him playfully. Then she noticed Leah inside the door and immediately sat back.

The young man pivoted and hastily stood as Leah approached. "Good afternoon!" he said, reaching to shake her hand. "Alex Duvall. How may I help you?"

"Ava Labanora. I have an appointment with, um"—she read the name on her mother's text—"with Attorney *Richard* Duvall—?"

The young woman glanced at her computer screen. "Back conference room." She met Leah's eyes before looking down, her cheeks tinged pink.

The young man lifted his elbow, gesturing for Leah to follow. "Richard Duvall is my dad. Come on back!" He threw the girl a sly wink as he turned to lead her down a newly carpeted hallway.

"How's your day going?" he asked over his shoulder, sauntering as if he very much enjoyed his suit.

"It's been interesting," Leah replied vaguely, offering nothing more.

"Well, here we are." He paused with his hand on the door's stainless-steel lever. "My dad's currently out of the office, but I expect him back any minute. I'll have one of our assistants bring you something to drink."

He swung the conference room door open, then turned to snap his fingers, calling out to a tall, sandy-blond girl working the photocopier in an open area off the hall. "Belinda! Hey, Belinda!" He jerked his head. "Take care of her!"

"Make yourself comfortable," he said, waving Leah in.

Chapter Two

Leah's mother, Lenore, was a serious woman and sturdy, her figure trim and muscular. Today she had on a yellow blouse with a navy zip jacket, her dark blond hair thick and wiry and fanned out around her shoulders. She and Leah's seventeen-year-old brother, Braydon, were seated at the long, polished mahogany table in the conference room waiting, and both looked up as Leah was shown in.

Immediately her mother's face puckered. "What the *heck* did you do to your hair?"

Yup, she'd called it. Politely Leah accepted the plastic water bottle offered by the attending office assistant and thanked her, then took a seat in the padded leather chair across from her mom and brother.

"Surprise!" she said lightly, flashing them a smile as the office assistant left the room. She was determined to remain positive. "It's my new look! Like it?"

"*No!* Good Lord, that looks awful! Why'd you go and do that?"

"'Cause I felt like doing something different." *Don't overreact*, Leah reminded herself, taking Pam's advice. She set her purse onto the chair next to her.

Slouched in his seat, Braydon stared open-mouthed, his own dark hair sloped over half of his face. "You got lipstick on your teeth!" he snorted, snapping a picture with his phone. He dropped his head, peering into the screen, his thumbs moving rapidly.

"Well, you've ruined it!" Lenore said sourly.

"She's trying to be hipster," Braydon said.

Leah wiped her thumb across her teeth. "I'm not trying to be anything! Can't a person do something new?"

"It looks ridiculous!" Her mother shook her head. "It looks—it almost looks *blue!*"

"That part is kinda cool," Braydon said, glancing up again. He sniffed.

Leah pulled her chair in closer to the mammoth table. "You'll get used to it."

"Seriously," her mother returned, "it looks ridiculous, Leah—and it's *way* too short!"

"Well, it's black with highlights now, and I happen to like it!"

"Well, if you had an ounce of sense—"

"Mom!" Leah set her hands on the table, her voice rising slightly. "It's okay if you don't like it—I don't care! But *I do* like it! Enough already about my hair!" So much for remaining positive and staying calm.

With a lift of her chin, her mother sat back. In the silence that followed, Leah opened her water bottle and took a drink. *Healthy boundaries*, she reminded herself.

"How long is this thing supposed to last?" Braydon asked, frowning into his phone. "My boss just texted that they need another driver."

"How would I know?" Lenore replied, glancing at the clock. She folded her arms, turning toward Leah. "Today's that day."

"What day?"

"The day you were jilted. It would have been your anniversary."

Leah's jaw grew slack. "No, Mother," she replied carefully, reminding herself to breathe, "*tomorrow* would have been my anniversary. And I was not jilted. *I* was the one who called it off—remember? I cannot *believe* you brought that up!"

"I ran into Evelyn DeSoto in the grocery store yesterday," she stated, as if that explained it. "She said that Jake and Rachel are having another baby."

Leah couldn't speak.

Her mother shrugged. "It only saved you from a divorce later on."

"Can we please not talk about this?"

"See? I'm telling you—it's the family curse!"

Leah set her water bottle on the table. "Mom—"

The door to the conference room suddenly swung open, and a middle-aged lawyer in a smart suit strode in with intention. He set a black leather portfolio onto the shiny table and extended a confident hand to Leah's mother, who straightened in her seat.

"Lenore Labanora?"

"Yes."

"John Ross." He shook her hand and reached toward Braydon for a handshake. "Hello."

"My son, Braydon."

The lawyer gave him a brief nod and turned to Leah.

"Ava Labanora," Leah said, shaking his hand.

"Ava," he said with a tip of his head.

"Her name is Leah—" Lenore began; however, Mr. Ross was already speaking.

"I must apologize. I know you were expecting to meet with my partner Richard Duvall, but Mr. Duvall is still in court. He fully thought he'd be here by now, but the case was pushed back into the afternoon. I'm very sorry." He sat down at the head of the large table. "Richard has asked me to either reschedule your family to meet with him at another time, or— if you'd prefer—for me to administrate this matter with you. With that in mind, I've taken the liberty to review your file, and everything looks pretty straightforward. I'm confident we can proceed." He gave Lenore an affable smile. "Ms. Labanora, since you've already had the initial meeting with your brother concerning your mother and father's will—"

"He was not my father," Lenore said, cutting in.

"Ah, yes. Your *step*father. Right." Mr. Ross nodded, glancing down at the orderly stack of papers before him.

"And barely that! He was my mother's husband."

Mr. Ross paused a moment, then raised his head, looking straight at her. "I apologize, ma'am. Would you prefer to reschedule with Mr. Duvall? I'm sorry for the inconvenience."

Lenore raised her brow as she folded her arms. "Well, I don't see much sense in that—we're already here!"

Leah cringed, noting the hardness of her mother's face framed by her thick mane of hair. Yikes! Apparently her mother was having one of her bad days. Leah wasn't at all surprised that her mom had gone off about her hair, as it always took her a while to warm up to new things, but to snip at the lawyer seemed especially rude. And Leah couldn't *believe* she had brought up Jake DeSoto! That was just mean.

"Do you know how long this will take?" Braydon asked.

Mr. Ross eyed the youth as he reached to remove a pen from his breast pocket. "If we get right down to business, I think we could be out of here before dark." He threw Leah and her mother a wink.

"Well, I hope we're not charged for the fifteen minutes we sat waiting for you," Lenore replied, missing the humor.

Leah pursed her lips, looking away.

Mr. Ross cleared his throat. "Right. Well, let's get started. This meeting is in regard to the property addendum of the last will and testament of Mr. Edward Keith Davison and his wife, Ava Jane Davison, or, as she was affectionately known by many, Mrs. Havi Davison." He gave a brief smile and shifted the papers before him. "First of all, I'd like to offer my condolences to you on your loss." He paused, looking at each of them. "It's hard enough to lose one loved one, but to lose two together would be especially difficult. I'm sure it was quite a shock." His voice was sincere, and Leah decided that she liked him.

"Thank you," she replied. "It was very unexpected."

"Well, it's been since January," Lenore said lightly. "It's not like it happened last week or anything."

Leah shot her mother a look.

"So," Mr. Ross continued, "as I was saying, since you and your brother, Richard—"

"Stepbrother," Lenore corrected.

"Since you and your stepbrother, Richard, already met with my partner Mr. Duvall concerning your mother and stepfather's will—"

"Just call him Ed."

"Mom!" Leah jerked her head, indicating she should let him talk. *Goodness—what was eating her?*

Mr. Ross leaned back. "Yes. All right—Ed."

Reaching inside his suit jacket, he extracted a pair of reading glasses and put them on to peruse the sheet before him. "According to the documents in this file, it appears you and your stepbrother, Richard, met previously regarding the will. So, I'll assume you're already informed about the will's provisions and the division of assets. I see here that Mr. Davison's shares of Seco Valley Copper, Inc., go entirely to Richard and his family, and then all your mother's and stepfather's—er, Ed's—real estate goes to you and your family." He paused, reading to himself briefly. "Which would be the Brownstone apartment complex here in Bridgewater, as well as the condominium in Mesa. All will, of course, continue under the same property management as before, but with *you* as the new owner." He glanced at Lenore over the top of his glasses.

Copper shares? Leah blinked in surprise.

Lenore gave a curt nod. "And the houses."

"And their homes. Correct," Mr. Ross replied, removing his glasses. "Which is the purpose of this meeting today—to discuss those properties, namely the Mesa home, the cabin on Pride Lake, and the two homes on Richmond Road in New Hampton."

The room was silent.

"Your, um, Ed—" Mr. Ross paused awkwardly—"perhaps we'll just call him Mr. Davison."

"He was Grandpa Ed to me," Leah offered hastily, "so Ed is just fine." Technically, he was her step-grandpa, but Ed had nixed the "step" part at her birth.

Mr. Ross's hand lifted slightly. "Right, then. So your Grandpa Ed"— he gave a nod toward Leah—"gave some specific instructions in the will for the disbursement of his homes, which we will review today."

"I've already decided what I'm going to do with them," Lenore stated crisply.

Mr. Ross turned his head toward her. "Right, but legally we must follow the protocol laid out in his will."

"It's not gonna make a difference. It's all just a bunch of jumbled legalese on paper."

"Nevertheless—"

"Mark my word—it's all gonna end up the same!" Lenore tossed her head.

The lawyer paused, looking downward.

Leah pressed her fist against her mouth.

Returning his eyeglasses to his face, Mr. Ross continued evenly. "Ms. Labanora, you'll receive a photocopy of this document, but for brevity of time, I'll verbally share the details of our business today." He took a sip of water. "So then, beginning with the two homes on Richmond Road. In accordance with Mr. Davison's—Ed's—recommendation in the will, and in the interest of overall fairness, your brother, Richard, has offered—"

"Stepbrother."

"—your *stepbrother*, Richard, has offered to transfer his ownership of 14628 Richmond Road—the smaller house to the west—to you, Ms. Labanora." He paused, raising his head to look at her. "Now you understand, ma'am, that he doesn't have to do this. He has every right to keep that house, as he built it, and it's already legally his. However, Mr. Davison—Richard—feels that since he lives out of state, and since the two homes are side by side and both on the original farmstead land, and because all the real estate was intended for you in the will, that it's only fair for you to have it." His eyes returned to the document. "Thus, he's transferring the deed of his 14628 Richmond Road house into your name, but with it comes the stipulation that his son, Martin Edward Davison, who's currently living on the property, be allowed to reside there for the duration of your ownership of it, renting now from you instead. Do you understand this?" He looked up at Lenore.

"So my cousin can stay there?" Leah asked.

"Correct. Except that your mother now owns it instead of your Uncle Richard."

There was a moment of silence.

"I'd like to sell it," Lenore declared firmly.

The lawyer gave a nod, raising a finger. "Yes, that *is* an option. In that case, Richard has stipulated that Martin be given first option to buy at its assessed value or fifty percent of its current market value, whichever figure is the lesser."

"*Fifty percent!*" Lenore protested. "It hardly seems fair for Martin to get a house for practically nothing! And I'm sure the rent he pays is dirt cheap too!"

Both Leah and the lawyer looked at her in disbelief.

"It's his childhood home, Mom! He grew up in that house! He should at least be offered to keep his own home!" She reached for her water bottle. "Besides, who's getting a house for nothing? I think it's amazing Uncle Richard gave it to you and not straight to Marty in the first place!" She unscrewed the lid and took a drink.

Lenore raised her chin and looked away.

Mr. Ross cleared his throat, his eyes dropping to where his pen held his place on the paper. "Moving on. Now regarding the other house on Richmond Road—"

"I'm planning to sell them both," Lenore voiced.

"Now hold on," Mr. Ross interjected, sitting back in his chair. "This is what I mean, Ms. Labanora. Mr. Davison has left specific instructions in his will for the dispersal of his properties—these homes. That's why we're here." He paused to smile politely before continuing. "Now according to this document, the other house, 14620 Richmond Road, is the original site of the Davison family homestead, and it was special to Ed. His intention is to keep it in the family as long as possible. So, as it stands, you, Lenore, are to be given first option to have it, and if you—"

"Why the heck would I want that house?" Lenore spouted. "Of course, I don't want it! It's my intention to sell *both* of them!"

"—and if you decline," the lawyer continued evenly, "it's to be offered to your oldest daughter, Leah."

Leah sat up with a jolt.

"Leah? Why her? She doesn't want that place!"

Mr. Ross lifted his eyes toward Lenore. "You have another daughter, I presume?"

"It's me," Leah said. "Leah's my first name."

But Lenore was shaking her head. "You don't want that house, Leah. It's a pile of junk!"

"Why wouldn't I?" Leah asked defensively. In a split second her mind was flooded with memories of snuggling in a crocheted blanket next to Grandma Havi on the brown living room couch where they'd read together. Dearest Grandma Havi, soft and plump and smelling of lavender and patchouli. She could almost hear their pendulum clock ticking softly on the wall above the television. Every memory of that house was a good one. And it was in New Hampton.

"And if she declines?" Lenore queried from across the table.

Mr. Ross adjusted his glasses. "Then the house goes into a trust until your son, Braydon, is twenty-four."

"Twenty-four?"

Braydon's head jerked up. "Wait—what house is this? Where's it at?"

Lenore scrunched her face. "That doesn't even make sense! He has no connection to it! We just need to sell it with the other one."

"If Braydon doesn't care to keep the house," the lawyer continued, "it is then to be offered to Richard and his family."

Leah's mom shook her head. "*Pfft!* That ain't gonna happen!"

Mr. Ross leaned his arms on the table. "Of course, you don't have to decide today, but to settle the matter with the 14620 residence, you'll need to choose, Ms. Labanora, whether or not you intend to keep it."

"Haven't you been listening? I'm *not* keeping it! I don't want the house! Period."

The lawyer paused, then swiveled in his chair toward Leah. "In that case, the offer now goes to you, Ms. Leah, er, Ava, if you'd want it. As with all the properties discussed today, it includes the land and anything on it, including the buildings and contents thereof."

"No!" Lenore said abruptly. "She doesn't want it!"

"You have time to think about it," he added to Leah. "Nothing needs to be decided today."

Leah swallowed. "I think I do."

Her mother huffed. "No, Leah—you *don't*!"

"Mother—"

"What would you want with that old house way down in New

Hampton? It needs all kinds of work, and it'd be way too far to commute to your job—"

"This isn't your decision, Mom! This is *my* decision." Leah could feel her cheeks growing warm.

Determined, Lenore shook her head. "You don't know what you're doing or anything about this! You don't need that house. That place is—"

"Excuse me, ladies!" Mr. Ross cut in, raising his hands. "Look—if you'd like, I could step out of the room and give the two, er, three of you some time to discuss—"

"Please do!" Lenore said.

The lawyer blinked in surprise, then leaned forward to rise, but Leah reached her arm toward him.

"That's not necessary, Mr. Ross," she said firmly. "You can stay put. The matter is settled. I'll take the house." She met her mother's challenging glare. *Boundaries*, Leah repeated to herself. *I am free to make my own decisions without being controlled by others.* She turned back to the lawyer. "Our next item of business, please."

"All right," Mr. Ross said, flicking an uncomfortable glance between the two of them as he settled back in his chair. He adjusted his tie in his shirt collar and took a drink. "The next property for discussion is the ranch house at 15436 Palo Verde Circle in Mesa. Lenore"—he gestured toward her—"again you have the first option to keep the house for your personal use or—"

"Well, I'm certainly not going to give that one to her too!" she said, shooting a hard look at Leah. "So far this meeting has been a complete train wreck! I can't believe this!"

Mr. Ross's eyes didn't leave the page. "If you decline to keep the house, Richard will have first option to buy at its fair market value. If he chooses not to, you're free to sell the property to anyone."

Lenore folded her hands in her lap.

"Like I said, you have time to think about this."

She gave a curt nod. "All right. And the lake house?"

"And finally, the lake home." He moved his pen further down the page. "Mr. Davison writes that the cabin on Pride Lake was one of Havi's and his favorite places. He hopes you'll enjoy it very much. You're free to do with the property as you wish."

He pulled his eyeglasses off, resting his arms on the table. "As I said previously, Ms. Labanora, you'll receive a hard copy of all that we've discussed this afternoon"—he glanced at his watch—"er, evening now, I guess. Do you have any questions for me?"

"No," Lenore replied. She shifted uneasily in her chair.

He turned to Leah.

"No," she echoed.

"All right. Just a few minor details before we can move on to getting signatures from both of you." He paged through the documents before him. "Now there were supposed to be a few envelopes in here—" He frowned, searching again, then slid back in his chair, holding up a finger. "Excuse me one moment."

After he stepped out of the room, Leah turned to her mother. "*Geez*, Mom! What's wrong with you? I can't *believe* how you're acting! You're being incredibly rude!"

"You just cool your jets! You don't understand a thing here!"

"That's no excuse to be rude! You're embarrassing me!"

"Trust me, Leah. I know what's best."

In less than a minute Mr. Ross returned with three white business-sized envelopes. "Sorry about that. Our new office assistant set them aside when she was scanning the file." He took his seat, holding up the top one. "All right. This goes to the new owner of the cabin on Pride Lake."

"I'm keeping that for myself," Lenore said stiffly.

He handed it to her.

"What's this?"

"I'm not entirely sure. My guess is that it's information specifically related to the lake home property—lake association dues, tax information, street assessments, and such. Mr. Davison was an organized man and very thorough."

He looked down at the next envelope. "Have you thought about the Mesa house, ma'am? Not that you must decide today, but I thought I'd ask."

Her head dipped in a nod. "I'm thinking of offering it to Richard. He expressed interest in buying the condominium, and I think he may want the house too."

"All right. We'll pass this on to him later." He set the envelope aside.

"And this"—he offered Leah the third envelope—"goes to the new owner of the old Davison place on Richmond Road." He smiled. "Enjoy it, Ava."

"Thanks," she replied, receiving it gingerly. She wasn't exactly sure what was inside, but she slid the envelope into her purse as if it contained a time portal to her grandparents.

"So"—Mr. Ross spread his hands—"before you go, I'll need a few signatures from each of you to signify that we've reviewed this. In a day or two you'll both be contacted to schedule appointments for the legal transfer of the properties. And unless you have any questions for me, I guess this concludes our business."

Sullen-faced, Braydon looked up from his phone. "What—seriously? I get nothin'? What the heck! I could have been at work this whole time!" He muttered something under his breath.

With a barely perceptible sigh, the lawyer turned to flip through his papers. "Here we are," he said, pulling out a sheet which he slid toward Leah's mother. "This document states you've reviewed this section of Mr. Ed Davison's last will and testament with me and that you understand the provisions therein. It's not a legal transfer of the properties, but it does bind you to Mr. Davison's wishes regarding the properties discussed."

Lenore perused it suspiciously, then signed without speaking. Leah signed it too, sliding it back to Mr. Ross with his pen, who slipped the paper under the clip of his portfolio.

Braydon frowned. "I don't exist or what?"

"You're a minor," his mother said.

Mr. Ross rose. "Again, I want to tell you how sorry I am for your loss. Mr. Duvall and I consider ourselves privileged to work with your family and represent your mother and Mr. Davison. Please feel free to call us at any time if you have questions." He reached to shake their hands. "Ms. Labanora. Braydon. Ava."

"Thank you very much," Leah said.

He nodded. "All right then—I'll be on my way. I wish you all a pleasant evening. We have nothing on the schedule, so feel free to remain here for a while if you'd like. Our assistant, Belinda, will show you out when you're ready." He smiled congenially and left.

The door closed.

Lenore broke the silence. "I'll bet he drives a Porsche."

Tiredly Leah rose and shouldered her purse so that the white envelope was hidden against her.

Braydon stood too. "Let's get out of here! I need to get to work. I knew we should've driven separately."

"Sit down, Leah," her mother said, not budging from her seat. "We need to talk about that house."

"It's already been decided, Mom."

"You're too young to make decisions like this! You're inexperienced, and I think—"

"Mom, come *on*!" Braydon cut in. "Can't you guys talk about this later? We need to go!"

Leah glanced at the clock above the door. "Um, I have to get going too. I have another appointment."

Her mother huffed. "Leah, if you take that house, you're not getting a dime from me to fix it up! Not one stinkin' dime! You mark my words!"

The ultimatum. Leah sighed, familiar with it. In the olden days those words would have provoked a fight, but Leah had learned not to be controlled by them. "Fine, Mom," she replied calmly, pushing in her chair. "That's your choice. I have to go."

"Well, we still need to talk about it! Will you be over this weekend?"

The question was a reference to the standing invitation to a casual lunch at her mother's every Saturday. Leah hesitated, her hands still on the backrest. It was always like that with her mom—one minute she was cantankerous and demanding, and the next moment acting like everything was normal. *You're not getting a stinkin' dime! Hey—stop over for lunch!* Conflicting guidance battled in Leah's mind all in a split second. She and Pam had gone over Leah's mother-issues plenty of times, and she knew what her counselor would say: *Rule number one: always think of yourself first. Be your own advocate. You're in charge of your own destiny—no one else. Give yourself permission to release relationships that do not build your self-esteem. Love yourself and set your boundaries!*

After a year of meeting with Pam, Leah was finally starting to get it. Pam would probably advise her to say no to her mother and say it with self-confidence. Besides, today her mother already had three strikes against her—first, insulting her hair, then throwing the thing with Jake in her face, and her obvious control issues with the Richmond house. Nevertheless, Leah had a nagging twinge of guilt—one that came with the strong obligation to respect her mom, even though stopping over there was the last thing she wanted to do. Thus, she had learned to delay hot decisions like this. So instead of saying *heck no* to her request like she wanted to, she defaulted to a standard evasive answer.

"Um, we'll see," she said. "I might be able to stop by for a little while. But I might have to work that morning." She never worked Saturdays, but saying it gave her time to decide later what she felt was the right thing to do, and then she had an out. "But seriously,"—Leah gestured to the clock, moving toward the door—"I do have to be somewhere. Maybe see you Saturday." She lifted her hand in a wave as she scooted out the door. "Bye, Braydon!"

❖ ❖ ❖

Chapter Three

Once outside the conference room, Leah spied a restroom off the hall and quickly ducked inside, locking the door behind her. The envelope from her grandparents was burning a hole in her purse, and she needed to open it before her mother remembered she had it, for surely she would insist on seeing it. She was that way. Setting her purse onto the marble sink, Leah slit the paper open with the edge of her car keys. Behind her she heard the voices of her mother and brother in the hall as they passed by.

Two letters were within, along with a plastic debit card. She fingered the card for a moment, noting the bank's swirly graphics on it, then turned her eyes to the top letter, a short note from her Grandpa Ed printed on Seco Valley Copper, Incorporated, letterhead. Crazy! She hadn't even heard of Seco Valley Copper before today. An online search was in order for the evening, no doubt!

Dear family, the note read.

Although I trust the Davison homestead has been managed by capable hands, I am not naive in my understanding of what happens to property under the occupancy of renters over a span of time. I have established a modest expense account for renovation, repair, and updating the house and property at 14620 Richmond Road, New Hampton, for the value listed below. It is my desire that the homestead remain in the family and that the new owner value the land as much as I, my own father, and my grandfathers did.

Best regards, Edward K. Davison.

Leah whistled at the figure written at the bottom of the page. Modest?

His modest amount was pretty nice! Was this for real? The scene of her mom declining the property replayed in her head, followed by Mr. Ross' magical words: "In that case, the offer goes to you, Ava." In one short sentence her life had changed—she had inherited a house in New Hampton! And with it a renovation account! Leah stared at the papers in amazement.

A second letter was underneath, also on company stationery, this one handwritten by Grandma Havi. Immediately Leah pressed it to her nose, searching for the slightest trace of her fragrance but found nothing. With a pang of grief she held the page out to read her grandmother's lovely cursive.

> *To the family member who inherits the house,*
>
> *It's strange to think I'm writing this for someone to read when I'm dead, so let's hope that's a long time from now! Regardless, I'll be with Jesus someday, leaving all my worldly possessions behind, whether many or few.*
>
> *Ed and I considered our family to be our most precious treasure. However, if you're opening this letter, our estate has now been divided and you've recently acquired another of our treasures—the Richmond house and the land that Ed's great-grandfather homesteaded. My dream is that you, Lenore, are reading this and are thrilled, but I won't kid myself—I know how you felt about it. It's a shame that a place Ed so loved be undesired by his son and my daughter. Yet after being in the Davison family for so many generations, we felt it deserved a chance, which is why we're requesting the family not to sell it. Ed was raised there on the farm. It was a part of him. And part of me too, as Ed and I built the current house together when I told that remarkable man that I'd marry him. Then afterwards, living there, God built me.*
>
> *So perhaps it's you, Leah, reading this, which makes me glad, as I know you held it fondly. Truly, the thought of any family member reading this gives me joy. Whoever you are, the Richmond house will be passed to you from the capable management of Martin Davison, to whom we are grateful for maintaining it as a rental.*
>
> *So it's yours, dear one, along with everything on that plot of land. We've also left items we felt belonged there—farm photos, tools, the canning equipment, antiques, etc., and things too much trouble to cart back and forth from Arizona to the*

lake house. Also with the house I leave my story, which lies within my journals, since most of the reconstruction of my heart happened there—a treasure you may think trivial, but I assure you that where it takes you will be worth your while and will offset any disappointment you may have about inheriting the house.

To be up-front with you, Ed and I have left some other valuables at the Richmond house specifically for you! We're not trying to be unfair to other family members but rather kind to the ones who invest themselves to seek them out. It's our feeble attempt to illustrate that treasures can be found in the most unlikely of places—even the Richmond house. I've spelled it out plainly in one of the journals, listing out—

Leah flipped the page to read on, but the backside was blank. Checking the other, she found the reverse side of Grandpa Ed's letter also blank, and nothing else was inside the envelope. Frowning, she read the letter again. What was she talking about? What of value would they have left at the house? Her jewelry? Wouldn't she have taken that to Mesa with her? Her spoon collection? Not exactly valuable. Was there some cash hidden away perhaps? Leah's brow rose at the thought. Now wouldn't *that* be a treat!

She sighed, checking the time. At any rate, it appeared Grandma had spelled it all out in one of her journals, and those Leah was eager to read regardless of what sort of treasures awaited her. She would figure it out later. And her grandmother was right—she *did* regard the Richmond house fondly and couldn't understand her mother's aversion to it. But for now, she needed to keep moving. Slipping the letter back into the envelope, she deposited it into her purse and exited the bathroom, stepping out right as Mr. Ross was passing by, briefcase in hand.

He smiled in recognition. "Miss Ava—you're still here!"

She gestured over her shoulder. "I was—in there. But I'm leaving now." She eyed his leather briefcase. "Heading out too? Boy, I bet you're glad to be done for the day!"

"Not quite yet! I have a little prep work to do before court in the morning. I was just about to grab a sandwich next door."

"Huh. Well, thank you for your time today, Mr. Ross. I understand now why you lawyers get paid so much."

"Oh?" He cocked his head, as if waiting for her punch line.

"For dealing with families like mine!" She gave an embarrassed smile. "I'm really sorry for all the rudeness in there!"

He laughed. "No judgment here!"

"There was no excuse for it! My mom isn't normally like that—truly. I don't know what her problem was! She was—well, she must have been having a *really* bad day. I apologize on her behalf."

"Hey"—he waved a hand—"like I said, no judgment from me."

"You're being awfully nice!"

He smiled again, and Leah thought his eyes looked kind.

"Well, I'm glad I ran into you. I was looking through these letters from my grandparents, and it appears we're missing a page." She extracted the papers from her purse and held them out. "We're missing the backside of this one."

Briefly he skimmed the document, turning the page to find it clean. "Huh. Well, I'll check if there's anything else in the file, but I'm almost certain this came to us sealed."

Leah nodded. "Yes, it *was* sealed. But I thought maybe—"

"No, I'm glad you said something. I'll definitely have our assistant check into it, and we'll call you if there's anything else in the file, but I'm pretty sure that's exactly the way we received it from your grandparents. Do you think perhaps your grandmother forgot to include her second page? But it doesn't matter. Like I said, I'll have one of the gals check the file, just in case. First thing in the morning."

"Thank you. I'd appreciate that."

"No problem." He folded the letters and handed them back. "I actually met your grandparents once—a few years back when they updated their will with Mr. Duvall. Both exceptional folks. And it's evident your grandfather was a wise investor."

Leah's eyes grew wide. "Honestly, I had no idea they were wealthy! None whatsoever! But it's kind of you to remember them—thanks for mentioning it. And yes, I agree—they were wonderful. I have so many great memories of staying with them in the Richmond house as a kid. That's why I'm excited to inherit it—I still miss them terribly."

Mr. Ross shifted the briefcase in front of him. "My wife and I have a little cottage down in New Hampton. Near the marina. It's a beautiful area."

"So beautiful! My grandparents' house is on the edge of a woods in the country less than a mile from the river. On one side of the road, it's all flat fields—cornfields, mostly. But behind them, it's grassy and hilly moving toward the river. They had a horse pasture that went all the way back to where the wooded bluffs start. Eventually it all drops down to the river—just backwaters, though, not the main current. So beautiful, as you say. Grandpa and I would sometimes hike down the ravine to fish. And there were always deer in their yard." She gave a wistful smile. "It's been a while since I've been there—probably ten years—but a place like that stays with you. And now I'm gonna own it! Pinch me, huh?"

He smiled, studying her face. "Miss Labanora, mind if I ask you a personal question? Is there a Mr. Labanora in the picture?"

"Like—my father?"

"Yeah. Have you thought of having your dad take a look at the property with you? Your mom made it sound like the house might need some attention."

"Oh, I already know what it looks like!"

"Yes, of course. But I'm talking about a set of eyes that might see some of the hidden things—you know, like structural or electrical issues. Someone to check out the furnace, air, water heater—all that stuff. You might want to consider it."

She nodded. "Okay—I get what you're saying. I mean, my dad's around—he lives here in Bridgewater, but I hardly ever see him. He's—" *He's had some issues staying sober*, she was going to say but realized she probably didn't need to tell him that. "He's not really in my life," she offered instead. Plus, he had another family now, which kept him busy.

"I see." He shifted his feet. "I have a daughter about your age, and I guess I was thinking of her. You're what—twenty? Twenty-two?"

"Twenty-six."

"Ah, then you're a few years older than her, but you remind me of her. She's got her hair all short and cute like yours." He gave a playful wink. "I guess I was imagining her in your shoes, inheriting a house."

"Right. Well, I'm not sure I could ask my dad that sort of thing anyway. The Richmond house is kinda my mom's territory, and the two don't cross over. She would freak if he got involved with anything remotely related to her." She gave a wry smile. "It was a nasty divorce, and they're still mortal enemies."

"I see. Is there anyone else that could take a look? An uncle, perhaps? Family friend? I think it might be wise."

Rocke. Rocke DeSoto appeared in her thoughts without warning or permission. Rocke, Jake's dad, had been that person, and her heart twisted painfully as she recalled leaning under the hood of her car with him on their concrete driveway as he taught her about her engine and showed her how to check her oil. Rocke, in his Saturday jeans, with oil-stained man-hands and his patient voice. He had been like a father to her. It still hurt.

Leah swallowed. "No. No one, really." No one in the last four years anyway, she added to herself. Before then there had been Jake and his family and all the wonderful people at their church. And her best friend, Rachel's, family too. But that was before—Leah cleared her throat and tossed her head, refusing to let her mind go there. "Nope, there's just me and my mom. And Braydon."

Mr. Ross lifted his fingers in acknowledgement. "Just a thought—that's all. So, you're moving down there then?"

She scrunched her shoulders. "Possibly! I mean, it's a house—and it's paid for!"

He laughed.

"It's all so new! I guess I haven't had time to think about it. But why wouldn't I?"

"Oh, I don't know. There's something to be said about being near your family and friends. Do you have any friends in the New Hampton area?"

Do I have any friends anywhere? "No," Leah replied.

"A good support network is important."

Leah was silent.

Mr. Ross slid a hand into the pocket of his slacks. "Ah, listen to me—I'm sounding old! I guess you caught me talking to my daughter."

She smiled. "That's okay. I don't mind. So"—she furled her brow looking up at him—"you would tell your daughter not to do it then? Not to take the house?"

"Oh, I'm not saying that. I guess if you were my daughter, I wouldn't want you down there all alone. Renting an apartment would be another story, but there are a lot of responsibilities that go with owning a home. And this sounds more like a farm. It'd be nice if you weren't by yourself."

"Right." She nodded. "But my cousin Marty lives right next door. I know I can count on him. And it's not really a farm anymore. It's two houses side by side in the country. All the out-buildings have been taken down, and all the land around it has been sold."

"Well, there you go then! That sounds more reasonable. I'm sure you'll do just fine there!"

"Thanks." Leah slid her purse strap farther up on her shoulder and suddenly remembered she was supposed to be somewhere. "Anyway, I should probably go. I have another appointment, and you probably want to get on with your work."

"Yeah, I suppose." He shook her hand again. "It's been a pleasure, Ava. Good luck to you."

Leah was almost to the foyer at the end of the hall when Mr. Ross called her name. She turned, discovering he hadn't moved.

"Hey, I should probably clarify something," he said, taking a few steps toward her. "I know I probably sounded a little negative about you taking the place in New Hampton, but on the other hand, Ava, it wouldn't be the worst thing for you to move down there. To maybe—you know—get out of town. A change of scenery might be good. And to have a little, ah—*space* in your relationships. I wanted to add that, for what it's worth." He smiled sheepishly. "Purely personal opinion."

"Thanks. I'll think about it."

"Have a good evening."

A little space in her relationships. That, Leah surmised, getting into her car, was undoubtedly referring to her mother. Taking a quick peek at her phone before heading out, she noticed a missed call from Chelsea, her dad's wife, and she chuckled in surprise. What timing! Chelsea's ears must have been itching when Leah and the lawyer were in conversation about her dad. Well, she couldn't call her back now. She tucked the phone back into her purse.

The Bridgewater Property Management office was still open when she arrived, but the front counter was without a receptionist. The clock behind the desk indicated that Leah was ten minutes late.

"Hello?" she called.

An elderly man poked his bald head around the corner. "I'm still here. Come on in."

"Sorry I'm late. I'm Ava Labanora. I'm here about my lease."

The man shook her hand at the door. "Bill Watters. Not a problem. Coffee?"

She declined, and he motioned her to a chair in front of his desk.

"It'll only take a second to pull you up on the computer, and we can get this taken care of quickly." He sat down facing his monitor and reached for his mouse.

After a brief pause, Leah cleared her throat. "Actually, I have a question."

"Hmm?" His head bobbed up and down from the screen to his keyboard as he picked at it with his fat fingertips. "What did you say your name was? Labanelli? I can't seem to find—"

"Labanora. And it's probably under Leah. Leah Ava Labanora." She leaned forward. "So I wanted to ask you—"

"Yes?"

"I'm, um, thinking about moving."

He stopped, his head turning in surprise. "You're *thinking* about moving? Or you *are* moving?"

"Well, I'm not totally sure yet. But I probably *am* going to be moving—to New Hampton."

His raised eyebrows seemed fixed. "Then you want to go month to month."

"No, I'd leave in a couple of weeks."

"So you *don't* want to sign the lease?"

"Well, I wanted to ask you about that." Leah slid a little forward in her chair. "You see, I have a roommate, and I don't want to leave her out in the cold. I haven't talked to her yet, but I was wondering if she could sign my lease for another year, since she's already living there."

Mr. Watters rolled his chair away from the desk. "We definitely could write up a new lease in her name, since yours is expiring."

"Okay. I guess I was wondering if the lease could simply be transferred to her without her having to lop down a chunk of money for a damage deposit. She's already going to have to look for a new roommate in a hurry, and I'm trying to be nice."

His brow furled in confusion. "You don't want your own damage deposit returned?" Before she could reply, his eyes narrowed and he added, "Or are you assuming it *won't* be, and you're working together to slip her in under the radar?"

"That's not what I'm trying to do!"

"Miss Labanelli—"

"Labanora. Lay-ban-*or*-uh."

"Yeah, er, Miss—" He shook his head, giving up. "There's a reason for damage deposits—"

"Yes, of course, I get that! Next month I'll have lived in my apartment for four years, and I've always paid my rent on time—except for once. I assure you I've taken good care of the place!" She suddenly remembered the dog and the carpet, and her eyes dropped guiltily to the desk. "I'm simply trying to be nice to her 'cause this is kinda sudden."

"Well,"—he shrugged—"you could keep the lease in your name and trust that she makes her rent every month and doesn't leave you hanging.

But I wouldn't recommend it."

"Can't she just take over my lease?"

He hesitated.

"Look—just click 'edit' on my account and we'll make a few changes." She pointed to the screen.

He blinked. "We can't do that."

"Why not?"

He folded his hands across his stomach, studying her. Finally he sighed. "Okay, if you're willing to forfeit your damage deposit, I'll draw up a lease for her and apply yours to her account." He shook his head unhappily. "You'll have to work out some kind of arrangement with her to get your money back."

Leah smiled. "Thanks. We'll work something out."

"I'm not thrilled about this. It goes against our policy. We should be doing a walk-through of the apartment together—"

"I'm really grateful, Mr. Watters. And I won't tell anyone."

"I don't think it's very smart on your part."

"Maybe not. But thanks." Leah stood. "I'll tell her to stop by. Her name is Celeste Dupre."

"All right. Tell her to come in soon. The property is changing ownership, and that's a fairly common time to see the rent bump up."

Changing ownership—a seemingly incidental fact that prior to her previous appointment would have gone unnoticed. The apartment would be transferring from her grandparents to her mother now, another fresh reminder of her loss.

She nodded, shaking his hand. "I'll let her know. Thank you very much."

"Have a nice evening, Miss Labanelli."

Grief, elation, fatigue—Leah felt the whole gamut on her drive home. And the day wasn't over yet. Pulling into her usual parking spot, she glanced up at their balcony to see lights on in the apartment. Good. Celeste was home. She hoped her announcement would be drama-free.

The apartment door gave its familiar groan as she pushed it open and entered. Noticing a dark clump on the carpet just inside, Leah recoiled in disgust as her shoe narrowly missed stepping onto another small dog "accident." Ugh. Not again! What was so dang hard about understanding that dogs needed to go *outside*? Leah gritted her teeth, trying not to retch. For certain, any remaining reservations about moving to New Hampton had vaporized!

This was her roommate's mess to clean up, she reminded herself. There was no need to unleash on her. Plus, their days together were numbered now. Leah would simply have to stick it out. Around the corner she could see the edge of the couch where Celeste sat watching television. Reminding herself to breathe, she hung her coat on the hook and stepped into the living room.

Celeste gave a startled cry, then covered her mouth with her hand. "Oh, geez! Man, you freaked me out for a second—I thought you were someone else! Your hair—it's—it's—wow, Ava, it's *dark*! Really dark! And short!" She stared from where she sat with her legs propped up and covered with a knitted throw, the dog nestled comfortably beside her. "I mean, you said you were getting it cut, but I never expected you to do all *that*!"

"Thanks. I know. My mom was a bit shocked too." Leah took a seat, adjusting the pillow behind her.

"I totally thought you were someone else!"

Perfect. Leah passed her hand through her hair with a little smile. "So, hey—I had an interesting day, and I have something to tell you. Something that's going to be a surprise."

Her roommate eyed her curiously. "Yeah?"

Leah nodded. "Yeah."

Chapter Four

Leah dreamed of Grandma Havi that night, and as happens in dreams, time was shaken together, and images of reality and unreality were all mixed and blended seamlessly.

They were at the Richmond house in the kitchen—Leah, her mother, and Grandma—back when Leah's heart was still able to sing. Every table and counter and chair in sight was covered with flowers, each blossom white and fragrant and full. And while the three generations worked on the arrangements, the sound of happiness filled the room, the occasion especially joyous, for even Leah's mother laughed freely as together they twisted wire and green tape around the stems, building large bouquets.

The flowers, she knew, were both for her own wedding and for Grandma Havi's funeral, but in the dream there was no sadness, for her grandmother looked with anticipation to her event with as much excitement as Leah did hers. "It's going to be such a grand day," she said eagerly, "such a grand day to finally be with him all the time!" Leah knew "him" to be her grandmother's divine bridegroom, Jesus.

And then Rocke came in.

Rocke knocked on the screen door and came in, and suddenly Leah was back at her own home in Bridgewater in her mother's kitchen, binding orange and pink gerbera daisies for her bridesmaids' bouquets. Rocke came in and made her sit down with her mother and her grandmother to share the terrible news.

That was when Grandma Havi took Leah by the shoulders and said, "Oh, darling!" Just those two words spoken—"Oh, darling"—but those two words spoke powerfully of love and understanding and comfort. No, those two words *gave* powerfully of love and understanding and comfort, conveyed it, passed them on to her, and she not only heard the words but also felt the substance of love and understanding and comfort enter her in a tangible way. And she wept in Grandma Havi's arms, wept and wept and wept as behind her, her mother began unleashing her awful tirade of anger fueled by her own festering reservoir of betrayal.

Di-di-dit, di-di-dit, di-di-dit—

Her alarm was going off. Jarred awake, Leah fumbled for her phone on the end table to hit the snooze, then fell back onto the bed with a groan. How in the world had she thought an early morning run would be a good idea? And now another disturbing dream—no doubt triggered by her excitement over the new house last night. Would she ever quit having them? Painfully tired, she rolled over, hugging her pillow while the images gradually faded, displaced by actual memories of that awful Friday, the day before her wedding.

They had indeed been at her home—Leah, her mother, and Grandma Havi—and they were working on the wedding flowers, trying to finish up. Leah was in a hurry to be done with them and get ready for the evening. Their whole morning had been spent decorating the hall for the reception, and she had yet to take a shower. Rehearsal was in less than three hours, and afterward was the groom's dinner, booked at the Blue Stallion. She was hoping for some time to relax—to get herself out of busy mode and mentally prepare to enjoy the weekend.

Systematically their lists of wedding tasks had been checked off one by one, and by the afternoon Leah was starting to get butterflies. It was finally happening—the culmination of months of preparation! In less than twenty-four hours she would become Mrs. Jake DeSoto! She checked her phone—she had texted that nugget to Jake over an hour ago, but he still hadn't responded. He was busy too. Perhaps Evelyn had him doing last-minute projects at the DeSoto house, getting ready for a weekend of guests.

"Here, hon—try twisting this stem a little to the side," her grandmother urged, tipping a blossom outward, careful of its delicate petals. "Yeah, like that—that looks nice."

Leah responded, adjusting the bouquet and moving her arms to give her grandma more room to work.

They had just finished binding all the bridesmaids' bouquets and had set them into shiny clean quart jars in the refrigerator when Rocke showed up, knocking briefly on the screen door and letting himself in.

"Leah, I'd like you to come down to the church," he said without his normal lighthearted greeting. "And you too, Lenore. Please."

Leah felt a rise of anxiety at his sober expression. "What's wrong? Did something happen to Jake?"

"Jake's—at the church," he said. "Just come down, okay? We need you there."

She got to the church in a hurry, her mind bombarded with a dozen morbid scenes. Had there been a car wreck? She'd heard of awful things like that happening before! Or had Jake hurt his knee again? She hoped he wasn't seriously hurt. Lenore and Grandma Havi pulled into the parking lot right behind her. As she reached the side entrance, Danny DeSoto, Jake's older brother, was coming out, his face dark with anger.

"What's wrong?" she asked in alarm. Oh, no—she hoped he and Jake hadn't butted heads again. Lately her free-spirited fiancé bristled whenever Danny came around, but she'd never seen Danny react quite like this.

He held the glass door for her and then left for his car without speaking.

Rocke entered right behind Leah and waved her to follow him to the prayer room. Entering, she spied Jake on the loveseat and let out a huge breath.

"Jake! Thank God you're okay! Holy cow—your dad was freaking me out! I was afraid something had happened to you!"

Pastor Reid was there too, and Evelyn, Jake's mom. And then across the room she noticed Mark and Anne Steinburg sitting with Rachel, who was crying, her mascara smeared badly down her cheeks.

"Rachel! My goodness—what's happened? Are you hurt? Was there an accident? What's going on?"

Pastor Reid directed Leah to an armchair. "Here you go. Have a seat, Leah."

Rocke pulled out folding chairs for Leah's mom and grandmother. The room was forebodingly quiet.

"What's going on?" she repeated, a dull pit in her stomach.

Pastor Reid spoke gently: "Leah, Jake's got something he needs to tell you."

That was when she found out that her best friend, Rachel, was going to have a baby—Jake's baby.

And that began the nightmare whirlwind of wedding cancellation. Of calling every single person on the guest list to let them know it was off. And calling the Blue Stallion to cancel the groom's dinner, and the hall to cancel the reception, as well as the dozen other vendors poised to execute their services on her wedding day.

"I should have known this would happen," her mom spewed angrily, yanking yards of tulle off the chairs on the center aisle and winding it around her arm. "You were born into this family and it's your fate! Don't think you'll ever escape it!"

That night Leah unpacked her honeymoon luggage. And the next day her mom and grandma and Braydon undecorated the reception hall, while her dad—who had showed up at the DeSotos' house livid when he found out—helped her move her stuff out of Jake's apartment, after they had spent all of the previous weekend moving it in.

After that followed a week of her and her mother sorting through wedding and shower gifts to return items to the people who had gifted them, fielding phone calls from nosy people who wondered what had happened, and refusing call after call after call from Evelyn DeSoto, deleting every message that she left. Leah wasn't going to talk to her.

Her grandmother had cried at that Friday meeting in the prayer room. Her mom had lost it and cussed Jake out bad—right in front of Pastor Reid. She didn't care who heard her—she was going to give him her piece. Leah felt as though she had fallen through the ice and sat stunned while the room spun around her. In retrospect, certain things made sense now—like why Jake had always been eager to include Rachel in whatever they did. Leah thought he was just being nice since she didn't have a boyfriend. It also explained why Rachel insisted the bridal boutique had gotten her size wrong when her bridesmaid dress arrived so much tighter than when they'd ordered it.

"What I don't understand," Grandma Havi said that night as she bagged up the gerbera bouquets with the trash, "is how that young man could still plan to go through with the wedding!" She shook her head, angrily clucking her tongue.

It was Danny who had brought it all to light, Leah learned from Pastor Reid a week or so later. Danny had come to him letting him know that he had given his brother an ultimatum to come clean or he'd go to Rachel's parents. But when the deadline passed, he'd gone to Pastor Reid instead. She shuddered to think of what might have happened if he hadn't done so.

Sleepily Leah yawned, stretching her legs beneath the sheets. Well, another would-have-been anniversary hadn't passed without reliving it after all. It looked like her hallmark of misery was going to continue dominating another year. With a sigh, she sat up and found her stylish running gear on the armchair and dressed in the morning light. Then quietly she let herself out of the apartment and headed for the footpath in the nearby park, having enough time to take it twice around before returning home to get ready for the day—where her black hair surprised her in the bathroom.

As predicted, her new hairstyle caused a stir at work, the drastic change the focus of confused stares and polite commentary as each of her eight coworkers arrived at the office. Most notable was the boss's son's reaction, who raved about Ava's new look and her appeal to younger clients, recommending that the company move her out of her cubicle right up to the front desk.

Leah was flattered, but it didn't stop her from giving her two weeks' notice at the end of the day. Concerned, her boss invited Leah to have a seat in his office, probing her as to what was going on in her life. The hardest part was convincing him that her move had nothing at all to do with her new hair and that the two were entirely coincidental. She could tell he didn't quite buy it, but in the end he agreed to give her a reference when she applied for a job in New Hampton.

Her counselor, Pam, was equally concerned about the move, but Leah's hair was a non-issue. Leah hadn't had an appointment scheduled for that day, but she stopped over anyway after work, hoping that Pam could squeeze her in for long enough to let her know what was going on. Plopping down onto the tan armchair in her office, Leah excitedly unfolded the whole story.

Pam peered at her over the top of her fuchsia reading glasses, her forehead wrinkled with apprehensive surprise. "Whoa now, Ava! I've heard *nothing* about this until now!"

"I know! Isn't it amazing? It all happened just yesterday!"

"Yes, but to make a decision like that in one day—it doesn't seem like good judgment!"

Leah shook her head. "Oh, I've been there and already know the house. I have a marketable skill, and I don't think it'll be hard to get a new job. Plus, my boss said he'd give me a good reference. I believe this is part of my Year of Freedom. I'm breaking out!" She laughed and gave her hair a little flip. "As you can see!"

"Well, all right then. Let's talk about this," she offered reservedly. "I'd like to ask you a few questions." Pam settled back onto the couch across from Leah, crossing her legs and centering her note pad on her lap. "Tell me what appeals to you most about this move, Ava."

"The house," Leah answered confidently. "Well, the whole place, really. It's been in my grandfather's family for generations. Every association I have about that place is good. My grandma was there for me when my parents went through their divorce. My mom would take me and Braydon down there—he was only a baby, like a one-year-old—and we'd stay with Grandma for a few weeks at a time. She was the best! She taught me to cook and sew and crochet, and I'd help her in her garden. And every night I'd help Grandpa Ed feed some calves he kept by the barn. Sometimes he'd take us out to ride the pony—when Braydon was older, of course." She paused, her eyes lingering on the trees outside the office windows. "He liked to sing a lot—Grandpa Ed. Songs from his church. They always took us with them when we stayed there." She glanced back at Pam, suddenly remembering the original question. "Um, the house definitely appeals to me the most. It's nice. And it's paid for."

Pam nodded thoughtfully. "And you're all right with going back into an environment with those religious ties?"

Leah gave her a questioning look.

"Remember your Year of Freedom? Part of what you're breaking out of is the burden of guilt you've carried from those religious influences. You were quite controlled by all that if you recall." Pam paused. "I believe it was your grandparents who got you connected to that cult here in town."

"It wasn't a cult."

"Sect, then."

"It was a *church*!" Leah clarified. "My grandparents had friends in Bridgewater who"—*who were believers*, Leah wanted to say, but Pam didn't care for that terminology—"who went to a church like theirs in New Hampton. Yes, they got us connected."

"And you got sucked in pretty deep, wouldn't you say? Summer camp and the whole nine yards."

"Well, yeah, but that was quite a while ago. I haven't been to Anchor Church in four years now." Leah folded her arms, bringing a hand to her chin. "But even back then it wasn't a *terrible* thing. I was really happy at Anchor. I mean, it was *good* there until—well, until it *wasn't* good."

Pam tapped her pen on the edge of the pad. "That's my concern, Ava. You still have a weakness for religion. Do you need to go back to the environment where it all started? I'm not sure that's healthy for you."

Leah was quiet, considering her words.

"My second concern is that every reason you mentioned that you like the place doesn't exist anymore! You can't go back in time. It's a heartbreaking reality, my dear, but your grandparents are no longer living."

"Of course, I understand that!"

"Right—but what I think I see is that you *do* want to go back to the past. You can't run away from life, Ava. You're trying to retreat to happy memories and hide there instead of moving on to make a new life for yourself."

Leah spread her hands. "But I *am* moving ahead! I *am* making a new life for myself! I just quit my job to do that very thing!"

"Okay, so how will your life improve there? How will this be moving forward?"

"Well, I'm going to find a new job, and I'll have a house to take care of." Leah paused, now defensive and unable to think. "I don't know! I'll find out when I get there, I guess!"

"Apartment living is different from home ownership. How will you handle a leaky water heater?"

Leah raised an eyebrow. "Pam, I'm twenty-six, not seventeen. I'll call someone and get it fixed!"

"Things cost money."

"I have a savings. And my grandpa left me some money to fix the place up."

"In the winter you'll have to shovel snow."

She laughed out loud. "Really, Pam! What's this about? You seriously don't want me to go!"

The counselor set her pad down and leaned in. "It's not that, Ava! I care about you! I don't want to see you sabotage a whole year of progress with one rash decision. You've come so far!"

Leah nodded. "I have—I agree! I've learned so much and I think so differently now. But I feel like I can never move on as long as I live here in Bridgewater! There's no letting the past fade away when I keep running into people I know. It's the one thing that snags me up!"

Both were silent for a moment.

"Look, Pam—I just want to move away to somewhere where I can start over. Somewhere where no one knows me, and I can put all the things you've taught me into practice. Somewhere I don't have to worry about running into Jake or his family or two hundred other people from their church who act overly thrilled to see me and tell me how much I'm missed. You can't *believe* all the connections this town has to that family!

"Plus, yesterday the lawyer hinted it might be good for me to have some space in my relationship with my mom, and I think he may be right. I'm only moving to New Hampton. It's not like it's Zimbabwe or anything. And I have options. If it doesn't work out, I can turn the house over to a trust for my brother." She took a little breath. "I really want to do this. I feel like I'm *supposed* to do this."

Pam gave a slow nod, the wrinkle remaining fixed on her brow.

"Okay—I can see you're determined. You don't need my permission, Ava. I'm just trying to help you think this through. Tell me some of the decisions you'll make to keep a healthy outlook on life."

"I'll watch two motivational videos per day."

Pam jerked her chin up. "Come on now—I'm serious."

"Well, like I said, I'll be getting a job, so I'll have a new network of people there. And I'll get to know my neighbors."

"That's a start."

"I'm not sure where you're going with this. Go ahead—tell me what's on your mind."

Pam clasped her hands. "You're going to step out of your cave and make new friends! You're going to take risks and not be afraid of people who are different from you! You're going to stay true to who you are and not be controlled by others! You're going to love yourself and put yourself first—all those things that we've talked about." She paused, tipping her head down. "And you're *not* going to get mixed up with narrow-minded people!"

"Narrow minded?"

"Religious!"

Leah let out a breath. "Right—but just for the record, there was nothing narrow-minded about my grandparents. My grandfather was a shrewd businessman. And they were a couple of the most warm-hearted, generous people I know. But as you say, they won't be there. So don't worry."

Pam glanced at the clock. "Oh, dear! I'm sorry, Ava! I have another appointment in one minute! We need to say goodbye, and I'm sorry it's in a rush."

"No—that's fine. I'm glad you were here and that I got to see you."

"Me too! I'm not sure when I'll see you again, but it's been a pleasure having you for a client. I wish you luck on your journey. I hope you won't give up on your Year of Freedom."

"Thanks, Pam. Maybe when I'm in town next I'll stop in and give you an update."

"I'd love that!"

If Pam had been vocal about her reservations, Leah knew her mother would be more so, especially with time to think since their day at the lawyer's office. Nevertheless, Leah decided to stop over on Saturday anyway so she could spend at least a little time with her before she moved, but it wasn't without some mental preparation for a debate that might occur and a strategic plan for escape if things went awry.

As expected, Lenore immediately brought up the Richmond house.

Leah sighed, shaking the water off some freshly rinsed lettuce. "Mom, I *know*—you don't like the idea. I'm already crystal clear on how you feel about it!"

"Well, I just don't want you to do something stupid like move down there. That property should be sold and done away with."

Leah had her back turned. "Why would that be stupid? What else is a house for? And why are you so adamant about me not keeping it?"

"Leah."

She knew that tone.

"You aren't moving there, are you?"

Here we go. Leah wiped her hands on the dish towel and faced her squarely. "Yes, Mom. I *am*. Tell me—what is it about that place you despise so much? Is there something wrong with it, or is it just that you never liked Grandpa Ed?"

"It's one and the same. I can't think of one good thing about that place! Mom and I should have never moved there to begin with."

"Well, I can't think of one *bad* thing about it. But either way, Grandma and Grandpa don't live there anymore. The past is in the past. Neither of us can go back even if we wanted to." She set the towel onto the counter, grateful for her previous conversation with Pam. "Time moves on, and things change. So from now on you'll have a good association with the place—me!" She threw a hand on her hip and smiled.

"Pfft!" Her mother shook her head. "You're making a bad decision!"

"It's one that's already made! Is that why you were so crabby the other day at the law office? Poor Mr. Ross—I felt sorry for him!"

"Ha! *Poor* Mr. Ross—right!"

"Well, I liked him. And speaking of—since when has our family been rich?"

Lenore's brow rose. "Whose family?"

"Well, Grandpa and Grandma. I mean, I knew they managed the apartments here in town, but I always got the impression that they were barely scraping by—like everything they made had to go back into Brownstone to keep it afloat."

"That's partly true, but the apartments *did* generate income. And you knew about the Mesa condo."

"Yes—but copper shares? Did you know about that copper company? That's pretty substantial!"

"Seco Valley. No, that was a surprise. But Richard knew—he said he and Ed had discussed it on occasion. Mom had hinted now and then that they were 'not in lack.'"

"Not in lack! So you knew all along that they had money!"

"Well, Leah, they owned three homes, the apartments, a condominium—"

"—and a partridge in a pear tree!" Leah shook her head. "It's so crazy! You'd have never guessed that about them!"

"Not to that extent. Richard and I were surprised too. They were *very* private."

"Apparently so!"

"That was Ed all the way." Lenore set a small bunch of scallions onto the counter and opened a drawer for a knife. "He was like that—so ultra-careful with his money. That guy had some funny ideas. A classic conspiracy theorist. Always so suspicious of the government and absolutely *convinced* of some impending economic collapse—staged by globalists, of course. Maybe because his relatives lived through the Great Depression—I don't know."

"Huh."

"But he also believed in good, honest, hard work. He didn't want either of us kids slacking, thinking we could get something for free. That was one good thing about him, I guess."

"I sure could have used a break with my apartment rent."

Lenore shot her a saucy smile. "And now you'll pay me instead!"

"Ah"—Leah lifted her finger—"but I'm moving—remember?"

Her mother huffed.

"Anyway, for a guy you never cared for, he sure was kind to you in his will. Holy cow, Mom!"

Lenore slid the onions off the cutting board into a bowl. "The bigger question is what they did with all those copper dividends over the years."

"What do you mean?"

"Well, there have been regular payouts for a considerable time. Large payouts. And the money went somewhere."

"More real estate we don't know about?"

She shrugged. "Possibly. No one has a clue."

"Let's hope for a beachside house in the Bahamas!"

"I'm with you there! But maybe Marty weaseled it out of them."

Leah shook her head in annoyance. "You know Marty's not like that."

"Or their church sucked them dry—that's a more likely scenario."

Leah had a hard time seeing her grandparents' generosity with their church as a negative. She folded her arms, watching her mom assemble their salads.

"So are you thinking this fall?" her mom asked after a bit. "Moving there."

"Nope. I already gave my two weeks' notice."

Lenore looked up in surprise. "What's the hurry?"

"Why not?"

"Well, that's one of the things I wanted to talk about today. I've met with a real estate agent, Leah, and the market is hot right now for selling. I really think you should reconsider—"

"Whoa, Mom—stop!" Leah broke in, raising her hands. "I'm enjoying being with you today, but we're not going to discuss selling the Richmond house. The subject is closed. So are two other subjects, and you know what they are." It was time to set her boundaries.

Lenore eyed her. "What's the third?" The subject of Jake DeSoto was a given.

"My *hair*."

Lenore's brow creased in displeasure. "Okay, I'll *say* it—it looks terrible! You look like a *rebel*! I sure hope you're not going back to those wild friends of yours."

"No, and I *do not*! Get over it, Mom! It's hair dye!"

"Well, don't start wearing black lipstick and all that!"

"Geez! See—this is what I mean! Subject closed!"

"The same for your tattoos. You just don't *think*, Leah!"

The floral array across her back and shoulders had been last spring's controversy. "We've been over this! I love my tatts, and we're done discussing it."

"Fine. You know how I feel." She handed Leah a bowl of bread croutons to put onto the table. "So what was in that envelope the other day?"

She sighed. "Well, if you must know, Grandpa Ed left me some money for repairs on the house. I thought it was extremely thoughtful of him."

"How much?"

"A thousand dollars," she said simply. Her mother didn't need to know how much.

She nodded in approval. "Probably Mom's idea."

"Yeah, maybe. Grandma said she left me some other stuff too—at the house."

Lenore laughed. "Oh, she left you stuff, all right! Plenty of it!"

"No, something valuable. I thought you'd maybe know what it is. She also said she left her journals for me."

"Oh, Mom and her journals—all her religious rambling! She had an over-inflated sense of self-importance when it came to that stuff. I wouldn't bother with them. Throw them away."

"I think I'm able to decide what—"

"If you move there, Leah, you'll see that Grandma had a peculiar sense of value. Remember that old rooster cookie jar? It was the 'most valuable thing in the world' to her!"

"Yeah, because you gave it to her!"

"Exactly! *That's* her idea of valuable! That's why I think you'd be better off selling while the market's good. A prime spot in the country like that and right along the river—"

"I'm not selling the Richmond house."

"But think of how you could get ahead! If you just looked into it—"

"Mom!" Leah opened her hands. "Look—I've asked you not to talk about this, and I'm really hoping I won't have to leave! That salad looks amazing, but I *will* walk out if I have to!" She met her mother's eyes with the challenge.

Lenore huffed in protest. "What else do we have to talk about?"

"Then we'll have a pretty quiet lunch, won't we?" Leah turned to pull two plates out of the cupboard. "So—what's going on at your work lately?"

Reluctantly Lenore dropped the subject and moved on, and Leah thought their lunch turned out to be nice—pleasant even. Braydon stopped by in the middle of their meal to change into his work uniform, but he made a face when offered a salad.

"I'll eat at work," he said, donning his pizza delivery hat.

After he left, Lenore turned in her chair. "Leah, there *is* something else I'd like to talk with you about."

Leah set her glass down on the placemat. "Yeah, what's that?" Oh, please—not the house again.

"This business of going by your middle name. What's that all about? It's odd, and I'm concerned about you."

Leah sat back tiredly. "We've talked about this already—remember? Plenty of people go by their middle names!"

"Well, I gave you the name Leah because I liked it and wanted to

66

call you that. I'm rather disappointed you've chosen not to use it all of a sudden."

"Nothing personal! You gave me the name Ava too—also a nice name. And it connects me to Grandma."

"You know what I mean."

Leah stared at her plate. After a moment she looked up. "Okay, you want to know why? I'll tell you—I just don't like the 'Jacob and Leah' thing."

"The what? You're not with him anymore!"

"Mom, anyone who knows anything about the Bible knows that Jacob and Leah are a pair. And not only that—Leah's sister, Rachel, was the pretty one whom Jacob preferred. So I'd be okay if I never heard those two names paired together for the rest of my life!"

Lenore made a face. "Oh, who knows any of that Bible stuff but you? It was *his* fault, Leah. You shouldn't have to pay the penalty in life for his mistakes!"

"Plus, our last name. In the Bible, Leah's father was named Laban."

Lenore regarded her, fork in hand.

"It's just—hard! It's constantly in my face!" She paused, then sniffed. "But fine—you can call me Leah. I'm all right with that. But can you please respect my choice to go by Ava with others? And try not to make a big deal about it around other people. It's something I need to do right now."

Lenore shook her head. "Okay, but I'm telling you—it's odd! Really odd! What do I tell people who ask me about it?"

"Tell them I miss Grandma."

Lenore paused. "I've also noticed you've been losing weight."

"A little. I've been eating better. Plus, I started running."

"Well, be careful. Don't get too thin."

"Don't worry, Mom."

"And that boy—" Lenore gestured with her fork. "He wasn't right for you."

Leah frowned, irritated. "I told you we weren't going to talk about him!"

"I'm talking about that Juan kid."

"Juan?" She laughed. "You mean Carlos?"

"Carlos—whatever. He wasn't right for you."

"Well, don't worry about that either! We haven't been together since before the funeral. I told you we broke up—I told you that a long time ago! Before Thanksgiving!"

"Well, he wasn't right for you."

Leah waved her hand. "I guess it doesn't matter at this point, does it?"

Lenore wiped her mouth with her napkin. "Well, we have a hard enough time with the family scourge as it is—you don't need to make it worse by picking some guy you're not compatible with in the first place. You need to make sure you have more in common. You should be friends first. *Good* friends."

Oh, the family scourge—as if she needed to be reminded of it. Leah bit her lip, saying nothing.

Lenore went on. "I'm just telling you so you don't repeat the same mistakes—both yours and mine. You're a pretty girl, Leah. There will be no shortage of men to ask you out. But be selective. You can afford to be a little choosy. Wait for the kind of guy that you can't live without. The kind you'd do *anything* to be with." She looked at Leah, then dropped her eyes, swirling the ice around in her water glass.

Leah supposed in the grand scheme of things—if she could step out of herself and view the exchange from a distance—that the conversation was normal. A mother giving her adult daughter counsel on affairs of the heart. But sometimes her mother mystified her—how she could be so motherly and encouraging on the one hand, offering earnest and sincere advice on love, and the next moment so adamantly pound the family curse down her neck. It felt a bit like being urged to go play in a minefield. Leah desperately didn't want to end up alone in life, but her desire for love was riddled with fear. Plus, Jake had corrupted her romance hard drive so completely—it was not surprising that she was wary.

Pam had dubbed her reservations as "trust issues" and said they were warranted but not insurmountable. "You'll learn to trust again when you find someone you feel safe with," she had said. But with the Corolla Curse hanging over her head, it was awfully hard to imagine trusting anyone again. After all, she had trusted Jake completely. Furthermore, after both Jake and Carlos, it was hard to imagine trusting *herself* again. No, at this point, if romance were to find her, it would have to practically run her down.

She pushed her plate slightly forward, leaning her arms on the table. "Thanks for the advice, Mom, but save your breath. I'm not going down that path anytime soon."

"Well, you're twenty-six. One of these days you'll start thinking about it again. It'll sneak up on you. Just be smarter next time."

Leah remained silent, as there was nothing good she could say.

Her mom's eyes flicked briefly to her hair and back to the table. After an awkward silence, she moved in her chair.

"I suppose we should clear these dishes."

"I'll help you," Leah offered.

Chapter Five

Two weeks later in the middle of the week, Leah's coworkers gave her a nice send-off on her last day of work with a cake and a card signed by everyone in the office and a large green plant for her new house. On the way out the door, her boss shook her hand, leaving a fifty-dollar bill in her palm.

"Good luck to you, kid," he said. "If it doesn't work out, call. I want you back."

The next morning Leah began her goodbyes, first wishing Celeste and her dog farewell, then secretly parting with her recently purchased apartment furniture—the latter a sore disappointment, but since there was no way of transporting it, she had to let it go. She was grateful for Celeste's offer to buy it, however, and decided that when she got to New Hampton, she'd see what was left of the furniture there or start again with new.

Leaving there, she stopped over for a late breakfast with her mom and Braydon, and then after gassing up her car and acquiring a fancy coffee for the road, she was on her way. With a tap she started her "Groovin' Tunes" playlist and turned it up. She was leaving Bridgewater on multiple levels, driving away from the suffocating blanket of DeSoto dysfunction and draining mama drama. Glancing back through the rearview mirror she paid her imaginary respects. *So long, Anchor angst! New Hampton, here I come!*

As she neared the turn to the main highway, however, she suddenly remembered her dad. Guiltily she paused at the corner. She should probably let him know she was moving. She saw him so infrequently that sometimes she forgot about him. The last time they had talked was right after the funeral when she called him to say thanks for the flowers he had sent to her apartment, a kind gesture on his part—or his wife Chelsea's, more likely, as she knew how much her grandparents had meant to her. Leah veered into the nearby gas station to call him.

As usual, his wife answered his phone.

"Hi, Chelsea. Is my dad around?"

Chelsea was ten years younger than Leah's mother and was as unlike her as a woman could be. Chelsea's disposition was cheerful and carefree, her bleached blond hair wispy and straight, in contrast to Lenore's stoic and sensible personality and her coarse lion's mane of hair that doubled in size with the slightest humidity. Everything about her mother was hard and sharp, including her tongue, whereas Chelsea was sweet and soft, body and soul, down to the two dimples on her porcelain cheeks.

For the first several years it was hard to warm up to her, and Leah referred to her as her "father's wife" rather than her stepmother. It was as though everything about Chelsea accentuated her father's rejection of her mom, and it was hard to forgive him, hard for Leah to open her heart to this beautiful new woman, hard for her to pair them together. And hard when they married, for it firmly closed the door to Leah's hopes of her parents ever getting back together.

She had been nine when the fighting began and ten when her parents separated, but she didn't really get what was happening, for her mother had taken her and Braydon to New Hampton to stay with Grandma Havi for a while. From Leah's perspective she was simply having an amazing summer vacation at the farm with loads of activities, enjoying her grandparents' doting attention day and night. Weeks later when they were brought back home to Bridgewater, she was told that her dad had moved out, and every other weekend after that she was dropped off to visit him in a stark apartment furnished with only an old couch, a small table and chairs, and his bed. A year after the divorce, her father married Chelsea.

Of course, Leah missed her father terribly and wanted to see him, but her visits were difficult. For one thing, there was not much to do at their house. Leah never went without a book or electronic device to keep herself occupied. Second, he was always busy. When he wasn't away on an insurance adjustor call, he was busy working in his den at home, or busy in the yard, or busy relaxing with a drink. She made what efforts she could, as she *did* want to spend time with him, but before long her dad and Chelsea had three little kids, and it was not Leah's idea of fun to hang out with tots or, as a teenager, get snagged into babysitting when she'd rather be out with friends.

At sixteen she decided to stop going altogether, drawing a line after one particularly tense outburst over breakfast at his place, which hurt her deeply. Leah dared not tell her mother about it, for it had to do with *her*, and heavens, she did *not* want to get in the middle of one of their arguments! She knew very well what it was like to get an earful about her mother from her father, and later upon returning home experience the inverse as her mother mercilessly lambasted her dad. She made herself a rule: whatever happened or was said at either place was best kept to herself.

Thankfully, her mother hadn't forced her to go after that, and her dad hadn't fought it. Besides, Braydon never had to go, even when he was little, and her dad hadn't argued that either. So the visits got farther and farther spaced apart until eventually Leah simply checked in with them a couple of times a year and at Christmas. Yet over time—they'd been married nearly fourteen years now—Leah had gained an appreciation for Chelsea, recognizing that it was she who made the efforts that at least kept her connected to her dad. Chelsea was the one who initiated calls and visits and remembered Leah's birthday. And the one who, like now, answered her father's phone.

"Hey, Leah! Nice to hear from you! Your dad's outside, hon, mowing the yard. Would you like me to get him, or can he call you back in a bit?"

"No, I can leave a message with you. I wanted to let him know—both of you—that I'm moving to New Hampton."

"You're moving?" Chelsea exclaimed. "When are you moving, dear?"

"Well, this week. Um—today."

"Is that so? Well, I'm sure your dad would love to hear the news directly from you! I'll have him call you back when he comes in."

"No, that's okay," Leah said. "I don't want to bother him. Just let him know." She fingered the bumps on the leather steering wheel, ready to finish the call and get back on the road.

"All right— I'll tell him." There was a slight pause. "So, how've you been? Things going okay? Are you excited for the move? What brought it about?"

Chelsea wanted to talk.

"Um, yeah—things are good. Just moving down to my grandparents' old house. Making a change. And yeah, I'm excited, I guess."

"Good! I'm glad for you! Your dad's doing well too. He just got his four-year sobriety pin!"

Leah had ceased being impressed with her dad's milestones. Earning sobriety markers had been a regular part of his life—earning the same ones over and over again in his AA group where he'd become a permanent fixture. Although four years was pretty good, she had to admit. His last bender—the one after her wedding fiasco—had landed him in treatment, and since then he had seemed to make real progress. She was glad he was still doing well.

"Tell him congratulations for me."

"I will!" Chelsea said. "Are you sure you don't want to talk to him? He was just mentioning you the other day. He's started this class at church, and we've been meaning to call you and invite you for dinner."

Church? Leah practically choked on her coffee. Had she heard that correctly? "Uh, sure—that'd be nice. We should plan it some time."

"Yes, hopefully soon! I've tried calling you a few times—"

"Oh, yeah—sorry I didn't call you back. I've been—packing and stuff."

"Well, we have so much to tell you! We've been going to your old church for about six months now—Anchor Church! And several people have asked about you!"

What? Leah blinked as her brain began to short-circuit.

There were two facets of her father's life that were an absolute given: his non-communicative manner and his disdain for the church—or religion, God, or whatever you wanted to call it, since they were all intertwined. She wasn't sure which was more startling to hear—the mention of her former church or that her dad was going there! *Her dad*—the one who had scorned her for attending Anchor youth group in high school. The one who had shredded the DeSotos after that terrible day and threatened to kill their son in a drunken stupor in front of their house until someone called the police. How could her dad be going to Anchor Church? The DeSotos and the Steinburgs still went there—wouldn't he and Chelsea have run into them? How could he even be in the same building as them?

She sat motionless in her car without the slightest notion of what to say.

"Hello? Leah, are you still there?"

"Er—yes. Excuse me, Chelsea, I'm getting another call, and I need to take it. Say hi to Dad for me, will you?"

"Okay—I'll let him know you're moving, and we'll be in touch soon. Nice talking with you!"

Leah set her thumb on the red end-call icon and stared at her phone. What the heck! Of all things, she would have never expected to hear her dad was going to a church *anywhere* period. But this was not just any church—this was the DeSotos' and Steinburgs' church. Crazy!

The people at Anchor were what she used to call—with admiration—"hardcore serious" about loving God and following Jesus. Sold out. And she had been one of them. She thought back to the days when her arrival there on Sundays would be followed by a dozen warm hugs from close friends all happy to see one another before diving into sincere worship. Church had been her favorite place to be, besides Jake's house.

Back then such news about her dad would have absolutely thrilled her. She would have called all her friends to tell them about it. But life had taken a cruel twist, and she was far from that person anymore. Her zeal for God had been snuffed out when he had left her high and dry. He had pulled the rug out from under her feet with Jake and humiliated her in front of a church full of people as the "cursed girl." And to think that her dad was going there now—? She couldn't fathom it!

Let it go, she told herself firmly, slipping her phone into her purse. *Boundaries, girl—remember? Physical and emotional boundaries!* He certainly didn't need her permission to go to church there or anywhere! Shifting her car into drive, she turned back out onto the highway. Her dad and Chelsea could do whatever they wanted; they could figure out what to do or *not* do with the Steinburgs and DeSotos. *Draw your circles*, Pam's voice said in her head. So she did, putting her dad and Chelsea in their circle. Disturbing as it was, this was *their* issue, not hers, and she would not allow herself to think about their choices or take them on as her problem. At least that's what she told herself. It took over half her drive, however, to emotionally get herself there.

The turn into the Richmond development was on the north side of New Hampton, just a mile or so outside the city limits. Leah knew the area by heart. She checked off the road signs in a mental countdown as she got nearer, her excitement ramping up as reality began to settle in: this was going to be her home! At the familiar exit she turned west onto Richmond Road, noticing at the corner an impressive cluster of new businesses and fast-food restaurants that had sprung up around the gas station convenience store since she'd been there last. Nice! New Hampton was growing! They had widened the road considerably too, she noted, transforming it from a narrow paved street to an efficient highway. She hardly recognized it!

She leaned forward, waiting with anticipation for the landmark that indicated her grandparents' driveway—the twisty tree across the road from it, thus named for the unique way the bark swirled up its trunk. She smiled, remembering the last time she had seen it. Braydon had been with her, and she'd made him walk out into the field to have his picture taken by the tree for posterity's sake, and he had gotten poison ivy in the worst of places—poor kid. That had been ten years ago already. The time gap was hard to believe. She had just gotten her driver's license that August, and at sixteen it had been her first solo road trip, driving down with seven-year-old Braydon for a long Labor Day weekend with Grandma Havi to help her pack for their move to Arizona and to say goodbye.

The area looked different now, she mused, navigating the road. Where there had always been fields of corn and soybeans to the right, an entire subdivision had sprung up, with row houses along the road and new streets branching off into whole neighborhoods. As she marveled at how built-up it had become, she was suddenly surprised to find herself at the end of Richmond Road at the entrance to the state park.

Feeling silly and a bit mystified that she'd driven right past the twisty tree and completely missed the house, she turned around. This time she proceeded more slowly, searching carefully to the right for the cream-colored ranch house with the long front yard—right next to Marty's neighboring rambler set perpendicular to it. A blanket of bewilderment descended on her as she found herself back at the corner of the main highway. Okay, so apparently the twisty tree was no longer there, but how had she passed the house twice without recognizing it? Richmond Road was less than two miles long from end to end—how could she miss it? With resignation Leah pulled into the convenience store to enter the address in her GPS.

It was the wall of overgrown shrubbery that had thrown her, she realized, finding the driveway at last via her electronic guide, confirmed by the reflective house numbers on the black metal mailbox. The tall arborvitae bushes hadn't been there last time—or if they had, they'd been much smaller. Comprised of two rows planted too closely together, the untrimmed shrubs had grown into an impenetrable hedge that almost entirely blocked the view of the house from the road. But there it was, tucked back in there—the Richmond house.

Excitedly Leah turned in, then immediately slowed her car, her jaw plummeting in dismay at the wildly overgrown yard surrounding the long, familiar rambler. Whoa! Had the lawn even been mowed in the last year? Perhaps it had, but currently it was an untamed field! Grimly she surveyed the weedy mess before her. Thankfully, the house itself looked fine, she surmised, though it was older and smaller than she remembered it, sprawling to the left of the garage with its full-length porch. But what had happened to all the lovely flowers in the front? All she could see along the driveway and the front of the house were tall patches of wild grass that had overtaken her grandma's flower beds, ruining the rock landscaping.

The most disturbing sight, however, was the massive dent right smack in the center of the garage door. With her car jolting over several deep ruts, she crept up to the house to park on the concrete slab where she stared at the gouge in the metal door. Whoever had rammed it had rammed it *hard*, and without a doubt the whole thing would need to be replaced.

Grieved, Leah sat unmoving in her car. Heads would be rolling if Grandpa Ed were sitting in this seat, she thought. Grandma Havi would be crushed. She wondered who was responsible for this—was it Marty? Wasn't he supposed to be the caretaker? Wasn't he in charge of renting it out? If so, he had obviously shirked his responsibilities for quite some time! What had once been colorful, beautiful, and manicured had fallen to woeful neglect. She found herself teetering between wanting to cry or swear.

Through her open window she observed the crushed rock areas meant to frame the now-scraggly, half-dead astilbe bushes. That weedy overgrowth hadn't happened just this spring. Sure, she would find someone to call about that garage door, but the yard—she bit her lip—holy cow, the yard was overwhelming! *Marty Davison, you owe me*, she scolded mentally. *You've got a little catch-up work to do here!*

Slowly Leah got out and leaned on the car door. Void of its former landscaping, the house looked—she frowned, struggling to describe it. *Plain* was all she could think of. She might have said *homely* had she not known its former glory. A simple off-white rectangle of a house boxed in by a thick double wall of hedges on every side. Yet despite its lack of aesthetic appeal, it appeared structurally fine as far as she could tell. The spindled porch railing was sorely in need of paint, but that was minor. The siding and windows seemed in good condition, dusty but unbroken. A few dark and curling shingles on the roof indicated it would need to be replaced sometime soon, but with her limited knowledge, it didn't appear to be urgent. Marty would help her figure that out.

Centered on the empty porch was the same red storm door that had always been there. To its right the living room picture window looked out over the space where Grandma Havi's ornate wrought-iron tea table and chairs had once been. Leah had entertained dozens of imaginary friends there on her little play dishes, supplied with graham crackers, frosting, and sprinkles from Grandma's kitchen. She smiled at the memory. On the opposite side, Grandma's white wicker furniture and hanging fuchsias had once adorned her restful summer haven, though it was barren now. Thoughtfully she studied the area, envisioning how it might look with new patio furniture and one of those cute outdoor rugs to cover the concrete. It was doable. It would look nice again!

Suddenly from beyond the thickness of the eastern hedge, a man's holler and squeals of children's laughter cut into the air. Unable to see them, Leah raised her head, listening. Wet footsteps thudded across what sounded like a pool deck. Then came a telltale diving board thump, a resounding cry of "Cannonball!" and a great splash into an unseen swimming pool.

More wild giggling.

"Again!" she heard a child beg with delight. "Do it again!"

A man's voice called out in playful response—it was hard for Leah to make out his words from where she stood. Then came another lively "whoop!" and another deep splash and the resulting outburst of children's crazy laughter. Again, the sound of water dripping onto concrete as feet padded quickly across a hard pool deck.

"Ha, ha—bet you can't get me!" a little voice taunted.

More swishing and the repeated thump of the diving board. The heavy splash. Playful shouts. Teasing growls with shrieks of children attempting to escape. The odor of chlorine was heavy in the air.

Then from somewhere nearby Leah heard the unmistakable sound of a patio door sliding open. A woman's voice interrupted the jovial play, calling out something that produced unhappy protests from the children. Mumble-mumble-mumble, *pleeease?* The "please" was delivered with a whining edge well practiced for maximum effect. The murmur of the woman's voice again. More disappointed groans as bodies exited the pool. Water splashing as feet pattered across the pool deck. The patio door opened again and closed, cutting off the little voices, leaving nothing but the sound of traffic on the road behind her and a few birds.

Well, Leah thought, leaning mesmerized against her car door, *now I know that a young family lives next door*. A young family with a pool. Her eyes flicked to the crushed-in garage door.

Her phone rang. Leah reached back into her car for her purse, fishing her phone out to check it. Her mother. Immediately she denied the call. Her mother would press hard for details, and she wasn't going down that road without a lot more preparation. Goodness, she would need to write a script for that call! She shook her head even thinking about it, then noticed that there was a message on her phone from her dad's number. Probably Chelsea again. She always made his calls. Leah tapped "play" and held the phone to her ear.

"Hello, Leah. This is Dad."

Her brow shot up in surprise.

"I'm, uh, calling you back." A pause. "Thanks for letting us know about your move, and congratulations on the house. So hey, if—if you need help or anything"—he cleared his throat—"um, I could help you. Like—like with lifting the heavy stuff. Or whatever you need. Just call, and I'll help you." Pause. "And Chelsea asked if you would text her your new address." Pause. "Okay. That's all. Call me if you need help. Bye."

Leah stared at her phone, regarding his offer with suspicion. What was *that* about? It was unlike her father to initiate a phone call, much less offer to help her! Not that he ever refused to—he just never had the time. The call coupled with Chelsea's comment about inviting her to dinner made her wonder if this was somehow related to their going to church. If so, it was unnerving. She shrugged. Time would tell. But it was nice of him to congratulate her on the house. Quickly she texted Chelsea her address before she forgot.

A blur in the corner of her eye caught her attention, and she turned, spotting a jet-black Labrador retriever nosing around in the grass between the garage and the western hedge that separated her and Marty's yards. Likewise startled by her movement, he bellowed out a series of deep, throaty barks, then stood erect, studying her for a moment. Finally he lumbered over to check her out.

"Hey there, big boy," she said softly, respecting his space.

He was short-haired and muscular. A young dog. He sniffed both her and the car, then stood nearby wagging his tail as if waiting for her attention. Cautiously Leah stepped forward to give his ebony coat a little pat. In response, the dog leaned in closer against her leg. She rubbed his sleek back some more, clearly gaining a friend. Reaching for the tag on his collar, she checked his name: Midnight. And on the back of the tag was engraved "Martin Davison" with a phone number. Marty's dog!

"Hello, cousin Midnight," she said, scratching his thick neck. He turned his panting head toward her and set his paw on her foot. Leah smiled. Marty's dog was a lover!

Marty. Leah entered his phone number into her contacts to save it. She was excited that they would be neighbors. As children they had played hard together, and their cousin bond went deep. Over the years they had drifted apart, but she still held him in her heart as one of her closest friends. Most recently they'd been together at Grandpa Ed and Grandma Havi's funeral, but they only connected briefly, as there were so many people to visit with that day. Before that, he'd come to her high school graduation party in Bridgewater, but she'd only said hi to him then, for she'd been too distracted by her handsome new boyfriend Jake and his entourage of friends to notice anyone else. She regretted that.

Marty was married now with two kids, and although Leah didn't know his wife, Tiffany, personally, she had attended their wedding and thought she seemed nice. Her fingers were crossed that Tiffany would be generous in loaning out her husband to her. With a glance toward the thick hedge separating their yards, she wondered if perhaps they were outside now, since their dog was. She couldn't wait to get reacquainted—except she did have a few things to say to him about the condition of her yard!

With the dog moseying along beside her, Leah rounded the corner of the garage to see if she could spy her cousin through the hedge, but she stopped short and groaned at a mound of debris which had been conveniently tucked out of sight. Was there no trash service here or what? A battered bed frame and old box spring were leaned against the side of the garage, next to which were piled more than a dozen swollen and tattered trash bags and decaying cardboard boxes bulging with who-knew-what. At the base of this weathered heap protruded the upholstered arm of what had once been Grandma Havi's favorite reading chair. Leah gave a cry of indignation. Grandma had read her Bible on that rocker every day after lunch! She stared at the dirty fabric in disbelief. It felt like a desecration!

Now alarmed at what the rest of the yard might look like, Leah made a wide circle around the garbage to the back of the garage—taking extra care not to step in the large deposits left behind by Marty's dog in the grass, who had trotted off without her, scooting through the narrow cut in the bushes up ahead on his way home. It was the same path she and Marty had used when they were kids and the house had been Uncle Richard's, except that there had not been such a formidable wall of shrubs separating their yards back then. With hands on her hips, she surveyed the expansive back lawn dotted with its few shade trees, feeling a measure of relief. Yes, it was beastly overgrown back there too, but she was over the initial shock of it now, and thankfully there were no other makeshift landfill surprises lying around for her.

Nevertheless, the yard was not the way she held it in her memory. There was no friendly red barn or corrugated tin machine shed. No silo, haystacks, or piles of corn. No horses, cattle, or chickens. Of course, Grandpa Ed had sold the livestock and taken down the old outbuildings and most of the wooden plank corrals quite some time ago, and she had been there several times since the change, but still she remembered it the other way.

Since she'd been there last, the clothesline had also been removed, as had the birdfeeders. There was no vegetable garden straight on ahead either, the plot that Leah had always been snagged into managing, one of her grandmother's clever strategies to keep her busy from seedtime to harvest. Leah chuckled, remembering how she'd teased her grandma about laboring on her chain gang.

Her eyes fell on the little wooden bench sitting forlornly alone in the vast yard a ways to the left of where the garden had been. She marveled that it was still there, mounted securely on its low base, beside what had been a special rose garden—a horseshoe-shaped semicircle of manicured rose bushes planted there by Grandpa Ed in honor of his rose-loving mother to commemorate where his childhood home had once stood, the original farmstead house.

Leah walked out to it, observing that the ground was no longer level where the roses had grown. Over the years it had sunken down considerably, creating a shallow depression in the lawn, which now looked a little odd in the otherwise flat yard. She would have to fill that in somehow. In its day, that oval of roses had been so lovely, the colorful blooms prolific and fragrant and humming with bees, but sadly, all the bushes were gone now and only a few dry and lifeless sticks remained, poking through the neglected grass in the broad dip. The lovely birdbath in the center had disappeared, but somehow the bench had survived, anchored securely on its peeling lumber slab. Leah gazed mournfully at its slats, warped, weathered, and bleached by the sun. The poor thing needed a lot more than a good coat of paint.

Brushing a few crumbs of dirt off the seat, she tested it to see if it would hold her weight, then gingerly sat to take in the panorama around her. If she'd been looking for privacy, the tall, thick hedges would have scored high, but that hadn't been on her radar. Nevertheless, here she was, tucked in her own little world.

Her eyes were drawn eastward to her favorite corner of the yard where the old climbing tree still stood, its fat and gnarly branches now towering majestically above the arborvitae. Thank God it hadn't gone the way of the twisty tree! She and Marty had spent countless hours playing in those wide limbs, which back then had morphed into limitless fantasy worlds—cowboy forts, pioneer shacks, pirate ships, space docks, even the secret intelligence headquarters for dangerous spy missions. Oh, she had been insanely jealous that Marty could play there with his friends whenever he wanted.

With the barn that had been next to the tree now gone, the thick carpet of rolling grassland behind it was open to view. At one time Grandpa Ed had grazed his few cattle and horses out there. It was still lovely—verdant and flourishing from all the spring rains, but dotted now with young trees, scruffy adolescent oaks probably planted there by busy squirrels and birds from the nearby woods. Her gaze lingered, feasting on the beauty. After she got settled, perhaps she would ask Marty or Tiffany to walk with her through the pasture and down the wooded ravine to fish in the river, as she had so many times with Grandpa Ed.

Inhaling the freshness of the air, Leah closed her eyes and leaned her head back, relishing the sun's warmth on her face. She was looking forward to going inside the house, but there was no hurry. There was no one she had to hurry for. No job to show up to or roommate to come home to. No one to meet for dinner. At the moment she was unhindered and completely free. And completely alone. On one hand it was kind of depressing; on the other, kind of nice. Kind of adventurous. *My slate is clean, Pam—my slate is clean.*

Disappointing or not, her fresh start had begun. The page was turned. A new chapter in her Year of Freedom had begun. From here on her changes could be deliberate, whether it had to do with her job, the house, or making friends—the latter an area she was very much looking forward to. Her loneliness in Bridgewater had been almost unbearable. Of course, all those things would take time, but she could steer things the way she wanted. And it was going to be good.

A little motion near the climbing tree brought Leah's attention to another dog that had found its way into her yard—a small dog this time, with a clean white coat, and it hadn't noticed her yet. Its tag jingled softly as it sniffed around in the grass, poking its nose busily here and there as it hurried from place to place. Unexpectedly it squatted and peed, then darted off back under the tree. With a sudden hunch, Leah peered at the weedy grass near her feet, observing the junior-sized dog bombs tucked here and there in the grass all around her. Well, well—her yard had become the neighborhood dog park! She sighed. At least she was getting to know some of the neighbors today. First Midnight, then—she tipped her head with amusement, making a wild guess—Snowball, perhaps?

Now wondering, Leah got up and slowly approached the dog where it lay panting contentedly under the tree, facing away from her. When it spied her, it sprang to its feet, exploding in a yapping fit. Patiently Leah hung back, letting it bark itself out; then under its wary eye, she inched forward to see if it would let her check its collar. She couldn't quite determine its breed—some sort of Westie terrier mix with fluffy white hair and tufted eyebrows freshly groomed. Now only a few yards from it, she stretched out her hand, speaking softly.

"Here, boy!"

That same second, Leah heard a patio door slide open, and a woman she couldn't see on the other side of the hedge spoke out: "Hey, bud—are you finished with your freezie?"

Leah jerked to attention, hearing a child somewhere nearby mumble out his reply. She remained motionless, unable to see anything through the thick foliage.

"Okay. Well, finish up then," the woman continued. "We need to get going. Where's your brother?"

Another soft reply.

"No, he's not in the house. He asked to go outside, and I told him to stay on the deck."

"I don't know where he is," the child answered.

Uttering an impatient sound, the woman called out, "Howie! Howie—it's time to go! Howie!"

A short silence followed.

"How-w-wie, where are you?" After a lull, the woman added, "Where *is* that kid? How-w-wie!"

A new voice was added to the mix. A man. "Are you looking for Howie? I don't think he's out here. I was down by the shed a second ago and didn't see him. Are you sure he's not in the house?"

"I just came from there!" An edge of worry crept into the woman's voice. "He said he'd be right outside near the deck, but that was a while ago!" Her voice rose again. "How-w-wie!"

The sliding door opened again, and now another woman joined them. "You can't find Howie?"

"No—he's disappeared! Howie!"

"I'll go look upstairs." The patio door slid closed.

"I'll check the pool," the man said.

The yard became quiet. As Leah contemplated the crisis next door, there was suddenly an abrupt rustling of leaves and snapping of twigs above her in the tree. Flinching, she looked up right as a little brown-haired boy leaped from a branch, plopping heavily to the ground in front of her, startling both her and the dog, who yiped and hastily scooted out of the way. Locking eyes, the two of them gaped at one another, his slightly built body frozen in a crouch from the jump. Leah guessed him to be around six years old.

"Howie Grant," the woman next door called again, "if you can hear me, you'd better get your little tail back here right this instant!"

Without a word the jean-clad boy shot for the hedge, scrambling through a narrow gap near the ground on his hands and knees. The little dog scurried through after him.

"I'm here!" he called on the other side. "Miss Kyla—I'm right here!"

A mild scolding ensued. "*You*, young man, are *so* in trouble! Where *were* you? You did *not* have permission to leave the yard!"

"I was in my fort!"

"I told you we were going! You were to stay on the deck!"

"I know, but it's right *there*! It's close!"

Her cry arose: "I found him! Hey, I found him! He's here!" Then she spoke more quietly: "Why didn't you come when I called? Howie, listen—you scared the daylights out of me! You can't go off like that without telling someone! Now hurry up—get your backpack and get in the car. Hank, you too. Get your shoes on and gather all your stuff. It's time to go. Your dad will be waiting!"

Leah stared at the little hole through which her trespasser had escaped, listening as the sliding door thumped again and the voices faded. A few seconds later another person crossed the deck, and the door opened and closed again.

She smiled, pleased that the old tree was onto another generation of climbers. Craning her neck, she looked fondly up into the broad cluster of branches where the lad had been, those leafy limbs as tame as a playground jungle gym, with its tangle of wide, fat boughs hanging so low. Eventually, when she met the neighbors, she'd let them know she was perfectly okay with their kids making it their fort. Like her grandmother, Leah wanted the reputation as the nice lady in the neighborhood who welcomed kids over to play. She sighed. So many memories in this place.

Of notable significance was the year Leah turned sixteen, when the climbing tree had also become an altar of sorts. That had been the same Labor Day weekend she and her brother had come to New Hampton to help Grandma pack and to say goodbye, only a few scant weeks after her life-altering August in which she had celebrated her birthday, acquired her driver's license, gone to Bible camp, and said "yes" to following Jesus.

Initially that summer, Leah had balked when her grandma brought up the prospect of paying for camp if Leah would go. In fact, she had given her grandma every excuse she could think of *not* to go. Why would she do something weird like that? Only dorky church kids went to *Bible* camp! Plus, it was an entire week, and she had a summer job! Yet somehow Leah had let her talk her into it and with great reluctance agreed to go. What a shock it was, then, for Leah to feel the tug of God on her heart there for the first time!

She told her grandmother about her decision during her Labor Day visit. Grandma Havi cried for joy and dropped the box she was packing to smother her with a hug.

"It's the best decision you'll ever make, Leah," she said.

Later that same afternoon while their dinner was in the oven and Grandma was reading to Braydon, Leah wandered out to the climbing tree to be alone and reminisce. And to pray. Pulling herself up into the tree, she found her favorite spot and leaned back against the trunk, still reveling in how wonderful it was to be forgiven and accepted by God. Gazing up through the leaves to the blue sky above, she imagined him up there somewhere looking down on her and listening attentively, and she poured out her heart to him, asking him for help to not be discouraged that others—including her mother—didn't share or even remotely understand her newfound desire for him. And she asked God for new friends who would.

The air was quiet, except for the gentle pattering of leaves, and enveloped by a sense of his presence, she closed her eyes as she soaked in the wonderful peace. As she rested there, an image appeared in her thoughts—a grand, white stucco house, quaint and old-fashioned, as in an old Italian countryside painting or something, and at its front was a beautiful arched door.

As she admired that distinguished-looking door in her mind with its rounded top, scuffed blue paint, and ornate iron latch, she suddenly felt that somehow that house was *her*—symbolically so—and that God was there desiring to enter. A prickle of goosebumps rushed up her arms as in her head she instantly swung wide the door, welcoming him. "I *do* want you in my life," she told him sincerely. The experience set off a big cry. Rather than being somewhere far away up in the sky, she felt as if God had come to *her*—as though he genuinely wanted to be with her. As though she *mattered* to him.

Grandma Havi told her to write it all down in a journal or on a piece of paper to save in her Bible.

"Always listen for his voice," she said. "But weigh everything according to this." She tapped the leather-bound Bible in her lap. "If it's contrary to God's Word, then you disregard it right away!"

A chorus of voices on the other side of the hedge pulled Leah back to the present. The neighbor children were calling out their goodbyes from the front of their house. Leah glanced in their direction for a moment, seeing only the green leathery branches of the thick shrubs. She turned back to the climbing tree.

A lot had happened since she was sixteen. She was a different girl now, ten years later. That scuffed-up door had long been closed—closed and tightly barricaded. And she'd become well-practiced at shutting God out. She tried to think of what she would say to that sixteen-year-old if she could step back in time and talk to her.

Those had been such sweet days, back then when everything was new. Back before she and Jake were a pair. Back when Evelyn DeSoto's patient listening ear and powerful prayers had supposedly broken the threat of the family curse Leah was so worried she'd inherited. She'd felt so free. How ironic that it would sink its poisonous fangs into her after all—by Evelyn's own son.

What would she tell that girl? *Don't do it—?* Would she tell her not to open herself to God like that? Leah was torn. It wasn't as though she didn't believe in God anymore. She *did* believe. She just—well, kind of like with her dad, she just didn't want to visit him any longer. Having him across town was sufficient. She folded her arms, mulling over her own question, and finally decided that no, she wouldn't discourage that sixteen-year-old from giving herself to God. But she would definitely tell that girl not to be so naive! She would tell that girl to be careful. Smarter. To not be so trusting of people and so trusting of—well, of *God*. She would tell that girl that the only one truly capable of taking care of her was—*her*.

Her phone rang again. Her mom. Leah knew she was dying with curiosity about the house. She sighed, denying the call and sliding her phone into her pocket. Still not ready. She was, however, ready to explore the inside of the house. *Her* house.

Chapter Six

Given the condition of her yard, Leah had no delusions about how she might find the interior of her house. Truly, the fat debit card her grandfather left her had already been a harbinger of what to expect, as was his cue that the house had been a rental. As she prepared to open the front door, Leah couldn't exactly say that she was ready for anything, but she was confident it wouldn't look like her grandparents' house.

And she was right.

A stale odor hung in the air as Leah stepped into the foyer—onto the same sculpted beige carpet from years ago, only it was older now and considerably more traffic-worn. In the sitting room to her right, a mammoth sectional sofa shouted "bachelor pad," the grungy, rust-colored furniture angled in an open square to face an oversized fake wood entertainment center that nearly eclipsed the entire far wall. Her best guess was that the previous occupants had been avid gamers with a dog or two, as indicated by the fur-caked dog bed and a tangled pile of discarded controllers on one end of the sofa. It also appeared they had been out of vacuum cleaner bags for an awfully long time—if indeed they had owned a vacuum.

Promptly Leah turned to open the window on the screen door, then pulled her cell phone out of her pocket and typed a few words into her search bar. Scrolling through the list, she chose one and waited for an answer.

"Yeah, I'd like to order a dumpster," she said to the woman on the other end. "And I think I'll need a big one."

It seemed like a necessary first step—and the sooner the better, she thought, eyeing the worn, malodorous furniture. She wasn't taking any chances of accidentally acquiring someone's left-behind pet hamster or boa constrictor or fleas or whatever else might possibly be living in that couch. She shuddered at the thought. However, in view that those two behemoth pieces were the only furniture in the room, Leah was mildly encouraged.

Once they were out, fresh paint, new flooring, and new furniture would transform the space.

Ahead she noted that the long table and elegant china hutch that had always graced the dining room were gone, and a dated swag light hung low in the center of the now spacious room. Heavy champagne-colored drapes shrouded the threesome of windows looking out over the backyard. She would replace those with blinds, she decided. She pulled the cord to open them wide, allowing in as much sunlight as possible, then cranked open the narrow window to the left. When she did the same to the one on the right, the handle came off in her hand. Stripped. She set it onto the sill and turned to the kitchen.

"Ugh," she muttered, taking in the room as she rounded the peninsula separating it from the dining room. What in the world had happened there? The lower cupboards in front of the sink were badly streaked and water-blistered, the casualty of some apparent sink overflow or multi-faceted plumbing disaster that had buckled the linoleum too, especially in front of the dishwasher, which sported a "do not use" sign in bleeding marker duct-taped to the front. The upper cupboards were only slightly better, with several having cocked doors or missing knobs. Between the stove and the sink, a dark scorch mark the diameter of a Dutch oven marred the countertop. Leah shook her head, trying to imagine a scenario that would cause that kind of damage. Boy, oh boy—she could only hope Marty had given the idiot who trashed the place a good tongue-lashing and more.

But this was what she had to deal with.

"Welcome home," she said dully, staring at the cupboards. There was no magic facelift that would remedy that kitchen. It would need to be gutted. *You don't want that house—it's a pile of junk,* her mother's voice chimed in an I-told-you-so fashion. Well, Leah thought defensively, perhaps her judgments were on point regarding the kitchen, but this was only the "before" phase. She checked the time, wondering when Marty got off work and how soon after that she could stop over without being impolite. Oh, she was going to need him, all right!

Opposite the cupboards along the wall where Grandma's kitchen table had always been, she noticed one lone spindle-back chair sitting forlorn against its antiquated wallpaper backdrop. Just one simple wooden chair—but something about it sitting by itself triggered a pang of grief. This was the same, exact wonderful house as all the other times she had been here, but today it felt so lifeless. There was no one to greet her, no sparkling eyes happy to see her, no warm hugs of welcome. Of course, *that* change had happened long ago when her grandparents had moved to Mesa, but today it sank in anew: her grandparents were gone forever. How long it would be until she stopped thinking of them every moment? She made herself move on.

Overall, Leah concluded that the bedroom side of the house would take minimal effort to update. The two bedrooms at the front of the house would be fine once she painted over the heavy burgundy and navy walls respectively, replaced the rug, and emptied the closets of plastic totes and tightly packed cardboard bankers' boxes tucked efficiently in every corner. The bathroom across the hall was slightly more complicated, needing its old-timey wallpaper removed and the shower and toilet replaced, but the woodwork, the countertop, and vanity were in remarkably good shape and neutral in color. She could live with both.

Similarly, the master bedroom needed new paint and flooring, but it also came with one sorry-looking king-sized bed, its warped mattress begging to be hauled to a landfill. Beside it an oak bifold closet door was leaned against the wall, broken. The nearby closet gaped open in its absence, revealing one entire side of the storage area crammed with boxes and plastic bins all labeled "Davison," leaving little usable closet space in the other half. *She left you stuff, all right*, echoed her mother's voice again. Leah wondered if whatever valuable things her grandparents had left her were somewhere within that column of storage. Or perhaps the journals were packed away in there, but she couldn't think about any of that now. First she had to figure out how to get that whopping mattress out of the house.

Odd trash was strewn about the floor—candy wrappers, a deodorant tube, stray socks, a broken leather belt, plastic shopping bags. Tiredly, she folded her arms, regarding the debris. No matter how much she wished for the house to be like a new apartment—cleaned, painted, and ready for the next occupants—*this* was her reality. Every square inch of this place needed work—hard work. Inside and out. It would require lots of time and muscle—*her* time and *her* muscle. She'd never had a project that required work to this extent. Was she sure about this? She bit her lip. Celeste's check for the furniture was still uncashed in her back pocket and her car still packed. If she were going to bail, now would be the easiest time to do it.

Perspective, she chided herself.

Yes, she'd done "hard" before. "Hard" was navigating a truckload of gloppy mental crud regarding Jake for four years. Comparatively, tackling a fixer-upper sounded a lot more enjoyable. Yeah, the yard was a beast and the kitchen a wreck, but those were *solvable* problems, and there was something satisfying about checking off a list of attainable goals, even if the list was long and might take forever. Plus, she wasn't alone. She had Marty. Thank God he lived next door! Talking to him was her first order of business.

In the meantime, Leah decided to set up camp. She paused in the hallway, vacillating between the two smaller bedrooms, then chose neither, deciding to make her nest in the dining room for now, out in the open part of the house so she could use the peninsula for her stuff. Eventually, when the bedrooms were painted, she'd pick one for herself.

On her trips in and out of the house to bring in her things, Leah could hear the neighbors outside again. Men conversing, and the metal-on-metal sound of a cover going over a grill. She paused at her trunk, inhaling the heavenly aroma of cooking meat. Burgers or steaks—it was one of the two, and the thought of either had her salivating.

A woman was there too—perhaps the woman with the little boys had returned home. Her voice rose cheerfully in the mix, followed by the oohs and aahs of the others for her apparent addition of some spectacular dish to the table, Leah guessed. Chairs were slid across a deck. Then out of the blue one of the men burst out in a loud guffaw, followed by the laughter of several people in response.

Leah turned in surprise toward the hedge. That laugh! That laugh was familiar! Someone from Bridgewater had a laugh like that—who was it? Automatically her mind flew to memories of all the mealtimes she had spent at the DeSotos', but quickly she caught herself. Nope—she wasn't going there! The boundary lines were drawn. She was *not* bringing that old stuff to New Hampton! DeSoto baggage was irrevocably confined to Bridgewater!

She turned back to her car, her stomach growling as she breathed in another tantalizing waft from the grill. Facetiously she imagined barging her way through the hedge for a conveniently timed introduction to the family next door. *Oh, so sorry—I didn't realize it was dinnertime! Join you? No, no—I couldn't! Well, all right—if you insist! You're too kind!* Self-amused, she hoisted up her last box and closed her trunk. It was time for a jaunt to town, anyway—first to locate the nearest source of steak tacos, then to find herself an inflatable bed, both of significant importance for the evening. At the porch steps she stopped to scoop up an empty aluminum can discarded in the weeds—someone's lime-flavored carbonated water. She popped it into her box on her way into the house.

After drafting a quick shopping list on her legal pad at the peninsula, Leah checked the time, calculating all her necessary stops in town to estimate when she'd return. She wanted to give Marty and Tiffany ample time to finish supper and put their kids to bed, and yet not show up too late either so that they'd have plenty of time to visit. Setting a ballpark hour to be back, Leah grabbed her purse and headed for the door.

On her way across the foyer, she happened to look up—right into the face of a dark-haired figure peering with cupped hands through the living room window. Instantly Leah shrieked, bungling her purse as she jerked in fright. In a flash the woman pulled away from the window to reappear slightly out of view beside the screen door where she gave a proper knock.

Leah stood, hand on chest, trying to catch her breath.

Another knock.

Bending, she gathered her purse from the floor, then shook herself and went to get the door.

The woman tapped vigorously again as Leah walked up.

"Sorry!" she blurted through the screen. "I'm *so* sorry! I totally didn't mean to scare you!"

The gal looked to be around Leah's same age—perhaps a few years older—and was slightly taller, with a large chest and long, thick hair dyed a pinkish burgundy with bright magenta ends. The mom next door, Leah surmised. Perhaps she would get an invitation for dinner after all!

"I'm so, so sorry," she repeated guiltily as Leah creaked open the screen door to greet her. "I shouldn't have been looking in your window like that—I probably scared the crap out of you! That was really—I'm sure that looked really, really bad! But I'm not a creeper, for real!" She talked rapidly, like she was nervous. Or just embarrassed.

"No, it's okay," Leah reassured. "I just wasn't expect—"

"I saw your car, and it looked like someone was moving in, so I thought I'd come over and say hello—introduce myself, you know." She extended her hand, revealing a sleeve of colorful tattoos adorning her arm from wrist to elbow. "Brindle Baylor."

Leah nodded. "Hello, Brenda. Yes, I just moved in. I'm Ava—Ava Labanora."

"It's *Brindle*," she repeated. "Rhymes with 'Kindle.' But don't worry—I get that a lot. I usually go by Brin. Or Brindie. But I get called Brenda, Bristol, Brittney—" She laughed. "I'm used to it."

"Ah—well, it's nice to meet you! It's a pretty name. All of them—are nice." Her eyes grazed the tropical palms and hibiscus blooms on her arm

91

and returned to her face.

The girl smiled, brushing her hair over her shoulder. "Yeah, thanks. So hey—I saw activity over here and thought I'd come offer to help you move in!"

"Oh! Well, thanks, but I'm already done—just finished, actually. I didn't bring much with me."

"Aww, bummer! Well, I'd be happy to help you put things away then. Or clean, maybe?" Her eyes darted past Leah into the house.

Clean? Was it that obvious? Leah hesitated, readjusting her purse on her shoulder. She didn't want to appear rude, but she wasn't exactly ready for anyone to see the inside of her house. Her yard was mortifying enough. "Uh, thanks, but I was just leaving. I'm running to town to grab a bite to eat."

"Oh, yeah, yeah—right! Not now, of course. I meant, like, tomorrow— or some other time."

"Oh, okay." Leah smiled, then added cordially, "Hey, whatever you were grilling over there sure smelled great! It made me hungry!" Inwardly she winced, hoping it didn't sound like she was hinting.

"Grilling? Oh, that wasn't me! But I could smell it too—so amazing!"

Leah cocked her head. "You're not from next door?"

"No—from the neighborhood across the street." She pointed behind her with her thumb.

"Oh!" Leah locked the door and pulled it closed behind her. "I thought you were the mom of the little boys next door."

"Little boys?"

Leah gestured toward the hedge on her right. "The family next door—I heard them in their pool this afternoon."

Brindle shook her head. "Someone must have been visiting them. No kids live there. Just an older guy with his daughter, and she's, like, kinda old too. Just the two of them in that big house. And a single guy staying in their cottage in the back—although *he's* not old. I met him the other day. He's quite hot, actually, and I've made it my goal to get him in the sack!" She winked, her lips curling into a devious smile.

Leah blinked in surprise, and Brindle gave a spurt of laughter.

"My gosh—you should see your face right now!" She bumped Leah on the bicep. "Come on, girl—we're all made of the same stuff! I know for a fact you're probably wondering who might live in the neighborhood for you to hook up with! Well, I'll tell you, and then you'll know! So"—she inclined her head to one side—"he's the hottest in my opinion, the one over there that I mentioned, but he's also super uptight. I threw the bait right out there the other day, and he didn't even *look* at me! There's also a single guy on the other side of you." She tipped her head the other way. "I've dubbed him 'Mr. Wild and Wonderful,' and he has prospects! I might get lucky there unless you get him first! And then across the street over by me is Mr. Suave and Studly. I'd like a piece of him too! And that's all I know so far."

"Whoa," Leah said lightly, stepping back. "I'm not—"

"Oh, come on! Wait until you meet Mr. Wild and Wonderful!"

"Uh, your Mr. Wild and Wonderful is my cousin! And he's *married*—with two kids."

Brindle's eyes grew large, then narrowed. "Oh. Well, that just makes it a little more challenging and a little more exciting!"

Leah gave her a sharp look.

The girl threw her head back in a laugh. "Hey—I'm *kidding*!" She laid her beautifully manicured fingers on Leah's arm. "Don't freak out now—I'm seriously *just kidding*!" Then she raised both hands, as if forcing herself to take a deep breath and pull herself together. "Okay, okay—I'm sorry! I know I've butchered the heck out of this meeting, and I've made a *terrible* first impression on you. But I really *am* serious about helping out." She paused for a second. "My job is only part time—I waitress. But when I'm not working, I could come over here. I could help clean, paint, move things—whatever you need. Next time I come, I'll behave—I promise! For real." She extended her little finger. "Pinky promise!"

Every boundary alarm was going off in Leah's head. "Um, right," she said. "Okay."

"Seriously, I have no filter sometimes," Brindle rambled apologetically, "but I *do* have a normal streak too—I do! And I know how to paint—if you're interested, that is. Not saying your house needs it—I've never been inside—but if you're going to do anything like that, I'd be glad to help."

Leah's head bobbed in a nod. "Okay. All right. Thanks. That's, um—good to know."

Brindle pointed her finger at her. "Promise me you'll give me another chance! I'll bring you something—a donut? Iced coffee?"

Leah gave a careful smile. "That's not necessary, and of course, I promise."

An awkward moment of silence passed between them.

"But hey," Leah said, "I should probably get going." She motioned toward her car. "I need to run to town for some stuff and get back soon.

I'm hoping to meet up with my cousin in a bit. It was nice meeting you, 'Brindle-rhymes-with-Kindle.'"

The girl laughed, tossing her pinky-burgundy hair over her shoulder. "Thanks. You too, 'Leah-rhymes-with—with nothing'!" She giggled. "See you later!" With a salute she turned to leave.

Leah stared after her as she sauntered down the sidewalk toward the older blue car parked beside her own. She frowned, calling after her, "How did you know my name was Leah?"

Brindle turned, her face wearing an unmistakable look of guilt.

"I introduced myself to you as Ava."

"You caught that. Crap—I'm so busted!" Brindle closed her eyes, swearing quietly. "Okay—I was looking through your mail. It was bad, and I'm sorry!"

Leah's head pulled back. "My mail?"

"In your mailbox. At the corner. I was curious to know who lived here, and I thought I'd be sneaky and find out." She squirmed. "I, um— sometimes I do stupid things like that without thinking. I'm really sorry!"

Leah eyed her warily. "Okay."

Brindle gave a nervous laugh. "Look—it was stupid! I was just trying to find out who lived here. You know, trying to read into the name a little—like if it's an 'Edward' or an 'Eduardo' or a 'Leonardo.' But it turned out to be a 'Leah.' So don't worry. I'm not psychic or anything." She laughed. "Totally sorry. Again. *Ava*." She cleared her throat. "Okay. See you around!" And with another jerky wave, she turned on her heel and continued to her vehicle.

"Yeah, um—see you around," Leah replied.

That was—interesting, Leah thought, watching the girl get into her car and drive away. Brindle Baylor. She wasn't quite sure what to make of the girl or that whole encounter, but she had met a neighbor. Albeit a slightly crazy neighbor, but a neighbor nonetheless.

Her phone rang as she was backing her car out of the driveway, and this time she *genuinely* couldn't take the call. Oh, her mother was *not* going to be happy when they finally talked!

The sun was setting when Leah made a beeline for the narrow path between the hedges that led to her cousin's house, her bags of groceries and purchases from town now haphazardly dropped in the middle of her dining room floor from her later-than-expected return from town. To her relief,

Marty's garage door was open, and a full-sized pickup truck was parked in their driveway, a good sign that they were home. She only hoped they weren't in their pajamas. Midnight was outside, his hind quarters swaying happily as he wagged his welcome in the dusky light. He followed her to the door inside the garage, where she pressed the doorbell and waited.

After no response, she knocked and turned to glance around, immediately noticing a powerful-looking riding lawnmower in one of the stalls. Nice! *That* would be put to good use soon! On the back wall the workbench was cluttered with tools. Near it towered a stack of what looked like moving boxes all packed to go, except that a few folding tables were leaned against them. Behind her, Midnight slimed her hand as he nosed her. Making a face, she wiped it on her jeans and knocked again.

Finally she heard the rapid footsteps of someone coming through the house, and the door jerked open, revealing Marty in cleats and a baseball uniform with the name *Comets* written at an angle across his chest. His striped pants were freshly smeared with dirt. The hall light shone above his head as he squinted down.

"Yeah?" he asked briskly. He was sweaty and dirty, with a telltale crease of a baseball cap across his sandy hair.

He didn't recognize her. Her hair, no doubt. She had been a blond at the funeral.

"Hi, cousin," she said with a little smile.

His head jutted forward. "Leah? What the heck are *you* doing here?"

"Hi, Marty!" she said, a little bugged at his sharp tone. "Sorry if I caught you at a bad time."

He said nothing, his forehead furled as he stared down at her.

"I'm here at the house—Grandma and Grandpa's house—and I wanted to stop over to see you and Tiffany."

"Well, that sure as heck didn't take long!"

Leah frowned. "What?"

He responded with a bitter laugh.

She drew back, confused. "Um, Marty, is everything okay?"

"'Um, Marty, is everything okay?'" he mimicked. "Why the hell would you ask me that? I suppose you're here to evict me!"

Her jaw fell open. "What? What are you talking about?"

"Oh, right!" he snapped. "Like you don't know! What *are* you here for—to scope me out and run and call your ma? Well, *both* of you can go to hell!"

With a powerful smack, the door was slammed in her face. She heard the clomp of his cleats as he walked away.

Leah's cheeks burned as she stood motionless in the dim garage. Her stomach felt sick. *Evict* him? What was *that* about? To scope him out and call her mom? Why on earth would he think—

She closed her eyes and groaned. Her mom. *Please, no—she didn't!*

Midnight had shoved his way in front of her to the top step, whining as he pawed at the door. With shaking hands, Leah reached up to open it and before she could change her mind, stepped in after him, nervously following the animal down the short hall to where it opened into the dining room. Marty was standing across the room on the opposite side of a cluttered table beside a desk-like counter scattered with papers, a beer tipped against his mouth. At the sight of her, his hand flew out to point the bottle at her.

"What the heck—? Get out of my house!" His face and neck were red.

"Marty! Hey, now—talk to me!" she pleaded with her hands in the air, glad for the table between them. "There must be some misunderstanding! What's going on? Did my mom call you or something?"

He scowled. "Right—like you know nothing!"

"I don't—she hasn't told me anything!"

"You know dang well what she's doing!"

Angrily he snatched up a nearby pack of papers and whipped them roughly across the table at her. They scattered, fanning across the floor, and from where she stood, Leah recognized the Duvall & Ross letterhead. Crud—she was right. Her mother was making Marty buy his own house from her, and she had wasted no time.

"Oh, geez—I'm sorry, Marty! I wasn't involved in that decision, and I never would have done it."

Without responding, he downed the remainder of his beer and angrily slammed the empty bottle into a nearby trash can. She flinched as the glass landed with an ear-busting crash atop several other glass bottles. Wiping his arm across his mouth, he turned toward the window, shaking his head as if trying to control himself.

Horribly uncomfortable, Leah stared at the number on his back, unsure of what to do or say. Her eyes flicked to the messy kitchen, noting a sink piled high with crusty dishes and every space of countertop packed with dirty pans and empty food boxes. Behind her the living room, too, was disheveled, though void of toys. The long wall above Marty's couch was bare, the paint marked with a faint outline of where a large picture had once hung.

"Marty, where's Tiffany?"

He turned, wild-eyed. "What the heck is that to you?"

"How long has she been gone?"

Ignoring her question, he retrieved another beer from the refrigerator, twisted off its cap, and guzzled a long drink. He paused a moment, then downed some more.

"I can tell things are really hard for you," Leah continued carefully.

Releasing a tremendous belch, he turned. "Hard. Yeah, that's right—things are a little freakin' hard!" He cocked his head, his face contorted with sarcasm. "It's been a little freakin' hard working my butt off to have my whole freakin' check go to child support! Yeah, it's been a little freakin' hard!" His body twitched agitatedly as he swore. "I'd say it's been a little freakin' hard to find out that my dad gave away—*freakin' gave away*—my house to your ma, who's making me *freakin'* buy it from her! What the freakin' heck! Like I can *freakin'* afford that too!"

Leah opened her mouth but couldn't speak. "I'm sorry," she said finally.

He turned, his eyes dark. "Get out of my house!"

"Marty, I'm really sorry. Is there anything—"

"Get out!"

"Marty—"

"Is there something-the-heck wrong with your hearing?" His hand whipped out in an angry gesture toward the back hallway. "Get the heck out! I don't want to see you!"

Leah swallowed, then gave a tiny nod and turned, leaving the same way she'd come, closing the door quietly behind her. By the time she got to the end of his driveway, her adrenaline rush had waned, and her whole body felt weak and rubbery, like she was walking on someone else's legs. Shielding her face from its branches in the evening dimness, she brushed quickly through the hedge, then cut across the dewy grass toward her back door. The motion set off a furious fit of barking from the little white dog who happened to be sniffing around in her yard again doing its business, its canine tirade persisting until she let herself in.

Her house was dark now, and Leah's hands shook as she fumbled to find the light switch inside the door. It didn't work. Using her phone as a flashlight, she made her way around the corner to the kitchen and found a light switch there, illuminating the center part of the house. She stood beside the peninsula, reeling. *Did that just happen? Seriously, did that just happen?*

Leaning on the counter, she dropped her head in her hands, feeling sick as her cousin's voice echoed over and over in her head—*Get out! I don't want to see you!* What on earth had happened to him? She'd never seen him like that! Certainly it had been a cruel blow to receive that letter from the lawyer on top of all his stress with his wife leaving—his anger was warranted, yes—but to unleash on her like that! *Oh, Marty!* she moaned, her hurt mixed with concern and disappointment. All her plans—all of them had crumbled! Could she do this without him?

Her phone rang. Her mother! Leah denied the call and set her phone onto the counter. Immediately it rang again.

"I don't want to talk to you!" she said out loud, turning off the ringer.

Oh, her mother! What a stupid thing to do! What a stupid, stupid, *stupid* thing to do—moving ahead to sell Marty's house without concern for his ability to buy it! Leah was both furious with her and ashamed of her. If she answered that phone, there would be a fight. She'd unleash on her and let her know what it felt like to have someone she loved spewing anger in her face because of her mother's *stupid*, selfish decisions! She would tell her what it felt like to be asked—no, *commanded*—to leave Marty's house when she needed him. She *needed* him!

After a brief silence, the phone pulsed with vibration on the counter. With a huff, Leah snatched it up to toss it into a kitchen drawer—when at the same instant she noticed a dotted trail of brown mud on the linoleum that went all the way back around the hall. She blinked in horror, lifting her shoe. *Oh, gag!* Now she could smell it! She clapped her hand over her mouth, trying not to retch. *Could she never escape dog poop in her life?* She pinched the phone to make it stop, staring at the floor and using every ounce of self-restraint to keep from screaming.

Again, the phone began buzzing in her hand. *Geez, Mom—get a clue!* Leah yanked open a drawer and dropped in the phone—then paused, noting a cellophane-wrapped package of mouse traps—in bulk.

"Oh, my word!" She closed her eyes. *What have I gotten myself into?* She closed the drawer.

Maybe it was time for a reality check. With Marty out of the picture, could she do this herself? Her mother's objections, Pam's hesitancy, and even the lawyer's urging to have a man's set of eyes look at the place—all of those came back to her. Her eyes rested soberly on the buckled linoleum in front of the dishwasher. Throwing some paint on the walls was one thing, but gutting a kitchen was quite another. She was twenty-six and knew *nothing* about home renovation, how to go about hiring someone, who to ask, or all the decisions involved, not to mention the costs. Could she do that by herself? Did she even *want* to do this without Marty?

Why was she even there? There was no one to prove anything to—except her mother, maybe, but wasn't that always the case? Seriously, what was her point? To start over where no one knew her and she wouldn't run into anyone from her past—? Wasn't that just trying to escape Jake again? How was living here going to fix anything and make her train wreck with him go away? That would always be part of her. She was shackled to it!

Maybe Pam was right. Maybe she *was* clinging to the past. Maybe keeping this house was her way of holding on to a tangible place where she had felt stability in her life for once when there hadn't been an ounce of it at home. Her grandma's love and steadiness had seen her through the awful fighting between her parents when her dad had betrayed her mom, her grandparents' home a place of refuge from the chaos of her own. And then later in her own nightmare of Jake and Rachel's betrayal, her Grandma had been the heart that understood, the arms that comforted, the voice that spoke hope that she would not die from the pain of it. Was that why she was here? To hold on to the thread of hope that it symbolized to her while she struggled to break free from her past?

Don't you cry, she warned herself, tossing her head in her effort to be tough. As a little girl, Leah had learned that crying never really helped a situation. No one ever showed her sympathy anyway, and it only made her face blotchy and her eyes puffy. She succumbed only when she absolutely couldn't help it—like when she learned her dad wasn't coming back home. And when she got the phone call about her grandparents. And at their funeral, especially at the end when they rolled their caskets out of the church. And on that awful Friday night when she learned what had been going on between her bosom friend and her fiancé and had to call off her wedding. Apart from intense times like those, crying was simply emotional weakness, and she had trained herself to suck it in, to steel herself and just deal with things as they were. *Work the problem,* was her motto. Stay in control.

But she was on the edge right now.

Take a deep breath, she ordered. *Breathe, count, say the alphabet—holy cow, do anything! Just hold it together! And do the next thing.*

Somewhere in that mound of merchandise lying in the middle of the dining room was a package of paper towels and some cleaning spray. Leah slipped her shoes off and found them. Then gagging repeatedly, she executed her grossly unpleasant task until the nauseating trash was gathered up in one of the plastic bags. Tying it shut, she lobbed it outside the back door. Glancing up, she paused in surprise at the tiny dots of lights flashing in the dark—lightning bugs. *Fireflies*, Jake's brother, Danny, had always called them. Her yard was full of them, and she lingered a moment to watch their random flickering.

"God, this is over my head, and I need your help," she whispered in the darkness.

Abruptly she caught herself. Praying, like crying, was another scorned character defect. What good did it do? And she was stronger than this. She went back in and closed the door.

There was no deadline, she told herself. She didn't have to decide anything right this moment. For now, there was nothing else she could do. She was staying there for the night, and that was that. So after scrubbing her hands with soap for what felt like ten minutes, she wiped them on a rag and turned to deal with the pile of purchases still waiting for her on the floor.

After an hour or so Leah had made some progress setting up house. Her food and cleaning supplies were stashed away in the refrigerator or cupboards. The card table and chairs she'd bought were erected against the wall in the kitchen, and with the chair already there, she now had a total of three. She inflated the new air mattress on the floor where the china hutch had been and made it up with a thick pad and new sheets, topping it with a multi-colored cotton comforter brought from home and her own pillows. Her suitcase and two clothes baskets of folded clothes fit nicely along the wall under the windows in front of the bed right where she lay her head, conveniently tucked out of the way. The room almost looked cozy, she thought when she had finished—which was at least *one* positive thing for a disaster of an evening. And it was a good place to quit.

Snatching her pajamas from a basket, she went to change in the bathroom, making another discovery as she brushed her teeth. The water coming out of the faucet had a distinct orangey hue. Rust. She cringed, letting it run until it cleared, mentally adding *drinking water* to her lengthening shopping list.

She jotted it on the legal pad when she returned to the peninsula, along with a broom and a dustpan, a trash can and bags to go with it, some flatware, and a small crate or shallow end table to put beside her inflatable mattress. And Kleenex. The list, of course, being subject to her decision to stay or not.

Prepared for bed, Leah hesitated, glancing around at the dark corners of the house. It didn't feel like Grandma Havi's house anymore. She thought for a moment, then, after confirming that both the front and back doors were securely locked, she leaned an old cookie sheet and a warped pizza pan up against them respectively, guaranteeing that any movement at those doors during the night would make a racket.

After a quick sweep of the garage, she did the same with the door into the house, balancing an aluminum pie pan atop a coffee can there. *Just for tonight*, she told herself, so she wouldn't lie awake with her ears on high alert. Rolling up a nearby rug, she propped it at the base of the door to the basement, and then she also left the bathroom light on with its door cracked for a minimal glow of light. Satisfied, she turned her music off and moved her phone to the outlet beside her bed.

To her delight, the inflatable bed was rather comfy, although it took some shifting around to find the right position. When she finally stopped moving, she was surprised to hear music coming through the open window above her. Someone's sound system, she thought at first, but soon it became evident that the music was live. Somewhere out there a man was playing a guitar and singing. Marty? Eh, probably not, she guessed, given his current mood. Whoever it was, his music was nice, even if his voice was faint and the words muffled. Leah lay still, relaxing to the pleasant sounds floating in. Then in a crescendo, the music swelled, and the words became audible:

Jesus, how we love you! Your name is beautiful, your name is powerful—

Oh, *great,* she groaned. They were *those* kinds of neighbors. Just what she needed! She was already struggling with the climbing tree dredging up memories of her past and now this! She recognized the song even. It rushed her straight back to Anchor youth group in the DeSotos' living room, worshiping with the brothers Jake and Danny and the rest of the gang while their dad, Rocke, led on guitar and their mom, Evelyn, played the piano. Her heart gave an involuntary twist as she remembered how she would pour her soul out to God. Following closely came the familiar stabbing ache of missing Jake's parents. He had wrecked her life, but after all this time, after all that had transpired, she *still* missed his parents. They had been so kind to her.

Stop it! she warned herself. *Don't you dare go there, girl! Don't start down that road again!*

But she was already well down that road. She sighed heavily, debating whether to get up to shut the window or not. Tonight, with the music wafting unhindered through her window, she could not divert her thoughts from God or the DeSotos. The memory of her youthful climbing tree declarations had blanketed her with guilt, and already emotionally fragile from her botched visit with Marty, Leah could not hold back her tears. It was as if God himself were all around her in the room, drifting in on the music, swirling all around. She could almost imagine his voice—

I'm here. Come back. Let me help you.

It scared her, but she resisted. How could she trust God after what had happened to her—after he had stood by powerless and let her heart get shattered like that? She had lost everything that horrid and humiliating Friday night—her fiancé, her best friend, her would-be in-laws, her church, her social network—everything except her own family. How could a loving God have led her down such a path?

Chapter Seven

Morning came early, heralded by what sounded like a million birds trilling and chattering with all their might right outside Leah's window. Rolling over, she cracked her eyelids a sliver to see a faint glow of light through the glass panes. The sun wasn't even up. Annoyed, she pulled her pillow into a hug, pleading with her body to go back to sleep, but after so long she knew her attempt was futile. The noisy birds had won. Resigned, she reached down to check the time on her phone. Yes. It was ungodly early.

Reluctantly she rose and stood tiredly beside the bed. The house was still dark, and there was nowhere to sit but on cold, hard folding chairs. With a wide yawn, she approached the window to view the sky lightening over the neighbor's hedge. She filled her lungs with the cool, damp air through the screen, the earthy scent a pleasant contrast to the asphalt and exhaust-tinged city smell of Bridgewater most mornings. If she stayed here, she'd be living in the country. Mostly. The neighborhood surrounding her was a lot more built up than she ever remembered, but at least her own backyard was still countryside. If she jumped ship and went back to Bridgewater, she'd forfeit all this.

On a whim, Leah grabbed her hoodie and slipped on her shoes. Since she was up, why not enjoy a sunrise? Outside, she cut across her yard in the direction of the climbing tree to the edge of her neighbor's hedges. As she climbed over the remnants of a low board fence into the grassy field, she discovered that she wasn't the only one up early. Nearby on the other side of the arborvitae she could hear the steady whoosh, whoosh, whoosh of water stirring. *Whoosh, whoosh, whoosh, whoosh.* She knew that rhythm: someone was swimming laps in the pool. Her neighbor was a swimmer. It reminded her that she was a runner now—she would have to explore and find herself a route.

The trek was worth her while, for the sunrise was stunning. She reached the crest of a little hill in the fragrant pasture while the horizon was still a vibrant orange. Moment by moment she watched its intensity fade as the sky grew lighter. Then, like a bulging dome of molten gold, the sun emerged over the edge of the world, fiery and alive. Contentedly she lingered, soaking in the lovely sight, listening to the jubilant birds as the landscape brightened with the lustrous glow of sunshine on the morning dew.

It was a nice house, she surmised on her way back, pausing to view her abode from afar. A simple house and by far the oldest home in the neighborhood, but it was still a nice house. More than adequate for her, certainly. It needed work, but improvements could be made—she would simply have to figure out how. *People do this,* she reminded herself. People remodeled kitchens. Elderly cat ladies who lived alone ordered new furniture and put new flooring in their homes. This wasn't impossible! She hoped she could stay. She wanted to stay.

Given her limited funds, she supposed that it would be smart to make an overall plan for her proposed improvements with a rough estimate of cost, which she would then weigh against the amount Grandpa Ed had left her. It had seemed like a lot initially, but now understanding the need, she wasn't sure. Furnishings, flooring, repairs, appliances, new cabinetry, labor and delivery costs—all were over her head! Nevertheless, her grandfather was her hero for his considerate provision. If he were there, she'd hug him—and then ask him for help.

Help. She sighed. That was the big question. With Marty out of the picture, she'd have to figure this out herself. Even simple things seemed daunting—like how to get that ginormous mattress and dowdy furniture out of the house into her soon-to-be-delivered dumpster. Her dad's offer crossed her mind, and she laughed out loud. Right! Her mother would absolutely turn inside out if her dad had anything to do with the Richmond house! Plus, there was their Anchor Church weirdness now. Calling *him* was as likely as calling Jake DeSoto himself to do it!

She glanced over at Marty's rooftop peeking over the west hedge. Her best scenario was for him to come over and apologize so they could return to Plan A. To maybe even hear him say he was glad to see her. She could only hope that he felt a little remorse for his behavior last night.

"God, it would really help if you could fix things with Marty," she murmured, then caught herself. *Praying* again! She shot an accusing glance at the climbing tree, knowing it was likely residue from her past being stirred up. That coupled with her constant thoughts of her grandparents had probably brought it forth. *It'll pass*, she told herself, although it was hard to escape the sense that God was near.

Reminded of her religious serenade the previous evening, she turned to observe her neighbor's backyard, wondering what the protocol was for meeting them. As a homeowner now, uncharted waters like this were all around her. Did she simply go to the door and knock? How intimidating could an elderly man and his daughter be?

Her eyes lingered on the roof of their brown-sided, story-and-a-half home. From where she stood, the hedge and a row of lilac bushes blocked her view of most of it—and the pool—but Leah's gaze was drawn to a small, rustic-looking cabin with a tiny porch in the far back of their yard. Hemmed in by the hedge, lilacs, and a sizable shed to the east, it was a quaint hideaway, open only to the pasture. The single guy's digs, she mused. The *hot* single guy, according to Brindle. Leah bet he was the singer and probably the swimmer too, who by the sound of it, she noted, was out of the pool.

Drawing in a full breath of fresh air, Leah turned for home at an invigorating pace. Of primary importance this morning was sanitizing her main living area. She could deal with old appliances, cupboards, and flooring—heck, she'd gone tent camping with the DeSoto family plenty of times, and this was more than a step up from that—but she could not handle grime. Regardless of its condition, that room was going to be *clean* until it was gutted and replaced.

Then with tenting on the brain, her thoughts wandered to a camping excursion at a state park with the DeSotos years back, when at the completion of one of their meals, Jake's older brother, Danny, had simply licked off his camp silverware and tossed them back into the storage box. He was teasing her, of course, baiting her for a reaction—and it worked, as she flipped out on the spot, horrified at what he'd done. He laughed with delight, and then in typical Danny fashion washed *all* the pieces to assure her they were clean. She smiled at the memory. He had always been so nice. They all had.

Leah groaned. She was thinking about them again!

Conquering the kitchen turned out to be an arduous task, with scrubbing everything mercilessly from top to bottom and scouring out the stove and the refrigerator. Upon completion, she had a pile of dead rags and had used up every one of the paper towels, but it was gratifying to have completed a task. She let out a long breath and wiped her brow. The room didn't exactly sparkle, but it had the bleachy-lemony smell of clean, and she felt a lot better about cooking and eating there. The only thing that would improve it at this point—besides having an entirely new kitchen itself—would be enjoying her momentary conquest with a satisfying cup of joe.

Mournfully she gazed at her new coffee maker on the counter. There was *no way* she was going to drink coffee made with the water coming out of those pipes, so until she made her next trip to town, there'd be no morning coffee for her. She supposed she could live without it for one day, but probably not for two. She upped her water quantity on her shopping list, then wrote "box fan" underneath, putting a star beside it. It would have a dual purpose, both circulating the air and covering the sound of her human and avian serenaders.

While at the peninsula, Leah started jotting down ideas for the house. Before long she was sitting at her card table with her feet up on the other chair in a brainstorming session. Turning her legal pad sideways, she took her pen and made four columns. In the first she listed tasks she could do—or learn to do—herself. Over the second column she wrote "hire out," listing her garage door, the kitchen, and the rusty water issue. The next column was for bigger items she'd have to purchase—appliances, furniture. The last column was for tallying estimated and actual costs.

If Grandpa Ed's renovation fund were not sufficient, she'd probably have to beg her mother for a loan—*beg* being the key word there, as her mother could be stubborn and had already warned her that *not one stinkin' dime* of hers would go toward the Richmond house. She wouldn't forget her promise—Leah was sure of it. But if it got to that, she would figure out something. It wasn't like her mom didn't have money now; it was merely a matter of how to shake it out of her.

Methodically Leah went through her pages, adding in items, making notes, using separate pages for the different areas of the house. Out of habit she reached up to pull her hair off her neck but felt nothing but the clipped ends of her bob. She still wasn't used to it.

Turning her focus back to the legal pad, she decided her first course of action should be to find a home improvement store where she could ask questions. At the top of her list of things to buy there was a hefty lawn mower, but she couldn't think of any possible way she could transport it home, and borrowing Marty's truck seemed out of the question now. She supposed she'd have to pay for a delivery service. Gazing unseeing at the floral wallpaper, she wondered how the elderly cat lady would do it; then she smiled, imagining herself using her womanly charms at the home improvement store to befriend some old duffer with a truck.

"Okay, God," she said flippantly, "if you wanna help me out, I could really use a handyman with a pickup. It'd be fantastic if you could arrange that for me!"

She gave an amused chuckle, then dropped her hand onto the table. Good grief! There she was—praying *again,* slipping right back into her old ways! She glanced at the dining room window with a shiver. It was as though God had invaded her home through the screen last night!

She threw up her hands. "Well, since we're on a roll, I may as well add some comfortable furniture to that list!" She felt a little guilty being smart-alecky with God, especially since she wasn't ready to get furniture until her floors were finished anyway, but her new folding chairs had almost no padding and her bottom felt it. She shifted uncomfortably on the chair.

The doorbell rang.

Brindle was there, done up with flawless makeup and lipstick, her thick hair pulled up in a loose knot so that the hot pink ends swirled together at the top of her head. She was wearing black slacks and a crisp white shirt unbuttoned one button too low, and in each finely manicured hand was a large to-go cup.

"Morning, Ava! Glad to see you didn't get axe-murdered in your sleep!" She handed off one of the coffees and stepped inside without invitation.

Leah stared at the paper cup in grateful awe as Brindle passed. A hot, amazing latte, right in her hand! "Uh, thank you! Please—come in! And yes, I'm very much alive."

"Just being neighborly," Brindle said. "And trying to atone for yesterday's awkward meeting—golly, that was *so* bad! Thanks for even allowing me in your house!"

"Well, of course! You didn't have to do this." Leah indicated the coffee, then gave a curious look toward the driveway. "I didn't hear you drive up. Where's your car?"

"Oh, I walked." She smiled, then glanced around, motioning with her coffee to the huge sectional across the room. "I see you're starting to get set up."

Leah's eyes widened. "What? No, that furniture's not mine! It was here, and it's going to the dumpster! Along with this carpet."

"Ah, I was wondering! It's a little on the dumpy side, I'd say. Maybe more than a little! But hey—I can't stay long 'cause I'm on my way to work, so how about a quick tour?" She craned her neck to see beyond Leah into the dining room. "I'd love to see what we're in for with this place!"

What *we're* in for. Leah's boundary alarms were ringing again.

"Look—I told you I was willing to help you with whatever you need around here," the girl continued, as if reading her thoughts, "and by the looks of it, you're going to ask me fairly soon anyway. So don't be shy about it!" She winked.

Caution, caution! hollered one part of Leah's mind. Brindle's forwardness had overtones of Rachel's bold and outgoing manner when they had met. Then immediately Leah heard Pam chime out from her beige armchair in her office—*You're going to step out of your cave and make friends! You're not going to be afraid of people who are different from you!* Leah blinked, regarding the assertive girl before her with her hibiscus tattooed arm and her perfect long nails gripping the cup.

She brought you a coffee! Pam's voice scolded mildly. *Why won't you let her help you? Don't you want help?*

With a decisive nod Leah plunged out of her comfort zone. "Okay then, one blitz tour coming up! But I'll warn you—the place needs work. Some parts are a bit trashed, so don't judge me."

"Hey, nothing can be as ghetto as that crater in your garage door out there!" Brindle gave a hoot of a laugh, then bumped her on the arm. "I'm kidding, I'm *kidding*! But seriously—it's *bad*! It needs to be fixed! So come on, girl—show me your place!" She charged forward into the dining room ahead of Leah, who took a breath and followed.

In a systematic but streamlined fashion, Leah took her from one end of the house to the other, starting with the area behind the kitchen first, quickly showing her the spacious utility room and bathroom opposite each other by the back door. After a brief glance into the garage, they passed by way of the kitchen through the dining room to the hallway, where they peeked into each of the bedrooms.

Brindle nodded approvingly. "Nice. Roomy." She crossed the room to yank open a closet door in one of the smaller rooms, gazing upward at the items packed tightly on the top shelf. "Lots of space in here too. Whose stuff is all this? It can't be yours."

"I'm not sure," Leah said, a little surprised at Brindle's action. "Probably my grandparents' or a previous renter's, maybe."

"Huh." Brindle nodded, studying the boxes.

"Like I said," Leah continued, from the doorway, "the house needs some work."

"Hey, if I owned a house, I wouldn't complain even if it *were* completely ghetto!"

"I'm not complaining," Leah said lightly, waiting for her to follow.

Brindle shut the closet and joined her in the hall. Extracting her phone from her bra, she checked the time before shoving it back in. "So what're you doing today?"

"I'm still figuring that out," Leah answered, moving to the dining room. "Right now I have more questions than plans, so probably nothing too exciting. Getting Internet set up—that sort of thing. I'm running to town soon for a few odds and ends, and while I'm there I'll try to get some leads on redoing my kitchen. That type of stuff. I'm not exactly sure where to start."

"I see." Brindle's eyes dropped to scrutinize her inflatable bed.

"I'm waiting on furniture," Leah blurted a little too loudly. "Right now I'm focused on getting a lawn mower."

The girl nodded, turning toward her. "Good idea! Seriously, the yard makes the place look deserted!" Her fingers popped over her mouth. "Oops—did I say that? Sorry. It does, though. I don't know how you can even sleep here! It looks—it looks—" She scrunched her nose, letting Leah fill in the blank.

"I know. I'm working on that. I was hoping to borrow a riding mower from my cousin next door, but—" She stopped, feeling uncomfortable to reveal her awkward conversation with Marty.

"But—?" Brindle's brow rose. "Mr. Wild and Wonderful won't let you borrow his lawn mower? That's not very neighborly of him!"

"It's complicated."

She shrugged. "Well, that's probably something everyone should own anyway, don't you think?"

Leah nodded. "I suppose you're right. So that's one of my goals for the day. But I only have my little car. I'm not sure how I'll get it to the house!"

The girl's eyes twinkled deviously. "Here's an idea—go stand out in the road in your underwear and offer your body to the first man who comes along with a truck!"

Leah shot her a look, then gave a spurt of laughter at the ridiculous image.

Brindle tipped her head in delight. "So, you *do* have a sense of humor! I was beginning to wonder!"

Leah started to protest, but the other girl continued abruptly, "Anyway, I need to get going. I may stop back later this afternoon." She started for the door.

"Okay. Maybe see you then. Thanks again for the coffee, Brindle."

She turned and smiled. "No problem—*Ava*." She waggled her fingers. "Too-de-loo!"

No sense of humor? Leah watched as Brindle crunched down the gravel driveway on her way home. Is *that* how she came across—as humorless and lame? She did too have a sense of humor! At least she *used* to—before it had gotten sucked out of her.

She took a drink of her coffee, hearing Pam's whisper again: *You're going to step out of your cave . . .* Leah sighed, reminded that "trust issues" were simply code for "fear." What was so threatening about Brindle? Okay, she was animated and bold—but wasn't she also nice and eager to help? Leah looked down at the disposable cup in her hand. The coffee had been a nice gesture. It probably wouldn't hurt to loosen up a bit. She popped the lid off and downed her last swig, then went to double-check her list for town.

Filterless. The word came to her as she slid the legal pad to the corner to neaten the card table. Brindle had no filter—that's what bothered her. Brindle spoke her mind, and she'd have to get used to that. Absently she fiddled with her pen, centering it on the binding of the pad, as was her quirky habit. And so bold! Yikes, who snoops in someone's closet like that? And to chide her about the house! *If I owned a house, I wouldn't complain even if it were completely ghetto!* Ghetto? Ouch! And did she think Leah was complaining? Plus, how did she know she *owned* her house and wasn't just renting? Her thoughts were interrupted by her doorbell again.

This time it was a woman in a salmon-colored blouse on her porch holding a small crockpot with both hands. She was older—maybe sixty-ish, give or take a few years—with kind brown eyes, lovely skin, and long, thick brown hair.

"Hi. I'm Jackie Burke from next door," she announced with a warm smile, tipping her head toward the sunrise hedge. "Just stopping by to introduce myself. I know moving's a chore, so here—I made you a meal." A small spray of arborvitae dangled out from her hair on one side.

"Oh, thank you! That's so nice! I'm Le—um, Ava. Ava Labanora." Problem solved. The neighbors had come to her!

"Ava—so nice to meet you! Welcome to the neighborhood!"

Leah reached for the crockpot. "Here—let me take that. Really, this is so nice of you!"

"Oh, it's nothing fancy," Jackie Burke replied, handing off the appliance and now propping the screen door open for Leah, who stood holding it. "It's a simple chicken-and-rice dish that we make for our church retreats. I hope you like it. I just assembled it, so plug it in, and it'll be ready in about three hours. A little longer is okay too."

"Thank you!" Leah repeated, then added, "Excuse me while I go set this down. Would you like to come in?"

"Only for a minute. I know you must be terribly busy."

Leah plugged the crockpot in on the peninsula and returned to the door where the woman stood.

"I live next door with my dad, Warren Glende," she explained, gesturing again. "He's eighty-two and needs a little help. My mom passed away last October, and since then my sister Susan has been stopping in to look after him. Susan Gordon from town here—perhaps you know her? Anyway, it's been too much to run over here all the time with her big family and cleaning business and all. I moved up here in February to stay with him, so I'm still new to the neighborhood myself. Although I *did* grow up in New Hampton. But I've been away for several years."

Leah nodded. "I see."

"And you're renting, I presume—? Did you grow up here in New Hampton too?"

"Actually, no. I, um"—it felt strange to say it—"I inherited the place. This was my grandparents' house. I just moved down from Bridgewater yesterday."

The woman's face brightened. "Is that so? That's wonderful! My dad talks so fondly of your grandparents! I've heard they were a wonderful couple, but I'd never met them myself." She made a sound through her teeth as she shook her head. "I heard they both passed away in an accident—I'm so sorry!"

"Thank you."

"Dad said they were his dear friends for years and years—ever since he bought our lot from them. He was so sad when they passed." She paused, studying her face. "He'll be delighted to meet you!"

Leah returned her smile.

"Well, hey," Jackie continued, "I won't keep you, but before I go, I want to give you this." She pulled an envelope out of her back pocket and handed it to her. "It's an invitation to a party we're having this Saturday afternoon."

"Oh?" Leah opened it and examined the card.

"Oh, yes! Every summer for I-don't-know-how-long my mom and dad have thrown this big neighborhood party. They invite everyone from all around here, and it's quite an event! Most everyone comes, and it's so fun. This is Dad's first year without Mom, so I'm stepping in to help. I know it's only a two-day notice for you, but I hope you can make it. It'd be a great opportunity for you to meet some people."

"Oh. Well, thank you. I'm not sure—"

"No pressure, no pressure!" Jackie's hands went up as she shook her head. "Don't worry if you can't make it! We'll have you over some other time so that you can meet Brother Warren. And soon, I promise!"

"Brother Warren?" Leah echoed.

"Sorry—I should have explained. That's what people call my dad. He's a retired minister—although he'd cringe if he heard me use the word 'retired'! He doesn't believe in it!"

"Ah." Retired minister. Late-night worship. Leah connected the dots.

"Yes, he's still very active for his age," she added, "traveling and speaking at area churches once or twice a month. You'll definitely want to meet him—he's very sweet! And he's writing a book—although he's mostly just talking, and the young man who's staying with us is doing all the work of writing. He's the one in the little cottage in the back." She looked toward the ceiling. "But I'm rambling! Seriously, I should go and let you get back to what you were doing."

"No, that's okay," Leah said. "Am I supposed to bring anything? To the party. If I can make it."

She shook her head. "Only if you want to. Some people like to bring a dish to pass. Or a pan of bars or something. But don't feel like you must. Just bring yourself!"

Leah nodded. "Okay—thanks for the invitation." She hesitated a moment, then smiled. "Sorry, but you, um—you have something in your hair. A leaf. Or something." She pointed to the sprig.

"Do I?" She pulled it off and let out a laugh. "Goodness—I'm wearing the hedge! Golly, what else is in there?" She ran a hand over her head. "The path between our houses is so overgrown. It hasn't been trimmed in years! I'll have to see if we can fix that. Anyway, it's time for me to get back. Welcome to the neighborhood, Ava! Come on over if you need to borrow anything—a cup of sugar, eggs, you know, that sort of thing. Or to hang out. Our door is always open!" She smiled and turned to go.

Leah went out on the porch to see her off. "Thank you. Nice to meet you too. And thanks again for the meal."

Jackie waved goodbye, and Leah watched her cross the pathetic lawn to somehow fight her way through the bushy hedge between their yards.

There was something so appealing to Leah about an older woman like that. Far beyond her outward beauty of lovely skin and hair, Jackie was a *lady*, and Leah couldn't help but note her similarities to her almost-mother-in-law, Evelyn, who'd been so gracious like that too. Jackie had a few more years on Evelyn perhaps, but she carried herself with the same air of confidence and spoke with the same manner of kindness as Evelyn had, qualities Leah had always admired in her. Her eyes dropped to the floor of the porch as she recalled one of her first heart-to-heart encounters with Evelyn DeSoto, that first fall after camp when she was sixteen and had just gotten to know them.

Leah's mother had gone away on one of her personal retreats for the weekend, as was her custom to do so fairly often—maybe once a month or so. Braydon was staying the weekend with a friend, and it was Leah's weekend at her dad's—back when she was still dutifully going there. She had slept over Friday night, and in the morning while Chelsea was serving up everyone's eggs for breakfast, Leah made the big mistake of mentioning to her father that her mom was away, taking a weekend to herself.

In hindsight, she kicked herself—hadn't she learned never to bring up the subject of her mother around him? And vice versa. His reaction was as if she'd poured two highly combustible elements together in a chem lab beaker. He swung his head toward her. "Right—a weekend to *herself*," he snapped, nodding sarcastically. Then he slammed down his coffee mug and pushed back from the table. Snatching up his breakfast, he walked over and chucked it—eggs, toast, plate, silverware, and all—right into the kitchen trash and abruptly left the room.

"David!" Chelsea cried after him in astonishment, the gallon of milk in her hand suspended in mid-air.

Leah couldn't breathe. All the kids around the table—her three step-siblings—stared at her, and the youngest began to cry. Chelsea couldn't speak either. She turned to Leah with a look of bewilderment.

Leah shook her head, clueless as to what had set him off. "I just—I—I'm sorry!" She wanted to throw up. Throw up or die.

"What in the world?" Chelsea plopped the jug onto the table. "Can you watch these guys? I'll be right back!"

Before she returned, Leah had thrown away her own uneaten food and retrieved her dad's plate and silverware from the garbage and put them in the sink. Then she collected her things and told Chelsea that she had to go to play practice and that she'd also made previous plans to spend the coming night with a girlfriend. Neither were true, but she couldn't stay there, even if Chelsea insisted that her dad's outburst had nothing to do with her. Her dad had never done anything like that before, but it didn't matter. Once was enough.

As it was still quite early that morning, Leah meandered around town in her car, trying to process what had happened. The way her dad had walked out of the room had cut her deeply, but there was no one to talk to about it. For sure not her mother!

On impulse she drove up the DeSotos' street and parked a few doors down from their house. Just a few days earlier that week, the youth group at Anchor had met there for a worship and game night, and Jake's mom had put out the offer for any of the girls to call or come over at any time if they ever needed to chat. Leah turned her car off and eyed their house through the rear-view mirror. Should she do it? It was still rather early to go to their door. And what would she even say? Letting out a deep breath, she leaned her head back to think.

Tap, tap, tap. "Hey, Leah! What are you doing here?"

Leah jumped, looking over to see Evelyn DeSoto rapping her knuckles against the window. She was standing on the grassy boulevard, leaning down to look in.

Leah turned the key to lower the window. "Oh, hi, Evelyn!"

"What're you doing out here?" she repeated. "Danny just got home from college for the weekend and recognized your car."

Leah put on her best smile. "Oh, that's cool! I was just, um—killing some time before my play practice this morning. I was early."

Evelyn raised her head. "I see. Mind if I join you?"

Before Leah could answer, she opened the car door and got in. It was then that Leah noticed Evelyn's teal jacket was actually a velour bathrobe—and she was wearing fuzzy slippers! Evelyn noticed Leah's surprise and laughed at herself. "I know! I must look like the neighborhood crazy lady—that's why I wanted to quickly get in! But I have time to hang out. I'll keep you company until you have to leave."

Of course, it didn't take long for Evelyn to draw it out of her, and Leah readily spilled. Evelyn was a good listener, waiting patiently through Leah's long and difficult struggle to tell her what had happened with her dad and how hurt she had been by her parents' long and relentless feud. Somewhere in the conversation Evelyn reached over and took Leah's hand. She simply held her hand and listened.

"You remind me of my grandma," Leah told her toward the end of their talk.

"I'll take that as a compliment," Evelyn replied. "So, hey—normally I wouldn't do this, but what would you think of skipping your play practice today and coming in to have breakfast with us? Rocke's cooking, and we'd love to have you!"

Leah felt her cheeks grow warm. "I don't have play practice this morning. I'm not even in a play. Sorry. I wasn't being honest."

"Ah, I see." The older woman gave a knowing smile. "So does that mean 'yes'?"

Embarrassed, Leah nodded. "Okay."

Rocke had delayed making their eggs and sausage until his wife's return, and soon they were all seated at the table, where he prayed, and the food was passed around. Leah eyed a plate of four luscious-looking sweet rolls in the center of the table, conscious that there were now five people sharing the meal.

"Why do you always get *your* favorites?" Jake asked Danny, helping himself to a frosted jelly-filled roll. "You never get the kind I like."

"Danny picked these up on his way home," Evelyn explained to Leah.

"*You* could do the donut run," Danny jabbed back playfully, "but that'd mean you'd have to drag your lazy butt out of bed before *ten!*" He held the plate out to Leah. "Here you go—help yourself."

Shyly she shook her head. "No, that's okay—"

"No, go ahead!" he urged. "I've already had mine."

"You have *not!*" Jake said, pausing with the pastry before his mouth.

"I did so! I—ate it in the car." Danny turned back, nodding again for Leah to take one.

As she did, Jake looked at her with a devious grin, his sandy bangs slanting down on one side of his forehead. "Hey, Leah—watch this!" Opening wide, he began to stuff the entire roll into his mouth.

Leah snickered, covering her mouth with her hand.

"*Jake!*" Evelyn exclaimed. "Honestly!" She shook her head, and Rocke frowned.

"Your manners, young man! There are ladies present!"

"Exactly," Danny said dryly.

Evelyn turned back to Leah. "Sorry about that. Do you have plans for the day? I'm making cookies for a bake sale tomorrow after church. Want to help me?"

"That'd be great!" Leah replied. With her mom gone, she had the whole weekend to herself.

"Awesome!" Evelyn said warmly. "I'd enjoy having you with me."

Now from where she stood on the porch, Leah's thoughts of Evelyn were interrupted by the ringing of her cell phone inside the house. Her mom. She was wondering when she'd start calling again. She hurried in, bracing herself for the conversation.

"Hi, Mom."

"Don't 'Hi, Mom' me!" her mother growled. "What's going on? I called you at least six times yesterday! Do you hear me? *Six!* Why didn't you answer? I was worried *sick* about you! I almost drove down there!"

Worried? Uh, probably not. Furious? Definitely! Although Leah couldn't exactly fault her mother's anger. After all, she *had* blown off answering her six times.

"Yeah—sorry, Mom. Thanks for calling."

"Why were you ignoring my calls?"

"I wasn't ignoring you! I couldn't answer when you called. I was driving."

"Not all day! You were *ignoring* me—admit it!"

"It might have been my service," Leah said, feigning confusion. "Maybe my phone was updating or something, I don't know. It seems fine today. Anyway, how's it going?" She hated lying like that, but she didn't know what else to say. Feeling guilty seemed a better option than telling her the truth.

"What do you mean, 'How's it going?' I want to hear about the house!"

"The house is good!"

Her mom made an impatient sound. "No—how's it look?"

"The house looks fine, Mom!"

"Is it trashed?"

Leah paused beside the counter. She knew it would be like this! That was why she had put off the call. Through the window she noticed that the little white dog was back. Snowball? Snowflake? Ivory?

"No, it's not trashed. I mean, it needs a little work here and there— mostly cleaning and painting and stuff. And new carpet. But it's okay. Mostly what I expected."

"So what've you been doing then?"

"Oh, just stuff. Odds and ends."

"Like what? Talk to me, Leah!"

"I've barely gotten here! Just getting set up, mostly." Leah turned from the window to face the kitchen. Her eyes dropped to the floor of the back hallway. "I've been cleaning some. And meeting some of the neighbors."

"Like whom?"

Midnight, Snowball, her mind listed, *the little boy in the climbing tree.* "Well, there's this girl my age who lives across the street who came over to meet me. She's nice. And an older gal named Jackie—a neighbor to the east."

"Jackie? Huh. I don't know her. Have you talked to Marty? I'm selling the house, you know."

"Yes, I talked to him, and yes, I heard that! He's pretty upset about it, Mom!"

She huffed. "Well, I don't know why he'd be upset! He's getting quite a deal, you know—fifty percent off market value! It's like I'm practically giving it to him!"

"Well, it's a terrible time for him right now. Did you know he just got divorced?"

"How should I know that?"

"Well, he did! And it's not a good time for him right now."

"There's never a good time for that, Leah. But it is what it is."

Leah rolled her eyes. "It sounds like he's really struggling—"

"Lots of people get divorced, you know. I've been there. He just needs to deal with it."

Leah turned in agitation. "For heaven's sake, Mom—don't make him lose his own home on top of everything else!"

"Oh, come now, Leah! It's hardly ever as bad as people carry on about! He's a grown man—I highly doubt he needs you to stand up for him. If he wants the house, he'll figure it out somehow."

Leah held her tongue.

"Hello? Are you still there? Don't you hang up on me!"

"I'm still here." Out of the corner of her eye, Leah noticed a movement and turned to see a large truck lumbering down her driveway. Who would have ever thought she'd give a cheer for a dumpster? Just in time. "I don't think you're doing the right thing, Mom. I think you should give Marty more time." Her mother started to reply, but she cut her off. "—But hey, someone just pulled into the driveway, and I need to go."

"Who it is?" she asked.

"Um—"

"Is it Marty?"

Leah blinked. "No. It's not. It's my trash service, and they'll be at my door in a minute. We'll talk later, okay? Say hi to Braydon."

Within minutes the dumpster was set in place near the side of the driveway, and Leah was on her way to town.

Chapter Eight

On her way home from New Hampton that afternoon, Leah was signaling to turn left into her driveway after the neighbor's stylish brown house—her new landmark—when she suddenly noticed that her mailbox was broken. She eyed it curiously as she pulled in, observing the black metal box tipped oddly downward at a near forty-five-degree angle. Whatever had damaged it had occurred since last night, for it had been fine when Leah had checked it last evening—after Brindle's guilty confession of snooping in it. Her paycheck from the accounting firm had been there. Had it been like that this morning though? She hadn't noticed anything, but then she hadn't thought to look. She frowned, parking her car to get a closer view.

As she touched the opening, the door flopped down loosely, and a few pieces of mail slid out. Quickly she snatched them up before they blew away—a pizza flyer, a car dealership advertisement, and a hunting gear catalog addressed to her grandpa. She shut it, tapping the loose door a few times to ensure it would hold, then looked around in the weedy ditch for any other items that may have previously escaped. Tucking the mail up under her arm, Leah lifted the box to level it on the pole, bending down to examine what had caused it to droop. That was the exact position she was in when a black pickup truck came barreling down on her.

Leah was certain she'd been well off the road, but the driver must have been distracted, not seeing her until the last second. Or maybe she startled him—perhaps it looked like she was about to cross the street or something—for he suddenly swerved the truck wildly out toward the center of the road and locked up his brakes, skidding to a halt at an odd angle in the middle of the road. Simultaneously, Leah flinched at the oncoming vehicle, recoiling further onto the shoulder, only to lose her footing and half-stumble into the ditch, the mailbox jerking noisily back to its original position. When everything was quiet, she pulled herself out of the weeds, craning to see the driver of the truck, who was also straining to see *her* through his passenger's window, shaking his head as if she were some sort of dolt. He moved the vehicle to the side of the road.

"Sorry!" she called lightly as he climbed out of his truck. "I didn't mean—"

The slam of his door cut her off. Determinedly he cut across the street toward her, an irritated scowl on his face. She swallowed, backing a step.

"What the *heck* were you doing?" he snapped. "I could have plowed right into you! Don't ever do that again! I didn't even *see* you—not until I was right on you!" He was thirty-ish maybe, wearing a camouflage shirt that looked a size too small on his intimidating frame, and his hands flung wildly as he talked.

"I wasn't even on the road! I was *way* over here!" Leah shot back defensively, pointing toward her mailbox. In midstream it struck her that she ought to be *de*-escalating the situation instead—after all, why would he have reacted so if he'd thought otherwise?

"You just popped up out of nowhere!"

"Yeah, yeah. I'm sorry—I really am! I thought I was far enough over! Truly!"

"You *thought*! Crap, I totally didn't see you! You were like a deer springing out of nowhere! I could have smoked you with my truck!"

Meekly she raised her hands. "I'm sorry! I wasn't trying to cause an accident. I swear!"

He looked away, as though getting a grip. "Okay. Just—just give me a second." Then as if really seeing her, he added, "Are you all right? You're not hurt?"

Leah shook her head. "I'm completely fine. And I'm sorry I scared you. I really am!"

He gave a nervous laugh, his brow softening a bit. "Okay—okay. I'm sorry! Holy buckets, you scared me! It would have been my worst nightmare to hit you!"

Her shoulders rose. "Mine too! And you kinda freaked me out as well!"

A brief silence passed between them, then he gave another laugh, visibly relaxing. "I suppose I did! Maybe I overreacted. I'm only glad I didn't ditch my truck! Do you mind telling me what you were doing out here?"

Leah gestured to the pathetic mailbox. "Just trying to figure that out.

And I thought I was well on the shoulder!"

Curiously, he surveyed the broken box. "Huh. What's going on here?"

"I have no idea! I was just coming home from town and found it like this."

"Well, let's take a look." The man bent down, then dropped to one knee to examine the mailbox from below. Righting himself, he stuck his hand underneath, then tipped his head to look again.

As Leah observed his muscular frame, her mind flashed to Brindle's summary of the neighborhood guys and deduced that this must be either her "suave and studly" candidate or the swimmer next door—although if it were the latter, he was also likely the singer, and she wasn't sure the song selection last night fit this guy. But whichever one he was, Brindle wasn't kidding—holy cow, was he hot!

"Okay, I see our problem. It's missing a bolt. There's a support bar here, and the bolt holding it together is gone." He pulled back, his tan work boot sliding across the gravel as he searched the ground. With a grunt he reached for a small piece of metal and held it up between his fingers. "Here we go! Now we gotta find the nut. It's gotta be here somewhere. And probably a washer too."

"Okay," Leah said, joining him in the search, though half-heartedly, for the ditch was terribly overgrown.

In less than a minute he snatched the tiny nut from the gravel and held it up victoriously. "Got it!" Then his expression changed as he fiddled with the two pieces in his hand.

Leah peered over to see what he was looking at.

He gestured, holding them out. "Look—it's the right nut, but it doesn't turn on here very easily. I should be able to tighten this right up."

"And—?"

"Well, that couldn't have just fallen off. I'd say this was removed by a person with a wrench." He turned to look at her, his blond hair light against his flushed face.

She returned his gaze blankly.

Wordlessly he righted the mailbox and threaded the bolt through the hole. He shook his head when he tried to screw on the nut. "Yeah, that definitely didn't just fall off. That took a wrench and some muscle."

"What are you saying?"

"Look," he said. "See this? There's rust on here where the nut sat before. That's normal. But see this?" He pointed. "These tiny scrapes on the edge of the nut—that's where a wrench was used. Those are fresh. And here too." He pointed to another spot, then tried to twist on the nut again. "Anybody got an ax to grind with you?"

"What?"

He faced her squarely. "I'd say someone was messing with your mailbox."

Leah straightened. "What? Why?"

He laughed. "Beats me! I'm just telling you what I see."

"Are you sure it's not just worn out?" She looked back at the mailbox.

He shrugged. "It's old, but I'd say it's extremely unlikely for this to happen by itself."

Leah didn't know what to say.

"Well, I wouldn't get too worried about it. And I've got my tools in the truck, so lucky you. I'll be right back!"

Leah frowned as he left to rummage in the back of his truck. Why would someone do that? Who even knew her here? Had she been pranked? After hearing the clatter of an unseen toolbox, she watched her rescuer saunter back with a crescent wrench, looking pleased to save the day. With a few cranks he completed his mission.

"Good as new!" he said, extending his hand with a smile. "Phil Crawford."

She returned the handshake, noting his bluish gray eyes. "Ava. Ava Labanora."

"You're new—just moved in, I see." He nodded toward her house, which suddenly made her ultra-conscious of her pocked garage door and rebellious lawn.

"Yesterday, as a matter of fact. So the place isn't actually abandoned anymore—it only *looks* like it!"

He grinned. "Well, one thing at a time! I'm in one of the townhouses a few blocks over. If you want, I could see who the association has do their lawn care. Maybe they could help you out."

"Lord knows I need it, but hopefully I won't have to take you up on that offer! I just bought a lawn mower in town this afternoon—a nice one. Delivery is scheduled for next week."

"Delivery?"

"As hard as I tried, I couldn't make it fit in there!" Leah waved to her car.

Phil looked at her vehicle for a moment, then back at her, his mouth curling into a smile. "Well, I might have a solution for that too. I happen to know a guy with a truck!" He shifted his weight, folding his arms.

"What—*you*?" Leah's eyes flicked to the truck and back to him. "I'd never take advantage of someone after meeting them so soon."

"Yeah?" His eyes twinkled. "Well, I think I'm pretty eager to be taken advantage of—unless I'm going to get the snot beat out of me by someone." He glanced over her shoulder to the house.

What a flirt he was! She wished she could keep herself from blushing. "I didn't mean it that way," she said, then added with a shake of her head, "but there's no one." It was a foolish admission, she realized after the fact.

"Well, then? I've got time right now if you want to go get it. Plus, I probably owe you for yelling at you like I did. I overreacted, and I'm sorry."

"Owe *me*?" She shook her head. "No, if anything, I owe *you*!"

"Right—so hop in then!" He smiled and nodded toward the truck. "Save yourself some money and time!"

Leah hesitated, rubbing her arm as she eyed him. This was stupid. She knew nothing about him. Absolutely nothing. This could be very foolish.

He spread his hands. "Do I look dangerous? Fine—call your mom or friend or whoever. Send them a picture of my driver's license—whatever you want. I'm okay with that. Or if you don't want to go, I'm okay with that too. But if you're feeling daring, we could have a lawn mower sitting in your driveway in less than an hour."

Looks could be deceiving. But he was a neighbor. And what were the odds of meeting someone with a truck on a day that she could really use one?

"I don't think it would take very long."

He lifted his arm. "Then let's do it!"

She gave him a timid smile. "Okay then."

It was like a dream come true—or like a prayer answered, Leah admitted a bit sheepishly, considering that a guy with a truck was what she had asked God for. Quickly she moved her own car to her driveway, and then the two of them headed back to town.

A few hours later they returned with not only a lawn mower, but with the back of the pickup stacked high and puzzled tightly with beautiful brand-new patio furniture that she had found on sale. In addition, four Boston ferns that Leah had found on clearance in the parking lot greenhouse were tucked on the back seat, chosen over the fuchsias, which had looked somewhat wind-tossed and scraggly. She hung the ferns on the hooks at the edge of the porch while Phil unlatched the straps that held everything securely in the pickup bed. Together they unloaded the truck piece by piece and assembled what needed to be put together. When finished, the furniture was arranged as she directed.

The small patio table and chairs went to the right of her front door, directly in front of the living room picture window, as Grandma Havi had always had hers. To the left of the front door, she unrolled the stylish jute rug on which she positioned a petite love seat and two matching armchairs opposite each another, complete with an ottoman in front of the chair farthest from the door. A coffee table and end table finished the set.

Pulling out two more large shopping bags from where they'd been shoved onto the floor of the backseat, Leah produced two colorful throw pillows for the chairs and a tall, decorative lantern for the end table, the latter of which came with a pack of size D batteries by which to power it. For the finishing touch, she unwrapped the cellophane from a shallow, multi-colored mosaic bowl, which she set on the center of the coffee table. With hands on her hips, she stood back to survey it all.

Phil shook his head, sipping his Coke. "Unbelievable! That looks fantastic!"

"Unbelievable is that we fit all of that in the back of your truck!"

"I had my doubts on that," he confessed. "But I could see you weren't gonna quit 'til it did."

"Now I *officially* owe you," she offered gratefully.

He raised the soda. "All I ask is that you stay off the road so you don't get smacked by a truck."

She smiled. "Deal! Would you care to sit down—now that everything's set up?"

He glanced at his watch. "Thanks for the offer. I'd like to, but I should keep moving. Maybe later when I swing by with gas for that mower."

"Gas!" Leah planted her palm on her face. "No, don't trouble yourself—I'll get that."

"It's no trouble! But I do need to head out." He started down the sidewalk and gestured toward the dumpster. "So what's with that? You having some work done inside?"

"I will be, yes. Just updating a few things."

"Yeah? Well, let me know if you need any help with that. I do a bit of handyman work on the side." He gave her a nod and turned for his vehicle.

Leah stared at his back. *For real?* "Uh, thanks—I will."

He paused with his truck door open. "If you don't mind my asking, what do you do for work? I mean, it can't be cheap buying a lot out here in a prime area like this." Then he shook his head. "Dang! You know what? Never mind! I'm an idiot! That's a personal question, and it's absolutely none of my business. I apologize!"

Leah smiled shyly. "No, that's all right. I don't mind. I'm an accountant. But I inherited the house, so that helps. And," she added candidly, "my grandfather left me a little stash for repairs and updating."

His brow rose. "Now *that's* helpful!"

"It is!" She decided to take a risk. "So, regarding handyman work—what sort of things do you do? Have you ever remodeled a kitchen?"

"As a matter of fact, I just finished one. Why do you ask?"

"Just wondering."

He gave a charming smile. "We'll talk."

She watched him leave until his truck rumbled away on the highway. Then she plopped herself down in the armchair nearest her. A handyman—with a truck! Could she get any luckier? This morning she'd left the house with nothing but a wish list, and now—she looked around, shaking her head in wonder—now after *one* day, here she was on new porch furniture with a new lawn mower sitting on her driveway! And not only had she met a handyman with a truck, but she had met *someone*. She could feel it. He was super nice and extremely helpful. Not to mention ripped. She waggled her head, smiling. Seriously, could she get any luckier?

The scuffling of Midnight's feet on the driveway alerted Leah of his presence before she could see him. A second later he bounded up the porch, depositing his slobbery jowls in her lap, his tail swinging wildly. She greeted him, directing his large head away, and with a surge of hope peered out to see if by chance her cousin was following.

He wasn't.

Resigned, she turned back to scratch the eager Labrador. Then with a final pat of his smooth coat, Leah pushed him away and stood, brushing his hair off her lap. She was hungry, and it was time to go in. She'd been gone since morning, and her car was still loaded with the goods she'd bought in town before Phil came along and fixed her mailbox. She frowned, hoping she hadn't left any cold food in there.

With her arms loaded, Leah unlocked the front door and pushed it open—only to be bowled over with the aroma of cooking food. *The crockpot!* Hastily she dropped her things in the kitchen and unplugged it, peering through the glass lid to check if Jackie Burke's chicken dish was burned, for she'd been gone much longer than its allotted cooking time. The edges were dark, and yet it seemed okay. But now, since she hadn't eaten since breakfast, the savory smell had her drooling. Hurriedly she retrieved the rest of her purchases from the car. Then she fixed herself a plate, and with a cold bottle of iced tea from the refrigerator, returned to enjoy her meal in her new outdoor room.

Wanting to face away from her unruly yard, Leah chose an armchair and put her feet up on the ottoman, surveying her fine furnishings. She was still amazed that in a matter of hours it had gone from bare to beautiful. Who would have thought that could happen? She knew her grandmother would have been delighted with her décor. Indeed, it exceeded her own expectations! The whole day had made her feel that even without Marty, everything was going to be okay. *I got this*, she told herself smugly.

Plus, she had met another neighbor—Phil Crawford. What incredible timing for him to show up like he had! And on top of that, here she was enjoying her supper in the company of a friend! She smiled down at Midnight, who panted contentedly beside her, his deep eyes gazing eagerly at her plate.

"Sit!" she commanded, and instantly his hind quarters dropped, his attention unwavering. "Good dog!" she praised, impressed, and he raised a paw, no doubt hoping for a treat. *Don't you dare start something*, she warned herself, resisting the urge to share her food.

The sunrise neighbors were having an early dinner too—or were about to, she guessed, hearing the clinking of dishes and movement of chairs out on their deck. She could now distinguish Jackie Burke's voice in the murmur of their conversation, and she heard that familiar laugh again—the same one she had heard yesterday. Was it one of her old high school teachers that it reminded her of? She wished she could recall, for she enjoyed the sound of it.

Savoring the overcooked yet delicious chicken dish, Leah reflected on how sweet it had been of Jackie to bring her the meal. The irony of church people living next door was crazy—after all her efforts to escape them in Bridgewater! And not just church people—a retired minister, no less! Given Brindle's hints and his song choice last evening, she didn't have to be a rocket scientist to figure out that the single guy in the cottage was also a Christian—but knowing it helped. If she ever met him, she'd be prepared. At least no one knew anything about her here. And now she had a box fan to block his singing.

On second thought, she supposed it was technically *possible* that the singer could have been Jackie's dad. But if that was so, he had a killer voice for being eighty-two, not to mention a nimble proficiency on guitar.

As if on cue, a voice next door suddenly rose in a clear melody, and another voice—or two, perhaps—joined in. Leah whirled toward the hedge, her fork paused in midair. She knew that song! She totally recognized it from camp when she was a teenager—one of the routine table prayers sung before meals there! Amazed, she listened to its completion, the cadence followed by a man in prayer. And then the talking and laughter resumed with the accompanying sounds of mealtime.

In milliseconds the song stirred up memories of the day she had met Rachel Steinburg on their first day at camp.

"Mind if I join you?"

Leah had been dying uncomfortable sitting by herself in the camp lodge dining room where everyone was gathering for camper orientation when she heard the voice. She looked up to see a pretty girl her own age with the thickest, curliest long hair she had ever seen standing with a backpack slung over one shoulder.

"Uh, sure," she said, scooting over a chair. "I'm Leah."

The girl blinked in surprise, then burst out a laugh. "Oh, my gosh—it's *destiny*! Hi, Leah—I'm Rachel!"

At the time Leah hadn't a clue what was funny or why it was suddenly "destiny." Even when the girl explained how their names were connected, she still didn't get it until Rachel went into a short explanation of the Bible story, and then, of course, Leah remembered the stories her grandma had read to her long ago. Before long they learned they were both from Bridgewater and attended the same high school too, although Rachel's family had moved there only a year previously, and they'd had differing class schedules. Furthermore, the two of them had been assigned to the same cabin for the week.

"Can you believe this?" Rachel exclaimed. "Put one here, camp sister! It was meant to be!" She raised her hand for a high five. "What church do you go to back home?"

Leah shrugged. "Nowhere. I don't go anywhere."

Rachel's brow crinkled. "Really? Then come to mine! I go to Anchor. Ouch—" She flinched suddenly, her hand reaching to the back of her neck. She twisted, looking briefly over her shoulder. Then it happened again. "Ouch!"

Leah nodded toward a cluster of teenage boys snickering at a nearby table. "It's those boys—they're throwing something at you."

Rachel turned, attempting to give the culprits a stern look, but it dissolved into a laugh and a wave. She turned back to Leah. "Those guys were all here last year. They're super great. The guy with the lighter hair is from home—the goofy one with the smirk on his face. He's my neighbor, and he goes to my church."

"He keeps looking over here!"

"Yeah, he's probably wondering who you are. His name's Jake."

Up at the front podium, the camp director's microphone screeched with feedback as he rallied the room's attention.

Rachel touched her arm, lowering her voice as the din in the room began to diminish. "The dark-haired one at the other end of the table is his older brother, Danny. I'll introduce you. They're nice."

A hush fell over the room, and the two turned obediently toward the camp director, who again thumped the mic before launching into his comedic welcome speech. Afterward he unfolded an animated account of the camp rules and gave the special announcements of the day, including instructions on dining room and KP procedures. Then he lifted his rich baritone voice to lead them in a table prayer song before their first camp lunch.

On her porch, Midnight gave a wet hiccup, bringing Leah back to reality. She moved her arm clear of him. The camp memory had stirred up unwelcome emotions, and she stared at her plate. It wasn't like Rachel had been some distant acquaintance or something. She had been her closest friend—her very *closest* friend! Leah still marveled at how secretive and deceptive she and Jake had been.

Zing! There it was—back to sting again! All the way from Bridgewater!

Why are you dwelling on that? Draw your circles, girl, Pam's voice urged in her head. *Make them stay in their own circle with all their unhealthiness! You don't have to have that in your circle!*

Right now everything about Pam's circles sounded absolutely stupid! Good grief—how was that even *possible* when they had been inseparable friends for so many years? She wouldn't be able to make a circle large enough to fit them in it! Jake and Rachel had been connected to every part of her life—starting first with camp, then every part of high school, church, and leisure time, not to mention also intertwined with her associations with God.

God. And there *he* was again too, barging in uninvited, invading her space—as if he had floated over the hedge in the table prayer song and joined her. She could almost *feel* him right beside her on her porch, like his eyes were searching her as he extended an invisible hand—

Come back to me, Leah. I'll make everything right!

Her heart beat faster. She knew that voice. He was there, like she'd felt him calling her at Bible camp, tugging at her, drawing her in so powerfully until she had surrendered to him—and willingly. She sat frozen with the plate on her lap, stubbornly resisting. No. It simply wasn't possible. Coming back was far, far, far too complicated! She could not open to him again! How could he have allowed a betrayal like that? How could God have put her through the awful embarrassment of cancelling a wedding and the resulting critical scrutiny of dozens of friends and acquaintances with their blaring unspoken questions: *How had she been so naive? How could she not have known that was happening?* As if she were some poor, stupid airhead! It had been utterly humiliating!

On top of everything was the stigma of the old family curse that her mother had reminded her of every time she turned around. *Mark my words, Leah—you're next in line!* It had been terrifying! She and Evelyn had prayed together against it, and it hadn't worked. God had not stopped it or kept her from a devastating heartbreak, and all her old friends saw her through that creepy filter now too—eyeing her pitifully, whispering behind her back: *She's the girl with that family curse—and look what happened!*

How was she supposed to trust God again—actually *trust* him? Of course, she understood that hard things happened in life to everybody— that was a given. It wasn't like she expected a perfect life or anything. But Evelyn had specifically addressed the Corolla Curse thing in prayer, and it happened anyway. It was like having a ceremonial prayer for safety, then immediately getting hit by a train. She couldn't get over it. How could she open her heart to God again when he had left her in the lurch like that?

And yet he was so powerfully there now, and his whisper was clear— *Come back to me!*

But I can't, she said inside, her heart burning, *I can't come back.*

A sharp shout rang out from the west side of her house. In a burst, Midnight scrambled to his feet, his ears erect. "Midnight!" the holler came again, distinguishable this time. Marty was calling his dog. Marty, who now despised her and wished she were gone. Instantly, the black dog shot off her porch, whisking across the driveway to disappear into the side yard. And Leah was alone.

She stared at the food on her plate now resting untouched on her lap. How could God want her back anyway? She had walked so thoroughly away from him. For certain he knew how far she had gone—after all, he was God, and he knew everything. And that meant he surely knew how angry she was with him still.

And yet she had asked him for a handyman with a truck.

The sound of footsteps crunching across the crushed rock of her driveway interrupted her thoughts. Leah leaned around the side of the chair to see Brindle approaching. She was still in her work uniform, her right sleeve smeared with a streak of ketchup.

"Holy cow!" the burgundy-haired girl exclaimed, mounting the steps, her jaw dragging as she surveyed the porch. "You've been Suzy Homemaker today! How in the *world* did you do all this?"

"Hello, Brin." Leah motioned to her new friend to sit down. "Welcome to my little piece of heaven!"

She shook her head in awe. "I'm serious! How did you *do* all this?"

Leah lifted her chin in an impish smile. "I took your advice—standing out on the road in my underwear. And it worked!"

"Yeah, right! Like I could see *that*—as uptight as you are!"

Leah let the zinger pass. "Well, I actually *did* meet someone on the road. Right at the end of my driveway, as a matter of fact. A super-nice guy with a big, black truck. And he helped me." She waved her arm at the furniture.

Brindle started, shooting her a bewildered look.

"Super-nice," Leah repeated, "and super-cute too! I'm pretty sure I met your Mr. Suave and Studly. His name is Phil Crawford."

Her mouth dropped open.

Leah noted her expression. "What's the matter? Are you jealous?"

Brindle waggled her head. "Pfft—I'm not jealous." She plopped down on the love seat and crossed her legs, looking up at the hanging ferns.

"Yes, you are—you are so jealous!" Leah laughed. "You're mad because I got to him first!"

"Who says you got to him first?"

Leah narrowed her eyes. "The look on your face does! Do you know him already?"

"No."

She set her plate onto the coffee table. "Well, don't worry—it wasn't earth shattering. We went to the store and back, is all. I'd say your chances are still pretty good." She gestured to her food. "Would you like something to eat?"

Brindle shook her head, regarding the rice dish. "I ate at work. Did you make that today too?"

"The lady next door"—Leah pointed to the hedge—"she brought it over. Really sweet lady."

Brindle gave a nod. "I've met her. Are you going to their party

Saturday?"

"I'm thinking about it. You?"

"I'll probably go for a while."

"Yeah. Maybe we could go together."

"Yeah, okay."

They sat quietly for a few seconds, while Brindle bounced her leg atop her other knee. She cocked her head. "So how'd you say you met this guy? You were on the road?"

"He stopped to help me with my mailbox," Leah said. "It was broken—falling off the post. He pulled over and helped me with it."

Brindle's brow wrinkled. "Weird. Did you fix it?"

"Yes." She eyed her, debating whether to share the bit about the bolt being tampered with. Did she want Bridle in her business?

"Huh. That's good." Absently she bounced her foot. "And he took you to the store? When was this?"

"This afternoon. Like I said, he helped me fix the mailbox, then offered to help me cart all this home." She waved her hand. "It was his idea—and it saved me a hefty delivery charge."

"Ah, I see. Nice!" She leaned back, lifting her arms in a broad stretch. "You know what? I'm beat. I think I'll head out. It was a long day at work, and my feet hurt."

Leah gave her a strange look as she rose. "You just got here!"

"I know. I wanted to stop in and at least say hi. But hey—your porch looks great! Good job picking everything out."

Leah opened her phone and held it up to her. "Here—put your number in my contacts. I'll text you so that you can have mine."

"Good idea." Brindle took it, then handed it back. "Okay, see you tomorrow." She waved and left down the driveway the way she had come.

Leah watched her walk away, reviewing their exchange. For all of Brindle's brusque exterior, she had shown a chink in the armor. She had been jealous of Phil, clearly. Leah knew it. Miss Bold and Brash, the tough girl who had the world by the tail, was suddenly threatened by Miss Tame and Timid. Leah realized two things. First, that she liked Brindle a little better for her weakness. She was much less intimidated by someone who on the inside was just like her. Perhaps they actually would become friends after all. And second, Leah noted that she felt unapologetic to herself about her hopes for Phil Crawford. She hoped he didn't forget about the gas he said he'd bring by for the lawn mower. She wanted to see him again.

Chapter Nine

The sound of Phil Crawford's truck rumbling into her yard was a bright spot in Leah's evening. Leaving her laptop on her new coffee table, she skipped down the porch steps to meet him in front of the garage.

"Here you go," he said cheerfully, lifting a brand new red gas can out of his truck bed with a strong arm. "A little welcome-to-the-neighborhood gift from me!"

"Thank you very much!" she said gratefully. "Although I think it may be more of a please-for-the-sake-of-the-neighborhood gift!" She laughed.

"Or that. But here"—he beckoned her to the mower, still parked in front of the garage—"let me show you how to get this thing running. It's right out of the factory, so let's hope it starts!"

After filling it with gas and oil, he gave her a short tutorial on the mower and coached her on a point or two. Then she took a shot at firing it up.

"You got yourself a nice powerhouse here," he praised, patting the handle. "Mind if I take it for a spin? We've got a little daylight." He glanced at the sky.

Leah sat hugging her knees on the porch steps, watching as he cut a narrow swath of grass near the road on the west side of her driveway, following the tree line back to the corner. He was *so* nice! Truly, how often did a guy show up and do all that for someone? And he had all but offered to help her with her kitchen.

It'll sneak up on you, her mother had said.

No kidding. This was the last thing she ever expected to happen, she thought, watching him double back. She remembered telling herself that if romance were to find her, it would have to run her down. She shook her head, marveling at the vision of Phil's black truck bearing down on her. What were the odds of that? Then she kicked herself for acting like a schoolgirl, crushing on a guy she hardly knew. *Don't be an idiot! For heaven's sake, Carlos had been super nice too!* Nevertheless, her eyes followed him.

Suddenly the machine's whirring was interrupted by a sharp report, and instantly the mower stopped dead. In the quiet she heard a string of profanity as Phil jerked the machine roughly back, leaning around to see what he had hit. Tipping it up, he examined the underside, tinkering briefly underneath, then he yanked the mower around and headed back to the house.

"You're not going to like this!" he called angrily over the clatter of the machine rolling across the gravel.

She met him in front of the garage.

"Lawnmower verses post!" he growled, muscling it onto the driveway. "Some kind of junk fence half buried out there! I was just mowing and—*smack*! No warning—I just drove right into it!" Another burst of expletives. "The sucker didn't budge, and now there's wire all wound up under there, and one of the blades is bent to heck!" He wrenched the mower onto its side. "You can't see *nothing* in that grass, it's so dang long! I rammed it square on, and this thing—" He gestured. "Heck—I think it's toast!"

Her hand went over her mouth at the sight. "What—you didn't see it at all?"

"I had *no clue* it was there!"

Dollar signs flashed before her eyes. She nodded, trying to remain calm. "Yeah, um, okay. Do you—do you think it can be repaired?"

Phil blew out his breath. "You could try, but heck, I don't know!" He set his hands on his waist, shaking his head.

Leah stared at the machine. *Was this really happening?*

Finally he spoke. "Man, I feel terrible! I didn't mean to do this."

Leah shook her head. "No—no, of course not! It was an accident!"

Another silence.

"If you want, I could maybe take it somewhere to be fixed. But I don't know."

She threw him a glance. "Do you think it's worth it?"

"They'll tell you if they can't."

She nodded. "Okay. Well, let's give it a shot."

With a heave, Phil righted the mower, dislodging several wet chunks of grass as it banged noisily onto the driveway. He shook his head again. "Dang, this sucks! Look, Ava—I'm really sorry about this! Crap, I trashed your lawn mower and then went ballistic on you—I apologize!"

"No—it's okay!" she assured, trying to be gracious. "I get it! You had no way of knowing it was out there." Right then her eyes landed on his grass-flecked boots, the leather stained a juicy green. She looked up at him. "Your boots!"

He gave a twisted smile. "I'd say this evening has been a bit of a train-wreck. We should call it a day!"

"Yeah?" She scrunched her nose.

"Yeah. So help me load this in the truck, and I'll make my escape."

After he had closed the end gate, he turned to her. "So hey—if you trust me not to blow up your house or anything, what d'you say we take a look at that kitchen tomorrow? I get off work around three."

"Deal!" She gave him a thumbs up. "After three would be perfect." Help with her kitchen? Suddenly a busted lawnmower seemed less of a problem! *And those eyes!*

"Good! And I'll let you know what they say about Old Chopper." He patted the side of the truck. "Hopefully it's not terminal."

"Yes, hopefully. See you tomorrow."

What a bizarre thing to happen, she thought, watching him drive away. Everything about it was awkward. She knew he felt bad. Maybe she should have offered him something to drink. Perhaps he would have stayed. He'd had a Coke earlier that day. She'd get some on her next trip to town.

She looked out toward the untamed yard where Phil had mowed. One way or another she supposed the situation would work itself out, but she hoped it wouldn't turn out expensive. She had already dropped a chunk on that mower. And now who paid for its repair? Him or her? Dang, why did things have to get weird? She sighed. Well, wrecked mower or not, he had made the first dent in that foreboding field, and a baby step was still a baby step. That was one positive, she thought, filling her lungs with the fresh evening air. Its fragrance was even sweeter now with newly trimmed grass. *Two* positives.

She paused beside the flower beds on her way to her porch, spying the long, flat leaves of a cluster of irises tucked in the weeds, the curled brown remnants of shriveled blooms still clinging to the stalks from a few weeks ago. Grandma Havi's irises. How amazing that those bulbs had survived so many years of neglect! Well, they would have to hang on a little longer, she mused, for she did not envision conquering those flower beds anytime soon, considering all she needed to subdue *inside* her house. She smiled, amusing herself with the notion of offering up another prayer to God. He had come through with the handyman and truck—what would it hurt to put in a request for a landscaper or gardener?

Her thoughts about God drew her attention back to the neighbors who were back out on their deck. She heard the low murmur of their talking with that distinct laugh mixed in every now and then. Leah eyed the hedge. Who would have ever thought that when she moved to New Hampton, God would be living right next door? That hadn't been on her radar!

"Do you fellas need anything out there?"

The voice was unmistakably Jackie Burke's. Someone gave a muffled response—and then came that laugh again. Was it Brother—she pursed her lips—golly, what was his name again? The retired minister guy. Brother Something. Eventually she would meet him. Leah wondered if he'd be at all like Reid Tanner from Anchor. An older version, perhaps, which would be okay. Pastor Reid had been a great guy. But he'd also been a little scary too, which was why Leah was somewhat nervous about the neighbor's party coming up. For four years now she had gotten good at avoiding God, but being invited to a place where he was obviously quite at home was another story. Her plan was to stick close to Brindle. Or Phil, of course, if he was going.

She let out a long breath and turned her head toward the other hedge, beyond which it seemed apparent God was *not* welcomed. Nor was she. Would Marty be going to the big party? Would it turn out terribly awkward if they were both there? Varying scenarios of how it might go played out in her head. Never in a million years had she ever thought her cousin would hate her! She wished it would all just blow over. Nevertheless, the mailbox incident made her wonder. Phil had been so certain someone had tampered with it. *Anybody got an ax to grind with you?* The only person she could think of was Marty, but why in the world would he do something like that? There was a lot she didn't get.

Around her, lightning bugs were beginning to twinkle in the damp air, and a flutter way too close to her head signaled bats above, swooping circles in the dusky light. She shivered. It was time to go in.

The water issue presented itself again when Leah did her dishes. Glumly she ran the faucet until the ochre-tinged water lightened. How was she to do laundry in that? Or shower? Yuck! Surely there must be some sort of filter system she could install—she would ask at a hardware store. She dried her hands and turned to write herself a memo.

She paused, her brow wrinkling. Her legal pad! Before she'd left for town that morning, she distinctly remembered leaving it at the upper left edge of the table, squared with the corner—she did things like that—and now it sat in the center of the table at an odd angle. Had she bumped it putting her leftovers in the frig? Perhaps she had dragged one of her shopping bags across the table after town.

Grabbing the pad, she flipped to a clean sheet of paper and reached for her pen—which wasn't there. She backed a step, checking the floor, then glanced around the kitchen. There it was—on the peninsula. She stared at it for a second, then looked uneasily around the room. It was a little thing, but she absolutely remembered setting the pen across the binding on the legal pad that morning, as she always did, and she was pretty sure she hadn't used it since.

At once everything around her seemed extraordinarily quiet. Leah glanced down the back hall behind her. Had someone been in her house? Hadn't she locked her doors? She looked back at the pen and pad, now questioning herself. She must have moved them without thinking—had she done it while talking with her mother that morning? She remembered fiddling with the pen and the legal pad—but had that been before or after she had talked to her mom?

Suddenly another thought struck her, and Leah swallowed, glancing in the direction of the bedrooms. Quietly she pulled out her phone. Poised for a 911 call, she stepped boldly into the living room and clicked on the light. Aware that the bare windows put her every activity on display for anyone outdoors, she peeked quickly but cautiously around the edges of the furniture, then jerked open the closet by the front door. Satisfied, she turned off the light and followed suit through that end of the house, even checking the shower.

Working her way back from the kitchen, she opened the hall pantry, broom closet, and utility closet, relieved that everything appeared undisturbed. The workbench full of tools and clutter in the garage seemed unchanged from the day before, as did the rug in front of the basement door—still curled up against it exactly as she had put it last evening before bed. But when she turned into the hall by the laundry room, she had her answer. Her back door stood open about four inches. She shuddered. So it was true—someone *had* been there!

Angrily she closed the door and locked it, then stood with her back against it in the dim hallway. Holy cow—what kind of neighborhood was this now? Her first day here and her home had been broken into! She was *sure* she had locked up. That meant the person or persons had actually picked the lock—and that was awfully disturbing. She shook her head in disbelief. Her only consolation was that she had nothing of value in the house to take—whoever had come in was likely the most disappointed thief ever!

With that thought, she scrambled to check her suitcase, kneeling to sift through her belongings to see if anything was missing. She wasn't exactly sure how she had left it all to begin with, so she couldn't quite tell, but it didn't seem like anything was out of place. The clothes in her laundry basket were still neatly folded. Even her laptop, which had been on the counter all day, had been undisturbed, except for when she had used it on the porch.

Then came another thought. Perhaps her thief had come in her back door while she'd been *there*—outside on her porch—for she'd been outside since she'd returned from town. She let out an indignant breath, feeling so violated. Something like this hadn't been on her radar either when she'd considered moving to New Hampton!

She sat back, resting her hands in her lap. Good heavens—it wasn't like her house was a beacon for thieves! What would anyone expect to find in an eyesore of place like this, with her wild yard and gouged garage door? Unless it was someone who knew the place and wanted something in particular, or someone who already had a key. Perhaps a former renter—or someone like—

Or someone like Marty.

Just the thought of it stung. Of course. He had keys to her house.

Then her brow rose with a thought: Had Marty come to see her? Perhaps—she had a surge of hope—perhaps he had come to make an apology after all! But just as quickly, her hopes were deflated. If he had come for that reason, why had he let himself in? Wouldn't he simply have knocked and left to return later if she weren't home? Unless—unless he had let himself in for some other reason. But why? To move her legal pad? Not likely. Or had he a more devious intention perhaps?

Anybody got an axe to grind with you? Phil's words echoed in her mind. *I'd say someone was messing with your mailbox.* She stared at the floor in thought. It was doubtless about her mom buying his house. Was he trying to frighten her? Pester her? Intimidate her? She had to know, because if that were the case, he was being nasty! She checked the time, ready to throw on her shoes and march next door—but right then her phone rang in her hand. She jumped.

It was her mother, calling to check in.

Ironically, Leah was relieved for the call, for it was like having another person in the room, and without even discussing her situation, she found herself suddenly gaining a new perspective that both cleared her jitters and relieved some of her ire toward Marty. First, there was no way to ascertain that it *was* Marty. Truly, it could have been random neighborhood thugs. But if it *were* him, and if he were trying to toy with her by coming in and moving things around, she decided she wouldn't be controlled by his scare tactics. If he wanted to be a jerk, that was his problem! And if he—best-case scenario—if he'd been coming over to make an apology, no doubt he would make the effort again. It had probably taken some humility to initiate such a gesture, so she wouldn't push it and risk driving him away. For now she'd let things be and see what played out.

Her mom was in a better mood than earlier that day, and Leah was happy to have something positive to share with her. She told her about the nice stranger with the truck who had helped her cart her new porch furniture home. She didn't tell her about the lawnmower mishap or that she now had a crush on the guy, nor did she tell her it appeared someone had been in her house that day—on the chance that her mother would use it as leverage for why she shouldn't keep the house. Leah was certain that battle was not over yet.

At the end of their conversation, her mother offered to come help her over the weekend. In a moment of panic, Leah put her off by making up that she had a few job interviews on Saturday and a big neighborhood party on Sunday. She felt like such a liar when she hung up, having fabricated and rearranged the weekend events, but she just couldn't handle her mom being there. Not yet anyway. Not until she had the place a little more under control.

Leah sighed, feeling conflicted. It bugged her that she could lie to her mom with such ease. It was like her conscience was just gone—only it wasn't. For the last four years she had told herself that God's opinion about her behavior didn't really matter, but if that were the case, why did she feel so guilty?

Religious confusion, Pam had declared it.

"You seem inordinately anxious about pleasing this God of yours," she had voiced to Leah with concern in one of their talks. "As long as you keep measuring your life against those standards, *of course* you're going to feel burdened with guilt! Goodness—who could ever measure up to all of that? It's impossible! Cut yourself some slack, girl! You don't need all that Jesus stuff to be a good person. Stop obsessing on right or wrong and do what's right for *you*! Put *yourself* first! Don't you think God would want you to be happy? If you're not hurting anyone, go for it!"

It sounded so reasonable. So simple. So easy. But for Leah it never quite lived out that way. It always left her torn on the inside.

She set her phone on the counter. At this point there was a myriad of reasons for God to be fed up with her anyway. For a girl who'd been crazy about him in her youth, she'd sure fallen away with gusto, and now there were too many strikes against her to count. She'd gone off the deep end after Jake, diving into the party scene with unreserved vigor, doing stuff she never thought she'd do. Then getting entwined with Carlos. Hating Jake DeSoto and her former best friend, Rachel, without qualms for what they'd done and refusing to forgive them ever, ever, ever. And lately shutting off the voice that kept calling her.

But still it came.

When she got into her inflatable bed that night, with her doors booby-trapped and the bathroom lights left on, and with her new box fan turned on low to drown out any sounds from outside, she could hear him in that quiet place inside her—

I'm your answer, Leah. Come back to me.

Sometimes she wanted to. Sometimes she wished she could jump back in time and skip over the hard parts and make them go away—to be with God as she had been at first. She pulled the quilt over her shoulders and tucked it in. It *had* been kind of him to send Phil with that truck. And her porch was a dream. She supposed she owed him thanks for that.

I'm your answer. Come—

I can't right now, she answered. Maybe once she got settled, she would be open to figuring things out. Maybe now that she was in New Hampton it would be safe to start back down that road, but it was too complicated to think about now. *I wouldn't even know what to do, God. But please watch over me tonight.*

The next morning Leah donned her running gear and crossed Richmond Road to explore the neighborhood behind the row houses. Partly she wanted to find a good route to run, but that wasn't the only reason. She also wanted to check out the area where Phil said he lived.

Since the entire development was less than ten years old, all the homes were relatively new, from modest family homes to cookie-cutter townhouses facing each other and—tucked farther back—wealthier neighborhoods that took Leah's breath away. As she trekked past the luxurious dwellings with their tall, magnificent windows and impressive stone or brick fronts, she was thankful that at least her humble ranch house was well hidden behind the dense wall of bushes across the highway. Nevertheless, the various styles of landscaping gave her aspirations of how she might improve her little place in the future.

It was wild to think that at one time the whole area had been lush fields belonging to her grandfather. Fields of rich black dirt that had produced corn, picked or cut for pungent silage each fall. Fields of rough stubble that her grandfather had trudged over while hunting deer so many cold Novembers. How much money had he made on this acreage? It couldn't have been an easy decision to sell it.

As she wound around another street, she discovered a delightful park with a paved walking trail encircling a pond. She slowed, noting the spread of lily pads peppering the ripply water near the edge. Several turtles dotted the side of a log, soaking in the morning sun. Mallards poked in the reeds near the shore, waddling into the water to glide away from her as she passed by. Leah found the trail so enchanting that she took another lap before heading home—where despite her water worries, her hair survived her first shower drama free.

Her agenda for the day was to flesh out some ideas for her house. Having spent hours on Pinterest the previous afternoon, she had gotten a good vision for what she wanted; now it was time to explore some stores. But first the crockpot. Leah wound the cord around the handle and replaced the lid. Returning it seemed the neighborly thing to do, given Jackie's big party tomorrow. What if she needed it? Reminding herself that neither the Steinburgs nor the DeSotos lived next door, she retrieved it from the peninsula and set confidently upon her errand.

After a hunt for the cut in the thick, double row of hedge, Leah shoved her way through the scratchy branches with the crockpot in her hands and made her way to her neighbor's front door. She rang the doorbell with her elbow, setting off an explosion of barking inside. In a moment Jackie appeared, wearing a colorful apron over a white blouse and jeans.

"Ava! Come in, come in!" she cried, holding the door wide, then she turned, scolding downward, "Oh, Angel—shush!"

The little dog quieted, pulling back from the door.

Angel. Of course. Leah smiled at the name, stepping in onto a bright foyer rug as the dog cautiously approached, his nose furiously at work. In the room hung the heavenly aroma of freshly baked cookies.

She handed off the crockpot. "I thought you might need this for your party. And thank you again for the chicken dish. It was amazing!"

"You read my mind!" Jackie replied with a friendly laugh. "I do—thanks for thinking of it! Please come in!"

Leah shook her head. "No, I can't stay. I know you're probably very busy—"

"We are *delightfully* busy!" she broke in. "We're having so much fun in the kitchen—I'd love for you to come see! Please—come meet my friend Kyla! Come, come! It'll only take a moment!" She gestured for Leah to follow.

It was not how she expected it would go, but compelled, Leah followed her across the polished hardwood floors of a spacious living room and dining room, both outfitted with lovely furniture. The dog trotted watchfully beside them as Jackie chatted on about how glad she was that Leah had stopped by.

"It smells wonderful in here!" Leah offered politely. Truly, her mouth was watering.

"Lemon Meltaways," Jackie said over her shoulder. "You'll have to try one. They're so delicious! And so easy. I'm into easy lately."

They entered a bright and sunny kitchen illuminated by southern patio doors where a pretty, young woman around Leah's age was frosting cookies at a kitchen island in the center of the room. Her long brown hair was pulled back in a ponytail.

Jackie set the crockpot on a nearby counter. "Kyla, this is my new friend Ava. She just moved in next door into her grandparents' old house."

Her new friend.

With a smile, the woman extended her hand. "Nice to meet you, Ava. I'm Kyla Watkins."

"Brother Warren knew them—Ava's grandparents—both dear, dear people. They just passed away recently."

"Sorry to hear that," Kyla said kindly. She had a smudge of flour across her belly, which Leah suspected was the beginning of a baby bump.

"Thank you," she replied.

Jackie pulled a mug down from the cupboard. "Do you drink coffee, hon? It's right here—I just made it!"

"Sure," Leah said timidly. "I'll have some."

"Wonderful!"

While Jackie busied herself at the counter, Angel fluffed his bed in the corner, spun a circle, and plopped down, resting his chin on the cushion to keep an eye on her. Grabbing the carafe, the woman continued: "Kyla

142

lives on the other side of New Hampton. Actually, she doesn't live all that far away—just on the other side of the river down there—but you have to drive all the way through town and around to get to her house."

"Have a seat," Kyla said, patting the chair next to her. "I have the morning off, so my husband and I came over to help these guys get ready for their party."

"Aren't they the best?" Jackie interjected, throwing an appreciative glance over her shoulder. "The men just ran to town to pick up the canopy tents for tomorrow—Kyla's husband and the young man who lives in our cottage." She frowned at Kyla. "I hope they have enough time to get them set up before you and Peter have to go!"

"Me too," Kyla replied, sliding back onto her stool, an enormous diamond in her wedding band flashing in the sunlight through the patio door.

Leah tried not to stare. Was that real? "Uh—do you work here in New Hampton?" she asked her, receiving the warm mug Jackie handed her. She murmured her thanks and took a sip.

Kyla slid the bowl of frosting between them and handed Leah a spreader, gesturing to a cooling rack of sugar cookie cut-outs. "Yes. I nanny for a professor at Taiton College. Two boys, ages four and six. He's got class in the afternoon today, so I've got to be back shortly after noon."

The boy in the climbing tree.

Carefully Leah frosted her first cookie. "I see. Do you watch them at your home or theirs?"

Kyla laughed. "Kinda both!" In one smooth motion she completed her cookie and reached for another. "It's one and the same."

Jackie laughed too. "Kyla and Peter rent a third-floor apartment in her employer's house."

Leah set the cookie in a row of frosted ones and took another. "Ah, I get it! That's convenient! But I bet you'll be ready for a larger place when your baby comes. When are you due?"

Kyla beamed, her cheeks a little pink. "Not until fall. But we're going to stay."

"Really? Yikes—my two-bedroom apartment in Bridgewater was so tiny. I'm sure a third-floor apartment has got to be tight quarters."

"It's not small," Kyla replied, swirling the frosting over another cookie, her ring glinting again in the kitchen light.

"But certainly you'll be a little more cramped with a baby."

"It's not small," she repeated with emphasis, a mysterious look on her face. "So you're from Bridgewater? I dated a guy from there when I was in college. And I worked there for two summers."

"That's cool," Leah replied. "Yes, I grew up there. But I just inherited my grandparents' house next door, so I moved here."

"How exciting! A time of new beginnings for you, huh?"

Nearby Jackie scraped a softened stick of butter on top of some sugar in a mixing bowl. "Yes, it'll be really nice to have someone living there again. Ava, do try those cookies! Don't be shy now!" She set the spatula aside and leaned into the refrigerator. "Okay, where are my eggs?"

Kyla's brow crinkled thoughtfully. "Who else do we know from Bridgewater? Just recently I was talking with some guy about being from there."

"From Bridgewater?" Jackie repeated, distracted. "What did I do with my eggs?" She straightened, an irritated look on her face. "Don't tell me I forgot to get eggs yesterday!"

Leah bit into a cookie, her mouth coming alive with its delicious sweetness. She brought her mug up for a sip.

"I wish you would have called me," Kyla said. "I could have brought you eggs."

"Oh, for heaven's sake! That was one of the main things on my grocery list yesterday!" Jackie turned to Leah. "You don't by chance have eggs at your house, do you? I know you just moved in."

Leah shook her head. "Sorry. I could run to town for you—"

Jackie threw up a finger. "Quick—let's call the guys!" She glanced around for her phone.

"I'm texting Peter right now," Kyla said, already holding hers up.

The older woman wiped her hands on her apron, shaking her head. "Thank the Lord for cell phones! All right, we'll wait on these." She covered the bowl and came to lean on the counter near the girls. "I'm sorry—where were we? Those are all looking great, by the way!"

"I forgot," Kyla said, back to work on the few remaining cookies.

Leah set her coffee mug down and turned to Kyla. "So, hey—I have a really great tree in my yard that's fun for kids to play in. You can probably see it from your side of the hedge. We called it the 'climbing tree' growing up, and it's bigger and even cooler now. Some of the branches are low and fat—perfect for climbing."

Kyla smiled. "Thanks! I think it's already been discovered. One of my boys keeps talking about his awesome new tree fort at Miss Jackie's house!"

"Well, they're welcome to play in it! You too, of course, since you'll probably come to watch them. Not that they can't play there by themselves, though. I don't mind."

"Aww, that's so sweet of you, Ava," Jackie said. "I bet you have so many wonderful memories there!"

"I do." A happy image of bouncing on a wide limb with her cousin flashed through her mind, followed by a pang of grief. Marty.

"They're at the corner!" Kyla announced, glancing at her phone. "Peter said they're stopping at the convenience store right now for eggs and do you need anything else?" Her eyes rose to the older woman.

"Oh, heavens—I hope I didn't forget anything else! Tell them just the eggs. I'm glad we caught them." She patted Leah's arm. "I apologize for the chaos here, Ava. Usually I'm a bit more together!" She laughed. "Okay, so where were we again? We keep getting interrupted. The climbing tree! Yes, that'll be nice for the boys to play in."

"It'll be nice to see a new crop of kids in it," Leah agreed, setting the last cookie on the cooling rack and sliding off her stool. "But I probably should be going. I'm about to head into town."

"All right—I'll walk you out," Jackie said. "It's probably going to get a little crazy here in a minute when the fellas come with those shade canopies. We'll have to have you over sometime when we're not rushed."

Kyla was smiling down at her phone but paused to look up. "Bye, Ava! It was nice to meet you! Hope to see you tomorrow!"

Leah followed Jackie back through the house while the woman chattered amiably on about how grateful she was for the extra help this summer from strapping young men. Angel tapped dutifully along with them, blinking sleepily at the door while they paused to say their goodbyes.

"So what do you usually do at your parties?" Leah asked. Fixed in her mind were the things they'd do at the parties after Jake. Ironically, all during college she would never go to any of "those" parties because she was a Christian and engaged to Jake DeSoto. Boy, had she made up for that! But she was positive this would not be one of those parties.

"Oh, we mostly hang out, but there's some yard games too for those who like to play. And organized games for the kids. And lots of food, of course! This year some jugglers from our church are going to put on a fancy show sometime in the afternoon. It's quite impressive! And then in the evening Kyla's going to share her story with the group."

Leah's brow rose. "Her story?"

"Yes! She has an amazing story of how her birth father unexpectedly showed up in her life after seventeen years, and how God—well, I don't want to spoil it. But I'm telling you—it's a really great story!"

"Huh. I look forward to hearing it."

"I'm glad you're coming!" She smiled. "Goodbye, Ava! Thanks for all your help with our cookies."

Protecting her face, Leah brushed back through the hedge. In some ways she regretted leaving so soon. She could have offered to stay and help them. There wasn't anything so important that she needed to get back to, but it felt strange hanging out there with women she barely knew. Not that they had made her feel uncomfortable—no. But she knew they were church people, and that made her cautious. Still, she could not deny feeling drawn in.

You're wanting Jackie to be Evelyn, she told herself frankly. *Knock it off!* Why did she feel the need to make a comparison? To be sure, Jackie had that same aura of warmth and sweetness as Evelyn, but she was a completely different woman. Jackie Burke was not, nor would she ever be, Evelyn DeSoto. Nor would there ever be another Jake—*thank God*! The DeSotos were in her past now—or would be if she could ever stop thinking about them! Wasn't living in New Hampton supposed to help with that?

At any rate, Leah felt a lot more confident about going to their party. It would be a good place to meet people. She'd go and stick with Phil or Brindle. And then perhaps if Marty showed up there, he'd be more willing to talk in a setting like that.

Chapter Ten

Leah spent the lion's share of her time in town that day—first being redirected around a home improvement store multiple times in a futile attempt to find answers for her house questions, then flipping through endless flooring samples of carpet, wood, and tile at a jackpot of a home interior store across town. Hours later, on her way home, her back seat was strewn with paint swatches and promising flooring possibilities, but she had a brain-overload headache that pleaded for a nap.

When she turned into her driveway, however, Brindle was in the middle of the road walking away from her house. Seeing Leah, she waved.

"Perfect timing!" she announced cheerfully as Leah rolled down her window. "Where've you been? I came to visit, but you weren't here!" She had woven her coarse hair into two, thick burgundy braids, the bright ends resembling fuzzy pink tassels. The low neckline of her tank top revealed another hibiscus tattoo that matched the colorful flourish on her arm.

"Hi!" Leah said. "Out getting ideas for my house. Floor samples and stuff."

"Cool. Well,"—she gave a little bow—"Brin Baylor at your service! I'm here to assist!"

"Oh, uh—that's great!" Leah held a polite smile. Had they talked about this? She didn't remember making plans. She gestured ahead. "Um, I should park."

"Oh, sure!" Brindle backed away from the window and waved her on, following the few yards to the driveway. "I have a couple hours before I need to get ready for work," she said as Leah got out of the car. "I thought I'd come help you get settled."

"I see," Leah said, trying to wrap her mind around starting some kind of activity with her.

Brindle was already in her back seat pulling out bags. "Whoa—new shoes! Nice! What'd you get?"

"Yeah, um, a splurge—running shoes. But hey—I'm a little brain-fried from shopping all day. I think I might take a rain check on your offer."

Her eyes popped in surprise.

"It was sweet of you to come over, but I think we'll have to do it another time. Sorry."

Brindle stared at her for a moment, then dropped her chin. "Ever hear of this stuff called caffeine? It's magical! You should have some!" Before Leah could respond, she waggled her head. "Are you serious? I broke my butt trying to get over here, and you weren't home! Then miraculously you show up—and now you're telling me that I rushed my tail off for nothing—?"

Leah gave a little laugh. "I didn't know you were coming! We didn't talk about this!" Her hopes for rest were fizzling.

"So? Oh, come on, Ava! It'll be fun! It's not like you have to *think*, and we can get to know each other! Two—" She held up a pair of fingers. "I have *two* whole hours before I work. We could *do* something!"

With her smile solidly fixed, Leah tried to determine if Bridle was being pushy or if she was simply an outgoing, overly eager helpful type. The line felt a little blurry. Yet at the same time she seemed nice—even fun. Pam's voice was talking in her ear again, making her feel like a stick-in-the-mud: *You're going to make friends with people who are different than you...*

Brindle flayed her hands.

Brindle was not Rachel Steinburg, Leah reminded herself. She gave a nod. "All right—you win! Although I'm not exactly sure what we'll do—I don't have a plan yet."

"Pfft! Since when is that a requirement?" She gathered up the shopping bags and headed to the house.

Inside, Leah grabbed a couple of iced teas from the refrigerator and offered one to Brindle, who was studying the living room with a manicured finger set thoughtfully on her chin.

"First off, this carpet needs to go! And that furniture. The place smells like *cat*." Her eyes met Leah's. "Sorry. Just being honest."

Or *something*, Leah corrected. "I think it's *dog*, actually, but I'm not sure the two of us have enough muscle to tackle that."

She shrugged. "Yeah, maybe. So let's clean out some of the smaller stuff instead—like all that junk in the closets or something. Or we could check out the basement—assuming there *is* a basement and stuff down there. I'm just guessing there would be, since there were millions of boxes left everywhere up here." She flashed a smile. "Where shall we start?"

Millions? Right. So Brindle was a free spirit with an unbridled opinion. In some ways Leah found herself irritated—like she was dealing with another controller like her mother, and it made her want to balk. Simultaneously she recognized her blaring trust issues manifesting again. No one was ever going to be perfect, she reminded herself. How would she get to know Brindle if she didn't give her a chance? She took a breath, making a deliberate choice to drop her guard.

"Let's take a stab at the master bedroom closet," she suggested. It honestly wasn't a bad idea, for she'd have to go through all that stuff eventually.

"Woot!" Brindle slapped Leah a high five and headed back, where upon entering the room, she cringed at the mattress dominating the area. "I totally get why you don't sleep in here!"

"Thus, the dumpster!" Leah flipped her thumb, indicating that the bed was going out.

"Well, for now it can be our sorting table."

"Good idea!" Leah nodded, turning to the closet. "Let's take down all these boxes and put—" She stopped, uttering a confused sound. The previous evening when she had searched her house fearing an intruder, she had purposely left the functioning bifold door of the closet wide open because its broken counterpart had already been removed. But now the door was shut. "That closet door!" she blurted.

"Is there something wrong with it?"

"Weird!" she exclaimed, glancing at Brindle.

Brindle gave her a sideways look. "What is? What's weird?"

"Well, I—" Leah gestured. "I opened that closet door last night! I'm *sure* I left that open."

Brindle eyed the door and looked back at her. "Okay. So—?"

Had Marty been there again? *Someone* had been there while she was out, and the thought of it was unsettling. She'd be talking to Marty now for sure! Why was he doing this?

"Did any friends pop in to see you?" Brindle asked. "Boyfriend? Family?"

"No boyfriend and no, I—" She hesitated. Should she say anything to her? Or would it freak her out? She met Brindle's eyes and smiled. "I probably just forgot. Anyway, it doesn't matter."

Brindle shuddered. "Yeah, but now you've given me the creeps! Look at my arms—I have goosebumps! What if there's a dead body stashed in there or something?"

At that Leah laughed. "Fat chance—there's no room for one!" She pulled open the bifold door to reveal a stack of boxes. "As I was about to say, let's pull all of this out and go through it on the bed." She scanned the shelves, but nothing stood out as different from before.

Brindle nodded, starting in. "Sounds good to me!"

Beginning with the top shelf and working their way downward, they removed cardboard boxes and plastic bins, setting them side by side on the edge of the mattress until they completely encircled the bed. Choosing a starting point, Leah began to open them one by one as Brindle hovered curiously nearby.

"Go ahead!" Leah urged after half a dozen boxes. "See what you find!"

As Leah had guessed, the closet had been packed snugly with a broad assortment of items belonging to her grandparents—winter clothes, knickknacks, games, puzzles, memorabilia, and the like. She wondered why their stuff was still there, given that the house had been rented out several years now. Those renters had doubtless been annoyed by so little usable closet space.

After working together for some time, Brindle held up a yellowed newspaper. "I feel like an archeologist! In this strata the Cardinals won the World Series! Looks like every inch downward takes us back about five years."

Leah chuckled, leafing through a box of loose papers. "I'm with you there! I might have reached bedrock! Look—my grandfather's grammar school stuff!" She held up a few tattered pieces of penmanship paper, then carefully paged through them to peruse his handwriting as a young student. "There's the whole gamut here—kindergarten through high school! These are *old*! And here—!" She held up another cluster of typewritten papers stapled together. "A high school report on copper mining—*copper mining*!"

"Is there something significant about that?"

"Oh, sorry—he owned shares in a copper company. Anyway, I bet when he wrote this, he never imagined he'd be making money from copper someday!" She looked up at Brindle, her memory suddenly jogged. *The letter from her grandparents!* She should be looking for what they had left her!

Brindle was unimpressed. "Or that his granddaughter would read it a century later! Why did they save all this?"

Leah shrugged, her eyes sweeping over the boxes Brindle was

looking through. "I don't know! But I'm glad they did. It's fascinating! Almost like a time capsule."

"And what are you going to do with it? Please don't tell me you're going to save your grandfather's school papers!"

"What's wrong with that?" Leah glanced down at the box and back up.

Brindle cocked her head.

"Well, I probably won't save *all* of this, but some of it I will. Why not? I want to at least look at his stuff before I get rid of it."

"If it were up to me, I'd walk most of this straight out to the dumpster."

Leah made a sound. "Well, it's not up to you!"

Brindle shrugged. "Okay, fine. So what about all this?" She held the flaps of a box down so Leah could see in. "A box of board games. Crusty old board games."

Leah stretched to see. "Some of those may be collectors' items."

Brindle stared at her a moment before moving on to another box. "Old blankets?"

"Those are my Grandma Havi's quilts. I'm quite sure she made them."

The girl frowned, unfolding one of them. "Here—this is the nicest one, if you ask me, but look—it's old and ratty. Tell me honestly—would you put this on your bed?"

Indeed, the quilt was worn, comprised of mismatched squares sewn together and tied with yarn. The colors didn't even coordinate. Leah screwed up her nose. "Probably not. I have nicer ones."

"Would you give this to anyone or use it for anything?" Brindle held it out questioningly. "Part of it's ripped."

"Um—" Perhaps Midnight would use it on her porch. "A dog bed or a drop cloth?"

Brindle tossed it to the floor of the closet and held up another.

With a sigh Leah came over and rummaged briefly through the blankets to make sure there was nothing hidden within. "Okay—get rid of the whole box! Take the whole thing to the dumpster and do it quickly before I change my mind! But Brindle, don't rush me through the rest of this. I know this is just old stuff to you, but these things belonged to my grandparents. This is *family* stuff! My Grandma Havi was super special to me!"

"Oh, I see," she said stiffly. "You know, Ava, not everyone is as privileged as you!" Snatching up the box, she marched out of the room.

Leah stared after her bewildered. What was *that* for? She looked back at the collection of boxes on the bed.

The girl remained aloof when she returned, poking through more boxes in stony silence.

Leah sighed. "All right, I'm sorry if I offended you earlier. I just wanted you to know this is important to me."

Her brow rose innocently.

Annoyed, Leah hit it straight on. "What's going on? You got mad and then you got quiet. And what did you mean by saying I was 'privileged'? What's that got to do with any of this?" She waved her hand.

Brindle shrugged.

Leah rolled her eyes. "*What?* I'm not going to try to guess! I'm sorry, but this stuff belonged to my grandparents! I want to look at it! Wouldn't you request the same for *your* grandparents' stuff?"

The side of her mouth rose in a twisted smile. "Oh, the irony! Yeah, I probably would."

"Well, then?"

"Okay, sorry. I'm just having one of those days."

"Then what's going on? Let's talk about it!"

She shook her head. "It's nothing. I'm just dealing with some—some sucky things in life." She took a long look at Leah, then dropped her eyes, letting out a long breath. "Okay, I apologize. I was rude. I'm—I guess I'm sort of a minimalist—that's all. I don't really have nostalgic things. I've never had anyone pass anything on to me, and I'm used to keeping things simple. So—sorry. I shouldn't have said anything. I'm here to help you, and you can do whatever you want. It's *your* stuff."

Leah nodded. "Thank you. But if I offend you, Brindle, I'm willing to talk about it." She couldn't help but think Pam would be proud of how she was handling this.

"I'm all right. Forget it." She smiled meekly. "But do you mind if I still look through some of this?"

Leah waved at the bed. "Of course, I don't mind! I'm simply saying don't rush me. And don't dump anything unless I see it first. Unless it's, like, old clothes or something like that. I probably wouldn't keep any of that."

"Yeah, okay. And if I find any live animals?"

Leah's head snapped up. "Live anim—"

Brindle laughed out loud. "I'm messin' with you! Just trying to lighten things up!"

Leah managed a small laugh in reply. "Good heavens—if you find any live critters, I'm out of here!"

"That'd be a lot more interesting than prehistoric school papers!"

"Knock it off! I'm going through each box, so get over it!"

"Whatever! But you don't have to save everything."

"True. But I'm still going to look. There might be things worth saving!"

"Riiight." Brindle nodded knowingly. "So far your life's been fine without any of it! So, what do you want me to do? I'm feeling pretty useless!"

"Um—maybe look for old photographs. I'd definitely want to keep them. And check what's in that box." Leah pointed to one with "for the girls" penned boldly across the top.

"Okay. In here we have"—Brindle pulled open the flaps—"white embroidered dish towels! A whole box of them." She held up a handful. "One for every day of the week for about—oh, maybe half a year."

Leah made a face. "Care to have a set?"

"No."

She groaned. "Oh, brother! It might have been a bad idea to start this!"

"Yeah." Brindle moved to the next box, murmuring under her breath, "It's too bad your grandma didn't keep a journal or something. Now *that* would be interesting!"

Leah's head popped up. "Wh—what made you say that?"

Brindle shrugged, glancing up at her. "I don't know. Just thought it'd be cool."

"Well, as a matter of fact, there *are* some journals! Now that you mention it."

Her head drew back in surprise. "Yeah? No kidding!"

"Yes! My Grandma Havi left me all her journals! I got a letter that said they went with the house, and I'm supposed to read her story. And supposedly she also left me some other—" She stopped. Did she want Brindle to know about her mysterious other valuables? She wasn't even sure what they were.

"Some other—?"

"Some other stuff. You know—stuff." She gestured to the boxes.

"Ah." Brindle lifted her chin. "So where are they? Have you read her story?"

"I haven't found them yet."

"Oh. Okay. Well, we'll have to keep an eye out for those, won't we? I'll be sure not to sneak them to the dumpster!" Playfully she winked.

"Don't you dare!"

"But first we need to find them, huh? Do you want me to bring in the stuff from the other closets? Or maybe quit here and go check out the basement—?"

Leah shook her head, holding up a hand. "Stop! One room at a time! This is overwhelming enough! Besides, Brin, eventually you'll go to work and leave me with this mess!"

"Oh, yeah. Work." Brindle sighed, checking the time. She turned to open the next box, tipping her head to read the name of a magazine. She pulled out an issue and flipped unhurriedly through its pages, plopping it back on top of the stack when she was finished. "Here's an entire box of *Ranch Life* magazines. Everything you'd ever want to know about raising livestock right here." She gave the box a tap. "Interested? Or dumpster?"

"Are you sure that's all that's in there?"

Brindle raised her hand. "Scout's honor."

At one time those magazines were important enough for her grandfather to box up and save. But for what? And now he was gone. Leah nodded. "Dumpster."

Leah offered Brindle a ride home later that afternoon. It was hot, and with the rising humidity, the cumulus clouds of midday had morphed into ominous, dark thunderheads, overtaking the sun and promising storms. Yet Brindle declined.

"I'm all right," she called back to Leah on the porch while she hurried down the driveway. "I won't melt if I get wet! Probably see you tomorrow."

Leah watched her for a few moments, then checked her phone, wondering where Phil Crawford was. He said he'd come after three, and he was well over an hour late! She put her phone back into her pocket and headed down to the slab in front of her garage door. Earlier that afternoon when Brindle and she had been sorting through boxes, Brindle had gone on a hunt for a good pair of scissors, and in the process she had found Leah's garage door opener. With the device in hand, Leah decided now was a good time to see if it still worked—and to test if the garage door itself worked or if its damage had been fatal.

After a quick jaunt back in to replace the batteries, Leah happily discovered that the electric door opener did indeed work; however, the crunched-in area stopped the door two-thirds of the way up, causing it to automatically reverse and grind closed again. With a critical study of the door's tracking, she experimented until she figured out how to freeze the door in the almost-up position. Feeling slightly victorious, she lowered it to try it once more, but this time it refused to obey her. She groaned, tinkering with it again for several minutes until behind her she heard the awaited sound of Phil Crawford's pickup crawling up the driveway. He stuck his hand out the window, flashing a broad smile. She cast a quick glance down at herself, wishing she weren't such a perspiring mess.

"Good news!" he said, swinging down from his seat and joining her where she stood with the garage controller.

She brightened. "They can repair the mower?"

He gave her a thumbs up. "You should have it back in about a week."

"Nice! And the cost?"

"Eh—" He scrunched his face a little. "Not such great news there, but hey—I was able to find you a loaner! Here—" He beckoned her to the back of his truck where the handle of another mower jutted out. "A friend let me borrow it."

"That's great!" Leah exclaimed eagerly, but as he dropped the end gate to slide the mower onto the driveway, she had to stifle her disappointment, for the replacement was not only ancient, but measly looking too, a fraction of the size of the one she'd had.

"Yeah, it's—old," Phil said somewhat sheepishly, looking down at it. "And kinda your bottom-line model, but I figured heck—it's a week!"

Leah nodded. "Uh—right. It's a week. Thank you."

He tipped his head. "Welcome. Let's make sure it runs, shall we?"

It was still kind of him to bring it, Leah thought. He wouldn't have had to.

"You're on your own this time," he called after they got it started. "I'm not taking any chances with this one. Plus, I'm wearing my good boots!" He scuffed his sole on the driveway.

Leah glanced at the sky, letting the mower die. "Looks like I won't be using it today! Maybe tomorrow. But my yard's certainly not going anywhere."

His eyes swept across the overgrown grass. "Sadly not. Anyway"—he gestured to the house—"how about that kitchen?"

"Yes!" she responded, maybe too enthusiastically. It was crazy how much a simple question could thrill her. It had been a long time since anyone had helped her with anything big like this, and now having someone like

Phil step in—well, it felt a bit like being rescued. She was excited, nervous, shy, intimidated—and also a bit embarrassed to let him see the inside of her house. But he was, of course, *nice*, nodding appreciatively as he looked around from the foyer.

"So here we are," she said awkwardly, acutely aware of her home's funky smell, the worn carpet, ghetto furniture, and her air bed in the dining room. Everything suddenly seemed a thousand times worse.

"Typical rambler," he said, his gaze moving from floor to ceiling, eventually landing on the rust-colored furniture. He jerked his head. "If we don't take too long, I could probably help you get that out of here too."

Leah's eyes widened. "Really? That'd be awesome!" Then she chuckled. "Do you have a habit of offering to dump people's furniture? I know it looks pathetic but—"

His mouth opened in surprise. "No! No, I thought—I thought—didn't you say something about getting rid of it? The other day. I thought you said you were getting rid of your furniture!"

Leah shook her head. "I don't remember saying that, but hey"—she waved toward it—"it *is* pathetic, and you guessed right—it's all going. If you could help, that'd be fantastic!"

"Yeah—yeah, sure. Let's do it." He met her eyes and looked away.

Okay, that went well. Leah kicked herself, wishing she hadn't said anything. She cleared her throat. "Um, the kitchen's over here."

With only a second's glance at her makeshift bed, he followed, rounding the peninsula with her.

"Holy—what the heck happened here?" he asked at the sight of the water damage.

"I couldn't even guess!"

He shook his head in disbelief. "Well, all of this needs to come out, of course"—he gestured to the cupboards—"but other than that, the space is loaded with potential. You could do a lot."

"I'm just hoping it's not too complicated."

Silently he turned to view the back hall and the wall against which Leah's card table sat. "You know," he said thoughtfully, "you could really open up this place. You could get rid of these hanging cupboards over the peninsula and even take out part of this wall over here by the table." He gestured.

Leah followed his gaze. "Really? I'm not sure that's necessary—"

"It'd give you more space. Think of how nice it'd be if you could see all the way to the front of the house! You'd be letting more of this great southern sunlight into the living room area. It'd open everything up and brighten it considerably in here!"

She tried to imagine it.

"I'd totally take out that wall," he declared. "Then I'd replace all these outdated cupboards and update your appliances, throw some new flooring down. Maybe add an island. This place could look really great!"

"And *you* could do all that?"

He gave a humble nod. "At your service!"

His eagerness blew her away.

"Mind you, I have a full-time job, so it'd have to be a side project. It wouldn't be done in a hurry—just so you're clear on that."

"I'll consider that," she said. She hadn't thought out the timing issue. "Everything else looks structurally sound—from here anyway."

"Yeah. That's what I thought."

He gave a charming smile, then folded his arms, looking at her in a way that caused a little stir inside. "All right—change of subject. I've been dying to ask, so I might as well get it over with. Would you be interested in going out sometime? Nothing super fancy—just a bite to eat somewhere. Maybe a few drinks."

It only halfway surprised her. She'd had a gut sense that things were moving that direction; she just hadn't expected it there and then or quite so soon. She returned his smile. "I'd like that. Sounds fun."

"Great! I've got to work this weekend, so not until Tuesday at the soonest. You don't mind going out in the middle of the week—?"

"I'm flexible."

He dipped his head. "Cool. I know this bar downtown with live music. Maybe we'll go there."

"Yeah. Okay."

He rocked back on his boots, looking pleased. "Awesome! Then sometime soon we'll talk about this project." He gestured to the kitchen. "You know—I'll do some thinking, and you do some thinking, and we'll come up with a plan."

Leah nodded. "Sounds good."

"Start by finding your look and your appliances and stuff. Don't buy anything yet, but find what you want, and we'll come up with some numbers. Then I'll need to order some things, so I'll need some cash up front—from your stash of cash." He winked. "But anyway"—he checked his watch and jerked his head toward the living room—"if we're gonna get that furniture out before it rains, we better do it!"

"Right." She sighed, eyeing the bulky sectional as they entered the room. "It'd sure be a lot easier if we had another hand, but I can't ask either of my neighbors to help. A guy in his eighties lives on one side of me and my cousin Marty lives on the other—Marty Davison. Maybe you know him." She nodded in the direction of his house. "I was counting on him to help me with the house when I moved here, but he's really ticked with my mother right now. And me." Outside thunder rumbled forebodingly, as if emphasizing her point about her cousin.

Phil glanced briefly at the window. "Yeah?"

"It's a family thing. He's kinda gotten the short end of the stick since our grandfather died, and now he doesn't want anything to do with me."

"Inheritance drama." He gave a wry smile. "Let me guess—*you* were the lucky egg."

"Something like that. It's complicated."

He was silent, and suddenly Leah felt embarrassed, like she had shared too much. Self-consciously she added, "I guess all that to say—I'm really grateful for your help."

"Of course! I'm happy to!" He bent to pull off a seat cushion. "And I don't think we'll need your stinkin' cousin anyway! Catch!" He flung the cushion at her hard, nearly knocking her over.

She cried out in surprise, then noted his teasing expression. "You! Oh—oh, you've just declared war!"

He laughed, firing another cushion at her.

But he was right. Phil had a two-wheel cart and some dollies in his truck, and although it was a laborious feat, the two of them managed to muscle the furniture pieces through the door to deposit them on the far side of the dumpster. Hot and sticky from the humidity, they paused after their second load to catch their breath, and Leah brought up the party next door.

"Maybe we could hang out—if you're going."

Phil drew his arm across his brow. "Wish I could. Gotta work tomorrow."

"It's no problem. There's another girl from the neighborhood who's going, and we talked about meeting up. Perhaps you know her—Brindle Baylor. She lives across the street too, somewhere in the same neighborhood as you."

He cocked his head, surveying the discarded recliner. "Does she have kinda bright reddish hair? Long?"

"Pinkish-red. Yes."

"Yeah, I think I know who she is. What'd you say her name was?"

"Brindle Baylor."

His chin rose slightly. "Brindle Baylor. That's right. Yeah, I think we've met." His mouth twisted into a little smile. "Well,"— he pointed toward the darkening sky—"we better keep moving!"

The impending rain held back until they had wrangled the last musty piece of furniture out and dumped it with the others, after which the sky burst forth with a pounding deluge, causing a rather unceremonious parting between the two of them. With a whoop, Phil scrambled for his truck while Leah dashed for the porch, screaming as she was pelted by the icy raindrops.

"—swing by—work—weekend," Phil hollered out the crack of his truck window.

She missed most of what he said, but she got the point—he wanted to see her again. She plucked her wet shirt away from her body, smiling dreamily as his truck turned onto the highway. She would be counting the days until Tuesday. Certainly she was smarter this time around! Her eyes dropped to the pitiful loaner mower pummeled by the roaring downpour in front of the garage.

Suddenly an earsplitting crack of thunder shattered the air as lightning struck somewhere nearby. Her peaceful reverie vanished, and she scampered inside.

Void of the sectional, the living room now seemed spacious. Leah gathered up the assorted trash left behind, hoping that perhaps when Phil was over next, they could remove the remainder of that titanic entertainment center on the far wall. She had already chucked its warped shelves.

On her way to the kitchen waste basket, she hit the light. Opening the cupboard, she emptied her load and was about to close the door when she paused, noting a lime green can in her trash—an empty carbonated water, exactly the same as the one she had found in her flower beds on the day of her arrival. Leaning over, she parted the trash—yes, there was the other one near the bottom. She straightened, staring perplexed. She hadn't recalled either Brindle or Phil bringing a drink. Instantly she was reminded of the closet door in the bedroom she had found closed earlier.

"Honestly, what's going on?" she sputtered.

She whirled to check her card table, noting with a measure of relief her legal pad lying undisturbed where she had left it. Turning back, she set the can beside the sink. *Who was doing this?* First someone coming in, then the mailbox—and now the closet door and this!

"That's it—I'm going over there!" she murmured, heading for her back door. No matter what his reaction, it was time to confront Marty! Yeah, maybe her mother had provoked his behavior, but this was getting weird!

But it was still raining. Leah opened the door to the downpour and closed it again. Not to be deterred, she raised her phone to call Marty instead. When he didn't answer, she left him a stern message that he was not to step foot inside her house again without her permission. She felt slightly bad when she hung up, for there *was* the chance that he'd been coming over for nobler reasons—it might have been his return attempt. The chance was slim, she acknowledged, but even so, it was still worth giving him the benefit of the doubt.

She sighed, throwing the empty can in the bin and tapping the cupboard shut with her foot. She wished there were some way to repair the relationship, some way to prove that she wasn't his enemy. Hopefully at the neighbor's party tomorrow she could initiate another conversation and work to that end. If he were there. Either way, they needed to talk.

With the pattering rain and soft thunder as a relaxing backdrop, Leah returned to poke through the boxes laid out in the master bedroom. Somewhere in that mess could be the valuables that had been left at the house for her, and she didn't want to accidentally miss whatever it was. Carefully she started through each box, perusing item after item, layering everything neatly back in when she reached the bottom. After a while she stopped, setting her hands on her hips, frowning thoughtfully at the daunting task before her. It couldn't be money she was looking for, she decided. Wouldn't they have put money or anything of real monetary value in a secure place? Like in a safe. Not in bins of memorabilia. She sighed wearily, knowing that nevertheless she needed to check each box just in case.

As she carried on with her chore, she admitted—with amusement—that it was a lot more enjoyable to work without Brindle's running commentary on every item she found. Her big question now was what to do with everything once she finished looking through it, and she concluded that unless Uncle Richard or Marty wanted anything specific, it would either be dumped or probably go back into storage for yet another decade. She stifled a yawn, checking the time. It had been a long day.

The box of embroidered flour sack towels that Brindle had found indeed contained more dish towels than one could possibly use. Leah lifted a few sets out of the box to admire the old-fashioned designs, fingering the fine, colorful needlework on the corners. Passing her hand through the box to make sure there was nothing else tucked within, she discovered a folded notecard that read, "A set each for Ava Jane, Lenore and her two girls, Richard's wife, Shirley, and Marty's new wife. Love, Aunt Hazel." Underneath her signature, Grandma Havi had penciled that Aunt Hazel was Ed's mother's sister.

Leah ran her hand over the soft, white cotton, wondering how long the towels had sat forgotten in that closet. She also wondered if it was too late to give them out. Ava Jane, her grandmother, was no longer living, Marty was no longer married, and she, Leah, was Lenore's only daughter. But she could still give a set to Marty, send one to her Aunt Shirley, and set aside another for her mom. On the other hand, would Aunt Shirley have any interest in Great Aunt Hazel's embroidered dish towels? Probably not. And wouldn't offering Marty a stack be like rubbing salt in his wound? Her own mother, she guessed, would react negatively—like she did with everything concerning Grandma Havi and Ed. No, for now the dishtowels could stay right where they were.

Leah closed the box and moved on to a nearby boot box, discovering within several bundles of letters bound together with thin, white string, most of which were addressed to Ava Jane Wilkes, Grandma Havi's first married name, at an address in Bridgewater. Slipping one out of a bunch, Leah scanned it, discovering it to be a love letter from Grandpa Ed to her grandmother during their engagement—mostly a mundane list of tasks he had done that week in the construction of their house, with gushing sentiments of affection at the beginning and end of the letter. Amused, Leah wiggled another letter out of the pack, finding its contents similar.

The electrical is in to where the sheetrock can go up. The cabinets were delivered yesterday and are waiting in the garage. Waiting, waiting—like me! I look forward to the day I wake with you next to me.
Until then, all my love, Ed.

Leah scrunched her nose, mildly cringing at the idea of her grandparents being romantic. She tried to calculate what their ages would have been. It was even weirder to think that this was their bedroom. She shuddered, glancing down again at the letter, noting a postscript at the bottom of the page.

P.S. How's Lenore? Perhaps you should consider taking her to a doctor.

That was another wild thought—imagining her mom as a teenager during that era—someone who got up and did her hair and went to school every day! Someone who got sick and needed a doctor. The first of the small bedrooms—the one directly across from the bathroom—had been hers. She knew her mother would hate these letters. Her mother bristled at *anything* related to the Richmond house.

Threading the envelopes back into the string-bound pack, she set them into the box and lifted out a lumpy manila envelope with *Ava Jane Davison* penned across the front. Above the name, in Grandma Havi's handwriting, the words "save forever" were underlined twice. Curiously, Leah opened the flap and tipped out the contents, a single paperback novel sliding into her hand, its pages dark and brittle with age. Charles Dickens, *Great Expectations*. She fingered the volume, wondering what was so precious about it that it should be saved forever. Fanning the pages, she discovered a little area inside that had been carved out in the shape of a ring. Tucked there was another letter to her grandmother from her grandfather, folded into thirds.

Darling, I thought this would be a fitting way to propose, as a reminder of how far you've come! You're no longer bitter Miss Havisham, with your similar pains and sorrows, but you're my sweet Havi, a name that means "bringing forth life and joy." And now you're soon to be married! That is, if you'll have me! I love you. Ed.

P.S. Thanks for embracing the hard work of forgiveness.

Leah's brow rose in disbelief. Seriously? *That* was how he proposed? Yikes! And *that's* where she got her nickname? From *Miss Havisham*? Ouch! Why in the world would he call her *that*?

Disturbed, Leah folded the yellowed note and tucked it back inside the book. She remembered *Great Expectations* from ninth grade lit class— with Miss Havisham, the old spinster jilted at the altar who refused to change out of her wedding dress, the bitter woman who refused to move on from her pain, staying emotionally stuck for years. And to hold her up as a comparison to Grandma Havi—? Especially since Grandma herself had been left standing at the altar on her wedding day! Wasn't that dangerously close to rubbing it in her face? How could the nickname "Havi" *not* be a constant reminder of her Corolla fate? Yet apparently her grandma hadn't seen it that way—otherwise she wouldn't have let him call her that, nor would she have "saved forever" the letter and the book.

She studied the cover, supposing that technically Ed had been right. Her grandmother *had* embraced the hard work of forgiveness, for she hadn't been a bitter woman. Still—how insensitive of him! Sadly, Leah recognized how *unlike* her grandmother she was in that respect. But she preferred not to think about it.

Her phone rang on the other side of the house. She glanced over her shoulder toward the door. Good grief—she never talked to her mother this much in Bridgewater! Her twisted obsession with the house was beginning to bug her. Reluctantly Leah dropped the package back in the boot box and went to get the call.

It was her dad's number. She gave another internal groan. It was probably Chelsea calling to set up a time to get together. Did she want to drive all the way back to Bridgewater for that?

But for the second time, it wasn't Chelsea.

"Yeah. Hi, Leah. I'm, um—just checking in."

Leah hesitated a moment, a little confused. "Dad? Hi—what's going on?"

"I'm just checking in," he repeated.

"Okay. About what?"

"Well, the—to see about the house and stuff. Didn't you get my message?"

Leah paused. He never called. He *never* called her! She pictured his tall, lanky body at his desk in his office at home where he liked to retreat to be alone. "Is there something wrong?" she asked outright.

"What? No, nothing's wrong."

Leah didn't believe him. "Dad, did you lose your sobriety? Or is it Chelsea?"

He huffed. "No, Leah. Why would you ask me that? And Chelsea's good."

"Well, you never call."

"I—I know. That's why—" He let out a breath. "I know. I'm trying to change that. I'm calling to offer you help."

Leah blinked. What in the world? Pigs were flying and hell was freezing over! "All right. Well, I think I'm doing fine."

"Okay. I was just—" He stopped to clear his throat. "Is—how is the roof? Does it need work? And if you need help with—like any repairs. If the house needs repairs, I could help you with that. Or the yard. Anything. Just let me know. Because I'd like—I'd *like* to help you."

"Okay," Leah replied warily. "I appreciate that." Why was he doing this? Was he sick? Dying? Maybe she should have stopped to say goodbye to him before she left Bridgewater. "Are you *sure* everything's okay?"

"Yeah, I'm okay."

"You never call me, and you're making me nervous. What's going on?"

"Nothing's going on! I just—I want to help you."

Leah was silent.

She heard him take a breath. "To be honest, I've wanted to talk to you, Leah. I've been thinking of calling you for a couple weeks now, but I'm not good at—at talking. We were going to have you over, but then you called to say you were moving. But I—well, I still want to talk with you."

"Okay," she said, still cautious. "About anything in particular?"

"Well, um—yes. I'm working on taking care of some bad decisions I've made. And that's why we were going to have you over."

Immediately her imagination zipped off in a dozen directions. Had he gotten a DUI? Or lost his job? Were they declaring bankruptcy? Was Chelsea leaving him? "And are these bad decisions somehow related to *me*?"

He gave a little laugh. "Well, yes! Leah, I've been a *terrible* father!"

She drew her head back in surprise. "What?"

"A terrible father! I've—I've messed things up pretty badly with you."

Leah didn't even know what to say. Was *this* what he intended to talk to her about?

"I'm trying to fix things in my life. I'm trying to fix—to change the way I am, trying to do the right—well, fixing my mistakes. I'm trying—"

Her hand went to her head. What in the world! She was half stunned and half squirming with embarrassment for him! She knew he disliked talking in general—that he "never had the right words"—and he was struggling now.

"Dad, no, it's okay—"

"—I'm trying to make amends. By God's help, I'm trying to make amends."

Trying to make amends? What? Unsure of how to respond, she

murmured, "Uh—okay."

"So, if I could help you—" he trailed off.

Leah nodded. "Okay. Well, thanks for offering. I *do* appreciate it."

"Okay. Okay—good. Because I *do* want to help you, Leah. I would be willing to come down there—whatever you need!"

"All right. Well, let me think. I'll look around and maybe see if I can come up with a few things—"

"Yes! Yes, you do that! You make a list! You make a list, and I, maybe Chelsea too—we'll drive down for a weekend. A weekend or even a *day*. If you make a list."

"Okay, I will."

"Okay, thank you! It would—it would mean a lot to me if I could—if I could—"

"All right, Dad," she cut in hastily, trying to save his dignity. "I'll see what I can do. Thank you for calling me, okay? I really appreciate it."

"Okay. Thank you for talking to me."

Leah nodded to herself, adding, "And say hi to Chelsea."

"Yes. I'll do that. Good—goodbye, Leah."

Good gracious, what was that? Leah pushed the red end call button on her phone and stood there, unable to move. That had been painful on so many levels—painfully difficult, painfully awkward, painfully pathetic, painfully *painful*! She'd never heard her dad like this—stumbling over his words, confessing that he had messed up with her! She rubbed her forehead. Trying to fix things and *make amends*? What in the world? Had Chelsea put him up to that call? If so, she was pressuring him! She was pushing him way too hard! It wasn't like him! It wasn't like him to be—Leah wiped a single tear that had escaped—it wasn't like him to be—to be like *that*!

She tried not to think about the past, when once upon a time she had been a Daddy's girl—before the divorce. It was the place her heart longed to retreat to—to the era before their relationship went dormant and Chelsea became his mouthpiece. She tried to recall the last time the two of them had actually *talked*, the last time they had intentionally done something together, the last time he had shown an interest in helping her with anything. Not that he deliberately refused to interact with her, but it simply wasn't a part of their relationship anymore. It hadn't been for a long, long time.

She brushed away a few more tears that threatened to spill over—tears from a capped off cistern deep in her heart, tears that *wished* for him to be in her life but had been taught not to trust, tears that were always followed by the deep breath of steeling herself for the inevitable disappointment just around the corner. Leah took that breath and stood in the dining room watching the drizzling rain on the window glass, asking herself—like every other time—*Did he really mean this?* Or would this follow suit as before? Would he remember this call? Should she even bother to make a list? Would he come if she asked him to, or would he be too busy? She could make her predictions, but there was no way to really know except to wait and see.

She set her phone back onto the counter. Somehow it seemed different with her dad this time—like he was genuinely trying. It almost made things worse, because then there was actually a thread of hope to hang onto. Chelsea had said they'd been going to Anchor Church, and in the back of her mind Leah wondered if that could be part of the equation. *Could it be?* Was there truly something going on with her dad and God? That was harder to believe than his calling to offer to help her! But she had to wonder. At any rate, she hoped he was all right and that there wasn't something deeper and scarier going on that they weren't telling her.

Chapter Eleven

Another runner was on the path ahead of Leah early the next morning when she went out, but it wasn't Phil—she could tell by his build—and he disappeared back into the neighborhood without seeing her after he rounded the pond. It was nice to know that others used the track. She almost hadn't gone, having had a restless night of invasive and puzzling thoughts about her dad and nasty Miss Havisham intermittently, but she was determined to keep up with her new fitness hobby. Wouldn't there always be a reason not to go? She pressed through even tired, and she was glad she did, for the morning was beautiful. The rain had stopped during the night, and the sun was now shining with brilliance, creating a shimmering effect on the damp grass and trees. Jackie Burke and her aged father certainly had luck on their side. It looked like a spectacular day for their party.

When she got back to the house, she discovered that her brother Braydon had texted.

"Heads up. Mom's on the rampage. Says you never call her."

Leah rolled her eyes, texting back, "Thanks for the tip."

She phoned her mother immediately and caught her by surprise, scoring high with the call. They chit-chatted about incidentals for a minute before Leah brought up the subject of her grandma's name while it was fresh on her mind.

"Did you know that Grandma Havi got her nickname from a Dicken's novel?"

"Oh, *he* called her that," she growled, referring to Grandpa Ed. "I always thought it was dumb."

"Well, apparently it meant 'life' or something, the opposite of what Miss Havisham was like."

"Who?"

"Miss Havisham. You know, from *Great Expectations*—the book."

"Never heard of it. Never knew why he called her that and didn't care to know. How'd you come upon that?"

"Oh, just some old letters in a closet."

"What letters?" Her tone sounded guarded.

"Just a few odd notes mixed in with a ton of other things left behind," Leah replied, keeping it minimal. "Board games, magazines. Stuff like that."

"He was so irritatingly religious—remember? I was never so happy to move out of there and back to Bridgewater."

Leah sighed and tried to steer the conversation to a more pleasant subject, but her mom was in the car on her way to the grocery store and had to cut their conversation short anyway.

Around noon Leah judged the lawn dry enough to mow, but because of the excessive length of the grass, there was still enough moisture deep down to gum up the underside of the little mower. She followed the edge of Phil's long swath over near the west hedge, being extra diligent to watch for remnants of the buried fence as she ran the mower back and forth over long, stubborn patches, but every twenty feet or so she had to stop and scrape the mash off with a paint stick from the garage. Nevertheless, she was determined to mow a little bit, even if it seemed like an exercise in futility.

Phil's mower accident, however, was both mystifying and somewhat irritating to her, for the post he had hit was protruding well out of the grass. He'd have had to been blindfolded not to see it! Her best guess was that he wasn't paying attention and was too embarrassed to admit it. Of course, she was confident he wouldn't have done it on purpose, but his fudging of reported details did lend a bit to cowardliness.

Hot and filthy, Leah returned the mower to the garage, satisfied to have finally made some forward progress on her yard. Pausing to cool off, she poked through the miscellaneous tools and equipment on the crowded workbench. Undoubtedly that disheveled surface had been more organized back in her grandfather's day, as indicated by the many empty hooks on the pegboard above. It appeared that most of the returned tools had been simply set down onto the bench to be put away later by someone else, and that person had not come along yet. Someday it would be her job to straighten up the area.

There was a lot in the garage that would need to be cleaned out and organized—a lot more than tools. Long shelves stacked with large, brightly colored plastic bins lined the inside wall to the right of the door into the house, several of which had sticker labels reading "crafts," "books," "kitchen extras," "miscellaneous," and "Christmas." Lots of Christmas. Eventually she would have her chance to sort through all those things too. Someday. But that was not today. She yanked her stretchy gardening gloves off and tossed them onto the corner of the workbench.

"Did you decide not to go today?"

Leah turned to see Brindle in a yellow blouse and cute white shorts duck under the partially opened garage door. "Hi. No, I'm going."

Her brow rose critically. "Like that?"

Leah brushed her hand down the front of her dirty T-shirt. "I'm a mess, I know! I'm running late—sorry. Mind hanging out while I shower?"

"Take your time. I don't exactly want to be the first ones there."

"Yeah." Leah gestured to her door. "Come on in. I won't be long."

That afternoon Leah and Brindle carefully struggled their way through the tight gap in the hedge, their arms laden with a platter of taco bean dip and a pan of chocolate chip cookie bars. On the other side, they startled a group of a half dozen people who were moseying along the sidewalk toward Jackie Burke's backyard.

"Excuse us—sorry," Leah said, raising her taco dip as she backed against the arborvitae to make room for them to pass. "Sorry."

"Sorry," echoed a young mom with a curly-haired baby on her arm. She turned sideways to move her bulging diaper bag out of the way, urging the preschooler in front of her to keep walking.

Cars lined both sides of the Glendes' driveway all the way to the street, and more people were arriving from where they'd parked along the road.

"Do you know any of these people?" Leah asked Brindle under her breath.

"Nope," she replied.

A middle-aged man with an official-looking lanyard over his black T-shirt stood near Jackie's front door, directing the newcomers alongside the house to the back, from where they could hear music and laughter. "Welcome, welcome! We're happy you're here! Go on back!"

Brindle threw Leah a look.

"It's too late—I already made the bean dip!" She jerked her head for Brindle to follow.

A narrow sidewalk between the house and the hedge led them to a large wooden deck off the back, the descending steps of which adjoined to a spacious concrete pool deck surrounding the long swimming pool that ran parallel with the hedge. Several happy children were already playing noisily in the water, their vigilant parents seated on plastic deck chairs chatting with one another while keeping a watchful eye on them. On the lawn behind the diving board, hefty speakers on tall stands boomed out energetic music to the crowd gathered there. Drawn into the celebratory atmosphere, Leah paused to survey the panorama before her.

On the poolside opposite the hedge, a broad, manicured lawn sloped gradually downward toward a sizable shed at the yard's edge, near which stood an industrial-sized stainless-steel grill and two enormous white shade canopies side by side. Beneath were rows of white plastic tables and chairs. Nearby a large, horizontal barrel released occasional tufts of smoke, causing Leah's mouth to water for whatever was cooking in there.

On the far opposite side of the yard, a temporary volleyball court was set up, its boundaries spray-painted hot pink on the grass. Some distance away were two sets of horseshoe pits dug into the earth, filled with fresh sand. All around the yard people were everywhere, spread out in little clusters playing yard games or standing or sitting here or there, some on lawn chairs, some on blankets, some at the table on the patio deck or beside the pool.

Jackie Burke was on the deck putting her dog in the house when she noticed their arrival. With a wave she closed the door and headed down the stairs to greet them.

"I'm so glad you made it, Ava! Thanks for coming!" She extended her hand to Brindle. "Hello! Not sure if we've met. Jackie Burke. I live here. Welcome to our party!"

"Brindle Baylor. From across the road."

Her head lifted in recognition. "Ah, yes—I remember! You were here last weekend to swim in our pool. You've changed your hair! I like it! It's nice to see you again, Brindle." She smiled. "Are you two related? Your eyes look alike."

"No," Leah said, glancing at Brindle for a hint of resemblance.

"No? Well, you ladies are so sweet to bring food—you surely didn't have to! Addie!" She beckoned to a preteen on the deck who quickly joined them. "Addie, hon, this is my neighbor Ava, and this is Brindle from across the street."

The girl nodded. "Hello."

"Would you be a dear and take their food into the house, please?" She turned back as the girl left. "We're keeping the food inside where it's cooler and away from bugs, but there're drinks on ice down by the tents. And snacks." She pointed. "Help yourselves, please. We've got a hog roasting, and we're grilling burgers around six o'clock, so there's plenty of afternoon yet before we eat. There's a bathroom in the house and one down in the shed. And a portable restroom by the horseshoe pit." She motioned to indicate its location.

Beside them a ruckus erupted as one of the adults jumped into the pool with an enormous splash. A little boy in the water screamed in playful panic, gripping the side near them as the man glided toward him. Behind him another child bounced up and down, waving his arms from the middle of the pool.

"Dad! Dad, come and throw me! Dad—over here! Throw me!"

Leah recognized his freckled face even wet—the little boy in her climbing tree.

"Dad! Dad! Dad! Dad—"

The father raised a dripping hand. "Hold your horses, kiddo! This shark can only gobble up one victim at a time!" He crouched low in the water, menacingly approaching his target.

Another wild shriek from the lad clinging to the side.

"Oh, dear—we're gonna get soaked!" Jackie warned, waving them out onto the grass away from the pool. "Did you bring your suits? You're welcome to swim—although there'll probably be tons of kids in there today. But you're still welcome to hang out in the pool if you'd like. Or beside it if you're into sunning or lounging. And there's volleyball, and they're setting up the bean bag toss—"

From across the yard Leah heard that familiar burst of laughter cut the air. She twisted, peering toward the volleyball court, noticing as she did so that Kyla Watkins was swiftly approaching them.

"That laugh—I know that laugh from somewhere!" she said.

"Oh, golly—I know!" Jackie grazed her fingers on Leah's arm. "Isn't it something? It's one of a kind! That's the young man staying in our guest house this summer. His name is—"

"Excuse me, Miss Jackie," Kyla broke in breathlessly as she arrived, her cheeks rosy. "Peter wants to know when you'd like him to start gathering the kids for the games." She smiled at Leah and Brindle. "Hi. Sorry to interrupt your conversation." Her hair was up, wound in a loose bun, and she reached up to tuck a loose strand behind her ear, her enormous wedding ring glinting in the sun.

Jackie frowned, glancing at her watch. "Well, I think it's still a little early yet. The kids will want to swim for a while, don't you think? I'd say wait at least an hour."

"Okay. He also said the jugglers want to know where you'd like them to set up and when you want them to start."

"Oh, all these last-minute things! I should probably go talk to him." Jackie turned to Leah and Brindle. "I'm so sorry—"

Leah waved her off. "No, we're fine—go on!"

"Thanks, girls. Enjoy yourselves today! Kyla, where now—?"

Kyla pointed through the yard. "Right there—waiting by the corner of the house."

Then as Jackie Burke left to traverse across the lawn, Kyla turned back to them. "It's Ava, right? Nice to see you again! And hello—I'm Kyla Watkins." She reached to shake Brindle's hand.

"Brindle Baylor—from the neighborhood across the street."

Kyla's eyes narrowed slightly. "Ah, we might've met! Weren't you here, like, a week ago? Swimming? Your hair was different. You went red. Or reddish, sort of. It's nice."

Brindle's chin bobbed. "Yes."

Kyla nodded. "I remember."

Brindle smiled.

"There are a lot of people here," Leah offered. "Jackie wasn't kidding when she said this party was a big deal."

"Yes, it is! Jackie's dad—Brother Warren—he started this a long time ago, and they have this party the same weekend every summer. People love it. Have you met him yet? He's awesome! But here's the deal—don't think that everyone knows each other already. You might feel like an outsider, but there's new people coming all the time. The whole idea is to meet people and hang out. This is only our second year here. We're not actually from this neighborhood, but I'm friends with Jackie and Brother Warren. We come over here a lot."

"We?" Brindle asked.

"Me and my husband, Peter. But mostly me and the kids I watch." Kyla gestured to the pool. "I watch a couple of boys, and we come here to swim. Jackie's become a dear friend. She's the sister of the lady who cleans the house where I work—Susan Gordon, who's like a mom to me. Anyway, I'm glad you're both here."

"Thanks," Leah said.

Kyla reached into her back pocket to retrieve a small stack of business-sized cards, handing one to each of the girls. "Did you get one of these?"

"Um, I don't think so—"

"I'm starting a Bible study here at Jackie's on Tuesdays. Ten o'clock. I know a lot of people work then, but if it works out, I'd love to have you both. Here's some info on it."

Brindle's eyes darted toward Leah.

Leah studied the card for a moment, then slid it into her pocket. "Okay, thanks."

"And after dinner tonight I'll be sharing the story of a miracle that God did in my life. I hope you'll stay to hear it."

"Yeah. Jackie said something about it the other day. Something about your dad."

Kyla's face brightened. "That's right! It's an amazing story! I've been through the most awful journey of rejection and abandonment, but God's done a miracle." She paused. "I'd tell you more, but it's complicated, and I'd really like you to hear all the details. I hope you'll stay for it tonight."

"We'll see," Leah replied politely without committing. Impulsively she added, "I just had a miracle *myself* with my dad—he actually called me last night!" She snickered. "I'm joking, of course. But it's true! He never calls, so it was a surprise!"

"Well, that's great!" Kyla offered with enthusiasm.

Leah shook her head. "No, it's really not that big of a deal. Sorry. I didn't mean to diminish your thing. It's just that my family is—you know—kinda the 'all American messed up' type. My dad and I haven't had a real conversation in, like, years!"

Kyla flicked up her hand. "I get it! Seriously, I get it completely! And as for families, no one has an odder family than mine—I guarantee you!"

The two girls laughed and turned naturally toward Brindle, who was gazing off into the yard, her arms folded.

"Well," Kyla said into the awkwardness, "I'm supposed to be helping around here, so I should probably go. Maybe after the kid games we can meet up again."

"Yeah, okay," Leah replied.

"Remember—don't be shy about meeting people! Just crash a group and introduce yourselves. That's the rule for the day! Truly!"

"All right—thanks."

"Bye," Brindle said simply as Kyla left.

Leah turned to her. "What's wrong? You got quiet all of a sudden."

Brindle gave a mysterious smile.

"Did she offend you? An invitation to a Bible study doesn't mean you have to go. You didn't need to be rude!"

Brindle shook her head. "You have *no* idea!"

"No idea about what?"

"You have no idea what you have."

"Me?" Leah's eyes widened in surprise. "What do you mean? How did this become about me?"

Brindle said nothing.

Leah opened her hands. "I don't get it—what are you mad about? That I took her card for her Bible study—?"

"I'm going to the restroom," Brindle said, and with a passive blink she turned to walk away.

"What the heck!" Leah muttered to herself, staring after her, wondering whether to follow her or let her be. "I'll be by the pool," she called. "Bring me a drink when you come back!"

Brindle didn't look back. Leah watched her cross the lawn toward the shed. She was learning that Brindle had a moody side, and it was a little disturbing.

Alone now, Leah scanned the yard. She wasn't exactly crazy about breaking into a group of strangers and introducing herself, but since it was the rule of the day and she was alone, she decided to comply. After all, she was genuinely new to the neighborhood and how else was she going to meet people? At the edge of the crowd on the far side of the pool deck she noticed a woman in a striking blue dress sitting by herself in the shade of the hedge, the table and chairs near her strewn with patterned beach towels and discarded bags, a heap of sandals near her feet. Target number one, Leah mused. Here goes—

"Hello," she said, approaching. "Mind if I join you?"

"Delighted!" the woman replied. Hastily she cleared a chair, tossing an armful of towels onto another seat, motioning. "Please, please!" Then she angled her own chair slightly toward Leah's. "Nice to have your company! Stellar day for a party, don't you agree?"

She was British, Leah determined by her accent, her voice pleasant and musical. Her eyes were hidden by a stylish pair of dark sunglasses and the broad brim of a sunhat, its ribboned band perfectly matching the blue of her summer dress. On her hand flashed a sizable diamond ring at least as large as Kyla Watkin's. Good heavens—that was *two* now, Leah observed with interest.

"I'm Ava. I live right next door on the other side of this hedge."

"Lovely! How do you do?" She extended a graceful hand. "Mary Grant. My husband, David, is in the pool with our boys. The shrieking ones, I'm afraid." She gestured toward a dark-haired man currently launching a crazily giggling child out of the water by his feet, crying "incoming!" and making the sound of an explosion as the lad splashed noisily back into the pool.

"Looks like fun! Nice to meet you, Mary. I just moved in, and this is the first time I've been to one of Brother Warren's parties."

The woman frowned. "Brother Warren—is that Mr. Glende? He's the elderly gentleman, correct? I've only met him this afternoon. Our nanny brings the boys here to swim frequently, but I've never visited here myself until today, so we were only introduced a bit ago. Kyla Watkins—I saw you talking to her a minute ago—she's our nanny."

"Ah, I see!"

"To be honest, my husband quite had to drag me here. I'm out of town on business for weeks at a time, and when I'm home I rather prefer to stay put. But this is very pleasant today. Excellent weather for a picnic."

"Yes, it is!" Leah agreed, adding, "You look so familiar—have we met? You're not from Bridgewater, are you?"

The lady smiled. "I get that a lot! No, I've never been to Bridgewater. Is that a city nearby?"

"My hometown, about an hour and a half away. Anyway, you look familiar. What do you do?"

"Oh, nothing too important, darling. But tell me about yourself—you said you just moved in. Do you have a family? A husband or children?"

"No, just me. I inherited the house from my grandparents recently—which is why I moved here. I'm not working yet, but when I'm settled, I'll find a job in the accounting field."

"That's grand! A versatile occupation, certainly. So tell me, since they lived next door, were your grandparents friends with this gentleman, Brother Warren?"

"They were!"

"Yes? Then perhaps you could enlighten me on this prefix 'Brother.' I've been wondering about it and haven't been sure whom to ask. Can you tell me if this is connected to a particular religion? I'm unfamiliar with it and am trying to determine if it's a Protestant or Catholic thing. Is it similar to a 'reverend' or a 'father'?"

"Well, um, I'm not completely sure. I think it's more like a title of respect for a preacher or a man of God."

"Oh, is that it?" She nodded thoughtfully. "I see, I see. And is it earned by a degree? Must they complete a course of education at a college or a seminary?"

Leah frowned. "I don't think so. But I'm not one hundred percent sure."

The woman leaned back, folding her hands in her lap. "It rather cheapens it, don't you think, when it's conferred without the proper education?"

"I've never thought about it."

"It's a curiosity. Do you practice religion, Miss Ava?"

Leah hesitated. There was the poke of that prod again. She knew what Mrs. Grant was asking, but she wasn't quite sure how to answer. Did she still believe in God? Yes. Did she still believe in the doctrines of Christianity? Technically yes, though admittedly she wasn't good at keeping even the basics. Was she walking with God the way Pastor Reid had taught them to—getting personal with him, reading the Bible, going to church, praying, and all that? No. She was avoiding him like the plague. Pastor Reid had always taught there was a vast difference between being religious and living as a child of God. But Mary Grant wasn't asking all that.

"Not really," she replied, but then recalling that just a day or so ago she had prayed, and God had answered, she added, "but maybe a little."

Mrs. Grant gave a nod. "And this Brother Warren—is he one of your friends too?"

Leah shook her head. "I've not met him yet. Only his daughter, Jackie. And briefly."

"Ah, yes—Jackie! Now she is a *very* kind soul! And quite beautiful too, given her age."

"Yes, she is!"

The woman gave an odd chuckle, dropping her arms. "Forgive me, but that's what's so confounding about my life lately! I'm surrounded by all these kind-hearted people who are obsessed with religion! It's a downright phenomenon!" She shifted, adjusting the skirt of her dress. "I've become the minority in my own home! My dear husband, our nanny, and our nanny's husband—they've all converted to practicing religion. And rather profusely, I'll add. And they seem to be entirely taken with this Brother Warren. It's bewildering to me, and I'm concerned!

"It's put a strain on our marriage too, I'll confess. Not that I can find fault in our nanny or her husband! You couldn't find a more wonderful couple, truly, and she adores our boys. But David has changed so much over the last few years. It's not *all* bad, mind you, but I hardly know him anymore! And our boys are growing up exposed to this! I'm quite at odds with what to do!" She flashed Leah a sudden look. "Sorry, love! Here I am unburdening myself when we've scarcely met! What you must think of me!"

Leah shook her head. "Don't be embarrassed! Your secret's safe with me!"

Her words were well-timed, as right at that moment Mary's husband joined them, fresh out of the pool and dripping across the deck. Leah slid her chair back to give him a little more room, observing the pink welt of a wicked scar on his upper right chest as he greeted them and rubbed himself dry with a thick towel from the pile on the chair.

"You should wear a shirt, darling," his wife cajoled. "You're getting pink! Ava, this is my husband, David Grant. David, this is Ava, who lives next door. Her late grandparents knew your Mr. Warren."

He lowered the towel and extended a damp hand. "Is that right? Pleasure to meet you. I never cease to be amazed at the breadth of Brother Warren's influence. Have you known him for a while then?"

"I've not actually met Mr. Glende yet. I just moved in."

"Ah, okay, okay. You most likely will meet him before the end of the evening. At any rate, I'm pleased you've met my wife." He exchanged the towel for a nylon golf shirt, pulling it over his head. Turning, he asked, "Hon, do you feel comfortable hanging out here with the boys? Dan's looking for a partner in shoes."

"Go on—I'm fine."

"Are you sure? Because I—"

"I'm fine, David."

He nodded. "Thanks. In a few minutes they should get out of the pool and get ready for the games. Make sure you give them enough time. And have them drink something. It's warm out here."

His wife shook her hand impatiently. "Yes, yes—go on now!"

He passed the towel again over his dark, wiry hair, which had wound itself into tight, damp curls, then hung it over the back of the chair. "I'll be on the far side of the yard." He tipped his head toward Leah. "Nice to meet you, Ava. We'll probably run into each other again today."

As he left, Mary added, "I think you're being beckoned too, my dear.

177

Looks like someone would like to play croquet with you."

Leah looked up to see Brindle on the other side of the pool wildly waving her arms to get her attention, croquet mallet in hand. Leah had guessed she'd be back. Part of her wanted to snub her in return by ignoring her.

"I saw you arrive together. Is she your sister?"

Leah shook her head. "Neighborhood friend. Sort of. We just met a few days ago. I'll go tell her no so we can finish our conversation."

"Oh, believe me, my dear—I am more than accustomed to living my life in interrupted intervals. In a short minute the boys will be out of that water and getting dressed. I'm quite content to have a moment to myself before that happens."

"But it feels rude just walking away. Perhaps later this afternoon we can chat again."

"Perhaps, love," she answered. "I would like that. But go on now—go enjoy yourself!"

Leah thanked her, then signaled to Brindle that she'd meet her on the grass near the croquet equipment.

A newly arrived pack of teenagers stood in a tight cluster at the foot of the deck stairs, blocking that way around the pool, so Leah headed the other direction, threading through the people seated on the deck chairs in the shade of the arborvitae to make her way to the grassy area behind the diving board. There she discovered a little rock pathway curling around the side of a grand row of lilac bushes that she guessed led to the quaint cabin she had noticed on her sunrise walk the other day. Hesitating briefly, she followed the stone walk past the lilacs for a peek, indeed finding the area to be a charming little nook, with its picturesque cottage hidden from the view of the main house and pool.

The cabin's boardwalk porch had an overhanging roof from which hung several bright red hummingbird feeders, each alive with a flurry of activity. Delighted, Leah paused to watch the jeweled creatures flit to and fro. Simultaneously she admired the cabin's rough-cut siding and mossy wooden shakes. At the base of the porch steps began a rugged stone patio, at the center of which sat a self-contained fire pit and a round glass table nearby with two chairs. The sizeable pavement was framed by a lovely shade garden which in turn was surrounded by the arborvitae and lilacs, although the far border opened to the field that adjoined her own.

As she stood appreciating the cozy area, she heard someone talking and with surprise noticed her cousin Marty suddenly appear around the back side of the hedge, having obviously cut across her yard on his way to the party. He was on his phone. Unaware of her presence, he paused with his back to her, facing the field to finish his conversation. Before she could even think of what she'd say to him, he slid his phone into his back pocket and turned to start across the stone pavement for the main area of the picnic. Only then did he raise his head—giving a start when he saw her.

"Hi, Marty," she said, her mouth terribly dry. "Hey—can we talk?"

He paused. "What's there to talk about?"

"You know—the thing with my mom. I told you before—I'm not in favor of what she's doing to you, but I can't stop her. So don't punish me for something that's not my fault!"

He screwed up his face. "What?"

"Well, I know what you're doing—all those little things over there! You can knock it off!"

He stared at her for a moment, then shook his head and began walking away.

"Oh, for heaven's sake, Marty—*please*!"

He spun on his heel. "Okay—what? You want to talk—talk!"

"I'm not your enemy, Marty," she appealed hastily. "I'm your cousin and your friend! Please remember that! This morning I was looking at all of Grandpa's tools and stuff in the garage—and I think they should be yours. Anything you want in there you're welcome to have. Take it all—I don't care! Except the lawn mower. I'm borrowing that."

He simply stood there. Dang it—couldn't he say *something*? Like maybe "thanks" or at a minimum "okay"? His cold manner stung.

"That's all," she said finally. "You can go. I'm sorry for how it's all turned out, but it's out of my control."

With a stiff nod he turned to go, trekking down across the lawn, right past Brindle, who stood watching the whole thing with one hand on her mallet and the other on her hip.

"Now *that* was interesting," she said mildly as Leah arrived. "Doesn't look like he cares much for *you*!"

"Mind your own business, Brindle!" Leah said, choosing a croquet mallet.

Her brow rose.

"Is it just us?" Leah asked.

"No, a couple more girls are joining us. They're getting their sodas."

"Okay."

Leah took her ball and went to stand by the starting point, lifting her eyes to watch Marty join the group of men at the horseshoe pit. Their exchange had been disappointing, but at least he had not cussed her out like before, nor had he reviled her for the peace gesture. Maybe there was hope.

Chapter Twelve

The afternoon at the neighbor's party flew by, and Leah immensely enjoyed herself—though at first she'd been on guard that the four girls who'd invited Brindle and her to play croquet were from Brother Warren's and Jackie Burke's church. As the game progressed, however, she soon discovered them to be friendly and harmless, and making a conscious effort to relax, she dropped her reservations and ended up having a ton of fun.

In the middle of the afternoon Kyla Watkins and her husband organized a wacky Olympics for the kids, which ended up being hilarious to watch because the kids were cute and funny, and after that three professional jugglers—also from Jackie's church—put on an impressive show near the house, delighting the guests gathered on the lawn for almost forty minutes.

By the time they were finished, the air was heavy with the aroma of roasted hog and grilled burgers, and every space on the serving tables under the canopies was loaded with food. Collectively the crowd rose from the grass and morphed into a slowly moving food line in which the two girls found a spot somewhere in the middle of where it snaked through the yard.

Brindle jabbed Leah with her elbow, nodding discreetly to where a few folks ahead of them in line, Kyla Watkin's tall, blond husband hugged his wife from behind, holding her pregnant belly and nuzzling her neck. With her hands atop of his, she nuzzled him back. Brindle threw Leah an amused look, who raised her brow and smiled in return. A moment later Kyla noticed them and waved. Motioning the people between them to go ahead, she took her husband's hand and joined Leah and Brindle in the line.

"We'll come back and stand with you so we can chat," she said happily. "Have you met my husband, Peter? Peter—Ava and Brindle. Ava's the next-door neighbor on the other side of the hedge. And Brindle lives in the neighborhood across the street."

Peter smiled. "Hello. I recognize your name," he said to Leah. "You're the cookie frost-er."

"I am! An impressive title for having frosted all of *four* cookies!"

They all laughed.

"Today's been a lot of fun," Leah said. "I'm really glad I came. Those jugglers were great! That was some serious talent!"

Kyla nodded. "They were—I know! And so are we! Last year we came as guests. This year we're helping, but it's still a lot of fun."

"Are you from the area?" Peter asked Leah.

"No, from Bridgewater. Born and raised there. Maybe you've already heard, but I inherited my grandparents' home, and that's what brings me here."

"I see. And are you working?"

"Soon. I'm taking a little time to fix up my house before joining the area workforce. Let me know if you hear of anyone needing an accountant. I'm going to need a job sooner or later."

"Will do! And how about you, Brindle?" Peter asked, turning to her. "Did you grow up in the New Hampton area?"

Brindle lifted a shoulder in a shrug. "Nope. Didn't grow up here. And I'm currently a part-time server at a local restaurant—so you can all assume I'm very wealthy too."

Another round of laughs.

"Yeah, no kidding!" Kyla interjected. "I've waitressed before, so I know how hard it can be. I'm sure you're working your tail off. You just moved here too, didn't you? I don't recall seeing you in the neighborhood until the other day when you were over visiting Dan."

"No, I haven't lived here that long."

"Where did you move from?"

She smiled evasively. "You know, I've moved enough times in my life to make your head spin. Right now I'm simply content to say that I'm from New Hampton."

Kyla's brow rose in surprise. "Okay!"

"Works for me," Peter said, folding his arms.

"A woman of mystery," Leah offered with an edge of sarcasm. Brindle's aloofness was starting to bug her a little. Raising her head, she tried to look around the people in front of her. "Is this line moving? It seems like we haven't budged from this spot."

"I know!" Kyla agreed, a little impatiently. "I'm so starving!"

"Oh, it's moving," Peter assured, peering over their heads. "My nose tells me it'll be worth the wait!"

Leah turned to him. "So how about you? What do you do?"

"He owns his own landscaping business," Kyla purred, taking his arm and beaming proudly up at him. "The kind of service that makes your yard beautiful. He partners with Watkins Nursery to 'make your landscaping dreams a reality.' That's his slogan."

Leah's eyes widened. "Seriously? Oh, man! You're just the guy I need but probably can't afford!"

Peter inclined his head. "Yeah? You starting a yard project?"

"I will be!"

"Wait—Watkins Nursery?" Brindle broke in, her forehead wrinkled.

"Yes," Peter said, "I partner with them as a subcontractor."

"Isn't that the place that was all over the news a few years back? With that one kid?"

"What kid?" Leah asked.

Brindle shook her head, as if it were obvious. "That Watkins kid. You know, the one that went off on his coworker there. It was a huge scandal! The media blew up with it."

Leah frowned, her memory faintly jogged. "Oh, yeah—Watkins Nursery! Wow—that was a long time ago already. But sure—I kinda remember it! Wasn't it the owner's kid? I think so anyway. Like the owner's son brutally murdered a guy and completely got away with it—or with a hand slap or something. Did you know him?"

Kyla's mouth dropped open with a squeak as Peter's arm came around her shoulder in a side hug. "Yes, I remember it too! That was several years ago." He tipped his head to look into his wife's face. "Kyla, honey, you would have been in Stanton at the time. You probably didn't hear about it. But I followed the case." He looked back at Leah and Brindle. "I followed it *very* closely, and he didn't get away with it—I can tell you that for sure. Justice was served."

"Really?" Leah said. "Well, that's good! I don't remember the gory details—just that it was bad!"

Brindle frowned, looking up at Peter. "You're a Watkins—you're not related, are you?"

Peter smiled. "I can assure you *that* guy is not around anymore! But yes, as a matter of fact I *am* related to the Mr. Watkins who owns the place, and I'm very grateful for our partnership. So, as you were saying, Miss Ava, you're planning a project in your yard—?" He kept his arm around Kyla, whose face was unsmiling and pink.

"Yes. I'm afraid my new home's been badly neglected since my grandparents lived there. It used to be so beautiful, and now it—well, to put it plainly, it's *not*! I could only dream of having it nice again, but at the moment I'm just trying to get the grass mowed. It's a hayfield!"

Peter raised his head in a laugh.

"I'm serious!"

"Oh, it can't be that bad!" he said. Then he looked up, lifting his arm to wave at someone behind her. "Hey!"

Leah turned to see Jackie Burke walking purposefully up to join them.

"Hi, guys!" she said, a bit winded. "I hope everyone's having fun!" She smiled kindly, then turned to Peter and Kyla. "Pardon me for breaking in like this, but I'm looking for Dan. Have you seen him? My dad's been asking for him."

"I thought he went up to the house already," Peter replied, gesturing. "That's where he said he was going."

Her shoulders drooped. "Really? When was that? I just came from there a minute ago!"

"It was right after the—" Peter stopped, holding out a hand. "Does your dad need help? You know what? I'll go!"

"Are you sure? You don't have to—"

"No, I don't mind helping your father!"

"I'll go with you," Kyla said to Peter.

He looked down in surprise. "Don't you want to eat?"

"I'm all right. I'll go with you."

"Are you sure? I thought you said you were starving!"

"I'll get something at the house."

He hesitated. "If you want, you could eat with these guys. I'll come back and join you as soon as—"

Kyla sent him a hard look.

"Okay, never mind—let's go! Ladies, enjoy your dinner!" With a playful salute the two left for the house.

"Thank you, Peter! I appreciate it so much," Jackie called as they departed. She turned to Leah and Brindle. "I just adore them! They're the sweetest couple. If I ever—" She paused, twisting to look behind her at someone calling her from under the food canopy. With a tired sigh she shook her head. "Ladies, next year I'm putting someone else in charge of this whole shebang! Honestly, I can't even finish a sentence without somebody needing me for something! I'm so sorry—"

The girls said goodbye as Jackie hurried off.

"She's going to need a spa after this," Leah said, watching her leave.

"It's the other one I'm concerned about," Brindle said. "Was it my breath?"

Leah frowned. "What?"

"Did you notice how quiet that Kyla girl got when we were talking about your yard?"

"What? No."

"Well, she sure didn't want to hang out with us anymore!"

"She's pregnant! Maybe she wasn't feeling well."

Brindle's brow rose. "I think maybe she didn't appreciate you flirting with her husband to get free landscaping!"

Leah's mouth fell open. "*What?* I wasn't flirting with him!"

She smiled and shrugged.

"I was totally *not* flirting with him! That's *not* what that was!"

Brindle lifted her chin in amusement. "Well, you could have fooled me!" The two of them stepped forward as the line moved toward the food tent. "Are you staying for her thing tonight?"

"I'm thinking about it. Are you?"

She laughed. "Heck, no! You get what this is, don't you?"

"What?"

"This party—this whole party! You know what they're doing, right? It's one of those 'lure 'em in' get-togethers. Lots of fun and free food— and then they'll pop the old high-pressure you-need-Jesus pitch. Mark my words—that's what it'll be!" Brindle gave a firm nod. "Some exaggerated story of how pitiful her life was before and how perfect everything is now that she has Jesus! I hate those things!"

Leah blinked in surprise, though suddenly acknowledging that her friend may well be right. "Well, I like her. She's nice."

Brindle huffed. "*Nice.* They're all nice!"

"Well, she is!"

"Whatever. But I'm leaving."

"Fine. Leave then."

"I will." Brindle smiled, folding her arms. "Right after I get my free food."

True to her word, Brindle was ready to go home after they finished eating. By now the sun had sunk below the western hedge, and the evening air had pleasantly cooled off. Leah strolled with her toward the house, scanning the crowd on the lawn for Mary in the blue dress, with whom she had visited earlier that afternoon, hoping to reconnect and finish their conversation, but she couldn't find her. Then, after another attempt to convince Leah to leave with her, Brindle gave up and headed down the narrow sidewalk on the west side of the Glende house.

Alone, Leah stood at the bottom of the deck stairs, now vacillating a bit. Perhaps it *would* be better if she left too, she considered. After all, if Brindle were indeed correct, an evangelistic talk was not something she was eager to hear and now would be the best time to slip out. Yet these were her next-door neighbors, and Kyla's "story" had been so amped up. Surely they would ask her about it when she saw them again, and if she said she'd left without hearing it, perhaps Kyla Watkins would feel obligated to share it with her one-on-one, and that could turn out to be even more awkward.

A voice spoke from behind her: "Hello! You can sit with me if you'd like!"

At first Leah didn't realize she was being spoken to until the man repeated himself, a little louder this time. "Hello, miss! You can sit with me if you'd like!"

She turned to see an elderly, white-haired gentleman on the deck seated at the patio table by himself.

He beckoned. "Come on up here and join me!"

Immediately she knew who he was. She'd been sort of dreading this moment, but she took the stairs anyway, slipping past the free-standing porch swing where it was positioned against the west railing, approaching him nervously. This was her neighbor—the great Brother Warren in the flesh—and they'd have to meet eventually. For being the touted Man of God, he was not as large a person as her imagination had made him out to be, being of average build with shoulders slightly rounded from age and a full head of snowy hair, parted and neatly combed. Before him on the glass top table was a Styrofoam cup of coffee and near it a watermelon rind and crumpled napkin atop a soiled paper plate, the only remnants of his dinner.

"You were standing there with that look of wondering who to talk to," he continued, waving her to the swivel patio chair across him. "I've been abandoned by all my friends, so here alone I sit. I'd be happy for some company." He had a prominent Roman nose and sharp, vibrant gray eyes.

"Thank you," Leah said, noticing then his foot in an orthopedic boot elevated on a chair. "I'm Ava. And I see you've had an injury."

"Yes, forgive me. I normally rise for a lady. Warren Glende." He reached across the table to shake her hand. "Welcome to my house! And I'm eighty-two in case you're wondering. No fantastic story to tell about that foot. I did something mysterious and awful to it getting out of bed the other morning, and my doctor insists I wear this silly thing until it heals. A little frustrating not to be able to walk around at my own party—but it's temporary, Lord willing."

"I'm sorry," she said, taking her seat.

"Thank you, sweetheart. I'd offer you a soda or a lemonade, but I'm afraid I couldn't deliver upon your request. Perhaps someone will come by soon, and I could have them get you something to drink."

Leah smiled. "I'm fine—thank you. But if *you* need something, I could help you."

He waggled a thick-knuckled finger at her, his eyes twinkling. "Ah, that's not the way it's supposed to work, but you're kind to offer. We have a capable and intelligent young man staying with us this summer who helps me with everything, but today he's been working double duty. My daughter's drafted him onto her picnic team. I'm seeing how much I depend on him! Have you met my daughter Jackie? She lives here with me."

"Yes, I have. She's a sweet lady."

"Yes, yes—Jackie is special. Very dear to me. She's walked a road of pain, that girl." He paused, his gray eyes resting on Leah's. "You've walked a road of pain too."

Leah stiffened, her stomach giving a twinge.

"Of course, everyone has," he continued, nodding soberly. "Everyone has a story of pain—although none of it surprises God. He can work it all for good, you know. God's very good at doing that. And he works through our pain. Even now—if I hadn't hurt my foot, I wouldn't be sitting here with you, hmm?" He paused, studying her. "You have very beautiful eyes."

Her cheeks grew warm, and she swallowed. "Thank you."

"Beautiful eyes." He smiled and shook his head. "Dear, oh, dear—did you know there was actually a woman in the Bible who was pointed out as having poor eyes? Yes—*weak* eyes, it says! Poor thing! How'd you like to have been her? Have you ever heard of Leah from the Bible? Never mind it—that girl found her destiny with God, and it was good. But as I was saying, your eyes are very beautiful. If your father never told you that, he should have. And not just your eyes. You are beautiful in every way. Excuse my faulty memory—what did you say your name was again? Kayla?"

"Ava," Leah squeaked out.

"Ah, yes, *Ava*! So, tell me about yourself, my dear."

Leah's pulse was racing. She took a deliberate breath, trying to hide her nervousness. "Um, well, I'm twenty-six. I grew up in Bridgewater, and I have a degree in accounting. I just moved to New Hampton this week—right next door, actually. I think you may have known my grandmother. I'm Ava Davison's granddaughter."

His face lit up as he drew back. "You're Havi Davison's granddaughter? I'm so honored to finally meet you! My late wife and I dearly loved your grandmother! She was a precious woman of God! She and Ed were such good neighbors—excellent neighbors! I was so sad when they started going to Mesa for the winters. And then to hear of their passing—" He shook his head. "Such a loss! My daughter Susan and I went up to the memorial service. Took another couple from the church with us who were close to them. They'll be dearly missed—both of them."

Leah nodded, trying to recall if she had seen them at the funeral. "Yes. It was unexpected. It's difficult to be at the house and not miss them."

"Of course!"

"The day of the funeral—that was not a good day for me. It was—hard."

"I understand," he said with a kind nod. "I laid my own wife in the arms of Jesus not too long ago. Seems like yesterday. Such a difficult thing. That's one blessing for your grandparents—to go together. It's hard being the one left behind—I can attest to that! That's why I'm so grateful my daughter moved down to live with me. She lost her husband too, you know—Jackie did. Some years back now."

"I'm so sorry for you both."

"Thank you, my dear. It's a temporary parting. Millie, James, Ed, and Havi—we'll all be together again in the presence of God someday, and I'm looking forward to that day. Are you looking forward to that day, Ava? The day you're called to stand before God in eternity? The day you'll see the lovely face of Jesus—?"

His question jolted her. "I, um—yes," she answered. It seemed like the correct answer, given who she was talking to.

"But we must finish our race first—run it faithfully to the end!" He paused, observing her. "Your grandmother was quite a lady. She had a transformed life. But I'm sure you're familiar with her story."

"Some. I'm not sure what you're referring to."

"Oh, well—someday Jackie and I will have you over, and I'll tell you the bits and snatches that I remember. I didn't know her before she came to Christ. I only met her after we bought the lot from your grandfather and built our house here." He looked downward, as if reminiscing. "She was the kindest soul. If she heard of anyone in the neighborhood who was sick or having a tough time, she'd make them a hot meal and take it right over. Everyone loved her—especially Millie, my wife. And she made the best homemade ice cream."

Leah's face brightened. "The best!"

"How I'd love some right now!"

"With her homemade fudge sauce."

"Yes! Oh, we're talking now! I could only hope you've inherited the recipe and have a little pity on us old folks next door!"

"I'll do my best to hunt it down," she promised with a nod. He was endearing, Leah decided. She had expected him to be intimidating, but he was not. It had been surprising, yes, that he had opened their conversation with the subject of pain—of all things—and had shot straight to Leah in the Bible, but she had navigated through it and regained her composure. She liked him.

"Did you know it was because of your grandmother that we have this party every summer?" He gestured toward the people in the yard gathering on lawn chairs in the diminishing evening light.

"Really?"

"Oh, yes! Back in the day the four of us would get together to play cards. One evening when she and Ed were over, she shared an idea to gather all the neighbors for an outdoor picnic with games, and then at the end of the night have someone share a testimony of what God has done for them. We had our first party that summer, and she was the one who shared. There were six couples who came besides the four of us—sixteen people in all." He waved. "Look at how it's grown! All this from a seed in her heart! They were lovers of God, your grandparents. Lovers of God."

Leah marveled at the connection to her grandmother and tried to picture her as the "Jackie" of days past.

The old man continued, "Tonight Kyla Watkins is going to share her story. Very soon, it appears, as it's tradition to do it at dusk. Have you met Miss Kyla?"

"Yes. We've talked a bit."

"She's a firecracker, that girl! I love the daylights out of her! And her husband Peter is as fine as they come! You'll enjoy listening to her. Her father abandoned her when she was young, and she lost her mother too. But then after seventeen years—oh, what am I doing? I'll let her tell it! I only hope they don't forget about me! Someone was supposed to come get me before she speaks. I'm on crutches because of this foot and have trouble walking on the uneven lawn. I'm still getting used to them." He craned his neck, looking beyond the deck.

Leah sat up. "Would you like me to help you? Or get someone? I could get Jackie—"

"Ah, here they come, sweetheart! I see my daughter and Peter on their way."

Leah saw them too. When she turned back, she suddenly noticed that Brother Warren was looking at her in a peculiar way. She leaned back in surprise. "Er—is something wrong?"

"No dear. But since we're about to be interrupted, may I share something personal with you?"

"Uh—sure," she answered hesitantly.

"It's just that when I look at you, this image keeps coming to mind, and I was wondering if I could share it with you."

"Okay—sure."

His eyes were penetrating but his voice gentle. "It might seem a little odd, but I keep thinking of a door—a old-fashioned wooden door—and tall. If I could describe it, I'd say it was bluish-colored—scuffed-like—with roughed-up paint and with a rounded top." He drew an arch with his hand. "Heavy iron hinges and an iron latch. Quaint-like. But what I noticed was that it was boarded shut. Not just locked, mind you, but it had several boards nailed across it." He stopped, tipping his head as he looked at her. "Does that mean anything to you?"

Leah's throat constricted and she couldn't speak. She could only stare and nod.

"I have some thoughts on what that might mean. Would you like to hear them?"

Her gut twisted. Now was the time she wanted to run away. Now was the time she felt lured in and taken captive, as Brindle had so accurately described earlier. But what could she do? He'd been charming! How could she jump ship and run now? No doubt he was going to tell her what a wicked sinner she was and how she needed to get right with God, or she'd go to hell. So here she was—stuck. *Just tough it out*, she told herself as she gave another nod and held her breath.

His eyes narrowed as though visualizing it again. "I may be wrong, but I'm wondering if that door isn't a picture of your heart." He smiled kindly. "Ava, dear, if you knew how much God your Father loves you and the good he has in store for you, I think you'd waste no time in pulling those boards off." He paused, nodding. "There's a beautiful life on the other side of that barrier! The Bible says that God's created you to do things for him which he's planned out in advance. Things that glorify him and bring life to others. Like he did through your grandmother. But I don't know—those are just my thoughts. You can pray about it yourself."

Then in perfect timing Leah heard Jackie and Peter on the deck stairs behind her. She let out a breath, hugely relieved and very much counting on their arrival to save her from further conversation with him. But as she started to turn, Brother Warren stretched his hand across the table for hers, bringing her back to focus.

"Just one more thing, Ava. I think God may have some surprises in store for you, sweetheart, but don't be afraid. You can trust him. Jesus will never fail you—you can count on that!" He squeezed her hand and repeated, "You can count on that!"

Letting go, he raised his head, addressing his daughter as she reached the table. "Jackie, my dear, where've you been? It's about time you came to get me! I was afraid I'd miss the main event at my own party! And I think you owe Miss Ava here a big thank you! If it weren't for this beautiful young lady, I'd have been sitting bored silly since my dinner! This is Havi Davison's granddaughter—did you know that? The Davisons, who lived next door!" His tone conveyed delight.

"Yes, I *did* know that, Dad!" Jackie bumped him playfully on the arm, smiling at Leah. "I hope he's been nice to you, Ava! He's been a pretty demanding invalid today!"

"Invalid?" Brother Warren gave a burst of laughter. "Now she's calling me names!"

"He's been fine," Leah replied, immensely glad for the interruption. "It's been nice hearing him talk about my grandma."

Jackie smiled. "How nice! I regret that I never met her. She's certainly a legend around here! But Dad,"—she looked down at her father—"about tonight. I have some good news for you. There's been a change in plans. The mosquitoes are a bit nasty down where Kyla was going to talk, so we're moving everybody up poolside where we sprayed this morning. She can stand here on the deck where everyone can see her, and that way you can stay put right where you are and hear everything. Dan's getting her set up for sound right now."

"What—*here*? No," he protested, "then I won't be able to see her!"

"You'll see her, Dad! You'll be right here, and she'll be right there!" She pointed toward the top of the deck stairs.

Determinedly Brother Warren relocated his booted foot to the floor and laid his hands on the table to rise. "I don't want to be looking at her back—I want to be down *there* where I can see her shining face! Peter, come help me! I'm moving down. And I'll need two chairs—"

"Yes, sir," Peter replied, throwing Jackie an amused glance and scrambling around the table to offer his arm.

Jackie sighed and shook her head.

Leah stood. "I'll get the chairs—"

"No, hon—you don't need to do that! You're a guest. We'll get them! Seriously—" Jackie laid her hand on Leah's arm. "Honey, let the boys do this." She turned, calling, "Dan! Dan—would you help me a sec?" She beckoned. "Sorry to interrupt your work! We need two chairs moved down on the pool deck for Dad. Would you help me, please? He insists on being down there!"

Leah continued to slide the bulky chair across the deck as a broad-shouldered man in a black T-shirt bounded up the stairs to take it.

"Thanks," he said distractedly, glancing up briefly. Then he started, turning his face fully toward her. "*Leah*?" He straightened in surprise. "Leah Labanora! What in the world—what are *you* doing here?"

A charge of adrenaline shot through her as she stared back. Why— why, it was Danny! *Danny DeSoto!* Danny with a beard and glasses, but unmistakably *him*—her almost-brother-in-law, the older and only brother of Jake DeSoto. All in a split second, Leah was sixteen on a tire swing at camp, and Danny was pushing her out over the edge of the short cliff, hollering the signal for when to let go and drop into the lake below. And then she was crammed like a sardine into the backseat of his car with several other girls from church as he and Jake did their bus route, giving rides to youth group. And then in another second he was scowling, holding the door on that awful Friday when she was called to the church.

Jackie's voice chattered through her blur. "—and finally, I can introduce you two, but I'll be brief, 'cause I know you're busy, Dan. I've mentioned you several times to Ava, but we've never had the chance for you to officially meet. Dan, this is our neighbor Ava. She just inherited her grandparents' house. And Ava, this is Dan, the young man who's staying in the cottage this summer to help us. He is—"

Jackie's voice went on, but all Leah was aware of was the cock of Danny's head, his confused expression, and the way he quietly repeated her name. "*Ava*?"

"Ava just moved in this past week," Jackie continued. "She's living right next door."

He drew back in disbelief. "Next door? Are you *kidding* me? You live *next door*?" He swung his head to look at Jackie, then back at Leah.

Jackie paused, looking from one to the other. "Do you two know each other?"

It was more than Leah could take. She took a couple of jerky steps toward the stairs, then swiftly turned to address Brother Warren, who was limping around the side of the table on Peter's arm. "Excuse me. I need to go! It was nice to meet you, Mr. Warren. Both of you," she added, shooting a brief glance at Peter. "I enjoyed our visit. And thanks for the, um, words. And Jackie, thank you for your hospitality. It was a fun party." Then without another look at Danny, she left, hastening down the steps and skirting around the pool deck to make her way down the path beside the large house in the dusky evening.

"Hey, wait!" He followed her, calling from the corner of the house, "Leah! Don't go yet! I want to talk to you! Leah!"

Leah did not stop, nor did she look back.

Chapter Thirteen

Blindly Leah tripped down the narrow sidewalk beside Brother Warren and Jackie Burke's house, her head spinning in disbelief. How in the world had Danny DeSoto ended up living *right next door*? At the front of the house she sought to find the slender gap in the hedge through which she'd come, futilely poking around in the dusk, but the branches were sharp, thick, and impassable. Casting a panicked glance behind her, she gave up and hurried along the paved driveway between the parked cars all the way to the street, where she turned left and power-walked the shoulder of the road the several yards to her own driveway.

Incredible. She bit her lip, shaking her head. There was *no way* this could be happening! No way! Honestly, how could Danny DeSoto live next door to her? *Right next door!* Through the air the screech of feedback echoed over a loudspeaker, followed by the magnified voice of someone at the party thanking the guests for coming and inviting them to move in closer to one another as they were about to get started. The emcee told a joke, and she heard that familiar laugh rise above the hum of the crowd. *Oh, for heaven's sake!* She brought her hand to her face. It was *Danny's* laugh! How in the world had she not remembered Danny's laugh?

From the corner of her driveway she could see a thin strip of light at the bottom of her garage door ahead of her, an apparent indicator that she'd left the light on after mowing that afternoon. As she hurried across the gravel, Midnight gave a wicked snarl from a dark corner of her yard where he was sniffing and burst out barking, and Leah shouted his name, fearing he'd rush her. Recognizing her, he loped up and trotted alongside her to the house, where with fumbling hands she retrieved the hidden garage door opener from under the porch railing. Pushing the controls, she waited as the giant door rattled upward. When it reached the three-quarter mark to stick at its usual spot, she dipped her head to pass under, then stopped short, gasping in astonishment. Her garage was bare!

"What the—" she cried. Her legs felt weak.

She'd been burglarized! While she'd been at the party, someone had completely cleared out the place! *Completely!* The workbench and pegboard above it were empty, entirely void of tools; all the plastic bins and boxes that had been packed tightly along the back wall had disappeared, and every tool that hung from the studs beside the bench was gone too— every rake, shovel, hoe, and potato fork. Everything had been taken— everything except her trash can, a few pieces of oily cardboard in the center of the floor, and her bright orange gardening gloves on the bare workbench exactly where she'd left them earlier that afternoon. There also remained one old misshapen metal rake with a split handle, placed next to her forlorn lawnmower—a cruel jab, as it dawned on her who it must have been.

Leah gritted her teeth, dropping her eyes to the dog panting peacefully beside her. What the heck! When she had invited Marty to have the stuff in her garage, she never expected him to do *this*! This was—why, this was insultingly low!

She tried to recall when she'd seen him last at the party—talking to Peter Watkins right before dinner, perhaps? He'd obviously ditched the party way early to do this, for it had undeniably taken some work—maybe even plotting from the moment she'd offered her garage contents to him! She shook her head in disgust. While she'd been savoring her barbecued pork sandwich on the neighbor's lush and weed-free lawn, Marty had rushed home for his pickup truck, loaded her entire garage, and disappeared—all in a matter of a few hours.

"You dirty rat!" she muttered, shooting a look to kill toward the black wall of bushes that separated their yards. He couldn't have been gone for long with that amount of stuff. She bet she just missed him, which was probably why Midnight was still there. She cocked her ear, listening for him unloading his truck, but all she could hear was Kyla Watkin's amplified voice breaking in and out of the evening air, and right now Leah wasn't too keen on tuning in to that.

Right that second Marty's sharp whistle pierced the night, and Midnight shot obediently across the driveway, disappearing around the side of the garage. Knowing her cousin was outside, Leah was sorely tempted to send a few choice words over the hedge, but given the crowd next door on the other side of her, she followed her better judgment and kept her peace. But Marty would hear about this! Oh, would he!

Perturbed, Leah lowered the electric door and entered the house via the garage, slamming the door hard behind her. She snapped on the light and kicked the grass-stained mowing shoes she had left lying in the middle of the hall out of her path on her way to the kitchen, where she paused by the card table, glancing around to see if anything else had been disturbed. Legal pad, laptop, clothes—at this point everything appeared to be as she had left it, but that was of little consolation to her.

She was so angry she could—*gah!* She kicked a cupboard door, the particle wood smacking the frame and bouncing open. She banged it shut again. This was like a bad dream, a *nightmare*—with Danny DeSoto living on one side of her and her skunk of a cousin on the other! A one-two punch! She had moved here to get *out* of Bridgewater and her Anchor-ville connections there, but there was no escape! Even in Bridgewater she hadn't had Danny DeSoto living *right next door*! Boy, oh, boy—

"Okay, you can knock it off!" she snapped at the ceiling. "I've had quite enough!"

That was the only way this could be happening, she knew. It *had* to be God! If he were trying to outwit her, he'd won hands down, for who could top this? Brother Warren had hit the nail on the head: *I think God may have some surprises in store for you.* Surprises—yeah, *no kidding!* It was uncanny! What else was coming down the pike? *Surprises* was plural! It scared her!

Danny would come over. She was sure of it. Absolutely sure of it. And probably even tonight, knowing him. That scared her too. He would come over and try to talk with her. Anxiously she paced the kitchen, rubbing her forehead in dread. She didn't want to talk to Danny DeSoto. She wished she could go somewhere to avoid him, but where? Not Marty's. Not Phil's. She didn't have his number. She halfway wished she knew where Brindle lived, but even if she did know, suddenly showing up at her place would be unquestionably awkward. She didn't know her that well yet. But what alternative did she have? To hop in her car and go home to Bridgewater? For how long? Anything she did simply delayed her encounter with him, unless she packed up and moved back to Bridgewater altogether, and she wasn't doing that.

She swung her head again toward the ceiling. "Why are you doing this to me?" She swore and turned on her heel, returning to the peninsula.

Danny DeSoto. Good grief! Of *all* people! She leaned on the counter, cradling her head in her hands. She supposed it could be worse—at least it wasn't Jake. She wouldn't want to see either of them, but of the two, she'd a thousand times rather deal with Danny. He was at least decent. And honest.

She had always liked him. He'd always been superior in character to his brother, but Leah had succumbed to Jake's irresistible charm.

Danny DeSoto. She breathed out a heavy sigh, unable to keep her thoughts from the past.

Everything had been so fun at the beginning—the whole time, really. Up until she'd been blindsided. The DeSoto brothers had been a dynamic duo: Danny, the dark and studious brother, two years older than sandy-haired, charismatic, and daring Jake. Though sparks often flew between the two, both had been super fun. Together they spelled a good time—and sometimes trouble. But Danny had always been more sensible.

The first year she had gone to Bible camp, they pranked her. The two of them had caught a young garter snake and sneaked it in on her bottom bunk sleeping bag. Unaware, Leah had hurried to her cabin after volleyball to change into long pants before the evening campfire, inadvertently tossing her jeans on top of it, so that when she grabbed them again, she touched the snake. The whole campground had heard her shriek. Danny had purposefully hung around to "rescue" her, but Jake had hightailed it to the campfire. When she arrived at the fire, she knew by the smirk on his face that Jake had done it. In the light of the crackling flames, she had view of him and his buddy on a giant log opposite her. He couldn't stop smiling at her all night.

That week of summer camp had forged an inseparable friendship between the four of them—Leah, Rachel, and the DeSoto brothers. Back in Bridgewater when they weren't working their after-school jobs, they did everything together—youth group, movies, swimming, chores for each other's parents, once even cleaning all forty-seven windows in the grand Steinburg home for Rachel's mom. That first fall Danny went away to college, but since his school was close, he returned home on most weekends for church and to hang out with them.

There was one particular weekend in August with the brothers that stood out in her memory. Danny had delayed leaving for college because it was Leah's eighteenth birthday, joining the bunch of friends who were going out for pizza after church that day to celebrate with her. At the restaurant Jake had tossed a witty card onto her pile of gifts that made her laugh out loud. Under his signature he had written in smaller print, "Wanna be my girlfriend?" but distracted by opening her presents with her friends all around, Leah hadn't noticed that part. The funny card was then passed around the table because everyone wanted to see why Leah had laughed, and so his little question became public to everyone but her. Jake had reveled in the attention, his eyes twinkling while Leah naively continued to open her gifts. When someone finally pointed out his question, her face turned bright red.

Danny hadn't cared for the joke. He punched his brother in the arm on the way to the car and called him a jerk. Jake just laughed and called him a loser back.

Outside, applause suddenly crackled through the night air. Leah eyed the open window, presuming Kyla had finished her story. Music began to boom out over the speakers with the muted voices of the crowd joining in a song—a worship chorus that rose in volume until it cadenced with more clapping. Then a man's voice—Peter's perhaps?—led the group in prayer. And then silence. The neighbor's party had come to a close. Leah bet Brindle's prediction was right—there was always an appeal to come to God at the end of church meetings like that.

She clicked her phone to note the time. Now would start the goodbyes, the putting away of food and packing up of equipment, the cleaning of the yard. Danny would have responsibilities there. She guessed she had about forty-five minutes to an hour before he came. Maybe more.

Restless, Leah brushed her teeth, then shut off the lights to wait in the dark on the floor against the peninsula. There was no use in going to bed. Even if he didn't come, she wouldn't be able to sleep anyway.

Danny DeSoto. She couldn't believe it.

She thought back to how he'd changed over those last years she'd been with Jake. For that matter, they'd *all* changed, but she'd only noticed Danny then. From the start he'd been like an older brother to her, someone she felt at ease to be herself with. They'd teased each other and annoyed each other like siblings. He helped her with homework and competed fiercely with her in board games. But after she started dating Jake, she felt Danny lost much of his playfulness.

Leah attributed some of it to having to focus on his studies at college, but also to her being paired with Jake now. The foursome still hung out, but Danny gravitated more to the serious side, being careful not to lead Rachel on, as if the two of them were a pair too, and deferring to his brother in activities with Leah. Jake didn't seem to care. He was all too willing for Leah to pit herself against his brother in H-O-R-S-E or in a cutthroat chess match while he killed time putzing with his car or something else. Leah especially enjoyed those times when Danny forgot himself and started having fun again.

Jake, now—he'd been the king of fun. He'd been such an exciting boyfriend back in the day—so spontaneous and doting. He'd do crazy things—like pulling over on the side of a road to pick her flowers from a field. He'd take her on a date two hours away just because she liked the chicken at a certain restaurant. Once he found out she had a favorite fragrance at a department store and secretly stocked her bathroom vanity full of it. He was always active, always moving, always engaged with people, always fun. Leah had loved living in his wake.

Danny, on the other hand, had been practical, reasonable, and responsible—sometimes frustratingly so.

"You guys shouldn't be alone in here," she remembered him saying once when she and Jake were hanging out in his room. Leah had been sitting sideways on Jake's bed leaning against the wall, scrolling through social media when Danny passed by and poked his head in the door.

Jake was trying out a new pedal for his electric guitar. "Why not?" he challenged.

"Because you're putting yourselves into a place of temptation. You need to move out to the living room."

Jake screwed up his face. "I'm playing guitar! Sheesh!" He rolled his eyes. "Don't worry, we're not gonna make out in here!"

Danny cast a brief glance at Leah. "Well, you're not being very smart. You should at least have the door open."

"He didn't want to be too loud," Leah said. "You can leave it open if you want."

Jake had already turned back to clicking the pedal board with his foot and picking his guitar strings, experimenting with his sound.

And then there were the fights. Leah remembered those clearly—the big altercations Jake had with his brother a few weeks before the wedding. Jake would never tell her what about, although eventually it all came to light.

"He's just an old grump," he would say, "Grumpy Danny." Then he'd laugh.

Leah hugged her knees in the darkness. Who would have thought that down the road Jake would find himself in a place that wasn't very smart with Rachel? It was her worst subject to think about—the day Leah found out what had happened, how it had happened, and where. And that it had continued. He had fallen in love with Rachel when Leah had been away at college. Not right away, but over time, he said. Jake had stayed in Bridgewater to attend the community college there, living at home. Rachel had also stayed in Bridgewater, training to be a beautician.

In hindsight Leah remembered how distant and distracted Jake had seemed in those final months before the almost-wedding. She'd been so focused on finishing school and wedding preparations that she hadn't given it much thought. She was simply waiting for the finish line when they'd finally be married.

A sudden brisk knock at her front door made her jump. Jabbed with alarm, she checked her phone—only thirty-two minutes had passed. Unmoving, she stayed where she was in the dark, her heart pounding, hoping he would think she was asleep, hoping he would go away.

But he kept knocking. Then he rang the doorbell and called her name. He called her name again and banged on the door. Then he tried the knob and knocked again. With a resigned sigh, Leah rose and slowly approached the door, mussing up her hair on the way. Clicking on the exterior light, she cracked the door open a few inches, squinting sleepily out.

"Who is it?" she rasped groggily, as if awakened from a sound slumber. She feigned a monstrous yawn.

Eagerly Danny leaned in to see her through the crack. "Hey—I knew you'd still be up! I can't believe it, Leah! I'm so glad to see you! Can you let me in?"

"I wasn't still up."

"Well, I'm glad you came to the door. Can we talk?"

She sniffed, continuing the charade. "No. No, I don't think so."

He jerked his head. "Oh, come on, Leah—please! I really want to see you!"

His body had filled out, his shoulders were broad, and with the beard and glasses Leah thought he looked so—so *adult*.

"I don't want to talk to you, Danny."

"What? No, Leah—please talk to me!"

"No. Good night!" She began shutting the door, but his hand shot up to catch its edge, holding it firmly open. He didn't say anything, but their eyes met and held. Her heart slammed in her chest.

"Leah, *please*," he said quietly. "I'm not leaving here until we have a conversation." He paused, then released the door.

"Go away, Danny," she said. And taking the opportunity, she shoved the door closed, turned the deadbolt, and clicked off the porch light.

Returning to the peninsula, Leah kicked herself for answering the door. *Where did you think that would go, you idiot?* Of course, he wanted to talk—what else? She slid to the floor, all her senses alive as she waited in the dark to see if he would knock again. Or try another door. Or try *something*. But he didn't, and the night grew quiet.

At last she allowed herself to breathe again. Certainly her year of counseling with Pam had paid off right there, she mused, and she felt like calling her to tell her so. Maybe she would in the morning. She had had her confrontation and won; she had established her boundaries and kept them. The door was closed, and Danny was on the other side of it. He had not knocked again or called her name through the barrier. Perhaps she'd have to do this a few more times before he got the picture—who knew?—but she didn't care. She would stand her ground.

The oak panel of the peninsula felt cold on her back. She shifted her position, still marveling that she'd been milling around a party the whole afternoon with Jake's brother there the *entire* time. The entire time! It was too wild of a coincidence to *not* be God! She'd been pursued in an invisible chess match as he'd patiently moved in on her piece by piece like a master strategist, until here she sat so decisively in check. He'd orchestrated her move to New Hampton in perfect timing for an innocent invitation to a neighborhood party. Then he linked her to Brother Warren by virtue of his relationship with her grandmother and brought her face to face with Danny, outsmarting her at every turn! Why was God doing this?

I think God may have some surprises for you.

She closed her eyes. And that Brother Warren guy—he was too much! Yeah, he was charming and everything but also completely scary! How could he have known what would happen? When she'd introduced herself to him as Ava, he had—of all things—jumped without pause right to the story of *Leah* in the Bible! Heavens, what were the odds of that? Of course, hearing him talk about Grandma Havi had been wonderful—that part was great—but when he got serious at the end of their conversation— oh, it was as though God *himself* were speaking to her! *God may have some surprises in store for you.* How uncanny, given she bumped into Danny not more than two minutes later! She tried to think of what else he had said— something about God never failing her or something. She could count on it. What was *that* supposed to mean?

And before that—his picture of the boarded-up door. She shivered. What he had described was almost exactly what she had imagined in the climbing tree as a teenager! How on earth could he have known it? Yet like it or not, she couldn't deny that it was a pretty accurate picture of her heart right now—closed and barricaded to God! Take those boards off? No, sir! She couldn't see that happening any time soon! A lot of trust would have to be restored before she'd think of doing that!

Automatically her memory skipped to the night long ago when she had confided in Evelyn—back when she was just getting to know the DeSotos after camp and long before dating Jake.

"I'll probably never get married," Leah had said to her out of the blue while the two of them washed dishes before youth group.

Evelyn set a freshly rinsed cookie sheet in the dish rack, looking at her in surprise. "Goodness, Leah—that's quite a statement! What would make you say that?"

Leah dried the pan. "Oh, you know—because of the thing in my family."

"What thing?"

Leah shared the whole Corolla drama with her, offering the woeful details about her mother's and grandmothers' plights, and then opened up about the impending doom she felt for her own future.

"Now hold on there, hon!" Evelyn broke in, pausing with her hands in the dishwater. "You know you don't need to live with that, don't you? We can pray to break that in the name of Jesus!"

Leah looked at her with surprise.

"Don't get me wrong—I believe you! Things like that happen— they're not uncommon—but we can pray against it! Jesus defeated every curse on the cross." She wiped her hands. "Repeated bad stuff like that— those are big clues of generational curses."

"Of what?"

"Cycles of bondage passed down from one generation to another. But Jesus paid the penalty for all that at the cross, and we can pray to break that off you. Would you like to do that?"

"Uh—like—*now*?"

"Why not?"

They went to the kitchen table where Evelyn took a piece of paper and drew a long, horizontal stripe across the page with her pen. "We'll call this your family line," she said, tapping it. "Let's say you were born here." She put a dot in the middle of the bar. "On this side of you are your parents and grandparents, etcetera—all who came before you. Just like parents pass on genetic family traits—hair color, body shape, that type of thing—well, there's spiritual stuff that gets passed down too. Things that you inherit spiritually from your ancestors. Those can be good things if you have godly parents, but if they weren't, sometimes *you* get snagged in the consequences of *their* sins. That's what we call a 'generational curse.'" She looked up to see if Leah was following her.

"You'll pass on stuff too." Evelyn moved her pen to the other side of the dot. "You'll either pass on a godly heritage or the baggage that comes with undealt-with sin. But when we plant the cross of Jesus here"—she drew a cross above the dot—"it becomes a stop sign for sin! All of those family curses were put on Jesus so that you could be set free from them—do you see?"

"Okay." Leah nodded.

Evelyn drew an arrow moving forward from the cross. "God wants to change your family history through you for the *good*—to pass his blessings down through you. All that old family baggage of yours—we'll address it right here and nail it to the cross!" She tapped on the dot.

"And that can stop it—the curse thing?"

"Absolutely! We're going to be specific and render it defeated at the cross!"

Evelyn led her through a prayer of repentance for her sins and the sins of her forefathers and mothers. Then they brought the specifics of the Corolla curse to the cross and proclaimed the power of Jesus over it.

"We declare this generational curse of being 'cursed in love or marriage' broken in the name of Jesus and by the power of his blood!" Evelyn said with authority. "The Bible says that 'Jesus redeemed us from the curse of the law by becoming a curse for us.' Leah, Jesus took this curse upon himself so that you might inherit the blessing of God instead! By faith we believe it, and by faith we declare it to be true over your life!"

The two sat quietly for a moment.

Leah looked up. "So that's it, then? It's done? So, like, even if my mom goes off on me about it, it's still done with?"

"Well, my dear, it's a matter of faith! We believe in the power of the cross to defeat every curse, but it's not a magic wand. You still have to walk it out. You have to follow Jesus and obey him."

Leah nodded thoughtfully.

"Let's say there's a generational cycle of abuse in a family. Or alcoholism. Or rage. It takes a lot of work to change those old engrained patterns and mindsets, but the grace of God is there to help if you invite him into your situation. And think of how it'll benefit the next generation if you persist in following Jesus and obeying him. So stick close to Jesus, Leah. He'll watch over you and help you. And when that fear comes again—which it probably will—you just remind yourself and the devil that the curse was defeated at the cross of Jesus Christ. Period."

A smile broke over Leah's face. "Thank you."

Evelyn smiled back, squeezing her hand.

She let out a long breath. "Seriously, I feel so much lighter right now, I can hardly believe it!"

Evelyn reached to give her a hug. "Well, *believe* it, girl! You don't have to live with that doom hanging over you anymore! It's not gonna happen!"

It's not gonna happen.

Leah stared into the dark room from beside the peninsula. She *had* believed it. Leah had followed Jesus and obeyed him. Leah had clung to Jesus and lived confidently without fear of the Corolla Curse—right up to the night of her wedding rehearsal when she learned about Jake and Rachel—in the prayer room at church, of all places! She'd been blindsided and betrayed by her best friend, her trusted fiancé, and God himself. Was it any wonder her heart was boarded up? Clearly, the family curse was still well in place. God had not prevented her fiasco from happening after all. On the contrary, he had pulled the rug out from under her feet and allowed her heart to get crushed. Faith was merely wishful thinking. Sometimes she doubted there even was a God.

But her doubts didn't last very long, for there was no question of his existence. Try as she might to make him go away, she *knew* God was real. He was like air—everywhere. She could feel him and hear him. He was like water, unstoppable when it came to seeping through cracks. As hard as she tried to keep him out, God was bigger and stronger and shrewder than her. He had a way of showing up on the inside of those boarded-up doors beyond her control.

Furthermore, there were things about God that Leah knew now that she simply could not unknow. Having read parts of the Bible before, she knew how things were *supposed* to be—how she was *supposed* to act or *not* act. Every day it was as though a war raged in her mind, an inner struggle between what she knew was right and the way she actually lived. Maybe it would have been better if she hadn't learned so much about God in the first place!

Like with Carlos, for instance, with all his pontificated opinions about God-this and God-that. She knew enough of the Bible to correct him—but she also knew that it was wrong for her to be sleeping with him in the first place—that is, if the Bible were correct in deeming sex outside of marriage to be sin.

Or like earlier that day at the pool when Mary Grant had asked Leah if she were religious. Leah knew following Jesus wasn't about being religious at all. It was about a real relationship with a living person—Jesus—but she was far from that kind of relationship right now.

Or like when Brother Warren talked to her like he assumed she was a believer. Oh, she had known exactly what to say. She could give all the right answers and bob her head in agreement. But she knew she was a million miles away from where she could be with God—by her own choice.

And then there was Danny. Leah knew it was God who'd brought about the astounding connections next door—as if he'd thrown a grappling hook from the neighbor's house and fixed himself to her, and she could not escape. It was God who'd determined her next-door neighbor would be a retired minister who'd been close friends with her grandparents. It was God who'd made the connections between Brother Warren and Danny DeSoto—whatever they were—so that he was living in their cottage for the summer. It was even God who'd crafted the timing of her bumping into him on the deck. Only God could have done all that!

If only she could escape him! But he kept calling! She could hear his voice in her heart.

Come, let me heal your wound—

Leah got a glass of water from the refrigerator and stood in front of the sink to drink it. Outside, Jackie Burke's dog sniffed around in the moonlight performing his nightly duties. Goodness—even the neighborhood *dogs* had a connection to her! Both claimed her yard!

She sighed. She knew where Danny would take the conversation if they talked. He'd ask her about her walk with God—Leah was *positive* about that. Danny was like that. He'd always been the one more serious about following God. Jake had loved God too, but in a more carefree way. He would often forget himself in the moment and get carried away. Danny, though, had been the moral compass, the one to steer the group from foolishness. "Hey—let's do something else," he'd say to the gang. "Why fill our minds with this garbage?" He was older and usually right, so they accommodated his opinion. But he was often heckled in the process.

A cool breeze blew gently through the window. Leah yawned, turning back to the dark kitchen. She had no aspirations for sleeping that night. Her mind wouldn't shut off. Nevertheless, she made herself change into her pajamas and lie down on the air mattress because it was more comfortable than the hard floor beside the peninsula. The box fan was left unplugged, however. She wanted advance warning if Danny returned.

The next thing she knew it was morning. Before even opening her eyes, Leah regretted her decision about the fan, for the chattering birds in the hedge were at it once again—with gusto. Rolling over, she pulled the blanket over her head to muffle their exuberant chorus, but after a restless hour she gave up. It was no use.

Once out of bed, she wasn't sure if she actually felt rested or if she was still adrenalized from the night before, but her body was wide awake and charged, as if she'd already had her first cup of coffee—which she was about to make, since she had bottled water now. She padded barefoot through the kitchen to get the pot brewing, her mind busily at work reviewing every detail of the previous evening. Had that all really happened? She wished it had been a dream!

She was not leaving there, she decided. No, it was not an option to move back to Bridgewater. She didn't care who lived or didn't live next door—she had the power to set her boundaries. The fact that Marty was being a jerk was disappointing for sure, but that was *his* problem, not hers. And Danny DeSoto—well, soon enough he'd get the point that she didn't want anything to do with him. Maybe she wouldn't get to know Jackie the way she'd hoped, but that was that. There would have to be some distance with her now, but there were plenty of other people in the neighborhood to know. There was Brindle and the whole neighborhood across the street, as well as thousands of other folks in New Hampton. Plus Phil Crawford. She had the distinct impression she'd be spending a lot more time with him anyway.

With coffee in hand, she headed to her porch to sit and figure out how to handle Danny when he showed up, for guaranteed, sooner or later he would. Flipping the deadbolt, she opened the front door and turned to push her way out the screen door with her back, taking extra care not to spill her mug. Letting the door fall shut behind her, she turned and gave a startled cry. Laid out on the floor of her porch and wrapped in a blanket was Danny DeSoto himself, camped out on the cushions of her furniture! At the banging of the door, he opened his eyes and lifted his head, his dark hair puffed out on one side.

"Wha—what are you doing here?" she sputtered.

"Morning!" he said groggily, raising himself to a sitting position. He rubbed his face, then extended his arms in a long stretch. "Nice to see you, Leah!"

"Who said you could sleep on my porch?"

"It wasn't too bad with these cushions. A little buggy 'til I got myself a blanket." He snatched his glasses from the table, then pulled himself to his feet and began sliding the cushions back onto the chairs.

"You slept on my porch!"

He smiled boyishly, wadding up the blanket. "Yeah, I told you I wasn't leaving 'til we had a conversation. I knew you had to open that door eventually!"

She stared at him in disbelief as he continued to put the chairs back together. When finished he faced her. He had on the same black T-shirt as the night before.

"So, hey—it was amazing running into you last night! You look good, Leah!"

Like they were there to talk about her looks! Caught off guard, all she could think of was her mother saying that her hair made her look like a rebel, and now suddenly self-conscious, she snapped back, "You don't have to lie."

"What's that supposed to mean? Why would I lie? You *do*—you look good!"

"I know you're judging me."

"I'm *judging* you—? For what?"

"For my hair." Her crazy black-and-blue hair, Carlos, and the million other ways she didn't measure up to his standard of moral perfection.

"Your—your *hair*?" He threw his head back, bellowing out his signature laugh. "Judging you for your *hair*?"

Instantly Leah acknowledged how ridiculous it sounded, but she was committed now. "You were cri—critical of everything, Danny! It's okay—I don't mind if you disapprove." Dang, she wished her heart would stop racing so she could think!

"Holy cow—why would I disapprove?" He glanced at her hair. "It's different, I'll admit. But it suits you. I like it! I'm certainly not *judging* you for it—I can promise you that!" He looked amused, standing there with his beard and muffed hair and sleeves tight around his biceps. He'd built some muscle in the four years since she'd seen him.

She held her coffee, having no idea of what to say.

"How's your mom?" he asked.

Leah stared at him, then shrugged. "Good."

"She's doing okay? Healthy?"

"Yeah, she's fine."

He nodded. "That's good. And Braydon?"

"Braydon's fine."

"Did he graduate this year?"

She shook her head. "Nope. He's only seventeen. He's got one year left."

"Ah! He must be driving then."

"Quite a lot, actually. He delivers pizza."

He smiled. "Good for him! And your dad—how's he doing? Are things any better with his drinking?"

Leah gave an impatient sigh. "My dad's fine, Danny. Chelsea's fine. Their kids are fine too. Everybody's *fine*! Is this what you want to talk about?"

His T-shirt was bunched up. He tugged it down around his waist. "Leah—"

"I've changed my name—*that's* something new! I go by 'Ava' now. You can call me that. It's my middle name."

He frowned. "Yeah, I was wondering about that. Why'd you do that?"

"Because I wanted to!"

He folded his arms. "Huh. Well, I like your name. To me you'll always be Leah."

"What do you want, Danny? Why are you here?"

"Well, for one, I want to know how you're doing."

She flayed her hands, the coffee dripping over the side of the mug. "I'm fine!"

"Come on—how are you *really* doing?"

"How is that any of your business?"

"With the Lord is mostly what I want to know—how's your walk with God?"

Oh, she had pegged him right, and he'd wasted no time getting to it! "I can see you haven't changed."

His brow rose as he waited for her answer.

"I'm not walking with God right now," she said finally.

"And why not?"

"'Cause I don't want to!" She tossed her head.

"And why's that?"

"Look—I don't owe you any explanations. And it's not like you don't know anyway, so I think this conversation's finished. I'd like you to leave."

"Well, I have something I'd like to say. May I?"

"No, thank you." She waved to the stairs. "You have nothing to say that I want to hear."

"I think you should hear me out."

"What part of 'no' don't you understand?"

"Leah, let me talk! I need to tell you something—"

"—Well, I don't want to hear it! Whatever you have to say will only make me feel bad, and I'm not going there!"

He spread his hands. "How do you know that? I haven't even said anything yet!"

"Because I know *you*! Every time you were around before the wedding, I could *feel* your disapproval! You used to be fun to be with, but it's like you got old and grumpy! That's what Jake used to call you— Grumpy Danny—because you were a *pill* whenever you came home!"

His expression changed. "Oh, yeah? Well, perhaps I should enlighten you on why—"

She put up her hand. "Stop it, Danny! I said I don't want to hear it!"

"I think you *need* to hear it!"

"I'm not going to listen!" She looked toward the ceiling, "La-la-la-la—"

"Oh, for heaven's sake, Leah—stop acting so childish!"

She drew back in surprise. He had never spoken sharply to her before—ever!

A mottled flush had crept up his neck. "Yeah, I was grumpy—I'll admit it—but it had nothing to do with *you*!" He paused as if to curb his frustration. "You don't think I struggled seeing what was happening between those two? It was terrible! I could see by the way he looked at her that something wasn't right—all their secret little glances they thought were hidden! I confronted him several times, but he denied it. Said I was reading into things, and I believed him at first. But then—" He shook his head, running a hand through his hair. "I warned him that if he didn't tell you *I* was going to.

"Anyway—" He stopped again and looked away. "Anyway, I wanted to tell you that I've been filled with regret for not saying something right away back then. Right away. I should have, and I'm sorry, Leah. Really sorry. It's been a huge weight on my conscience all these years. I know it would have been hard any way you look at it, but it was much worse the way it happened. I should have said something immediately, so I take responsibility for that. Please forgive me."

Leah gave him an incredulous look. "*That's* what you need to tell me? Wow, Danny—you're only four years too late! I can hardly see it's helpful now, as it doesn't change anything! Thanks a lot for the fresh reminder of those miserable days! I hope your conscience feels so much lighter!"

He fell silent at her eruption, chewing his lip. "All right, look—it goes without saying that my brother was a complete idiot. I can't imagine what you went through. We were all furious for what he did to you, but you know what, Leah? *You* weren't the only one hurt in that whole ordeal!"

"Oh, is that right?" For a second she was tempted to throw her coffee at him.

"Yeah! *You* ran away. *You* disappeared. Poof! You were gone from our lives without even a goodbye, and my mom"—he shook his head—"Leah, my mom died a thousand deaths! It was awful! She was so humiliated and ashamed of Jake, but she was devastated to lose you too, and you wouldn't return any of her phone calls! My dad had to make her stop calling you! Why wouldn't you talk to her? She *loved* you, Leah! She mourned for you! She cried for *months*! And Dad—" He looked down then back up at her. "Honestly, it was like you had died."

Leah sniffed.

"And Jake and Rachel—yeah, they blew it—they blew it bad! But let me tell you—they've had a rough time of it! Their wedding was like a funeral—seriously, a funeral! But no wonder—from the get-go they've lived under a cloud of guilt, not to mention the disapproval of every single person close to them! I pitied her, the poor thing. The doofus father of her child would have gone ahead and married her best friend—how do you think that made her feel?" He snorted. "What a heck of a way to start a marriage, huh?"

He paused reflectively, his voice softening. "They had a little girl. I don't know if you know that. Her name's Anna Lisette, and she's an absolute delight—the light of Mom's life, really. God's used her to bring a lot of healing to our family. She's three now, and they're having another baby in August." He gave a thin smile.

"Oh! Well, isn't it *wonderful* everyone's lived happily ever after?" The dagger was cruel, she knew, but it just popped out.

Danny stared, then dropped his head. "Okay, I'm done. I said what I needed to. I should get along home."

"So soon? Aww, I was just about to invite you for breakfast." She gestured with the mug.

His tone remained unaffected. "I'd stay, but I don't want to be late for church. I need time to help Brother Warren get ready. But we'd wait for you if you'd care to come with—?"

Leah looked away. "No thanks. I'm pretty sure I'd not be wanted there!"

"Not be wanted by whom?"

"By *God*." She wanted to spear him with her words.

"Why do you say that? You know that's not true!"

"Doesn't matter."

"Yeah, it does. Because *you* matter. More than you know."

Leah swallowed, uncomfortable and utterly frustrated that she couldn't intimidate him.

"Don't make Jesus out to be the bad guy here, Leah. He loves you! He always has and he always will."

"Oh, you know everything, don't you?"

He shot her a look. "No, I don't. But I can tell you with absolute certainty—"

She rolled her eyes, cutting him off, "—Didn't you say you had to leave?"

Danny suddenly looked tired. With a curt nod he pulled the blanket off the chair. "Yeah, okay. See you 'round."

"Goodbye," Leah said dully.

He took the steps in a single bound and cut through the weedy flowerbed. Halfway to the hedge he stopped and swung around.

"Just one more thing, Leah," he said calmly, meeting her eyes. "I'd like to remind you that I am not your enemy. I'm your *friend*. I always have been. I'm very sorry for all that has happened, but I can't change any of it. It's out of my control." He paused, then added, "And in case you might have gotten confused, *I* am not Jake."

Chapter Fourteen

The moment Danny was out of sight Leah kicked the chair beside her, the hot coffee sloshing up onto her hand. Angrily she whipped the contents out toward the yard—and missed, the dark brew splattering against one of the painted pillars, dripping onto the floor. What business did he have coming over to share all that with her?

She was *glad* Jake and Rachel had had a "hard time of it," as Danny had put it—glad, and she didn't care what it made her look like! They *deserved* a miserable start, and she hoped it never got better for them! She hoped Rachel was plagued with terrible guilt every single day of her life! Leah had absolutely no sympathy for her!

Oh, she could get it that some guys stumbled with lust—not that it made things any better, but she could at least understand that it could have been a factor for Jake. But best friends—best friends were the ones who were supposed to stand guard for you, weren't they? The ones who fought for you and defended your territory—who stood for you in the gap. Best friends were the ones who reamed your boyfriend out for you when he was being a jerk. Best friends were *loyal*. Years of shared everything—memories, dreams, secrets, and clothes—all had gone down the drain with Rachel's cruel and selfish choices. Leah hated her. Loathed her. And she hated times like this when she couldn't block her out of her mind and was forced to deal with her.

Her avoidance techniques had been confronted in counseling.

"Look, Leah—you can't just decide to *not* think about them," Pam's voice resonated in her mind. "Ignoring the problem is denial, and it'll keep you stuck. You need to address what happened or it'll fester inside of you. So that's what we'll do—we're going to look this thing square in the face and call it what it is. Then you're going to pull from your inner strength and rise above it. You already have all the power you need within you. You're going to draw healing from your core. I'll walk you through it. We humans have amazing abilities within!"

"I can't forgive her," Leah warned her frankly.

Pam's hand on her arm was comforting. "Let me assure you that's *not* going to be a requirement. I believe there's other ways to come to a place of serenity."

"Other than forgiveness?" Her memories of Pastor Reid's sermons begged to differ.

"Yes—you'll see! Don't worry—we're not going to gloss over what Rachel's done. We'll put her on a dartboard or whatever you need to come to terms with this. But *then* you'll be able to move on."

Leah had listened. With Pam's help she had faced it. They had "gone there" full bore together in her office with an entire handwritten page of ways Rachel had violated her trust. Then they did the same for Jake. For months she had practiced Pam's empowerment exercises, struggling to be the victor, not the victim. And for the most part the exercises helped—until times like *this* when it all flooded back again. And then here she was—right smack at the starting line.

And now thanks to Danny DeSoto her whole day was ruined—or thanks to God, rather, since it was he who had sabotaged her again! Holy cow—it felt like her life was careening out of control! She sniffed, standing in her pajamas on the porch rug.

It was times like this when she ached from loneliness. There was no one to talk to. No one except Pam, whom she had paid handsomely for her scant fifty-five minutes every other week. Her old roommate Celeste never understood her, and then it was worse for Leah to have to explain herself and try to prove her point. Both were back in Bridgewater and were of no help today. Besides, Leah was trying to move on from there. Should she call her mother? Heavens—that would only send her on a rant! Brindle? Leah hesitated. She was still figuring Brindle out. She was temperamental and outspoken; yet it was her rawness that Leah could appreciate. There was nothing proper about Brindle, but she was *real.*

Oh, why not? Tucking the empty mug under her arm, Leah pulled out her phone and pressed her number, gazing out across the yard while it rang. Shortly a woman mumbled out a sleepy "Hello?"

"Hey," Leah said. "Can you come over?"

There was a pause. "Who's this?"

"Ava."

"*Who?*"

214

"Ava. Is this Brindle?"

"Ah—I think you must have the wrong number."

With an awkward apology, Leah hung up. Now wasn't that her luck? To finally call a friend—only to find Brindle had messed up entering her own phone number!

The screen door banged shut behind her as she went back in the house to restart her day with another cup of coffee—her first cup, actually, considering she hadn't even tasted her first pour.

Danny.

Mug in hand, she leaned against the sink and stared into the backyard, pondering his need to sooth his conscience after all these years. Good grief! Had he really thought it necessary to dump all that about Jake and Rachel on her? And to point out that she wasn't the only one who'd been hurt! *Oh, right*—like she was supposed to feel guilty now for not sticking around to comfort everybody else! Was he that clueless? Had he no idea how humiliating it had been to phone a couple hundred guests the night before her wedding to cancel?

At least it was over with, Leah reasoned. Danny had come and said his piece and gone home. She pictured him whirling on the lawn to face her. *I'm not your enemy—I'm your friend.* Some friend he was—waiting all night on her porch to grind in her past!

She abandoned her coffee and went to take a shower. She wasn't enjoying it anyway.

Later, to keep her sanity, Leah attempted to salvage her day's sour beginning by scrawling out a to-do list on her legal pad: *mow lawn, do laundry, clean, sort through boxes, call Pam*. She paused, considering her last item, then crossed it off her list. Her monumental boundary win last evening had been shot to smithereens this morning, and there was nothing left to report. It would only be an embarrassment. Plus, it was the weekend; she wouldn't be in the office anyway.

Since it was too early to mow for a Sunday, Leah focused on keeping busy inside, for there was plenty to do. Her eyes fell on the dried grass clippings strewn all over the floor in her back hallway, where she had so angrily kicked her shoes aside coming in the door last night from the emptied garage fiasco. She shook her head, still in disbelief at what Marty had done. Coupled with running into Danny at the neighbor's party, the two events had practically put her over the edge. But that was last night. And this was today. She would live through this.

Resigned, she pulled the broom from the closet off the dining room and slid the chairs away from the card table, prepping to sweep. With vigor she began working her way from the edge of the dining room through the kitchen on her way toward the back hall, her thoughts automatically reverting to obsess on Danny. She couldn't help it. What he'd said about his parents wouldn't leave her mind. *It was like you had died!*

Regrettably, Leah *did* feel bad about Evelyn. Terrible, in fact. Maybe she should have taken her phone calls. And Rocke. She hadn't really thought about them hurting for *her,* grieving their loss of her, like she had grieved her loss of them. But it was too late now. Nothing could be done, and besides, they were certainly well past it now. But she did feel bad.

Danny.

Now that she had gotten over the initial shock of actually talking to him, she sort of regretted being so mean. She wasn't proud of that. In all the years she'd known him, he had never been unkind to her. He hadn't deserved how rude she'd been, but being put on the spot like that, she had reacted. Reacted poorly, she admitted, although she couldn't think of how else she could have faced him. His parting words swirled through her head. *I'm sorry for what has happened, but I can't change any of it. I am not your enemy. I'm your friend. I always have been.*

Hadn't she said practically the same thing to Marty yesterday in her appeal to him at the party? Almost exactly. She paused guiltily with the broom. It was weird how similar the situations were, given that what had happened between Marty and her was her *mother's* fault, not hers. She stared unseeing at the floor as Danny's words echoed back: *In case you might have gotten confused, I am not Jake.*

No, Danny wasn't Jake. Her issues were with Jake, not him. Could she wave the white flag and surrender? Could she lay down her arms, empty out her arsenal, and be cordial to him? She sighed heavily. It just wasn't that simple! Good guy or not, Danny represented the DeSoto *family,* and relating to him was way too close for comfort! She didn't want to deal with that. Furthermore, Danny accentuated the rift between her and God, for it was clear that following Jesus was still what he cared most about in life—she could tell. Did she want to subject herself to that? Internally she groaned. Why the heck did this have to follow her all the way to New Hampton? It was so dang much work to wade through it all!

She leaned on the broom, wondering if Marty might be having a similar conversation in his head about her. Not likely, she mused. No, he was probably over there gloating about all the booty he had acquired from her garage.

Her gaze dropped to the door of the garage and her old running shoes lying haphazardly in the middle of the hall. Simultaneously she noticed the rug in front of the basement door and stiffened. *The rug!* She stared at it, stupefied. The rug that she had rolled up and put at the base of the door had been moved! And not just moved but scrunched up back against the wall, as if it had been pushed there by the door being opened! Her stomach gave that sick lurch again. Clearly, someone had been in her basement. Someone—

A sharp tapping shook her screen door, and she gave a cry, her hand flying to her chest.

"Anybody home?" Brindle called through the house.

"Back here!" Leah called, her heart racing. What timing!

Brindle came around the corner into the kitchen, looking freshly showered and dressed in her work uniform, her white shirt tucked neatly into her black pants. Her hair was wet. Leah was hugely thankful for her presence.

"So, did you get saved?" she asked.

Leah threw her a strange look. "What?"

"At the party last night! Did they give the hard sell at the end of the night?"

"Oh—I didn't stay."

"You didn't stay? Why not? I thought you were going to!"

Leah let out a breath. "It's a long story. I ran into someone I knew. Maybe I'll tell you later. But right now, I'm glad you're here! I just discovered that someone was in my house last night, and I got a little spooked! It's so freaky! I'm pretty sure it was while I was next door at the party."

Her eyes grew large. "Are you serious?" She flashed a look around her. "That's crazy! How did you find out?"

"Oh, it's obvious! I know exactly how I left things before I went!"

"And you're sure?"

"Absolutely certain!"

Brindle stared at her for a moment, then guiltily raised her hand. "Okay—it was me."

Leah drew back in surprise. "You? Why? What were you doing?"

"I'm sorry! You were in the shower, and the string broke, and the letters scattered everywhere. I picked them up, but I couldn't put them back the way they were. Geez, I knew you were picky, but I didn't know you were *that* particular about stuff!"

Leah frowned. "Letters? What are you talking about?"

"The letters in the box in the bedroom—your grandma's letters. I was bored waiting for you, and I snooped."

Leah gave her a bewildered look. "But—so you weren't downstairs?"

"No, in the bedroom." She gestured.

"Well—well, someone was in my basement! Sometime yesterday afternoon or last night. I'm not exactly sure when."

"Don't you lock your doors?"

"I *did* lock them!"

"Did they take anything?"

"I don't know. I haven't been down there yet."

"Then how do you know someone's been down there?"

Leah set the broom against the wall and pointed to the floor. "Because that rug was pushed up against the wall. I had rolled it up and laid it in front of the door the other day. But not like that. It's definitely been moved!"

Brindle stared at the rug. "Okay, that's, ah—creepy! I'd call the police!"

Leah nodded. "It's crossed my mind! But I'm pretty sure I know who it was."

Her head rose. "You do?"

"My cousin Marty. At the party I told him he could come and get some of our grandpa's tools from the garage. Well, he cut out early to do it, and when I got here the place was emptied out! He took *everything* out of there before I got home! And not only that—I think he helped himself to more!" She waved toward the basement. "But I only now discovered it."

Brindle whistled. "Wow! Things aren't good between you two, are they? What's up with that? Maybe you should report him."

"Right. The thing is—I told him he could have it all. The stuff in the garage. But not the stuff down there."

"Okay, so let's see what he took!"

"That's the weird thing. I wouldn't even know. I haven't been down there since I moved here."

"For real? Why not?"

"Well—" Leah squirmed. "I don't know! I've not needed anything down there."

"What? I can't even believe that! Are you afraid of going down there?"

"No, I'm not afraid of my basement!"

"Right!" Brindle laughed and with one smooth motion opened the door and flicked on the light. "Come on—I'll go with you!"

"I *do* know this place, Brindle. It's not like I haven't been down there before. I've spent lots of summers here. It's just that I haven't had a reason since I moved in."

"Uh-huh." Brindle nodded dubiously. "You're funny! Come on— let's go see what your crazy cousin was up to."

At the bottom of the stairs Leah hit a switch, illuminating a long and minimally finished room, in the center of which stood a faded ping pong table. Other than an old five-piece beginner's drum set in a corner and a portable electronic keyboard leaning against the wall beside it, the room was bare.

"Your grandparents were rockers, I see," Brindle commented. She raised her brow and turned to Leah. "I'd say either your cousin took everything or there was nothing to take."

"There used to be some old junky furniture in this room. If he took that it'd be a good thing!"

"What else is down here?" Brindle gestured questioningly to a door to the right of the stairs.

"Not much. This is an old bedroom," Leah said, opening the door to reveal an antique bedroom set, the ornate bed topped with a vintage chenille bedspread. In the corner beside the matching dresser stood a spindled back chair like the one in her kitchen. "I'm pretty sure this furniture was from the original farmhouse, but as far as I know, no one ever slept in here."

Brindle screwed up her nose at the musty odor. "Allergy central!"

"Yeah," Leah agreed. "But I've always loved this set!"

Brindle pointed to a black-and-white 1800s-era family portrait on the wall. "Are those your dead relatives?" She shivered. "This room's like the set to an old horror film, if you ask me—their eyes follow you around!"

Leah laughed. "That would always freak us out as kids! I have no idea who those people are!"

Brindle turned to Leah with amusement. "This could be your new bedroom!"

They both laughed, and Leah led her to the next door a few yards down.

Observing a dark and narrow room lined with shelves, Brindle gave a playful cringe, jumping into a dramatic stage voice. "'Horror movie scene two—the torture chamber! Soundproofed to stifle blood-curdling screams!' Okay—I'm beginning to see why you don't want to come down here!"

Leah chuckled. "Grandma's canning cellar." Now this was the fun side of Brindle, she mused, the side she enjoyed having around.

"Ah, the canning cellar!" Brindle perked up with sudden interest, curiously leaning in to look about. Well-labeled boxes of quart-sized mason jars filled one wall of shelves, and on the far wall straight ahead were several dark ceramic-coated canners, along with ample boxes of canning supplies.

Leah tapped the door frame. "Lots of memories in this room—mostly good ones. It was my job to haul the jars of fruits and vegetables we canned down to put them away."

"Huh," Brindle said simply, eyeing the shelves.

Leah found the next door on the far end of the basement locked.

"Shoot!" she said, jiggling the doorknob. "I hope there's a key to this somewhere. The furnace is in there."

Brindle gave Leah a sideways glance. "Do you have a pen I could take apart? Or a hairpin? These are super easy to open." She cast Leah a dark look. "Now don't judge me! In one of the places I lived as a kid, I was always locked out of the bathroom. I had to figure out how to get in to use it."

Leah stared at her in astonishment. "That's terrible! And what do you mean—how many places have you lived?"

A single eyebrow went up. "Too many!"

"What's the story with that?"

She shrugged. "Eh, tell you some other time. But here—perfect! This'll do!" She snatched up a stray piece of wire from the floor and carefully wiggled it into the knob. It gave a pop, and she pushed the door inward. "Ta-dah! Am I good or what?"

Leah's eyes widened as she turned on the light. "Oh, you've got to be kidding me!"

Brindle paused beside her. The whole length of the room was filled with row after row of metal racks, each with a narrow aisle between them and reaching from the floor to nearly three-quarters of the way to the ceiling. Each shelf was tightly packed with plastic bins, cardboard boxes, and loose items, all puzzled neatly together, a claustrophobic library of stuff. In stark contrast, the furnace stood off to their right in a cleared corner all by itself, dwarfed by the rest of the room.

"Holy mackerel—your grandparents were hoarders!" Brindle blurted.

Leah shot her a defensive look. "They were *savers*, not hoarders! It's clean, it's orderly, and it's—it's—" She sighed. "It's a *lot* of stuff!"

Brindle glanced wordlessly at her and back at the room.

That, of course, was an understatement. The storage there was excessive, but as she'd said, it was orderly. On the rack nearest her, she spied a foot spa and an old electric typewriter nested vertically side by side next to some kind of large musical instrument in a case—an accordion, perhaps? An old liquor box overflowed with jumbo boiled wool pumpkins and long, artificial branches of colorful fall leaves. Next to that—an electric ice cream maker in its box. Then a compact humidifier and dehumidifier, side by side. A row of old white-painted windows, possibly from the old farmhouse. Several pairs of hip-wader boots and a camouflaged jacket lay across an open box. Camping equipment. The variety was endless.

"Kinda looks like an estate sale that shoulda happened and never did!" Brindle said.

"Yep," Leah echoed. Looking at it made her tired.

"Or like the back room of some thrift shop."

"Yep."

"And it looks like they had a fetish for plastic tote bins!" Brindle reached over to click her nails on the side of a blue plastic tub.

"Yep, that too," Leah nodded, stepping into the room. "This is probably where my grandparents put all the stuff they didn't want to move to Arizona." She looked at Brindle. "They bought another house in Mesa some years back."

"Ah, I see. And then locked this to keep the renters out."

Leah nodded. "Probably. Wow—more stuff that I get to decide what to do with!" And sift through to find her mysterious valuables. This was nuts! Why would her grandparents do this to her?

"Well, hey—I'm willing to help!" Brindle gave a winsome smile. "Lucky you!"

With that, Brindle proceeded to wander through the racks of storage, tilting her head at odd angles to read the labels stuck in various places on the tightly packed bins.

"Toys," she read. "Crafts. Crafts. More crafts. Quilting hoops and supplies. Kitchen items. More kitchen items. Keepsakes. Carvings and wooden toys. Antique camera." She turned to Leah. "Well, if you were going to steal anything in particular, you'd know right where to find it, wouldn't you?"

Leah smiled at the humor. "I guess it doesn't look like anything's missing. Especially since that door was locked. Unless our bandit was someone sneaky like you!" She winked.

"Ha, ha!" Brindle said, looking amused.

Leah observed the bins on the shelving nearest her, noting her grandmother's handwriting on the boxes. Piano books. Ed's Army mementos. DVDs. Old telephones. She shook her head. Going through everything would not be fun.

"This box says 'Lenore,'" Brindle said from across the room.

Leah turned in surprise, glancing over. "That's my mother!"

Brindle snickered. "Ah, so your grandma saved other people's stuff too!"

"Apparently."

"Mind if I take a look?"

"Knock yourself out!"

Nimbly, Brindle swung the bin to the floor while Leah turned to examine an interesting old globe. A lighted globe, she determined, noticing its cord. She went to find an outlet, noting Brindle fan through the pages of a yearbook, stopping every so often to study a picture or two. In a bit she set it aside and returned to the bin, pulling out a bright blue-and-white cheerleader sweater and skirt with matching pom-poms. She held the sweater up, peeking at its size before tossing it beside the yearbook. Bending back over the bin, she carefully sifted through the layers below.

"I thought you hated that sort of thing," Leah said, looking up from testing the globe.

"I do! It makes my nose itch."

The globe didn't light up, but Leah wasn't sure if it was the actual globe, the bulb, or the outlet. She gave up and put it back into its box, then turned to read through the titles of some antique-looking books packed away on a lower shelf. Out of the corner of her eye she noticed Brindle suddenly straighten, staring down into the bin.

"What?" Leah asked.

Brindle didn't reply but quickly leaned forward to move a few things around.

Curious, Leah went to see what she'd discovered. Spying a knitted baby blanket, she made a little sound. "Aww—you've found my childhood!"

Reaching past Brindle, she plucked up the afghan, fingering the soft pastel yarns. "I bet my grandma knitted this for me! Isn't it sweet?" After briefly looking it over, she folded it roughly and handed it off to Brindle, reaching for another blanket. "Wow! I don't remember seeing these! This is beautiful!"

Fascinated, she spread open a pink-and-white patchwork quilt, admiring its finely embroidered alphabet letters and animals on the cotton squares—*A* for Alligator, *B* for Bee, *C* for Cat, and the like. She passed her hand over the retro designs, a little surprised to find the quilt here at her grandma's house, as she had another similar box at home with her childhood relics.

"It's like new," she observed. "It can't have been used much." She gave it a sniff. "Nope—it definitely doesn't smell like baby anymore!" She draped the quilt over her arm and smiled up at Brindle, who stood by quietly, holding the knitted blanket. "What else is in here?"

"Just normal childhood stuff," Brindle said with a shrug. "School papers, keepsakes—that type of thing. But you know what? We should go." She folded the knitted throw in quarters and dropped it into the box.

Leah looked at her in surprise.

"This is overwhelming! I've reached my clutter maximum, and it's starting to get to me. It's evident your cousin wasn't in here, so we should go back upstairs and tackle this another day." She reached behind her for the sweater and pom-poms.

Leah nodded, surveying the room. "You're probably right." After one day of going through closets upstairs, this was the last thing she wanted to do. She folded the quilt, and Brindle layered it in with the rest of the items, repositioning the lid on top when finished.

Leah smiled. "Okay, so don't gloat, but I'll admit—you were right about my grandparents being packrats! I can't believe all this." She waved her hand. "I don't remember them like this."

Brindle shelved the bin and stood with her hands on her hips, silently studying the racks.

"But yeah," Leah continued. "You're right. Not today. We should go."

Brindle nodded, turning for the door.

"We can leave it unlocked."

"Okay," Brindle answered simply.

Leah frowned. "You okay? You got quiet. What's wrong?"

She shrugged. "Nothing. Just ready to go."

Not this again. Now what? Had she offended her? Leah turned off the light and closed the door, trying to think of anything she might have said that may have bugged her.

At the top of the stairs, Brindle finally spoke. "So—if your cousin was down there, do you think he was looking for anything in particular?" She turned to eye Leah carefully.

Leah hit the light and closed the door. "Well, I'm guessing he'd want all the tools of Grandpa's he could find."

She gave a slow nod, as if satisfied by her answer. "Yeah. But nothing down there seemed disturbed."

"Well, maybe he took something, maybe he didn't—I don't know. There's no way to tell. It's been years since I've been here, and I have no idea what might have been down there. What bugs me is that he came in without asking me!"

"Right. But what's weird to *me* is that there's no sign of anyone being down there at all. How are you so sure he was?"

"Well, I'm not. But I *am* clear on this: I had this rug a certain way, and it was moved." She waved her hand toward it. "Marty definitely opened this door!"

Brindle nodded, her brow creased in thought. "Right. But I don't know—something feels funny about this. Like—what if it wasn't your cousin?"

Leah cast her a doubtful look. "I think it's pretty likely it was Marty. He was here to get everything else. Who else would it be?"

"I don't know." Her eyes flicked over Leah's shoulder toward the dining room. "You hear of strange things happening sometimes."

Leah twisted to look behind her. "What do you mean?"

Brindle shrugged. "You know—crazy stuff."

"What are you talking about?"

"Well—like weird things. You said you left your closet door open yesterday and then found it shut. I've heard of bizarre things happening to people before—stuff being moved, strange sounds, pictures falling off the walls. And things like this—" She pointed to the rug.

Leah gave an involuntary snort. "What are you saying? That my house is haunted? That's stupid!" Nevertheless, a shiver went up her spine.

"It happens!"

Leah batted her on the arm. "Stop it! My house is not haunted!"

"That bedroom down there—it gives me the jitters!"

"Hellloo! It's antique furniture, and it's been there since I was a kid! For heaven's sake, Brin—knock it off! You're scaring me!" Indeed, disturbing images had begun flicking through her mind: her legal pad moved, the back door found open, the can in the trash, her closet door—

"Go ahead—make light of it," Brindle continued, "but it *is* a possibility! I personally know people who have had some awfully freaky things happen to them. A friend once told me about this apparition she called 'Gertrude' that would appear in her house. She could tell it was coming because her dog would start growling out of the blue—just out of the blue the hair on his neck would stand up, and he'd start to growl! They never could actually *see* her—Gertrude—but they'd find things out of place. Little things."

"Well, not *that*!" Leah pointed to the rug.

Brindle's hands rose in innocence. "Don't get mad! I'm just saying it's a *possibility*—that's all. If you have any other weird stuff happening, I'd definitely think about it!"

Other weird things. Leah hesitated, debating whether to say anything about the other odd things she'd experienced. "Well, I *have* had—" She stopped mid-sentence as her phone began to ring on the peninsula. She glanced at it and back at Brindle. "It's probably my mom. I'll call her back."

Brindle jerked her head. "You can answer it."

"It can wait."

"Go ahead! I don't mind!" She waved her on.

Indeed, it *was* her mother, who immediately charged in with a question. "So how'd your interviews go yesterday?"

Leah blinked. "My interviews?"

"Yes—your interviews! I thought you said they were Saturday afternoon."

"Oh, yeah!" Leah frowned, trying to remember what she'd told her mom previously. "Yeah—um, they called to reschedule them."

"*Both* were rescheduled?"

"Postponed. Yeah. Same company. Different departments."

"What company is that?"

"Um, I don't remember exactly. I'd have to check." She scrunched her face, suddenly conscious of how her mother's voice carried. Even across the room Brindle was undoubtedly able to hear most of the conversation.

Lenore gave a cynical laugh. "Now that sounds promising! I'd figure that out before your interview!"

"Well, there were so many." Leah met Brindle's eyes and looked away. "I'll let you know when it is. But anyway, I have someone over, so I can't talk now."

"Oh? Who's there?"

"My new friend Brindle."

"Who?"

"Brindle Baylor—the neighbor girl I told you about."

"Brindle—what kind of name is that? Sounds like the name of a dog or something!"

"Geez, mom!" she said through her teeth, throwing a covert glance at Brindle lingering near the garage entrance.

"Has Marty been over yet?"

Leah smiled at the irony. "As a matter of fact, he has! Marty stopped over last night, but I wasn't home."

"Well, don't get yourself all sucked up in his drama! If he can't handle his life, that's his problem, not yours!"

Leah didn't respond.

"Anything else new?"

"Nope," she said simply. She couldn't imagine how her mother would react to finding out that Marty had cleared out her entire garage last night—or that Danny DeSoto was living next door!

"Okay. Well, call me to let me know how your interviews go."

Leah nodded. "I'll try to remember. But I should go."

After hanging up, Leah turned back to Brindle, who now stood with folded arms and a smug look on her face.

"That wasn't exactly private. You were lying to your own mother, weren't you? Shame, shame! What's with that?"

"Yeah. She wants to come visit me, so I made up some stuff to put her off. I'm not ready." She gave an embarrassed smile.

Brindle raised an eyebrow.

"It's complicated. You'd have to know my mom. She can be—difficult. And for some odd reason she despises this place."

"Oh? Why's that?"

"Beats me! She won't say. It's like she has really bad memories of living here or something. Bad associations—I don't know. She hates everything about this house and is bugged that I inherited it. And as you can see,"—she gestured—"it's pretty beat up, and the yard is horrendous, so I'm trying to get it at least a bit more presentable before she shows up. Hopefully that will help things a little."

Brindle stood expressionless a long while without speaking. Then abruptly she dropped her arms. "Yeah, I get what you're saying. I don't know how you can live here. It's about as ghetto as they come, and not only that—it's creepy as hell!"

Leah started. "Ouch! What was that for?"

She tossed her head. "Just agreeing with you."

"But you didn't have to be nasty! Geez, cut me some slack! I can't help what it looks like now! It's going to take some time!"

"Well, good luck with that! I'm leaving. My advice is for you to start locking your doors. And if that doesn't solve your problem, you might want to call a *priest*!" She gave a firm nod with the pronouncement like it was a done deal, then walked briskly past Leah for the front door.

"What the heck is wrong with you?" Leah called after her. "Brindle!"
But Brindle did not stop or look back.

"Brindle!" she yelled again, as the screen door banged shut. "Fine—
be that way!" she huffed, throwing up her hands, although Brindle was
already out of earshot.

Who knew what *that* was about? It was like she had flipped a switch
and had gotten mean. Had she overheard her mother's rude comment about
her name? Possibly. It was hard to tell. At any rate, she was beginning to see
how emotionally volatile the girl was. Truly, she didn't know anyone on the
planet as temperamental as her. Well, maybe with the exception of—Leah
shook her head, suddenly marveling. Goodness! Brindle was so much like
her mother! The more she pondered it, the more remarkable the similarities!
Both had the ability to go from kind to caustic and back within the matter of
a minute! Both could be fun and enjoyable, and then instantly moody and
erratic. Why, Brindle even kinda *looked* like her!

Oddly, Leah found the discovery helpful. Brindle's unpredictable
manner wasn't pleasant to deal with, but she was certainly used to it
with her mom. And with her mom she'd learned that most things—*most
things*—generally blew over quickly. Perhaps it'd be the same with Brindle.
Nevertheless, at this point it looked like the relationship might remain
guarded and shallow for a while. Or it could even be done with—that was
a possibility too. Overall, Leah was disappointed. She had begun to like
Brindle.

Guarded and shallow. She glanced toward disheveled rug piled
against the wall by the basement door. That was at least better than hostile.
She pulled up Marty's phone number, pushed "call," and waited. This
deserved a conversation. This *required* a conversation—if only for her
peace of mind. Though outlandish, Brindle's suggestion of paranormal
activity had genuinely snagged her anxiety, but she had caught herself. She
knew better than that—but still, she needed to confirm that it was Marty.

Once again, her cousin didn't answer. Leah sighed. Why wouldn't he
pick up? It was Sunday morning, for heaven's sake! Where would he be?
She could guarantee he wasn't at church!

The thing that bugged her the most about the garage ordeal was his
incredible rudeness—clearing everything out of there before she was even
home from the party! Seriously—couldn't he wait until the next day and
load his truck up in the daylight? Oh, but then he would have to *see* her and
possibly *talk* to her! And the boundary issue too. She had told him to take
the stuff from the *garage*, and he had gone far beyond that into her house.

It wasn't right! But what could she do about it now?

"Stupid jerk," she muttered to herself, tossing her phone onto her bed.

Dang. How was she going to keep her sanity with Marty, Danny, and Brindle all cycling through her brain? Life back in Bridgewater suddenly seemed like a piece of cake! Mentally Leah drew a broad circle and plopped the burgundy-haired girl down in the center of it, commanding her to stay put. Her life was nuts enough today without having to deal with Brindle's issues too! She attempted the same with the other two as she took the broom and determinedly finished sweeping the floor.

After cutting one final swath of grass, Leah let the puttering lawnmower die and leaned on the handle, filthy and hot. Though far from reaching her goal of what to conquer before lunch, she had given it her best effort. As with her previous mowing experience, the grass was so long the tiny mower merely pushed it over instead of cutting it, and she had to go back over it several times. Now her accomplishment needed a good raking—or yet another mowing to mulch up the grassy debris. One fact was glaringly obvious—Phil Crawford's loaner mower was grossly undersized for the job!

Her momentary quiet was disrupted by the frenzied yapping of Angel as Jackie Burke happened into her driveway right then, the dog pulling hard against his leash as he furiously scolded a squirrel scampering for refuge in the hedge. With a cake pan and a platter tucked awkwardly under her other arm, Jackie tugged back on the strap, coaxing him along. Her face brightened when she noticed Leah in the yard.

"Howdy, Av—"

Angel's barking escalated as the squirrel taunted him from the shrub.

"Angel! Angel, *enough*!" Jackie scolded. "For heaven's sake!" She turned back to Leah with a laugh. "Golly—it's like I brought my own crier to announce my entrance! Angel, come boy—Angel, *come*!" With another yank, the dog relinquished his quest and reluctantly followed.

"Hi," Leah said, dropping her arms from the mower handlebars. *Great.* She wondered if Jackie had come to talk about her abrupt exit from last night's party.

"Beautiful day, isn't it?" the woman said sweetly. "I'm doing my rounds through the neighborhood—making deliveries." She indicated the dishes under her arm.

"Oh, thank you."

"No, thank *you*! It was so nice of you to bring food yesterday. I was so glad you came." She held out the platter. "Would it be all right if I left Brindle's pan with you too? I'm not exactly sure where she lives."

"Sure, that's fine." Leah said, receiving them both. "I'll probably see her. She's over quite a bit." She *hoped* she'd be back.

"Thanks. Be sure to thank her for me, will you?" Jackie smiled and looked around, taking in a deep breath. "Ah, nothing like the smell of fresh-cut grass! But boy—you've got your work cut out for you with that little thing! You've got quite a yard here!"

"Yeah. My, um—my other mower's in the shop. But hey—I just finished for now and was about to get myself a drink. Care to join me on my porch?" It was probably best to get it over with.

Jackie declined. "Thank you—you're so sweet—but I've got a few more things to drop off across the street. Plus I've got him." She gestured to the dog panting at her feet. "He needs to burn off some energy."

"Oh, sure." Inwardly Leah sighed. Jackie had probably already gotten an earful from Danny anyway, and the longer she waited the harder it would be. She charged in. "Um, Jackie, I want to apologize for the way I left your party last night. Walking out like that was very rude, and I'm sorry. I'm sure by now you've heard all about it from Danny."

Her forehead puckered with concern. "Oh, hon, of course! You're so forgiven! And no,"—she shook her head—"Dan hasn't said anything to us. Not anything!" She paused momentarily, then added, "Well, he did mention *one* thing—but that's all. He told us right away that you had a valid reason for not wanting to see him—but that's it." She nodded kindly, eyeing her. Unable to hold back, she continued, "I'm sorry, Ava dear, but I'm very curious. If it's not too private, do you mind telling me what he did to you? He's staying with us, you see, and if there's something we should know—?" Her eyes were round and questioning.

Leah shook her head. "It's not a secret or anything. I was engaged to his brother."

"Oh." Her chin rose, then dipped in a quizzical nod. "And Dan did something to harm that relationship?"

"No. No, there's nothing with Danny. It was his brother, Jake. He, um—we had to break it off."

"Oh, I'm sorry!" She frowned sympathetically. "So—Dan didn't cause it?"

"No. It was all Jake, his brother."

The woman looked relieved, then confused. "And you're upset with Dan because—?"

"Family association, I guess." Leah shifted uncomfortably.

"Oh, I see, I see. I'm sorry—it's really none of my business."

"No, it's okay. It was a pretty tough breakup. We were all very close. Danny's a fresh reminder of how awful it was."

"Oh, I see, I see." Her head bobbed. "I see. It must have been terribly difficult."

An awkward pause followed in which the two looked at each other.

Jackie took a quick breath. "Ava, would you like to come over tonight? We have a lot of leftovers, and we're just hanging out."

It bugged Leah when people went into fix-it mode. Clear as day, Jackie was on a mission to patch things up between her and Danny. *Tell her straight out,* the thought came. *Tell her and set your boundaries!*

"Sorry—I'm really not comfortable around Danny."

"Oh—it's just the girls!" Jackie returned eagerly, patting Leah's arm. "Just girls, I promise! Kyla Watkins is coming over. My sister too. Maybe." She frowned. "Did you meet her yesterday—Susan Gordon, my sister?"

Leah shook her head.

"Anyway, Dan's taking Dad to a church meeting up in St. Cicerone, and Peter wanted to go along. We girls decided to relax and put our feet up while they're gone. Actually, we're taking care of the party food first, but after that we're going to rest. It might be nice for you to hang out with friends. To forget about all the other stuff for a while." She smiled, her brow raised expectantly. "We'd love for you to join us."

Leah nodded hesitantly. "Um, okay. I'm not sure, but that might work. I'll see. What time? If I come."

"Oh, not until later. They're leaving around dinnertime, so in the evening. And if you see Brindle, tell her she's welcome too!"

"Okay. If I see her, I'll let her know."

"Great!" Jackie jiggled the leash, and Angel sprang to his feet. "All right, Ava dear. I'm going to keep moving. Hope to see you this evening. Have a restful afternoon."

That was another thing, Leah thought, watching her leave. Danny had called her "Leah" at the party, and everyone had heard it. Somewhere down the road Jackie would probably want an explanation for that too. She sighed, pulling off her gloves and stuffing them into her pocket. Then she hiked the cake pan and plate under her arm and pushed the mower one-handed to her barren garage.

Chapter Fifteen

Phil Crawford stopped by later that afternoon while Leah was sipping her iced tea on the porch—"for no particular reason," he said. Glad to see him, she offered him a cold can of Coke, and he settled in for an hour or more, entertaining her with dramatic tales of his high school football heroics, as well as a few hunting exploits on her grandfather's land behind her house, even candidly admitting having bagged a few off-season trophy bucks.

"The first was mostly an accident," he confessed guiltily at her look of surprise. "I was hunting pheasant, but I saw those antlers and—well, it was an opportunity I couldn't pass by." With a sideways glance, he added, "I hope I won't have to kill you after sharing that nugget."

She pulled an invisible zipper across her lips. "I won't tell the warden." She wondered if Marty were aware of Phil's hunting excursions.

Eventually the subject changed to her kitchen, and both shared ideas for the project. She told him she hoped to do the homework of mulling over cupboard styles and picking out appliances soon.

"I think I'll have fewer distractions this week."

"Hey—no hurry," he assured. "You've been busy." He lifted his soda toward the front yard. "You've made some progress out there, I see. Bet that was fun!"

"Ha, ha—so much fun! Case in point for 'distractions' right there!"

They both laughed.

"Man, I still feel terrible for wrecking your mower. But I've got to hand it to you—you've got some spunk taking on a house like this, especially with all that needs to be updated! Most people wouldn't have the patience for a fixer-upper. Or the money, honestly."

"Well, it was my grandparents' home. My motivation is strongly sentimental."

He gave a mysterious smile. "My guess is that there must be other motivations too. Being the lucky egg has its advantages, I hear."

Leah eyed him. "I'm not sure what you mean. I suppose it looks like I have everything going for me, getting a house and all, but hard work and elbow grease count for something. It wasn't handed to me on a silver platter. I wish I had a money tree, but who gets one of those?"

Phil dipped his head. "Yeah, I suppose you're right."

"At any rate, I feel pretty fortunate to have run into you! I can hardly believe my luck to find someone so close to home who can help me with all this!" Especially since Marty was out of the picture, she added to herself.

"Yeah. I'd say we're both pretty lucky, eh? You were lucky to run into me, and I was lucky I *didn't* run into you!"

Again they laughed.

"You still up for going out this week?" His eyes shone with the question.

"Of course!"

"I'm officially good for Tuesday. Does that work for you?"

"Sure."

"Good." He downed the last swallow of his Coke and set the can onto the coffee table as he pulled himself to his feet. "All right, then. As always, Ava, it's great seeing you. I'm looking forward to Tuesday night. I'll pick you up around six-thirty."

"I'll be ready."

She walked him to his truck. "Out of curiosity, where do you live?"

He jerked his head. "In the development across the road."

"I know—you mentioned that before. But where? I've gone running over there, and I thought it'd be kinda fun to see your place. Since you've seen me in all my glory." She gestured to her house.

"Ah, right, right. On Forrester Street—number 417. I'll warn you, though—I'm hardly ever there. And when I am, I'm usually sleeping."

She gave a timid smile. "Warning taken. Don't worry—I won't stop in unannounced. Especially at six am."

He winked. "See you Tuesday!" With a wave he climbed into his truck and left.

After an afternoon of fitful consideration, Leah decided to go to Jackie Burke's that evening—oddly mostly because of something Danny had said earlier that morning about his parents. To learn she'd been mourned by

Rocke and Evelyn meant a lot to her. Indeed, her bond with the two had been so deep—deeper perhaps than with her own parents. Certainly they hadn't replaced her mom and dad, but Rocke and Evelyn had showed her care and affection in a way that her own parents never had. She felt bad making the comparison, but it was true. Of course, the DeSotos were out of her life now, but part of her hoped that maybe, just *maybe* she'd be given a second chance for another relationship like she'd had with Evelyn through Jackie. A new and entirely different relationship, yes, but a chance for something nonetheless. It was a risky step, but why not try it, she told herself, even if Danny lived there. Wasn't it her year for reinventing herself? What would it hurt to get to know some new ladies? And since Danny was guaranteed to be gone for the evening, the coast was clear. And so she opted to go.

Jackie was out on the west side of the house watering her narrow shade garden when Leah rustled through the layers of hedge, sending Angel into one of his fevered barking fits.

"Angel, shush!" she scolded, turning off the sprayer. "Hi, hon! Good to see you! Did you have a nice afternoon?" She looked genuinely happy to see her.

"It was okay," Leah answered, letting the dog sniff her.

"Good—I'm glad. You're here in the perfect time! The fellas left a bit ago. Kyla's inside, but my sister couldn't come." With the hose directed away, she quickly uprooted a few weeds and tossed them aside, startling the dog, who skittered back. "I had a short snooze after I saw you earlier, but I thought I'd better get out here this evening to give these poor plants some attention. We've been so busy they've kind of been neglected." She moved the hose to another plant. "Just look at these hostas—they should have been divided weeks ago! They're overtaking the place!" She looked up. "Could you use some hostas, dear? I could get a shovel right now and throw them in a box for you!"

Leah shook her head. "As much as I'd like to say yes, my yard is nowhere near ready for plants. It needs a complete overhaul. But this"— she gestured, admiring some delicate periwinkle flowers that looked like bells—"this all looks very beautiful."

"Oh, yes, yes—you'll get there. All in its time, hon, all in its time. And thank you. Do you like to garden?"

Leah shrugged. "I haven't done much, really. I mean, I've pulled weeds for Grandma Havi as a kid, but that's about it. My mom liked to garden alone—so she could think, she told us. I was a chatterbox."

"Oh, dear!" Jackie chuckled, dragging the hose along.

"My grandma, though—she was an avid gardener. She had that place over there looking so beautiful! The whole front of the house always had something in bloom. And in the backyard my grandpa planted a rose garden in a big oval and mounted a special bench on a wooden platform so they could sit and enjoy them. It was so pretty. But the roses are completely gone now, and the area looks pathetic. There's a big dip in the yard back there—you've probably noticed it. Everything's been neglected. It's a sorry sight—all dead or overgrown."

Jackie made a sympathetic sound.

Leah continued, "I'll confess I was disappointed when I drove up and saw the yard for the first time. But I'll figure it out. I'll have to, I guess!"

"Of course, you will!" Jackie nodded.

Finished, Jackie cranked the spigot shut, and Leah helped her wind the hose on the rack attached to the side of the house.

"There," Jackie said, wiping her hands on her thighs. She clicked her tongue at the dog now busily scratching at the dirt under a shrub, burying imaginary bones. "Angel—come now! Let's go in!"

"Um, Jackie—"

The older woman turned questioningly.

"I was wondering—does Kyla know about last night? The thing with me running into Danny on the deck. Does she know about that?"

"Oh, I don't think so, hon. But I don't know for certain. I'm not sure what she saw or heard. But I wouldn't worry about it."

"Well, if it's all the same to you, do you think we could maybe not talk about it? It's a little embarrassing."

Jackie nodded kindly. "Of course, sweetheart. I won't bring it up."

"Thanks." Leah gave a sigh of relief. The fewer questions the better.

They entered the kitchen through the sliding door on the deck, finding Kyla leaning on the kitchen island in the center of the room, on which sat three disposable tin pans heaped with leftover meat, each covered with clear plastic wrap.

"I just brought the last of these up from the refrigerator in the shed," she told Jackie breathlessly as they entered. "If you tell me where your plastic bags are, I could start bagging this. Oh, hi." She glanced briefly at Leah and looked away.

"Hi," Leah returned.

"My goodness!" Jackie exclaimed. "You did all this already? Oh, Kyla, I would have helped you—those were heavy! How many trips did you make? And being pregnant! Thank you!" She waited for the dog to enter, then closed the door. "I invited Ava to join us."

"Okay." Kyla gave a nod and turned back to the pans without looking at her.

"We're dividing up the leftover pork," Jackie told Leah, "freezing it in quart-sized bags." She eyed the pans tiredly. "Do you think I might have over-judged the quantity of meat for last night? I couldn't find Mom's notes from previous years."

"It'll keep," Leah said.

"Oh, definitely. And with the three of us, we'll have this bagged up in no time! Are either of you girls hungry? Cause now's the time to fill your plates! Take as much as you want! We'll sit down when we're finished."

Suggesting an assembly line, Jackie held the bags open for Kyla, who filled them with meat. Leah squished out the air, then flattened and sealed the bags. Before long they had several stacks of meat ready for the freezer. When they had finished cleaning up, Jackie waved them to the dining room table.

"Bring your sandwiches, girls! It's time to relax!" She set out the remnants of two leftover cakes and two partial tins of pie on the table. "Anyone want coffee or a glass of water?"

"I'll have coffee," Leah said, stealing a look at Kyla as she brought her plate. She had barely spoken to or even looked at her since her arrival.

"Water for me," Kyla said.

Jackie slid into her chair and turned to her. "You feeling okay, sweetie? You're awfully quiet tonight."

Kyla shrugged, focused on her sandwich. "Just tired. Didn't sleep too well last night."

Jackie nodded. "Yes—well, you were probably worn out from yesterday! I imagine you were plenty adrenalized after sharing your story. You did such a fine job!"

"Yeah, I guess. Thank you."

Leah shot an apologetic look across the table. "Sorry I didn't hear it. I—had to leave early."

Kyla's eyes flicked up to hers and back down. "That's okay."

The look said all Leah needed to know, confirming her suspicion that Kyla Watkins had heard all about it from her husband. All evening she had gotten the cold shoulder from her, and Leah concluded that either she was being punished for her rude exit from the party last night—and consequently missing Kyla's speech—or it was a case of Leah infringing on Kyla's territory with Jackie Burke. Perhaps three was a crowd. Either way, she'd already played mystery mind games with Brindle earlier that day and wasn't eager for another round. But she *did* intend to be polite.

"Maybe some other time you can give me a shortened version."

Jackie swung her face towards Kyla. "Why, that's a great idea! It'd be good practice, hon! You've mastered the long version of your testimony, but you could share the shortened version with Ava right now!"

Kyla gave Jackie a long blink, then slowly and deliberately set her fork down, her diamond flashing in the light.

Jackie turned to Leah with a smile. "Would you care for some of this cake, hon? It's really good!"

"Um, sure." Feeling Kyla's displeasure, Leah shifted in her chair, awkwardly receiving the slice Jackie offered.

Kyla sniffed and started in, speaking rapidly with little expression. "Okay, so I grew up in Stanton, and my mom died when I was twelve. I was raised by my stepdad who legally adopted me before she died. His name is Kendall, and I call him my dad."

"You may have heard of him," Jackie broke in, laying her hand on Leah's arm. "Kendall Lee?" Her brow rose questioningly. "He's running for state senator."

Leah shook her head.

Kyla cleared her throat. "So my birth father—before my dad Kendall came along—he left when I was five, and I never saw him again until the day I graduated from college. He found out I got a job working for Professor Grant at his house here in New Hampton and followed me here, leading me to believe he wanted a relationship with me.

"All my life I'd been bitter at God for taking my mother and giving me such an odd family—I'll explain some other time—so I had a really negative attitude toward God and religious people in general. Anyway, at Professor Grant's house I really tried to figure out things with my birth father, but trying to relate to him was so confusing and hurtful to me. Come to find out, he was actually *using* me to try to steal some valuables from the professor's house. My own father!" She paused for a breath.

Leah nodded, trying to follow.

"At the same time, I was getting to know Susan, Jackie's sister. She also worked for Professor Grant, and she helped me work through a lot of my anger with God and talked to me about the power of forgiveness. God opened my eyes to see my own sin and faults and my need for a Savior. I asked Jesus to forgive my sins and make me his child. Then because I understood that God had forgiven *me*, I made a deliberate choice to forgive my birth father for all the hurt and disappointment he had caused me—not to mention the feelings of abandonment I had carried with me through my life."

Kyla paused, then gave a nod to indicate she was finished. She picked up her fork to try her pie.

Jackie frowned in surprise. "Well—there's so much more than that!"

She shrugged. "You said to give the shortened version!"

"But tell her what happened!" Jackie urged. She turned to Leah. "Her dad, like she said, was a—"

"—No, my *birth* father!" Kyla held up a finger, interjecting through a mouthful of pie. "There's a *big* difference between my dad and my birth father!"

"Like she said," Jackie went on, "he was a professional thief and was searching to find some valuables in the professor's house! It even got to the point that their lives were in jeopardy!" She laid her hand on her chest. "It's so frightening to hear her tell it! He ended up going to prison!" She jerked her head at Kyla. "Tell her what else!"

Kyla swallowed her food and paused with her fork loaded for another bite. "So after my father went to prison, God gave me grace to go visit him. On my seventh visit I was able to pray with him to receive Christ as his Savior."

Jackie turned to Leah. "Isn't that *wonderful*? I'm telling you—there is power in forgiveness! You just never know what doors it's going to unlock!"

Leah nodded happily in agreement, though inwardly she was recoiling. Four years ago Kyla's story would have thrilled her, even in its abbreviated version. Now anything remotely connected with the subject of forgiveness made her grossly uncomfortable. It was her least favorite subject in the world.

Jackie grew serious. "Just recently they found out that her birth father has cancer." She sat back, shaking her head. "Lung cancer. And the outcome doesn't look good."

Kyla sipped her water and set her glass down. "I don't know if I'll ever *love* him—you know, like, feel affection for him—but it doesn't really matter. God's Word says to honor your father and mother, and I forgive him. Truly. I'm able to go see him with a free heart, without any of those ugly feelings inside." She gave a twisted smile. "Of course, it helps that we're only allowed to talk for half an hour at a time. And Peter helps by giving me a list a mile long of questions to ask him and subjects to talk about."

Out of the corner of her eye, Leah could see how Jackie was beaming at Kyla.

Kyla continued, "I know I haven't given you very many details, but probably the biggest thing I learned through my experience was that the thing I was so very bitter at God for was the very thing he had put in my life to keep me from greater harm. I thought he'd been cruel to me—that *he* was the one making all the bad things happen in my life. But I learned that God never causes evil. I've had some tough situations to navigate, but God has preserved me from what would have been more trouble. So I'm thankful. I wasted a lot of time scorning the God who only wanted to rescue me and bring me into a place of more love than I've ever known."

Leah had nothing to say, and they were all silent for a moment.

Kyla looked up. "So what about *you*?"

Leah's eyes widened. "Me?"

"Has there ever been a time when you've asked Jesus to forgive your sins? Have you surrendered your life to him?"

She should have seen it coming. "Yes," Leah answered just as boldly. "At Bible camp when I was sixteen. My grandma sent me there, and I prayed to receive Christ."

"Oh." Kyla blinked and sat back.

Jackie smiled at Leah. "That was so wise of your grandmother—to send you to Bible camp!"

"Then how about your dad?" Kyla asked.

"What about him?"

"Have you ever forgiven him and released him from his faults?"

The question seemed odd. Forgive her dad? Release him from his faults? Her father was the last person on her radar. Over the years she had come to peace with the way he was. Being upset with him was never going to change him, so she had learned to deal with it. Her glaring need for forgiveness was for Jake and Rachel's stuff—that was clear as a beacon in the night. During Kyla's story, every mention of the word *forgiveness* had brought a zing of conviction, but Leah refused to go there. She just couldn't do it right now, and no one was going to make her.

Leah shook her head. "I'm not mad at my dad for anything."

"It's not about being mad. It's about *forgiving* him."

"Well, my dad has his issues, but they don't upset me anymore. I've learned to deal with them."

Kyla's head drew back indignantly. "It's not about feeling bad toward him. It's about releasing him for his sins of wrongdoing in your life, regardless of how you feel!"

"Wrongdoing?"

"Yes! Extending forgiveness for how he's wronged you. Surely he must have done things that have hurt you."

Leah found herself getting defensive. "Well, what father hasn't? But I'm not angry with him!"

"Well, yeah, but—"

At that moment Angel sprang to his feet, barking wildly in the direction of the front door.

"Who could that be?" Jackie mused, rising. "Angel—shush!"

As she spoke, the door opened, revealing Brother Warren, who hobbled inside on his crutches, singing happily to himself about Jesus.

Bewildered, Jackie glanced at the clock, then back at her father. "How can you guys be back already?"

"The meeting was cancelled," he said, closing the door. He repositioned the crutches and carefully made his way across the room. "They have a flood. We got up there right as Pastor Tim called it off. Most of the men from the church were over sandbagging at the riverfront. But it was a nice drive."

A pang of anxiety hit Leah. She knew that Danny probably wasn't far behind him.

"Where's Peter?" Kyla asked.

"Outside. He and Dan are throwing the basketball around. What do we have here?" He paused at the table, smiling at the ladies. "Has that slice of pie been claimed by anyone yet?"

"It's yours," Kyla said, sliding the tin toward him as he lowered himself onto a chair.

"I'll get you a plate," Jackie said, setting his crutches against the wall.

"No, just get me a fork," he replied. "I'll eat it straight out of here." He looked at Leah and smiled. "How are you doing tonight, my dear?"

Leah nodded. "Good."

"Am I interrupting anything? Or were you gals just trying to enjoy all these desserts without having to share them?" He threw Leah a wink.

"Kyla was just sharing her testimony with Ava," Jackie said, handing him the utensil. "And Ava was about to tell us about her father."

Brother Warren turned to Leah. "Sorry to interrupt! Please—" He gestured with his fork. "Carry on!"

As all heads turned toward her, Leah uttered a sound of protest. "I'm not sure what you want me to say! My dad is—I mean, my dad's got his issues, but I don't take those on, so it's not like it's a big deal. I don't see him very often. In fact, I don't have much of a relationship with him at all. Hardly any."

Kyla frowned. "But surely you must have *some* hurts—"

Leah shrugged. "Well, yeah, maybe a few. But not a lot. I ceased caring long ago. I mean, I love him and everything—he's my dad—but I've learned to quit expecting things from him because he can never deliver. I just know that about him. He used to drink a lot, and it was harder then. I guess it's gotten better, but his issues are *his* issues. Like I said, I just can't take that on. He's got another family now. So, it's not like I have a truckload of resentments toward him.

"If anything, it's more my *mother* that I probably need to forgive. My mom is, um"—she paused, considering how to describe her—"*challenging*, I'd say. Kind of an angry person—maybe *contrary* is a better word. Not all the time, of course—I don't want to give the wrong impression. And I love her too. I love her a lot! But sometimes she can be difficult. There's been a lot of hurts with her. But I don't want you to think that I'm mad at her all the time either, because I'm not. She can be really great!"

Brother Warren swallowed a mouthful of pie. "Hmm. Why is your mother angry?" He turned to his daughter. "Jackie, dear, would you get me a little cup of coffee? Decaf, please."

Jackie rose to fill his request.

Leah let out a breath, thinking. "I don't know. Probably because she's been burned by a lot of men in her life—my father being one of them. It's kind of a trait with the women in my family—to be unlucky in love."

Brother Warren made a little sound in his cheek. "There's no such thing as 'luck.' There are reasons these things happen, but it usually boils down to two words—*sin* and *selfishness*. And various expressions of them both. Tell me—did your parents divorce?"

Leah nodded. "When I was nine or ten. Maybe eleven. I can't remember. That's when my mom would bring my brother and me to stay here in New Hampton with Grandma and Grandpa."

"I'm sure that was very difficult for you—your parents splitting up."

Leah shrugged. "It was what it was. My dad moved out. Of course, it was hard, but you just deal with it and get used to how it is. I accepted it. I learned to leave it alone—to not make it any harder than it was. I just lived my life and did what I had to do. For the most part he's a nonissue to me." She lifted her eyes to Kyla. "So to answer your original question—no, I've never specifically forgiven my dad and released him from his faults."

Kyla raised her chin in a challenge. "Well, maybe you should!"

Brother Warren set his fork down onto the pie plate. "Oh, I think this little lady hears the voice of God." He smiled kindly at Leah. "I think she can hear exactly what the Holy Spirit is calling her to do. And I think she's probably already asked the Lord for help in being willing to forgive. He does that, you know, sweetheart—he helps us. The Word says he works within us both to *will* and to do the things that please God. Your mother, your father—whichever, it doesn't matter—God will show you exactly where to start. I wouldn't worry about it. Why don't you just ask the Lord Jesus what he has on his heart for you? Then do what he says."

His eyes. Leah's heart was pounding out of her chest. It was like he could see all the way inside of her! Could he see what a hypocrite she was? Surely he could tell! Surely he knew that she'd never *consider* asking God to make her willing to forgive!

Jackie dropped a coaster onto the table in front of her father and set his coffee on it.

"Thank you, Jackie." He looked up at her. "Have I told you how much I love you today? You're a delight to my heart!"

"Thank you, Dad." Jackie slipped into her chair. She smiled at Leah. "Will you be—"

Her question was interrupted by another of Angel's barking fits as the front door opened once again. Leah dropped her head in dread. It was Danny. She stared at her plate, letting out a long breath. Sitting around a table with him was the epitome of what she had *not* wanted to happen tonight! But she couldn't get up and leave. She had played that card already.

Danny paused at the corner of the table between Brother Warren on one side and Leah on the other. "Hey guys! Looks like a party's happenin'!"

"Join us," Brother Warren said, pulling out the chair beside him. "Those desserts are disappearing—get 'em while they last!"

Danny shook his head. "Thanks, but no. I'll let you guys talk. I'm going back to have a little time to myself before the new week starts. But enjoy yourselves." He turned to Brother Warren. "Give me a call when you're ready to turn in. Good night, everyone!" He looked down and gave a nod. "Leah."

Although enormously relieved to see him go, Leah was soon conscious of all eyes upon her in the silence that followed the closing of the patio door.

Brother Warren cleared his throat. "So your name is 'Leah'?"

Leah nodded. "Yes. But 'Ava' is my middle name, after Grandma Havi. I go by that now. I have for some time." Somehow she felt guilty, like she needed to justify herself. What should it matter to them what name she called herself?

"And how do you know Dan?"

Leah's eyes flicked around the table finding everyone curiously dialed in. Each of them had witnessed or heard about her reaction to meeting him by surprise last night. *Just tell it like it is. Tell it all and be done with it.*

She took a breath. "I was engaged to his brother, Jake. I broke it off the night before our wedding when I found out he'd been sleeping with my best friend, Rachel, and they were going to have a baby."

Kyla's jaw dropped.

Jackie brought her hand to her mouth. "Oh, dear!"

Brother Warren pursed his lips thoughtfully, his eyes still fixed on her. "So—Jacob and *Leah*, Jacob and *Rachel*. Is that why you go by your middle name?"

Leah nodded.

"I see." Brother Warren was silent for a moment. Suddenly he looked down, the pie untouched before him. "Holy Spirit—Holy Spirit, come. Come with your comfort, come with your healing. We love you!" Then he gently patted Leah's arm. "I'm so sorry for what you've been through. It grieves my heart, and it grieves the heart of God."

Leah swallowed, and another long silence ensued. Across from her Kyla stared at the table, and Jackie reached behind her for a box of tissues.

"Tell me, Leah—how did your father respond to what happened?" Brother Warren asked. "Was he a strength to you?"

Tell it like it is. She sighed. "Well, he wasn't there for the actual confession—thank God!—but when he found out, my dad drove over to the DeSoto house and sat on the hood of his car drinking his booze and cussing them out loud enough for the whole neighborhood to hear. One of their neighbors finally called the police. It earned him a night in jail. And a stint in treatment."

"Hmm," he said, nodding thoughtfully. "That's tough. You were his little girl. He might have been defending you in his own way—who knows? But God knows every part of what you've been through." He pushed the pie plate away from him, turning to look intently at her. "Leah, let me tell you something: you're a beautiful girl, and you have a beautiful name. It was given to you by God."

Leah knew exactly where he was going and had already practiced this line of logic with her mother. "Thank you. But so is my middle name. It's a nice name too, also given to me by God. I like it 'cause it's a special connection to my grandmother."

"Yes, you're right!" Jackie broke in sympathetically. "Ava *is* a nice name! And a beautiful name too!"

"Thank you!" Leah said, grateful for her support. "Lots of people go by their middle names! Like Danny, for instance—did you know that Danny's first name is actually 'James'?"

Kyla's forehead wrinkled. "What? I didn't know Daniel was his middle name!"

"It's not—his middle name is Danforth. James Danforth DeSoto. Go ask him!"

Brother Warren had not moved from where he leaned in toward her. "But Dan's not running from anything."

Leah met his eyes and looked down.

"Leah, God's pursuit of you is because he *loves* you." He tapped his finger on the table. "You know he's pursuing you—don't you?"

Thankfully, Leah didn't have to answer because for the third time that evening Angel announced the opening of the front door with a flourish as Peter Watkins came in and made his way over to his wife. He was sweaty, with rosy cheeks.

"Ah, I see what's going on here!" he said, eyeing the desserts.

Jackie handed him an empty plate and fork. "We have a leftover problem, Peter, and we're hoping you'll help us out!"

"Happy to oblige!" he said with a grin, immediately scooping up a large piece of cake. He looked up at Leah. "Hi—it's Ava, right?"

Leah nodded. "Yes. Hello."

"What happened to your mailbox?"

She blinked. "What? Is something wrong with it?"

"It's broken." He motioned with his hand. "The box is hanging down with the front wide open." He speared a chunk of cake and popped it in his mouth.

A shiver went through her body. "Like—a couple days ago?"

He shook his head. "Just now."

"I wasn't aware of that!" Good grief—how in the world could that happen *twice*?

He wiped a crumb from his lip. "I noticed it when we got back tonight and ran over to check it out. Didn't see any mail on the ground, though. Looks like maybe one of the bolts came out underneath or something. If you want, I could fix it for you in the morning. I'll be working nearby, and I could swing by on my way. I'd do it now, but we have the car, and my toolbox is in my truck."

"That'd be nice—thank you very much," Leah replied, her thoughts spinning. Apparently, whoever had done it the first time thought he needed to emphasize his point. Unless, of course, Phil hadn't fixed it properly and it broke again by itself. Either way, it was awfully strange to happen twice.

"Honey, we should probably go," Kyla said up to him. "As soon as you're finished."

He nodded, taking another bite.

"I should too," Leah said, anxious to escape. She moved to rise. "Thank you for inviting me."

Hastily Jackie hopped to her feet. "One moment, both of you! Kyla, I want you to take some of that meat home for the Grants and you. And I have a package for you too, Leah. Um, *Ava*—sorry." She threw her a look of regret on the way to the refrigerator. "And I set this aside for you too." She brought Leah a large plastic bowl with a lid. "It's leftover watermelon— would you eat it?"

Leah brightened. "Yes—thank you! I love watermelon!"

Jackie tipped her head. "Yes, that's what Dan said." She smiled.

Brother Warren extended his hand. "Come closer, my dear. I have one more thing to say, and I can't follow you to the door with this boot."

With apprehension Leah stepped up.

"We serve a great God, Leah. The Bible says he gives us beauty for ashes and the oil of joy for the spirit of mourning. What the devil meant for evil in your life God will use for good. I'm praying for the Father to redeem all those places of pain in your heart and make things better than before." He squeezed her hand. "Your Heavenly Father loves you, precious Leah—he loves you!"

She could barely squeak out her response. "Thanks."

Chapter Sixteen

Angel ambled sleepily along as Jackie walked Leah to the front door, his nails clicking across the wood floor. Squeezing Leah in a warm hug, the older woman reiterated that she was welcome to visit any time. Leah simply nodded her thanks, her throat too tight to speak. It had been forever since she'd had a hug like that. Since she'd had a hug period.

Outside in the deepening dusk, she couldn't find the break in the hedge again; plus, her arms were laden with the food from Jackie, so Leah chose to walk around the long way. But she didn't mind. She needed to think. *Your Father loves you, precious Leah—he loves you.* Brother Warren's words resonated within her, and combined with Jackie's show of affection, Leah found herself stifling the urge to weep. It was good to walk a little.

I'm praying for the Father to redeem all those places of pain and make things better than before.

Bother Warren was—was—wow, what was it about him that affected her so? His words—it was like they went *in*. Permeated, like oil on cloth. She couldn't brush them off or reject them; they soaked in deeply, her heart tingling at the thought of them. *Your Father loves you, precious Leah—he loves you.*

Ahead she spied the broken mailbox from the street, its metal box tilted at the same odd angle as on the day she had met Phil. She stopped and examined it with the light of her phone. Indeed, the support underneath was gone again. She could see the scrapes on the rusted metal where a tool had been used.

She straightened, looking toward Marty's. What had been strange the first time felt eerie the second. That kind of underhanded hostility made her nervous. If that's what he was going to be like, then perhaps it was best their relationship stayed distant. Inarguably she needed to either call him again or go over there, but that sounded about as fun as going to the dentist. She was thankful that Peter had offered to fix the box in the morning. At least she had people like him and Phil to help her out. Hopefully Marty would eventually get a clue and stop his childish antics.

Unless it was someone else.

Uncomfortably she glanced at the shadowed hedges nearby and at the homes across the street. It seemed like an awful lot of work to do for a prank— to get down under there to remove a rusted bolt, especially on a busy road where anyone could see it. And to do it again! If someone besides Marty had deliberately done this, then who? Who on earth would want to harass her? Who else even knew she lived here? Unless it was some random punk neighborhood kids who thought it was funny. She shuddered and hurried up her driveway.

Soft music filled the air—the same type of music she'd heard her first night there, and this time she knew who it was. But Danny wasn't merely strumming his guitar and singing. He was worshiping God. She leaned over the rail at the far corner of her porch to hear him better, listening as the tune rose and fell in the evening air. It was unmistakably his voice—and unmistakably like him to do what he was doing. He'd always been that way. And now his melody was swirling through the arborvitae, bringing Brother's Warren's penetrating words back.

You know God is pursuing you, don't you? God is pursuing you because he loves you.

Yes, she knew it. She'd known his pursuit for four years now, and it was hard work keeping him barricaded out. The question was—how did Brother Warren know it?

Your Heavenly Father loves you, precious Leah.

Leah heard the patio door suddenly open next door, and Jackie Burke called out. The guitar stopped. Leah waited in the silence watching the fireflies blink until the neighbor's door slid open and closed again. Brother Warren was about to get ready for bed, and Danny would help him. How humbling, she thought, imagining what he might be doing in that process. Humbling for both of them. The more she thought about it, the more she had to admit—Danny was a good guy. He hadn't changed in that respect.

At least he had been considerate and had left her alone tonight—that was a relief! He hadn't joined them at the table or pursued conversation with her, nor had he announced to his friends that the two of them had already known each other for ten years. For that she was grateful.

The mosquitoes were out in full force. Leah slapped one buzzing her neck and went in, pausing behind her door with her ears on high alert for the slightest sound of movement in her house. She couldn't help but feel a little on edge, for twice now someone had come in while she'd been gone. How did it help to double-check her doors with someone around like Marty, who had keys and zero qualms about trespassing? Who was to say he wouldn't come in during the night and do something crazy? Of course, she'd never think *that* about Marty, but she wouldn't have thought he'd come to mill about when she was gone in the first place. Plus, the repeat mailbox thing made her extremely uncomfortable. What was that supposed to be—some kind of warning or something? She glanced over at the spacious and bare living room, glad to no longer have the massive boxy sectional to feed her fears of someone lurking behind it.

The glow from the light above the sink illuminated her way to the kitchen, where she hit the main light and put away her food. Closing the fridge, she began her nightly check through the house, breezing quickly through each of the rooms, from the laundry side of the house to the master bedroom, where the boxes still lined the perimeter of the bed. Nothing appeared disturbed apart from the bundle of her grandmother's letters in the bedroom—the evidence of Brindle's confessed poking around the previous day. Leah's brow rose at the scattered mess of envelopes beside the box. She was a snoop for sure, but at least she admitted it. She wondered when— or if—she'd be back.

Giving herself the "all clear," Leah returned to her dining room camp to organize her stuff and change into her pajamas. The mound of clothes accumulating on the floor indicated her need to do laundry soon, but she was hesitant, not knowing the condition of her washer or the water going into it. She sorted out her lights and darks, determining that tomorrow she'd try to find an old bed sheet or something in the basement to run a test load, rather than risk wrecking her clothes. If that were a fail, she'd find a laundromat.

Ready to unwind, Leah grabbed a pillow and took her spot on the floor beside the peninsula, making herself as comfortable as the hard floor and cushion would allow. Her mind was overflowing with a million things from the evening next door, and she needed to sort them out. Her thoughts lingered on Brother Warren, the kind yet frightening old man with his snowy white hair and intense eyes. He made her so *nervous*! It was like God was *in* him—like he was going to call out her sins right then and there in front of everybody at the table. Like he knew what an absolute phony she was, nodding and smiling to all the God-talk around the table.

And yet the way he had looked at her and had spoken to her—he was so—so—Leah bit her lip, contemplating his manner. Maybe what she was trying to describe was the way she *felt* being near him. He was so kind. So very kind. She decided it was *love* that she felt, scary as it was. But strangely it didn't feel contrived or syrupy. It was as if he genuinely loved her—but more than that, it was as though when he looked at her, she could feel his *affection,* like she was his favorite girl or something! How was that possible with a person she'd met only twice, and briefly at that?

And what a contrast from that ice block Kyla Watkins! Holy cow— what had changed from their meeting in Jackie's kitchen when she'd seemed so friendly? All night she'd been short and aloof, giving Leah the clear impression the girl did not like her whatsoever! It was obvious she'd been completely annoyed at having to review her story *one more time* with the heathen neighbor girl who hadn't bothered to stay to hear the main event when it was given—like Leah had personally insulted her or something.

And then there were Kyla's barbed statements to Leah about forgiving her father. She'd been so insistent about it, like she had almost *wanted* her to feel hurt by her dad or something. What was Leah supposed to do? It wasn't like her dad was evil or anything—he was just messed up! She didn't hate him for it or anything. Things weren't perfect, and there were hurts, of course, but life went on, didn't it? What would it help to dwell in the past? Why had Kyla made such a big deal about it?

On top of that, Leah knew Kyla had been surprised to hear that she had once prayed to receive Christ. Kyla's doubtfulness was glaring, and it kinda stung. Yet on the other hand, she had been simply judging her by the outward evidence of her life, so how could Leah blame her for that? What would make her think otherwise? She wasn't even *trying* to follow Christ now anyway.

Leah sniffed, fiddling with a loose thread in the carpet. She *hoped* she was still saved, despite how she was living. Was it possible to keep living in sin and still believe in God? Would he cast her off or punish her? Send her to hell? And was it okay to believe in God and yet want him to leave her alone? She sighed, dropping her head in her hands. It was so hard to navigate through all her twisted thoughts. So hard to admit that she *needed* God yet wanted him to stay away. And at the same time, she didn't really want him to stay away—she just wanted him to do what she wanted him to do and not cross any of her boundary lines! Leah rubbed her forehead. This was the type of thing she would talk to Pam about, although Pam had strongly cautioned against her religious bent. Leah wondered what Pam would think of Brother Warren.

What the devil meant for evil in your life, God will use for good. I'm praying to the Father to redeem all those places of pain and make things better than before.

That would be a dream, Leah thought—for things to be better than before. But it was highly unlikely—impossible, even. She couldn't imagine anything good coming out of the Jake DeSoto fiasco. Not one single thing. And worst of all was that times like this made her think of him again, and then she ended up wasting a truckload of mental energy on a skunk who didn't deserve to have a place in her thoughts.

Hoisting herself up from the floor, Leah wandered to the refrigerator to pop the top off the watermelon bowl, stabbing a sizable chunk to relish its cold sweetness. Danny had remembered she liked watermelon. She leaned on the door recalling the time she had taken an elbow in the face during a high school volleyball game. Knowing the off-season fruit would be a special treat, Jake and Danny and Rachel had searched the entire town to find some, so pleased to present the little plastic container of cubed melon to her that night. Danny had been thin and wiry back then, she remembered. He had certainly filled out. He looked strong now. She speared another chunk and closed the refrigerator.

It was then that she noticed the rug—the same one in front of the basement door—and she froze in mid-bite, wondering how she had walked past that earlier. That same rug was now folded in half the short way with her tennis shoes set neatly on top of it, heels against the wall. She stared, unable to breathe. *What was going on?* She had locked—had *absolutely locked* her doors! Marty? Why would he come in *again* if there'd been nothing down there for him the first time? What was his point?

Or—the wild thought struck her—or had Brindle done this? Brindle was the only one who would have known about the rug thing earlier—had she gotten into the house somehow and tried to scare her? Was this some kind of mean joke? Was this related to her stinky attitude earlier that day, some sort of passive-aggressive punishment for something?

Or was it someone else entirely?

Or some*thing* else?

Goosebumps prickled up her arms as she remembered Brindle's words: *stuff being moved, strange sounds, pictures falling off the walls.* She shivered. The idea of paranormal activity in her house was extremely unreasonable, but all rational thought had vaporized. She wanted only one thing, and that was to get *out* of there!

Jackie, she thought, lobbing the fork in the sink. She was going next door, and she didn't care how crazy it made her look.

Snatching up her phone, Leah hustled across the dewy grass for the cut in the hedge, but while searching for it with her phone's flashlight, she spooked herself with the thought that her intruder might still be lurking in her yard somewhere—maybe even watching from some hidden pocket in the dense foliage! After all, someone had felt pretty comfortable tinkering around with her mailbox on a busy road. She swung around, shining the light back toward the house, but her jitters were only heighted by the dark edges and shadows deepened by the yard light on the far side of the house. Nope, she was getting out of there.

Just get to Jackie's!

Bolting in the direction opposite her mailbox, Leah hastily followed the hedge back past the climbing tree until the row ended, then came up the other side to the stone pavement in front of Danny's cottage. His windows were dark. Quietly she tiptoed across his patio to the lilac, where the little stone path led to the main house. There she paused, crestfallen. The patio doors on the deck were black and all other lights in the house extinguished. *Shoot!* She gazed thoughtfully at the swimming pool shimmering in the yard light, weighing out the likelihood that if she knocked at the house, she'd awaken first Angel, then Jackie, and probably Brother Warren too. She eyed the dark hedge, debating. Could she go back home? Sleep was out of the question. She'd be a nervous wreck on the floor beside the peninsula all night long.

Dismayed, she turned to the little cottage.

Nope. She shook her head. *Absolutely not!*

A scant forty-five seconds of deliberation felt like an hour as Leah stood by the lilac glancing back and forth between the two dwellings, the crickets chirping rhythmically in the damp air. Finally she conceded, telling herself that desperate measures were in order. She stepped onto Danny's porch.

He pulled open the door after her second round of knocks.

"Leah! What are *you* doing here?" He pulled on a T-shirt as he spoke.

"I'm having a little emergency," she told him.

"Yeah? What's going on?" Behind him a lamp illuminated the cabin with a golden glow.

"Someone was in my house. Or some*thing*—I don't know. I had a rug by the basement door, and my shoes were on it, and *I* didn't put them there!" As she spoke Leah realized how stupid it sounded.

His face puckered in confusion. "What?"

"No, I know it sounds crazy, but I'm serious! Someone was in my house!"

"Do you need me to call the police?" He gestured behind him, as if to get his phone.

"Police? Um—I don't know." She fidgeted nervously with her hands.

"Is someone there right now? Is someone in your house?" He glanced toward the hedge.

"No, not now—I'm pretty sure no. I mean, I looked before, but then I saw the rug and it freaked me out. I didn't leave it like that!" At his silence she added, "I was coming to get Jackie, but their house was dark."

"Should we call it in?"

"Well—well, I'm not sure." She looked up, feeling foolish.

"Okay. Well, what would you like me to do?"

"I don't know." She put a hand to her forehead. "I'm just—I don't know. I'm scared! Brindle—this girl from the neighborhood—was over today, and she said she thought my place could be haunted, and I'm beginning to wonder!"

"Right." He sounded amused.

"No, seriously—because the rug was moved *earlier* too! Someone came into my house yesterday while I was over here at the party. And before that someone moved my legal pad."

"Legal pad—what? This sounds—" He shook his head. "Okay, are you missing anything? Was there anything stolen from your house?"

"Not that I'm aware of. But I don't have much stuff."

"And you have no idea of who it is?"

Leah hesitated. "Well—it might be my cousin Marty. I guess it's *likely* my cousin Marty, but I'm not sure."

"Ah, there you go. Have you talked to him?"

Leah shook her head. "No."

"Why not? Call him up and ask him!"

"Well, it's late, for one thing. And second, I've tried. He won't answer my calls. He's not really talking to me right now. He's—he's angry with me."

Danny studied her in the dim light. "So what do you need me to do for you, Leah?"

That was a good question. Leah rubbed her arm in the cool air, unsure herself. "I don't know. I'm just—afraid. Could you—could you maybe come over? Like, walk through the house with me just to make sure there's no one there and then maybe—I don't know—like, pray or something?" She couldn't *believe* those words had come out of her mouth! What was happening to her?

Another silence. "*You* can pray, Leah. You have authority in Christ."

She shook her head.

"Yes, you do."

"I've got nothing. I'm not in a good place right now."

"God's not going to reject you if you call out to him. He loves you."

Leah huffed. "Can't you just come over? I'm scared, Danny!"

He sighed, shaking his head. "I think you should go home and pray yourself, and Brother Warren and I can come over in the morning. Or me and Jackie."

"Why not tonight?"

His hand twitched as he shrugged. "I don't know—I don't think it's a good idea for a guy to go to a girl's house in the middle of the night."

"Are you kidding? Danny, it's *me*!"

"I know. But it's a matter of principle."

Leah stared at him. "You're serious—you won't come over?"

He simply looked at her.

Leah blinked, observing him thoughtfully. "Okay. All right. Could I have a blanket then?" When he didn't move, she extended her hand, repeating herself, "Could I borrow a blanket, please?"

He frowned. "Why? What do you need a blanket for?"

"Because I'm gonna sleep right here on your little porch if you won't come over. I'm not going home! I'm not sleeping there!" Two could play at that game, she figured.

Danny first drew back in surprise. Then he tipped his head back, letting his laugh ring out in the night. "Oh, man, have I missed you! All right, Leah Labanora—you win! I'll come over. Wait here."

Leah laughed a little too.

In a few minutes he appeared dressed in jeans and a T-shirt, fiddling with his phone.

"Who are you calling?" she asked.

"It's late. I'm texting Peter to let him know what we're doing."

Leah rolled her eyes. "Good heavens—you're still doing that? You haven't changed, Danny! Your 'principles' are still terribly annoying. And you know what? It's not even *near* the middle of the night! Look—it's barely eleven-thirty!"

He finished and slid the phone in his pocket. "It *feels* like the middle of the night! Last night was a little rough. Those cushions kept coming apart at my hip."

She smiled. "Good! So apparently your rigid principles didn't apply last night."

He cast her a glance. "On the contrary! I had Brother Warren's encouragement. So all right—around the hedge or through?"

They went around and cut through her backyard.

"Check your shoes," she told him as he held the door for her. "Angel and my cousin's dog visit my yard daily. And heads up—the place has been abused by renters. It needs a lot of work."

"I'm not here to inspect your house," he said, examining the underside of each foot.

They paused in the back foyer.

"Okay—so tell me again what's going on. What's all this drama with your cousin?"

Leah nodded. "Okay. So you know my grandparents used to own this house, right? Well, Grandpa Ed had one son—Richard—who built the house next door. He moved away, but his son, my cousin Marty, continued to live there and rent from him. Grandma Havi had my mom. So when they divided the inheritance earlier this year, Uncle Richard got all of Grandpa's copper company shares, which was a lot, and Mom got their real estate, which was a lot too. To even things out, Uncle Richard deeded Marty's house to Mom, and now she's selling it."

He raised his brow. "Ouch!"

"Yeah." She nodded. "He's been given first option to buy, but he's struggling financially, and there's things with his marriage—" She opened her hands and let them fall.

"Okay—I get it," Danny said thoughtfully. "And did you say there was something with a—what was it?—a *rug* or something? What's that about?"

Leah pointed to the rug in front of the basement door. "That!" Involuntarily she shuddered. "So my first night here I was a little nervous, so I left some lights on and put this rug in front of the door in such a way"— she gestured—"because I hadn't been down there yet."

He cocked an eyebrow. "What was the rug supposed to do?"

She closed her eyes, embarrassed. "I don't know! I don't know what I was thinking. But here's what happened: after the party at your house, I discovered it was moved! I'm certain of it! Someone came into my house and went down there because the rug was pushed up against the wall. However, I'm pretty sure it was Marty because he was here to take some stuff from the garage that night—stuff I said he could have, although he *didn't* have permission to come in the house. I also think it was him because—well, he has keys."

"Okay—you need to talk to your cousin!"

Leah held up her finger to finish. "So tonight after I got home from your guys' house, it was *folded* just like that with my shoes on it and still pushed against the wall. I did *not* put my shoes there today! Someone has been here this evening, and the house was definitely locked!"

"Okay. Sounds likely that it's him." He looked from the rug to Leah. "Does Marty have a girlfriend?"

Leah's brow crinkled. "What?"

"Well, typically guys couldn't care less about a rug and how it's put back. If Marty was here, maybe he brought someone with him."

She shrugged. "I don't know. He was alone at the party."

Danny nodded. "Okay. Carry on."

"So I got thinking about weird things happening in the house—you know, like spooky stuff, because there's been a number of strange things happening. I found my door left open the other day and some stuff was moved. Little things. And a closet door that I was sure I had left open was closed the next day. Anyway, I know how I left this rug, and I was at Jackie's for only two hours tonight. It happened during that time. It scares me! It's either Marty going psycho or—or it's something demonic! I'm serious! Maybe this place *is* haunted!"

He chuckled. "Not to make light of it, Leah, but I don't think the devil folds up rugs nice and neat like this. A *person* did that. What's down there?" He pointed to the door.

Leah flayed her hands. "Nothing! I was down there this morning! It's just an old basement with a plethora of plastic bins filled with my grandparents' stuff. Nothing of great value—monetarily anyway. And the only girl that's been around is Brindle, but she's here a lot! There'd be no need—"

"Brindle—the new girl?"

"Yes, Brindle Baylor. Have you met her? She welcomed me to the neighborhood and comes over almost every day to help me out."

"Yeah, I've met her." He lifted a finger. "Ask her."

Leah shook her head. "No, seriously—she's over a lot. There'd be no need for her to sneak in here. Plus, she helps me. In fact, she went downstairs with me this morning. She's got her quirks, but I'm positive it's not her—not unless she's playing some kind of really bad joke on me."

Danny looked dubious. "I'd still ask her. Ask her directly about it."

"Well, do you understand why I'm a little freaked out?"

"Yeah, I get it, I get it."

"Plus, the mailbox thing. That happened again tonight too, and it's unnerving!"

"What's the 'mailbox thing'?"

"Yeah, so like the first day I was here, I came back from town and found my mailbox broken on the pole with the whole box part of it hanging down. Just suddenly broken! A stranger stopped by to fix it for me and told me that a bolt holding the support underneath had been removed. He said he thought it looked intentional because the bolt was rusted and would have needed quite some torque to loosen it. Then tonight Peter said you guys noticed it broken again—the very same way! Something like that doesn't happen twice. It's creepy!"

Danny gave a groan of disbelief, shaking his head. "This all—this all sounds so weird! So high school! Someone around here is obviously trying to pick on you!"

She spread her hands, as if he'd proved her point. "That's why I think it's Marty. He's the only one I know who's got an issue with me, and I'm beginning to think he's, like, *really* unstable!"

Danny lifted his head to glance around. "Well, I'll talk to Peter about the mailbox in the morning and see what he thinks. But I'd suggest you call a locksmith—tomorrow if possible. And if I were you, I wouldn't tell anybody about it. Not anyone."

Leah nodded.

"I think maybe it's time for a heart-to-heart with your cousin."

"Oh,"—she shook her head—"I've tried, and it didn't go well! Not at all! He cussed me out. And he won't answer *any* of my calls."

"Well, you gotta talk to him. That's your first step. I'll go with you."

She looked at him a moment, then nodded. "Okay. I'd appreciate that. That just might help. Thank you."

"And if nothing comes of that, maybe we go to the police."

A little silence lapsed between them.

"Well, how 'bout we look around? And then we can pray."

Leah let out a breath. "Okay."

"And I think we should start by taking a look down there—" He gestured toward the basement.

Agreeing, she followed him down and switched on the lights.

"Anything changed from when you were last down here?" he asked, surveying the area.

She shook her head. "Not that I can see. We didn't do much—just peeked in all the rooms. The back one's chock full of stuff left by my grandparents, but I doubt anything's worth much or they'd have taken it to Mesa or their lake home." She swung open the door to the furnace room, revealing the rows of boxes and bins puzzled together on the shelves. A few tassels of the pom-poms pinched by the lid hung over the side of the bin that she and Brindle had looked at earlier.

Danny glanced around briefly. "By the looks of it, I'd say your grandparents were planning to move back here eventually. That's my guess anyway."

"Huh," Leah echoed, considering it. He was probably right. It seemed a reasonable explanation.

He backed out, and they shut the door.

"So nothing's different?"

"Nope!" she said, but then she noticed the cellar door standing open a crack. "Wait—I thought I'd shut this!"

Danny's head perked up. "Let's take a look!"

"It's the old cellar," she said, pushing open the door. "All the old canning stuff."

He turned on the light and glanced about. "Anything changed?"

Leah frowned, scanning the quart and pint jars evenly lined up along shelves. Her eyes dropped to rest on a large canning pot on the floor. "Uh— *yes,* as a matter of fact! That canner was on the shelf earlier today! I could swear it!"

Danny shot her a look, then followed her to discover a round area on the wooden shelf void of the thin layer of powdery dust everywhere else. "Is your cousin into preserving foods?" he asked. He looked inside the kettle, finding it empty, then returned the lid with a clatter.

"I have no idea!"

"Hey now—take look at this!" He slid the canner out to reveal a broken jar hidden in the corner behind it.

Leah stared. "Okay, that was *not* broken this morning! This is bizarre!" Her eyes swept around the room until she met his gaze. "See— this is the type of stuff Brindle was talking about! Things broken or moved! I'm telling you, Danny—this is weird! This scares the daylights out of me!"

Danny waggled his head. "No, Leah—someone was in here. Look here—the handles of this pot have been touched. You can tell by the dust. Someone broke a jar and tried to hide it. But the question is—*who?*"

"Well, probably Marty—"

"Then *why*? Was there something in here he'd want?"

Leah opened her hands. "Beats me! Nothing I can think of!"

"And nothing's missing? Anything that was here this morning that's not here now?"

Again she shook her head. "I don't think so." She shuddered. "I can't take this! I'm ready to move!"

"Hey, now—don't freak out! I'm sure there's a logical explanation. We'll talk to your cousin—that's our first step! Maybe there's something specific he was looking for."

"He could at least *ask* me for what he wants! He's being such a jerk!"

"Well, I'd say talking to him is a pretty high priority! Come on now—let's pray."

And he did so, pleading the blood of Jesus over each room and asking for God's cleansing presence to fill each part of the basement. Afterward he motioned to the stairs. "One floor down and one to go. After you!"

Then, starting at the back of the house and moving all the way through to the bedrooms, he did the same, praying over each room, making a special point to pause by each of the entrances to her house to ask God to guard and protect her home from evil. Along the way Leah prayed with him, although in a slightly distracted way, as her eyes kept searching for anything else out of order. Finally they ended at the front door, where he turned and laid his hand on her shoulder and prayed for her too, thanking God for her and for their lives intersecting again.

"Pour out your Holy Spirit on Leah, God, and bless her with every good thing that you have for her in Christ Jesus. In Jesus' wonderful name we pray. Amen." He smiled and squeezed her shoulder.

"Thank you," Leah said meekly. She was undeserving of his help but sincerely grateful.

He dropped his hand, and the two of them were quiet.

In the silence Leah studied him, marveling that a DeSoto was standing in her foyer. She would have never imagined it! She recalled how Danny had inquired about her family that morning on the porch and thought perhaps she should reciprocate by making some kind of polite conversation. But she didn't want to ask about his family.

"Um, so what are you doing now?" she asked finally. "Helping Brother Warren can't be your permanent job."

"Nope. I'm teaching history and phys ed at a private high school in St. Louis. I've been there a few years."

"Still teaching, huh? How'd you end up in St. Louis?"

He shrugged. "Just found a job there, I guess. And then Pastor Reid got me connected with Brother Warren for the summer. He's working on a writing project, and I'm helping him."

"So I hear."

"And what about you?"

"Still in accounting. I hope to get a job with a local firm after I get my act together with this house. My old boss in Bridgewater said he'd give me a good reference."

"That's great! You must enjoy it."

She nodded. "I do. At least I did at my old job. I had a great boss."

"Good."

Another silence.

She calculated his age, adding up from her own. She couldn't get over how different he looked from four years ago, with his full beard and broad swimmer's shoulders. She let out a breath. "Geez, I can't believe I'm standing in the same room as you!"

He smiled. "I guess the Lord works in mysterious ways."

"I guess! So you must be about thirty now, huh?"

"Not quite."

"And still single? What's with that, Danny?"

He shrugged. "Still waiting for the right girl."

"Picky, picky! Are you dating anyone?"

"Nope."

"Are you waiting for anyone in particular? Holding out?"

He didn't answer, but she noted his expression change slightly. She narrowed her eyes. "Ah, so you *do* have someone in mind! Would I know her?" She tipped her head, watching his face. "I'll take that as a 'yes.' Let me guess—Kaylynn Wallace? Cassie Schrader?"

He laughed. "Kaylynn isn't around anymore, and Cassie is married to Brandt Werner with two kids. Don't even go there, Leah—I wouldn't tell you even if you were right."

She snickered. "Well, I don't envy whoever you end up with! I can't imagine the pressure of dating *you*! You'd have to be next to perfect! I'd feel sorry for the girl!"

He threw her a look of annoyance. "Oh, knock it off!"

"No, seriously!"

"So how about you?" he returned.

Leah assumed he'd probably already heard about Carlos, so she tried to spin it in a way that didn't sound like an epic failure. "I was in a pretty serious relationship for a while, but it didn't work out. I broke it off. I'm not dating anyone now, although I have a prospect this week." She lifted her chin proudly. "The guy who's going to redo my kitchen asked me out."

He raised his brow. "Oh, really? And who's that?"

"His name is Phil Crawford. He lives nearby."

"Black truck?"

"Yes."

"Okay. Yeah, I know who he is." He nodded thoughtfully. "Yeah, he looks like the kind of guy who would protect your heart."

"*Right*—says the expert on dating who's thirty and can't get a date! I think I can handle it, Danny. I'm not completely stupid!"

His hands went up. "You're right! Never mind! I'm sure you know how to make good choices. So what are you doing to your kitchen?"

Leah turned toward it. "Gutting it and starting over. A major overhaul on cupboards and appliances. And Phil suggested taking out this wall here to open up this whole area!"

"This wall?" Danny asked, pointing to the center wall.

"Yes. It would let the south light spill all the way to this side of the house! Wouldn't that be nice? Put a little crown molding up arou—"

Danny burst out a laugh. "Are you serious? Does this guy have credentials? That's a supporting wall!"

"Well—"

"That could structurally damage the house! I've done enough work with my dad to know that!"

Leah glanced up to where the wall and ceiling met, not knowing what to say, but Danny's hands were already in the air.

"Okay—I'm sorry! Sorry to burst your bubble! It's none of my business. I'm sure if this Phil guy is qualified, he'll have a plan that'll open up the area safely. I shouldn't have said anything. Sorry."

She shrugged. "It's okay—you're entitled to your opinions. But Phil's *experienced*."

Another silence.

Danny checked the time on his phone. "Well, since we're finished, I should probably go. It's getting late. Are you comfortable here? Because I could call Jackie if you'd like."

She shook her head. "No, don't wake her. I think I'm okay. But thanks for coming over. I really appreciate it—truly I do!"

"I'm glad you felt you could ask."

"It was a risk, but I figured I could trust you."

He looked surprised. "Well, absolutely! Of course, you can!"

"And I'm sorry I was rude to you this morning. And last night. I was caught off guard and freaked out."

"I understand. You're forgiven." He smiled and held out his palm.

She shook his hand.

He chuckled, extending his hand again. "Thanks, but I was about to ask you for your phone. Let me give you my number. That way you can call me if anything else weird happens tonight. I wouldn't want you to have to handle a rouge rug by yourself." He winked.

With a sheepish smile she handed over her phone.

"So I don't know if you were told about this," he continued, looking down as his fingers busily typed, "but Kyla Watkins is starting a Bible study at Jackie's on Tuesday mornings."

"I was already invited."

"Awesome! You going?"

Leah shrugged. "I don't know. Like I said, I'm not in a good place right now. Plus, she doesn't like me."

His head popped up. "Why would you think that?"

"She was rude to me tonight. Very unfriendly!"

Danny studied her a moment. "All right, ordinarily I would stay out of people's business, but—well, I heard you offended her yesterday at the party."

Leah's eyes widened. "Me? I offended her? How so? What did I do?"

He hesitated.

"Did she think I was flirting? Brindle thinks I came across as flirting with her husband, but I swear I wasn't! I was inquiring about his business—that's all! I didn't do anything to her, and she was super cold to me tonight, flashing that big rock around on her hand like she got it from the queen of England or something!"

Danny's jaw dropped in surprise. Then he threw his head back to bellow out a laugh. "I'm sorry, but that was *funny*!" He laughed again and held up a hand. "Okay, so apparently yesterday at the party there was some mention of the Watkins Nursery assault some years back."

Leah blinked. "How is that funny?"

He shook his head. "Sorry. The joke had to do with her ring. Ask her about it sometime. Seriously, ask her where she got it. But the Watkins Nursery thing—Peter Watkins, Kyla's husband, whom you met—*he* was the guy who did it. He did time behind bars for that!"

Leah gave him a confused look. "What? Peter Watkins is a murderer?"

Danny handed her phone back, shaking his head. "No, no! The victim was *assaulted*, not murdered! But you accused Peter of murder, and that's why Kyla was offended."

Leah frowned, trying to remember the conversation. "I still don't see what I did. I didn't know Peter did anything, so how could I accuse him of murder?"

He made a little sound. "Never mind. It's too complicated to explain, and I wasn't there. But it'll be okay. Give Kyla a chance, Leah. Trust me— she's super nice, and she's *real*. I think the two of you would hit it off. You should go to her Bible study. You already know Jackie, and you'll have a chance to meet some other girls too. Just go!"

"But it's a *Bible* study, and I'm not—" She paused, struggling for words to convey how worthless she felt. How marred. Turning her back on God had absolutely destroyed her spiritual life.

"You're not what?"

She gave a mournful groan. "Danny, I've been so far away from God. I've done things I never thought I could do. I don't belong there."

"Nonsense!"

"No, seriously—you would hate me if you knew the stuff I've done! You wouldn't even want to be around me."

"That's silly! I could never hate you!"

"I wouldn't be too sure about that! I've messed up pretty bad—you have no idea! I don't even know if I can come back."

Danny bumped her on her arm. "Hey, now—don't you be talking like that! The prodigal son messed things up pretty bad, and you know how eager his father was to have him home! You know the story! And remember the verse—'A bruised reed he will not break and a smoldering wick he will not snuff out.' You've been bruised, Leah, but you're healing. And you still believe—otherwise you wouldn't have asked me to come over here and pray, right?" He raised a hand as if stopping himself. "Anyway, I think you should go, but I'm not going to push you—I promise. I'm simply happy to see you."

"I appreciate that. And yeah—you too." She nodded.

Danny put his hand on the door. "Okay, this time I'm *really* going. You're all locked up, so you should be good, but call me if you need to. Good night!"

"Good night. Thanks again for coming over. For everything."

He left out the front, and Leah closed the door behind him. After a moment she quickly opened it to call after him, "Hey, Danny!"

He turned at the corner of the house.

"Don't forget to text Peter that you're back! I'd hate for you to be grounded!"

His guffaw sounded again, and Leah laughed with him. He left, and she went back into the house feeling lighter than she had in a long time. It was strange, but somehow it was like having her own big brother back in her life again.

Chapter Seventeen

Jumbled images swirled though Leah's dreams as she fitfully tossed in her sleep. Heaping bowls of watermelon. Chocolate cake. Pie in a tin. Danny DeSoto leaning over the table to hand her a fork. And someone knocking at her door—knocking, knocking—

Knocking, knocking.

"Who could that be?" Grandma Havi asked, glancing up from her hand of playing cards to the others gathered around Brother Warren's dining room table. Grandpa Ed was seated next to her.

"You need to get the door, Leah," Kyla Watkins declared firmly.

"She's right, hon," Jackie Burke agreed kindly. "You need to answer that."

Beside her, Brother Warren squeezed her arm. "Leah, God's pursuit of you is because he loves you. He'll show you exactly where to start. Ask him what he has on his heart for you."

"Okay," she said rather timidly, rising from her chair.

Then, as if the two locations overlapped, Leah was in her *own* home. Her front door was heavy—a great arched beast of a door with an iron latch requiring tremendous effort to pull back. She opened to a barricade of musty old scrap boards. Her screen door was boarded shut.

Knocking, knocking. Persistent knocking.

You need to get the door, Kyla urged from somewhere unseen.

Yes, hon—you need to answer that, echoed Jackie.

Bending, Leah peered through a crack in the rigid slats into the brightness of the outdoor light. Someone was there, all right. Did she know him? His face was bright and features hard to distinguish. Why, it almost looked like—she craned her head, trying to see. Had Rocke DeSoto come to see her? Yes! She felt a momentary excitement as she saw him lift his hand to acknowledge her, but no—as she looked more closely, she realized it was Danny—*Danny* reaching out to her. And then in another second, he changed again, taking on the appearance of—it was almost like—wait, was it—was it *Jake*? And as quickly as she recognized him, the figure's face morphed again to become *Jesus* knocking on the boarded slats.

You need to get the door!

She's right, hon—you need to answer that.

Leah, God's pursuit of you is because he loves you—

Leah stood paralyzed. No! She couldn't do it! Why should she open that door if Jake might be on the other side of it?

Steady knocking, knocking.

I love you, Leah. I'm the answer. Come back to me.

I can't! I can't open that door.

And now there was a commotion as someone else arrived—another man coming swiftly up the porch steps, making his way straight to the door to look in at her through the barricade.

"Um, Leah, if you need help, I'd like to help you." It was her father peering in! The slats disappeared as he laid his hand on the nylon screen between them. "If you need help—like with repairs. I could help you with that. Anything. Just let me know. I'd like to help."

Bam, bam, bam!

Bam, bam, bam!

Leah's eyes popped open to the sound of someone pounding hard on her door.

Bam, bam, bam! The screen door rattled.

Adrenalized, she slid out of bed, shaking herself awake as she hurried across the room to answer. Through the window she spied Brindle trying to peek in. Quickly Leah dismantled the cookie sheet and pop cans propped against the door, opening it as Brindle tried the knob.

Her eyes dropped to Leah's pajamas. "What's wrong? Are you sick?"

"No—no, I'm not sick." She ran a hand through her hair, still separating herself from the dream.

"It took you forever to come to the door!"

"Sorry. You woke me." Leah gave a quick yawn into the back of her hand. "What time is it?"

"It's after nine!" Brindle said. She was in her work uniform.

"Really? Man, I must have needed the rest! I was up kinda late last night."

Brindle bent down to pick up two monstrous coffees, handing the one without lipstick on the lid to Leah. "Well, good morning. May I come in? I can't stay long, but I wanted to bring you this."

"Thank you. Of course!" Leah took the coffee, moving aside as Brindle stepped past her into the house.

"You're welcome."

Leah took a sip, the last remnants of unreality fading. "I'm actually surprised to see you this morning. I wasn't sure you'd be back to visit a trash heap like this again." She spoke lightly but looked her full in the face.

A hint of shame grazed Brindle's eyes before she looked away. "Yeah, sorry. I came to make an apology. I was having a really bad day yesterday."

Leah raised her brow. "Oh, was that it? And when you have a bad day everyone else gets to have one too? Is that how it works?"

Another brief glance. "Maybe. Sometimes." She gave a wry smile. "I'm sorry. I got a little irritated at something and lost it." She brought the coffee to her lips.

Leah nodded, observing her. "Yeah, I assumed that was the case, but I had no idea what happened. I'm not that scary, Brindle—just talk to me! Don't get mean and stomp off!"

Her head bobbed. "Yeah, yeah—I know—of course! I apologize. That was kinda rude. But I'm fine now, so don't worry about it."

"So what was going on?"

"It doesn't matter."

"Well, apparently it *did* matter, so I'd like to talk about it."

"Well, it really *doesn't* matter, so I'd prefer *not* to talk about it." She lifted her chin and turned to look around, obviously done discussing it. "So why were you up so late?" Her eyes dropped to rest on the baking sheet in Leah's hand. "And what are you doing with *that*?"

Leah looked at the pan for a moment, then leaned it against the wall. "It's my redneck security system. I booby-trapped my doors last night. With those." She pointed to the pop cans. "It helps me sleep better with what's been going on lately."

Brindle glanced at the cans with a laugh. "Holy buckets! You haven't had another visit from 'Gertrude,' have you?"

Gertrude. Leah stared at the cup in Brindle's hand, her thoughts racing. It was wild, but *what if*—? What if Brindle *was* behind the rug thing after all and not Marty? What if *she* had somehow come in last night and visited the cellar? Had Brindle laid her shoes on the folded rug? Was she trying to scare Leah for some reason? Why else would she bring up 'Gertrude'? *Ask her,* Danny had said. *Ask her directly.* Why had he said that? Had he some reason not to trust her?

But Leah hesitated. Things between them were already a little fragile. What if it came out wrong and she was offended again? Or what if Brindle was simply into ghosts and *liked* that sort of thing—or what if she had been genuinely afraid her house might be haunted? Any of it was possible.

In the long quiet, Brindle tipped her head questioningly.

"Nope, no Gertrude," Leah responded evenly, concocting an experiment in a flash. "I slept like a baby. And I was up late chatting with a friend. But hey, I have an idea—let's have our coffee outside!"

Brindle looked surprised. "Out there? It might be a little chilly."

Leah opened the door and took a deep breath. "Naw, it's nice out!" She gestured. "Come on—let's get some fresh air! You can have the chair in the sun."

"Yeah, all right," Brindle agreed, returning to the porch.

Leah waved her to the corner seat and sat across from her. If Brindle had *intentionally* tried to frighten her with the rug business, she would certainly want to know if her antics worked. If they were inside the house, Brindle would see the rug and might possibly point it out and make a bigger deal out of the spooky stuff. But outside, she'd have to find out about it some other way. And if she started probing the subject, Leah decided she'd do what Danny suggested and ask her directly about it.

"So what do you have going on today?" Leah asked.

Brindle gestured to her uniform. "Work. Same as every day. How about you?"

"No plan yet—although laundry, for sure. I'm running out of underwear."

Brindle threw her a look of amusement, shaking her head.

"What's that look for?"

"You have a pathetically easy life, you know. Most people don't get to lounge around all day. Us poor folk—we have to work!"

Leah snorted. "Are you insinuating I'm rich? Believe me—I'm quite familiar with work! And look around—" She waved. "This isn't exactly a mansion! I'm not sure where you got the idea that I lay around all day. I'm usually up early. And I'm getting a job eventually—I'll *need* to get a job! It's just that I'm hoping to get started on my kitchen soon, and I think I'll need to be here initially. After that I'll be nine-to-fiving it like everyone else. In the meantime, I have a ton of work to do. So no guilt trip, please!"

Brindle waggled her head. "I know—sorry! I'm just yakking. I didn't mean anything by it. I'm only part time myself. And I *am* serious about helping you with whatever you need. I'm available any time, except when

I'm working, of course. If we teamed up, we could get a lot done! We could get all that old stuff out of the bedrooms and then paint. It'd be fun!"

Leah sighed inwardly. Brindle was a little stuck on helping her with those closets, but she could see she was sincere. "Okay—thanks. So, you like painting then—?"

"Sure! I've painted before!" She crossed her legs and bounced her foot. "In fact, we could be going through some of that stuff right now! I have a little time. Why don't we go empty the two smaller closets before I leave for work?"

Leah shook her head, intent on her experiment. "I just woke up. I'm not ready yet. The only thing I want to do is enjoy this"—she held up the coffee—"and the morning air. So let's get to know each other. Tell me about yourself!"

Brindle's eyes grew large. "Me? Oh, what you see is what you get. Not much to know."

"I'm sure there's a lot to know! Where'd you grow up?"

"Everywhere."

"No, really—I'd like to know! Where'd you go to high school and college and stuff? Tell me about your family. Yesterday you referred to living in many places—what did you mean by that? Have you moved a lot?"

"Oh, yes. Yes, I have. I've moved a lot!"

Leah nodded. "Okay, so tell me about it! Were your parents in the military? Or were you in foster care or something?"

Brindle's hand suddenly twitched, bumping against her coffee which then plummeted off the arm of her chair, bursting open as it hit the floor. She swore as she sprang to her feet.

"Sorry! Quick—get a towel! Crap—I hope I haven't ruined your chair! I'm *so* sorry!"

Hastily Leah ran inside for handful of towels from a kitchen drawer, but Brindle, on her heels, cried, "*Paper* towels! *Paper* towels! Those'll get wrecked!"

"Here!" Leah snatched a roll from under the sink and handed it off, and together they dashed back to sop up the mess.

"It doesn't look *too* bad," Brindle said when they had finished. She gathered up the soggy wad with two hands and stuffed it into the plastic bag Leah held open for her. "I'm so relieved it missed your new chair! Sorry I was such a clutz!"

"No, it's okay," Leah assured, tying up the bag ends. "Only a tiny bit of the rug got splashed, and it doesn't even show."

Brindle gave a heavy sigh. "This is *not* my day. I should probably just get out of here."

"Why? You don't have to go—you just got here, and it was an accident! Isn't there a saying—'Don't cry over spilled coffee'?"

She pulled herself to her feet. "Well, I need to go to work soon anyway."

"Brindle, it's *okay*—forget about it! Here—I'll split my coffee with you. It's huge! Way more than I'd drink anyway."

She shook her head. "No, I should go. Maybe I'll stop by this afternoon. If I'm not too tired." Abruptly she turned down the steps to leave.

Leah called after her, "Brindle, wait! What are you doing tomorrow morning?"

She turned. "Tomorrow? Tomorrow's my day off! Are you thinking of doing closet stuff?"

"Um, well—I was going to ask if you wanted to go to Kyla Watkins' Bible study in the morning. I've decided to go, and I wouldn't mind having a friend there with me."

Her brow went up. "You're kidding, right?"

Leah gave a half-shrug. "I thought I'd try it once."

Brindle eyed her. "Okay. I don't know. I'll have to think about it. I'm not really into that."

"All right—think about it. And let me know. What time do you get off work today?"

"Three."

"Okay, good. Maybe see you then."

Leah plopped back down onto her chair and put her feet up, watching Brindle from her perch until she turned onto the street. She sipped her latte, her eyes dropping to the damp corner of the rug. With the coffee accident, her experiment had been a bust, but there was always the afternoon. Brindle would be back, and Leah would see if she brought up "Gertrude" again—although she was starting to feel guilty about even *considering* that Brindle would want to scare her. The way she had left—beating herself up like that for an accident—it made Leah feel sad for her. Sometimes Brindle appeared so unsure of herself. Like inside she was begging for a friend.

She checked the time. This morning she needed to call a locksmith. And then she'd go gangbusters clearing out boxes in her upstairs closets. She wanted to be completely finished and prepped for painting before Brindle came back to "help," and she had only five and a half hours to do it. If Brindle wanted to paint, then she'd let her paint! It was better than her pawing through her stuff.

Yet mesmerized by the beauty of the morning, Leah lingered a moment longer, enjoying the coffee while still in her pajamas. She laid her head back, now hearing the quiet, rhythmic swish of water next door, presumably Danny swimming his laps. He was in the pool much later this morning—probably because he'd been up late with her.

Danny. Wow—this was Jake's brother, for heaven's sake! And she'd sought him to come to her house to *pray*, of all things! She didn't know whether to pinch or slap herself! Her God-boundaries were getting a little permeable! Never in a million years had she seen that coming, but strangely it felt—she gave a resigned sigh—it felt right. It felt *good*, in fact. Lifting her phone, she pulled his name up in her contacts. To have a DeSoto in her phone again was a miracle, although it was just Danny. Danny was safe. Truly, of all the guys on the planet, he was the safest she knew. On a whim she sent him a text.

"I survived the night! Thanks again for coming over. Any word from Peter on my mailbox?"

There was no reply, but Leah knew there wouldn't be. He was swimming.

Relaxed in her chair, Leah searched online for a locksmith and chose a random company. To her delight, the owner offered to send someone out late morning. Checking the time, Leah decided she had enough of a time gap to make a lightning jaunt to town and back before they arrived. Downing the last swallow of coffee, she scrambled inside to throw on her clothes and head for her car. It made sense to get her shopping out of the way first.

After purchasing and filling her car with several large plastic bins similar to the ones her grandmother had used, she swung by the paint store to pick out a neutral-colored paint for the bedrooms. She bought several gallons of it, along with ample painting supplies. When she was in the parking lot ready to leave, she remembered something and returned to the store a second time to buy a step stool and a couple packages of plastic drop cloths, just in case—although on the way home she regretted the drop cloths. The old carpet in those rooms would not need any sort of protection from splattered paint, plus she had all the old blankets that they had discarded.

At the turn onto Richmond Road, Leah gassed up at the convenience store and picked up some milk and bananas. While paying, she noticed that Danny had texted a while ago to say that Peter had been there early that morning and had fixed her mailbox. It was after-the-fact, since she had already noticed the repair, but he added that now she wouldn't have to worry about missing any pizza coupons or mattress sale flyers. She chuckled, considering the irony that a mattress sale flyer might possibly be helpful to her in the near future.

Once home, she dragged the bins into the large bedroom where she'd been previously working. Her mission, she told herself, was not to look through things too thoroughly but rather to *sort* stuff. With a permanent marker she labeled one bin for items she wanted to keep, another for stuff for her family, and a third for things to go to Marty. Anything else either went in the dumpster or on a "donate" pile in the garage.

From that point, Leah's sorting went more smoothly, although she was embarrassed at how similar she was to her grandmother in the use of plastic bins. It felt a little crazy to be moving items from one plastic box to another, yet it seemed the most logical way to get rid of a lot of unnecessary stuff and still save what she should look through later. In a short while both the closet and the mattress were completely emptied of keepsakes. Apart from needing to get rid of the old bed itself and fix the broken closet door, bedroom number one was done and ready for paint!

From there Leah slid the totes into the hallway and emptied the closets of the two smaller bedrooms, taking a break midway through to greet the old locksmith who had arrived to change her locks. He was an old, bent-over man, well past retirement age and eager to chat, having known her grandfather back in his farming days. He leaned against his truck rattling off stories of the olden days and memories of when her house had been built.

"Ed and I were classmates," the old man reminisced. "Both of us ran cross-country. For a while he and his first wife lived somewhere in Indiana, but she died young from cancer—poor thing. He stayed out there for a while with his boy but then moved back when his mother passed away. A few years later he married a gal from up north—a real nice lady. She had a daughter the same age as mine. I remember that 'cause both of our girls ended up in the family way at the same time—and much too young!" He clucked his tongue. "But life moves on, doesn't it?"

It was no secret that her mother had been pregnant as a teen. Leah gave him an amused smile, opening her arms. "As I'm living proof! Lenore was my mother, and guess what—I'm the daughter in the oven back then!"

His face brightened. "Is that right? Well, nice to meet you! That was a long time ago!"

"Twenty-six years, apparently."

"Twenty-eight, I thought. My grandson just had his birthday. I don't know—I could be wrong. I'm starting to forget things. At any rate, time flies!" He shook his head. "Seems like yesterday I was standing right here in this same driveway visiting with your grandfather."

"Yes, time does fly."

"And speaking of time"—he threw her a wink—"I'd better get busy before you file a complaint with my boss!" His twinkling eyes told Leah he was self-employed.

"You could be in big trouble!"

He cackled in laughter that ended in a rough cough. Then he waved her off and told her he'd come get her if he needed her for anything.

By the time the locksmith was finished, Leah, too, had completed packing the remainder of the bedroom closets into bins. The old man brought her to see and approve of the new locks, and she paid him in cash before he left.

Once he was gone, Leah muscled the plastic totes she intended to keep all the way through the house to the garage and hefted them onto the empty shelves that had once held the bins now somewhere at Marty's. Her heap of discards was hauled out to the dumpster and the giveaway pile relocated to the long empty wall in the garage. Then she carried all the painting supplies from her car to the bedroom hallway and deposited them there. In triumph she found that she still had an hour before Brindle got off work. She had done it!

Tired but satisfied, Leah stuck the rest of Jackie's leftover rice into the microwave for a late lunch. Waiting against the counter, she toyed with her phone.

"Mission accomplished," she texted Danny. "Locksmith just left."

He texted an immediate thumbs-up. "Did he drive a Kia?"

Leah smiled, texting, "LOL, Danny!"

Her lunch was as delicious as the first day, and it felt good to sit. Reviewing her morning, she thought about her declaration to Brindle about attending the Bible study and shook her head. Some crazy things were happening! Of course, she would *never* have considered it apart from Danny's encouragement. It'd be risky—intentionally subjecting herself to church people and the Bible—and it had the potential to go very, very wrong. But in that case, she wouldn't have to go back. On the other hand, her encounters with Brother Warren or Danny hadn't been *so* terrible, so all things considered, things could go very, very right. Or at least in the right direction. The wildcard was Kyla Watkins. If she still had an attitude, things could be awkward. Leah bit her lip, trying once more to remember what she'd said at the party that had been so offensive to her.

Thinking of Kyla brought to mind the tangled images of her strange dream that morning: that great arched door again and Kyla's urging to answer it, the multi-identities of the man knocking, the barred screen door, her dad showing up at the end. Pam had once told her that dreams were the brain's way of defragmenting—similar to a computer's process. Perhaps that's what was happening. She thought back to the conversation at Brother Warren's table the previous evening, reviewing his pointed comments about God pursuing her, as well as Kyla's strong opinion of Leah's need to forgive her dad.

What was there to forgive? She was used to things now. It wasn't like his mistakes caused her an enormous amount of pain. Besides, Brother Warren had spoken up in her defense, telling Kyla that Leah could hear the voice of God and that she would know what she should do.

God will show you where to start.

Leah scooped up her last bite of chicken. Right now, the starting point with her dad seemed hazy. What was there to say to him? What was there to do with him? Not much! Forgive him?

"Yeah, okay—I forgive you, Dad," she said flippantly. Now what? What was the big deal about it?

Anyway, regarding Brother Warren's comment that she could hear God's voice, Leah was highly doubtful of her ability to hear God speak to her about anything. Why would he bother? She didn't deserve to hear from God. She didn't deserve anything from him.

Filling herself a little bowl of watermelon, Leah leaned on the peninsula, enjoying her dessert. Her mound of laundry on the floor sat waiting, but she couldn't stop thinking about her dad in her odd dream—the way he'd reached out his hand to her as he'd peered through her screen. *Maybe I should call him.* She paused, staring at the watermelon, a mix of memories stirring in her mind.

When she was little—back before he moved out—she would nestle into him on his lap while he read the newspaper in his recliner, her favorite place in the world to be. She'd study the ads and pictures and ask him questions—or sound out the headlines—until he'd tell her to sit still and not talk so much so he could read. And then she'd "pretend read" to herself until he'd turned the page and she had something new to look at. She simply liked being there, snuggling with him, with the smell of his soap and shirt, the newsprint, and coffee. It was never the same after he left. For one thing, she was older then and too big for his lap. And there was no recliner at his new place. But also, *he* had changed.

"Dad, what time are you picking me up this weekend?"

"Uh, Chelsea'll be there around ten."

"Dad, I need ice skates for gym."

"Your mother can take care of that."

"Dad, wanna play H-O-R-S-E with me?"

"Not right now. I have an important phone call to make."

"Dad, I need a ride to work."

"Uh, yeah—Chelsea'll do it."

"Dad, can you help with this biology assignment? It's dominant and recessive genes. How do I chart out our family traits when none of them make sense?"

"Now *that* would a good assignment for your mother to help you with!"

"Dad, I need money for a church retreat."

"The heck I'm wasting money on that!"

Her gradual pulling away was only natural, as was her new bond with Rocke and Evelyn, who had welcomed her into their hearts. Although when it came to her wedding, Leah had determinedly put her foot down.

"I have one request, Dad, and you *can't* say no: I want you to walk me down the aisle!"

After a brief hesitation he nodded. "Uh, okay. You'll have to let Chelsea know what I'm supposed to wear."

Maybe I should call him.

He *had* made a deliberate effort to contact her last week. Leah set her bowl down. Had he really meant it when he offered to help her with the house? Because she really could use advice. Yeah, she'd have Phil, but it'd be nice to have her dad's input too. What would it hurt to call him? If he weren't sincere, he'd have some excuse for why he couldn't come, and that would be that. Then at least she'd know. And besides, maybe this was her "place to start," as indicated by Brother Warren—whatever that meant.

Out of habit she opened her contacts to Chelsea, then catching herself, switched to her dad's number, pushing "call" before she talked herself out of it. Her hands were sweating—a familiar reaction to ramping herself up for the unknown. She had her hopes up again, and rejection always stung.

He answered right away, surprising her. After a short exchange of greetings, Leah got straight to the point.

"So. Dad—about that offer to help me. I'm going to need some major work on the kitchen here, and I was wondering if you could come look at it. I'd like your opinion."

"My opinion, huh? Are you sure you want it? I've thought about this a little, and I'm not sure it's the best idea."

A shot of disappointment zinged her. She *knew* it! He was all talk, backing out like usual. But then, almost as quickly, a light went on and she understood.

"Right, Dad—I know what you're saying, but look—this is *my* house now. Mom doesn't need to know about this. I won't tell if you won't."

Another pause. "Are you sure? I don't want to get you in trouble! You could be taking your life in your hands, Leah girl!" He laughed.

Leah girl! She cocked her head in surprise. Not only had he used her childhood pet name, but he'd remembered it! "Well, you offered," she said smoothly, knowing he was right. It wouldn't be pretty if her mother found out he was at the house. "It'll be risky, but we'll both be daring. It'll be a clandestine operation!"

He chuckled. "Yeah! After I called you the other day, I thought maybe I was overstepping my bounds, but yeah, okay—let's do it! When?"

"Well, how soon could you come?"

"Let me talk to Chelsea and get back to you, okay? I'm thinking this weekend."

"Really?"

"Too soon? Perhaps the next—"

"No! This weekend would be awesome! Thank you, Dad!"

Hanging up, Leah marveled. How could a simple phone call feel like a breakthrough with him? But then doubt swung in. Was this for real? He wasn't putting her on, was he? She hoped this whole thing wasn't some sort of Anchor Church assignment or something—a box on a worksheet to be marked off upon completion: *Make amends with Leah. Check.*

And yet his voice—his tone—there had been an eagerness there. She heard it. She *felt* it. Plus, he had called her *Leah girl.*

She speared another chunk of watermelon, wondering if *God* had directed her to make that call. She found herself wanting to tell Danny about it. Of all people, Danny would understand. He knew their relationship. He knew the dynamics with her dad, and he'd totally get what a feat this was for both of them.

Leah was scrutinizing one of Aunt Hazel's embroidered dish towels for rust stains when Brindle joined her in the laundry room after work. Spying the clothes piled on the floor, she chided Leah for just now getting to her laundry—the one thing she said she'd do that day. As if properly baited, Leah gloated when she showed Brindle the empty bedroom closets. The look on Brindle's face was priceless.

"Okay, maybe you're *not* a total slacker!" she teased. "But where did you put everything?" She glanced around.

"Well, about half of it went in the trash or on a pile for Mom or Marty. And I saved the other half to look through later."

"And did you find the—um, anything cool?"

Leah looked up. "Find the what? What were you going to say?"

Brindle shrugged. "Oh, you know. You were looking for old pictures and stuff. And journals."

"No, none of that. But enough flour sack dish towels to start my own store, thanks to Great Aunt Hazel!"

"Impressive! She was a busy lady!"

Leah gestured to the paint. "So we're ready to go!"

Brindle looked surprised. "Now? But I'm in my work clothes! I can't paint in these."

"Want an old shirt?"

She shook her head, slapping her slacks. "No. These are my only work pants, and I can't afford even an accidental speck of paint on them. But if you want, we could look through basement stuff—"

"No!" Leah nearly shouted, holding up a hand with a laugh. "Absolutely not! I've had my fill of filling totes today! Besides, you were so eager to leave yesterday when we were down there."

Brindle huffed. "Well, it was a little freaky to hear that your rugs were slithering across the floor by themselves! It made my skin crawl! You haven't had any other weird stuff happening around here, have you?" She looked up at Leah.

There—for all practical purposes she had brought it up! Leah had been somewhat waiting for it, yet the way it came out was still a surprise. She hesitated, meeting Brindle's eyes, debating whether to go for it or not. Flipping an imaginary coin, she took the plunge.

"As a matter of fact, yes! I noticed how you folded the rug nicely this time and put my shoes on it!"

Brindle's eyes widened. "What? What are you talking about?"

"Like you don't know! Were you wanting to look at something down there? You could have just asked me, Brindle."

"What?"

"You've been in my basement!"

Her brow furled in confusion. "I haven't a *clue* what you're talking about! You think I went—what would I want down there?"

Leah folded her arms. "I don't know—you tell me!"

Brindle's head jerked forward. "You're serious? You think I was in your basement? When? When would I do that? I've been at work all day! And for what? Crafts? Dusty Christmas decor?"

Leah waited.

The girl rubbed her forehead. "Geez! Okay, I don't know what this is about, but I have a sudden headache. I'm going home. Great job on all your progress today, Ava." She spun on her heel to leave.

"Brindle—"

"I'm outta here."

"Wait—seriously, Brindle, *wait*! I want to know if you were down there—just tell me!"

Brindle spread her hands, her cheeks red. "Is that a question or an accusation? I don't know what this is about, but it sounds like you're insinuating I've *stolen* something from you! I can't believe that! Honestly, why would you even *think* that?"

Leah couldn't tell if she was guilty or simply indignant. "I didn't say—"

"—What are you missing?"

"Nothing! I didn't say you took anything. But someone's been down there! And this time the rug was folded with my shoes on it!"

Brindle's eyebrows rose.

Leah let out a breath. "I don't know. It's just that—I don't know—you've always seemed so obsessed—so *eager* to go down there. And, well, I thought that maybe you went down there while I wasn't here."

"Yeah?" Brindle set her hands on her waist. "Okay. For what? Maybe I appear eager because I want to *help* you. Have you thought of that? Holy crap, Ava—this whole conversation is bizarre! Do you realize this is all about a *rug*? This is so—dumb!"

"Well, I know, but"—Leah faltered, losing confidence—"but I know how I left that rug. And demons don't fold rugs," she finished, borrowing Danny's wisdom.

Brindle stared. "Well, I'm sorry I can't help you. It all seems pretty strange if you ask me. What would I want in your house? What would *anyone* want in here? That's what I'd like to know. What's the point?"

"I don't know." Leah shook her head, feeling a little foolish, unsure of where to proceed from there. And yet there had been a broken jar in her cellar. *Someone* had been there! "Well, sorry," she said awkwardly. "Never mind. It doesn't really matter. You're right—it's silly. And it was probably Marty anyway. He's—well, it doesn't matter. I guess I'm just weirded out, and I don't really know what to think."

"That makes two of us!"

They stood facing each other, Brindle looking as if she was trying very hard to process what just happened. It was becoming apparent she knew nothing about any of it.

Leah sighed. "Okay, look—can you still come over tomorrow? Come over, and we'll paint together, okay?"

She nodded tiredly. "Yeah. We'll see."

"And Kyla Watkin's thing starts at ten."

Her lip curled slightly. "If I come, it'll be *after* that! Goodbye."

Leah felt terrible watching her leave, having all but declared to Brindle that she didn't trust her, which was practically the same as telling her she didn't like her. Or that she didn't want her around. Yes, Brindle was quirky, but now Leah felt like a jerk. She sighed, fingering her phone, wondering if Danny was around. She debated whether to call or text him to come over. Or to simply go over there herself.

She decided on the latter, closing up with her brand-new locks and pocketing the shiny key before brushing through the tangle of arborvitae. Hearing voices outside, she went straight back to the deck, where she found Brother Warren and Danny sitting together at the table, the older with his booted foot propped up and Danny leaning back with his ankle on his knee, his arms behind his head. A note pad rested on his lap. Observing that they were praying, she stopped, but Danny saw her and hastily rose.

"Leah!"

"Sorry. This doesn't look like a good time."

Brother Warren craned his neck to see her over the rail. "Why, hello there, sunshine!" He waved. "No, no—come on up and join us! Please! We were just finishing."

"I was coming to—" She paused, supposing it would sound funny to say she was coming over to see Danny.

"Jackie's at her sister's," Danny said, laying the pad of paper on the table. "It's just the two of us tonight."

"And we were about to decide which of the leftovers we can still tolerate," Brother Warren added. "You're welcome to join us if you'd like. Come, come—sit down!"

Leah took the stairs, pausing in front of the swing. "Thanks. You don't have to feed me. I had a late lunch."

Danny pulled out a chair for her. "So did I."

"To what do we owe this honor?" Brother Warren asked.

"Oh, it's nothing really. I, um,"—it seemed embarrassing now with Brother Warren there—"I was just going to tell Danny that I took his advice today." She looked at him. "Brindle came over, and I talked to her. I confronted her about being in my house."

He looked surprised. "*Did* you? And how did she respond?"

Leah shook her head. "It wasn't good. I was *way* off, and now I feel like an idiot." She glanced at Brother Warren. "Sorry—there's a whole saga that goes with this."

"Yes, yes—I've gotten a little synopsis. That girl"—he shook his head—"she needs a father!"

"Sorry to hear that," Danny said. "So, it wasn't her then?"

"Definitely not! She seemed really hurt when I asked her about it. I apologized, of course." She was conscious of Brother Warren's eyes on her, and it made her nervous. Was he about to say something to her again?

"That's too bad," Danny said. "And I'd have to agree with Brother Warren. I think Brindle's a lost and lonely soul who's desperate to belong. It's nice that you're a friend. Just keep being kind to her—and lock your doors." He gave a playful grin.

"*If* she comes around again! We've had our moments lately!"

"Oh, she'll come around."

"Yep, I think so too," Brother Warren agreed, bringing his boot down as he rose and reached for his crutches. "Well, I'm going inside for some dinner."

Danny moved to stand. "I'll give you a hand."

"No, no—you have a seat with this delightful young lady. I'll fend for myself tonight. I can handle it." He winked at Leah before hobbling his way into the house.

"He's very sweet," Leah said after the sliding door closed, "but to be perfectly honest, he scares the daylights out of me!"

Danny chuckled. "Yeah, he can be a little intimidating. I'm privileged to help him this summer. Any glitches with the new locks going in?"

"Nope. Everything went slick. And turns out the guy knew my grandpa, so that was kind of fun. He had all kinds of stories."

"Cool. It'll be interesting to see if the new locks make a difference."

"I know! I hope so! So there was something else I wanted to tell you. Do you remember how my dad was back in the day?"

"What—his drinking?"

"Yeah, but more than that. How distant and uninvolved he was in my life. Well, something's going on with him, I think. The day I moved here, he called and left a message offering his help. Then he called me a second time, this time apologizing over the phone for being a bad father and offering *again* to help me!"

"No kidding!"

"It's quite unlike him! I didn't give him much consideration, but last night Brother Warren and Kyla Watkins said some things that got me thinking. I felt like I should call him back and take him up on his offer. So this afternoon I did. And guess what? He might come up this weekend! And he sounds excited about it!"

"Is that right? Wow—that's great!"

"Yeah—it was pretty crazy! It's like *he* took a step toward me, and then *I* took a step toward him. Something's happening, I think."

"That's great!"

She nodded. "I thought so. I know it's only a couple of phone conversations, but it's something. A start."

He raised his hand for a high five. "Way to go, Leah!"

Leah slapped his hand, returning the smile. What a relief to finally have someone to talk to—although she was still pinching herself that it was *Danny* and that they were hanging out on her neighbor's deck together. The new version of him looked so different with his glasses and beard. But he had aged well, she thought. He looked good.

"Hey—I need to ask a favor of you."

"Yeah?"

"I don't have a Bible. Could I borrow one? For the Bible study tomorrow."

He frowned. "You have a Bible—you have a nice Bible! What happened to it?"

Leah squirmed. "I threw it away." At his look of surprise she added, "I was mad at God."

He bellowed out his hearty guffaw. "Well, you showed him, didn't you?"

Though embarrassed, she laughed too.

He held out his hand. "Here—let me show you an app you can use, and I'll let Kyla know to bring you a Bible tomorrow."

"Thanks." She handed her phone over and watched as he navigated it. "So does the offer to come with me to Marty's still stand? I absolutely dread going there, but I think I need to talk to him."

"Yes, of course! I'll go with you, Leah—whenever you'd like."

She nodded. "Thanks. How about tonight? The sooner the better. I'm more than ready to be done with all this stupid drama!"

Chapter Eighteen

After the fourth time of Leah buzzing Marty's doorbell without a response, Danny suggested they leave and come back in an hour.

"But his truck's here," she said, knocking again and straining to see interior lights through the dark window in his front door. "He might be in there. Maybe he's in the shower." Having psyched herself up for the mission, she didn't want to walk away. "Let's try the garage door."

"His garage is closed, Leah."

"I know," she said, hopping the stairs and cutting across the lawn, "but that's where I went in before. Remember how people would always walk into our garage at home?"

The garage side door opened easily, but she stopped short when she stepped inside.

"What the—"

"He's getting ready for a garage sale," Danny said, arriving behind her.

"Yeah—with *my* stuff, that snake!" She set her hands on her hips. "Well, my *grandparents'* stuff."

Leah had already braced herself to find the collection of bins and tools taken from her place on the night of the party, but she had not anticipated the extent of nor the degree to which the items were organized. Several long, white tables had been set up end to end across both car stalls on which various power tools were crammed side by side, filling every inch of available tabletop. Other items were crowded in a similar fashion on the floor around the perimeter of the room, with only a small pathway between the rows. The plastic bins that had once lined the back shelves of her garage were now shoved underneath the tables.

"Unbelievable! It wasn't like this the other day! He's intentionally selling what he took from my place!"

Without speaking, the two surveyed the cluttered area, noting how similar items were grouped in little clusters—dishes, pans, kitchenware. Blankets, rugs, couch pillows, throws. Hunting gear. Sports equipment. Car accessories. The variety covered the entire garage floor.

Eventually Danny gestured toward the house. "You should probably knock."

Leah made a sound of disgust. "I don't think I can face him right now!"

"Go on—just knock."

But there was no answer.

"It might be best to come back later," she said, dropping her arm. "I'd probably spew on him if he were here! I'm *not* happy about this!" She turned to Danny, who stood nearby studying the room with his hands in his pockets.

"I can't get over how organized he is," he said.

"I know!"

"No, check this out!" He pointed toward a small black table on which two desk lamps with bendable necks were positioned to light a cordless drill. Walking over, he clicked on one of the lamps. "It's a photo station! And look—he's got a log going!" He paged through a spiral notebook lying open on the table.

"He's selling stuff online," Leah stated.

"That'd be my guess." He flipped through a few more pages, then snapped off the light. "All right—let's get out of here."

"See what I mean about him, Danny? This is a new low!" Leah waved her arm. "To clear out my entire garage like he did and then turn right around and sell it all—what a rat he is! This is what I'm dealing with!"

He nodded. "Yeah."

"Oh, geez, look—" Leah frowned, spying a cluster of pocketknives on the floor. She stepped over several pairs of mud boots to get to them. "The guy has no sentimental value whatsoever! He's even getting rid of Grandpa's knives! I'm taking these for Braydon!" She scooped them up, tucking them in a pouch made by cupping up the bottom of her shirt. "When did my cousin turn into such a skunk? I can hardly believe this!"

Danny beckoned. "We should go."

"I know, but I *gave* all this to him! If he didn't want it, he should have told me, and I would have kept it!"

"If you gave it to him, it's his to decide what to do with." He jerked his head for her to walk ahead of him. "Let's go."

Leah rolled her eyes, stepping over an old suitcase as she made her way to the door. "You know, sometimes I wish you'd keep your opinions to yourself."

"It works both ways, Leah. You're in his garage! If you want him to stay out of your house, you need to respect *his* space!"

She turned to face him. "I don't think you get it. It's not about the stuff, Danny—I don't even want it!"

"Well, I can see you're upset—"

"Yes, I *am* upset! It's his disrespect that upsets me—the disrespect he's showing toward our grandparents by turning around and selling all their stuff like this! And the disrespect he's shown to *me*! Who acts like this? Marty and I—we used to be close! We used to be good friends! I don't understand why he's so hostile to me—doing all these crazy things to harass me! Sneaking in my house—"

"—Settle down, Leah! You have no idea what's going on in his life. There's no sense in making a judgment 'til you talk to him."

She looked at the ceiling. "You're *defending* him! Open your eyes, Danny! I'm sorry, but I don't have to know what's going on in his life to know that my cousin Marty is a first-class *jerk*!"

Danny's eyes suddenly flicked over her shoulder in surprise. Leah twisted to see Marty standing in the doorway behind her, his shoulders thrust back and his arms out at his side.

"What's going on?" he demanded, glancing between the two of them. "What are you guys doing in here?"

Her voice stuck in her throat and her cheeks burned. Behind him Midnight suddenly burst through the doorway, knocking against the trash can with his tail flinging side to side. Spying Leah, he nosed happily up to her, then swung his head to sniff Danny. Stepping around the dog, Danny moved beside her and extended his hand.

"Hi. Danny DeSoto. We met playing horseshoes the other day. I'm a friend of Leah's, and we came over so she could talk to you."

Marty ignored his hand, his eyes boring into Leah. She knew he'd heard what she said, and she swallowed, trying to remember why she was even there. Midnight shoved his wet nose under her hand. She pulled it away.

"You're selling—why are you selling all of Grandpa and Grandma's stuff?" she croaked.

He shrugged defensively. "I have no use for it!"

"But—but you took everything, and now you're getting *rid* of it?"

"You *told* me to take it! 'Take it all,' you said! That's exactly what you said! So I did! But mind you—I never touched your fancy lawnmower, did I?"

His mockery smarted. "What's happened to you, Marty? You've gotten mean!"

He gave his hyphenated laugh. "Right! If you want to talk about *mean*, let's talk about your ma! That woman is one—"

"Hey!" Leah's hand flashed up. "That's enough! Yeah, okay, Marty— she's mean, but don't take it out on *me*! I agree—you don't deserve what she's doing, but look at what you're doing to *me*—trashing my mailbox and slinking around in my house when I'm not there! I said to take stuff from the *garage*! Stay the heck out of my basement!"

His face puckered. "What the devil are you talking about?"

"Oh, don't try to deny it! I know you've been in there! You've come in a number of times, and I want you to knock it off! If you want something, ask me directly! As I told you before—I'm not your enemy! And knock off the juvenile mailbox stuff!" As she spoke, Leah was conscious of Danny's hand on the small of her back. She jerked a quick glance at him.

"I haven't been in your house!" Marty retorted.

"Marty, I'm not stupid! Just *ask* me if you want something, but don't come in if I'm not there!"

Marty narrowed his eyes. "Leah, I haven't been in your house! I don't know what you're talking about, but *think* about it! I grew up here. I've had access to that place as long as I've been alive. Believe me—anything I've wanted from that house I could have taken long ago. All that's down in that basement is *junk*—box upon box of it! Same with most of the stuff in the garage! I don't need any of it!"

"Then why'd you take it?"

He threw up his hands. "To sell it! Isn't it obvious? I sure as heck could use the money! I'm broke! And you should talk—who's snooping around here?"

Leah swallowed. Beside her Midnight gave a noisy yawn and wagged his tail.

Marty suddenly reached up and pounded his fist on a control button near the door frame. Noisily, the garage door rattled up, the room brightening with the evening light. Briefly he surveyed the garage and turned back to Leah. "And what *about* your stupid mailbox?"

"Can we cut the charades?"

"I don't know what you're talking about!"

Danny spoke up from beside her. "There's been someone tampering with the support bar underneath it so that the box falls forward."

"It tips down," Leah added.

Marty folded his arms, looking between them. "What the heck—like I've got time for that! What would *that* accomplish?" He gave his hyphenated laugh again. "Believe me, I'd do a lot more than that if I was going to get nasty!"

"Well, you *are* being nasty! You won't even answer my calls!"

"What calls? You've never called me!"

"Oh, yes, I have! I've left you several messages!"

He shook his head. "I've not gotten *one* phone call from you! How would you even have my number?"

"From Midnight's tag!"

"Midnight—?" He snorted. "That's Tiffany's old number!"

Leah stared, then let out a long breath. "Okay—whatever. It just caught me off guard that you're selling all this stuff. It seems really dishonoring to Grandpa and Grandma."

"Dishonoring?" He dropped his arms, casting a look around him. "Like how?"

"Well—" Leah shrugged. "I don't know. I didn't even get to look at what that stuff was! There might have been something of theirs that I wanted to keep."

Marty blew out his breath, nodding. "I see. It's all about you! Fine. You can have it back. It's all yours. Come and get it."

"No, no—I get what you're saying! It was the *way* you took it—coming over like that when I wasn't even there. It just caught me by surprise, is all. And honestly, Marty, I just went through a bunch of stuff today in the closets that I could bring over to add to this. I know what you're saying. It's mostly old stuff, and I don't need it either. But there's a few things—" She stopped.

Marty's eyes flicked down to the bulge in her shirt.

"Well, like these," she said showing him the knives. "I thought Braydon might want these."

He nodded. "Fine. Have them. But the mother-of-pearl one is the only one worth giving him, and one of its tips is broken. The rest are junk. If you haven't noticed, Leah, Grandpa and Grandma had a hard time throwing stuff away, and anything worth anything they took with them to Mesa or up to the lake." He sniffed. "But, yeah—take whatever you want. I don't care. Take whatever you feel you need in order to *honor* Grandpa."

Leah threw him a look. "Well, don't make me feel bad about it! You got to see them all the time, so I get that you don't really care about this stuff. But I rarely did!"

He gave a laugh. "And didn't I hear about that too! Believe me—it was made clear who the favorites were!"

Leah's mouth dropped. "That is *so* not true! Whenever they were in Bridgewater, Grandma couldn't stop talking about you! I was always jealous because you got everything all the time!"

"Oh, right! I got everything!" Marty swept his arm toward her house. "It all comes out in the wash, doesn't it?"

Leah cocked her head. "Okay—look. I know you're furious with my mother for selling your house, but I'd like to remind you that it was your own father that gave it to her in the first place! Have you had that conversation, Marty? Because all your anger flying around probably originates right there!"

He closed his lips and looked away.

Danny tapped her back again. She glanced up to see him tip his head like they should go.

She gave a heavy sigh. "Okay—we'll get out of your hair. Where would you like me to put the other stuff from the house? I'll bring it over tomorrow afternoon."

"I'll leave the door open," Marty replied stonily.

She nodded. "Okay. I'm—I'm sorry everything's gotten so weird." Holy cow—it had to be the tenth time she'd told him that!

Marty said nothing, his expression unchanged.

Danny pulled a money clip out of his jeans pocket and wiggled out a business card, holding it out to Marty. "Part of the reason I came with Leah was to give you this. Peter Watkins is looking for some extra help. Just part time, second-job-type stuff."

Marty took the card, regarding it suspiciously.

"You may have met him at the party—a tall, blondish guy. Landscaper. But maybe not. He said to give him a call if you're interested."

"Okay—thanks," Marty said, reluctantly shaking Danny's hand.

"See you around." Danny gestured to Leah. "Shall we?"

Midnight trotted out with them as far as the hedge.

On the other side of the arborvitae, Leah covered her face with her hands, groaning in a hushed voice, "That was awful—so awful!"

Danny waved her toward the bench in the backyard. "Hey—let's go talk that through."

"Just awful!" Leah repeated, shaking her head as she followed him across the dip in the yard where the old rose garden had been.

He brushed the seat off, indicating for her to sit, then joined her. "I think you nailed it with the thing about his dad. That was revealing! Did you see his face?"

"He has changed so much," she mourned. "I feel like I don't even know him!"

"And he seemed more open at the end. I was very encouraged!"

Leah scrunched her face, looking at him. "Are you kidding me? He was downright cold! I found it very disturbing!"

"What's disturbing is that he obviously has nothing to do with the mailbox antics. Or coming into your house. It's not him, Leah."

"But—but then, who else? And why?"

He raised his shoulders.

"Seriously, who could it be? It's not Brindle! She looked genuinely hurt that I accused her today."

"She could be acting."

"*Acting*? Why? Geez—do you have something against her? It's like you're determined to not like her or something! How do we know *Marty*'s not acting? Honestly, I feel like I don't even know him!"

"It's not that I don't like Brindle. It's more a matter of trust. We don't know her either. And she exhibited some poor moral character beside the pool at our house last week that I prefer not to talk about."

Leah threw him a look. "Listen to you! Poor moral character? Look who's making judgments! Danny, you're so weird! You wouldn't want to be around a sinner now, would you?"

His lips grew thin. "No comment. Just keep—I don't know—just keep your doors locked, okay? We don't know who this is. It could be anybody, really! A former renter maybe? Have you thought of that?"

"It's crossed my mind."

"Well, it wouldn't hurt to look into it! Hopefully things will change now that your house is rekeyed—but call me if there's anything that makes you feel uncomfortable. Or text me. Or Jackie. Someone. I mean it, Leah! I want you to."

She nodded. "All right. But aside from that—"

"—Aside from that, I thought we made some real inroads with your cousin."

Leah frowned. "What? Inroads?"

"Yes! He was angry, but he was honest. It's clear he's struggling financially. And I would guess—as you so accurately put it—that there's some big issue with his father. He was quite open to taking Peter's card at the end there. Did you notice that?"

"I already told you he was angry and struggling before we went! That's not a new discovery! And what the heck—offering him a job working for Peter? What's the deal with that? Right, like Peter asked you to give him his card! I can't say I've ever seen you dishonest like that before, Danny!"

His head drew back. "There's nothing dishonest about it! Peter and I have a standing agreement. He's always willing to hire guys for odd jobs if he can spend some time with them and share the gospel. His landlord, Professor Grant—I don't know if you've met him—he's got a retaining wall down by his shoreline that Peter's dismantled and rebuilt at least four times now with the help of guys like Marty!" He laughed.

Leah blinked. "What? Peter hires guys for work that's bogus?"

Danny shrugged. "Oh, it's real work, all right, and he pays them well. If they stay on with him, he tells them it was training. If they don't, they don't need to know. But either way, he has several hours to talk with them." He checked the time and glanced at the sky. "You said you had some stuff you were going to deliver to him tomorrow?"

"Yeah."

"Let's take it over tonight."

"Why? I told Marty I'd bring it tomorrow afternoon. Besides, I do want to add stuff from the basement, and it's not ready."

He nodded. "I know, but let's take what you have over to him tonight. Then not only can I help you with it, but maybe we can make another connection with him. And then we'll bring the rest of it over another time. It will be another excuse to go over there."

She leveled her eyes at him. "Has my cousin become your project now? What are you trying to do?"

"He's an eternal soul, Leah, someone that Jesus loved enough to give his life for! I'm not happy that he's struggling, but these difficulties might make him open to receive the gospel. Who else does he have that's going to share that with him?"

Leah stared at him for a moment, then looked away.

"What?"

She groaned. "Why are you even sitting here with me? You are so— you're such a saint! You're good and nice, and you care about people's souls. I am *so* not like you! I don't even deserve to be in the same room— the same backyard—as you! I'm barely even saved—that's if I even *am*."

"Then what are you waiting for? It's not as complicated as you think. One simple, heartfelt prayer could change everything for you, you know. It's called *repentance*. It turns everything around. You need to get yourself right before God!" At her silence he continued: "Don't kid yourself, Leah. Sin has consequences! The longer you wait, the harder it'll be. You'll reap what you sow—it's a spiritual law."

"You're lecturing me."

"I'm *appealing* to you to save you from more pain!"

She didn't know what to say. She wished she could articulate the list of "yeah, buts" in her head, but it was five miles long. It'd take a year. She sighed. "You haven't been in my shoes, and it's not as simple as you make it. I went off the deep end after Jake, and it wasn't good. Then I met this guy—Carlos—who got me somewhat straightened out, and I asked him to move in with me. We lived together for two years, and that wasn't good either. I *know* it costs. I *know* it costs a lot to sin. I'm feeling the loss. I'm just not sure I can ever be, you know, like I used to be."

"Uh-huh. I see." He nodded, studying her. "You seem pretty convinced your sins are too big for God to forgive. You know how ridiculous that sounds, don't you?"

"It's a lot more than that. I know what the Bible says about forgiveness—that if you don't forgive your brother from your heart, God won't forgive you. And that's where I'm at. I don't want to forgive, and I'm mad at God." She met his eyes and then looked away. "So there!"

He leaned back, resting his arm on the back of the chair. "Okay. I appreciate your honesty. But let me ask you this—apart from forgiving my brother, why are you so mad at God? Because what happened wasn't about you, Leah. *Jake* was in the wrong, not you. Why are you stiff-arming the one who loves you?"

"Because I feel like he betrayed me."

"God betrayed you? How so?"

"I can tell by your voice you disapprove, but that's how I feel!"

"All right—so tell me!"

Leah sighed. "It's complicated."

"I've got time."

She paused, struggling to untangle it all. "Okay, way back before Jake and I were dating, I told your mom about this curse thing in our family—"

"Curse thing?"

"Don't you remember—the Corolla Curse?" Leah hated that name. Every time she said it, it repulsed her more. "That big generational thing with the women in my family."

"What does that have to do with my mother?"

"If you let me talk, I'll tell you!" Leah said, shooting him a look. "So it's true—the curse thing. My grandma was left at the altar. When she did eventually marry, her husband was unfaithful, and they divorced. My mother's had guys step out on her twice, both very ugly divorces. And then there's me. Your mom said we could pray to break the family curse, and I *did* that with her. We prayed in your kitchen, and it was a big deal. We 'took the whole thing to the cross'"—Leah held her fingers up in quotes—"and I was told it was broken and gone, but it quite obviously didn't work. How can I trust a God who doesn't keep his word?"

He observed her silently.

"He didn't! So I'm doomed! I'm one of the cursed Corolla girls."

"Pfft—stop! That's ridiculous! You are not!" His head swung back and forth.

"I knew you'd say that!"

"Leah, you've got to trust the *Lord*! It's not a matter of being lucky or unlucky!"

"Right, Danny! That's what I believed about Jake!"

"Jake was in *sin*! That had nothing to do with you or your family curse!"

"But still, God didn't save me from it!"

Danny frowned. "How do you know that? Leah, have you ever considered that what happened might have been the best thing for you? That God *did* save you from that family curse? Have you ever thought of how it grieved him to see all that was happening? He *knew* what was going on! God gave Jake so many chances to come clean—I know he did, because that's God's way! But Jake chose to keep his sin hidden. I think it was God's mercy to save you from that!"

"Oh, right!"

"I'm serious! You were saved from marrying him!"

Leah rolled her eyes as she folded her arms.

He let out an exasperated breath. "Knock off the victim attitude, would you? Do you know what you're like? You're like a child pushed out of the path of a Mack truck, and now you're sniveling 'cause your arm got broken in the fall! For heaven's sake, get some perspective! God's not against you, Leah. He's *for* you!"

"If he were *for* me, he wouldn't have let me be humiliated like that in front of all my friends and family! Anyway, I'm too far gone to turn things around."

"That's just not true!"

"You don't understand—I can't just walk back into my old life after all that's happened!"

He shook his head. "You got it wrong, Leah. You're thinking wrong. Jesus is a *person*, not some kind of venue—like you can decide when to go back into the building or something. He's a real person full of grace and mercy who wants to help you out of this. He *loves* you!" He paused a moment. "Look—I know you've been through a lot, and there's much I don't understand, but I'm concerned for you. I hate to see you stumbling over this. God *is* for you, whatever you think, and you can't just turn him off like a movie you don't like. He's *real* and he's coming back." He gestured to the sky. "But he'll respect your boundaries. He won't force you to do anything. But you're missing out. I'm warning you—don't wait too long!"

His tone made her shiver. "I'm just afraid to trust him again," she said finally.

"That I can definitely see. Do you trust *me*?"

It took her a little while to answer. "Yes, Danny, I do. You're probably the only person in the entire world that I trust right now. I know I don't have to pretend anything with you."

"Well, good. I'm glad to hear it! Would you let me pray for you?"

She gave a defeated shrug. "If you think you need to."

He laid his hand on her. "Father, in Jesus' name, would you show Leah the path home to you? Dismantle any lies she's believed about who you are and what you're like. Convince her heart of your trustworthiness and your love for her. Help her receive the forgiveness found in your Son, Jesus Christ. Help her, God, and restore the joy of your salvation to her. Amen."

A long silence lapsed between them.

Finally he bumped her with his elbow. "Come on—let's get your stuff and take it to Marty's."

Her mouth curled into a smile. "You have a one-track mind!"

"Do you have anything really heavy? Because it'd be great if we needed him to help us carry something. Asking for help can open doors in a relationship."

"Seriously? Who thinks of things like that? No, I don't. And everything's already in my garage."

They used her car, cramming full the backseat and trunk. When they arrived at Marty's, the garage door was still up, but his truck was gone.

Danny's disappointment was only momentary. Together they unloaded her car, placing everything neatly in one corner near the house door where Marty would see it. Afterward Leah glanced around.

"All these things make me miss my grandparents." She shot him a look. "Don't even say it!"

Danny straightened in surprise. "Say what?"

"You were going to tell me that these are just *things,* and that things aren't people."

"You aren't always right, you know. In this case you missed it by a mile!"

She folded her arms. "So what *were* you going to say?"

"I wasn't going to say anything!"

"But it's what you were thinking, wasn't it?"

"You want to know what I was thinking? I was thinking that Brother Warren is going to need me in about twenty minutes to take that boot off his foot, and sometimes that foot doesn't smell too great!" He smiled and waved toward the stuff in the garage. "Have at it! It doesn't matter to me! Take what you want! Marty already gave you permission. I'll help you haul it back."

Leah paused, then dropped her arms. "Thanks. I'll try to be quick."

She strolled through the tiny aisles exploring the debris on the floor, every now and then plucking up an item or two, collecting them in a small box that she had emptied of other things. Under one of the tables she found a nice set of copper mugs that interested her, but then she put them back. She didn't recall Grandma or Grandpa ever having copper mugs, and it was likely they were Tiffany's. It'd be weird to take something of hers and Marty's. In another area she found a nest of retro Christmas ornaments that she remembered on her grandparents' tree. Besides those, she salvaged a set of salt and pepper shakers, a decorative plate, a wooden lamp hand-carved by Grandpa Ed, a set of canisters, and an umbrella—which she also put back because one of the ribs was bent.

"I'm done," she announced, approaching Danny with her booty.

His eyes dropped to the box. "You don't have to hurry. I'll wait for you."

Leah shook her head. "No, Marty's right. Most of this stuff isn't anything special. But I do have some fond memories attached to *these.*" She raised the box a little.

"What's this?" Danny lifted a plastic bag tucked inside her box.

"Just trash. I'm ready. Let's go."

He pulled the bag out and walked it to the garbage bin. Lifting the lid, he tossed it in, then paused with the hinged top up, staring downward.

Leah noticed. "What is it?"

"Books," he said reaching in.

She groaned. "Figures! Marty doesn't have a sentimental bone in his body! It's probably more old school stuff. I already found a box of my grandpa's childhood in a closet over at my house. Truly, they saved *everything*. And I'm torn—I mean, some of it is interesting, but most of it's just *old*."

"Look!" he said holding one up. "It's a journal!"

Leah gasped. "My grandma's journal!" She all but dropped her box on the floor to take it from him.

"More than one," Danny said, digging another out of the trash. "These are all journals. I'd say there's close to a dozen in here—maybe more!"

She peeked over the edge of the receptacle at the heap of discarded books. "Oh, my gosh! Hold on—" She cracked open the one in her hand, immediately recognizing her grandmother's handwriting. "Oh, they're definitely hers! I want every single one!"

He passed them off to her in handfuls.

"An interesting find in light of garbage collection in the morning!" he mused, stretching in for another stack.

"No kidding! Know what? I was *supposed* to have these! They were specifically mentioned in the will!"

"In their will, huh?"

"Yes!" She clutched the new volumes he handed off. "They are to go to whoever gets their house. So that's me!" She grinned as they stood with their arms full. "Danny, I could hug you right now for finding these! Let's get a box—quick, before Marty comes home again!"

"I'm guessing he won't care, since they're already in the trash!"

Leah emptied a large purple bin she found under a nearby table, and together they packed it full of the recovered journals. Then Danny tipped the trash container, shuffling through the remaining contents for any other miscellaneous treasures that might have been tossed. When they were both satisfied they'd gotten everything, he fitted the lid on the plastic box and loaded it into her car.

Back at her house, he carried it in for her and deposited it where she directed—in the corner under the window at the head of her inflated bed, right next to the laundry basket where she kept her clothes.

"It'll double as an end table," she said, "and keep the journals near so that I can read them at night. Plus, it'll help keep my pillows from falling off the bed!"

Placing her other keepsakes on the peninsula, she turned happily to him. "Thank you so much! That was practically miraculous!"

His head bobbed in agreement. "And to think we might have left that little bag of trash in your box and brought it *here* to throw it away! Pretty amazing, I'd say!"

"And I didn't even want to go over there again tonight! If it weren't for your urging, we wouldn't have!"

"Don't you see, Leah? God did that for you! He orchestrated all that just for *you*!"

She eyed him thoughtfully. "You know, Danny, finding out you lived next door was the shock of my life, but I have to say that it's been really nice having you around. You've been a good friend."

"Thanks. I'm pretty glad about that too!"

"It's too bad that—" She stopped.

His head tipped questioningly. "That my brother is Jake?"

It was the stain that wouldn't go away. Leah shrugged, saying nothing.

Danny folded his arms, leaning his hip against the peninsula. "You know what? I don't think you would have been happy with him."

Automatically she tensed.

"I can almost say with certainty you wouldn't have been happy with him. He wasn't right for you. You'd have been lost in that marriage."

She groaned. "Moment spoiled. Is there a reason we need to go here?"

He rubbed his beard, as if debating whether to continue. "Leah, I love my brother. He can be a lot of fun. But Jake was—and typically *is*—always about Jake. He's *always* been that way. He's the center of his world, and everything and everyone must revolve around him. What he decides to do is what's going to happen, and everyone else gets dragged along with him. Who you are, Leah, would have disappeared with him."

Her forehead crinkled. "So you're saying you're glad it fell through?"

"No, I'm not *glad* for what happened. But like I said before, in some ways I think it was the grace of God over your life."

Leah closed her eyes and gave a heavy sigh. "Okay—maybe you're right. But maybe you're wrong too—who knows, huh? Because it never happened! Yes, Jake has his flaws, but he's not the only one! You know what's irritating about *you*, Danny? You're always so doggone reasonable and always so right! You know everything!"

"Why do you always say that? That's certainly not true!"

"Stop!" Leah shook her head. "I refuse to argue with you because no matter what, I lose! And right now, I want to make one thing clear: you're not free to bring up the subject of Jake around me anymore. Period! I'm not going down that road with you! It's off limits!" She gave a stern and decisive nod. It surprised her a bit, having come out so naturally. Sometimes setting boundaries felt good!

Danny remained silent, studying her from where he stood, and suddenly Leah felt a little bad. But only a little.

"Look," she went on. "I want to be friends, Danny, and I think we could manage it if you could do that for me—just avoid the topic of Jake altogether, okay? Like *forever*." She paused. "And it might help if you could maybe dial your zeal for God back a couple notches too. I'm just not there. I can't—" She sighed. "I'm not like you, Danny. I can't live up to all that!"

He raised his hands, as if in surrender. "Okay—I'll admit I could have kept the comments about Jake to myself."

"Yes—thank you! You definitely could have!"

They hadn't turned on the lights, and the kitchen had grown dim.

"I get where you're coming from, Leah," he continued, "but let me remind you that Jake is my brother. It's a fact I cannot change—ever! He can drive me crazy, but warts and all, he'll always be a part of my life, and I'll not tiptoe around him. So no deal on that. And second, to love Jesus and please God is why I live." His hand went to his chest. "This is who I am. You get what you get with me. As for you, I give you the freedom to be yourself—to not have to pretend anything around me and to be completely honest—like you were just now. I don't mind. So can we be friends? Yes, of course! I think so. I hope so. But that'll be for *you* to determine, I guess."

Always right. Case in point. Leah blinked. "Okay, Mr. Wise Opinion—thank you for ruining a perfectly good night!"

He gave a little smile. "Oh, come now! Has it been ruined for you? Because it hasn't for me! Your grandmother's journals were marvelously rescued from the trash, and you've had an honest conversation with a friend you can trust. I'd call that a pretty good night!" He reached up to tap her arm. "I need to go help Brother Warren with that foot of his, so you go on, get yourself a healthy snack, and enjoy reading about your grandma. And don't forget to lock your doors. Good night, my friend Leah."

He left via the back door. Leah watched him through the dining room window as he sauntered back toward the climbing tree in the dusk. Leaning in toward the screen, she cried out impulsively, "Danny, check your shoes before you go in!" She couldn't help it.

Chapter Nineteen

A s Danny had suggested, Leah fixed herself a snack that doubled as a late dinner and sat at her card table mulling over their conversation.

He'd been right in his characterization of his brother, certainly. Jake had indeed been the type of person who could walk into any room and become the center of everything. But that had been an attraction for Leah. She had loved that about him and loved the flurry of activity surrounding him. He'd made life exciting! *You'd have been lost in that marriage.* Really? Leah paused, pondering it, her sandwich suspended in midair. It was speculation, of course, but Danny was hinting that she hadn't truly been herself with Jake. Was that true? She thought it had all been good— Jake had been the leader and Leah the follower. It had worked for them. At least that's what she thought at the time.

Apparently Danny didn't agree. Not that it should matter now, she told herself, for Jake was out of her life for good. Yet it *did* matter, for although it annoyed her very much that Danny was right all the time, she did respect him because—well, because he *was* right most of the time. Not every single time. But enough that his opinion was one she listened to, even if she did so reluctantly. Perhaps her individuality *had* disappeared with Jake. If only Jake had been more like his brother, she mused, more God-conscious and careful with people. Indeed, if Jake had been like Danny, they'd have been married four years already!

Setting her plate into the sink, she turned to explore the journals. Choosing one at random, she opened it and found herself moved by the familiar graceful lines of her grandmother's cursive. Fondly she rested her hand on the page, then raise the book to breathe its scent. What a treasure their find had been! To think the journals might have been lost! She pressed the book to her chest, acknowledging that of all her grandmother's possessions left behind, these volumes were the truest prize.

"Thank you, God," she murmured softly. She owed him that at the very least.

Emptying the bin, she spread the journals out across the countertop, counting twenty-one of them, each of them unique, an assortment of sizes, colors, and patterns—from elaborate and beautiful hard bound volumes to plain and flimsy spiral-bound notebooks and everything in between. Going by the date at the top of each first page, Leah laid out every journal, lining them up chronologically, overlapping as many on the counter as she could. Those that didn't fit she arranged across the card table and the bed. Once in order, she numbered the upper left corner inside each cover with a black marker, then returned them to the bin, aligning them consecutively and saving out the first two to pore over when she finished. The plastic cover went back onto the bin in the corner.

Dressed in her pajamas, she nestled into her pillows on her floor spot bedside the peninsula and opened the first journal, a slim, red softcover with an old-fashioned typewriter embossed on the front. As she began to read her, grandmother's voice silently filled the room.

March 14. I've never owned a journal before. It feels strange to put ink on an empty page, like I'm writing a book or something that should be important. Ha, ha. Who am I writing to? Myself? God? Someone else? Heavens, I hope not! Anyway, this fancy journal is from Mary McAllister, who saved my life. (Older hostess lady at work.) She says I'm beginning a new life now, and I should record my journey. Not sure what that means, but it was nice of her to give it to me, so ta-da, here's my first entry. Mary's been at Grady's the longest. I've always thought her nice, but we've never really been friends. Last week she had the courage to get religious with me and tell me the truth about sin. My sin. Not that I'm worse than anyone else, and she didn't grind it in or anything. I guess I've been accustomed to playing the victim for what everybody else has done to me, which is a lot. Everybody meaning Mom, Dad, Marcus, and Curt. (Turns out Mary M is second cousin to Marcus. Says the rat is back in Bridgewater now with a different girlfriend! Figures!)

Anyway, Mary listened to me whine about how miserable my life is because of all the junk that's happened to me. Actually listened. Then she prayed for me right there in the kitchen.

She was so nice that I waited for her to finish counting the till to walk out to our cars together, and we ended up talking out in the parking lot for a long time. She told me about the greatness of God. How perfect and good he is. How he has the right to set the standard for right and wrong because he made everything and knows how it should work. It made sense the way she told it, and it's all from the Bible. Things I maybe knew subconsciously but never ever thought about.

Leah turned the page.

But her words about sin made me uncomfortable. She explained to me what sin was and how we're all guilty before God, who is holy. What person in their right mind could deny it? Sexual sin, hatred, lying, greed, envy. I had to say "yes" to doing all of it, but I honestly didn't feel too bad about it because that describes everybody, right?

But when she started talking about the consequences and penalties of sin—that there would be an eternal punishment for it—something crazy started happening. My heart started pounding. It's like it all sank in—that I am responsible for my own sin, that I've made choices that I alone will answer to God for. To God himself! Some stuff seems petty. I mean, who doesn't lie sometimes? But still, they're all choices against God that I'm accountable for. No one else. There'll be no blaming Marcus for the hatred I've let steep in my heart. He'll have to answer to God himself someday for leaving me standing at the altar. And Curt too, for dumping me and Lenore for Kendra S. And that sleazebucket will have to give an account to God too. Everybody will. I guess what hit me is that all their wrongs against me didn't negate that I will have to answer to God for my own sin. Period. For the first time ever, I'm not as good as I thought I was.

Leah flopped the journal back onto her lap, squirming. *Here we go again*—with God invisibly staring at her from across the room! Was the whole journal going to be preachy like this? She flipped to the middle, eyeing the handwriting. Hopefully it was just the beginning part. She turned back to her place.

If I'd have to sum it up, I think I've made life all about me. Like I'm the center, and God exists to serve me and make my life good. I've been furious with him for all my hurts, like somehow he owes me or has done me wrong. I hadn't a clue of how my own sin separated me from him. I honestly thought that God would cut me slack because I was the innocent victim who was wronged.

When Mary pointed out the eternal destiny of all sinners, I was shocked. I always thought hell was figurative, not a real place. She said there'd be no distinction between "good" people or "bad" people. All people are sinners, and all people will answer to God for their own sins, big or small, including me.

Then she explained that Jesus died on the cross in my place so that I could be forgiven—he actually paid for MY sins— beaten, punished, put to death, sent to hell. If I believe that and put my trust in Jesus, he will pardon my sin and give me life. She asked if I'd like to pray to ask God to forgive my sins, and I did! It made sense to do it, and did I ever feel relieved! I was embarrassed at how much I cried.

That was last week, and this week she gave me this journal and a Bible and said she'd like to help me learn what it means to follow Jesus. I don't exactly recall signing up for that, but she said that it was not only a matter of God forgiving you for your sins. She said I need to learn how to live to please him. I told her that I didn't want to do anything weird. She just laughed. I'm not sure if that means she agrees with me or not. She's nice, though, so I think it'll be okay.

Leah closed the journal on her thumb and stared at her bed, feeling as though the decades overlapped and Mary What's-Her-Face was speaking directly to *her*. So much of the writing resonated with her own life— surprisingly so—*uncomfortably* so—even down to what Danny had said about Jake living as the center of the world. But if Leah were honest, wasn't *she* the same way? Wasn't *that* why she'd been so angry—because God *owed* her? She'd been hurt and life had gotten hard—and didn't God exist to serve her and make her life good? She much preferred to believe she deserved a difficulty-free life, but who got one of those?

A rush of memories flooded back from her past life at Anchor Church, moments of kneeling at the altar making earnest commitments to love God and serve him no matter what—*no matter what*—for all her life, and yet here she was, stuck in this miserable pit. Her grandma's sobering words were nothing new to her. Leah *knew* all that already. She simply refused to listen to it. Instead, she'd attempted to seal her rebellion away in a vault of denial and blame it on others. But the Holy Spirit was speaking to her from inside of that vault right now.

Yes, it was a matter of repentance—she knew Danny was right. Yet it scared her. She knew she needed to change. She knew she needed to do *something*, but whatever step she took would be a step toward pain. How was she supposed to navigate that? *Don't wait too long*, he'd said. The thought of taking that step was terrifying. *God, how do I turn this around?* she asked him silently. *Show me the way out of this ugly mess.* She could not see an answer.

Stretching her legs, Leah adjusted the pillow behind her back and resumed reading.

March 25. I'm reading the book of Matthew. Mary says to write down thoughts about what I read, but I keep forgetting. She's been so sweet. She gave me a box of clothes for Lenore that her daughter outgrew. Nice clothes. Expensive brands. Lenore feels like a million bucks in them, which helps her feel better about herself around the "popular girls" who she says are mean to her.

On another note, I waited on a nice guy at work today. He was alone and very talkative. A notch above your average guy. And he left a nice tip.

March 26. Same guy was back tonight. He said he was in town for business this week. We chatted again. Another nice tip.

March 27. Mr. Nice Guy's name is Ed.

Leah smiled in amusement. Grandpa Ed!

This is the third night he's eaten at Grady's. I can't imagine he prefers the food there over any other place in Bridgewater! He asked my name and told me his. When he left he said, "See you tomorrow." What am I supposed to think about that?

March 28. He didn't come in today. I don't even know who this guy is, but I felt stood up! I told Mary about him, and she reacted kinda weird. She said I shouldn't be thinking about guys right now but focused on getting to know Jesus. I almost felt scolded! I don't even know the guy! Mary seems convinced that if I keep my eyes on Jesus that God will take care of everything else. She obviously doesn't get what it's like to be alone.

March 31. What an awkward night at work! Mary got on me again about looking for a man. She says I shouldn't even consider going out with an unbeliever. That it will only take me down the same path of pain I've gone down before. I get what she's saying, but I can't see that there's many choices in her world! If I can't even date, I'm not sure I want to be a Christian. She prayed for me and everything, but I was a bit mad at her. More bummed than mad. It's hard! Lenore's all attitude lately, and there's never a break financially. I'm always broke and always working, and there's no one to talk to. Mary says, "Talk to God." Okay, God, I'm talking! If there's such a thing as a nice guy who follows you, send him my way! I could use the help, not to mention some romance. And maybe money too. And if there aren't any Christians available, at least send someone who's nice.

April 14. I keep forgetting to write in this book. Finished Matthew. Started Mark and Ephesians. Lordy, the wind is whipping hard today. Practically blew the hair off my head.

April 29. Finished Mark. Finished Ephesians and Colossians. Starting the next book after that. I've been going to church with Mary for several weeks now. I like it. Surprised to find that a lot of "normal" people love Jesus. Ha, ha. There are even some single men in the bunch, all younger than me except one. The older guy's okay, but I'm trying not to think about him. Mary may be right. I might have a few issues to work out before I think about dating again.

May 29. Pastor Chet asked Mary if I'd be open to a blind date with a friend of his from New Hampton. I said yes, but now I might cancel. The whole thing feels weird, like I'm some kid who can't make choices for myself. I don't know. Supposedly he's nice. His wife died of cancer a few years ago. But shouldn't going out with a guy be natural? Like you meet each other and have an attraction and go out together. A blind date just sounds so awkward, like there are all these expectations that everyone else has. And on top of that you're being watched! I don't know. I think I should cancel.

June 11. It's Thursday, and the blind date is tomorrow night. I don't ever remember being so nervous! Mary says I'm making too big of a deal out of it. I should relax and enjoy myself. I feel like her and Pastor Chet's social experiment. She's offered to pick Lenore up from cheerleading practice for me, so now I don't have an out.

June 12. Okay, I'm writing this before I leave for this stupid blind date. Today, of all days, that guy showed up at the restaurant again! The same super-nice guy who came in three days in a row back in March. He asked the hostess to seat him in my section. Yes, he specifically asked for me! We talked, and when he left, he left a little card with a Bible verse on it with his tip! A Bible verse!

This is where I'm struggling! This is exactly the kind of guy I'd want to go out with, but what am I supposed to do about it? Would it be strange for me to ask him for his phone number? I didn't, but what if he comes in tomorrow? I'm afraid to ask Mary what she thinks because she'll probably get weird. But I like him! God, how can I get to know this guy? And is it wrong to wish I was sick so I don't have to go on this blind date? I really don't want to go. Maybe I should fake a headache. But then I'd feel guilty for lying.

A bold line was drawn across the middle of the page.

I'm back. It's three hours later, and a true miracle happened tonight: It was him! I about fell over when I saw that my blind date was Mr. Nice Guy from Grady's! He had no idea it was me either! Both of us laughed. It was so much fun. At the end of the night, I told him how much pressure I had felt going into the date and how relieved I was that it was just him. He said he'd felt the same way. His name is Ed Davison, he's from New Hampton, and he loves God! Best of all, he asked for my phone number! And now here's to you, God: thank you, thank you, thank you! We'll see where this goes!

June 14. Ed Davison was at church today. Turns out he was there in March too, but I hadn't started coming with Mary yet.

June 25. Mary asked how I'm doing reading my Bible. Not very good. It's hard with having to work all the time and then taking care of Lenore and everything. She loaned me the Bible on cassette to listen to while I'm getting ready for work in the morning. Also, Ed called to say he's coming to Bridgewater this weekend again and asked if I would want to go out.

June 28. Great weekend!

June 30. Ha, ha. Mary McAllister is something else! I think I wouldn't like her if I didn't know she loves me! But I know she truly does. Today at work she took me aside and encouraged me to do my best to put God first. She said a man will never fix my problems, whether he's a Christian or not, and whether I'm married to him or not. Married? Whoa! I've had two dates with Ed Davison! Just two! Always put Jesus first, she says. I know she wants the best for me, and I know she's right. It's just not always so easy. Did I mention that Ed has a son? His name is Richard, and he's a little younger than Lenore.

Pausing, Leah flipped back to the front to check the year again. With some quick subtraction she determined her mother would have been a teenager—fifteen, maybe just turned sixteen years old at that time. And raised by a single parent, as she herself would later become. What had life been like for her? She knew her mom had clearly balked at Grandma's newfound faith. In fact, Leah remembered once inviting her mom and Braydon to Anchor Church with her, but she coolly declined, declaring, "There are some things in life even religion can't fix."

Leah inhaled, enjoying the sweet smokiness of someone's campfire wafting into the room. Probably Danny's. He was outside on his guitar again, likely by his fire pit in front of his cabin, and she only now noticed the music. She glanced toward the dining room window listening to his voice fade in and out, his worship a fitting backdrop to her grandmother's story. Stifling a yawn, she adjusted herself on the pillows and turned back to the journal. It wasn't late, but reading made her sleepy. She kept going, however, until she finished it entirely. Then snapping off the light, she crawled into bed, leaving her fan off this time to fall asleep to Danny's music. He had a nice voice, and Grandma Havi would have liked his singing.

Those birds! The chirping army in her arborvitae burst forth their morning chorus with fresh zeal. Leah cozied into her quilt, wondering if her grandma had ever been annoyed by the ancestors of those same creatures. Probably not, she mused, opening her eyes to the morning light. She couldn't remember Grandma Havi ever annoyed at anything. At any rate, it was Tuesday, and the countdown was on—only twelve hours until her date with Phil Crawford. Time couldn't pass quickly enough.

Resolutely she rose and dressed in her running gear, intent on starting her day with a lap or two around the pond. When she got there, the same runner as before was out ahead of her again. Instantly she recognized his form and slowed. When had Danny DeSoto become a runner? He was unaware she was behind him, and she didn't call to get his attention. She simply watched as he rounded the pond and turned off toward home at the trail entrance. Had he continued, he would have had the similar surprise discovering *her* ahead of him on his next lap. It was probably best he hadn't seen her anyway, she decided, as she preferred to be alone this morning. There was a lot to think about for the day ahead, the first of which was the Bible study.

Now, on the heels of reading her grandmother's first journal, the event had somewhat changed perspective, mostly because of someone she had never met—the woman Mary McAllister, her grandma's coworker-become-mentor back when. Though penned secondhand, her words still had power—specifically her words about being accountable for choices. This Bible study, she realized, was more than just a social call with Kyla Watkins and Jackie Burke. They'd be reading the Bible and discussing it, and that meant she'd have choices to respond to accordingly. Ms. McAllister's pointed warning on choices and consequences had made her wary.

Her words on dating stirred within Leah too, but those were met with irritation. She wasn't cancelling her date with Phil Crawford by any means, whatever Mary McAllister's stuffy opinion was! Phil was super nice, and it wouldn't hurt anything for her to go out with him. She wouldn't be hopping in the sack with him right away—that was certain. She had learned that the hard way with Carlos, so Mary McAllister needn't worry herself! Why did it feel like her grandmother's mentor was peering over her shoulder?

Now with Phil Crawford on her mind, Leah slowed at the pond trail exit to check street signs. Unfamiliar with the neighborhood, she slipped her phone from the belly pocket on her shirt to type 417 Forrester Street into her GPS. To her surprise, the app showed Forrester on the opposite side of New Hampton. Had she spelled it wrong? She tried several variations, but nothing came up in the area. She glanced around. Perhaps his dwelling was too new to show up on the GPS. It would be a conversation topic on their date.

After studying the street layout on her phone, Leah turned down a quiet street to try a new route home. Though initially it would take her out of the way, eventually it would zigzag over a few blocks and bring her right back to the crossing on Richmond Road. As she turned onto the third street, she found herself between two rows of tall, identically built townhouses across from each other. There parked in the last driveway on the left was a big, black pickup truck—Phil's truck! Delighted, she jogged toward it—although she reminded herself that he wasn't the only person in the world with that model and make of pickup. Having ridden in it, though, Leah made a quick jaunt up to peek in the passenger's window to confirm that yes, it was indeed his truck!

That solves that, she told herself, pausing to take a good look at the numbers on the front of his townhouse: 417. Now she knew where he lived. Not wanting to appear nosey, she continued on to the next street, but as she rounded the corner, she just happened to notice the corner signs—Pierce Avenue and Reed Street. Stung, she stopped, glancing back at his truck. Had Phil put her off and given her the wrong address?

She bit her lip. She supposed it was possible he lived across town on Forrester Street but was staying here with someone else. Yet given the house number was coincidentally 417, it seemed rather unlikely. Even allowing him the benefit of the doubt, either scenario made her feel funny, and she thought about it all the way back to her house. If Phil was being dishonest, then—then—well, Leah didn't even know what to think! Doubtless this would be a topic of conversation *before* their date!

Showered and dressed, Leah lounged on her porch in the crisp morning air, passing the time until the Bible study, wondering how soon Kyla Watkins would arrive next door. Their misunderstanding weighed heavily on her, and she hoped to clear the air beforehand if possible. Not that she knew what to say, but something needed to be done.

Absently she fussed with the Bible app Danny had downloaded on her phone, not wanting to look stupid, as though she'd never used the app before—which in this case was true but about to be remedied. It had been four years since she had read the Bible, but she imagined that navigating it again would be like riding a bike once she had the app down. She wasn't a scholar, but she knew enough about God and the Bible to fake her way through most things if she had to. It was good to have a little knowledge to hide behind. Nevertheless, she was still a little nervous.

Before long, the slam of a car door and the chatter of voices next door caught her attention. Glancing at the time, Leah noted that Kyla was early, exactly as she'd hoped. She calculated that going over there in about fifteen minutes should give her the time she needed to talk to her without crowding the start time of the meeting.

In preparation, Leah went to use the bathroom and then ended up changing her shirt three times before settling on what to wear. Then she tossed her bed together, slipped the two journals onto the bin in the corner, and got her purse. Halfway to the door she decided against the purse and put it back on top of the journals. A purse felt way too formal for going next door. Her keys and phone would fit in her pocket. Anything else—a pen or tissues—anything else she could borrow there.

Noting it was time to go, Leah locked her door and started for the hedge, looking up to see its branches shaking as Kyla Watkins and her two young charges noisily pushed their way through it.

"Ouch! Hey—careful now! Hold that—Howie! Don't let that—I told you not to let that snap back in his face!" Kyla's back was turned, both of her arms holding branches taut as she guided the boys through. Turning, she saw Leah standing there and gave a start. "Oh, hi!"

"I was coming over early," Leah said.

"Great!" she said, smoothing a hand over her hair and straightening her shirt. "I'm glad you're coming! I was just—" She gestured to the boys. "I have these guys today, so I was going to ask if they could maybe play in your tree—if you think it's safe by themselves. I wouldn't be here to watch them, but we'd be nearby. One of the moms was going to bring her older daughter, but they had to cancel."

"It's safe," the older boy insisted, "safe for *me*!" He cast a condescending glance toward his little brother, whose eyes were fixed warily on Leah.

Leah swept her hand toward the tree. "Let's walk back. I'll let you decide! But watch your step—dog bombs!"

"I already know what it's like," the same boy announced. "I've been in it, and I know it's safe." His eyes flicked to Leah's. At her wink, he looked away.

Kyla took the younger boy's hand. "Have you met these guys? These are Professor Grant's boys—Howie and Hank. And boys, this is Miss Leah—er, sorry—Miss *Ava* Lay-von-obra." She glanced up apologetically. "I butchered that."

"Labanora." She shrugged. "I know—it's a mouthful. And you can call me Leah."

"No, I'm sorry—I'll get it right!"

Leah shook her head. "It's okay. It's simpler."

Kyla turned to the boys, her voice a little breathless. "Okay, boys—this is Miss Leah. She lives in this house, and this is her tree, so when you're here you have to listen to what she says. Do you understand?"

"Nice to meet you, boys," Leah said. "I'm glad you like my tree."

Howie eyed her curiously. "Why do you have two first names?"

"That's a private question, Howie," Kyla answered. "Besides, you have two first names, right? Howard and Howie. Sometimes three when your dad calls you Howard David!"

He shrugged and took off to impress them with his climbing skills. "Miss Kyla, watch how fast I can get up there!"

His younger brother followed, struggling hard but unsuccessfully to pull himself up the trunk into the lowest branches.

"Hank's the one I'm concerned about," Kyla said, peering up the tree at Howie with her hands on her hips, her round belly protruding. "He tries so hard to keep up with his brother, but he's only four."

As if to prove her point, Hank dropped his arms in frustration. "Argh! I can't do it! Can you lift me up there?"

"No, Hank. I won't be here to help you. You need to be able to do it yourself to play in the tree. Howie, stop—that's high enough! Don't go any farther up than that!"

Hank's lip turned out in a pout. "What can I do, then?"

Kyla uttered a sympathetic sound, tousling his hair. "Sorry, Hank. I guess you'll have to play quietly by me with Jackie's Legos or something."

He made a sour face. "I *never* get to do anything!"

"Sorry, bud. If you can't get up and down by yourself, it's not safe. You have to be big enough for both."

The boy's shoulders slumped. "Then can I bring my dump truck over? I'll stay by Howie, I promise!"

Kyla nodded, looking relieved. "Yes—that's a wonderful idea! You can play here in the grass and dirt." She glanced at Leah. "Providing you're okay with that."

"Of course!" Leah nodded.

The boy folded his hands, pleading, "Can Angel come too? Please?"

"Angel's already quite familiar with my yard," Leah said before Kyla could respond. She met Hank's brief and happy peek with a smile.

"Great—thanks!" Kyla said. "I'll confirm with Jackie that it's okay. Good." She checked the time on her phone. Then with a deep breath, she glanced at the boys and turned awkwardly to Leah. "So, um, I was also hoping to talk to you a bit before the study this morning."

For a split second, Leah tensed for a scolding, but Kyla shoved the phone back into her pocket, raising her eyes sheepishly. "I've been kind of a brat to you since the party, and I want to apologize."

Leah straightened in surprise. "What? No, I was coming over early to apologize to *you*! What I said about Peter Saturday—I had no idea what I was talking about! I'm sorry I was so stupid."

"Well, you didn't know."

The two looked at each other, and Kyla gave an embarrassed laugh. "I was *so* rude to you when you were over the other night. I felt like a total jerk sharing my testimony with you—expounding on the power of forgiveness when I had such a stinking attitude toward you. I'm *really* sorry!"

"No, I deserved it," Leah replied. "Truly! I was an idiot!"

"I was much worse—I was an idiot on purpose!"

"Well, I didn't even have to try!"

Kyla smiled. "Okay, so in fifth-grade fashion—" She held out her hand. "Friends?"

Leah took it. "Friends."

Kyla threw her other hand to her chest and let out a laugh. "Oh, my gosh! I feel so much better! I was miserable preparing for this Bible study and so afraid you wouldn't come because of me! And all that terrible stuff that happened to you—man, I felt *awful* you had to go through that! I couldn't believe what you told us—it's the type of thing that only happens in really bad chick flicks! It must have been a total nightmare!"

"Thank you. And yes, it *was* a nightmare, but don't worry about it. And I want to apologize for not staying to hear the real version of your story the other night. Maybe sometime you can give it to me unedited."

"Absolutely!" She nodded. "And for that matter, Peter's story too. Then you'd have the full facts! It's pretty interesting!"

"Yes, I'd like that."

"Awesome! But aside from that, I was wondering if you'd ever want to hang out sometime. I'm over here at Jackie's a lot, and I think it'd be fun."

"I'd like that! I don't really know anyone around here yet."

"Well, great!"

Leah hesitated, then gestured to her house. "Are you busy later today? I'm painting some bedrooms this afternoon with Brindle. You'd be welcome to join us."

"This afternoon, huh?" Her brow creased in thought. "That might work out perfectly. I'll need to run these guys home after the study and give them lunch, but I could change and come back. Yeah, I'd be up for that!"

Leah smiled. "Nice!"

"Yeah, great!" Kyla gave a happy sigh and looked down at Hank. "Whew! Now that I survived *that*, I should probably get these guys situated." She laughed.

Leah laughed too. "I hear you! Anything I can do to help?"

"Oh, I've got it. You can walk over to the house with me. Jackie's already on the deck. We're meeting out there this morning so I can ensure these boys don't go near the pool." She faced the hedge. "Um, how do we get back?"

Leah pointed to where she'd come in. "Either back there or we walk all the way around to Danny's cabin and up to the house."

"Or you can crawl under," Howie said from his perch on the branch above them, pointing to the break in the branches near the ground through which he had scrambled on Leah's first day there.

Kyla raised her brow, glancing at Leah. "Let's go around. You can hang with Jackie, and I'll join you as soon as I get Hank his dump truck. Boys, you can stay here. I'll be right back!"

"Don't forget Angel," Hank piped up.

As it turned out, Jackie Burke was no longer on the deck, but Brother Warren was. He was at the table by himself, freshly shaven and in a short-sleeved dress shirt, reading his Bible with his arms folded in front of him. Initially—when they had first met—Leah had thought of him as frail, but she was beginning to see how strong he was for being eighty-two. Apart from his foot.

"I'm waiting for my ride," he said to Leah as she came up the steps, "so don't worry, I won't be sitting in with you ladies—I promise. How are you this morning, my dear?"

"I'm good," Leah answered. "And how are you? Is your foot

improving?"

"Better than I deserve, surely, and yes, my foot seems to be healing!"

"That's good."

She took the chair across from him, noticing that he was looking at her again with that sharp-eyed look of his, like he *knew* things on the inside of her. She met his eyes briefly and looked away.

"I'm having one of those crazy thoughts again," he said with a kind smile. "Would you humor an old man?"

She gave a nervous shrug. "Sure."

He nodded. "I certainly don't want to weird you out, but when you came up the steps I started thinking about gold—specifically that gold is underground."

Leah blinked, unsure of how to respond.

His brow knit together. "Does that mean anything to you?"

Leah gave a faint smile and shook her head. "No."

He rubbed his chin, studying her. "Okay. Perhaps it's a reminder that you'll have to look for Jesus if you want him." He paused a moment. "You have to *seek* him, you know. He hides himself so that you'll search him out—like gold that's underground. It's not just lying in the open. You have to dig for it. He's worth finding—Jesus is. He's the treasure of treasures. The Word says, 'In him are hidden all the treasures of wisdom and knowledge.' And he wants to be found, so if you seek him, you'll find him."

Leah nodded. "Okay."

His eyes didn't leave her, and Leah squirmed a bit, her heart beating faster. Brother Warren was clearly not finished.

"It's not so much buried," he added thoughtfully, "as *underground*. The gold is underground."

Then he took a breath and shifted in his chair, as if letting the thought go. "Jesus was buried, you know. Completely dead and buried. But He was raised up from the grave to live forever. That's where life is, Leah—in Jesus, the resurrection and the life. But you gotta die to yourself. If you die to yourself and are buried with Christ, you'll find new life in him." His gaze lifted over her shoulder. "Ah—here's Dan! That's a good man right there! He is *steady*! Steady Dan!"

Leah turned as Danny swiftly took the stairs to join them. "Morning, Leah! Did you have a good night?"

His eyes were alive. He always looked happy, Leah observed. Well, maybe not *happy* in particular, but he certainly looked pleasant most of the time, like he was at peace with himself. This morning he had on jeans and a blue T-shirt that fit snugly around his biceps. He was doubtless proud of those muscles, she thought, considering his slight build when she had known him years ago. On second thought, he wasn't the vain sort, so his frame was probably a nonissue to him.

"Good morning. Yes, I did."

"And the journals—find anything interesting?"

"I did! I already finished the first one!" She hoped she could tell him about it soon.

"Nice!" He nodded amiably and turned to Brother Warren. "Ready when you are, Captain!"

"Then let's go!" The old man rose to his feet, and Danny stepped up to help him.

Behind them the patio door suddenly opened and out came Jackie, chattering away with two other ladies with her. Following them—Leah gave a start—was Brindle Baylor, who threw her a smirk.

Brother Warren turned to greet them. "Morning, ladies! Welcome! What a beautiful day to enjoy the Word of God out on a patio!"

The door thumped closed, and Jackie turned. "Dad, have you met Megan and Lauren? And Brindle. You remember Brindle, don't you? She was at our party. And here once before that."

Brother Warren tipped his head to all, reaching out his hand to the latter. "Sure, I remember Brindle!" He looked into her face, not letting go of her hand. "Yes, yes, Brindle. Brindle, whom the Lord loves!" Brindle pulled back awkwardly, but Brother Warren had fixed his gaze on her. "A lovely lady who's searching. You're searching, aren't you? I'll tell you a secret, lovely lady—your Father is searching for *you*! There's a story in the Bible of a woman who lost a coin, and she searched and searched until she found it. Then she rejoiced. You are much more valuable than coins, my dear Brindle—much more valuable! God is seeking you because he *loves* you!"

Brindle looked stunned.

"Dad, stop! You're making her uncomfortable! You forget that these ladies don't know you!" Jackie laid her hand on Brindle's arm. "I'm sorry, hon. Ladies, this is my dad, Warren Glende. And our friends Dan and Ava."

Murmurs of greeting were passed around, but Brother Warren's eyes remained fixed on Brindle, who was now very pale. After a moment he turned back to give a long look at Leah, who waited uneasily. Was there more to come?

Right then Kyla trotted nimbly up the deck. "Hey—thanks for

coming, everyone! Looks like it's gonna be a great group! Let's all have a seat. Sorry, fellas, but this is for girls only! Move along now!" She brushed the air as if shooing them away.

"We're leaving, we're leaving!" Brother Warren said with a chuckle, turning for the steps. "Enjoy yourselves, ladies! Dan, would you fetch me my glasses from my desk? I'll meet you up front."

"I'll do that," Danny replied, taking his arm, "but let me walk you to the car first."

"Stop—stay right there! I'll get his glasses *and* his crutches," Jackie said, heading back into the house. "He's supposed to be using them!"

As the men changed direction to follow Jackie, the other ladies gathered around the table, resuming their conversation. Kyla turned to rummage through her shoulder bag as Brindle slid onto the chair next to Leah.

"You didn't wait for me!" she said under her breath. "I went to your house, and you weren't there!"

"You said you weren't coming!" Leah countered.

"I changed my mind. And that was the *freakiest* thing that's ever happened to me! What the heck was he doing?"

"I'm not sure," Leah replied quietly. "It's like God puts thoughts in his head or something." She looked at Brindle. "Did that mean anything to you?"

Brindle's head jerked back. "No! Why? Should it?"

"I don't know! He's asked me that a few times. And sometimes what he says really hits home."

"I have *no* idea what he was talking about!"

Kyla plopped a short stack of study books in the center of the table, along with a handful of pens. Then she slid a Bible with an embossed purple cover over to Leah. "Dan said you wanted to borrow a Bible. You can have this if you'd like. Jackie's sister, Susan, gave it to me at a very confusing time in my life, so it was special to me. It was originally her daughter's. But Peter gave me a new one, so I don't use it anymore."

"Thank you."

"I could get one for you too," Kyla added, glancing at Brindle.

"I'm—not sure yet," Brindle said.

"She can share with me today," Leah said.

"Okay," Kyla said. "Just let me know."

Chapter Twenty

The subject of the Bible study that morning was God's kindness, the first chapter of a six-part series on the love of God. Kyla opened by asking each woman to think about the kindest person she knew. Then one by one they went around the table describing qualities that set their person apart as being kind.

Leah picked Evelyn but she used a fictitious name for her in case the subject came up some other time when Danny was present. She shared how Evelyn would always greet her with a warm smile and questions about her well-being whenever she'd go to the DeSoto house. Often she would take Leah's face in her hands and look in her eyes and tell her how special she was, and that God had destined her to do great things for him. And although Grandma Havi probably technically loved her more, Leah felt that Evelyn trumped her on expressing kindness.

From there they opened the study books, which led them through a series of scriptures on God's kindness toward mankind. When finished, Kyla asked each woman to share her reflections of the lesson.

Jackie pulled off her reading glasses and set them aside. "I was really struck by the verse that says, 'It's God's *kindness* that leads us to repentance.' When you really see all that God has done for us, why would we resist him? Yet we do sometimes! I'm amazed how he still keeps wooing us to him despite our stubbornness!"

Heads nodded around the table.

"That hit me too," the woman named Lauren offered. "God shows us mercy even when we don't deserve it! When I've been wronged by someone, I don't typically respond with kindness. That's not my nature. But God *loves* to show mercy!"

"And he keeps pursuing us!" Jackie reiterated.

"Yes, but you can refuse it," the girl Megan added. "I can't imagine what that feels like to him—to have so many people refuse him after all the kindness he has shown us!"

Lauren agreed. "But it's out of ignorance, I think. They simply don't know how amazingly good God is."

"I can personally attest to that!" Kyla said. "I had this notion that God was against me—that *he* was the one causing every bad thing in my life! I was completely blind to his goodness!"

Leah stared at the corner of her booklet as the conversation passed around the table. Was this a script? Had Danny staged this? She knew it wasn't possible, but nonetheless, she wanted to yell out, "Stop pressuring me!"

Her arguments for "stiff-arming" God were quickly unraveling. Maybe Danny *was* right! Maybe God had indeed rescued her from the family curse that awful Black Friday night at Anchor Church, humiliating as it was. Maybe it was time she accepted that. Even so, she still had to deal with Jake. She gnawed on the side of her thumb, self-absorbed as the other women talked. All paths of surrender converged on one big hurdle: forgiving Jake DeSoto and his deceptive sidekick, Rachel. Was it even possible?

"Any thoughts you two ladies would like to share?" Kyla asked, turning toward Leah. "Brindle?"

Brindle plopped her folded arms onto the table, her tropical tattoos on display for curious scrutiny. "Honestly, I'm not quite sure what I think. Everything makes sense here, of course, but this discussion is so one-sided. I don't necessarily believe God is always kind. There's a lot of things in life that just plain suck. Terrible things happen all the time—natural disasters, people dying of starvation, poverty, cancer, children beaten or sexually abused. Where's the kindness of God in stuff like that?"

All eyes turned to Kyla.

Bravely she met Brindle's glare. "That's—that's a good question! I'm not sure I can answer that adequately here, but what I can say for certain is that God never causes evil. The devil causes evil and death, but God is always good. *Always.* Even in the worst of circumstances, the Bible says that he can work all things together for good for those who love him."

Brindle's hand twitched. "Well, slogans like that sound nice, but they don't really cut it with me. A kid gets molested—but hey, 'God's going to make it all good somehow!' I don't believe that! Not to rock the boat here, but in my opinion Bible ditties don't help anything. They have absolutely no bearing on stuff that happens in the *real* world."

Kyla paused, regarding her thoughtfully. "Okay—I hear you. I'm sorry—I wasn't trying to shut you down. Your questions are valid. I guess I'd like to hear more about where you're coming from personally. Maybe we could talk about this later, like when Brother Warren gets back. He's way better at explaining things than me, okay? I *do* want to connect on this! I promise you—I do." She offered Brindle a sober smile, then turned to Leah. "Anything you'd like to add about what we learned today?"

"Uh—" Just say *something,* she told herself. It didn't matter what. "Well, I appreciated the Bible verse about God sending rain on the just and the unjust—that he shows kindness to *all* people, not just some." She threw a sideways glance at Brindle, who raised her brow and looked away.

Before Kyla could respond, an unseen commotion erupted next door beyond the hedge. First, Angel burst into one of his furious barking frenzies. Then, as all the ladies' heads turned in question, the dog's tirade suddenly gave way to a tremendous and pitiful *yelp*, at which both little boys instantaneously screamed out the dog's name. The glass table rocked as both Kyla and Jackie shot to their feet. At the sound of crying, Kyla sprinted down the deck steps.

"Jackie—close in prayer—" she called back.

But Jackie was at her heels.

The boys' weeping escalated into full out bawling. Leah and the other ladies rose in alarm at the sight of wailing Hank crawling out from under the hedge on his hands and knees. Running up, Kyla caught him by the shoulders and dragged his body out the rest of the way. Behind him came Howie, hobbling through on his knees with one arm hooked around little Angel, struggling to keep a grip on the wiggling animal. With a cry, Jackie anxiously scooped up her dog, while Kyla helped dust-covered Howie to his feet. Both boys blubbered on hysterically, pointing back through the hedge, although from Leah's position on the deck, none of their words were intelligible. Dropping to her knees, Kyla wrapped her arms around them, and Jackie's concerned gaze bounced back and forth from the boys to craning her neck to see through the thick branches into Leah's yard.

When their cries finally began to diminish, Jackie turned her attention back to her dog, worriedly checking him over as she made her way back to the deck.

"My goodness—what happened?" one of the ladies asked. "Did one of the kids fall on the dog?"

That was Leah's guess too—that Howie had fallen out of the tree and landed on Angel, but Jackie shook her head with disgust.

"A man over there kicked Angel—kicked him *hard*, they said, and he was limping badly!"

"*What?*" Leah's face snapped toward the arborvitae.

Jackie lifted the dog to examine his belly. "I can't even believe someone would *do* that!"

Brindle swung her head to look at Leah.

Leah shivered. *Her intruder.*

"Sorry, ladies," Kyla called from across the pool deck, guiding her distraught charges by the hand. "We've had a little incident! Some guy over there kicked Jackie's dog, and unfortunately the boys saw it!"

"Who would *do* such a thing?" one of the ladies echoed Jackie indignantly.

"Well, I don't know!" Jackie murmured, her eyes grazing Leah's as she continued toward the patio door. "I'm putting him in the house to watch him. Hopefully it won't mean a trip to the vet!"

Leah shook her head. "No one's over there! I'm not even expecting anyone!" As Kyla and the boys returned to the table, she urged them to tell what happened. Hank's cheeks were dirt-streaked from tears, his breath coming in little jerks. Behind him Howie sniffled and wiped his nose with his sleeve.

"Unbelievable!" Kyla said sliding back onto her chair. She pulled Hank onto her lap and drew Howie near, embracing him with her arm. "Hold on, sweetie. We'll wash you up in a minute, all right? No one's going to hurt you—I'm right here!"

Hank threw Leah a dark look. "Your dad is mean!"

"Hank!" Kyla whispered into his neck. Her eyes met Leah's. "Sorry—"

But Howie chimed in too. "I *saw* him do it! He kicked Angel hard—like this!" He swung his leg.

Leah remained standing, frowning at Kyla in confusion. "My dad's from Bridgewater—"

"No, like the 'dad' of the family," Kyla interjected. "You know—like your husband or boyfriend."

"Of which I have neither!" She turned to Howie. "What did he look like?" All she could think about was Marty Davison, her scoundrel cousin. Oh, if it was him, she was calling the cops!

"Go on—tell Miss Leah," Kyla encouraged.

"It was a grownup," Hank blurted out. "Big—like my dad!"

Leah nodded, asking more earnestly, "And what did he look like?

What color was his hair? Was he wearing glasses?"

Hank sank back against Kyla, but Howie shrugged. "Maybe. I don't remember. He was knocking on your door, and Angel went up and started barking at him. Then the man got mad and kicked him. I heard Angel cry when he did it—like it hurted him *bad*!" His lip quivered, and he tipped his head against Kyla's arm, fighting back tears.

"Your dad is *mean*!" Hank repeated, staring at her.

"It's not her dad, Hank!" Kyla chided softly. "We're pretty sure it was someone she doesn't know."

He sniffed, turning his face upward. "What about my dump truck? Is he going to steal it?" Bursting into tears, he buried his face into Kyla's chest.

"I'm going over there!" Leah announced. She pushed her chair up to the table and bumped Brindle on the shoulder. "Come with me!"

Brindle drew back. "*Me*?"

"Yes, you!" Leah said, jerking her head. "Come on! I'm not going over there alone! Ladies, it's been a pleasure."

The women shifted uncomfortably, murmuring their concern.

"Can we pray for you?" Lauren asked, but Leah was already heading down the steps. Reluctantly Brindle rose, trailing behind.

"Are you sure about this, Leah?" Kyla hurriedly hefted Hank into her arms, following to the edge of the deck. "This might not be a good idea! I mean, someone who kicks a dog—!"

"I'm gonna find out who this is!" Leah called back.

"Well, be careful!" Kyla hollered after her. "And call me to let me know what happens, okay? Oh, never mind! I'll just see you this afternoon!"

As they got to the gap in the hedge in front of Jackie's house, Brindle grabbed Leah by the arm. "Hold on! Wait! My God, Leah—Ava—or *whatever* you're called now! We should think about this!"

Leah turned in surprise. "Why? Let's find out who did this!"

"I—I don't know! It scares me! Who knows who this person is and what he might do! Maybe we should call the police!"

Leah hesitated.

"I mean, geez—I'm a little creeped out! What if—what if—" She lifted her shoulders.

Leah considered her words, but only momentarily. Her intruder would be long gone by the time any police arrived if he weren't already. Plus, this was Leah's chance to find out once and for all if it was Marty.

She nodded. "Fine—stay here if you want, but I'm going over! If you hear me yelling, then call the police!"

"What? No, Leah, wait—"

Decisively Leah pushed through the hedge.

As she suspected, no one was in the yard, front or back, nor were any vehicles in her driveway except her own. Determinedly she made a beeline to the path that led to Marty's house—first to see if he were home, and then, if so, to confront him. His garage door was closed, however, with no truck parked in front.

Bypassing the front door, Leah went straight to the unlocked side entrance of the garage. Midnight was there inside the door, sprawled out on a dog bed. With a startled "woof" he raised his head, then sleepily pulled himself up to stretch and amble along after her as she navigated around the clutter on her way to the house door. Despite several hard knocks, there was no answer, and when she tried the knob, it was locked. That helped, she thought, letting out a long breath. Now she was almost certain the person who kicked Angel wasn't Marty. Yet it was *someone*, and the fact that weird things kept happening at her house was disturbing!

Awakened from his nap, Midnight was eager to go outside. Leah stood by the door, waiting as he sniffed around, taking his time finding the precisely perfect spot in his yard on which to relieve himself. She folded her arms, pondering on little Angel catching her Mr. Snoop at her back door. No doubt he had noticed the changed locks. Would he try something else now? Leah shuddered. This craziness was getting more and more uncomfortable.

Finished, Midnight bounded up, and after an affectionate scratch, Leah put him back into the garage. Shaking his loose hair off her hands, she returned home the way she'd come, where she tested her back door. Thanks to the elderly locksmith, it was firmly locked.

Satisfied, Leah rounded the back of the garage to confirm that her porch door was also securely locked, but as she came around the corner toward the driveway, she stopped in her tracks, observing an unfamiliar navy crossover vehicle now parked beside her own. Someone had just arrived. Cautiously she continued across the driveway, craning to see the porch. Sure enough, she spied the tall figure of a man—right as he turned away from her front door to take the steps. As he did so, he looked up to meet her eyes.

Leah blinked in astonishment. "*Dad!* What are *you* doing here?"

David Labanora paused with his foot on the stair. "Oh, you *are* here! Great! I was afraid I'd missed you!"

"What—what are—" Her voice caught.

"I know—sorry. You weren't expecting me!" He came down the rest of the way to meet her. "Sorry to surprise you like this! Turns out I have an appointment here in New Hampton in an hour or so, and I thought I'd come down early—just a quick stop in to see what we might be doing this weekend when I come down to help."

Leah stared, unable to speak. There were too many possibilities whirling in her head.

He frowned. "Leah? Good heavens—are you all right? Here—sit down!" He gestured to the step.

"No, I'm—all right. Sorry." Hastily she pulled herself together.

"Are you sick?"

She shook her head. "No, I'm—I'm fine. I just came from the neighbors' where they've had a bit of a crisis. Someone kicked their dog this morning and hurt it very badly." She watched his face.

"Really? Ah, I see." He shoved a hand into his pocket. "Yeah, sorry—I probably should have called. The appointment came in late last night, Otherwise I would have said something when we talked yesterday. But I decided to take a chance anyway and stop in. I didn't want it to be a big deal, which is why I *didn't* call. I wasn't going to say anything if you weren't here. But I'm glad I caught you."

Why was he *really* there? She cocked her head. "And everything's all right at home?"

"Home? No, nothing's happened at home." He shook his head. "No, I just stopped in. Sorry—I should have warned you. But I can't stay long."

Leah nodded. "Okay. It's just a surprise—"

"Yeah, yeah—I know. Is it all right?"

"What?"

"The neighbor's dog. Is it okay?"

"Oh—well, they don't know yet. When I left, they said they were going to watch him. I was over there at a—um, over there with some friends this morning. Hanging out."

He nodded. "Well, that's too bad about the dog. It's sad there's people like that."

"Yeah."

It seemed weird to let him know she had been at a Bible study. They had never related well before over that subject. It was even weirder that he would show up right then, right after what had happened to poor Angel. She could hardly bring herself to consider it could be him, but the timing! Yet right now she needed to do something other than stand and look at him.

"So—" Awkwardly she turned to encompass the yard with her arm. "Here we are! Impressive, isn't it?"

Her father cast a polite look around. "It's—maybe gone downhill a bit over the years."

She laughed. "Quite a *lot,* Dad! Especially since *you've* been here. You probably haven't been here in, what, seventeen years? Probably not since Braydon was born."

David Labanora's eyes flicked up to hers, then fell. "No. No, I haven't." He put a hand on his belt and turned away, examining the roof and the gutters. He was tall and trim and well dressed in his dark blue dress shirt and charcoal slacks. His dark hair was a lot grayer at the temples than she remembered.

"What time is your appointment?"

"One fifteen. But I'd like to be early. I'll need to leave by one."

Leah checked the time on her phone. "Okay. That gives us an hour and twenty minutes. Would you like some lunch? I have leftover pork sandwiches and watermelon. It wouldn't take long to fix."

He nodded. "Thank you! That sounds great!" He followed her to the door, waiting as she unlocked it. "I was actually here earlier this morning, but you weren't around. So I went back to wash the car at the station out on the highway. It's built up nicely there. This whole area is all built up!" He gestured across the road.

"Yeah—I hardly recognized it," Leah agreed. "Did you, um, try the back door—earlier when you came?"

He gave her an odd look. "Why would I go to the back if you didn't answer in the front?"

She lifted her chin. "Yeah. Yeah, right."

"Do you leave it open?"

"No, just wondering." She pushed open her door and stepped in. "So don't freak out, Dad. This place needs some work."

He nodded as he looked around. "It's not bad! It's not bad at all! It's mostly cosmetic, and that's easy to take care of. It just costs a little."

"Yeah, well, wait 'til you see the kitchen! That's what's going to cost me!"

Leah led the way, noting his expression when he saw the cupboards.

"Yeah, this," she said grimly. "I'll let you think about it while I use the restroom."

Quickly Leah ducked down the hall into the bathroom, where she pulled out her phone to text Kyla. "K, big favor: ask the boys what color the man's shirt was and text me back. It's important!"

Kyla's instant reply was an automated response that she was driving.

With a sigh, Leah washed her hands and rejoined her father in the kitchen.

"Well, there's no way around it, Leah girl—this room needs to be gutted," he told her. "You might be in over your head with this!"

Leah girl. As she turned to look at him, she was caught off guard by the twinkle in his eye as he smiled.

"Grandpa Ed left me some money for upgrading the place," she told him. "This room's priority, of course, but I'm not sure how much'll be left after that."

"Oh, I bet your mother didn't like that!" Then he shook his head and raised his hand. "Sorry! Sorry, I had no business saying that! Forgive me! It was thoughtful of him to leave you some money."

Leah gave another smile. "I'll make lunch." Without a doubt, something had happened to her dad! Whatever it was, she liked it!

As she reheated the leftovers, he offered to investigate replacing her garage door, at which she more than happily gave the green light. Then she brought up her water issue, and her dad recommended a type of filter system, another area that he volunteered to explore for her. Next he gave her several recommendations on the overall kitchen project. Leah slid him the legal pad and pen to record his suggestions in bullet points so that she didn't forget. When she had finished constructing their sandwiches, she handed him a loaded paper plate and a glass of iced tea.

"Here's a question for you, Dad—what's your opinion on me taking out this wall and opening up the whole center part of the house?"

He pivoted to study the area, then shrugged. "Oh, I suppose it's possible. You'd be taking out a supporting wall here, but there's ways you could make it work. Keep in mind this is an old rambler, Leah, not new construction. You never know what you might run into when you start pulling out walls. Or parts of walls. You've got a limited amount of money, so if I were you, I'd keep it simple. Plus, I think you'd regret losing that storage space." He lifted his iced tea to point to the closet.

Her eyes followed. He was probably right. There wasn't a huge amount of storage space in the central part of the house.

"What you might want to consider is adding on a deck and putting in a door right there." He pointed to the dining room windows. "Just a thought, since you'll be ripping out those cupboards. It'd be smart to do it all at once."

Leah nodded thoughtfully. "Thanks. That's not a bad idea! I think I'd like that—if I can afford it. I appreciate the advice." She gave a wry smile. "And speaking of limited amounts of money—Dad, I'm lost with all of this! I need your help from start to finish. There's a great guy in the neighborhood that's offered to help me, but—"

"—but he's going to charge you, and I'm free." He smiled. "Count me in, Leah girl! I'd be glad to help in any way I can."

"Thank you!" She gave a breath of relief, feeling the wonder of the moment. Then her father shifted his feet, still balancing the paper plate on his hand, and Leah motioned with her head. "I usually eat out on the porch."

As they were seated, Leah was about to check the time when her phone chirped in her hand—a text from Kyla. "Howie says the guy's shirt was 'darkish-red.' Be there in 30–40."

It was nice to receive her text, but the description wasn't really necessary at this point. Her dad had never been mean to animals in the past, and his manner today—his kindness, openness, and eagerness to help—had more than convinced Leah he'd had nothing to do with Angel's misfortune. She set her phone down and took a huge bite of her sandwich, glancing up to notice his plate resting untouched on the coffee table. He was looking at her with an expression that gave her a knot in her stomach. Okay—so something *was* coming! She knew it—there was something wrong after all!

"Leah, can I—can I talk to you?" He paused, clearing his throat. "Your phone call yesterday—I want you to know it meant a lot. And this"—he gestured, indicating the two of them sitting together—"this does too. Thank you."

Leah set her sandwich down, still chewing her mouthful.

"I need to tell you something—to *ask* you something, really."

She moved her plate from her lap to the table. Was it cancer? Here it comes—he was about to tell her he was dying from cancer.

He leaned forward, his fingers touching as he rested his elbows on his legs. "I guess there's really no way to go here except to jump in. I, uh—I dropped the ball with you, Leah. When you were growing up, I dropped the ball and failed you as a parent. I was a *terrible* dad! After the divorce I just"—he shrugged—"I just checked out! There was no excuse for it. I closed off and checked out. Before the divorce too, I guess."

What was he doing? Leah swallowed, wiping her mouth with her napkin. Hadn't he already gone here in their previous phone conversation? "Dad—"

"No, please—I need to say this. Just hear me out, okay? Please, Leah."

She studied his face. Was he drinking? She hadn't thought so.

He noticed and smiled. "I assure you I'm completely sober. It's the God-honest truth! This has been the best year of my sobriety yet! But that's not what this is about." He glanced at his watch and looked back at her.

"So, Leah. All along I blamed your mother for why I bailed on you as a parent, but it wasn't her fault. And it certainly wasn't *your* fault either—not at all! I'm here to take"—his words suddenly grew raspy, and he looked downward—"I'm here to take responsibility for neglecting you as my daugh—as my daughter. You have every right to be angry with me—or even *hate* me. I could never make up for how I neglected you. I never parented you. I didn't take care of you. I completely missed out on knowing"—his voice cracked, and again he had to pause—"on even knowing who you are as a person, but that's my loss. That's *my* loss. And I'm not asking for you to do anything except to forgive me." He met her eyes. "Leah, from the depths of my heart, I'm sorry for abandoning you. For the thousand things I've missed in your life, and all I *should* have done for you and didn't—I'm so sorry."

Leah stared at him dumbfounded, her heart slamming in her chest. What had happened to her dad?

"I don't deserve it, but I'm asking—I'm asking, Leah, for you to forgive me."

She opened her mouth, but he held up a hand to stop her. "No—wait! Just wait, please. I'm not asking for you to say anything right now. Truly. You had no warning this was coming, so you don't have to say anything." He pursed his lips for a second. "In fact, I wouldn't be surprised if you found yourself angrier than you've ever been with me. It's okay. I deserve it. But I want you to know that I *am* sorry! I'm sorry I was such a terrible father, and I deeply—I deeply regret checking out on you."

Leah blinked, looking down at her plate, her mind reeling in the long silence that followed. Was this really happening?

Her dad reached for his iced tea and took a sip.

"Dad, I haven't"—she paused, struggling—"I haven't been a very good daughter either. I could have done *much* better, and I'm sorry too!"

He gave a twisted smile. "I appreciate that, but I could hardly hold anything against you, Leah girl. But don't turn this on you. This is about *me*. I'm asking you to forgive *me*. I can't count the ways I've failed you."

Her throat grew tight. "Of course! Of course, I forgive you, Dad!"

She couldn't say anything more, as she was working very hard to choke back her tears.

His eyes grew red, and he gave a stiff nod. "Thank you." He sniffed, reaching up to wipe his eyes.

And then neither of them could hold it in. As a few tears slipped down Leah's cheeks, her dad rose and extended his hand. "Come here, Leah!" She stood and he pulled her into a hard embrace, and both of them wept together. At first it was strained and awkward, but soon her stifled tears gave way to crying freely—the noisy kind of crying—and he just held her crushed against his chest for a long time, stroking her hair.

After what seemed like forever, Leah finally gained some composure and was able to breathe again somewhat normally. Eventually she moved and he let her go, looking down on her with his own tear-stained face. Reaching back, he retrieved a handkerchief from his pocket and offered it to her.

"I can't remember the last time I hugged you," he said, brushing a hand across his cheek.

"I can't either," Leah squeaked in a nasally voice. She wiped her eyes with the hankie, alarmed at the dark smears of mascara on it. "Oh, brother—I must look horrible!"

He gave a short laugh. "Well, you'll need to fix your makeup. At least you don't have to meet with a client!"

Her eyes rose to the wet blotches on his chest. "I've wrecked your shirt!"

He pulled at the damp fabric. "It's just tears, I think. It'll dry."

"I hope so." She blew her nose.

"Leah, I apologize for coming unexpectedly like this. I debated calling you. I know this has probably been the surprise of your life, but this weekend Chelsea might be with me, and I wanted time with you alone, even if it was short."

"I get it. Thank you. It means a lot to me."

He blew out a long breath, as if relieved that he had accomplished his mission.

"You should probably eat," Leah said, conscious of the time.

His eyes dropped to the plate. "I suppose."

They sat, and he started in on his sandwich. Leah watched him, no longer interested in her own food. He was different. He *looked* different— different than she remembered him. His face—how could she describe it? Fewer lines, fewer creases? He looked—he looked happier, more at peace.

Less—she had to say it—less like a chronic drunk. He looked *normal*.

"You look good, Dad," she said.

His head bobbed as he swallowed his food. "Thanks. So do you—apart from—you know." He motioned to her streaked mascara. "When did you change your hair? It's really cute!"

Leah's hand went to it automatically. "Oh, thanks. A few weeks ago."

He took another bite.

Leah sighed. Since they were having a heart to heart, she might as well go for it. "Dad, do you mind if I say something?" She didn't wait for his answer. "I don't ever recall asking for your side of the story after the divorce, and I'm sorry. I've only heard one side, and that's my whole perspective on things."

He looked at her but continued to eat.

"I'm just letting you know that I'd like to hear your side sometime."

He took a drink and set his glass on the table. "Thanks, but that's no longer important. I don't think there'd be any benefit in dragging that up." Taking his fork, he started in on his watermelon.

"Okay. Well, since we're on a roll, I forgive you for all of that too—all your cheating on mom and your affair with Chelsea. I want to say it out loud to make it official. All of it—I forgive you, Dad!"

He stopped with his fork in midair, then dropped it back in the bowl and set the watermelon down unfinished on the table. With a napkin he wiped his face and laid it beside the bowl. "Thank you," he said stiffly, offering nothing more.

She checked her phone. "It's almost time for you to leave for your appointment."

"Yes, I suppose it is." He stood. "If you don't mind, I think I'll go throw a little water on my face."

"Sure," she said as he went inside.

When he returned, she walked him to his car, and he hugged her goodbye.

"I wish this hadn't been so hurried," he said. "I debated over and over about whether to stop or not. I knew we wouldn't have much time."

"I'm glad you did, Dad. And I'm really looking forward to this weekend."

He kissed her forehead. "Me too! I'll come up Friday morning. I'm taking the whole day off work. I'll grab some tools from home. Maybe my chainsaw. And mower if I bring the truck. Maybe Saturday we could visit a kitchen store."

"That'd be perfect!"

He got into his car and strapped on his seatbelt. Through his open window, Leah noticed a book atop his briefcase on the passenger's seat, and her eyes about bugged out when she recognized it was a Bible! He tapped its leather cover, smiling sheepishly. "No, you're not seeing things! That's another apology I owe you, Leah girl! Believe it or not, I've finally embraced what I've fought so hard all my life. The song is true: I once was blind, but now I see!"

She stepped back from the car. "Amazing. Goodbye, Dad."

"See you Friday, Leah."

She watched him drive away and stood unmoving on the driveway for a long time.

Pinch me, somebody! Tell me I'm not dreaming! He had *kissed* her! He had called her "Leah girl" and kissed her head! A jumbled tide of emotions surged and rolled: happiness, amazement, hope, and a gritty undertow of wariness—although it was diminishing more and more. Of all the people in her life, she would never have imagined her dad to become a Christian! He ranked rock bottom on her list of people who could change. And now— more than merely going to church, her dad was following Jesus—no doubt about it! Yes, he was right! This *had* been the surprise of her life—him showing up with what he'd come to do. *Another* surprise of her life, given that only days ago she'd discovered Danny DeSoto lived next door!

She raised her brow. Now *that* would have been an interesting piece of information to share with her father, but she hadn't thought of it until now, and their time together had been so brief. She wondered how he'd react to the news when she told him Friday. All bets were off. There had been too many remarkable changes in him to make any predictions on that!

Her phone chirped in her hand. Another text from Kyla.

"Hey, I forgot Hank's truck by your tree. Can you send a photo to quell his panic?"

And Kyla Watkins. Just yesterday Leah had been so perturbed at Kyla's persnickety urging to forgive her dad. Who could have foreseen what would unfold? Leah shook her head in amazement. Furthermore, something had happened in that handshake with Kyla before the study. *So, in fifth grade fashion—friends?* Was it that easy?

Hearing a sound behind her, Leah turned and started in surprise at Brindle sitting on the porch steps hugging her knees. "Geez—you're quiet! Where'd you come from? How long have you been there?"

She shrugged. "Who was that guy?"

"My dad. He's got an appointment in town, and he came down early to see me."

"Ah. Did he do it?"

"Do what?"

"You know—the thing with the dog."

Leah shook her head. "Not in a million years!"

"Huh. Well, what happened? You were crying—both of you. Did someone in your family die or something?"

Leah had mixed feelings about Brindle spying on her time with her dad. "No, everything's cool. We had a talk. It's—personal."

Brindle tipped her head expectantly.

Leah simply wanted to be alone. "Hey, Brin—do you mind hanging out here on the porch a bit? I need a few minutes alone. I'll be back soon."

She pulled herself to her feet. "I can come back later. Are we still on for painting?"

"Yeah, we'll paint. Maybe in an hour. I just need a moment. Thanks."

As Brindle left, Leah headed around the side of the house to the climbing tree. Under it was now a maze of primitive roadways winding around in the dirt and grass with boundaries of tiny rocks and sticks laid end to end. Scooping up Hank's dump truck from the dirt, she turned to survey her house and yard, trying to imagine the scene that morning. Mr. Darkish-Red Shirt would have had to come around the garage side of the house. She frowned, picturing it. Then slipping the truck under one arm, she snapped a selfie with it and texted it to Kyla.

"Here you go. Ask Howie if it was a T-shirt or a dress shirt with buttons."

She was beyond sure that Mr. Darkish-Red Shirt could never have been her dad. Or Marty either, unless he'd driven away lickety-split before she made it over to his place. Regardless, *someone* had been lurking around—someone with a mean streak. Perhaps Brindle was right. Maybe it was time to call the police. If there were a neighborhood stalker, she might not be the only one being harassed, and it was probably better to be safe than sorry.

With a guilty sigh, Leah glanced toward the hedge separating her yard from Brother Warren and Jackie's house. It was all too quiet over there now, like no one was home. Poor Angel was likely on his way to the vet. If Danny were back, she'd ask him what to do about that. Plus, she'd tell him everything about her dad. He would totally get how she was feeling.

She closed her eyes, still trying to wrap her mind around what had just happened—her dad showing up like that for the sole purpose of talking to her alone. And not just a random 'hi-how-are-you' visit. Her dad had sought her out deliberately to make an apology. No—Leah shook her head—no, what he had done was above and beyond a mere apology. An apology was what Jake had made that awful Friday night: "I'm really sorry, Leah. I know you're *probably hurt*…." No, her dad had made a *confession of abject guilt*. It wasn't a glossing over of a few mistakes. Nor had he thrown out any lame or even valid excuses for his faults. No, he had pulled out all the stops and humbled himself with sincerity, embracing the scope of his wrongs, validating any feelings of anger that she might have had. And why? Why would he do such a thing unless he *loved* her and genuinely wanted to fix things between them?

She wished he hadn't had to leave for an appointment. The ten-year-old in her would have liked to ask if she could sit on his lap and have him hold her there for a long, long time. And now simply acknowledging it allowed her to feel the cavernous emptiness of her adolescent heart. The cistern of hurt she had so carefully kept buried was wrenched open, the painful wounds emerging with a fresh bite. Her heart pulsed with the ache, and for the second time that day, Leah sank to her knees beside the climbing tree and let her sobs come forth without restraint, howling into her hands, crying harder than she knew was possible.

Her dad's handkerchief was now soggy beyond use, and she resorted to wiping her nose with her shirt. Suddenly self-conscious of kneeling out in her open yard, she glanced around, hoping Brindle wasn't still watching from some hidden corner. It was hard enough blubbering like an idiot—she didn't need an audience! Taking a few breaths, she shimmied up the climbing tree, hiking herself up onto the fat, curvy branch she remembered from days past. The bark was smoother there from all the visitors over the years, the seat wide enough for two—two children at least, she realized today, for her hips fit more snuggly since she'd been up there last. It wasn't as comfortable as she remembered, but it didn't matter today. She needed to be alone. She needed to think.

Alone. She swung her feet considering it. No, she wasn't alone. In all her running away, she hadn't ever been alone. She had simply been closed. Closed to God. Shut up tight and offended by his painful intervention in her life. But everything lately—everything—was speaking to her—no, more like *shouting* to her—that God was *for* her and not against her. Without warning her dad had burst into her life as a genuine believer! And here she was in this place with all these people—Jackie Burke, and Brother Warren, and Kyla Watkins—all of them strangers, but already they felt like family. And she *wanted* to come back. God had been kind to her—so, so kind. Kinder than Evelyn. And like her dad, he *wanted* her! How could she refuse him?

"All right, God—I'm done fighting you. I surrender. Whatever I have to do, I'm willing." Her voice was muffled by the leafy branches.

Chapter Twenty-One

On her way down out of the climbing tree Leah's phone rang. Dropping the rest of the way to the ground, she wrangled it out of her pocket, hoping it was Kyla calling about the darkish-red shirt. She frowned, recognizing her Bridgewater counselor's number.

"Pam?"

"Ava! Glad I caught you! How are you doing?"

"Hello!" Leah pictured her behind her desk in one of her smart linen pantsuits, her hair pulled back, and bright red reading glasses resting far down on her nose. "I'm great—although I'm back to using 'Leah' now. The name thing didn't work out."

"Yeah? Well, hello, *Leah* then! You've been on my mind the last few days, and I felt the urge to check up on you. How are things going with the new home?"

"That's nice of you! Things are going well!"

"Glad to hear it! Is it all that you expected?"

Leah brushed the tree crumbs off the back of her legs, glancing at her house. "Well, to be perfectly honest, it wasn't nearly as nice as I remembered it. It needs a ton of work, but it's okay. I'm fixing it up, and it'll be great when it's finished!"

"Really? That's too bad. But you're getting help from your cousin, right? I know you were kind of depending on him."

"Ah, things with my cousin didn't work out either. But it's all right. My dad's gonna help me."

"Oh, that's nice! Wait—your dad? How did *that* come about? I thought you didn't have much to do with him!"

"Yes, but he's, um—well, he's made some effort to connect, and he offered to help me."

"No kidding!" Pam returned. "I'll bet that was unexpected!"

She had no idea. "It was! In fact, just this morning he stopped in to look around, and we had a good talk—a *great* talk! I've never seen my dad like this, Pam. He's really changed—like, *really* changed! It's pretty incredible!"

"Interesting. That's rather sudden, isn't it? How do you account for it?"

"He's become a—" She suddenly remembered that Pam wasn't keen on religion. "—Um, he's following God now."

There was a pause. "Huh. Doesn't that seem out of character for him? Are you sure he's not just moving in for control now that you own some property? I'd be careful if I were you!"

"No, that's definitely not the case." Leah scooped up Hank's dump truck and began strolling toward the house.

"You never know! I'm only offering a perspective that you might want to keep in mind. So what else have you been doing? How's the job search going?"

"I'm waiting on that. I'm getting the house remodel started first."

"Okay. Uh-huh." Another silence. "Well, just remember, Leah—good nutrition is important for good mental health."

Leah frowned. "I'm sorry, Pam. I'm not seeing the connection between that and a job."

"Lots of people eat junk when they're broke. I'm saying you need to be proactive in keeping a healthy diet."

She raised her head. "Ah! Got it." There were a lot of assumptions packed in there that she'd let pass.

"Have you gotten to know any people in the area yet?"

"Yes!" She glanced at the hedge that separated her yard from Jackie's. "There's an elderly gentleman and his daughter who live next door. He knew my grandparents way back when, and they have younger friends my age that I'm getting to know." She paused, debating whether to tell Pam about Danny DeSoto. Her pathetic DeSoto saga had been stuck on repeat over the last year. Would Pam wig out if she were told she and Danny were now friends? She might. "There's also this girl across the street—Brindle. She and another gal are painting with me today."

"Wow—good for you! You surprise me, Leah!"

"Thanks. It's not been without challenges, but I'm managing."

"And how about setting boundaries?"

"I think you'd be proud of me, Pam! I won't go into it, but I *have* had to put your wisdom into practice." Not that she'd been terribly successful at it, Leah acknowledged to herself. Yet she *had* changed the locks on her house, and technically that qualified. She decided to leave it at that.

"Excellent! I'll confess I was a little worried about you, which is why I called. I don't normally follow up with clients like this."

"I'm honored. Thanks for the call." She had reached the line in the grass that was becoming a path to the neighbor's, pausing halfway between her porch and the hedge.

"Just one more question, Leah. In the past when we've talked, I know you've had a propensity to bend to religious influence. Any struggles with that?"

Leah hesitated.

"Uh-huh. Want to talk about it?"

"No—it's—I'm doing fine."

"Does it have anything to do with your father—because he's religious now?"

Leah shook her head. "It's with no one. It's between me and God. It's personal, and I'm working things out."

"All right, all right. I can respect that. Although in my opinion, religious decisions hardly ever happen in a vacuum. I find there's usually someone applying a high degree of influence, if not pressure. I'd hate to see you get mixed up in that again. You were terribly confused when we started meeting. Do you remember that, Leah?"

"Yes, but that's because I was hurt. I was fighting God. I was resisting him. But I'm not anymore. I guess I'm seeing he's *for* me and not against me."

There was another pregnant silence. "Who have you been talking to, Leah?"

"Well, the—er, neighbors. They—well, it's complicated. But I'm doing good. I am! Better than I have in a long, long time."

"Uh-huh. All right." Her tone was dubious. "It's your choice, really. Your health all around is your responsibility."

Leah was quiet.

"So I need to go, but—"

"Thanks for the call, Pam."

"—could I share some parting wisdom with you?"

She nodded. Pam wasn't finished. "Of course."

"Like you said, Leah, religion is a personal thing. It's between you and God, and I'd advise you to keep it that way. Whatever *you* decide is fine. However, I'd highly encourage you to put some space between you and the religious people who are pushing their views on—"

"—I'm not being pushed by anyone, Pam!"

"Now don't get defensive! Just listen to me, dear! If I were you, I'd put some space in those relationships. I guarantee you'll have less confusion in your life—truly! Less guilt. Less tension. Who wants to live with all that? You need to go after peace of mind, girl! This is your Year of Freedom! Life is about *you*—remember? *You* are the center of your world! Get out there and conquer! Do what's best for *you* and quit trying to please God or anyone else!"

The center of your world. Leah could see so clearly where being the center of her world had brought her, and there was no happiness or peace of mind associated with it.

"Thanks, Pam." Leah didn't want to be impolite, but she was ready to move on from the call.

"You're welcome. I'm proud of you, Leah! You can do this! You just need to toughen up those boundaries in a few areas."

"Right. Well, thanks again for the call."

Leah slid her phone into her pocket. Over the last year she'd learned a ton from Pam, but her advice on religion wasn't sitting right with her anymore. In all her awful four years since her painful betrayal, staying away from God was the worst thing she had done. It had only opened the way to worse and worse places for her. But today was a new day.

Instead of returning to her porch, Leah dropped Hank's truck in the middle of her lawn and turned determinedly for next door. It felt like the appropriate thing to do—to go tell Danny right away that she had prayed to surrender to God. Plus, she wanted to find out how the dog was for she felt partly responsible for his suffering.

Brother Warren was on the deck rocking gently in the covered porch swing, singing quietly to himself.

Leah greeted him at the base of the stairs. "Hello, Mr. Warren. Is Danny around?"

"No, my dear. He went with Jackie to take the poor dog in."

"Oh." Leah felt a lurch in her stomach. "I'm so sorry!"

The old man frowned and beckoned. "You're upset! Come up here, child—come, come! Let's talk!"

Leah approached. "I feel terrible about the dog!"

He grimaced. "Oh, I know! It's too bad, isn't it? But that wasn't your fault. Is that why you've been crying?"

Her mascara. She'd forgotten about that. She probably looked frightening with her blotchy face and puffy eyes, but it didn't really matter now, for suddenly she found herself choking back a new batch of tears, and she didn't know why. "That's part of it. It's been a crazy morning—with the Bible study and the dog and all that. And I got this phone call from my old counselor. And then my dad—my dad—" Her hand went to her forehead as a whoosh of emotions tumbled forth. "My dad came—" *Why was she crying again?* It was as though a geyser had erupted from inside of her!

"Oh, dear!" Brother Warren exclaimed, struggling to get out of the swing.

She shook her head, trying to pull herself together. "No—no, don't get up! I'm sorry—"

He reached out. "Give me your hand, sweetheart!"

Leah helped him up and held his arms while he steadied himself. Then he changed his grip to grasp her arms in his. "Now tell me—why are you crying? What's happened with your father?"

There was something about his presence, something about his genuine care that made maintaining control a lost battle. "Well, he—it was so unexpected! He showed up at my house this morning right after the Bible study. He had an appointment in town and came early to see me and to ask me—um, he came early to ask me—to ask me to forgive him for neg—neglecting me as a child!"

The dam had burst.

Overwhelmed, Leah laid her head against his chest and let the emotional squall blow. With a sympathetic grunt, Brother Warren cradled her against him, patting her while she cried like a little child, unable to stop. Eventually the intensity began tapering, and embarrassment set in. Good heavens—she was bawling her eyes out on a neighbor she hardly knew! Catching her breath, she awkwardly pulled away, wiping her cheeks with her hands.

"Oh, gosh. I'm so sorry about that! I don't know what's wrong with me—why I keep crying! I mean, it's a *good* thing that my dad showed up—I'm glad, and I forgive him and everything. But I can't stop crying!"

"It's okay! It's okay, Leah! You go ahead and cry—cry it all out!"

His voice. His voice was so kind, so full of love. It set her off again, and for the fourth time in the space of an hour Leah had another gut cry, weeping on Brother Warren's chest with heavy sobs coming from the deepest part of her. He simply held her, saying nothing while years of deep disappointment and hurt rushed to the surface.

At last her tears subsided. With a deep breath she backed away again, wiggling the soggy handkerchief out of her pocket, but Brother Warren offered her a clean hanky of his own.

"Thanks," she said, dabbing her eyes. "That was the strangest thing—crying like that. But I think I'm okay now." She yawned to pop her ears.

He nodded. "There may be more of that to come. It's okay. God's healing your wounded heart, dear girl. Sometimes pain gets stuffed way down in there, but he's bringing it out."

Leah sniffed. "Maybe." As a staunch conscientious objector to crying, she'd made up for her deficit in a short time! With a timid smile, she brushed the hanky across her face again.

A silence passed between them. He was waiting for her.

She let out a long breath. "So it's pretty obvious that my dad has turned to God—and in a *big* way. His wife told me they've been going to church, which is new for them. And when I moved here, he called me to offer to help with the house, which is also a new thing, since we ordinarily don't talk much. And then after my conversation with you and Kyla in your dining room the other night, I decided to call him back. He totally floored me by apologizing to me for his failures as a parent—right over the phone! That enough was a surprise, but today"—she shook her head—"today he took it to another level and asked me to forgive him for emotionally checking out on me after the divorce. It was—well, a shocker, for sure, but it was also good! Amazingly good! Things are—wow—things are so different! *So* different! I can't even say!" She looked up at him. "I'm just blown away by it all!"

Brother Warren smiled. "Praise God!"

A week ago that expression had irked her. She nodded. "Yeah. He actually had a Bible in his front seat! That was unheard of before! I'm telling you—my dad has changed!"

He grinned, making a sound through his cheek. "That's awesome, Leah! Would you care to sit with me?" He gestured to the swing.

"Sure!" It sounded like a wonderful idea.

She steadied the frame while he lowered himself onto the cushion, then joined him, leaving a space between them. Gently she rocked the swing with her foot.

"I guess I'm a little nervous about all of this. Excited too, of course, but I don't really know him, so I don't know what to expect. I'm not sure what our relationship is supposed to look like now. What do I do? I don't know how to swim in this pond! He's coming up again this weekend, and I'm glad—but I'm scared!"

Brother Warren laid his hand on hers. "Well, my dear, he's probably nervous too. He doesn't know how to swim in your pond either, as you put it. But I think it's going to be okay. I think you're both going to love learning to swim. This is a God thing, you know. It's *God* that did this, because his heart is for fathers to love their children and for children to love their fathers. It's biblical. It's not gonna be perfect, but let it unfold. God's going to help you both every step of the way."

His hand was comforting. It made her feel safe. Loved.

"I'll be honest—I was so perturbed at Kyla Watkins the other night— how she was urging me so strongly to forgive my dad for his 'wrongdoings' in my life. I had no idea!"

He smiled.

"So I suppose I should probably forgive my mom too, huh?"

"Do you need to forgive your mom?"

Leah looked away. Yikes—going *there* would be a huge, complicated mess! How could she begin to explain it? How could she express what it was like to be emotionally yanked around by someone she loved? She *did* love her mom, but sometimes it wasn't fun living a guarded life with such an unpredictable person, not knowing from day to day which she would get— the nice mom or the angry one. There were lots of faults and weaknesses to forgive, but unlike her dad, her mother wasn't asking to be forgiven. So why go there? Leah was well accustomed to the lack of stability in the relationship, and going down that road sounded like a recipe for pain. Maybe the bigger issue was for her to stop wishing her mother could have been like—

Like Evelyn DeSoto.

Leah gave an internal sigh. Or Jackie Burke. Or *anyone* who showed her an ounce of warmth and affection. Who knew which woman would be next in line for her to hope to fill that void? She knew it was understandable, given her mother's personality. Yet right now Leah felt a tug of guilt for rejecting her.

"Well, I know there's a lot to forgive," Leah told Brother Warren, "but I think for today I simply want to say that I'm glad I *have* a mom. She's got her issues, but she's the mom God gave me, so I'm at least grateful for that. I can't go beyond that right now. Not today anyway."

He nodded. "We'll trust the Lord to lead you on that."

After a short lull between them, Leah turned to him. "Brother Warren, how do I get back with God?"

He tipped his head inquiringly.

"I've been—" She paused, unsure of how to continue. "I've done some horrible things, and I know God must be utterly disgusted with me. I've been so far away. So hypocritical and hard-hearted. I've asked God to forgive me, but I want you to know it's my desire to be right with God—really, truly, and sincerely right with God. Just tell me what I need to do. I'll do anything!"

He squeezed her hand. "Your Father's arms are wide open, Leah. He hears your voice. He sees your heart. Just be completely honest with him."

"I have been! I surrendered to him in the climbing tree right over there a bit ago. But it scares me how far away from him I got."

"And he was loving you the whole time, my girl, drawing you back. Waiting for the moment when you'd say 'yes' to him again."

"Well, I'm saying 'yes'—I'm saying 'yes' right now!"

"That's wonderful!" His eyes shone with happiness.

She smiled back.

"You know there's a huge celebration in heaven right now, don't you? The Bible says the angels in heaven rejoice when one sinner repents."

"So is that enough? Do I need to do anything else?"

"Enough?" He opened his hands. "Yes and no! It's both enough and never enough! God's after your heart, my dear. He wants to be close to you. He wants you to live with your heart always open to him—that's the secret of living to please him! Keep taking steps *toward* him, never in the other direction. And all those good disciplines—praying, reading your Bible, going to church—those are very important, yes, but keep your heart wide open to him." He patted his chest. "Ask the Holy Spirit every day to show you who Jesus is and why he's so worthy of your love and devotion. Ask him to fill your heart with the revelation of Father God's love for you. Obey him—but from the standpoint of staying in his love, rather than performing to be good enough for him. Do you hear what I'm saying?"

Leah nodded. "I think so."

"Saturate yourself with his Word, and above all, *relate* to him, Leah. Spend time with *him*. Get to know him as your Daddy, your Savior, your Comforter, your Shepherd, your—" He chuckled. "Oh, dear—now you've got me preaching!"

Leah smiled. "I don't mind. I like it. I was wondering—would you pray for me?"

"It'd be my delight!" He squeezed her hand again, then lifted his to rest it on her head. "Father God, bless this beloved daughter of yours with the assurance of your love and forgiveness. Show her the love and beauty of your Son, Jesus Christ, and rekindle her first love. Fill her with a hunger and thirst for you and your righteousness. And for your Word. Help her by the power of your Holy Spirit." He paused to take her chin in his hands and look into her eyes. "Daughter, be restored in Jesus' name!"

More tears spilled as Leah reached to give him a hug. "Thank you!"

"My pleasure," he said happily. "Will you be hanging around until Dan comes home?"

She shook her head. "No, I can't. This afternoon Kyla and Brin—oh, shoot!" Quickly she snatched her phone out of her pocket and groaned. "I completely forgot about the time!" She pulled herself out of the swing. "Kyla and Brindle are coming over to my house to help me paint this afternoon. They may even be there already waiting for me!"

He waved her on. "Oh, you better go then!"

"I should! Thank you so much for all your help! I'm really sorry to rush off."

"My privilege. I love you, Leah, child of God! You have a marvelous day!"

"Thank you! I'd love a report on how Angel is when you hear. Will you have Danny call me?"

"Yes, yes. Angel will be okay. We prayed for him. Go on now and join your friends. I don't want to keep you."

Leah blew him a kiss and skipped down the steps, no longer ashamed of her emotional meltdown there. Brother Warren had been a spiritual paramedic in the right place and time.

Leah walked in on Brindle and Kyla taping off the window trim in the large bedroom. Immediately she apologized for her absence, but neither seemed to mind too much.

Kyla smiled. "I'll admit when I first got here, I was a little freaked out to see Hank's truck right smack in the middle of your lawn. I was afraid our evil dog kicker had nabbed you, but then I heard you over there with Brother Warren." She tipped her head toward the neighbor's and met Leah's eyes. "Everything all right?"

Oh, brother! The whole neighborhood had probably heard her! Leah gave an embarrassed smile. "Yes, everything's good. Everything's very good!"

"Wonderful!" By her tone of voice and the way she smiled back, Leah guessed that Kyla understood when it came to spending time with

Brother Warren.

Brindle looked between them, saying nothing.

"Any word on Angel?" Kyla asked. "I've texted Jackie but haven't heard back."

Leah shook her head. "Not yet. Brother Warren said they're at the vet. I'm wondering if I should report the incident to the police. Unless it turns out the dog's totally fine. I don't know—either way, it's just not right!"

"No, it's not," Kyla agreed. "That was cruel and uncalled for! The boys were so frightened—they couldn't stop talking about it! And to answer your question about the guy's shirt—neither boy could say whether it was a T-shirt or otherwise. They were focused entirely on poor Angel."

Leah sighed. "So crazy! Anyway, thanks for coming to help me paint. I hope you guys haven't been here long."

"It was Brindle's idea to start," Kyla said, casting an appreciative look at her on the step stool. "She was here before me."

"Nice! Well, I'll go change and join you." She turned to leave, calling back from the hallway, "And since you two are so hard at it, I think I'll take my time!" She heard Kyla's amused chuckle behind her.

Finding an old T-shirt and shorts in her clothes basket beside the air mattress, Leah quickly changed and then laid her earrings on the counter. Ready to return, she grabbed her phone, when out of the corner of her eye she spied a small envelope at the end of the peninsula—sealed, with her name on it. Pausing, she picked it up, finding a folded notecard with neatly printed handwriting inside: *Ava, sorry I missed you. I stopped by to tell you that I've been called in to work tonight. Not sure when we can reschedule. So sorry. Phil*

With a cry Leah flipped the card over and back again. Stuffing it back into the envelope, she brought it to the bedroom and held it up.

"Where did this come from?"

Kyla peered across the room. "What is it? I know nothing."

"That was stuck in the door when I got here," Brindle said. "I put it on the counter for you." She turned back to her taping.

Leah gave a disappointed sigh, shoving the note into her back pocket.

Kyla looked at her curiously.

"This guy I like cancelled on me tonight."

"Huh."

"I'm really bummed! He was super nice."

"I see. He's a believer then?" Her brow rose with the question.

Leah looked away, guessing by her expression that Kyla shared Mary

McAllister's take on believers and unbelievers dating. "Um, I'm not sure yet. But he's nice—super nice and handsome too! I was really looking forward to going out with him."

"Huh." Kyla nodded and turned back to her work.

Brindle looked down and shrugged. "Sorry it didn't work out. Could you hand me that other roll?"

Leah handed up the tape, then opened a playlist on her phone and set it onto the mattress.

"He had my phone number—I don't understand why he didn't *call* me. A note on the door seems lame!"

Brindle stretched a piece of blue tape off the roll and extended her arms to the top of the window. "It's not so lame. At least you weren't stood up."

"No, it's *lame*—it's definitely lame! But—oh, well." She brought the paint cans to the foot of the bed and knelt to open one.

Kyla tore off a strip of tape. "It's probably no consolation, but Peter and I were wondering if you're busy tomorrow evening. Around seven."

Leah looked up. "I'm not. What's up?"

Kyla gave a mysterious smile. "Good. Reserve the evening for us, and you'll find out tomorrow! Brindle, you can come over too."

Brindle threw her a look. "Come over where?"

"Right here."

"Why all the secrecy?"

Kyla raised her brow. "I guess you'll have to come find out, huh?" She smiled. "Leah, I could start cutting in when that paint is ready."

"Well, now you have us both curious! It's ready, but let me give it a quick stir first."

When she was finished, she handed Kyla a small container and a brush. "So hey—the dog thing interrupted us, but I wanted to tell you I liked the Bible study this morning. It really spoke to me."

"Cool! Does that mean you'll come back?"

Leah nodded. "Definitely. I'm coming back—on multiple levels."

Kyla's eyes brightened. "I'm so glad to hear that! And how about you, Brindle?"

"What?" She was moving the step stool to tape along the edge of the closet doors. "Oh, yeah—maybe. We'll see. It depends on my work schedule. We've been kinda busy lately."

Leah found herself exchanging a glance with Kyla—as if intuitively, and it surprised her. It appeared that their mutual faith had already formed an invisible bond.

"So I never heard what happened after you left Jackie's this morning," Kyla said. "I take it there was no one around then—?"

Leah shook her head. "Nope. The guy was gone. I went over to my cousin's next door, but he wasn't home either—to my relief, I guess. I sure didn't want it to be him!"

"Weird!" Kyla said. "It's so unnerving if you ask me! Who'd treat a dog like that? A delivery guy maybe? Were you expecting any packages?"

"No—and they wouldn't go to my back door anyway. But I did have another big surprise! My dad showed up out of the blue—which had nothing to do with the dog, by the way!"

Kyla turned, her eyes questioning.

"It was the strangest thing—coming home from Marty's to find him on my porch! I don't see him very often, but he had an appointment in town with a client and came by early to talk with me. It turned out to be amazing—especially in light of our conversation at Jackie's the other night! All I can say is that God is working in our relationship!"

"Wow!" Kyla exclaimed. "Tell us about it!"

Leah hesitated. "Well—I'm not quite ready to talk about it. I'm still processing things. Maybe give me a day or two."

"I get it! I understand completely."

Brindle glanced over but remained quiet.

"But how about you, Kyla?" Leah asked. "Now might be a good time for us to hear your story, since we both missed it Saturday night—that is if you can talk and cut in at the same time!"

Kyla laughed. "That's asking a lot, but I'll give it a try!"

Starting in, Kyla shared her drama as together the three of them worked and chatted well into the middle of the afternoon, conquering the master bedroom and making good progress on the smaller bedrooms. Eventually Brindle checked the time and said she had to go.

Kyla, too, checked her phone. "Hmm. It's already three o'clock. I should probably go too. I see Peter texted me an hour ago concerned about me being around paint fumes. Is that a pregnancy thing?" She shrugged. "Too many things to know!"

Ready for a break herself, Leah walked the girls out together and said goodbye, then fixed herself a drink and went to relax on her porch. She texted Danny to inquire about the dog, but he didn't answer. A moment later she looked up to see Kyla's car speeding back down her driveway, jolting across several potholes, and pulling up to park on the concrete slab in front of the garage. The girl hopped out of the car and hurried so determinedly up the walk that Leah stood in alarm.

"What's happened?"

"I'm glad you're out here!" Kyla said, pulling her phone out of her back pocket. "Sit down, Leah! I need to show you something!"

"What?" Confused and a little worried, she lowered herself onto the love seat.

Kyla plopped down beside her, opening her phone to a photo which she held out for Leah to see.

Leah narrowed her eyes. "What am I looking at?"

Kyla zoomed up on the photo and held it out again. Leah could then see a blurry image of two people standing close together.

"Who is it? Is this supposed to mean something?"

"Look closer!"

Leah gasped. "Oh, my gosh—it's Phil! And he's with someone!"

"Who's Phil? Leah, it's *Brindle*!"

Leah's eyes grew round as she scrutinized the photo again. She couldn't see Brindle's face, but now she recognized her clothing. It was definitely her—with Phil Crawford.

"You're kidding me!"

"You know him?"

"It's my date—Phil Crawford! The guy who cancelled on me tonight! I didn't know they were friends!"

Kyla grunted. "Close friends, I'd say! They were kissing!"

"What?" She stared at Kyla. "How did you get this picture? Did you know this before?"

Kyla took her phone back and peered at the photo again. "No. I didn't know who he was. I followed Brindle just now when we left. I wanted to see where she lived so I could go over there this week—you know, just pop in. I wanted to try to talk to her more about the questions that she had this morning at the study because I suspect she was referring to herself. I thought maybe she'd open up if it was just me and her. Anyway, I saw them together from a distance and took this photo."

Leah dropped her head. "I feel so stupid right now! Why the heck didn't Brindle say anything? That little stinker was holding out on us! When we were talking about him cancelling on me, she totally acted like she didn't know him!"

"I'd say she acted pretty calmly considering the guy was stepping out on her!"

"No kidding!"

Kyla eyed Leah. "Do you still have his note? Can I see it?"

Leah pulled the card out of her back pocket and handed it over.

Kyla read it thoughtfully, nodding. "Yeah."

"What?"

"*She* wrote this!"

Leah glanced again at the note, then quizzically back at her.

"I'll bet anything you she did! Tell me one guy in the whole world who carries a notecard with an envelope in his vehicle! Right—like he stopped by to see you—then supposedly wrote this note and left it in the door—?" She shook her head. "No way! His note would have been on the back of a receipt or on a Burger King napkin or something, definitely not on nice stationery like this with an envelope!"

"Maybe." Leah frowned, considering it. Then she huffed, tossing the note onto the coffee table. "Then that means *she* cancelled for him!" Her shoulders slumped. "Oh, brother! Why didn't she just say something if she didn't want me going out with him? She talked him up as one of the hot guys in the neighborhood! She called him Mr. Suave and Studly!"

Kyla let out a giggle.

Leah also laughed. "Danny was one of her hot picks too! So was my cousin Marty."

"Well, she's right about Dan!" Kyla winked.

Leah sighed. "She's been after Phil this whole time, the little sneak! We've been in competition, and I didn't even know it! This must have just happened 'cause the last time I talked to him he wasn't exactly sure who she was. That's so wild! Well, I'm curious what she'll say when I ask her about it. And Phil too! I wonder if he'll come by to reschedule with me. Probably not if *she* has anything to say about it!"

Kyla lowered her chin. "You're not wanting to go out with him still, are you? Leah, let him go! You should trust the Lord for a believer."

Leah rolled her eyes. "You sound like Mary McAllister!"

"Who?"

"My grandmother's mentor. I was reading one of my grandma's journals last night. But never mind."

Kyla looked at Leah. "Plus, there's the other thing."

"The other thing?"

Kyla held out the photo again. "His shirt! That's why I took the picture in the first place!"

Leah zoomed up to examine the photo more closely, then looked questioningly at Kyla, who raised her brow.

"See what I mean? It's red!"

Leah frowned. "It's brown."

Kyla shook her head. "Reddish brown, if you ask me. From where I took the picture it definitely looked *red*!"

Leah checked again. "Um, I'm seeing brown. That's not even close to 'darkish-red.' It's brownish brown. And his hair is blond."

"Yeah, blond-*ish*. To a little boy that's brown! This could be the guy who kicked Angel!"

Leah shook her head. "You're stretching things! There's no way! He's *way* too nice!" She looked up. "Seriously, Kyla—I've met him. The guy is super nice!"

"It's just a possibility."

Leah studied the photo again. "I'm not seeing it. Plus, he works during the day. What would he be doing at my house in the middle of the morning? And at my back door. He told me he gets off work at three." She blinked, adding, "Which, coincidentally, is when Brindle was ready to leave today."

"Well, that's a good question, isn't it?"

Leah's mind was spinning with new crazy thoughts—one of which was the home address he had given her. "That'd be so weird! And completely disturbing!"

"Definitely."

Nervously she tapped the cushions. "He'll be coming around to talk about my kitchen remodel soon. What do I say to him?"

"I'd be very careful with that guy, but I'd definitely bring it up!"

"Like how? What am I going to say?—'Hey, I just found out you're schmoozing my friend Brindle! And by the way, did you kick a little white dog at my house?'"

"That might be a little awkward! Maybe you could drop something out there like 'Hey—I thought I saw you with my friend!' Or 'Hey—I thought I saw you leave my house this morning.' You know—something like that. See what he says."

Leah nodded. "Yeah, maybe. But you should for sure show this picture to the boys. See if they recognize him—even if his shirt is brown."

"I definitely will."

Leah sat back, adding glumly, "If Phil Crawford kicks dogs, boy, have I been a poor judge of character." And not only that, if it was Phil Crawford coming in her house this whole time—Leah shook her head at the outlandish thought. It was so out there she didn't even want to consider it; yet it was disturbing enough that she had to.

Chapter Twenty-Two

By dinnertime Leah still hadn't heard anything about Jackie's dog, and she was becoming worried that perhaps there was bad news and they didn't want to tell her. After she cleaned up her dishes, she headed next door to see if there was any word. Just as she cleared the hedge, Danny was exiting the Glendes' front door.

He lit up when he saw her. "Hi! I was just on my way over!"

Leah folded her arms. "You never texted me back! How's Angel?"

He waggled his phone. "I know—sorry! I just got your text! I had to run back to town this afternoon, and I forgot my phone in Jackie's car from the vet thing earlier. The dog's going to be okay."

"For real?"

"He's bruised, but there's no broken bones or internal bleeding, as far as they can tell. He's currently glued to Jackie's hip on the couch. He'll be sore, but the vet thinks he'll recover just fine."

Leah dropped her arms, breathing a sigh of relief. "Thank God! You should have heard the poor thing, Danny—it was the awfullest sound! I can't understand why someone would do that!"

"Which is why I was coming over." He joined her on the narrow walk. "Too many strange things have been happening over there, Leah, and I don't like the idea of you staying by yourself."

"And my alternative?" She spread her hands. "I know *you're* not offering to stay with me!"

"I've talked to Jackie and Brother Warren, and they're in complete agreement with me. You're to stay in their guest room."

"That'd be imposing!"

"Nonsense! You're like family! You could come and go as you please. I'd feel much better if you were here."

Her reluctance diminished rapidly. "Well, okay. I appreciate that. But for how long? I mean, I'll want to be in my own home sooner or later!"

"Yeah—so Peter knows a guy who works for a security company. He could take a look around for you."

"I don't know—it's all so crazy! Nothing like this has ever happened to me before. Plus, it sounds expensive!"

"Well, at least consider it." He slid his phone in his pocket. "Anyway, I just brought home a pizza for dinner, and there's plenty for all of us. Would you like to come over?" He gestured toward the house.

Leah shook her head. "I just ate. You go ahead. I'll go get my stuff and meet you in a little bit."

He nodded. "All right. Get your things and come back. And by the way, Brother Warren tells me you've had a big day, and I should ask you about it."

She gave a cry. "He told you?"

"No! He wouldn't tell me anything!"

"Good." She lifted her chin. "Danny DeSoto, I can't wait to tell you about my day!"

He gave a curious smile. "Well, then, Leah Labanora, I can't wait to hear about it!"

He left, and Leah returned to gather her things from home. She grabbed a small laundry basket and threw in a couple changes of clothes, some pajamas, and her makeup bag, adding her running shoes on top as an afterthought. It'd be a fun surprise to join Danny on a run in the morning. On top of that she deposited her new Bible and the little study booklet from Kyla and the legal pad with her notes on the house. At the last minute she picked up Journal 2 of her grandmother's from the top of the corner bin and slid it down the side of the clothes. It would be good reading material before bed.

Before she left, Leah set the basket down and went to inspect the day's work once more. With hands on her hips, she viewed the clean, smooth walls of the master bedroom. It and three-fourths of one of the smaller bedrooms were finished, and the hallway was cut in and ready for the roller. She'd also gotten the other bedroom taped and ready to cut in— perhaps she'd finish it tomorrow. The smell of fresh paint signaled progress, and happily she breathed it in. Once she got the old bed out and replaced the carpet, the master bedroom would look like new, apart from the broken closet door, which she hoped would be an easy fix for her dad.

Carefully she tugged at a short piece of the painter's tape, which peeled easily off the wood trim, leaving a crisp, clean edge. Pleased, she pulled it off the rest of the room, letting it drop in long strips to the floor. When finished, she gathered it into a big wad and threw it away next door in the bathroom—the location of her next major project. She sighed. Removing that wallpaper would not be a pleasant task. One room at a time, she reminded herself.

Ready to go, Leah retrieved her basket of belongings to head to Jackie's for the night. On a last-minute whim, she decided to grab the next two journals, as the volume she had read last night had gone rather quickly. Lifting the plastic lid off the purple tote, she snatched the two at the end of the row and placed them on top of her Bible. Snapping the lid back down, she turned to go. As she lifted the basket, she noticed Brindle topping the porch steps to knock on her door.

Seeing Leah, she came right in. "Howdy! I thought I'd stop by to see if you got any more done this afternoon." Her eyes dropped to the clothes basket. "What are you doing?"

"Hi! Going over to Jackie's. I'm spending the night there. And yes— I've got the whole hallway cut in and ready for the roller, but I had to quit. It's been a long day, and I'm beat!"

Brindle blinked. "Staying at Jackie's? Why?"

"They invited me. The dog incident made everyone feel a little weird. And some other stuff. They didn't want me staying here alone."

Her head pulled back. "You should have asked *me*! I would stay with you! I would totally stay here with you!"

Leah cradled the basket on her hip. "That's sweet of you, but there's only one bed. One decent bed. And there's no way two of us are sleeping on that!" She nodded toward the air mattress. "So how was your afternoon, Brindle? Do anything interesting?"

She shrugged. "No. Just normal stuff. I took a nap."

"Uh-huh. And connected with friends and such?"

"What?"

"Did you meet up with any friends?"

Brindle cocked her head, confused.

"Like—Phil Crawford, maybe?" Leah gave her a knowing look. "Your ruse is up, girl!"

Brindle's eyes grew round, and she couldn't speak.

Leah sighed. "Seriously, Brindle—I don't get why you couldn't just say something!"

"H-how did you—?" Her face was pale.

"You were seen with him this afternoon after we painted," Leah said.

"It was *you* who cancelled my date tonight, wasn't it? You didn't want me going out with him. Am I right or what?"

Brindle stared, and Leah thought she almost looked frightened.

"We're not seventh-graders. Geez, I can take it that you like him. You should have said something—you didn't need to keep it a secret!"

Brindle hesitated, regarding her carefully. "Uh, yeah."

Leah raised her brow.

"I didn't—I didn't want to hurt our friendship."

Leah leveled her gaze at her. "All right—let's talk about friendship. Honesty goes a long way in a friendship, Brindle. You should have let Phil cancel with me himself!"

"Sorry." Her eyes dropped penitently.

Kyla sighed, shifting the basket on her hip, the journals sliding across the top of the Bible. "Do you get where I'm coming from? It just struck me as odd that you never let on about anything this afternoon when we were talking about it. You should have said something *then*."

"Yeah, I get it—you're right," Brindle agreed, suddenly eyeing the basket. "I'm really sorry." She looked up at Leah. "What do you have there?"

Leah tipped the basket out. "I told you—I'm staying at Jackie's."

"No, those."

"Oh. My grandma's journals. I finally found them—did I tell you?"

Her face brightened. "Really? Where were they?"

"At Marty's house—in his garage! He had thrown them in the trash!"

"Marty's?" she repeated. "How in the world—?"

"I know!" Leah nodded. "It's a complicated story, but yeah— amazing, huh? I'm bringing them with me. I thought I'd read a bit tonight at Jackie's."

Brindle's brow rose. "Ah, that's cool! I'd love to have a look at them too if you wouldn't mind. I think they'd be fun to read."

"Yeah, sure. Maybe when I'm finished."

"Or if there's one you're not reading now—?"

Leah smiled, feeling a bit possessive. "Um, maybe sometime. But not tonight, okay?"

"Oh—right. Yeah, that's fine."

A little silence passed as they stood together. Brindle glanced awkwardly around the room. "Well, I'll leave then."

"I'm leaving now too," Leah said, moving with her out to the porch.

Brindle waited as Leah locked the door behind them. "So how'd it come about that you saw Phil and me?"

Leah slipped her keys into her pocket and hoisted the laundry basket up from the chair. What could she say that wouldn't give away Kyla's reason for following her? Nodding toward the shoes in the basket, she said simply, "I'm a runner. There's a trail over there." So much for honesty in friendship, she mused.

"Ah."

Together they turned to leave the porch.

"So you and Phil—" Leah asked in turn, "how long has this been going on?"

Brindle paused at the edge of the sidewalk. "It's complicated. Let's just leave it at that."

Leah rolled her eyes. "Brindle, *you're* complicated!"

She smiled. "You've got *that* right! Sorry for stealing your man."

Leah shrugged. "It never had a chance to start. Sorry for infringing on your territory."

Brindle gave a sudden laugh. "Now *that's* an interesting way to put it! You have a good night!" With a little salute she left down the driveway.

Leah rapped her knuckles on Brother Warren's front door and let herself in, calling to Jackie that it was just her and not to get up. The older woman was cozied on the living room couch watching television with her feet up on the ottoman. Tucked tightly beside her was Angel, who lifted his head momentarily to acknowledge her entrance. When she came to pet him, he gave a tired whimper, nestling his nose next to Jackie's leg, who lifted the remote to pause her show.

"He's just bruised—thank God! The vet says he should get his zip back in a day or so."

"I'd like to help with the bill for that," Leah offered, tenderly stroking his ears.

Jackie waved her off. "It wasn't *your* fault, hon! I'm more concerned about *you*! Thanks for coming over to stay here tonight!"

"It's generous of you to ask me."

"Of course! Dan is quite bewildered at all the little things happening over there. I had no idea! But we prayed for you."

"Thank you."

"Now forgive me if I don't get up"—she gestured to the dog—"but the guest room is down the hall past the bathroom to the right. Can you manage? I'm going to sit tight if you don't mind."

"I'll figure it out. Where's Danny?"

"Well, Dad went out to dinner with an old friend tonight, and I'm snuggling with my baby, so the poor guy took his dinner back to the cottage to eat by himself. He said to tell you to join him."

"Great. Thanks." Leah picked up her basket of belongings.

Jackie smiled. "Dan's a great guy."

Leah nodded. "He really is! He's like the gold standard of what a guy should be. I never thought I'd say it, but I'm so grateful to have him back in my life! We've been friends for a long time, and he's like a brother to me."

"How wonderful!" She toyed with the remote. "Well, hon, I'm going to continue my show. Enjoy your evening!"

The shadows of the arborvitae stretched long across the yard when Leah went out to the cottage to find Danny. From the edge of the lilac, she spied him at a small table near his fire pit gazing thoughtfully into his laptop. A pizza box was balanced partially off the back edge of the table, its lid loosely closed, and beside him the pages of his legal pad fluttered gently in the light breeze where they weren't weighed down by his plastic water bottle. He didn't see her at first, and she watched him work, glancing back and forth between the pad and the screen as he typed. After a while he paused and removed his glasses to rub his face, looking up to notice her there.

He smiled. "Hi!"

"Hi," she said, approaching. "Nice office!"

"Nicest I've ever had," he agreed, rising to his feet.

"What are you working on?"

"Brother Warren's book—the whole reason I'm here this summer. Well, the main reason. I've set some deadlines for myself so that I finish before I have to leave for school, but I'm falling behind. I've had an entire week now of interruptions. First with his foot thing, and then the big party and"—he shrugged—"and everything."

"Me," Leah said flatly.

"Yeah. But you're the best kind of interruption. Come and sit down. I have the fire ready to light, and you can tell me about your big day."

He closed his laptop and pushed in his chair, motioning to a pair of lawn chairs near the fire ring. As she sat, he knelt to put a match to the crumpled newspaper beneath the pile of kindling, tending the flame until it was burning well. Gradually he added larger pieces of wood. She couldn't help but think back on their camp days.

He glanced up. "By the way, I ordered you a security camera for your porch tonight—one that'll synch to your phone and notify you if it detects movement or light. Should be here in a few days."

"Cool! How'd you think of that?"

"Just poking around online." He topped the fire with one last log, then dragged the other lawn chair to sit at an angle beside her. "I'll get it rolling for you when it comes."

"Thanks. Let me know what I owe you."

"Sure. If we like it, I'll get another for your back door. Or garage. You can still connect with the security company about an alarm system inside if you want."

"We can play it by ear."

"Yeah, that's what I thought." He leaned back and crossed his feet. "Okay—shoot, girl! What's your news?"

Leah smiled, folding her hands in her lap. "All right—here goes! Tonight's top story is that Leah Labanora is no longer stiff-arming God, as you put it so eloquently last night. I've surrendered, Danny! Fully and completely!"

Danny grinned, raising an arm to give her a high five. "Best news ever!"

"Yeah. I guess miracles can happen, huh? A week ago this was not on my radar—nor were *you* on my radar!" She waggled her head in disbelief. "I'm honestly *relieved* to be back, and I'm absolutely humbled by God's forgiveness. Let me tell you—I certainly don't deserve it!"

"I couldn't be happier!" With a broad smile he tipped his head back on his chair and closed his eyes, as if sending up a silent prayer. "Tell me how it came about."

Kyla stared into the fire. "Well, it was a combination of things. Our talk last night really made me think. And then reading my grandma's journal—some of her mentor's advice was what I needed to hear. And then Kyla's study and several things Brother Warren said. And talking to you."

"I'm happy to be a part of it."

"So that's not all that happened today, but can I just say two things before I go on to tell you my next news?"

He looked at her expectantly.

"I've made a couple of very personal decisions today, and I want to tell someone to make them official. So first off, I want to say out loud that I'm even willing to forgive Jake and Rachel. Mind you, I said *willing*, because I'm not entirely there yet." As she spoke, a lump formed in her throat, and she had to pause.

He nodded. "I hear you, Leah. That's a huge step. I understand it's hard, but I think God is pleased by your willingness."

"And the other thing—" She covered her face with her hands. "This is a little embarrassing!"

"What is?"

She faced him squarely. "Okay, I was supposed to go on that date tonight—remember? It got cancelled in a way that was out of my control, and I think it was a God thing."

"Okay—?"

"Well, in my grandma's journal, her mentor talked about not being 'unequally yoked' in relationships. She said it's only an invitation to pain. I'm kinda thinking it would be smart for me to take her advice."

"That sounds like wisdom."

"Right. But I don't want to be single forever, so if you know any guys you trust, I wouldn't mind if you set me up with one of them."

Danny blinked in surprise. "Set you up? Why would you ask me to do that?"

"Because I don't want to be old and without anyone."

He laughed. "You're not that old!"

"You know what I mean! I don't know anybody, and I have no idea of how I'd find someone."

"I wouldn't worry about that."

Leah threw him a look. "That's easy to say, but look at *you*—you're almost thirty!"

He winced. "Ouch! You keep rubbing that in!"

She flashed an impish smile. "Well, you know me better than anyone, Danny! I would totally trust your judgment! Besides, my grandparents met on a blind date, and it seemed to work for them."

"Yeah?" He eyed her thoughtfully. "Well, I'm flattered that you trust me, but I think I'd defer that responsibility to Brother Warren."

"Brother Warren? Why him? He hardly knows me!"

Danny shrugged. "He's a pretty good judge of character. I'll let him know you're looking. Better yet, just pray and trust the Lord. He's the perfect matchmaker. So anyway, what else happened today?"

Leah leaned forward in her chair. "Okay—are you sitting down?"

Danny folded his arms and leaned back. "Let me have it!"

From there Leah gave him the play by play of what happened with her dad—every detail, including her time with Brother Warren after her time in the climbing tree. She was surprised at his initial reaction, which was to shed some tears himself. Then he shook his head in amazement, wonderfully excited for her. That led to her sharing all about Kyla's morning Bible study too, followed by the dog incident, and then the girls coming over to paint her bedrooms with her in the afternoon, which led her to also share what Kyla had discovered about Brindle and Phil Crawford afterward.

"And the worst part of it—it might have even been him who kicked Angel, because in Kyla's photo he had on a T-shirt that could possibly be construed as red! Maybe." She frowned. "Which completely floors me because he was so nice! Seriously, he was so nice that I can't help but doubt that it could be him. Plus, he works until three. But still, it's a possibility—it *could* have been him."

"That is—interesting," he said thoughtfully.

The fire popped and sizzled, and they were quiet for a moment, watching it. It was nearly dark, and Leah noticed the bats circling above.

She sighed. "I guess I'm starting to wonder about Phil Crawford. He told me he lived on Forrester Street, and there's no such street over there. But I saw his truck at a townhouse, which I'll bet is where Brindle lives—whom, incidentally, he led me to believe he didn't know. But I really wonder now."

"Have you ever considered that *he* might be the one coming in your house?"

"It's crossed my mind—yes. But look—he's been super helpful to me. He fixed my mailbox the first time, helped me set up my porch, offered to help with my kitchen—all that. Plus, I was under the impression that he *liked* me—he asked me out, for heaven's sake! I thought there was something there! I don't know why he'd do that if he was sneaking into my house after something. Unless he's some kind of—you know—serial killer or something."

Danny choked, jerking forward in his chair. "Whoa, Leah—that's a little extreme!"

"I'm just pointing out that it's not likely him! I had no idea that Brindle had pegged him for herself, and it was a little awkward getting caught between the two!"

"No doubt. I'd still be cautious, though—with both of them."

"Of course." She nodded, then threw him a smirk. "Incidentally, my dad didn't think Phil's construction ideas were very smart either—although Dad was nicer about it than you!"

They laughed together, then fell into another natural silence, their eyes lingering on the fire.

"So regarding Brindle," Leah began after a bit, "another interesting thing happened today. During Bible study she kinda spilled some hints of some major hurts in her life. I felt sad for her. I think she's hurting and genuinely looking for a friend. She just has some, you know, issues. And who doesn't?" She glanced teasingly at him. "Except maybe *you!*"

He lifted his hands. "What can I say? It's hard to beat perfection! Lucky *you* for knowing me!"

Again they laughed.

"Anyway, my heart goes out to her. She's quirky and moody as heck, but I kinda like her."

Danny simply nodded.

The subject then turned and meandered through a dozen different topics of mutual interest, punctuated with laughter and thoughtful lulls, as happens when friends converse around a fire. Leah lost all awareness of time, but after a while she shivered and mentioned that the air felt damp. Danny rose, indicating that he should put his laptop inside.

"I suppose we should call it a night. I have a lot to do in the next couple days. Brother Warren and I are leaving town for a conference on Thursday."

"You're not going to sing?"

He looked up in surprise.

"I can hear you from my house, and I like it. You have a great voice! And it's been meaningful to me."

"Is that right?"

"Well, *now* it is. It was highly annoying at first. I even bought a fan for white noise! But that was so *last week!*"

Danny guffawed. "Yeah, so *yesterday!*"

"Right! So get your guitar! We're out here in the open where everyone can see us, and we're not breaking any of your rigid principles." She gestured to the fire.

He gave another hearty laugh. "All right, here—help me carry this stuff in." He handed her his laptop with the papers piled on top. "I'll get the rest and fetch my guitar."

"Thanks." She smiled. "Grab me a sweatshirt too."

In the flickering firelight Leah watched him tune his instrument as he strummed a few odd chords, tuned it again, and got situated in his chair. But when he began to sing, her focus drifted from him. She stared into the flames, breathing in the sweet smokiness, contemplating her day and God's overwhelming kindness toward her. With her heart she took hold of the music, turning it upward to God in genuine thanksgiving. It was the first time she had worshiped—truly worshiped—in a long, long time. Her heart felt clean. Clean, full, and contented.

Leaning her head back on her chair, she closed her eyes and simply relished the moment. The barricade of boards was removed, her heart's door opened wide again. God was there, fully welcomed in. Remembering Brother Warren's words, she thought about Jesus and the angels celebrating her return. For all her wandering, he had not cast her off or rejected her but had cleansed her and drawn her to him in love. She wanted to linger in that place forever.

But eventually the music stopped. She opened her eyes to find Danny watching her.

"It's time," he said simply.

She nodded, and he walked her up to the house.

On the deck she paused. "Danny, can I tell you something? I feel terrible about your mom. She didn't deserve how I treated her. And your dad too."

He took his time responding. "It was hard on everyone, Leah. They knew how devastated you were. They knew it wasn't about them."

"Well, it scares me to even say it, but I think I'd like to see them again. Especially your mom." She found herself blinking back tears.

Danny was silent.

"I'd just be nervous of what they'd say. I can't imagine what they must think of me!"

"I already know the answer to that—they'd be thrilled to see you! But don't take that on tonight. God will bring it about at the right time."

She took a breath. "Yeah. You're probably right."

Through the patio door they noticed Brother Warren arrive at the kitchen sink to fill a glass of water. Danny slid open the door for her.

Brother Warren turned, lifting his glass to greet them. "Hello there! Good evening, lassie! How's my favorite girl? Mr. DeSoto, did you hear what happened to this young lady today? She's had a monumental day!"

Leah smiled. She wanted to hug him.

"I did!" Danny replied, latching the door behind them. "It's pretty awesome!"

"Get some rest now, my dear," the old man told her. "You've done a lot of work today in your soul."

She nodded. "I'm about to. I'm very tired. Thank you for all your"—
she searched for the words—"for all your wisdom and help. I don't even
know how to say it. Thanks for listening to me. And for letting me stay
here."

"You're more than welcome!" His eyes shone, and Leah felt every
ounce of his sincerity.

She looked back. "Good night, Danny."

He tipped his head. "Good night, Leah."

Then he turned to Brother Warren. "All right—shall we see about
that foot? Sorry I'm late."

Leah went to her room and stood in the middle of the floor. Her heart
felt so full, like it had expanded to double its size. How would she be able
to sleep with all that was bursting within her? But she washed her face,
donned her pajamas, and slid beneath the comforter.

Leah.

She hugged her pillow and pulled the blanket up around her shoulders.

I'm watching over you. I'll never leave you, never forsake you.

Where she lay it was as though she could still hear Brother Warren's
voice in her head. Only it sounded as if the words were from God—as if
God were speaking to her like a father. And not just a father, but as God, *her*
Father. She could feel the warmth of his love covering her, almost pulsing
around her, and she snuggled more tightly in the blankets, enjoying the feel
of it. How could it be that in one day something she had only known before
as a concept had now become a reality? It was as though she had tasted
something real—though *barely* tasted it—and it made her hunger for more
of him.

I am with you. I'll never leave you.

She couldn't help but think about her dad, who'd left her both
physically and emotionally in life. She had gotten entirely used to living
without him. And in an odd way, it was almost as if the reconnection with
her dad that morning had been a precursor to experiencing this new deluge
of God's love. Or like the key that had opened her up somehow. As if her
forgiveness and acceptance of the gross failure of her earthly dad had swung
wide the door for something greater to flow in.

Who would have thought when she took that first little step to phone
him that the results would be beyond her imagination—that he'd come to
see her face to face out of desire to mend their relationship? She never
would have dreamed she'd stand on her porch weeping in his arms. Her dad
had failed her beyond what she had allowed herself to acknowledge. And

yet if an imperfect man who had given most of his life to work, isolation, and booze could change and pursue her, how much more could a perfect God? If a flawed and broken vessel still had love to give, how much more an immense God without any flaws?

I'll never fail you.

Leah readjusted her pillow. It was almost as though she could hear God say that he'd never fail her as a father. She was still trying to wrap her mind around that, for it was entirely unlike her own dad. Their initial talk had been a breakthrough certainly, but Leah knew the dad she'd be getting to know wouldn't be perfect. He was off to a good start—especially being sober now—but he was coming from behind. Doubtless there were issues and faulty mentalities that had kept him in his addiction for years. Those patterns didn't go away overnight. Until now the whole of her relationship with him had been dealing with truckloads of broken promises and disappointments until she'd taught herself to stop caring altogether. She'd have to learn to care again. And she'd have to learn how to handle his mistakes. How would it be different this time?

I'm your Father. I'll never leave you. I'll never fail you.

What did it even mean when God said he wouldn't fail her? All she knew for sure is that he wasn't going to quit on her. He wasn't going to stop being her father if she made a mistake. He wasn't going to stop caring for her or parenting her in his perfect God-way of being a father, and for that she was glad. And knowing God wasn't going to fail her would help her if—more like *when*—her father made mistakes.

She yawned, feeling sleepy in the soft covers. Yes, God would help her. She could trust that God as a father trumped her earthly dad's efforts. The enormous, holy God who created the universe—this God truly cared about her and wanted to be her Father far more than her earthly dad was capable of. He wanted to pour his love out on her. To draw her near to him in an invisible embrace that was as real as her earthly father's arms around her. It was beyond her ability to understand. Why would a God so great pursue an awful sinner like her? Exhausted from an emotional day, Leah drifted off to sleep.

Chapter Twenty-Three

Having slept on an air mattress for the last week, Leah was reluctant to budge from the divinely comfortable bed in the Glendes' guest room the next morning, except that she remembered her plan to surprise Danny on his run that morning. Hurriedly she threw on her shorts and T-shirt, opening her bedroom door to the tantalizing waft of freshly baked biscuits and brewed coffee. Brother Warren sat in an armchair in the corner of the living room quietly reading his Bible, while Jackie bustled about the sunny kitchen cooking breakfast with Angel's adoring gaze fixed on her from his padded bed.

The woman greeted her cheerfully as she whisked the eggs. "Good morning, hon! Perfect timing! Dan just got back from his run and went to shower. By the time these eggs are done we'll be ready to sit down. Are you okay with scrambled eggs and sausage?"

Leah eyed the amount of food with alarm. "You're not making a special breakfast on account of me, are you?"

"No, no—this is our daily routine!"

Leah nodded in relief, casting a brief glance outside toward the cottage. "In that case—yes, that sounds perfect!"

"Good. Help yourself to coffee." She gestured with her elbow.

Leah poured herself a cup and brought it to the dining room table, which was set and ready for their meal.

"How's Angel?" she asked, noting the dog's ears twitch at his name.

"Spoiled rotten!" Brother Warren piped up from behind her as he hobbled across the room to join them. "That little dog gets more attention from Jackie than I gave all of my eleven children combined!"

"Oh, go on!" Jackie protested over her shoulder. Then she laughed. "You know, Dad, that could make you sound like a terrible father!"

Brother Warren gave an amused chuckle.

"And to answer your question, Leah, he's doing fine. This morning he has a bit more pep. He'll be himself in no time."

"I'm so relieved!" Leah responded.

"We raised eleven kids here," Brother Warren said, setting his half-filled coffee mug beside his plate. "Jackie is my youngest."

"Not *here*, Dad," Jackie corrected. "You and Mom didn't move to this house until all us kids were gone."

"Yeah, yeah—I meant here in New Hampton."

Jackie threw a glance at Leah. "He loves to boast about raising such a large family."

Leah raised her brow. "That's a lot of kids! That's not very common. Sounds like a ton of work to me!"

Jackie raised her spatula. "Oh, yes! My mom was one busy lady!"

"Oh, she bragged about it too," Brother Warren said. "It was a lot of work and a lot of fun." He smiled at Leah. "Were you comfortable last night, dear?"

"Very," she answered. "Thanks again for letting me stay."

"Oh, look—here's Dan already!" Jackie announced as Danny slid open the patio door.

He was freshly showered, his cheeks still flushed from his run. Jackie slipped a spoon into a bowl of fruit and held it out to him as he passed the kitchen island on his way to the dining room. He set it on the table, nodding his greeting.

"'Morning, Leah. Did you sleep well?"

"Like a rock." Leah decided she liked his beard. It fit him well. He looked smart and healthy. Even handsome.

Jackie followed with a jar of salsa and a plate of biscuits. "Dan, I don't know what we're going to do around here when you go back to school!" She glanced at Leah on her way back to check the eggs. "He's been worth his weight in gold this summer! There's no way I can do all that needs to be done around here."

"We'll find someone else," Brother Warren said.

"Well, I don't know who we could get! It's hard to find someone who doesn't already have a full-time job. I simply can't keep up with the yard anymore. Or that pool—"

"Oh, there'll be someone," Brother Warren assured her.

Danny took a chunk of napkins from the holder in the center of the table and handed them around. "No sense in worrying, folks. I'm not gone yet. We still have a good six weeks."

With a sigh Jackie set the eggs and sausage on the table and slipped onto her chair. "That's still too soon. Dad, would you bless the food?"

Brother Warren gave thanks, and Jackie began passing the dishes around.

"So what do you have planned for today, Miss Leah?" Brother Warren asked.

"I'll probably finish painting," she replied. "Although if there's anything I could do for you, Jackie, I'd be happy to lend a hand."

Jackie looked up from her plate. "Oh, heavens—I hope you didn't think I was hinting! No, no, no—we're fine, hon! I'm just anticipating pool maintenance after Dan leaves."

"I'll have my boot off by then," Brother Warren said.

Jackie scowled. "*No*, Dad—you're not going to be—" She huffed and shook her head, throwing a look at Leah. "You can't reason with him! He doesn't listen! This spring I came home to find him up on a ladder cleaning out the rain gutters—by himself!" She turned back to her father. "Part of the reason we need someone here is to keep an eye on *you*!"

Brother Warren laughed, turning to Leah. "She exaggerates! What are you painting, sweetheart?"

Leah spread a layer of jam across her biscuit. "A hallway and bedroom. But Jackie mentioned caring for the yard, and I have yet to conquer mine. If it's nice out, I might devote part of my day to that."

"No!" Jackie and Danny stated at the exact same time.

Leah straightened, looking at them in surprise.

Jackie shot a look at Danny. "Didn't you tell her?"

"Kyla said she'd take care of it," he replied.

Leah looked from one to the other. "Tell me what?" At their silence she added, "She asked me yesterday if I was available this evening. Does that have anything to do with it?"

"Don't work on your yard," Jackie said simply.

Leah looked at Danny, who smiled and turned back to his plate. She set her biscuit down. "All right—what's going on?"

The three were silent. Leah folded her arms and sat back.

Brother Warren chuckled. "You'll have to tell her *something*!"

Danny paused with his sausage-loaded fork in hand. "A few of us would like to come over and help you with your yard tonight."

Leah cocked her head. "A few of us?"

"Well, *us*. And Peter and Kyla. And some others."

She stared.

Jackie placed her hand on Leah's arm. "It's sort of like a housewarming. It's our way to bless you and say welcome to the neighborhood."

Leah shook her head. "My yard is—it's *so* bad! Really bad! I'd be embarrassed! And I'd hate to have anyone in the house. It's so—oh, man, it needs so much work!"

"Nonsense, dear," Jackie said, giving her a pat.

"Our small group does things like this periodically," Danny added. "But don't worry—it's just us."

Leah crinkled her forehead at him. "Was this your idea?"

He shook his head. "Wish it were! It was Peter's actually. He brought it up the night of the party when we were cleaning up."

Leah held his eyes for a moment. The night of the party—when she had insulted Peter by insinuating that he'd murdered someone. She covered her face. "Now I feel even worse!"

"Just receive the blessing," Brother Warren said. "You'll have your opportunity to pass it on soon enough."

Danny nodded in agreement. "Peter's bringing by a trailer with some equipment around noon today. He'd like to park it in your yard." He took his bite. "Just letting you know."

Leah protested, "I'll die of embarrassment!"

Brother Warren tapped the side of his head. "Perspective, Leah! What a shame to feel embarrassed when you could feel so loved—as you are!"

She looked down, not knowing how to respond.

Jackie dished a spoonful of fruit onto her plate and turned to Leah. "I wanted to tell you I'll be at my sister's for lunch today and part of the afternoon. Do make yourself at home here. Help yourself to food—whatever. The guys will be around. And Kyla will probably bring the boys to swim. She typically does on Wednesday afternoons."

Leah nodded. "Thank you."

"If I were you, I'd take the afternoon off and get in the pool yourself. It's supposed to be a nice day!"

"Maybe I'll paint this morning then."

Danny paused with his coffee mug near his mouth. "Let me know when you're going over. I'll go with you to check things over. Just to be sure that there's nothing—you know." He shrugged.

"Okay—thanks." She gave a reflective sigh. "I just don't understand why all this stuff is happening! I didn't think I had any enemies!"

Brother Warren clicked his tongue, and Leah looked at him. He had that look on his face again. She tipped her head questioningly, and he smiled.

"Do you have something to tell me?" she asked.

"Nothing new. Only a reminder that Jesus will never fail you."

Leah gave a nervous laugh. "Uh, something about that kinda scares me!"

"Why? Your safest place is with him."

Jackie set her hands on the table. "Dad! Now you're scaring *me*! I don't think you should be saying things like that!"

Brother Warren gestured innocently. "I don't mean to scare anybody! God intends for her to feel secure!"

She looked at him sternly. "Yes, but the way you go about it!"

"How was that scary? It's true—it's only with him that we're safe!"

"But the way you say it insinuates something bad is going to happen! You could say it in a way that doesn't sound so foreboding!"

Danny winked at Leah from across the table, and Leah smiled, glad he was there.

After breakfast Leah tidied the kitchen with Jackie while Danny helped Brother Warren get ready for the day. Then Danny left to do other chores around the yard.

"This might be a nice time to read your Bible," he suggested on the deck. "Before we go over to your house. It's good to give God the first part of your day."

His comments annoyed her, even if she did agree. "What about *you*?" she jabbed back, but his expression told her he'd already accomplished that for the day. She frowned. "What time do you get up?"

He smiled. "Early. I'll meet you here when I finish taking care of a few things. Should only be an hour or so."

Leah retrieved her borrowed Bible from her room and cozied herself on the deck swing. After brushing her hand across the faux leather cover with its nubby floral embossing, she opened it, reading the name "Samantha Gordon" in the upper right corner. Jackie's niece. Bravely she flipped to the middle and began to read in the Psalms, taking her time to savor the verses that today seemed alive with meaning. She paused, looking unseeing across the yard. How had she convinced herself she didn't need this for so many years? Even now she knew her soul was sick, having been spiritually starved. It was going to take some time to recover, but today was a starting point. Making herself comfortable, she turned to the New Testament and began reading the gospel of Matthew.

After a healthy space of time, she went in for a quick shower—in wonderful, crystal-clear water, which gave her hope for her own. Then she scooped up the next of her grandmother's journals on her way out to wait for Danny on the deck. She had no sooner gotten settled in the swing again when she realized she had grabbed the wrong one. What she had thought was Journal 2 turned out to be Journal 21–her grandmother's final volume. Apparently she had taken from the wrong end of the purple tote when leaving her house last evening, inadvertently taking the last two instead of Journals 3 and 4. The morning was so pleasant, however, and the swing so comfortable, Leah didn't want to move. She opted to stay put rather than go switch them out. Though vastly out of order, Journal 21 would have to suffice.

Danny's tasks took longer than expected, but eventually he joined Leah on the deck, hauling with him a large box of miscellaneous items left over from the party. He shoved it in a corner of the deck to deal with later.

"Sorry to make you wait," he said. He was standing with the sun behind him.

Leah squinted up. "I'm in no hurry. I'm enjoying another one of my grandma's journals. Her final one, actually—at least of the ones we found. She even mentions me in it." She closed the book, holding her place with her thumb.

"Let me guess—you were getting into trouble, right?"

"Now why would you think that?" She laughed. "I just read about her 'concerns' for me as a teenager. She thought I was heading in the wrong direction, and boy, was she right! She wrote that she was praying for me but was encouraged because I had just agreed to go to Bible camp."

Danny's brow went up. "For real? Well, how about that! That's where our lives intersected! Think about it—we might not have met if she hadn't prayed for you!"

"True—although it would have been okay with me if that had never happened."

He shot her a look.

"I meant that about Jake, not you."

"Ah, I see. So, what else have you learned?"

She gave the swing a tiny push. "Well, something I didn't know was that my Grandpa Ed was an avid coin collector."

"Yeah? That's cool. Like rare coins?"

Leah frowned. "I'm not sure what they were, really, whether they were old or rare or what. But he bought a lot of them—like, a *lot*! I was reading about it just now. They're called kurigrans or something. Um, kugger—" She held the journal up with her finger on the page, spelling it: "K-r-u-g-e-r-r-a-n-d-s."

"Krugerrands," Danny said, leaning over to read it.

"Yeah, that—whatever those are."

"Gold coins. From South Africa, I believe." He pulled out his phone to do a quick search and held it out for her to see. "'Krugerrand—a South African gold coin.' Says they were first minted in 1967 but got popular in the late seventies and early eighties."

Leah let the journal drop to her lap. "Well, there you go! According to my grandmother he was buying them left and right."

Danny continued reading his phone. "Hah!" He gave an exclamation, holding the phone out to her again. "Check this out—look at their current value!"

"Whoa! That's four figures!"

Danny gave a wide-eyed nod. "That's for *one* of them! Leah, your grandfather wasn't a coin collector, he was buying gold—as an investment!"

"Really? Do you think so?"

"That'd be my guess!"

She let out a breath. "Oh, geez! I wonder who got all those? Probably Uncle Richard since I've heard nothing about them. I had no clue my grandparents had so much money. I can't relate!"

He laughed. "Right!"

"I mean, they drove modest cars—everything! Their lifestyle was so unpretentious—just look at that house over there!" She waved her arm, looking up at him. "I had no clue!" She paused with an amused smile. "I never gave much thought to the fact that they owned *three* homes!"

"That might be above average." He returned his phone to his pocket.

She sighed. "I've been stressing all morning thinking about people coming over to my ghetto house tonight, but I guess I shouldn't complain. My grandparents' lives were not about their money, and I guess mine shouldn't be either—even if I don't have much. Although that's not exactly true. I have a house that's been given to me free and clear with a renovation fund besides. I have it pretty good, even if it's in its raw, unfinished form."

"Good point. You've been here how long—a week? Enjoy this, Leah! Enjoy the process. How many people get to do this with someone else's money?"

"I know. I'm just trying not to think about when the money runs out."

"Then you live like the rest of us!" He gestured toward the hedge. "Come on—I'll walk through the house with you, and then I need to get to work on my writing project—er, Brother Warren's writing project."

Leah swung her legs down, and he pulled her to her feet. Then he leaned down to pick up a piece of paper that had slipped out of her journal. As he handed it back to her, he stopped and frowned, unfolding the sheet to study it more closely. His head went back.

"Holy cow—you're not kidding! He *did* buy a lot of them!"

Leah leaned in to look, discovering that the paper was a detailed list of the coins her grandfather had acquired with invoice numbers and dates that they had been purchased.

"Good heavens—look at this!" Danny said in amazement. "There must be easily three hundred coins listed here! More, surely!"

"What? Oh, wow!" She read over his arm, waggling her head in wonder. "See what I mean?"

"And look at this—" Danny pointed at her grandmother's handwriting at the bottom of the page.

"'These are the coins in the cellar safe,'" she read, noting a numerical combination below it. She frowned, looking up at him.

"Did your grandparents keep a safe in their cellar? That's what it sounds like, although I'm sure the coins wouldn't be there now. They would have taken care of that long before they moved."

Leah's hands flew to her cheeks. "Oh, my gosh, Danny! Maybe they're still there!"

"I wouldn't think so." He shook his head skeptically.

"No—" She grabbed the paper from him and stared at it. Could this be what her grandparents had left her? "We need to go over to the house right now! I have a letter that I was given at the lawyer's office—it was part of the will. It says there are other valuables that come with the house!"

"Valuables?"

"Well, I'm not sure what they are, but *this* could be what she's talking about!"

"I'd highly doubt they'd leave coins worth that much lying around."

She folded the paper and tucked it back into the journal. "Well, I want you to read the letter." She poked his chest with her finger. "Come with me, mister!"

He grinned. "Let's go!"

They cut through the arborvitae near the front of the house, where Danny was proud to show her that he had trimmed back the branches to make a neater part in the hedge. Though distracted, Leah thanked him politely as she hustled through it and across her yard to her house. Once inside, she knelt beside her bed, rummaging through her belongings until she finally produced a large manila envelope.

"It's in here!" she said breathlessly.

She plopped it on the peninsula and pulled out a stack of papers from within. On top was the smaller white business-sized envelope she was searching for.

"This!" she said removing its contents. "Okay, so Grandma mentioned things that they left here at the farm—like tools and canning stuff, farm photos. But listen to this—" She unfolded the letter and read out loud, "'Also with the house I leave my story which lies within my journals, since most of the reconstruction of my heart happened there—a treasure you may think trivial, but I assure you where it takes you will be worth your while and will offset any disappointment you may have about inheriting the house. To be upfront with you, Ed and I have left some other valuables here at the Richmond house specifically for you! We're not trying to be unfair to other family members but rather kind to the ones who invest themselves to seek them out. It's our feeble attempt to illustrate that treasures can be found in the most unlikely of places—even the Richmond house. I've spelled it out plainly in one of the journals, listing out—'" She stopped, looking up at Danny, who was listening carefully.

"Go on," he urged.

"That's where it ends!"

He took the paper to read it himself, flipping to the blank side when finished. "Where's the rest of it?"

"That's all I got!"

"But it doesn't say what it is! It could be anything!"

"Well, yes, but with the list we just found—and it was in the journal—!" Leah jerked her head to make her point.

Danny smiled, handing it back, and she smiled in return.

"I suppose it's possible!"

"Possible? I mean—what else?"

"There's only one way to find out. Let's take a look in the cellar!"

"Yes!" Then she gasped. "Oh, my gosh, Danny! What if—what if all this weird stuff going on is about this?" She waved the letter.

He raised his brow. "Interesting thought! Remember the big kettle thing that was moved—? Do you think someone else could be looking for those coins?"

Leah glanced toward the basement door. "I wonder! I mean—the rug—it was moved twice, like someone went down there. It could be! I mean—what if?"

"Yeah, what if? Who all got this letter?"

"Just me. It came in a sealed envelope as part of the paperwork for whoever got the house." Her forehead creased in thought. "How would anyone else know about this? Unless—" She met Danny's eyes. "Unless Marty knew Grandpa was investing in gold."

Danny nodded at the idea. "That could be. But remember what he said? He's had access to this place for years. Why would he all of a sudden—"

"—Because he didn't know where they were! And then when he took the stuff from my garage the night of the party, he discovered the journals! He found that list of Krugerrands!"

"Then threw the journals in the trash?" Danny shook his head. "No. I think he tossed those journals out 'cause he couldn't care less about them. If he'd found that sheet about the Krugerrands, he never would have put it back in there before he threw it away. No way. I doubt he even *looked* at any of those."

Leah held her chin, thinking. "You're probably right. Something about this doesn't make sense. The rug was disturbed the same night he took all the stuff from the garage. He wouldn't have even found the journals at that point. Plus, the mailbox thing—how would it even relate?"

"Right!"

She sighed. "Well to begin with, let's go see if there's a safe downstairs in the cellar."

"Or if there *was* a safe. I didn't notice anything down there before."

"Yeah, I had the same thought. It could be long gone. This letter was dated a while ago. Who knows—my grandparents might have changed their minds and cashed it all in already. Maybe they forgot about the sheet in the journal."

Danny caught her arm. "Before we go down, let's do a quick walk-through. Just in case."

"Yeah," she agreed, thankful for the suggestion. He was great like that—careful and protective. Plus, she was happy to show him the newly painted bedrooms.

Sufficiently satisfied no one had been there since she'd left the house the previous evening, they moved on toward the basement. Danny opened the door.

"After you, my dear."

Leah shook her head. "I'll follow this time if you don't mind." As he started down, she added, "I hope you know how much I appreciate this—your coming over here and everything. You certainly wouldn't have to do this."

"It's no problem."

"Well, I'm grateful. Yesterday Jackie mentioned what a great guy you are, and I completely agree. I only hope to find someone as nice as you someday. It's my dream!"

He threw a startled look over his shoulder. "Er—thanks!"

There was no safe in the cellar, however. Nor was there evidence of there ever having been a safe in the cellar. The two of them moved items around on the shelves to examine the walls for any sign of a concealed area or an area that had been mudded in, but there was nothing. They even checked the furnace room next door, searching the room to the corners, but no coins or safe were to be found anywhere.

"They're gone," Leah said in resignation. "We were right—either Grandpa and Grandma moved them or cashed them in. Or Marty found them first."

"Eh, I highly doubt Marty found them," Danny remarked. "At least recently anyway. Sounds like the guy's swimming in debt! He's selling Christmas decor online, for heaven's sake! For a guy that's a little humiliating! I think you're right. They must have moved them—perhaps to a bank. Didn't you say that they rented the place out?"

"Yes—maybe a renter found them!"

"Sure. But then there'd be an empty safe."

"True." Leah nodded.

"No other family members saw your letter? Father, mother, brother—?"

She shook her head. "If Mom had known about this, she would have rushed up here immediately. Possibly Uncle Richard—maybe he knew about the coins somehow and came to get them right after the accident. Or years ago, for that matter—but then again, as you say, the safe would still be here." She heaved a sigh.

"Well, I'm sorry about your inheritance. It would've been a blast to find those coins. I know it must be disappointing."

Leah shrugged. "I'm okay. Earlier today I was simply trying to be grateful for a house, fixer-upper or not. So I guess I'm back to square one. It's about what I *have*, not what I *don't* have."

He bumped her fist with his. "*A* for attitude right there! But that still doesn't explain why someone's been sneaking into your house or vandalizing your mailbox."

"Right. Or why someone was trying to get in my back door and kicked little Angel!"

Danny chewed his lip as they fell silent.

"You know what?" he said finally. "You should lock up and spend the day next door. I don't feel comfortable with you here. Kyla Watkins will most likely be over this afternoon, and you can hang out with her by the pool. In the meantime, we'll pray that whatever's going on will be exposed and brought to light!"

Weary of the drama, Leah didn't protest. "Sounds good—although for the record, I haven't had any problems inside since I've had the house rekeyed. But I'm not going to argue with you! Let me grab a few more things upstairs."

"And I wouldn't worry about your house, Leah. We'll help you with your yard tonight. And maybe next week I can help you inside."

"Yeah. And Dad's coming this weekend. Maybe Chelsea too. I know it'll be okay."

"It will." He nodded. "They can stay in my cabin. I'll get it ready for them."

Leah frowned. "Your cabin? Where will *you* be?"

"Cantonville. I told you. We're leaving tomorrow—remember? Brother Warren's speaking at a conference there."

She blinked. "Tomorrow? What'll I do over there all alone?"

"What do you mean? You said your dad was coming. And Jackie's around. You won't be alone."

"I know." Leah agreed reluctantly. "But *you* won't be there. When will you get back?"

"Sunday late afternoon."

"Then you won't even be here when my dad is here."

Danny tipped his head. "Did you *want* me to be?"

"I think it'd be a lot different than the last time you saw him!" She smiled.

His brow shot up. "I have no doubt about that! Come on—let's go upstairs! You can collect anything else you want to bring next door." He gestured for her to go ahead of him.

Chapter Twenty-Four

Kyla and the boys arrived at Jackie's shortly before noon. Leah had just applied the topcoat to her fresh pedicure out on the deck when Howie appeared around the side of the house lugging an enormous blue-and-white striped canvas bag over his shoulder. Behind him walked Hank with a colorful life jacket hooked on each arm, their straps dangling and dragging on the ground. Seeing Leah, he paused, eyeing her guardedly.

"Keep moving, Hank," came Kyla's voice from behind him. "Howie, set that up on a chair so our stuff doesn't get wet!"

"Hi, guys!" Leah called.

"Hi!" Kyla responded, finally stepping around Hank, her arms loaded with a jumbo-sized pizza, a four-cup beverage tote hanging on one side, and a plastic grocery bag hanging down on the other. "Lunchtime!"

"Nice! Thanks! Let me help you!" Leah hurried to take the pizza.

"Bribery," Kyla said under her breath. "Neither of them wanted to come today because of—you know—*yesterday*."

"I'm sorry."

"No—no one's blaming you!" Kyla exclaimed, following her up the stairs and setting the drinks onto the table. "But I was able to persuade them with pizza and ice cream sandwiches and promising to play with them in the pool."

Hank trailed Kyla onto the deck, standing closely behind her. She snatched the life jackets and tossed them onto the swing.

"Thanks, bud. Have a seat at the table, please, and I'll get you your pizza!" She grabbed the plastic bag. "I'll put these in the freezer and get some paper plates. Do you want your pizza cut up or whole? Howie! Remember we're eating first, before we get in the pool!"

"Whole," Hank murmured quietly, slipping onto a chair while Kyla disappeared inside the house.

Leah smiled at him. "I like pizza too."

He blinked, asking soberly, "Did Angel die?"

The question sucked her breath. She shook her head. "No! The vet says he'll get better soon! He's in Miss Jackie's bedroom taking a nap."

"Can I see him?"

Leah nodded, noting his relief. "Yes, probably—as soon as Miss Jackie comes home."

"Where is she?"

"At her sister's."

"Miss Susan's?"

"Yes," Leah replied, recalling that Jackie's sister was their housekeeper.

"When will she get back?"

"I'm not sure. This afternoon sometime. You'll probably still be here."

Hank's eyes dropped to the pizza box then flicked up again. "Do you have my dump truck?"

"It's in the corner right behind you!" Leah gestured toward its place on the deck. "I've been guarding it."

He turned, giving a hint of a smile as he spied it.

Howie tromped noisily up the deck and slid away the chair next to Hank to reach the lid of the pizza box. "Yes!" He gave a fist pump and turned to Hank. "She got pepperoni!"

Hank uttered a cry of disappointment. "I said *cheese*!"

"You can pick them off." He glanced at Leah. "We brought enough for everyone, but I can eat a lot. I can eat two whole pieces. Sometimes three!"

"So can I!" Hank echoed.

"No, you can't!" his brother corrected. "You can barely eat one! He can only have one."

"Uh-huh! I can have *three*! Miss Kyla says!"

"No, you can't!"

"Uh-huh!"

"It's nice of you to share," Leah broke in. "And I'm sure both of you can eat a lot. You look like you're growing."

Howie drew back his shoulders. "Yep, I know!"

"I am too!" Hank said. "I can ride a two-wheel bike!"

"Can you?" Leah exclaimed.

"But you can't climb the tree yet!" Howie jabbed. He threw a look at

Leah. "Miss Kyla said we can't play in the tree fort today. But I don't want to anyway."

"Oh. Well, that's good, 'cause I wasn't going to let you play there—not 'til they catch the bad guy who hurt Angel. But it appears he's gone away. For one thing, he's certainly not here at Miss Jackie's house!"

"I already know that. Miss Kyla told us."

"Ah, I see!" Leah smiled, admiring the sun-darkened freckles on his nose.

Kyla returned with a short stack of paper plates and two plastic tumblers for the kids. After praying to bless the food, she let them each choose their slice while she split one of the drinks between the smaller cups and set them in front of the boys. The patio door opened, and with a cheery fanfare, Brother Warren joined them, making the little boys giggle by asking each if he were married and by complimenting them on their impressive muscles. The boys adored him, crowding together on the same chair to be near him and jostling for who got to sit the closest, until Kyla moved to the other side of the table to let each boy have his own chair on either side of the old man.

Danny, however, did not join them for lunch. He replied to Leah's inquiring text that he was on a roll with his writing and still had leftover pizza from the previous evening. Leah brought him an ice cream sandwich anyway after they finished eating.

His eyes lit up when he saw her, and he rose from his computer. "Ah, two of my favorite things!"

"Two?" Leah asked, handing him the treat.

"Yeah—ice cream and sandwiches! What did you *think* I was going to say?" He grinned.

She batted him and went to join Kyla poolside where she was drilling the boys with the rules of the pool. Before Leah could sit down, however, Peter showed up, looking for her. He was dressed in his work clothes, his leather gloves hanging out of his back pocket.

"You may have already heard," he said. "I'd like to park some equipment in your yard. Does it matter where I put the trailer?"

Leah could feel herself blushing. "You don't have to do this! I'm so embarrassed for what I said about you the other day—I'm really sorry!"

He shook his head. "Don't worry about it! How could you know? And we're all looking forward to tonight."

"Well, I'm humbled by your kindness. You can park anywhere you'd like."

He kissed his wife and patted her baby bump before he left, and the girls then positioned their deck chairs in the sun. Kyla shed her sundress, exposing her cute maternity swimsuit, and Leah also stripped down to her one piece and made herself comfortable beside her new friend.

"Don't let anyone tell you parenting isn't a real job," Kyla said, shooting a glance at the boys. "Some days these guys are a ton of work!" She rummaged in her bag for a tube of sunscreen and began rubbing lotion on her arms and legs.

"They look like great kids, though."

"Yes, they *are* great kids! They listen to me, so that's good." She finished and handed the tube off to Leah.

"How long have you been their nanny?"

"A little over two years. Initially I was hired for a summer because their mom was away on a long-term job, but they kept me on when she came back. She's typically gone a few months at a time. She's back again now, but she still prefers me to watch them quite a bit."

"What does she do?"

Kyla looked away. "She's, um—involved in movie production."

"What does that mean?"

"She's an—well, her work, um—it varies, actually. And she travels a lot."

"Huh." Leah finished with the sunscreen and handed it back. "I feel like I know her from somewhere. I met her at the party Saturday, and she's super nice." She grabbed her T-shirt to clean a smudge of lotion off her sunglasses.

Kyla nodded. "Yeah, she's great! But pray for her—pray for both her and David, the professor. It's tough for them. They have vastly different lives."

"She said something about that. Their religious differences."

"That'd be an understatement."

"Well, I get that!" Leah held up her glasses to check the lenses. "Seriously, why do I feel like I know her—like we might have met before? It's so weird!"

"Huh."

Leah wadded the T-shirt into a makeshift pillow. "You know what else is crazy? She totally reminds me of that actress in that movie *Galleghent*. Don't you think so? She looks just like her! Have you seen that movie?"

Kyla chuckled.

"What's her name again? Something Montayne. They could be

sisters!"

"You think so?"

"Totally!" She held up a finger. "Marilee—that's it! Marilee Montayne! She looks just like Marilee Montayne!"

"You think so?" Kyla repeated. "Like how?"

"Well, everything! Her voice for one, and her—" Leah glanced over toward Kyla, who had an amused expression on her face. "What? Why are you looking at me like that?"

"Looking at you like what?"

Leah blinked. "Wait—no way! Is that—?"

Kyla simply raised her brow.

Leah threw back her head. "No stinkin' way! Mary Grant is *Marilee Montayne*?" She brought her hand to her face. "Am I an idiot or what?"

Kyla laughed. "She likes to keep a low profile, but word is trickling out!"

Leah shook her head in amazement. "You gotta be kidding me! I sat beside a swimming pool visiting with actress Marilee Montayne! Somebody pinch me!"

Kyla dipped her chin. "And I *work* for her! Double pinch me!"

"Oh, my goodness! What's it like?"

"She's a regular person, Leah. Down to earth and super sweet. And yes, she *does* need your prayers. She's having a tough time right now."

"Right—I'll pray for her!" She laughed again. "Marilee Montayne—I can't believe it! So, tell me—do you two shop at the same jewelry store or something? You both have the most enormous diamond rings I've ever seen! Is that rock real? Sorry if I'm being nosy!"

Kyla laughed. "I don't mind! It's real, but I do have a fake version of it too—for security reasons, depending on where I'm going. And as a matter of fact, Marilee and I both received our rings as gifts from the same person—as rewards for the missing valuables we found in Dr. Grant's house."

Leah's eyes widened. "Yikes! That's some reward! Tell me more!"

She gave a mysterious smile. "Someday I will. But hey—change of subject. I have something to tell you."

"What's that?"

Kyla reached into her bag for her phone. "Okay, so about Phil Crawford. My dad is close friends with a detective in Stanton, and I asked him to do a little research for us."

Leah inclined her head with interest. "Ah, it's about *who* you know!"

"Precisely! So I found out that Phil Crawford's home address is 417 Reed Street in New Hampton."

"So it's true then. How bizarre! He told me he lived on *Forrester.* Ouch!"

"Yeah, ouch."

"I thought maybe he was staying at *her* house—Brindle's. It must be the other way around."

Kyla nodded, looking at her phone. "Apparently. And we don't know where *she* lives—officially. Maybe there. The other thing is that he has a squeaky-clean record. He's single and has lived at his residence for a year. Grew up in New Hampton but lived in Bridgewater a short while before moving back here. Works full time at an appliance manufacturing company." She set the phone down beside her.

"Not cabinetry or woodworking?"

"No. Not to say it's not his hobby, which is possible. Maybe his dad or uncle does cabinetry and he's helped him with projects before."

"Huh." She'd already had her suspicions about Phil, but nevertheless, the news was deflating.

Kyla turned back to watch the boys in the pool.

"How about my cousin Marty?" Leah asked. "Is it possible to find out about him?"

Kyla raised her phone. "It doesn't hurt to ask! Full name please?"

"Martin Edward Davison." Then Leah supplied his address and added that his birthday was sometime in June.

"Okay, we'll see." She sent off the text, then lowered the phone to eye Leah curiously. "Sleuthing on your cousin, huh?"

Leah opened her hands. "Well, there's been a few other things besides the dog incident. Nothing super big. Just weird little things—like someone coming in multiple times when I'm not there, but nothing's missing. And my mailbox being vandalized—you know, like what Peter discovered the other night. Except that it's happened before exactly the same way."

"How strange!"

"I know! It's unnerving!" She fingered the edge of her towel. "Danny ordered a security camera for my porch, and I can hardly wait for it to arrive. I want to see for myself what's going on."

Kyla frowned. "Don't get me wrong, but I can't see your house as a huge attraction for thieves."

"Right! But there's something else." Leah swung her feet to the pool deck to face her. "Danny and I learned something this morning that might factor into this, but you'll have to swear to secrecy."

Kyla raised her right hand. "I swear on a stack of Bibles!"

Candidly Leah shared what they had discovered in the journal about the gold coins, including a synopsis of her grandmother's letter and Danny's and her futile search of her basement.

Kyla turned toward her. "Wait—so do you think whoever's been coming in there has been looking for those coins? What did you call them?"

"Krugerrands." Leah shrugged. "Well, that's what you'd think, wouldn't you, but I don't see how it could be possible. How would anyone know about them? Unless it was—"

"Marty," Kyla said in unison with her. "He's family, and he lives here. That's just logical. But why the mailbox thing? And Angel—"

Leah threw up her hands. "My head hurts trying to figure it out! And meanwhile I feel like my house isn't safe!"

Kyla frowned, her hands resting on her round belly. "What about Brindle?"

"What *about* her?"

"Could *she* be sneaking in to look for those coins?"

Leah shook her head. "How would she possibly know about them? And she was here with us at Bible study yesterday during poor Angel's ordeal. No, I'd highly doubt it. Although granted, she can be a little 'out there' and mysterious. Maybe you should pass her name on to your dad's friend too."

"I already did."

Leah threw her a look. "And?"

"The name comes up unknown."

Leah drew back. "Really? Now isn't that interesting?"

"Yeah, interesting."

As they looked at one another, a boisterous commotion unexpectedly erupted on the far side of the pool. Both girls burst into laughter at the sight of Danny in swimming trunks, snorkeling mask, and flippers suddenly appearing from around the lilac, growling ferociously and wildly flailing his arms as if they were claws. Roaring, he flapped his way across the lawn, the boys shrieking in panic as they scrambled for the pool stairs. At the diving board Danny threw off his accessories, shouting that he was going to gobble up two little boys for a snack. Then he vaulted into the pool with a tremendous cannonball splash.

Kyla giggled with her hand over her face. "Oh, my gosh! Dan is the absolute *best*! They just *love* him!"

Leah watched the boys flee their snarling pursuer, lunging hand over hand along the side of the pool, screaming in anxious delight. "He is," she agreed softly. "I seriously forgot how much fun he is!" She grinned and stood up from the lounge chair.

"Where are you going?" Kyla asked.

"I'm joining them! I'm going to play!"

Kyla leaned back happily and waved her on. "Great! You and Dan can fulfill my end of the bargain with the boys! I'll stay right here in my comfortable chair!"

"Happy to help," Leah said, sloshing into the pool.

Willing laborers started to trickle in at Leah's house shortly after six o'clock, much sooner than she was told they would come. Peter was already there with his pickup truck parked in her driveway when Danny walked her over after dinner. Kyla arrived in her car a few minutes later and began making introductions as people came so that Leah could learn everyone's names.

At first there were about seven people who stood chatting together in a little cluster, but by the time Peter looked at his watch and decided it was time to start, the haphazard group had more than doubled in size. Danny introduced Leah as a dear friend from his past, and she thanked them all for coming. Then Peter briefly let everybody know that the night's objective was to bless Leah by cleaning up her yard and doing anything else she needed done.

From there Peter began handing out assignments. A trio of men trudged off with a chain saw and a lopper to clear out dead brush, starting from the tree line along the highway and working as far back as they could get in a night. Another man offered to mow with Peter's zero-turn mower, and another claimed the weed whip to edge along the house and the hedge. Jackie showed up in bright yellow rubber gloves and a face mask, toting a mechanical grabber and a black trash bag.

"I hear Angel frequents your yard," she said meekly. "I've never paid attention to that—sorry!"

"It's no problem," Leah told her, but she *did* warn her about Midnight's contribution to her yard too, so that Jackie was not surprised.

Then Peter beckoned Leah to the back of his mulch-filled truck, where tucked inside the tailgate were four cardboard boxes overflowing with dug up plants. He explained that one of his crews had inadvertently switched an order, putting in the wrong plants at a job site. The mistaken order was rejected, but Peter requested they salvage the plants rather than throw them out—and would Leah like them?

"This wasn't in my original plan tonight," he said, "but I think I have enough manpower to pull out the loose rock and weeds along the front of your house and come up with something nice-looking. If you're not crazy about these plants, you could always switch them out with something better down the road."

"I'm not picky." Leah said humbly. "Thank you! I can't believe you're doing all this!"

Out of the corner of her eye she saw a movement and looked up to see Marty walking up with work gloves on—Marty! She gaped at him in surprise. The same instant, Peter noticed him and extended his hand.

"Hey—thanks for coming, man! We could really use your help. I'm going to need a partner for this area." Peter removed his hat, indicating the overgrown flower bed, then rubbed his forehead, returning the hat to his head.

Marty gave his assent, his eyes darting to Leah. He dipped his head in greeting.

"Hello, Marty," Leah returned, too shocked to even think of thanking him for coming.

"One second—" Peter raised his arm to hail Danny, who was passing by. "Dan! Hey—can you lend me a hand?" He extracted a roll of plastic from the back seat of his truck. "I need you and Leah to cover everything on the porch with this. I'm going to bring around the skid loader, and it's going to get dusty. When you're finished, you can help me and Marty clear out the front of the house. We're digging all of this out." He motioned with his hand.

"Got it," Danny said.

Leah left to assist him with the plastic, but another man who'd just arrived—who she learned later was Peter's father—stepped in, leaving her standing on the steps without a job.

Kyla approached her with a group of ladies. "Not to invade your house or anything, but we're all looking for something to do. They're wondering if they can paint."

Leah smiled timidly. "Sure. Come on in!"

On the floor right inside the door, Leah discovered two ice cream buckets heaping full of homemade chocolate chip cookies.

"Goodness—where did these come from?" she asked, her mouth

watering.

Kyla cocked an eyebrow. "Don't ask questions!"

Leah showed a few of the ladies what was left to be painted on the bedroom side of the house. Then she had two others start taping off the woodwork in the laundry room to prep that area for painting too.

Kyla offered to work in the living room, so Leah brought her the supplies, partnering with her there. She liked her. The two of them had spent the entire afternoon together at the pool, and, as Danny had predicted, they'd hit it off, enjoying each other's company and finding much in common. Leah had even divulged her whole history with Danny's family to her, sharing honestly about her dark plunge away from God and her fresh desire to come back. Kyla was a sincere and engaged listener, both crying and laughing at times, and asking Leah if they could pray together before she had to dash home to change her clothes for the work night. Now together again, Leah knelt beside her, wiping off dust around the windows.

"Look—Brindle's here!" Kyla said quietly, gesturing through the broad picture window as the burgundy-haired girl walked up the driveway. She watched her for a moment, then crouched to finish taping along the baseboard.

"What's happening?" Brindle asked Leah, stepping inside after navigating around the porch plastic. "I'm on my way home from work but thought I'd stop to find out what Kyla's big secret was yesterday."

Kyla leaned out and waved from where she was working. "Hi!"

"Oh, hi!" Brindle said. "I didn't see you. So what's going on?"

"It's a work night that Peter and Kyla put together for me," Leah said. "They're helping me with my house and yard."

"Who are all these people?"

"Friends of theirs. And new friends of mine, I guess."

"We know each other from church," Kyla explained, now cross-legged on the floor. "Want to join us? We gals are puttering around in here while the guys are out doing the dirty work. Your job could be guarding those cookies so the pregnant lady doesn't snap and devour them all!" She laughed.

Brindle smiled. "They do look tempting! But hey—I can't stay. I've had a long day, and my feet are shot." She turned to Leah, crinkling her brow. "Your cousin's out there!"

Leah nodded. "Yeah!"

"I thought you guys didn't get along. He wouldn't talk to you at the party!"

"I know! Can you believe it? Things are changing, I guess!"

"Huh."

"Pretty great, isn't it?"

"Huh," she repeated, then smiled. "Well, sorry I can't stay, but I'm happy for you. I'm sure the place will look a lot better when they're done out there."

"In here too!" Kyla chimed sweetly.

"Yeah, of course. Anyway, see you later!"

As she turned to leave, the earth shook as the rumbling skid loader suddenly began digging in front of the porch. Leah pushed the door shut.

"Yikes, that's loud! Sorry, Brin! You'll need to go out the back!"

"Sure. Goodbye!" She waved and left through the kitchen.

"See you later, Brindle!" Kyla called.

Leah paused, gazing thoughtfully after her. When she turned, she noticed Kyla watching *her*, and the two exchanged a look.

"You know what I've noticed about her? She always walks here, and I find that odd."

Kyla frowned. "How does she get to work then? She can't be walking all the way to town!"

"Oh, she has a car—it's blue. I saw it the first time we met. But ever since then, she's walked here."

"Huh. Maybe she's getting her steps in. You know—exercise."

"Yeah, that's probably it. She probably has a tough time getting all her steps in—you know, as a waitress. With sore feet."

Their eyes met.

Kyla sighed and held out her hand. "Here—help me up, and I'll tell you something else you probably don't know."

Leah pulled her to her feet. "What?"

"Did you hear? Peter talked to Marty for over an hour this afternoon! Right out in your backyard while we were at the pool!"

"No way! About what?"

She shook her head. "I don't know! He wouldn't say, but it must have been good, because Peter's a busy man—he doesn't give time away like that to just anyone."

"So *that's* why he's here! I about fell over when I saw him!"

Kyla nodded. "Yep. As you said, maybe things are changing. And while we're alone, can I bring up something else?"

"Sure."

"That bed in the other room—" Kyla motioned across the house.

"What about it?"

"Have you ever thought that maybe—like, maybe the reason it's still here is because it's *supposed* to be here?"

"I'm not tracking."

"The coins," Kyla whispered. "Maybe they were hidden in the mattress!"

Leah eyed her skeptically. "Now that's a wild thought! A safe, a mattress—same thing!"

"You know what I mean! It's possible they were removed from the safe and hidden or something. Let's see if Peter and Dan would take it out tonight!"

"They wouldn't want to do that."

"Sure they would! Why wouldn't they?"

"They'll be worn out! These guys have already put in a full day's work before coming here to work on my yard! They'd hate me! 'Hey, want to lug a ginormous, smelly mattress out of my house for me?' Right!" Leah shook her head. "There's no way I'm asking them to do that tonight!"

"Oh, I don't think it'd take much to sway Dan." She raised her brow.

Leah shrugged. "Perhaps. He's always been great like that, but I'd hate to take advantage of him. Let's play it by ear. But aside from that, right now I'm feeling a little guilty for ditching the other ladies who are working away while we're chitchatting out here."

Kyla giggled. "Me too! We'd better go—'cause I'm dying to snitch one of those cookies!"

They both laughed.

Moving toward the hallway, Kyla added, "Okay, how about this—I'll tell the guys you *suggested* moving that mattress out tonight. That way you're not saying that they have to do it, but it'll for sure happen."

"That *I* suggested it? You stinker!"

She spread her hands. "Come on! Aren't you curious? Strategy, Leah! You're not directly asking them. It's just a hint, and it gives them an out. But take my word for it—Dan'll do it for you in a heartbeat!"

"I know! Every one of them out there would. It's embarrassing the way they're all serving me!"

"That's exactly the point, girl! They're *serving* you!" She nodded. "Okay—I'll mention it, and watch—it'll happen!"

Leah gave up. "Fine, go ahead—and I don't doubt it. Now save your baby from these paint fumes and go outside!"

"I believe I will. It's between helping Jackie and picking up brush."

Leah screwed up her nose. "Ugh. I'd choose the brush if I were you. Here—I'll loan you a long-sleeved shirt so you don't get scratched up."

By the end of the evening, Leah's house and yard had been transformed. Inside, the bedrooms, hallway, and laundry room were completely conquered with a fresh layer of paint, with more areas prepared for cutting in. When some of the men had finished their outdoor projects, Danny recommended they remove what they could of the old carpet, and they went gangbusters at it, dragging it out and piling it into the dumpster. Several of Leah's new friends confessed their envy that her house was getting not only a new kitchen but a complete overhaul! Some even volunteered their assistance in removing her bathroom wallpaper when she got to it.

Though still dominated by weeds, her vast lawn was neatly trimmed all the way to the edges of the overgrown arborvitae, a great improvement. The dead branches near the road were cut out and collected in a burn pile, as well as other scraggly brush throughout. And although it had taken the entire evening, Peter, his father, Marty, and Danny had removed all the patio rock and overgrown weeds from along the front of the house and tilled the soil before planting Peter's discarded plants in the ground, along with a few of Leah's they'd been able to salvage. When finished, they blanketed the whole area with a thick layer of rich, dark mulch. Leah was thrilled.

"It's beautiful!" she gushed to Peter, who, though modest, was also pleased with the result.

"You'll need to keep those plants well-watered," he cautioned, wadding up the plastic that had protected her porch furniture. "They've been in the open air in my truck all day, so there's no guarantees on them."

"They'll do fine," Kyla affirmed. "He has to say that, but he's good at what he does. I think they'll fill out nicely, and you're going to love them when they bloom." She had the cookie buckets and was directing everyone to the front of the garage to end the night.

"I already do," Leah replied.

The only negative of the entire evening was that earlier that day when Peter had brought the equipment over on his trailer, he had done a broad U-turn in the backyard and had parked the trailer right over the little depression where her grandparents' rose garden had been. Leah was dismayed at first when she saw it, for it felt like a desecration. She quickly let it go, however, as truly there were no living bushes remaining that would even indicate it ever had been a rose garden, so how could Peter have known it? Apart from the dip in the ground and the prominent placement of the bench, not even she would have recognized it as such. The ground was soft there though, she noticed. One of the trailer wheels had sunk into the lawn some. It would leave a rut when the trailer was removed.

After disposing the plastic drop cloth in the dumpster, Peter joined the happy crowd on the driveway as they visited and enjoyed the chocolate chip cookies. Eventually he had everyone gather around Leah to pray a blessing over her, which made her cry. When they had finished, she thanked everyone for coming and cried once again. Then Peter officially called it a night, and her new friends came to say goodbye, many hugging her before they left, although Leah noted that Marty had disappeared before the prayer. Jackie, too, had gone home early to help Brother Warren with his boot before bed so that Danny could stay.

When all but Peter and Kyla had departed, Danny turned to Leah. "One last task, I hear! I'm told there's a lumbering mattress to be searched before it takes a trip to the dumpster!"

"We don't have to do it tonight if you're tired," she told him.

"Are you kidding me? Why not? It makes more sense to do it while Peter's here than to wait. Plus, I'll admit—I'm curious!" He gave a boyish grin.

Kyla smiled, folding her arms.

The two men lugged the enormous mattress off the bed and hoisted it up against the wall. Then the four of them thoroughly scrutinized its underside and rigorously knocked against every square inch of its surface. Kyla insisted they examine the box spring, too, before it left the room, but they uncovered nothing.

"Sorry I made such a big deal out of it," she said to Leah, but Leah shrugged.

"What did it hurt to check it out? And now it's out of my house!"

The yard light was coming on when Peter and Kyla hugged Leah goodbye. Danny stayed to close the house with Leah, waiting on the sidewalk while she killed the lights and locked up. Coming out the front, she paused with the porch light on, gazing out at the beautiful new landscaping at the bottom of the steps. The air was rich with the fragrance of freshly mown grass and the earthy smell of mulch. She shut the door and came to join him.

"This is a bit overwhelming for me," she said. "I don't deserve this. I don't deserve *any* of this!" She felt that tightness in her throat again.

"It's called 'grace,' Leah! No one deserves it."

She nodded. "I know. But it's not like I'm brand new to this. These people have no idea of how ugly rotten I've been. I used to look down on backsliders like me with such disdain." She gestured to the new landscaping. "It's not only this I don't deserve, but it's *them*. If they really knew me—"

"Don't even go there," he said quietly, cutting her off. "You're back with Jesus, and that's what counts. The past is on the cross. Leave it there. Every one of them understands."

"I suppose." She sniffed. "But they were so kind. So willing to help me. So—" She couldn't finish.

Danny handed her his handkerchief. "That's the body of Christ. When you get to know them better, you'll find they're imperfect people just like yourself. They make mistakes and sometimes hurt people. But nevertheless, the church is a beautiful thing."

"Yeah, I guess I forgot that. It's good to be back." She blew her nose, then gave a nasal laugh. "I can't believe you carry a handkerchief in your pocket! You're so much like Brother Warren and my dad!"

His laugh rang out. "Hey—you never know when you might get stuck with the neighborhood crybaby! I have a Kleenex too if you'd prefer. It might be a little damp and crumpled though."

She made a face.

He smiled, beckoning. "Come on—let's go."

Leah threw her arms around him in a quick hug. "I can't even tell you how grateful I am for you, Danny. I know I keep saying it, but thank you—thank you for everything!"

"It's what a brother does."

"Well, you've been more than a brother—you've been a true friend!"

"You're welcome." He hesitated, as though he had more to say but seemingly changed his mind, gesturing toward the hedge. "Okay—well, let's go."

Chapter Twenty-Five

Leah.

Leah stirred, snuggling into the soft blankets.

Leah!

She was back in her childhood home—in her mother's kitchen—with her mom there and Grandma Havi too, who was comforting her in her arms. Behind her the back door stood open, and someone was standing there knocking—knocking and knocking and calling her name. She could hear it clearly enough, but she couldn't move from where she stood weeping on her grandmother, weeping and weeping, like she couldn't ever stop, and her grandma hugged her tightly, weeping with her. Leah didn't want to move from her arms.

But as the knocking persisted, she heard a voice from within urging her: *You need to get the door!* Grandma Havi also whispered in her ear, *Yes, darling, it's time! It's time to answer that.* Reluctantly Leah broke from her grandmother's embrace, wiped her tears, and turned to see who was there, turned to see who was so irritatingly relentless in his or her knocking. Why couldn't the person leave her alone? Couldn't the person see how much she was hurting—that her heart had been broken?

Immediately Leah was perturbed to recognize Jake DeSoto—Jake!—filling her entire doorway, staring soberly at her, his cheeks blotchy and red, as if stained from shame. What was *he* doing there? Was he that clueless to think that he'd be welcome at her house? How dare he show up anywhere near her! Her temper flared as she prepared to unleash on him—but her verbal daggers fizzled as another figure suddenly appeared with him, stepping out in front of Jake at that exact moment, stepping boldly out in front of him like a shield or a buffer, like a barrier for all she wanted to say and send his way.

Leah!

Frightened, she drew back. *This one* had been the voice calling her name, not Jake. His plain features, his form, his humble attire—none were recognizable to her, but when he turned his face toward her—when he turned, Leah knew at once who he was! With a rush of dread, she crumpled to her knees, unable to look at him; yet she knew his eyes were locked on her, for she could *feel* them—she could feel his terrifying gaze piercing her, laser eyes cutting into her with an intensity of purity and kindness that both drained her of strength and filled her with life. No words came from his mouth, but his words were everywhere, exuding from his presence all around him, as his burning eyes bore into the very depths of her.

I've carried the full weight of sin, beloved. I bore the punishment. It is finished!

The words reverberated through her, passing over and through her body like vibrations. She heard and felt them as she bowed frozen on the floor, unable to make a sound, unable to lift her head.

My blood cleanses, Leah. Let it do its work. Let it cleanse the guilt. Let my blood do its full work.

And then a hand of scarred flesh reached out.

Leah gasped in her bed, jerking awake from a painful shock, as though she had just been zapped with a jolt of electricity. Her pulse was racing—her heart slamming so hard she could practically hear it. Confused and frightened, she sat up, daring to peer across her room in the dim morning light, fully expecting to see him. It was a dream, she knew—a *dream*. Yet it felt as though Jesus was still in the room with her.

Her body tingled, the vivid images lingering. She had *felt* him speak, and his *eyes*—she couldn't stop thinking about the way he had looked at her. Oh, he had certainly seen everything. All her pain *and* all she had done out of anger and depression in the last four years—all of it. He had seen *all* that was in her heart with nothing hidden! Every ounce of hatred for Jake and Rachel, all her desires for them to be miserable in life—all had been laid bare before those burning eyes!

A weight of guilt pressed heavily on her. How was a blemish like her not completely swept away by the purity of his presence? How was she still alive and breathing? And yet the way he had looked at her—those eyes had not condemned! His eyes had radiated love—a pure and frightening love so full of kindness. Overwhelming love and kindness! Eyes of mercy, she realized. *Mercy.* She could barely comprehend it!

It was a *dream*, Leah reminded herself, her heart burning within. With a deep breath she pulled the sheet up to wipe her eyes, her limbs still rubbery with adrenalin. She was wide awake now, and one big question gnawed at her: Had Jesus been defending her or defending Jake? It wasn't quite clear. The Jake in her dream had been undeniably steeped in guilt; he wore it all over his face, like he knew a scourging was coming. Then why did it seem as though Jesus was defending him?

It scared her, as though for a moment it appeared Jesus was taking Jake's side—standing with *him* and abandoning her! Yet when that scarred hand had touched her—when it touched her Leah knew with certainty that he was *for* her. Wholly for her. She could *feel* it through and through—and with it was a promise of justice! Nevertheless, what humiliation she felt when those penetrating eyes had looked so fully on her dark, dark heart. How could this man Jesus show her so much kindness?

I carried the full weight of sin. I bore the punishment.

Bit by bit, reality settled back in. Leah shifted in her bed, mulling over the words—not only what he said, but the way he'd said it, right before he touched her. Full work? What did that mean? Yeah, she got the words, but what was he *saying*? Would Brother Warren understand? Would he think her strange to have such a dream? Perhaps Danny could explain it—if he believed her! She craned her head to see the time on the nightstand clock. It was almost time to get up—which reminded her that she had set her alarm to go off a little earlier to surprise Danny on his run. The thought woke her up completely. *Perfect.* She would ask him on their run!

Hastily Leah cancelled the alarm and dressed in her running gear. Quietly opening her door, she hurried silently through the house, intent on waiting on the deck until Danny came out of his cabin, but through the patio door, she saw that he was already in the pool swimming laps. Disappointed, she paused with her hand on the latch, watching him glide back and forth in his steady rhythm—whoosh, whoosh, whoosh, whoosh.

For a moment she debated whether to go for her run anyway or to go back to bed, but then she decided it wouldn't be the same going by herself. If she did, she might bump into Danny afterward and have to explain it all—that she was a new runner now. It would lose the surprise. Why not wait to catch him another day and make it fun for them both?

As she stood there, she heard a movement behind her and turned to see Brother Warren in athletic pants and a T-shirt carefully limping into the kitchen in his stocking feet, minus his orthopedic boot. He smiled at her, his eyes flicking briefly over her shoulder to where Danny swam in the pool.

"Good morning," he said. "I was hoping to make it bootless to the coffee pot without getting caught. You'll have to promise not to tattle on me."

"Good morning." Leah hastened to pull out one of the kitchen island stools for him. "Have a seat! I won't tell Jackie if you let me make your coffee."

Gratefully he took the chair. "Oh, you're a good girl! I accept. Thank you!"

Leah found a package of ground coffee and some filters in the cupboard above the pot. She scooped the rich grounds into the basket, and the machine began clicking softly as it started to brew. Brother Warren leaned cross-armed on the counter watching her.

"You're a gift from God, Leah. You're a beautiful girl with a pretty face and a sweet spirit."

Leah lifted her eyes to him. "Thank you." Was this about to go somewhere?

He waited for her to return the pouch to the cupboard before resuming. "Did you know I named one of my own daughters Leah? It's a lovely name! It rolls right off the tongue! A lovely name for a beautiful woman of God! I'd love for you to meet her."

She leaned against the other side of the counter, facing him. "I think you're trying to make me feel better about a name I don't care for. It's okay. Somehow I've managed to live with it." It occurred to her that since they were alone, she might have an opportunity to bring up her dream.

"Ah, of course—you saw right through that!" He smiled, folding his hands. "But I *do* have a daughter named Leah, and she *is* beautiful. She'll always be beautiful in my eyes because I'm her father. But I'd hate for you to live your life not liking something so close to your identity as your own name." He reached across the counter. "I woke up praying for you today. Come—give me your hand."

Her stomach gave its familiar twist. Good heavens—her day had barely started, and he was going to do his thing again! She had not expected this when she had offered to make him coffee. Cautiously she stretched her arm across the counter and placed her hand in his. He covered it with his other hand.

"So this friend of yours—Rachel. She spoiled your name for you?"

"Well—yeah. I mean, she spoiled a lot more than that!"

"Yes, she hurt you very badly, didn't she?"

Leah nodded.

"And nothing can fix it?"

She shrugged. "Well, there's no changing what happened!"

"Nope, there's no changing the past—you're right about that! But the *future* can change. Forgiving her can set a new course for your life."

Leah sighed. "I know. I'm having a tough time with that. I want to—but at the same time I don't. It's hard!"

Brother Warren nodded, squeezing her hand. "Yes, it's hard."

"I know I need to forgive her, but she got everything she wanted. I struggle with her getting away with what she's done—like it's no big deal. It seems wrong to just let her go free!"

"On the contrary, my dear, it's *you* who would be going free!"

"But then what about *her*?"

"Leah, Leah," he said kindly, "as long as you hold grievances against her, you make the choice to stay connected to her. It's like refusing to uproot a poison ivy plant from your garden—pretty soon you're going to have a whole patch of it, and *you're* the one who'll be miserable! Do you want to contend with this your whole life? It'll turn you bitter, and your bitterness will spread to others. Forgiveness is plucking that thing up and getting it out of your life."

"Right. I know. But then *she* gets off."

"Ah. So you think she should have to pay—?"

Leah hesitated. "I'm not sure I'd use that particular word, but—" She shrugged.

Brother Warren frowned thoughtfully. "Right, right—so let's talk about this. Would it make you feel better if she were somehow punished for what she's done?"

"Well—" Leah shifted uncomfortably against the counter. "Sort of. I mean—yes. It seems only right that there should be some consequences."

"Yes—and fitting for the offense, right?" He nodded. "So how about if someone deceived her in return—would that help?"

She squirmed. "Maybe. What are you saying? It's not like we can arrange that or anything."

"I know, but bear with me for a second. How about if she was betrayed—betrayed by one of her closest friends? Would that fix it for you?"

Leah was silent, observing him.

He met her eyes. "How about if she was spit on and mocked and then beaten with a rod? How about if she was stripped naked and publicly humiliated? Given an unfair trial and sentenced to death—?"

Her jaw dropped. "Okay—I see where you're going with this, but it's not the same! Jesus was innocent! He didn't do anything wrong. Rachel—Rachel was *not* innocent!"

"If he was innocent, why did he go through all that?"

"Well—Pilate. Because of Pilate and the Pharisees and everybody—they ganged up on him and put him to death."

"And God his father didn't stop that from happening—? Whyever not?"

"Well, he was *willing* to. Jesus *chose* to go through all of that to die for our sins on the cross. It was God's plan. I hardly see how this applies!"

"So Jesus was punished for sins he didn't commit? The sins of others—?"

She eyed him, offering the obvious answer. "Yes."

"Ah. *Whose* sins was he punished for?"

She gestured. "Everybody's."

"Whose in particular?"

"Okay—mine. And yours."

"Okay. So if innocent Jesus was punished for *my* sin, could we say that everything that happened to Jesus—that that's what *I* deserved for my sin?"

"I've never thought about it like that, but I guess so."

"It should have been *me* then. It should have been *me* to be betrayed, beaten, mocked, humiliated, and put to death. Yet Jesus took what *I* deserved. He took *my* punishment for me." He paused for a moment. "So tell me again, dear girl—whose sins was he punished for?" His brow rose with the question.

"Mine."

He nodded. "And—?"

She swallowed, knowing he was waiting for her to say it. "Okay—Rachel's sins too."

He nodded, speaking gently. "Yes, child. Jesus carried the full weight of Rachel's sin too. All of it—my sin, your sin, Rachel's—*all* of it has been fully punished on the cross. Remember what he said? 'It is finished!'"

The full weight of sin. Fully punished. Leah blinked, stunned at his words. "But—but still, what about—shouldn't there be some sort of consequences for doing wrong? What she did to me—"

"—what she did to you was *very* wrong, Leah. No argument there! And consequences do come—no doubt about that! I guarantee she's suffered them. I've had my own hard knocks in life because of my sins, but by God's mercy I've not gotten what I deserve. But listen—you're not in charge of Rachel's consequences! Give that over to God! Give *her* over to God! He knows exactly how to deal with her. Untie yourself from her!"

Her heart was beating hard.

He patted her hand. "Don't be afraid. The Lord sees you and loves you and wants to make everything right. He's not going to miss a thing. There's so much power in forgiveness, but to choose *not* to creates a hindrance to the power of God working in your life—and in hers too!"

Leah nodded, trying not to cry. "Okay. I hear you. It's just—hard."

"Of course. It's a step of faith." He smiled. "I woke up with this on my heart this morning and need to tell you: the blood of Jesus cleanses, Leah. It cleanses guilt, it cleanses shame. Let it do its work. Let it heal your heart. Everything your friend Rachel did that hurt you, everything she did that spoiled your name—Jesus bore it all on the cross. Let the blood of Jesus do its full work. Rachel deserved to be punished—as did you and I—but Jesus took her place. He bore the punishment. Forgive her! Let him remove the shame from your beautiful name! Let it be cleansed by his blood so you can wear it like a crown. You're God's beautiful one, his own daughter!"

Leah couldn't even speak. She had meant to ask him about her dream, and here he was—speaking to her as if he'd witnessed it! Even now the same burning finger reached down to touch an open wound in her heart. How could Brother Warren have known it? *He bore the punishment. Let the blood do its full work.* She hadn't been prepared for this—for a challenge to forgive Rachel—and yet as she stood there beside the kitchen island, she could still feel those fiery, permeating eyes on her—the kind eyes—and she knew there was no excuse. He was calling her name.

Leah!

Right then, in his customary ill timing, little Angel suddenly burst onto the scene, scampering noisily across the living room floor and through the kitchen on his way for the patio door. Both Leah and Brother Warren turned as Jackie emerged from the hall in her robe. Seeing them, she glanced up at the clock.

"Goodness! Everyone beat me out of bed today! Good morning!"

She followed to where Angel pawed the glass and let him outside. Turning, she noted Leah's athletic wear and tennis shoes. "Aww, you look cute! Are you going out for a run, sweetie? It looks like a nice morning. Dan runs too—did you know that?" Her eyes landed on her dad, and she suddenly frowned. "You're not supposed to be putting any weight on that foot without your boot!"

Brother Warren let out a howl, squeezing Leah's hand and letting her go. "You caught me, sunshine girl! But it's not as bad as it looks! Leah, here, has been making my coffee while I sit and enjoy her company."

Leah had already blinked back her tears, but the tender wound inside still pulsed. "I made him sit down right away."

Jackie clicked her tongue. "I have to watch you like a hawk! You'd better behave while you and Dan are away!"

He waved his hand. "Of course!"

She dug her hand on her hip. "You *have* to if you want that foot to heal properly! Let me tell you—a walker will be more inconvenient than a boot!"

"You're right, you're right!" he said penitently. "I was up early and impatient to get my coffee."

Jackie glanced back at the deck.

"Looks like Angel's feeling better," Leah observed.

"Oh, yes—amazing, isn't it?" She opened the door to let the dog back in and offered him a tiny treat from a decorative tin on a nearby shelf. "You'd never know how injured he was, would you? Such an answer to prayer!" She approached them at the counter. "So—are you heading out or are you back already?"

Leah smiled sheepishly. "Neither actually. Danny doesn't know that I run, and I was going to surprise him by joining him. But he's swimming, so I'll wait for another time. Brother Warren and I were, um—hanging out." She threw him a glance.

"I see!" Jackie lifted her head knowingly. "Well, I'll let you continue your conversation. Dad, stay put! I'll bring your boot when I'm dressed."

"I love that girl," Brother Warren said as his daughter left. "I don't know what I'd do without her. I might have died of a broken heart if not for her. I still miss my wife terribly, but Jackie's a blessing. She takes care of me so well. She helps me do all the things that are good for me that I'd prefer to skip—as you can see!" He winked.

Leah smiled. "Yes, I see that. I'm happy to know her. She's very sweet. And so are you. Thank you for your kind words and all your help. And again—for letting me stay here with you. You have no idea what it means to me."

"Of course! Dan wouldn't hear of anything else. And I hope you take what I've said to heart. Life is filled with enough pain as it is—there's no need to reject *yourself* on top of it. Do you hear me? Take back your name! Forgive that girl and set yourself free!"

Leah took two mugs down from the cupboard and poured their coffees.

"Creamer?"

"Just a little milk, thank you."

She gave him a spoon and put the milk back when he was finished.

"So about my name."

Brother Warren brought his cup up for a sip. "Yes, what about your beautiful name?"

"I get what you're saying about forgiving Rachel, and I *will* take it to heart. But one thing that's always been a bummer for me is how the Bible paints Leah as the ugly sister. The unwanted one. That alone was hard enough to deal with before everything happened, and then when Jake and Rachel—" She shrugged. "It put me over the edge! Like I'm *destined* to be rejected. Like my own name dooms me. Plus, there was the family curse thing. It was a one-two punch."

"Uh-huh," he said thoughtfully. "So let me ask you a question. I lost my wife, Millie, in October. Why shouldn't I just go find another girl named Millie and marry her and go on as before?"

Leah opened her hand, as the answer was plain.

Brother Warren raised his eyebrows and gave an exaggerated nod.

"Okay, so you're saying I'm not her—the Bible Leah."

"Exactly! Same name, but you're not her. Nor will you *ever* be her! You couldn't be her even if she were someone you admired! You're *you*— body, soul, and spirit. Your looks, your personality—everything!" He set his mug down onto a napkin. "Nor are you intended to be like her. You're intended to be like Jesus! And your destiny is not linked to her either. Your destiny, Leah, is linked to *Jesus*!"

His words were so simple, but there it was again. The burning finger touching the hidden places of her heart, like it was pointing to the pain and commanding love to be there instead. Leah swallowed.

"You get it?"

"I get it."

"Good." He leaned in eagerly, his elbows on the counter. "By your logic, every girl named Leah is ugly and doomed! That's ridiculous! Stop taking that on, dear girl! God broke the mold after the Bible Leah, and he broke the mold after you! There's no one on earth like you, and no one to do the work God has assigned to you but *you*! Your purpose in life is to make the Lord Jesus known in your own special way. And when you start to understand how special you are and how much the Lord loves you, it'll set you free! You are *loved*—believe it!"

She wiped her cheek. "You have the gift of making me cry."

"That's the Holy Spirit touching you with his love. He's setting you free!"

"It *is* my Year of Freedom," Leah said without thinking. It just seemed appropriate to say right then, but she knew Pam would shudder if privy to their conversation.

Brother Warren tipped his head in agreement. "Indeed! What an excellent declaration! And doesn't freedom feel good?"

"It's starting to—yes."

He smiled and raised his coffee to his lips. Leah realized she hadn't even tasted hers yet. She took a sip and held the warm cup with both hands.

"So let's talk about the other thing. What's this family curse about?"

Leah set the mug down, weary to explain it yet another time. "Okay, as far as I know, it started back with my great-grandmother Marlena Corolla, Grandma Havi's mother. Her husband abandoned her for another woman in her first year of marriage, leaving her with a baby girl—who was Grandma Havi. Then she—my grandma—was left standing at the altar at her first wedding. The next guy divorced her for another woman—before she met Grandpa Ed. And the same with my mom. My dad left her for another woman. She married again later, but it didn't last very long. And then there was me, and you know what happened there. It's part of my family tree. My mother says the Corolla Curse dooms the women in the family to be cursed in love."

He nodded thoughtfully. "I understand your concern."

"Totally! Yes, I *am* concerned! I've been personally affected by this, and it terrifies me!"

Brother Warren set his coffee down and leaned his arms on the counter. "I have a hard time believing your grandmother hadn't prayed to break that thing over your family already. She was a godly woman and understood things like this."

"Well, perhaps she did, and it didn't work."

He shook his head. "Your grandma had an excellent marriage with her husband, Ed. She certainly wasn't 'doomed.'"

"Then what about my mom? And what about me?"

"Every generation is responsible to hold onto their freedom. If you're not careful, you can keep that garbage alive and keep passing it down. I don't know anything about your mother, but listen to me now, Leah. Jesus said the devil comes to steal, kill, and destroy, but *he,* Jesus, came to bring life—and abundant life at that! You need to understand that this curse is not a part of God's plan for your life, okay? And if it's not a part of the plan of God for your life, you need to reject it. You need to believe by faith that through the cross of Jesus Christ, this curse can be broken off your life. Jesus—"

"—paid for my curse?" she interjected.

He paused to smile. "You got it! Jesus *is* the Great Curse Bearer! But more than that, dear girl. Let me explain something. You see, the power of a curse is linked to sin. No sin, no curse. The Bible says that Jesus *became* sin on our behalf so that we might become his righteousness. Jesus bore all the curse of sin in his body on that cross so that we might receive his righteousness and inherit his blessings. It's *finished*, Leah. He's already done it! You simply receive it by faith.

"But when a family doesn't follow Christ, as is the case with so many, many people, there are sins and consequences thereof that get passed down the family tree from one generation to another. These are generational curses—people reaping from sin—and these curses keep people stuck in a lifestyle contrary to the kingdom of God. It's bondage. Are you with me?"

Leah nodded, trying to understand. "I think so."

"It can involve anything—big or little. The Bible says that God punishes the sins of the fathers to the third and fourth generation of those who hate him, but he *blesses* those who love him to the thousandth generation. Sometimes it's clear where the curses got started; sometimes it's not. When we know the origin, we confess that sin and get it to the cross. When we don't, we put it on the cross by faith and call for the life and blessing of God to flow from that place instead. Your destiny is *kingdom* life, Leah. You're destined to live by the ways of Jesus and under his blessing. Just because every person in your family has an issue, it doesn't mean you're doomed to have it too. You can break the cycle in Jesus' name!

"So with this thing in your family,"—he gestured—"you confess those sins to God, and the sins of those family members before you too— that you know of—and by faith reckon those things as paid for at the cross. The power of his broken body and his blood spilled for you breaks the power of the curse. You've died with Christ, my friend, and you've been raised to life with him. You share in his inheritance of blessings, one after another!"

She sighed. "That's part of the problem. You make it sound so easy. I don't want to sound contrary or anything, but I've done this already. I've prayed to break this curse thing once before, and I still ended up getting slammed by it."

He nodded sympathetically. "Yes, hon—I'm so sorry for what you went through. I'm sure it was horrible." He was quiet, studying her. "But you say you prayed through it beforehand with someone?"

"Yes. With Danny's mom, Evelyn. Just like you said—we did all that."

He frowned. "That's interesting. Perhaps, Leah—perhaps it was already broken over your life."

"Apparently not. Look what happened!"

"Right, but think about it—it wasn't your sin."

"Well, I was affected by it nonetheless! Hugely!"

"Yes, but you weren't 'in sin.' You were sinned *against.*"

"Same difference! It still happened!"

He nodded. "I know. I'm not saying terrible things won't ever happen. I'm just saying that maybe what happened to you wasn't from reaping the family curse over your life."

"Then what was it?"

"Well,"—he smiled kindly—"perhaps it was God's goodness in disguise, painful as it was. Look what was going on! It needed to stop, and God saved you from much worse."

She looked at him in bewilderment. "It could hardly be *worse!*"

He patted her hand. "Now, now, dear. I don't understand why God allows things like that to happen, but I've learned to trust him even in the darkest storm. His goodness and his mercy are always there in plenty, and he's able to work all things for good. He's never failed me yet. Your situation was painful, but the love of God was evident in it nonetheless."

She eyed him soberly. "That's what Danny said too. Not exactly in those words, but that was the gist of it."

Brother Warren raised his brow.

"He said it's like I was pushed out of the path of a Mack truck, and I'm whining because of a broken arm."

"Well, I think he may be right." He moved his cup to the side. "But the arm is healed now. Or at least it's on its way. It's time to move on."

Yes, darling—it's time. Leah felt a shiver, recalling her grandmother's whisper in her dream.

"Regarding that curse—what did you call it again?"

"The Corolla Curse."

"Okay, let me ask you this, Leah: Is there any sin in your life right now that would give that old curse permission to remain? Because you can let it stay or invite it back."

She shook her head. "I don't think so. There was for a while, but not anymore."

"Okay." He nodded. "Do you believe that the Corolla Curse is part of the life that God has for you?"

She gave him a meek smile. "No."

"Do you want it hanging over your head anymore?"

"No."

"Are you sure? Because some people like the novelty of things like that. It gives them a twisted sense of identity, sort of an excuse to live less than God intends. And it's something to blame their sin on so they don't have to take responsibility."

"I don't want it."

He nodded. "Well, okay, then—let's pray."

Leah reached out her hand, but Brother Warren leaned forward and put his hand on her head. "In the name of Jesus, I break the power of this curse off Leah and any fears associated with it! Let it dissolve right before her eyes! Jesus, you became the curse on her behalf so that she might be your righteousness and inherit your blessings. I speak fullness of life over her. Show her the reality of who she is in Christ, your perfect and precious son. In Jesus' name. Amen." He dropped his hand to squeeze hers on the table.

"Thanks," she squeaked.

"Leah, God has *good* in store for you! You're a blessing, and you need to believe that about yourself!"

She wiped the tears off her cheeks—again. "Thanks."

Behind them they heard Jackie humming as she returned, going straight to the cupboard for a mug. "My, my—you two are chatty this morning!" She poured her coffee and returned the carafe to the warmer. "I feel like I'm missing out on something special here! Or like I'm slacking, one or the other! Thanks for getting this started."

Angel clicked dutifully past Jackie to his dog bed, making three rotations before dropping onto the cushion. Resting his furry chin on the edge, he fixed his gaze on her as she brought her coffee up for a sip.

"I still can't believe I'm the last one up!" Then she noticed Leah's face. "Oh, hon! Are you all right? You're crying!"

"They're good tears," Leah said. She blew her nose, then smiled at Brother Warren. "And it *has* been special. I can't say I've ever had a conversation with anyone that's been so affirming."

He smiled warmly in return. "Let me tell you a secret, lassie! When you spend time with the Lord each day, you'll start hearing him speak to you directly! He'll build you up every day! Remember—you gotta *relate* to him, not just learn about him! He's most certainly alive, just as real as you and me!" Then he lifted his eyes to his daughter. "But don't worry, Jackie dear—no one can make ham-and-cheddar omelets like you!"

Jackie's brow wrinkled in confusion. "*What*? Now there's a nice subtle hint! Is that your request for breakfast this morning?" She shook her head, glancing at Leah. "He's got a smooth way of getting whatever he wants around here. Oh, and that reminds me—Dad, I forgot your boot!"

He leaned in toward Leah. "Wait 'til you have one of her omelets! You'll see for yourself how wonderful they are." Then he reached out an arm to stop his daughter. "Don't trouble yourself, Jackie! Dan'll get it—he's on his way."

Leah's eyes darted outside to where Danny walked briskly alongside the pool, now fully dressed and heading toward the house. She straightened and set her cup onto the counter. "Excuse me. I'll be right back."

When she had changed out of her workout clothes, she returned to find the men side by side at the table before Danny's open laptop. He smiled in greeting and gestured toward the screen.

"'Morning! Just tweaking the slides for his message tonight. We're trying to get a jump on the day. There's a lot to do before we leave."

Leah peeked over their shoulders, then glanced down at Danny's shirt, noting he was wearing a short-sleeved button-down with his shorts instead of his usual T-shirt.

"Golly, Danny—you look like a million bucks! Did your mom buy that for you?"

Danny gave his jovial guffaw. "I'm almost thirty, Leah! You don't think I can pick out my own clothes?" Then he grinned. "Actually, this shirt *was* from Mom! How'd you guess?"

She laughed. "I couldn't see *you* buying it. But it's sharp—you look good!"

He looked down at it. "Thanks."

Leah left to join Jackie at the stove, where she was artfully folding an omelet with a spatula. Carefully she slid it onto a plate and returned the pan to the burner.

"What can I do?"

She gestured to the finished plates on the counter. "I'm on the last one. You can set those on the table. And there's some leftover cantaloupe in the refrigerator."

When breakfast was ready, Jackie sat down, and Danny moved to his place across from Leah. Brother Warren said grace and complimented his daughter on the fine presentation of the meal.

"Thank you, Daddy, but be careful—you're getting awfully close to flattery!" She gave him a teasing smile.

Danny also nodded appreciatively at his plate. "This *does* look fit to eat! Thank you, Jackie!" He picked up his fork and turned to Leah. "So hey—I found some extra hose that I'll hook up for you to water your new plants. I hear it's supposed to warm up this weekend, so it wouldn't hurt to water them morning and evening, just to help 'em out a little."

"Okay. Thank you."

He took a bite and nodded his approval again to Jackie before turning back to Leah. "On Sunday you could ride to church with Jackie if you want. I was hoping to be there with you your first time, but Kyla and Peter will be. Don't stress about it—it'll be fine. You'll enjoy it. And don't worry about what to wear. It's like Anchor—you can wear anything."

Leah looked at Jackie, who nodded. "Of course. You can definitely go with me!"

Leah took a breath, looking back at Danny. She wished he would be around for her first time back.

"Do you have any plans for the day, hon?" Jackie asked.

"I haven't really thought about it. My dad's coming tomorrow to help me on the house."

"Yes, how nice! I'm looking forward to meeting him!"

Danny wiped his mouth with a napkin. "Be sure to have him stay in the cottage. And your stepmom, too, if she comes. It'll give them some privacy, and they'll feel less like they're imposing. I'll have it ready for them."

Leah nodded. "Thanks. I really appreciate that."

"You should call him today to tell him that. And be sure to let him know what we got done last night too so he doesn't collect a bunch of tools for something that's already finished."

"Right. Good idea. I will!" Leah sipped her coffee. "I suppose I could do more painting over there."

"You should wait with that."

She shot him a look. "And do what instead?"

He shrugged. "You could do a million things! Go to the library. Go to the mall. Call Kyla and go shopping for your new furniture or something."

Her eyes lit up. "Great idea! It'd be fun to shop for furniture with her! I'll see if she's free today."

"But you should spend some time in the Word this morning."

"Already planning on it." Leah cast a glance at Bro Warren, who was heartily enjoying his breakfast. He pointed his fork at her and winked.

Danny continued, "Then maybe afterward you could relax at the pool and read more of your grandmother's journal. You might find out more about—" He raised his brow.

"Yes!" She gave him a knowing look, leaning back in her chair. "Another great idea!"

She glanced at Jackie, who was looking at Brother Warren with a smile on her face. Her eyes met Leah's.

"I'll be here all day," she said sweetly. "Just let me know if you need anything. Would anyone like some melon?"

"I'll have some," Danny said, taking the bowl from her. "And I'll remind you, Jackie, of the business with my car this afternoon."

Jackie nodded. "Oh, yes—I remember!"

"What business with your car?" Leah asked.

"Someone's borrowing it for the weekend," Danny said simply, spearing a chunk of cantaloupe. "But Jackie's on it."

"Yes," she affirmed with a thumbs-up. "I'm on it!"

"I think we should leave no later than noon," Brother Warren offered. "I'd like a little time to get settled before the meeting."

"Noon it is," Danny agreed. He turned to Jackie. "Jackie, you've outdone yourself this morning! Thanks again for the breakfast."

"Yes, thank you," Leah agreed, and Brother Warren nodded his approval.

"It was excellent! Plus, you grow more beautiful every day. You're a joy to my heart!"

Jackie gave an embarrassed smile. "You're pouring it on rather thick this morning, Daddy!"

Brother Warren laughed, and everyone laughed with him. But Leah agreed: Jackie was beautiful.

Chapter Twenty-Six

After arranging an afternoon of furniture shopping with Kyla via text, Leah went to help Jackie clean up after breakfast, but she discovered Jackie had already finished loading the dishwasher and was wiping down the countertops.

"Sorry. I meant to help you!" Leah said regretfully.

"No worries, hon," Jackie returned. "But here—" She opened a cabinet and waved to an overflowing trash basket beside a recycling bin. "If you want to help, I'll gladly let you take care of this."

"Whatever you need!" Leah responded, pulling out the bag to tie it up. "Please—assign me chores or something! I feel like a kid on summer vacation with nothing to do. Hopefully I'll get a little more direction this weekend when my dad comes." She shook open the new bag to line the bin.

"Oh, I'm sure you will," Jackie said, hanging her damp dishtowel over the oven handle. "I'm curious at what he'll say about what's been happening over there."

"No kidding! Me too! This goes to the garage, I assume?"

"Yes. There's a box near the trash for the aluminum cans—you'll see it. The other recyclables go in the bin with the yellow lid." She rubbed in a squirt of hand lotion. "I'll be upstairs, hon. Let me know if you need anything."

"Got it."

Awkwardly Leah waddled her way to the garage carrying everything at once. She chucked the heavy bag into the open garbage can, lifted the lid to toss the lighter one in the recycling, then turned to dump the aluminum cans into the designated oversized box nearby. Bringing the waste bin down, she turned to leave, then stopped, looking curiously back over her shoulder at the mound of aluminum cans. Out of the dozens of assorted cans collected there, one stood out among the rest—a single bright green can. One lime-flavored carbonated water can just like the one she'd found in her yard her first day there—and identical to the one she'd found in her trash at her house. She eyed it for a moment, then stretched to pick it off the pile.

When Leah returned the plastic bin to the kitchen, the men were entering the living room. Brother Warren was freshly showered, his snowy hair damp and neatly combed to the side. Dressed in charcoal slacks and a dress shirt tucked in, he let himself down onto the couch and raised his foot to the ottoman, where Danny knelt with the boot. Noticing Leah across the room, he smiled at her as he fitted the plastic casing around the old man's pant leg, strapping it snugly with the Velcro strap.

"I'm counting the days until my good riddance ceremony for this contraption!" Brother Warren announced. "Won't that be a fine day?"

Danny gave the boot a tap. "I'll join you in that celebration! Anything else you need before I go pack for myself?"

"My dress shoe for my good foot," he reminded, gesturing downward with his gnarled finger.

Danny fetched it from his bedroom, then helped him to his feet, offering him his crutches.

"Thank you, son. Now where did you put my Bible?"

"It's still at your desk."

"Okay. I'll study until it's time to go."

"All right," Danny told him. "I'm going out. See you around noon."

"You're my hero," Leah declared quietly as Danny paused with her in the kitchen.

He shook his head modestly. "It's an honor. But he *is* quite a character!"

She smiled. "He is! The two of us had another talk this morning while you were in the pool. A great talk—with prayer."

"Is that right? Excellent!" Then he spied the aluminum can on the counter. "Hey—I'll have one of those!"

"It's empty." She lifted it and set it down again.

"Oh. Did Jackie pick some up? I like that kind, and I keep forgetting to buy more when I'm in town." He opened the refrigerator to peek inside.

Leah blinked, staring at his back.

He closed the door. "Where'd you get that?"

"The garage. It was in the recycling."

He looked at her a little confused. "What are you doing with it?"

"Uh—nothing." She slid open the cabinet and dropped it into the bin.

"Okay. Well, I need to keep moving. See you later!" He waved as he went out.

"See you later," she echoed. But when the patio door thumped shut, Leah retrieved the can and turned for the stairs. Thoughts too wild to even consider were baiting her. She needed to talk to Jackie right now.

When she topped the stairs, the woman was exiting the bathroom with an iron in her hands, the cord trailing along the carpet.

"Why, hello!" she said. "Do you need something, dear? I'm about to press Dad's shirts for his trip." An ironing board was erected in a wide part of the hall behind her.

"I'm fine—thanks," Leah said. "Just a quick question. Does anyone around here drink this?" She revealed the aluminum can.

Jackie glanced at it. "Just Dan. I don't care for those."

Leah's head swung back and forth in disbelief, her mind barraged by crazy scenarios as her week replayed in her head.

"Goodness, Leah! What's going on?" Jackie asked, giving her a strange look.

"I found a carbonated water identical to this in my trash last week— same brand, same everything—and *I* didn't put it there. Whoever's been coming in my house did."

Jackie's eyes grew wide as she lowered the iron. "Are you insinuating that Dan came in your house when you weren't there?"

"Well, I don't know!"

Jackie looked stunned. "He would *never* do that! Have you asked him about it?"

"No. I didn't want to. I was afraid that—" She stopped, unable to finish.

"Well, go *ask* him, for heaven's sake—right away!" She waved urgently. "Although I can already tell you what he'll say! He'd *never* go in someone's house without them knowing it!" She let out a breath. "Are you telling me you've saved that can for *days* only to bring it up now?"

"No! I noticed it in your garage with the recycling this morning. It was the only one like it in there."

"Oh, that one!" Jackie brought her hand to her chest. "Well, that's a relief! That's not one of ours!"

"It's not? Oh, yeah—the party! I forgot about that!"

"Oh, no, hon, I found that in your yard. I picked it up last night when I was cleaning up after my dog. It was with a bunch of other trash in your shrubs along the driveway." She frowned. "Oh, dear! I hope that wasn't from your prowler too! Well, whoever he is, I'll guarantee you it's *not* Dan!"

In the shrubs along the road. Leah nodded. "You're right. Thank you."

Jackie lifted the iron, drawing up the cord. "You tell Dan about this right away! I don't want you thinking funny about him." Then she gestured. "I'm going to finish Dad's shirts."

Thanking her again, Leah went downstairs and tossed the can back into the recycling. Then she washed her hands and went to get her Bible.

Making herself comfortable at the deck table, she spread out her books and with her pen promptly inked, "Relate to him!" across the cover of her study booklet from Kyla, then opened to her homework. Her first instructions were to copy the day's theme verse in the version of the Bible she liked best. Feeling app-savvy, she quickly found Romans 2:4 on her phone and tapped open a number of versions, settling on her favorite: "Don't you see how wonderfully kind, tolerant, and patient God is with you? Does this mean nothing to you? Can't you see that his kindness is intended to turn you from your sin?" Leah scrawled out the words and added a couple of stars in the margin. It would make a great reminder card for her mirror.

Her next assignment was to read the story of the woman caught in adultery. She paged through the book of John to find it, then made a point not to hurry reading it, deliberately envisioning the scene. Her eyes lingered on the page. There was no question of the woman's guilt. The gathered crowd could rightfully accuse her, but when Jesus stepped in, he caused her accusers to see their *own* guilt. "Has no one condemned you? Then neither do I condemn you. Go now and leave your life of sin."

There was that overwhelming kindness again! In the space given, Leah jotted her thoughts: *Jesus, your kindness wasn't simply being "nice." You weren't naive. You saw her guilt without ignoring or glossing over it. True mercy. You knew what she was, yet you released her from her debt of sin.* Yes, his love saw the full scope of her debt and he took it as his own—and with no guarantees for what she would do in turn.

She paused, recalling with shame the reckless abandon with which she had given herself to Carlos and so many other men, a defiant path chosen in her inability to deal with her hurt. *How is it, Jesus, that you do not condemn me?* she wrote. *That you can look at me and set me free? I'm like this woman. Her name could have been "Leah."*

Or—the thought rushed in—Rachel.

Leah sat back, eyeing the page. Caught in the act. Clearly in the wrong. Unquestioned guilt. Rightfully accused. Her heart burned. *Don't you see how wonderfully kind, tolerant, and patient God is with you? Does this mean nothing to you? Can't you see . . .*

After what felt like an eternity, she spoke it out: "Okay—I *see* it! *You* don't condemn *me,* and so *I* won't condemn *her.* I have absolutely no kind feelings toward her, but I forgive her, God. I forgive Rachel Steinburg." With a flourish she wrote it out in her book, underlined it, and dated it. Then she slapped the pen down onto the table, unable to continue working on her study. The Bible pages fluttered gently in the breeze as her thoughts raced in every direction—her dream, Brother Warren's words, her excuses and objections, the scriptures—everything was jumbled messily together.

"You gotta take it from here, God," she said in resignation. "I don't know how to deal with this."

Finding herself too distracted to read the Bible, she went to get her grandmother's journal that she had started yesterday and went out to sit beside the pool. As the final volume, it was a quick read, comprised mainly of thoughts and mixed emotions about their move from the family homestead to their new home in Mesa, but nothing more was mentioned of the Krugerrands or any other valuables. Leah studied the inserted printout that listed them out again, along with her grandmother's letters from the lawyer's office, but there was no new revelation about where the coins might have gone. Tucking the papers inside the cover, she trekked back to her room to switch it out for Journal 2, leaving the finished one on the corner of her dresser before returning to her deck chair beside the pool.

Well, it happened! We're engaged! Saturday morning Ed surprised us by showing up at our apartment, then "kidnapping" us and bringing us down to New Hampton, where I had the surprise of my life! He's been building a new house on his family homestead without my knowledge of it! At first it scared the daylights out of me. I thought it meant that Lenore and I weren't going to continue to be a part of his life, but he assured me he was building the house for us. Us together. And then he proposed to me in his Ed sort of way. I never dreamed that something like this could ever happen to me. I feel like Cinderella who has met her prince. He's such a wonderful man! (And the new house will certainly be a palace compared to our apartment!)

Lenore, on the other hand, has been an absolute pill. I can't understand what's gotten into her! She is sassy and sulky to me and terribly rude to Ed and Richard. I'm not sure what's going on. Ever since she's made cheerleader her whole attitude has changed. I think it's because of one of the girls she hangs out with. Ed thinks moving to New Hampton would do her good. I'm not so sure. Mary McAllister encouraged me to have her spend more time with her dad, but he is not the best influence on her either. Mary also insists I should bring Lenore to church every Sunday and not let her sleep in. And that I should pray for her daily. Honestly, I feel like there's so much I should be doing that I can't keep up with it all! The nice thing about Mary, though, is that she doesn't just dole out her opinions. She really does care about us. She's taken Lenore out for treats on several occasions. Even shopping. Lenore kinda rolls her eyes and asks if she has to go. I guess I'm open to anything right now, as I'm rather worried about her.

Out of the corner of her eye Leah noticed Danny come out of his cottage and gather up a roll of garden hose from his small porch. He disappeared around the backside of the shrubbery, and Leah knew he was going to her house to hook it up so that she could water her plants. That she had even *considered* he could be the one coming into her house brought her shame. He was so good to her. So thoughtful in so many ways. She stared at the hedge thinking of him. Her eyes dropped back to the page.

For all her hovering, I have to say that I am thankful for Mary McAllister in my life. She has been my mentor, my teacher, and my friend. She mothers me and smothers me. She pushes me and sometimes annoys me too, but she has taken me into her heart "for the sake of the Lord," as she puts it. I don't know what I'd do without her. She cares about one thing and one thing only in life, and that's pleasing God. I have learned so much from her and can only hope to have the same love and grace that she has extended toward me to share with someone else that God puts in my path someday.

Danny was back, empty-handed. Leah watched him come around the arborvitae to his cottage, but he passed it and walked on to the shed in broad steps, where he disappeared inside. In a moment he came out with a caddy in one hand and a long pool net in the other, striding determinedly across the yard toward where she sat.

"Will I disturb you if I skim the pool?" he asked.

"Not at all," she replied, observing as he knelt to test the water and measure out the chemicals to add in. Then he stood and swept the skimmer slowly back and forth, shaking the debris out the net every so often. He looked good in his gray flecked shirt and shorts with his loafers.

He was like the male version of a Mary McAllister, Leah thought. For all the time she had known him, his one goal was to please God too. He had extended love and grace to her when she had been in a bad place. He had pushed her and annoyed her too, but always for her good.

He glanced up. "Anything interesting in the journals?"

"Yeah. It's been good. Slow, though. A little hard to focus."

He knelt to check one of the filters on the far side of the pool, then went back to skimming.

"It's like you live here," she said. "You do a lot of work around this place."

He chuckled. "Yeah. I want to help Jackie out before I leave for the weekend. I'm afraid this place might be getting beyond what the two of them are able to maintain."

"What do you mean?"

"Oh, you know—" He waved out across the yard and back to the pool. "He can't keep up with this, and it shouldn't be Jackie's responsibility. Sooner or later, they're going to have to think about selling."

Leah gave a cry. "Sell the house? No! They can't! They're my neighbors!"

He threw her a look.

"Can't *you* stay on and help them?"

"I have a job, Leah. This is my summer break."

Her shoulders fell. "All right—now my day is totally wrecked! Seriously, if *they're* gone, and *you're* gone—" She opened her hands. "That would be so depressing!"

He shook the net out once more and set the pole down on the pool deck. "Well, don't get worked up before it actually happens! Who knows—maybe they have other plans for the place that we don't know about."

"Like what?"

"I don't know! Maybe one of their kids or grandkids will come live with them or something. Don't borrow grief from tomorrow."

Leah sighed.

"Did you call your dad yet?"

"Oh. No, I forgot." She sat up in the chair.

"You forgot?" He smiled at her as he picked up the caddy and skimmer. "All right. I gotta keep moving. See you later!"

"Danny, wait! I need to tell you something."

He turned.

"That empty can I had this morning—the carbonated water—well, I learned that Jackie found it in my yard last night. In the bushes by the driveway near the road. It matches the one I found in my wastebasket last week."

"Is that so?" He looked surprised at first, but then his brow furled. "So then our guy either threw it out of his vehicle or he—"

"—was walking there," Leah finished for him.

He nodded thoughtfully, and the two of them were quiet.

"Don't go over there alone," he said finally, turning for the shed.

Leah called her dad right away, her eyes following Danny across the yard while she held the phone to her ear. He didn't answer, so she hung up and called Chelsea.

"Sorry, hon—your dad's not around this morning," Chelsea said. "He went to take care of some business and probably has his phone on silent or left it in the car."

Leah debated leaving a message with her, but it seemed rather complicated to communicate it all. "Maybe I'll just call him and leave a message on his phone," she told her, but immediately she realized how unfriendly it sounded. For so many years she had shut Chelsea out of her life. It was time to open her heart to her. "I wanted to tell him that some people from"—how could she explain it? How did she explain where the army who descended on her yard had come from?—"from my new church came and did a ton of work at my place. I wanted to let Dad know so he didn't get a bunch of tools together unnecessarily. Could you maybe tell him to call me sometime today and I'll explain it all? I'm really grateful he's coming, and I'd love to have you too, Chelsea, if you're able to."

Chelsea paused a moment. "Thank you, Leah. I appreciate the invitation. He's really looking forward to helping you too, but I'll need to stay home with the kids this time. I'm excited, though, to hear you have a church again. Your father will be glad to hear it too. I'm not sure if you know it, but we've been going to your old church—Anchor Church. We go every Sunday."

"Yeah, you said something about that."

"Things have changed around here. So much! Your father's a new man! He's—well, both of us—we're following God now!"

"I could tell," Leah said. "I could tell when he was here. I think it's great!"

"Oh, that day—you wouldn't believe how *happy* he was when he came home! I could tell something really special happened when he was with you."

How strange, Leah thought, that Chelsea's words could cause a physical sensation in her body. "Yeah," she agreed, feeling tender toward her dad. "It was good!"

"Your dad's in a recovery group at church, with a mentor and everything. They're in a new unit where he's encouraged to repair damaged relationships. In fact, that's what he's doing this morning. He said when he was with you the other day that you mentioned something to him about your mother that got him thinking. He went over there this morning to talk with her."

What? Her hand went to her forehead. "Dad went over to talk to *Mom*?"

"Yes, hon. He went to try to catch her before she went to work."

Leah felt a pit in her gut. What a foolish thing to do! There was nothing good that would come of that—nothing! Why in the world would he go poke at a hornets' nest?

"Leah? Hello?"

"Sorry—I'm still here."

"Yeah, so he'd probably appreciate some prayer. He was determined to go."

Leah pressed her eyes closed. Prayer was the very minimum of what her dad was going to need! "Yeah, okay. I'll pray for him. But look, Chelsea—I should go. Will you have Dad call me, please?"

"Sure. I'll tell him as soon as he gets home. Goodbye, dear!"

Leah hung up and sat with her face in her hands. One thing she had learned in her twenty-six years was that things never went well in discussions between her mom and dad. *Never.*

"What's wrong with you?" Kyla's voice broke in from behind her, making her jump and twist around.

"Oh—you scared me!"

"Sorry," she said. "I can't stay. I'm just swinging by for Hank's truck. We forgot it *again*, and he insists he needs it today! Are you all right?"

Leah nodded. "Yeah, I'm okay. It's right there." She pointed to the corner of the deck where Hank had left it. "I just got off the phone with my dad's wife, Chelsea. She told me that my dad went over to talk to my mom this morning—back in Bridgewater. That doesn't happen!"

"That's cool!" Kyla said eagerly, then cocked her head at Leah's expression. "Right?"

"No! That's *not* a good thing! They don't get along at all! The sparks are gonna fly!"

"But what does that have to do with you?"

"No, I'll—I'll hear about it! Believe me—I will hear about it!"

"So?" Kyla walked over to where Leah sat and put her hand on her shoulder. "Lord Jesus, give Leah your peace and use this situation for your glory, in Jesus' name! Now, I'd advise you to give it over to the Lord and let them duke it out! This is *their* thing, not yours."

She was right, Leah acknowledged. It was genuinely a matter of boundaries. She nodded. "You're right! I'll try. Thanks. Where are you off to?"

"Dental appointments, then home. But guess what?"

"What?"

"My dad called me back about your cousin!"

Leah sat up. "Yeah? What'd you find out?"

"Two words." Kyla looked around her, lowering her voice. "Gambling addiction. That and all kinds of issues related to it. Apparently, it was a *huge* part of his divorce!"

Leah's eyes widened in surprise. "Whoa. I would have never guessed that! How do they find out stuff like that?"

"I'm not sure, but understand that this is confidential! Dad's a bit upset with me for taking advantage of his relationship with his friend—especially because he's running for state senator now. So mum's the word on this, okay?"

"Absolutely!" Leah agreed. "A gambling addiction! So *that's* probably why he's so broke! And that would explain why my Uncle Richard wouldn't give him the house in the first place!"

"Maybe! But there's something else you should know."

"What?"

"Peter said your cousin texted him last night about Brindle. He told Peter to tell you to tell your friend—Brindle—to stay out of his garage!"

Leah frowned in confusion. "What?"

Kyla jerked her head, pausing to let it sink in. "Brindle went to Marty's last night after she left your house. Marty walked in on her looking through the stuff in his garage!"

"What the heck! What for?"

"I don't know, but there's something up with that girl! I think Brindle's the one who's been in your house!"

"I'm starting to wonder! I just don't get *why*. She wouldn't know about the coins—*I* didn't even know about the coins until I read the journal!"

"Maybe it's unrelated. Maybe she's a kleptomaniac or something!"

"She's *something*! And yet she was here when the Angel thing went down, so she's not a part of *that*."

"Phil." Kyla nodded briskly. "They're in this together—that's my guess anyway."

"In *what* together? You just said he checked out squeaky clean! Plus, he actually *helped* me with my mailbox!"

Kyla raised a skeptical brow. "Eh, I don't know! Something's up with them!"

Leah gave a grunt. "That security camera can't come soon enough!"

From a distance came the sound of the Grant brothers hollering for Kyla. She smiled and rolled her eyes. "Yes, get that camera up as soon as possible! But hey—the kids are in the car. I told them to count to one hundred and then call for me if I wasn't back. I gotta go. See you around two!" She snatched Hank's dump truck off the deck and left around the side of the house.

Leah sat back mulling over her newfound information about Marty, thanks to Kyla Watkin's help. Danny had been right about the two of them connecting well together. For so long she'd gone without any friends at all, and now she didn't know what she would do all weekend without Kyla there. Who would have thought that she could find such a great friend in New Hampton in such a short time? It was another blessing from God in her life, and all those blessings were beginning to overwhelm her. She recalled Brother Warren's words in their very first conversation: *If you knew how much God loves you and the good he has in store for you, you'd waste no time in pulling those boards off.* Leah laughed to herself. No kidding!

And that reminded her that Brother Warren had been right about God having "surprises" in store for her too—both with Danny and her dad! How could he have known what was coming in her life? But not only surprises—there was also the promise that Jesus would never fail her. She wasn't exactly sure how that applied, but since Brother Warren seemed to know what he was talking about, she supposed she should embrace that part too. At the minimum it was a good thing to think about—that God was not going to let her down. She might as well learn how to relax and trust him.

Sighing contentedly, she slid down in the chair and put her hands up behind her head, the journal resting upside down on her belly. She wondered how the conversation between her mom and dad had gone. She couldn't even imagine how furious her mother must have been with something like that popped unexpectedly on her in the morning! She hoped her dad survived to make the trip to help her in the morning! But Kyla was right—this was *their* deal, not hers. In her mind Leah drew an imaginary circle around her parents, decidedly keeping herself out of that sphere.

Yawning, she picked up the journal and found her place.

> *I had to stay home from work today. I think Lenore has the flu. She was so sick this morning, poor girl. Couldn't keep anything down.*

But the day was perfect. The sun warmed her skin deliciously with just enough breeze to keep it comfortable. Leah yawned again and leaned the journal back, closing her eyes to rest another minute, the pages crinkling as the light breeze waved them back and forth. It was hard to focus with everything else going on—her parents sparring in her head, the new discovery about Marty, Brindle's weirdness, and Danny leaving for the weekend. She wished he didn't have to go. She liked being with him. Briefly she peeked toward the cabin to check if he were outside yet, but she couldn't see him. He was still packing.

With effort she tried again with the journal. Paging back to find her place, her eyes fell at the top of a random page along the way.

> *—so angry with her! Here all this time when I thought she was hanging out at her friend Jody's house, she was with him instead! Todd Caratta is his name. She's not very far along, but Ed and I plan to meet with Todd and his parents soon to talk about it. She's only sixteen!*

Leah's eye paused on the words. Not very far along? Curiously, she turned to the previous page.

> *After three weeks of Lenore puking and feeling perpetually run down, I finally took her to the doctor. I thought maybe she had mono. About fell off my chair when the doctor announced*

that her pregnancy test came back positive! I was completely blindsided. And Lenore sat there looking at me with that poker face of hers—like she didn't have the slightest clue how it might have happened! I could have killed her right there, but I had to be nice in front of the doctor. I couldn't believe it! I was so angry—

Leah sat up, bewildered. Her mother's teenage pregnancy wasn't a surprise, but Todd Caratta—? Who the heck was he? She stared at the journal in disbelief. Someone named Todd Caratta was her—her *father?* Impossible! How could that be?

Hastily she flipped back to the last recorded date, and a cry escaped her lips. There—that explained it, but it added to her amazement: the entry in the journal had been made *two years* before Leah had been born! Her mom had been pregnant with another child before her! Why had she never said anything about it? What had happened to the baby? Had it died? Had there been a miscarriage or—or an abortion perhaps?

Adrenalized, Leah straddled the chaise lounge with the journal between her legs, haphazardly turning the pages as she skimmed her grandmother's handwriting. Hastily her finger followed the words toward the end of the volume.

Well, if today wasn't a day to beat all days! Here it is—my wedding day, the day of my dreams, and my pregnant daughter is throwing a fit and screaming at me because her dress is too tight, and she doesn't want to move away from Bridgewater. She hates Ed, hates New Hampton, hates me, hates her life, hates everything! And I'm trying to hold it all together as I've packed up our entire apartment in preparation for our move and prepared for our wedding on top of it. Ed is convinced moving is the best thing to do, to get her away from Todd, but our lives have been sheer hell in the process. I really can't see how to fix any of this. I've cried on Mary, cried on Ed, cried on God, but I guess we're simply going to have to ride out this storm. We haven't even begun to think about the baby itself. Lord, have mercy!

Leah bit her lip and shook her head. *No wonder!* No wonder her mother hated the Richmond house! It made all the sense in the world now!

But Leah had reached the final page. She closed the cover, rising off the chair. Journal 3 was still in the purple bin at the head of her bed over at her house, but she wouldn't go alone to get it. She needed Danny—not only for safety's sake, but something else had occurred to her too, and she wanted him there.

Chapter Twenty-Seven

The cabin door was open, and Danny was inside zipping up his duffel bag when Leah topped the steps and knocked on the door frame.

He straightened, flashing a broad smile. "Hello!"

"You wouldn't *believe* what I just discovered!" she burst out. "My mom is pregnant!"

He jerked. "*What?*"

"Not *now*, silly! In Grandma's journal! But it's *not* with me! There was *another* baby before me!" Before he could comment, she continued: "So I'm reading along, and I find out my mom's pregnant and only sixteen—and this is right at the time my grandparents are getting married. She didn't want to move here *at all*, which explains a lot. I totally get why my mom hates this place so much!"

He stood fixed beside the table. "Wow!"

"Yes, 'wow'! And I need you to go with me to get the next journal."

He nodded hesitantly, his eyes darting to the clock. "Right. Could Jackie maybe go over with you? I'm leaving here in a minute."

Leah shook her head. "Nope, 'cause we have to go to the basement for something, and I'd like you there."

"Well, I want to, Leah, but we're supposed to roll out of here at noon, and I don't want to be late."

She raised her phone in a challenge. "It's not noon yet. We have half an hour, and this is important!"

He paused, giving way to a crooked smile. "Well, since it looks like I don't have a choice, we'd better get moving!" He grabbed his bag and scooped up his guitar case, starting toward her. "I'll drop these off at the car on the way and set an alarm on my phone."

"Pfft—set an alarm! You're so funny, Danny! I'd hate for you to go against your principles and be a few minutes late!"

He pulled the door shut. "It *is* against my principles! What's wrong with setting an alarm?" But he gave his hearty laugh.

"Come on—let's hurry then!" She ran up the path ahead of him.

After depositing his things in Brother Warren's car, they cut across her yard. Hastily Leah took the porch steps, unlocked the door, and made her way to the bin of journals in the corner under the window of her dining room camp.

"Want me to pull that whole thing out of there?" Danny asked, watching her dig.

Leah found the third journal and began paging through it. "Um, I think I have what I'm looking for—but yeah, sure. I might want to keep going after this." She moved aside to let him get to the bin.

He hefted the tote out of the corner and set it in the center of the room. "You know, Leah, it may be simpler to call your mom and ask her directly about this."

She nodded. "Oh, yes—we will *definitely* have something to talk about! But not quite yet. I'd like to know Grandma's perspective first. My mom's never spoken a single word about this! Not a word. Nor did Grandma."

"There might be a good reason for that."

"You could be right," Leah agreed. "I hope she didn't lose the baby. That'd be so sad!" Moving to the counter, she continued to scan the book page by page.

Danny shoved a hand in his pocket, peering out the window as he waited. "Looks like there might be a problem with Peter's trailer back there."

Leah glanced up briefly. "Huh? What's the problem?"

He leaned closer to the pane. "I'm not sure. Earlier when I brought over the hose, it looked like it had a flat tire, but now from this angle, it looks sunken down in the dirt. Like it's up to the axle!"

"It sunk?"

"Well, like the ground's soft there—like it's in mud or something."

"How could that be? It hasn't rained."

"I don't know. A spring maybe? Anyway, that can't be good. I'll call Peter. He should move it."

"Okay," Leah said, focused on the journal.

Danny turned from the window. "Time is ticking, Leah. You said there was a reason you wanted me?"

"Hold your horses! I have to find it in here first." Swiftly she skimmed paragraph by paragraph, drawing her finger down, murmuring as she went, "Still pregnant. Still pregnant. Still pregnant. Yes—here—I found it!" Excitedly she tapped a line of handwriting. "It's a *girl*! It's a girl, Danny DeSoto!" She whirled to look at him. "Well, what do you know? I have an older sister!"

Danny came to peek over her shoulder. "Congratulations! What's her name?"

"Hang on—I don't know yet." Leah flipped to the next page. "Here— here it is! Ta-da! Her name is Belinda—Belinda Ann Wilkes!" She was silent, reading to herself. Then she let out a long breath. "Oh my—this is brutal! They're placing her for adoption." She looked up at him. "My poor mother! Holy cow—I bet that was tough!"

He tipped his head in agreement. "Yeah."

"It's what I suspected, but still, it's so sad. No wonder she never talked about it!" She patted the journal. "All right—I *do* want to read this, but it'll have to wait. I'll probably be crying. But now that I *know*, come downstairs with me. Brindle and I found some baby stuff in a box down there, and I'll bet you anything it's baby Belinda's!"

He gave a curt nod and gestured. "After you."

Leah found the plastic tote marked "Lenore" in the furnace room storage area. There beneath her mother's old cheerleader sweater, pom poms, and other high school memorabilia were the knitted baby blanket and embroidered block quilt that she and Brindle had found before.

"I bet old Aunt Hazel embroidered these for her," Leah said, running her hand over the pink-and-white blocks. "When we found them, I thought they were mine. But I'll bet they were hers—Belinda's."

"Want me to carry the bin upstairs for you?"

"Oh, no—no, I just want to confirm it's hers." Carefully she set the blankets aside and shuffled through old photos and large packets of keepsake papers. Further down she found a shallow box with baby graphics on it. Inside was a small baby book with a padded satin cover. Gingerly she lifted it open to reveal a decorative copy of a birth certificate, complete with a tiny ink footprint.

"Jackpot," she said, gazing at the document in awe. "This is what I was hoping to find. Goodness—she was so teeny! Not even seven pounds! And look—a curl of her hair! So delicate! I bet Grandma saved all this for Mom." She looked up at Danny, who stood nearby. "It kinda makes me want to cry! I wonder what happened to her. She'd be twenty-eight now. But know what? It all makes sense! The old locksmith who knew my grandpa said his daughter was pregnant the same time as my mom—twenty-eight years ago. I thought he was off, but he was right!"

Danny nodded thoughtfully. "That can't have been easy to go through as a teenager."

"No kidding! But I so *get* why she hates this place—I get it! I hope she'll be willing to talk about it." Leah sighed and began packing everything back into the bin. "Okay, I met my objective. It's time to go." She snapped the lid back on and stood. "How are we doing for time? Your alarm hasn't gone off yet!"

"We have six minutes."

"Great! Let's go up and grab that bin of journals and be done!"

"Cool—let's do it! Who knows what else you'll learn?"

Leah laughed. "Oh, golly—I don't think I could handle any more surprises!"

Danny closed the door at the top of the stairs.

"So why'd you need me here again?" He pulled his phone out to cancel his alarm.

"Just *that*." Leah gestured to the basement. "Thanks for going with me."

"Seriously? That's all?"

"Yes—I didn't want to go down there alone."

He gave an amused chuckle. "You goofball! You said you needed me for something Jackie couldn't do! I was expecting to fix something or lift some heavy object for you!"

Leah narrowed her eyes. "*No*, I told you I had to do something in the basement, and I wanted you to come with me!"

"Yeah, and Jackie could have done that!"

"Yeah, but Jackie doesn't know my family like you do! Or me. I wanted *you* because you get it! But I'll let you lug that tote of journals back for me, if you'd like to carry something heavy." She gave an impish smile.

He howled out a laugh, his eyes shining. "Leah! You are something else! But we should get going."

"Yeah," she said with a wistful sigh. "I wish you didn't have to go."

"You'll have a great time with Kyla this afternoon—and Jackie tonight! And your dad'll be here in the morning."

Leah nodded. "I know. It'll all be great. I just wish you were here too."

"And why is that?" His eyes rose to meet hers.

The realization crashed in all at once, taking her breath away as it spread with a lovely tingle in her belly. Holy cow—she *liked* him. She liked being with him, liked his sense of humor, his manner—everything about him. Heavens—she more than liked him—she *loved* him. She stood there, charged with a flustered happiness, her cheeks aflame. How had this happened—that her friend and brother had become so much more to her? Steady and dependable Danny. Smart and kind, strong, athletic, and so much fun. And now as she struggled to answer him, holding his gaze made it even harder, for there was a spark in those eyes looking back at her.

She swallowed, attempting to appear nonchalant. "So, um—so you could be a part of everything."

"Leah," he whispered, stepping closer.

And then he kissed her—a little kiss at first. But as she responded, he kissed her again, hungrily this time, the kind of kiss that sent electricity rushing through her body. And Leah knew he wasn't kissing her for fun—as for the pleasure of simply kissing a girl. For all the years she had known him, Danny DeSoto was never one to lead a girl on, never one to mess around and play with a girl's heart. It was against his principles. For him to kiss her now was no thoughtless whim, and in it, she marveled: How could it be that *he* had feelings for *her*?

Her heart was racing when he let her go. "What just happened?" she breathed.

He gave a crooked smile. "I believe I just kissed you! And I'd like to again, if you'll let me."

She needed no urging. Returning his smile, she raised her face to his, but now her thoughts went careening down a panicky trail. If Danny didn't play with girls' hearts, then Danny was kissing her because he loved her, and there was only one place that would go. And if she were going to marry Danny DeSoto, she would *become* a DeSoto, and that meant she would be connected to Jake forever. Jake would become her brother-in-law. And that meant every holiday they would see Jake and Rachel—not only see them, but see them together as a married couple, with their kids besides. There would be no escaping them, no evading the relationship, no letting them fade from her memory with time. Oh, she wanted him—she wanted Danny enormously—but it all boiled down to one quite simple equation: If she were going to be with him, she would have to deal with—

"—Jake," she said mournfully, pulling away.

He drew back, looking down at her. "It's Danny."

"What?"

"My name's *Danny*." He dropped his arms.

Leah's mouth opened. "No, I know! What I meant was—"

The chime of the doorbell suddenly cut in from across the house. Both of them turned their heads. Crud—it was probably Brindle. Leah sighed in irritation. Like she wanted to deal with her right now!

Danny looked back. "Leah, you're killing me! I cannot live my *entire* life under the shadow of my brother!"

"What? No!" She held up a hand. "No, Danny—it's not that! It was just, I mean, I was thinking that if we—you know—if I were to—to be with *you*, then I would have to deal with the stuff with Jake. And Rachel. All of that."

He gave a deliberate nod. "Yes. Yes, you would!"

The doorbell sounded again, followed by a sharp rapping on the door.

Danny gave an incredulous shake of his head. "Unbelievable! Leah, I'm sorry! We can't do this now. You need to answer your door, and I've got to go. Brother Warren's expecting me."

"*What?* But—"

"—I'm really sorry! Look—it's probably good to be away from each other this weekend anyway—to think and pray about things."

Leah felt a stab in her gut. "Danny, wait—you can't just leave! We're not done talking!"

For the third time the doorbell rang.

"I know. But we'll have to finish later." He closed his eyes, shaking his head again. "I'll carry the journals over for you. My place is all ready for your dad. Tell him hello from me—will you?" He caught her hand and squeezed it. "Leah, truly—I'm sorry! We'll talk when I get back. I promise. Go get the door, and when you're finished go right back to Jackie's."

Leah watched in disbelief as he retrieved the bin and crossed the kitchen on his way to exit out the back. More rapping. Numbly she turned for the door. Honestly, Brindle was the dead *last* person she wanted to see right now. She didn't trust her one iota. Not one. As she reached to open it, the knob twisted and the door swung wide, and there stood her mother— her *mother*—with her thick hair down around her shoulders and an ornery expression on her face! Leah gaped.

"Mom! What are you doing here?"

"So what now—you don't answer your door anymore?" Lenore stepped inside, letting the screen door bang shut behind her. "What took you so long? Were you still in bed or what?"

"I—I didn't know you were coming! I wasn't expecting you!"

"That's no excuse to leave someone standing outside!"

Leah made a sound, moving aside. "I'm—I'm sorry! I was—busy." It was hard to think. Her head was spinning, though not only at seeing her mother. She couldn't believe Danny had left like that—that he had just *walked out* after what had happened! After kissing her! And now what was she supposed to do? What was she supposed to think? And with a promise to talk *when he got back*—? That was Sunday night—like, four days from now! And with no offer to *call* her! What was wrong with a phone call? Had he even considered it? Or didn't he want to?

"There's a dumpster out there!"

Leah blinked. "Uh, yeah. I got rid of the old carpet and stuff. Furniture." She waved toward the bare and echoey living room. *Why did he leave like that?* And what did her mother want?

Lenore turned to scan the room. "I see you've done a little work in here and out in front, but that garage door definitely needs to be replaced! What did you do—hit it with your car? It's not the greatest impression when you drive in—with your mailbox laying out in the middle of the road and your garage door all crunched to heck! Neighbors care about that sort of thing, you know. You gotta keep the place up!"

"I know, Mom. I'm working on it—" She stopped, shooting her a look. "My mailbox? Is it, like—leaning forward?"

"It's broken off! Laying out across the driveway, and I almost ran over it coming in! That should have been taken care of! It might have damaged my car!"

Leah felt a sick lurch in her stomach. Someone was dead serious about getting a message across. "I—I didn't know about it! So why are you here?" Her best guess was that it had something to do with her dad.

"What—a mother can't visit her own daughter?"

"For real, Mom—what's going on?"

Lenore folded her arms. "*You* tell *me*! I'm here to get a straight answer from you!"

Leah opened her hands. "Tell me where to start, and I'll tell you what I know."

"You've been lying to me! Your father's been here, and you've been hiding it from me!"

Leah groaned inwardly. "I haven't been hiding anything! I haven't talked to you for a day!"

"Right—and on purpose! You've been avoiding me!"

"I've been busy!"

"Busy, my foot! I want to know what you've been telling your dad about me!"

"Nothing! We don't talk about you!" Oh, she had called it! The moment Chelsea said her dad had gone over there, Leah *knew* it would come back on her somehow!

"That's not what *he* said!"

Kyla's poolside counsel popped into her head. "Don't put me in the middle of your beef with Dad. That's between the two of you! You guys can duke it out yourselves!"

"You put *yourself* in the middle when you told your father whatever you told him!"

"I'd prefer to stay out of it, Mom. You're a bitter woman, and I don't need your 'poison ivy' spreading all over my life too!" As she blurted it, Brother Warren's analogy rebounded to smack her. Surely, if there were any generational issues going on in her family, wasn't it this—*bitterness*? Wasn't she just like her mother—only with Jake and Rachel, not her dad? And she had a choice to keep it alive in her character or not!

Lenore's gaze bore into her. "You can skip the insults, Miss High and Mighty. I simply want to know what you said!"

Helplessly Leah shook her head. "I don't know what you're referring to! He's going to be helping me with the kitchen, and he stopped by to see it, and we talked. It was *good*. He wasn't drinking. I guess he's taking this class or something that's helping him repair relationships—something like that."

She paused, eyeing her. Should she go for it? Would she pay if she tried to disentangle herself from their feud? Recklessly she plunged ahead. "He asked me to forgive him for failing me as a father, and you know what? *I do!* I don't care what you say—I *do* forgive him! And I told him that! And he didn't bring it up, but I also told him that I forgive him for his affair with Chelsea and for cheating on you too. All that stuff. I know it probably makes you spittin' mad, but this is where I'm at! So deal with it!" There—she had set *somewhat* of a boundary! And now she braced herself for the backlash.

Her mother simply lifted her chin. "So what did he say after that?"

"After what?"

"After you said you forgave him for cheating on me."

Leah raised her shoulders, trying to remember. "Uh, I think he just said, 'Thanks.'"

Lenore stared.

Leah sighed, eager to eject herself from the argument. All she could think about was Danny being away until Sunday night, which seemed like a year away. "Mom, I don't want to be rude, but I'm in a bind. I need to run next door to take care of something super important. I'll come right back—I promise—and then we'll talk. I *do* want to visit with you. We'll finish this conversation, and I'll show you around and tell you what I've been working on."

"What's so urgent?"

Leah hesitated. "Uh—I'll tell you when I get back. I'm hoping to catch some friends before they leave on a trip, but I'll have to hurry because they're leaving, like—right now!"

Her mother nodded grudgingly. "Fine then."

"Thanks." She gestured to her porch. "Sorry—out there is the extent of my furniture. Make yourself comfortable. I'll be quick."

Leah cleared the porch steps in a single bound and sprinted across her lawn. She just wanted to tell him *one* thing, and she didn't even care if she had to say it in front of Brother Warren. She'd do it! She wanted Danny to know she was committed to forgive Jake and Rachel and letting it all go no matter how hard it was, no matter how long it took, no matter if she had to go to counseling for a hundred years. She would face it all and go through it—not only to have him, but to be free from the poison of bitterness. If her dad could navigate those difficult waters, why couldn't she?

But Brother Warren's car was gone. Danny's was there, but Leah knew they had taken the old man's vehicle. She let out a defeated sigh, staring down the driveway. She could call him, but he'd be driving, and they'd be on speaker phone and it wouldn't be the same, especially with Brother Warren in the car next to him. And then later he'd be in conference meetings. Who knew what his schedule would be? A text conversation wouldn't cut it either. No, she'd have to wait.

She did have one short thing to say, however. Resigned, she pulled out her phone, texting, "Danny, you jerk face!"

She didn't expect him to text back, but he did—right away. "Acknowledged and deserved. Sorry. Driving. Call you tonight."

Well, she reasoned, considering it was against the law *and* his principles to text and drive, his response was encouraging. Tonight. They would talk tonight. She glanced at the time. The thought of him not wanting her because of her baggage with Jake was frightening. She didn't know anyone she was as comfortable with as him, nor anyone who understood her like him—nor anyone she admired and trusted as much as him either.

And to be without him—Leah couldn't even imagine how miserable she would be!

Shoving her phone back into her pocket, she blew out a long breath. How had this happened? How in the world had she fallen in love with Danny DeSoto, of all people on the planet? Yes, it was sudden, but it wasn't as though they had just met or anything. They'd already been close friends for ten years, minus the last four. The most incredible part was that she hadn't seen how perfect he was for her until now! How had she been so blind?

"Oh! Hi, Leah! How long have you been here?"

Leah turned. Jackie had come up the side of the house to water her plants and just now noticed her in the driveway. She had a canvas gardening pouch over one arm. Nearby, Angel nosed around in the grass.

"Hi," Leah responded, motioning to the driveway. "I see the guys left."

"Yeah, Dad was anxious to get on the road. It's a four-hour drive for them. Did you get what you needed?"

Leah tipped her head. "From the house?"

"No, from Brindle—the stuff that Brindle came to get for you."

Leah frowned. "What?"

"Well—" Jackie paused, giving her a confused look. "She just left a moment ago. She said you sent her over to get something for you from your room." She gestured toward the house.

Leah made a little sound. "What? I didn't send her to get anything for me! I haven't even seen her today!"

Jackie's head jerked back in surprise.

"What did she want? Did she take anything?"

"Um, I—" Her lips moved as she considered it. "I don't know. I don't remember her leaving with anything."

"Oh, man!" Leah put a hand to her forehead. Could it be any clearer? Danny had been right all along. And Kyla. *Brindle* had to be the one who'd been snooping in her house from the beginning. What was she up to? Somehow she had to be related to the mailbox vandalism too. "I'm gonna quickly check my room," she told Jackie, taking the stairs to the front door. "But my mom stopped in unexpectedly, so I'll need to get back to the house right away."

"Oh, your mother's here? How nice!"

"Yeah."

"How sweet of her to visit you!"

Leah lifted her hand to acknowledge Jackie's comment, but she was certain her mother had never had the description "sweet" associated with her in her entire life.

Once she was in her room, Leah knew exactly what Brindle had come to find, for her grandmother's journal on the corner of the dresser where she'd left it had obviously been repositioned. Furthermore, upon closer observation she found that the sheet of paper with the list of Krugerrands was now tucked inside a different journal—the one Leah hadn't read yet. Not only had Brindle seen that list, but she had tried to make it look like she hadn't.

"Well, well, well," Leah murmured, glancing around to see if anything else had been disturbed. "Look who knows about the gold coins!" If Brindle didn't before, she did now.

Quickly she did an inventory of where the other journals were. Besides these two, she'd left one poolside on her chair before getting Danny. It was probably still there, but she'd check for sure. Danny had brought the whole purple bin of them back to Jackie's from her house, but if Brindle had taken any or taken the bin itself, surely Jackie would have noticed!

Her eyes returned to the volume on the dresser. There was no way to tell for sure, but it certainly appeared Brindle had been intentional about what she'd come for. And now she not only knew about the list of coins, but also the combination to the safe, scrawled across the bottom of the page. She had likely taken a photo of it. That little sneak! She shook her head.

Wrenching her phone out of her pocket, she called Kyla, but it went directly to her messaging.

"Call me right away when you get this—*right away*!" Leah said into the phone. Then she also texted her the same thing, adding, "It's important!"

Eyeing the journals, she huffed, recalling Brindle's multiple inquiries about them. How obvious now! Of course, she'd been looking for them, sneaking into her house to search for them—and Marty's garage too! But how in the world could she have known about the printout tucked away in that volume? Or had she stumbled upon it accidentally just today? Leah frowned. If it were the cache of gold coins that she was ultimately after— seriously, how on earth could she have known about it?

Somehow she would have to confront Brindle on this—to tell her she knew what she was doing and what she was looking for—and that did not promise to be a pleasant task. On the upside, if Brindle *were* searching for a safe, then she'd find out soon enough that both it and the coins supposedly within it were gone. That helped the situation at least. But if Leah told her that, would she even believe her? The mailbox antics also crossed her mind and she shuddered. If intimidation were the goal, Brindle had hit the mark. Leah swung her head, contemplating her crafty friend. Oh, she'd been slick!

Just like Rachel Steinburg!

First things first, she told herself. She needed to deal with her mother. She sighed heavily, wondering how long she was planning to stay—perhaps even overnight, for all she knew, which would mean that she'd have to call her dad to postpone his trip up to help her. And that reminded her that she would have to cancel with Kyla for the afternoon as well. She turned to go, but before she left the house, she scanned the main floor for the purple bin, finding it quickly in the corner of the kitchen, right inside the patio doors. On it was a note folded in half with her name on it. She knew Danny's handwriting.

"Leaving you like that was so bad. Forgive my idiotic timing. D."

"I'll say!" Leah breathed, pocketing the note. But it made her feel a lot better.

She pulled the cover off the bin to find the collection of journals undisturbed. Securing the lid, she peered through the glass toward the chaise lounge beside the pool. Yes, she could see the edge of the journal on the chair. That was good.

Jackie was weeding when Leah came up the walk. She straightened. "Was everything okay, hon? Your friend didn't take anything from you, did she?"

"No, nothing was taken," Leah replied, debating if she should tell her anything. How would it be beneficial for Jackie to know what was going on? It would only make her worry.

Her breath rushed out in relief. "Oh, that's good! I felt so bad! If Brindle comes back, would you like me to tell her anything?"

"Yeah—yeah, tell her to come talk to me. Don't let her go in the house—tell her I already have everything I need over at my place."

Jackie gave a sincere nod. "All right, dear—I will."

"I'm going back to hang out with my mom." She gestured.

"All right, hon. Have an enjoyable time together! I'd love to meet her if it works out."

Leah smiled. "Thank you. We'll see." Enjoyable—*right*! Her mother was in such a mood! Leah wondered if she dared bring up what she knew about her pregnancy and the baby.

Lenore was in the kitchen looking through the cabinets when Leah got back.

"I thought you said you'd be quick," she said as Leah came in. She closed the cupboard doors and turned to face her.

"Yeah, sorry. I had to"—had to run and check something in her room next door? How would she explain that she was staying at the neighbor's?—"um, had to cut a long conversation short. But I'm here." She smiled.

"Whose trailer is that out in the yard? Marty's? It's wrecking the lawn, and it'll surely cave everything in back there!"

"It belongs to my friend's husband. He's coming to move it soon. He used the equipment for some work on the yard last night."

"Yes—well it should be moved off there right away! And you have no furniture here! None at all! And *that* doesn't count!" She pointed to the inflatable bed.

"I know. Once I get the flooring replaced, I'll get a real bed and a couch and stuff. Soon. But that air mattress isn't terrible. I've been painting though—as you can probably tell. We've gotten a lot done!" She gestured, sniffing the air.

But Lenore had turned back toward the cabinets. "There's nothing salvageable about these. Looks like Marty completely destroyed them!"

Leah faced her tiredly. "Marty lives *next door*, Mom. He always has. He's *never* lived here!"

"Yes, but wasn't it his responsibility to watch this place?" Her eyes flitted around the room. "And you said your dad is going to help you replace these? Who gave him the right to step foot into this house?"

"Knock it off, Mom! I asked him for help 'cause Marty hates me now—and that's because of *you*!"

"And whose money is paying for all of this? Don't come running to *me*—I already warned you about that! A new kitchen, carpet, furniture—that can't be cheap! Is your dad paying for this?"

"Grandpa Ed left me some money for renovation—remember? But I won't turn Dad down if he offers!" As she spoke, her phone chirped in her pocket. A text! Hopefully it was from Kyla—but it could be from Danny too.

"I'm sure half of that thousand bucks you said your grandfather gave you flew out the window on that patio set. What were you thinking to blow the whole wad out there? You have no common sense!"

"Well, I lied. He gave me a lot more than that, but I knew you'd have a fit about it. So yeah—this is my house, and this is what I'm doing! End of story." She flayed her hands.

Her phone sounded again. Wiggling it out of her pocket Leah saw that Kyla had texted twice for her to call.

"Would you put that away?" her mother barked. "Honestly—we're talking here! You and Braydon both! I don't understand why you two can't carry on a conversation with another human being without having to be constantly on your cell phones! It's so rude!"

"Mom, *please*! Would you chill out? Just one second!" Quickly Leah typed a reply: *Can't talk. My mom's here. Have to cancel. Will call soon.* She pushed "send" and slid it back into her pocket. "Okay. Let's go sit outside. Would you like something to drink?" Almost immediately she heard another text come in.

Lenore rolled her eyes. "Fine. I'd have some of that iced tea you have in your refrigerator. If any of your glasses are clean."

Leah took a long, controlled breath. Geez—her mother was crabby! Right now the thought of bringing up the knowledge of her previous pregnancy seemed like a suicide mission.

On the way to the porch with their drinks, Leah's pocket chirped and vibrated as two more texts came in.

"When did you do all this?" her mother asked, indicating the new plantings and the fresh mulch.

"Just last night," Leah replied. "My friend Kyla and her husband and some other friends came over to help me."

"Who?"

"My friend Kyla Watkins and her husband, Peter. He's a landscaper and had some throw-away plants that he offered me. A few other friends came to help too. They did a lot of work for me, and I think it looks really nice!" She shuddered at what her mother would have thought of the yard if she had come only yesterday!

"Watkins?" She frowned. "I sure hope it isn't anyone related to that Watkin's Nursery ordeal years ago. I'd be careful about that! One of those Watkins boys assaulted an employee. It was shocking! They were from New Hampton, you know."

"Huh." She looked away, letting it pass. "Well, I love my little garden."

Once again, her phone chirped with a text, and her mother cast her a look of annoyance. Leah squirmed uneasily. Hadn't Kyla gotten her message? Why did she keep texting? Then her phone began to ring.

"I'll put it on silent," she said, pinching the ringer off through her pocket, but when she got it out, she saw Kyla's last text on the face of her phone.

"I need to talk to you RIGHT NOW! Please! Go somewhere private!"

Leah set her drink down onto the coffee table. "Excuse me, Mom. I'll be right back. I need to use the restroom."

Chapter Twenty-Eight

Kyla answered Leah's call immediately, her voice breathless. "Leah—oh, my gosh—do I have something to tell you! Where are you? Why didn't you answer your phone?"

Leah closed the bathroom door. "I'm at my house. Didn't you get my text? I couldn't! My mom's here! She showed up unexpectedly!"

"Well, I found out something, and you need to sit down!"

"What?" Leah asked, alarmed at her urgency.

"She knows! Brindle Baylor is *definitely* looking for those coins!"

Leah's head bobbed in agreement. "I *know*! I was going to call you too! While I was over here with Danny, she showed up at Jackie's saying I sent her to get something from my room. She saw the sheet from the journal—I know it for sure! She saw all the stuff about the Krugerrands!"

"Interesting! Well, there's a lot more than *that*!"

"What?"

"Okay—so when I left Jackie's this morning, I still had some time before the boys' dental appointments, so I went over to Brindle's place. I was planning on stopping over there anyway this week to talk to her about the stuff she shared at Bible study, and I thought why not probe a bit—? Who knows what might come out?"

"What do you mean you went to her place? We don't know for sure where she lives!"

"We do *now*! It's pretty obvious she's living in that town house with Phil! His truck wasn't there, but a blue car was, so I texted my dad a picture of her plates—"

"Kyla, you're a genius! What'd you find out?"

"Thanks—tell you in a sec! But first—while I was on my way to her front door, she suddenly came out of the house and started walking toward *your* place—she just appeared! I was right in front of her garage, but she

437

didn't even see me!"

"Seriously?"

"I stood there 'til she was gone, and then on my way back to my car I happened to glance inside *her* car, and Leah, I found something!"

"What did you find?"

"Some papers! There were these letters on the passenger's seat, but it was the letterhead that caught my attention! And since I knew she was gone, I opened her car door to get a closer look—"

"You went in her car?"

"I know! I'm feeling pretty guilty about it, but you need to see what I found! I took some photos, and I'm texting them to you right now!"

"Well, hurry up! My mom's waiting for me on the porch. I'm in the bathroom, and I can't be gone that long!"

"Okay. I also found a key on a plastic key ring with the name 'Ed Davison' on it! I took a picture of that too."

"Oh, geez! What on earth!"

"Yeah, she got a key to your house somehow—maybe from your garage or Marty's—who knows?"

Leah's phone vibrated as several photos arrived, and she switched to speaker phone to open them. Her jaw fell open.

"Those are mine!" she exclaimed, immediately recognizing the Seco Valley letterhead. Here were the letters she had received from both her grandparents at the law firm! "Oh, that *rat*—she's been in my stuff! What the heck! That rat went through my stuff and stole my—*What?*" She gasped, enlarging one of the documents. "It's the second page! I've never seen this! It's the page I've been missing from my grandma's letter! How did *she* get it?"

"I thought you'd find this interesting!" Kyla said. "Do you recognize the return address on the envelope?"

Leah zoomed up on the last photo. "Duvall & Ross, Attorneys at Law—our family lawyer."

"Ha! Is that so? Okay, so get this, Leah—I used to work there! I used to work at Duvall & Ross, and I know Richard Duvall personally because I dated his son in college!"

"No stinkin' way!"

"Right! So when I saw this, I called Richard right away—"

Leah gave a disbelieving shake of her head. "Are you serious?"

"He knew no one by the name of Brindle Baylor, but while we were talking, my dad texted me back to let me know that Brindle's car is registered under the name of Belinda Taylor at a Bridgewater address. So I called Richard right back, and he said they had an office assistant named Belinda Taylor who worked for them earlier this year. She quit about three weeks ago because she was moving to—get this—New Hampton!"

Leah huffed. "No kidding! So Brindle Baylor is Belinda Taylor! She's been using a fake name!"

"That's my guess!"

"And she got my stuff at the law office!"

"Yup! Belinda Ann Taylor—age twenty-eight."

The words struck her like a punch in the gut, sucking out her breath. Leah stared at herself in the mirror as a hundred details all shimmied into place.

"*Oh, my God!*" she sputtered. "Oh, my *God*!" Her hand popped over her face.

Kyla made a little sound. "Leah, you're using the Lord's name disrespectfully and you shouldn't do that. What's going on? Do you know her?"

"Oh, my God! Oh, my—"

Bam-bam-bam! Several sharp knocks rattled the bathroom door. Leah gave a startled cry, twisting around toward it.

"Everything all right in there?" her mother called from the hallway.

Leah stared at the door with jelly legs, trying to catch her breath. "Sorry, Mom—I'm not feeling that great!" It was completely true.

"Well, holy smokes! What's taking so long? We can't wait all day out here!"

"Be out in a minute!"

A silence.

Kyla spoke, "That was your mom?"

Leah lowered her voice. "Yes—hold on." She put the phone down, listening carefully to assure that her mother had left. "Okay—we need to hurry, but listen, Kyla—*listen*! I've got to tell you something—something so incredible! Oh, my God!" She ran her hand through her hair, pacing in front of the sink. "This morning when you came, I was reading one of my grandma's journals at the pool—"

"Yes—?"

"Well, shortly after you left, I read about my mom getting pregnant while she was in high school. This is two years before I was born, and no one in the family has ever mentioned it! Ever! So I found out she had a baby girl, and guess what they named her?" She paused with another incredulous shake of her head. *"Belinda Ann Wilkes.* Wilkes was my mother's maiden name. They placed her for adoption."

There was a long space in which neither of them spoke.

"Could it be?" Kyla finally asked.

Leah closed the lid on the toilet and sat down. "I don't know! I mean, what are the odds of it? How—how many girls do you know with the name Belinda? It's not a very common name!"

"No, it's not."

"And the age is right. And the same middle name too. And she just moved. Oh, my God, Kyla! Brindle Baylor could be my—could be my—"

"Leah, don't dishonor the Lord like that! It looks very—well, like it could be a good possibility, but you don't know that for certain. It could still be a coincidence."

Leah stared dazedly at the shower doors ahead. "It's possible she doesn't even know! I mean, *I* wouldn't have if I hadn't read it in the journal this morning! So maybe she has no clue about that part either. You know, that we're—that we could be—the part about being—sisters." She swallowed, trying to take it in. "I mean, she could have simply stumbled upon those letters at the lawyer's office and thinks she's going to find some gold coins at this random place in New Hampton and get rich."

"Maybe."

"But they don't even exist—that's the crazy thing! There's no sign of them anywhere and no safe to be found—but wouldn't she know that too if she's been looking?" She was babbling, she realized, her thoughts tumbling out of her mouth.

There was another pause.

"Do you know anything else about her?" Leah asked finally. "Could you maybe have your dad ask for a background check on her too?"

"Already asked, and I'm still waiting for him to get back to me. But my dad's getting a little bugged. He says we should go to the police if we have concerns. Maybe we should, Leah. Have you thought of that?"

"I have. It's just that everything's been so vague and hard to explain."

"I know, but maybe it's time."

"Yeah, maybe it's time," Leah echoed. "My mom told me that when she arrived this morning my mailbox was sheared off and lying in the middle of the driveway."

"What?"

"I know! This is getting scary! What's the point of that? It must be Brindle—don't you think? But what's she doing? After my mom leaves, I'd like to go to the station."

"Shouldn't you tell your mother about this?"

"There's *no way* I can tell her about this, Kyla! Think about it!"

"Right," she murmured thoughtfully. "Well, for now, is Dan with you? I think you should go get Dan!"

"They left—remember? They're on their way to Cantonville for their conference."

"Oh, yeah. Well, let me think. I'd come over, but I'd have to bring the boys. I got wrangled into watching them again because their mom's not feeling well—I would've had to cancel this afternoon anyway. Maybe you should take your mom and go to Jackie's. This whole thing makes me nervous. What if Brindle shows up there? She's been *so* deceptive—I don't trust her at all!"

"I'm with you there! I could bring my mom over to meet Jackie, but anything beyond that would be weird—how would I explain it? It's not like my mom would want to hang out there. Plus, she's going to have a heart attack if I even begin to let her know what's going on!"

"I'll call Jackie right now and explain it all. Maybe she could cook a meal or something to keep the two of you there for a while."

Leah shook her head. "No, Kyla—Jackie would give it away in a second! Plus, I don't think my mom would go for it. Is Peter around? Could he come over? Danny wanted him to look at his trailer in the backyard. Apparently it's parked on some soft ground or something."

"Peter's in St. Cicerone. He took his crew up to help with the flooding relief, and he's gone until tonight. I'll see what time Dr. Grant gets out of class. Maybe he could swing by."

"For what reason? How would I explain him showing up to my mom?"

"It doesn't matter! I don't want you there alone!"

Leah sighed. "Fine. We'll figure something out. But I really should go. I've been in here way too long, and I'm sure my mom is quite irritated with me."

"All right. Text me if you find out when she's leaving, and I'll try to go to the police station with you. And keep your phone with you, okay? I'll text you anything more I find out about Brindle."

After she hung up, Leah splashed her face with water and buried it in a towel. Brindle Baylor—that conniving rat! All her joking banter flooded back with biting overtones of Rachel Steinburg's smooth duplicity. Leah set the towel aside, meeting her eyes in the mirror. After all she'd done to accommodate her—inviting her in as a friend, letting her poke through her grandma's stuff, putting up with her moodiness, chumming together at the neighbor's barbecue—oh, she wanted to punch that girl in the face right now! If she came waltzing into her yard this afternoon, Brindle was going to hear it!

Blowing out her breath, Leah snatched her phone and reached to open the door—but then paused, remembering her grandmother's letter. She supposed she should know what the whole thing said, since Brindle already did. Her mother would have to wait another two minutes. Quickly she tapped the photo of the letter and zoomed up to read it again, this time continuing to the second page:

> *To be upfront with you, Ed and I have left some other valuables at the Richmond house specifically for you! We're not trying to be unfair to other family members but rather kind to the ones who invest themselves to seek them out. It's our feeble attempt to illustrate that treasures can be found in the most unlikely of places—even the Richmond house. I've spelled it out plainly in one of the journals, listing out—*

Leah switched to the next photo.

> *—the entire treasure trove of Ed's Krugerrands by the year we purchased them and their total weight, along with the combination to the safe. Buying gold was his way of putting his copper dividends to good use. Plus, he got a kick out of earning money from one metal to invest in another. I thought we should put the coins on deposit at the bank, but Ed insisted it was important to have a little wealth in reserve out of the knowledge and hands of anyone. His theory was that being tucked away in the cellar was better than the bank if our economy would someday fail. I suppose they're just as secure there in the safe as any other place. They will surely go unnoticed.*
>
> *So now you have incentive for plowing through my journal ramblings! Do put your inheritance to good use but stay humble in your wealth. As long as I have breath, I'll be praying for you to come to know Jesus our Savior, and when my life is over, I'll be with him, waiting for you to come and worship with me. Fondly, Havi Davison.*

Question answered, Leah mused, clicking off the screen and dropping her phone into her pocket. Sure enough, Brindle had found out everything at the law office! Thus, her eagerness to "help" with the house and her interest in old photos and journals. And her curiosity with the basement—especially the cellar. It all made sense. But did she know about—Leah frowned, recalling the moment in the furnace room when Brindle found the bin with the baby things inside. Leah nodded to herself. Oh, *yes*! Oh, yes—Brindle absolutely knew they shared the same mother!

For the first time, Leah considered what it might be like for her mom if Brindle did indeed show up while she was there. What if it all came out? Her mother would be completely unprepared for such a bombshell—finding out some random stranger was the child she had placed for adoption! That can't happen, Leah thought, her hand resting on the bathroom door. Perhaps Kyla was right—maybe she should get her mother out of there. Take her over to meet Jackie or something. If only Danny were around. She could really use his wisdom. Yet that might even be worse, considering how her mother might react to him. She would not take kindly to seeing a DeSoto!

She checked the time. Typically Brindle stopped by in the morning on her way to work and then again afterward. Given that she had already sneaked into her room over at Jackie's, it was possible—likely even—that she wouldn't come over at all. She could only hope for that to be the case! One thing for certain—while visiting with her mom, there'd be no talk of her mother's past, no mention of the journals yet or of Baby Belinda. Now was not the time!

With a deep breath Leah reached for the doorknob. Her mother would be livid if she took any longer. As she headed to the porch, she wondered what in the world they would talk about. She was going to have to be creative.

"Sorry, Mom," she said, pushing opening the screen door. "I feel so much better now. So I was thinking that maybe the two of us could go—"

Her voice caught as she looked up into the eyes of Brindle sitting in the armchair across from her mother. Her legs were crossed, and she was bouncing her foot as usual.

"—Oh, hi," she choked.

"Hello," Brindle said simply, raising a bright green can of carbonated water to her lips.

Lenore was finishing her iced tea, and she set her empty glass onto the table, smacking her lips. "Your friend was nice enough to keep me company while you were off homesteading in the bathroom. Holy cow—

what took you so long? That was an excessively long time!"

Leah rolled her eyes. "I'll spare you the details. But thanks for standing in, Brindle. I see you've met my mother. Do we need to make formal introductions?"

She looked toward Lenore with a pleasant smile. "Yes, I have! And no—we've introduced ourselves. We've had quite a nice chat already!"

Leah swallowed. Was it her imagination or was Brindle looking at her mother funny? Ready or not, it was time to go to Jackie's. She cleared her throat. "Um—that's great! As I was about to say, Mom, I was thinking that the two of us could maybe go"—in the last second, she upped her game—"out for lunch somewhere special. You know, since we don't see each another very often now." She cast a sheepish look at Brindle and shrugged. "Sorry." It was outright rude, yes, but what else could she do?

Her mother's eyes darted to Brindle and back to Leah. "That sounds great, given you have no food in the house—but let's invite your friend!" She gestured.

"No, no!" Brindle's hands flew up. "No, I've already eaten. And I wouldn't want to intrude on your special time together." She smiled at Leah and looked away.

"You wouldn't be intruding!" Lenore insisted, but Brindle declined.

Her smile was so plastic, Leah thought. That girl was a living lie. Moment by moment things were coming into focus. Brindle had known their family connection all along. No wonder her frequent moodiness! No wonder she had gotten snippy when Leah had talked about her family! But it seemed as though Brindle thought she was the only one who knew. Lenore, on the other hand, hadn't a clue, and Leah intended to keep it that way.

"You don't have to work today?" Leah asked Brindle, studying her features carefully for the first time. Her eyes—yes, there was something about them that were like her own. And the set of her chin which was like her mother's, without a doubt.

"Nope!" Brindle took her last swig of water and set the can onto the table, rising to her feet. "But I *do* have some other business I need to take care of, so I'll let you go. I hope you have a nice lunch!" She lifted her arms in a stretch, filling her lungs with fresh air. "Golly—what a beautiful day! You two should do something fun—like go to a park or get pedis or something after you eat. Take a day to relax!"

Leah nodded. "Good idea. Thanks."

"All right—see you later! It was nice meeting you, Lenore! Too-daloo!" She wiggled her bright fingernails in a wave as she turned to go.

"Nice to meet you too," Lenore replied. "Goodbye!"

"Maybe see you later," Leah said after her, although she sure hoped not! She was getting a stress headache from the charade! Her mind was racing for ways to stay in town all day.

She turned to her mother, who was watching Brindle leave. "Are you ready to go? I'll get my purse."

"Who is that girl?" Lenore asked in a low voice.

Leah shrugged. "A neighbor."

"Doesn't she have a car? Look at her walking—I feel like we should offer her a ride somewhere or something."

"She doesn't live very far away, and she prefers to walk." And keep her car out of sight so that she can't be identified, Leah added silently to herself. "I'll go get my purse."

"It seemed kind of rude to exclude her," Lenore added. "And right in front of her face like that! I think you should have invited her along. She was very pleasant to visit with."

"I'll get my purse," Leah repeated. "Your car or mine?"

Leah had never had an exercise in intentionally killing time before, but today she wanted to stay as far away from running into Brindle again as possible. Plus, she wanted to draw out her time with her mom and fill it with so much chatter that by the time they returned she'd be all talked out and eager to get back to Bridgewater. Then Leah would call Kyla and decide where to go from there—whether to file a police report or what.

Thus, Leah chose a restaurant on the far side of New Hampton to extend their drive, firing off as many conversation-starters as she could think of along the way. When ordering off the menu, she stalled, asking the waiter to come back twice before she was ready to place her order, and when she finally did, she chose what she thought would have the longest preparation time.

Over fresh chips and salsa, her mom caught her up to date on Braydon, relaying a play-by-play of his fender-bender last week, backing into a pole while he was in a hurry on a delivery, followed by the resulting sagas of insurance claim technicalities and marks against his record. Then she gave Leah a thorough description of Braydon's new girlfriend, Carae, the younger sister of his friend Tyler, which led to an acrid denunciation of young people gaging their ears and getting foolish tattoos. Leah listened for a while, but the subject of Braydon having a girlfriend made her think of Danny, and she found herself distracted with the new prospect of how to explain her sudden friendship with him to her mother. Sooner or later, she would have to know.

When their food arrived, Leah baited her mother with questions about her work, which had short-term success in keeping her talking—until it backfired as Lenore began asking Leah about her progress in getting a job. Eventually the conversation rolled around to her ire with her dad helping her with the house again, and "poor, poor Marty's" misfortune with the sale of his house, and unending reasons why Leah should sell her house and be completely rid of it.

Leah was weary of the argument. "Mom, I can't sell it anyway. It goes into a trust for Braydon—remember? That's the end of it!"

"Oh, there's always ways around things like that! Mom and Ed are no longer living—they'd never know!"

Leah paused between bites, gingerly broaching the subject. "Mom, tell me what it was like for you when you moved here."

Lenore looked up in surprise.

"I know you've said every association with the Richmond house is a negative, but you've never explained why. What was it like? I'd like to hear about it."

Her mom pursed her lips, shaking her head.

Determinedly Leah waited.

"It's best not to talk about it."

"I'd have to disagree. You were how old—sixteen? It must have been a hard move. I bet it was hard to leave your friends."

Lenore met her eyes and looked away.

Leah added gently, "Mom, I'd like to know."

Her mother set her hand on the table. "Stop pressuring me, Leah! I don't care to talk about it, and I'd like you to accept that!"

Leah nodded. Subject emphatically closed. In the awkward silence, she decided to wade into another topic, hoping it would eventually lead to Danny. "So I've been getting to know my next-door neighbors to the east."

"Oh?" Lenore threw her a questioning look, turning back to her plate.

"There's an elderly man in his eighties—a widower—and his daughter Jackie, who's also a widow. Both super nice."

Her mother finished her bite and swallowed. "Ed made a *fortune* selling off all that land around there! That was the first of it—that lot to the east. But when they platted out the field across the road—" She shook her head. "Oh, his father would have rolled over in his grave if he had known Ed sold all that good farmland for a housing development!"

"He must have struggled with the decision—don't you think? Parceling out the family farm like that. I bet it was a difficult thing to do."

She shrugged. "Maybe. Maybe not. One thing for sure—Ed was as shrewd as they come when it came to money. His biggest struggle was probably hoping to sell before the price of land went down again. He was an opportunist. A brilliant investor, though a hard person for me to warm up to personally. He was a lot older than mom."

The strain between the two of them was old news, but her mother's admiration of his business sense came as a surprise. It made her suddenly wonder if Grandpa Ed might have also sold the alleged Krugerrands in an upturn of the gold market. Perhaps the financial climate had turned out exactly right for a windfall. It was a plausible idea worth consideration. But that's not where she was trying to take the conversation when she'd started.

"So as I was saying, I'm getting to know my neighbors. Both of them are really nice. Jackie—the daughter—brought me some food the first day I arrived—a crockpot meal. We've become friends. And that's how I met my friend Kyla. She goes over there to swim in their pool with the two little boys she watches."

"I see." Lenore nodded.

"The older gentleman is a retired pastor. He's writing a book, and guess who is—"

"That's not the girl who was over this morning, was it?" Lenore broke in. "What was her name again?"

"No, that was Brindle," Leah explained quietly. "My other friend is named Kyla Watkins. So this retired pastor is writing a book, and—"

"Yes, *Brindle*—that's an unusual name—don't you think? She came right up on the porch and introduced herself. Said, 'You must be Leah's mother—she looks just like you!'"

"Huh." Leah turned back to her plate, picking up a dab of refried beans on the end of her fork. "As I was saying, this pastor guy is writing a book—"

"Yes, yes, I heard you! He's writing a book! On what?"

Leah paused. "Um, I'm not sure what the book is about. I've never asked."

"Oh. Well, it's noble of him to write a book in his old age, whatever it's about. I'm glad you're getting to know your neighbors. Brindle said the two of you have been doing a lot of work together on the inside of the house."

Inwardly she sighed. Dead end on bringing up Danny from that angle. "Yes, she's helped me some. We've cleaned and painted together."

"Ah, good. She told me about her interest in old farmsteads."

Leah frowned, looking up at her. "Her what?"

"Her interest in old farmsteads. Says she's studied places like ours. She had all kinds of questions for me."

"Questions like what?"

"All kinds of questions."

"I know, Mom, but *what* questions?"

She paused with her glass in mid-air. "Goodness, Leah—chill out! She was very polite! She wanted to know if there was ever a barn on the place, and if so, was it red or white. And did we ever have a vegetable garden, and did we can vegetables in mason jars. Stuff like that."

"And?"

"That's all! Stuff like that!" She took a drink and set her glass down. "She was particularly interested in the cellar. She asked if a farm like ours ever had more than one cellar, and I told her—"

"No!" Leah's hand dropped to smack the table. "You're *kidding* me!"

Lenore recoiled in surprise. "What's wrong with *that*?"

"What did you tell her?"

She opened her hands. "I showed her!"

"Showed her what?"

"The storm cellar! She wanted to know if farms like ours ever had more than one cellar, and I told her about the old storm cellar that Ed kept."

"Old storm cellar?" Leah could feel her heart begin to race. "Where's that?"

Lenore's face puckered. "What's *wrong* with you? You're acting testy! Since you took so eternally long in the bathroom, we walked around to where that fool parked his trailer. It's caving in the roof, you know!"

"What?"

"He parked right on top of it!"

Leah blinked. "There's a cellar there?"

"*Storm* cellar—you know, for taking shelter. It's underground there on the site of the old farmhouse—where the original one was before Ed built the new one. When he took down the old house, they kept the old cellar and put a new roof on it. Covered it all with dirt. That's why he planted that rose garden there, you know—right over top to mark it. But you'll probably have to fill in the whole thing now because of that machinery. It's certainly damaged the roof!"

Brother Warren's white hair and intense eyes instantly flashed before Leah. *The gold is underground. Does that mean anything to you?* Her mouth hung open. "I—I never knew about that! How do you get in?"

Lenore smiled. "The bench."

"What?"

"The bench! The whole thing's attached to a door! You pull it back to open it. It was very clever, although I'm sure that door is quite weathered nowadays. Probably close to rotted out."

Leah laid her hands on her cheeks. "And you showed Brindle this?"

Her shoulder twitched. "Well, we were standing there looking at that trailer halfway falling in there!"

Leah groaned, setting her napkin onto the table. "Mom, we have to go." She raised her hand to a server passing by. "Excuse me—could we please have our check?"

Lenore stared at her in surprise. "What's going on?"

Leah pulled out her phone to calculate how long they'd been gone. In the back of her mind she saw Brindle relishing the fresh air, encouraging them to go do something fun together—go to a park, go get pedicures. She wanted them away from the house!

"Crud!" she said under her breath.

"What's going on?" Lenore repeated.

It would all come out eventually, Leah realized. Her only struggle was whether to tell her mom everything or mostly everything.

"Mom, you know those envelopes we got at the law office that day—? Well, in mine was a letter from Grandma that said that whoever got the house got some gold coins left in a safe in the cellar. Like apparently a lot of them. They're called Krugerrands. Grandpa Ed bought them as an investment in gold."

Her eyes widened. "And you never bothered to tell me about that?"

Leah let that pass. "I didn't know about the storm cellar. I looked in the canning cellar and there was nothing there, so I thought they were gone. But this whole time they could have been in that storm cellar!"

Lenore gave an excited nod. "Well, when we get back, we can go check if they're there!"

"Yes, but there's a problem. This girl, Brindle—" Leah paused, looking at her mother's questioning face. "She, um—I found out that she, um—" Her stomach twisted. She couldn't bring herself to tell her mother anything about Brindle.

"For heaven's sake, Leah—*what*?"

She swallowed. "Um, there's the possibility that she may have—may have overheard me talking about the coins to someone. So, um, she might be looking for them too. Maybe."

"That nice girl?"

"That's part of the problem. I'm not so sure about her. She might have been playing you."

At first Lenore looked stunned. Then she shook her head. "Leah! Honestly, Leah—sometimes you do not *think*! Why in the world wouldn't you keep your trap shut about something of value like that?" Angrily she slid out of the booth. "Let's go!"

Lenore continued in full rant the whole drive back to the Richmond house until Leah finally put a stop to it.

"Mom, there's a whole lot more to this than you know!"

She threw Leah an icy look. "Well, I think it's pretty obvious you've been holding out on me! You should have let me know what was in that letter in the first place! If those coins are gone when we get there—" She shook her head, her jaw set hard.

"Then what, Mom? They were given to *me*!"

Lenore huffed. "*See?* You don't even care! What is it with you? It's like your whole generation has no appreciation for the hard work of those before you!" She folded her arms and with a toss of her head turned to face the windshield.

Leah gripped the steering wheel more tightly, struggling with how to navigate the mess they were in. She fully expected Brindle to be there when they got back, and she had no idea of what to do or say to her! If she called Kyla, she'd have to be so careful of what she said with her mom in the car. To call the police would open a can of worms with her mother too. If only Danny hadn't left! What in the world was she supposed to—

God may have some surprises in store for you, but don't be afraid. You can trust him. Jesus will never fail you. You can count on that. You can count on that.

She shook her head in sudden amazement as Brother Warren's words slipped through her mind—the words spoken on the first night she'd met him out on his deck at their party that beautiful summer night, right before she'd met Danny.

"God *knew*!" she murmured.

Lenore turned. "What'd you say?"

"Nothing."

She bit her lip. Yes, God *knew* this would be coming! He had known about *all* her surprises! And he was telling her to trust him! God was not an absent father. He was *with* her and *for* her, and he would not fail her.

Okay—help me, she entreated him silently. *Show me what to do, and send someone to help! Anyone—I don't care who. Just send help!*

Chapter Twenty-Nine

Butterflies churned in her belly as Leah exited the main highway onto Richmond Road. She was now less than two miles from home.

Lenore fidgeted in the passenger's seat. "If that girl Brindle has tried to take those coins, I am going to have some words with her!"

"If she's there," Leah cautioned. "And that safe could be long gone, you know."

"Oh, it's there! I'm sure that beast is right where it's always been." Her leg bounced restlessly. "By golly, if she was pumping me with all those questions just to get information—oh, I will have words with her! I promise you—I will have *words* with her!" She clicked her tongue.

"You need to let me handle Brindle."

Her mouth curled with scorn. "*Right!* When it comes to confrontation, my dear, you are *way* too timid! You did not inherit my gift!"

Leah slowed and signaled on the highway before her driveway, waiting for an approaching car to pass before turning in. Off to the side was the lopped-off mailbox, which she had dragged out of their path on the way to town earlier.

"No, I did not. But I know her a lot better than you."

"That's beside the point!" her mother began—but then she gave a start, twisting to look back at the car that had just passed. "What the heck would *he* be doing here? That looked like one of the DeSoto boys! Leah, you aren't seeing Jake again, are you? Good Lord—please don't tell me you went back to him!"

Leah's eyes flicked to the rear-view mirror where she saw a car the same color as Brother Warren's—and yes, it was turning into the Glende driveway! Her heart leaped. Was Danny back? Kyla must have phoned him! *Oh, thank you, God!* she rejoiced silently. What an answer to prayer!

He was absolutely the person she needed right now!

"It's his brother, Danny," she said, "and as a matter-of—"

"—It looked like Jake!"

"It wouldn't be Jake. I didn't tell you, Mom, but Danny DeSoto lives next door."

Lenore swung her head to face her. "You told me an old man lived there! A retired pastor."

Leah nodded, turning into her driveway, her car bouncing over the ruts. "Yes—and Danny DeSoto is helping him write his book."

"Well, I could have sworn it was Jake!" Her face suddenly soured, as if Leah's words had just sunk in. "Good Lord—how on earth did *he* end up living here of all places? What a nightmare! Thank God for those hideous shrubs between your yards!"

"It's a long story, but like I said, you need to let me take care of this."

"Well, keep in mind age has its advantages when it comes to—oh, now look! Someone's dog is loose! I hate it when people don't leash their pets!"

Eagerly Midnight loped up to meet them as Leah parked in front of the garage.

"It's Marty's. He's friendly," Leah said, getting out. She closed the door and leaned back in the open window. "Wait for me on the porch, Mom, okay? *Promise me* you'll wait! I'm running next door for one second, and then we'll walk back to the storm cellar together."

Her mother produced an unhappy response, but Leah didn't wait around to argue. Hastily she took off for the split in the hedge, and with an excited yip, Midnight leaped to follow.

The instant Leah saw the figure poised to knock at the Glendes' door she knew it wasn't Danny, but it was too late to turn around, and in the commotion of her hurried arrival through the arborvitae, she startled the guy. He turned in surprise, then jerked again as he recognized her. Leah, too, stared in dismay. Her mother had been right—the driver of the car had been the one and only Jake DeSoto!

After a moment of mutual stupefaction, Jake stammered, "I'm—I'm only here to switch vehicles! Danny's letting us borrow his for the weekend. More room for stuff. We're, uh—going on vacation." He motioned to the driveway.

Leah couldn't breathe, much less speak. Midnight nosed her hand, but she pulled it away.

"I knew you were here" he blurted. "Danny told me, but he forbade me to see you, which I wouldn't of, truly. I was only letting the lady of the house know I was here to take the car, and then I was leaving." His hands went up, as if swearing his innocence.

He was bigger, Leah observed, maybe forty pounds heavier or more, and like his brother, he also wore glasses now—rounded black frames with a flashy red interior. He looked so much older—older than Danny. Awkwardly he shifted his feet on the Glendes' welcome mat, clearing his throat and adding, "Your, um, hair—it's really—um, *different*. I almost didn't recognize you."

Unbelievable! Of all people, what were the odds of *Jake* showing up at a time like this? Her mind spun. In all the four years since she had last seen him, the only interaction she had ever imagined with him was spewing out her anger on him, truly letting him know in full force how much he had hurt her and how humiliated she had been by him—how he had *ruined* her life! She had wanted to see him devastated, thoroughly punished, and humiliated—to get everything he had coming. Yet strangely, right now all she could think of was an odd mix of Brindle poking around in her backyard and her frightful dream that morning.

I bore the full punishment. Let my blood do its work. Let it cleanse his guilt.

His face. Jake looked just as he had in her dream—scared silly. Defenseless. Completely vulnerable and fully at her mercy, like he knew exactly what he deserved. He looked ashamed. And in her memory loomed the other image—humble Jesus, with fiery, kind eyes, stepping in to shield Jake from *her*, just as Jesus had saved the woman caught in adultery from her accusers.

Let my blood do its work. Let it cleanse his guilt.

She knew what she needed to do. She had already *decided* she would do it. She just hadn't been prepared to do it *now*.

It helped to know that what Jake had done hadn't been glossed over or ignored. His debt of wrongs was great and glaring; he *did* deserve to pay—except the guiltless One had stepped in to pay it in his stead. His wrongs were fully punished. Just as Jesus had taken what *she* deserved. And Rachel. Hadn't she just been over this with Brother Warren? Who was *she* to negate Jesus' work on the cross? Hadn't justice been served? To refuse them forgiveness would be to refuse the kindness offered *her*. To refuse them forgiveness gave fertile ground for bitterness to multiply in her heart, the deadly poison she had seen so taint her mother's life. To refuse them forgiveness would swing wide the door to reap back the consequences of sin not only on herself, but also—possibly—onto generations after her.

It stung, but here was her time to deal with Jake—right here—which in fact meant dealing with *herself*: to choose to let him go whether he was sorry or not, to give up her right for revenge, to lay down hate, and to choose—and to choose *mercy* instead. To show him kindness as it had been shown to her. Here was her time to face the insurmountable hurdle, to run toward it and not away, and to take her leap of faith. Here was her time to fight her battle and win, and to clear the baggage out of her future with Danny. There was nothing complicated about it anymore. The opportunity had come to her. Jake wasn't ninety miles away at his apartment in Bridgewater; he was standing right in front of her. And Jesus had promised to help her. Already a deep calm had settled over her.

But the timing.

Jake squirmed, looking uncomfortably toward his car and back. "Look—yell at me or whatever. Don't just stand there, Leah!"

The dog wagged his tail, whining up at her, but she ignored him. "Jake, this is—this is *very* unexpected! I'd like to talk with you sometime, but I can't right now."

His hands went up again. "Nope! I'm not asking for that! That's *not* why I'm here."

"I know. I'm hoping we can, though. I *would* like to talk. Really, I would. But listen—I'm in a weird situation right now, and I need some help. Are you alone? Or do you have Rachel and your little girl with you?" She threw a quick glance at his car.

"Alone," he said cautiously.

She studied him a moment longer. Asking him was a risk, but what were her options? "I, um—like I said, I'm in a bind. A bit of a crisis. Could you help me?"

"You're asking *me*?" He looked utterly confused.

She nodded. "I know. It's crazy. I thought you were Danny coming home, and I was running over to get him. I need someone to come with me to my backyard. Right now." She gestured behind her. "This girl from the neighborhood has been sneaking around, and we think that she might be after some, um—after something maybe valuable in the old storm cellar—this underground cellar that's in my backyard."

"Okay. So you need me to—?"

"Just walk along. I simply need you to walk back to the cellar with us. If the girl is there, then I want someone else with us. A third party."

He frowned. "What—is she dangerous or something?"

"I don't think so, but I'm not sure. I don't trust her. I need you, Jake."

"Uh, okay. Who's with you? You said 'us.'"

"Um—" She hesitated. "Well, my mom. She's here visiting me today, and—"

"Oh, now that's *great*!" he huffed, throwing his head back as he shoved his hands into his pockets.

"Yeah, I know! But I just learned about this storm cellar from her today—and so did this other girl, so it's a little urgent. It's—" She paused, jerking her head in frustration. "Jake, it's way too complicated to explain right now! Trust me! We need to get over there quickly! I know it sounds crazy, but I *promise* you that afterward we'll find a time to talk."

He stared at her.

"Please!"

He shook his head. "No—no, I better not. Danny threatened me with my *life*! I was not to see you or talk to you!"

"He would *definitely* want you to do this—I promise you he would!"

"I already know what's gonna happen. Your mom's gonna shred me. She's gonna pulverize me with her tongue!"

Leah nodded. "Yeah—you're probably right! But you're going to have to put up with it, and she's going to have to get over it when she sees you. And you and I—eventually we're gonna talk. We'll have to!" She paused, leveling her gaze at him. "Jake, listen to me. I'm going to marry your brother Danny, so we're going to have to figure this thing out. But right now I have this weird situation in my backyard with this girl named Brindle. Are you coming with me or not? Because if you won't, I'm going to have to take care of it myself. It can't wait any longer!"

He blinked in astonishment, then closed his lips and gave a stiff nod. "I—okay."

"Then let's go!"

Halfway to the porch Leah realized her mother wasn't there. She stopped, annoyed at her stubbornness. No doubt she'd taken a jump on having her words with Brindle, but the prospect made Leah nervous. Who knew where that could go? Beckoning, she hurriedly led Jake around the side of the house toward the now-lopsided flatbed trailer parked on the camouflaged roof of the hidden cellar. As she had feared, the garden bench had been pried loose and tipped backward to rest upside down on the ground, and starting down the gaping hole that led inside was her mother.

"You were supposed to stay on the porch!" Leah called, shuffling across the lawn, her eyes scanning the yard for Brindle. "What are you doing? Get out of there!" A crowbar lay on the grass near the now hacked and broken overturned bench. From the opening descended a series of ten or so steps leading to a dark cellar opening at the bottom. "Did you do this? Did you take this door off?" She looked around her again.

Before them, the cocked angle of Peter's long trailer gave clear indication that the ground underneath it was giving way. On the trailer bed, the skid loader and industrial mower leaned precariously to one side, their chains taut and strained. She should call Peter, Leah thought. She should call him now! He was going to lose everything! She pulled out her cell phone.

"Good grief—it took you long enough!" Lenore growled. "A person can't sit around waitin' forever, and no, I did not open this! Thanks to your big mouth, that girl was here ahead of us!"

"Is she in there?" Leah squinted down past her, noting the musty, earthy odor wafting up.

"No, she's not, and if you hadn't—" Her jaw drew slack as she suddenly noticed Jake's arrival behind Leah. "What the—" She looked back at Leah in disbelief. "Good Lord—I was right! You lied to me! You *are* seeing him again!" She shot Jake a wicked glare.

Leah groaned. "Oh, stop! Of course, I'm not! For heaven's sake, Mom—he's married. Remember? I went next door to get Danny, but it was Jake. He's borrowing his brother's car. I asked him to help us."

Her face puckered. "Help us? What the heck for? We don't need no little boy cowards! Run on home, you—you—!"

Nope, Leah decided firmly. She wasn't going to hear it! Jutting out her chin, she raised her finger. "Stop it right there, Mother! Not another word about Jake—do you hear me? Not *one*! Now come up out of there! It's not safe!" Her arm flew in an angry wave. Whoa—that was one more to add to her tally of surprises! She had actually defended Jake DeSoto!

Lenore, however, set her jaw hard. With a dark look, she turned to descend the rest of the way to the bottom where she leaned into the black cavern. Extending her hand, she called up, "Leah, bring me your phone. I need a flashlight."

Leah huffed, staring down. "Are you crazy? You're *not* going in there!"

Jake gave an involuntary grunt behind her. "What's she doing? Don't let her go in there! Look at it, Leah—the whole thing's caving in! You gotta call someone! Whose equipment is that? They need to get it off there—right away!"

It was likely already too late, Leah observed.

Lenore wagged her hand from below. "Your flashlight, Leah!"

Leah cast a glance at Jake. "It's my friend Peter's. He's away in St. Cicerone today."

"Well, you gotta call someone! That's not good—not good!"

"Honestly, can't you hear me?" Lenore called again. "I'm talking to you!"

"Mom, get a clue!" she snapped impatiently. "You're not going in there! It's not safe!"

Lenore dug her hand into her hip. "Dang it, Leah—bring me your flashlight! If that Brindle girl was down here, I want to know if she got to the safe or not!"

Leah hesitated, glancing at the precariously cocked equipment and back to her mother. She was torn—yes, bursting with curiosity like her mother, but she didn't want to be an idiot. She swallowed, sweeping the yard again for any sign of Brindle, then reluctantly took the steps to join her mother.

From above, Jake swung his head, urging her not to go in.

"Jake, I know. I'm just looking."

Lenore snatched the phone from her hand and shone it into the old cellar, illuminating a large portion of the ceiling that was grossly sagging. Two large beams hung down at a forty-five-degree angle in the center of the room, nearly touching the dirty concrete floor.

"Oh—oh, no!" Leah exclaimed, shrinking back. "Mom, that's barely holding!"

"I know that safe is over there—I can't quite see—" Lenore tipped her head from side to side looking across the cellar. Stretching her arm into the room, she shone the light from another angle. "Those blasted beams are in the way! It's in the far corner on the other side. If we could get around—" With a brief glance at Leah, she took a cautious step into the room.

"Oh, geez," Jake groaned from above. He shoved his hands into his pockets, pacing nervously. "I wouldn't go in there, Mrs. Labanora! Don't do it!"

"Oh, just watch me," she muttered under her breath.

"Mom, you should listen—"

"—It held just fine for that conniving friend of yours apparently," Lenore cut in. "What kind of friends do you hang out with anyway? And what are you doing with *him*? Honestly!"

"I said *enough*, and I mean it! Now give me the phone. You're not doing this!" Leah reached to take it from her.

Lenore yanked her arm away, taking another determined step.

Leah shook her head. "Mom, you're being stupid! You could get killed! Please—let's call someone to get this trailer off here, and then we'll deal with the safe!"

"All I want is to *see* it. I just want to see if she's opened it—that's all!" Illuminating her way with the flashlight, she sidled closely along the dank wall at the perimeter of the room.

Leah twitched anxiously. "Mom, you're scaring me! Seriously, it's not worth it! Come out!"

With a sudden dip of the light, she ducked and disappeared to the other side of the drooping beams. "Oh, yes—it's here all right!" she hollered, then burst into a howl of laughter. "Well, if this isn't providence!"

Leah threw a look up at Jake at the top of the stairs, where he swung his head from side to side. "This is nuts! You guys are—you—" He shook his head. "This is *nuts*!"

"What's providence?" Leah called back, unable to see anything now but a strip of light on the far side of the cavity.

"It's blocked—completely blocked! If there's money in here, I'm sure it's all accounted for! There's a big old beam hanging down right in front of the door—just far enough down to block it! There's no way she could have gotten in!" She gave another cackle.

"Okay, so you know—now come out!"

Waiting, Leah glanced apprehensively at the bowed lumber of the dark ceiling, but her mother did not reappear. Frowning, Jake hurried down to join her at the bottom of the cement steps.

"What's going on? What's she doing in there?" he queried, peering in.

"I have no idea!" Leah answered in frustration. "What are you doing, Mom?"

"I'm gonna try to move it," she called out.

"What?"

"I'm seeing if this beam will move—if I can push it up out of the way. It's loose."

"No! Come on, it's not sa—"

Her voice was cut off by a slight downward shift of the sagging beams.

"Mom!"

Over the pattering of crumbling of dirt came a resounding shriek of pain and a string of cursing. "Help me!" Lenore cried. "I'm pinned! I'm—" Another furious blast of cursing. "I'm pinned! My hand is pinched under— ouch! This blasted—"

Above them the ceiling gave another menacing creak, followed by a large chunk of dirt breaking way to explode on the floor into a thousand tiny crumbs rolling in every direction. Leah screamed in unison with her mother.

"Jake, it's gonna fall!"

"Help me!" Lenore bellowed across the darkness, "I'm pinned! I can't pull my hand out! It's stuck!"

"I'm coming!" Leah shouted, but Jake grabbed her shirt and wrenched her back.

"*Stay here!*" he commanded, slipping past her into the dark and musty room.

"Hurry!" Leah urged. "Use your light!"

"My phone's in the car. I got hers."

With his belly pressed against the wall, he inched his way around the sagging debris back to where Lenore's flashlight glinted. Leah held her breath, straining to see through the hanging beams.

"Is she okay? Jake, is she okay?"

"Got her!" he yelled, ordering sternly, "Hold still, Lenore—*hold still*! I can't help you if you don't hold still!"

Then apart from the drone of her mom's pitiful whine, the cellar was quiet—forebodingly so, Leah thought, holding her breath as she eyed the fragile ceiling. The seconds ticked by. One minute felt like an hour. If only she could help—or at least *see* them!

"Jake, *hurry*!" she called worriedly. "Can you please hurry up?"

Over his reply, Leah heard a familiar voice above her.

"Why, hello down there!"

Leah's head snapped up to see Brindle peeking down the concrete stairwell with a look of amusement on her face.

"Hey, what's going on?"

Right, Leah thought. Happy and cheerful Brindle. She was so done with pretending. "Oh, I think you already know!" she retorted.

Brindle's brow furrowed innocently. "What do you mean?"

Leah's eyes flashed. "Cut the crap, Brindle! I know *exactly* who you are and what you want!"

Her smile disappeared. "You think so, huh? I'm sorry, but you know *nothing* about me!"

"I wouldn't be so sure about that, Belinda Ann Taylor!"

Brindle stiffened, and in the silence that followed, the two locked eyes, as if sizing one another up.

"Who's out there?" Lenore called from across the cellar. "Who are you talking to, Leah?"

"You were pretty darn smooth," Leah continued boldly. "I know you worked for Duvall & Ross, and I know what you're after, but you're not getting' them!"

"Oh, yeah?"

"Yeah. The safe's completely blocked anyway, so let it go. If I were you, I'd look at the bigger picture. You have an opportunity here—a chance for something a lot more valuable than what you're looking for." She gestured inside the cellar, indicating her mother.

Brindle did not respond.

"Who's out there?" Lenore called again.

"Think about it," Leah said. "I know it's awkward right now, but we can work it out somehow. You owe it to yourself to know your own family."

"Leah!" Lenore's voice rose with irritation. "For heaven's sake, answer me! Can't you hear me? Who are you talking to? It'd better not be that manipulating friend of yours! You have no judgment when it comes to—*ouch*! That's my *hand*, you idiot!" Another series of expletives went flying.

Brindle's lip lifted in a smile, and she looked away.

"She doesn't know who you are yet," Leah said. Behind her she could hear Jake raising his voice at her mother to hold still. "And she doesn't know that I know anything about you. If she were to know who you really are, Brindle, I'm sure she'd—"

"Oh, save your breath, Leah," Brindle interjected. "You're trying way too hard!"

Leah shook her head. "I want to *help* you. I want to help you connect to her."

She gave a short laugh. "Believe me—I don't need your help!"

"Seriously, Brindle—this is your mother! You should make the connection."

Her eyes narrowed as she leaned downward, her thick pinkish-burgundy hair falling forward. "Since you think you know everything, let me enlighten you on my reality! Let me tell you that I've spent the last eight years of my life looking for that woman, and when I finally found her, she wasn't across the country or even in the next state over or anything. She was right across town. I called her at least a dozen times, and she didn't respond to even *one* of my calls! Then I set up a third party to arrange a meeting with her and she declined! Save your energy, Leah. That woman wants nothing to do with me!"

Leah's mouth opened, but she didn't know what to say.

Brindle gave an odd chuckle. "Know what I thought was funny? The day of the party—that Jackie lady asked us if we were sisters! Did you catch that?" She shook her head. "And how ironic that when we met, *both* of us were using phony names—doesn't that strike you as odd? Here I drum up a clever name and finally meet my sibling, and what do you know? *She's* using a fake name too! Who would have guessed sisters to have *that* in common?"

"It wasn't fake," Leah returned defensively. "Ava's my middle name—after my grandma."

"Right—your precious grandma! Hey—guess what—? She's *my* grandma too! And know what else? I believe this house was legally set up to go to Lenore's oldest daughter. That'd be *me*, wouldn't it?" She gave Leah a condescending smile. "I thought you should know I'm in the process of working that out!"

Leah stared. Behind her, her mother continued to call out in a shrill voice, demanding to know whom Leah was talking to. Brindle sniffed and suddenly looked around the yard, first one way, then the other. Leah felt a twinge of uneasiness.

"Brindle!" Leah called up, ignoring her mother. "You can take whatever legal action you want—it's still going to bring you face to face with the woman who gave you birth. Is that how you want to meet her? It doesn't have to be that way!"

"It'd be my pleasure to see the shock on her face!"

Leah shook her head. "No, Brindle—give it up! It's not worth it. You've lost the coins. You would despise this house. Every road for you is a dead end. If you're not willing to try again with Mom, then it's time for you to walk away."

The girl was silent, gazing down at her. Leah shivered at her expression.

"Think about it, Brindle. We could work things out so that the two of you could talk. We could do it today. Or sometime soon. Or you could leave if you want—you could walk away and go home, and I wouldn't tell her anything about this."

Brindle backed a step, looking around her again.

"Brindle!" she called, trying to keep her attention.

She laughed, shaking her head. "Dang, Leah—you're so smart, but none of your options really jive with me. I've got something else in mind, and it works out nicely that you're together!" With that she stepped away from the opening and disappeared.

Leah kept looking up, waiting for her to reappear, but after a minute of nothing happening, she set a hand on the wall beside her and made herself breathe again. Was she gone? It looked like whatever Brindle's "something else" was, she had taken her wiles elsewhere to do it. The house, perhaps? What would she try there? Or—or would she vandalize her car? That might be a more fitting expression of animosity! Leah closed her eyes. Crud—he'd left the keys in it when she'd run next door.

Behind her, her mother carried on in her ruckus while Jake fired back.

His voice rose. "Leah, where'd you go? You still out there?"

Leah turned to squint through the hanging debris. "I'm here! For heaven's sake, Jake—what's taking so long? We need to get out of—"

"Go get help! Hurry! I can't get her arm out. I'm calling 911, but I need you to get—"

Boom! An enormous thud suddenly shook the ground above her. Flinching, Leah shot a look upward. Brindle was back! She came into view, squatting near the top of the stairs, straining to lift something heavy.

"What are you doing?" Leah called in alarm. Simultaneously she recognized that Brindle was hoisting the heavy platform door of the cellar. "What are you—*Belinda!*"

With a great heave, she rolled the wooden platform with the attached bench to the mouth of the stairs where it banged down with another heavy thud. Seeing what was about to happen, Leah felt a stab of panic.

"Belinda, *stop!* Don't do this!"

Without hesitating a second, Brindle determinedly muscled the huge platform in a final shove over the edge into the stairwell.

"*Belinda!*" Leah shouted as the brittle door crashed downward, splintering to fill the cavity, and sliding down the stairs in a rush to knock her backward into the dark cellar. As she landed on her seat, the sharp edges of smashed door fragments slammed into her legs. Across the room, Jake was yelling her name while her mother shrieked, and in the blackness Leah heard the ceiling shift. A shower of dirt pattered her head.

"*Leah!*" Jake shouted again.

"I'm okay!" she called, wrenching her knee out from the busted wood to grab her shin. She curled onto her side, wincing in pain.

"Get out! Get out of there!"

"I can't—it's blocked." She coughed, tiny beads of dirt flinging from her hair. "The door's wedged in the stairwell!"

"Then get over here! Get out from the middle of the room!"

Gingerly Leah moved to pull herself off the floor.

"*Now*, Leah!" Jake commanded. "If that trailer goes, it's coming down on your head!"

As if confirming his warning, the beams above her groaned again, pelting her with chunks of debris as she scrambled to the wall. She followed it with her hands as Jake lit her path, urging her to hurry.

"Oh, my God—it's going!" Lenore cried. "We're gonna die! We're gonna be buried alive down here!"

With another ominous creak, more rubble crumbled to the floor.

Jake reached for Leah's arm, yanking her in behind him. "Get in beside the safe—get in tight! It might protect us if it goes." He pushed her against a cold, hard wall. "Was it that girl?"

Lenore was on the edge of hysteria, breathing hard. "We're gonna die! God is judging me, and we're gonna be buried alive!"

"Hang in there, Mom," Leah said, trying hard not to panic too. "Yes—she's blocked us in, that lyin' snake! Holy cow, Jake—how are we going to get out of here? We'll have to dig!"

"Leave me," Lenore whimpered. "Just leave me and go!"

Jake huffed. "Shush! I'll get you out!" He shoved the flashlight in Leah's hand. "Hold this!"

"Get a knife then—just cut it off!"

"Mom, stop!" Leah said, trying to keep her hands from shaking as she directed the light.

The trouble was clear. Lenore stood at the corner of a tall, dark safe—a steel safe, a good four feet wide and as tall as Jake—with her arm awkwardly extended upward where a large four-by-four beam pinned her hand against its door. The other end of the culprit plank, however, was butted tightly at an odd angle against another beam that was precariously holding up a section of the ceiling. Leah watched as Jake ventured out, cautiously lifting two loose boards from the floor. Immediately Leah knew he'd try to brace up the second beam with the scrap boards so that it'd be secure enough to remove the one against her mother's hand. Nothing looked stable.

"Oh, be careful," she murmured.

"We're gonna die," Lenore repeated dully. "God is judging me!"

"Mom, stop *saying* that! It's not helping!"

"But it's true! There's no way we're getting out of here alive!"

"Well, it'd help a lot if you kept your mouth shut while we try!"

"Leah—the light," Jake said.

She turned back to refocus the flashlight.

Another major dirt clod dropped from the ceiling, blasting apart in the middle of the room. Jake froze, his shoulders around his ears. Then casting her a look, he slowly and carefully proceeded to lodge the two-by-four between the ceiling and a stack of boards on the floor.

Leah heard a sniffle. Looking over, she observed tears on her mother's face in the poor light. She stared, stunned. Her mother *never* cried!

"Mom, we're working to get you out," she said more gently. "Jake's trying his best. Is the pain unbearable?"

She shook her head, wiping her face with her free hand. "I heard what you said. I heard you."

"Heard what?"

"You said her name. Over there—you said her name."

Leah paused, feeling a stab of self-reproach as she studied her face. She'd been careless. "I was—talking to Brindle, if that's what you mean. We were right—she *was* intent on those Krugerrands, and she was the one who threw the door in to block us in here." She shot a quick glance back to steady the light on Jake.

"No—I heard you say her name."

Leah met her eyes in the dimness.

"You said 'Belinda.'" She sniffed, adding meekly, "Was that—*her*?"

Leah hesitated, then nodded.

A new batch of tears spilled. After a long silence, she asked, "How in the world did she get connected to you?"

"She handled our file at the lawyer's office."

She let out a breath. "And how did you find out?"

"Grandma kept some journals, and I came across it this morning—just this morning! I was hoping we could talk about it. That's why I kept asking you those questions at the restaurant."

Lenore looked away, weeping silently, her hand still stretched upward, wedged by the beam. "God's judging me," she said finally, "and I'm going to die here."

Leah was fighting to have compassion, but her patience was wearing thin. "Mom, *please*! Please stop saying that!"

Barely had the words escaped her mouth when from behind them came the sharp report of busting wood—a dull, echoing pop—and with it the horrifying thunder of the ceiling disintegrating. With a holler Jake dove toward them as everything above finally gave way, a reverberating crash of wood, metal, concrete, and earth all collapsing upon them. Leah's screams were muffled as she shielded her head from the falling debris.

Chapter Thirty

Dazed, Leah lay in eerie silence, enshrouded in dirt, unable to budge. Everything was black. An enormous weight pressed heavily on her, pushing hard against her chest, pressing down, down, down, pinning her hard against the cellar floor. I'm dead, she thought. Yet her lungs could burst.

Then a movement. Something shifted, freeing her arm but not relieving the pressure—excruciating pressure—and she thrust frantically against it. It was Jake, she realized—the suffocating weight was Jake lying on her, trying to move and fumbling with his hand to scrape debris from her face. She jerked her head away and gasped, inhaled dirt, and tried to cough, but now Jake was coughing too, each motion a sharp, punctuated blow against her chest, crushing her. In a choking panic, she shoved furiously against him until, with a wince of pain, he slid off. Sucking air, she turned on her side, coughing violently until she retched.

"Your shirt," he rasped between coughs, "breathe through your shirt!"

But Leah had already yanked it up over her nose, hacking, hacking, and hacking until the spasms began to subside. Dirt gritted in her teeth. Her throat burned.

"Are you hurt?" Jake squeaked. He coughed and tried to clear his throat. "Your mom—can you check—?"

Her mom. She thought of her the same instant and called her name. There was no response. Now wedged side by side up against the safe, there was a little more headroom in the cavity where Jake had pushed her in his desperate dive. Laboriously, Leah drew her legs up in the complicated process of flipping herself, working and wiggling her torso around to face the opposite direction. Then sliding with her belly against the cold steel, she stretched her arm around the edge into the dark rubble, feeling in the blackness for her mother, calling her, patting chunks of dirt and concrete until she was rewarded by a handful of coarse hair.

"I got her," she mumbled to Jake through her shirt. "Mom!"

"Airway!" Jake said, his voice coming from her feet. "Help her!

"Mom!" Urgently she strained to reach further, but as she brushed her mother's face, Lenore suddenly grasped her hand. She gave a weak cough followed by a groan of pain.

"Leah—my arm—my arm and my back!"

"I'm here, Mom!" Leah squeezed her hand. "Jake, she's breathing!"

"Good," he called. "Now get the phone!"

Lenore coughed again, then moaned in agony. "My back! I can move my legs, but my shoulder and my back—oh, my back!"

"Don't move. Lie still and breathe through your shirt," Leah urged.

"The phone, Leah!" Jake repeated.

Leah squeezed her mom's hand again. "We're right here, Mom—we're right here!" Then she turned to call to Jake, "I don't have it! It was knocked out of my hand!"

"Look for it! We've got to call for help!"

"Didn't you already? I thought you were calling 911!"

"But then everything happened! I didn't call."

In the black stillness, her mother moaned.

A harsh reality suddenly crashed in. Leah felt herself gripped with a claustrophobic panic as the thick darkness, nauseating odors, pressing closeness, dirt in her mouth—as everything around her closed in. Breaking into a cold sweat, she pulled the neck of her shirt down and vomited until her body had nothing left to give. As she lay panting, Jake spoke her name again, bringing her back.

The phone. Yes, she needed to find the phone. Wiping her burning eyes with her shirt, she forced herself to focus and tried to recall where she'd been during the collapse. Slithering back on her belly, she retreated to pat the dirt in Jake's and her tiny pocket of space. He shifted his weight to give her more room.

"Are you all right?" he asked. "Are you hurt?"

Everything hurt, she acknowledged, conscious of her body for the first time—but she could move. "Uh, I think I'm okay."

In contortionist fashion, she twisted herself back around so that she lay parallel to him again and then pawed through the dirt on that side. But no phone was to be found.

"I can't find it, Jake. Did you check all around you?"

"Yeah."

Leah paused, suddenly aware that he hadn't budged from his position. "Jake, are *you* hurt?"

"I'm all right."

He was lying. She could tell by his breathing. "What's wrong?"

"I'm okay. My leg's pinned, but I can move my toes. Look again."

"What?"

"Find the phone!"

His tone made her worry. Leah groped through the debris with more diligence, following an invisible grid to carefully feel every square inch within her reach, digging her fingers as deeply into the dirt as she could.

"A lot of good they did in the safe all these years!" Lenore's voice cut eerily into the darkness.

Startled, Leah turned.

"Really, they're worth nothing if they're never used! Absolutely nothing! But 'one must *always* be prepared'! Oh, yes, the economy might crash—you better be prepared so you don't lose everything! And now we're going to die with his stinkin' loot! We're gonna die with it! Oh, God, my back—!"

"What the heck is that about?" Jake asked in a low voice. "She's delirious!"

"She might be," Leah whispered back, wondering if she should try to wiggle down to lie by her mother to comfort her. Yet the phone—finding it was crucial. "She's talking about my grandfather. He bought gold—as an investment. There's coins in this safe, we think. It's what that girl was looking for."

"Oh, someone *do* something!" Lenore wailed miserably. "Please! My back's killing me!"

"Hang on, Mom!" Leah called. "We'll call for help as soon as we can!"

But after several more minutes of earnestly scraping through the dirt, Leah gave a bleak sigh. "Jake, I've searched and searched—I don't know what else to do! It's buried out there somewhere!"

He grunted in resignation. "Okay—take a rest, and we'll look again later. Who all knows we're here? How long do you think it'll be before someone looks for us?"

Leah pressed her back against the safe wall mentally checking through a list of names. Danny and Brother Warren were gone and so was Peter. Neither Jackie nor Kyla knew anything about the cellar, so even if they discovered it was caved in, they wouldn't know they were in it. Marty was at work. No one but Brindle knew where they were. Anxiety nagged as she battled with her dismal conclusion. Part of her wanted to lie to give him some kind of hope, but it would only prolong the inevitable.

"My back!" her mother whimpered again. "I can't take it! I can't *take* it! I'm gonna die!"

Leah was direct. "Jake, we have to pray. Only Brindle knows we're here—the girl who shut us in."

Jake swore under his breath. "Crap! This isn't good, Leah, this isn't good! We can't survive down here! There's no way!"

"I know—but we can pray."

He didn't respond.

"We should pray, Jake!"

"Go for it," he said without expression.

He didn't *want* to pray, she realized. He didn't believe. Oddly, she understood. Jake had been on his own wandering path. It was only the grace of God that she wasn't still in that dark place herself—recoiling at the idea of prayer, deeming it weakness or wishful thinking. Did she believe it would make a difference now? It felt like the wrong question. *He* was her answer. After experiencing God's kindness at every unexpected turn, Leah found herself counting on the One who said he'd never fail her.

"We're going to pray and trust God, Jake."

"Yeah, that's fine."

She charged in. "Jesus, you said you wouldn't fail me, so send someone to help us right now! *You* see us, even if no one else knows we're here, so save us, God—save us somehow! Thank you that you're always good." She paused, then added, "And God, forgive Brindle. Have her call someone to help us or something." Another pause. "We pray in Jesus' name. Amen."

A long silence ensued. Beside her Leah heard the controlled rhythm of Jake breathing through his teeth to manage his pain. She hoped his injuries weren't too severe. For certain she was indebted to him. He had shielded her from the falling debris—saving her from being pinned by whatever he was lying under now. Or from being crushed to death.

"Jake," she said in a hushed voice.

"Yeah?"

By now the dirt had settled somewhat, and she lowered her shirt from her face to speak to him. "I *do* trust that God won't fail us, but that doesn't mean he's got to do things our way." She paused. "I'm just saying that there's still the possibility we could—you know—that we might not make it. So, if that happens, I don't want to die with some things on my chest. I want to officially go on record by telling you that I forgive you for everything you did to me. Both you and Rachel, but specifically you, since you're here." She took a breath. "I forgive you, Jake. From my *heart*, I forgive you."

He was silent for so long that Leah wondered if he was ignoring her or offended. Then she heard his breath catch in a quiet sob. He was crying. Her gut twisted with the surprise of it. Unsure of what to say, she touched his arm and squeezed it, then let go.

"Thank you," he squeaked through his tears, his voice high pitched and jerky. "My God, Leah—I don't deserve that! I've made a complete mess of my life. I've made a complete mess of everything!"

"Well, it's one less mess for you to feel guilty about now." She drew back, repositioning herself on her elbows in the dirt where she lay, pressed between him and the hard safe.

"It should've never happened! I'm so sorry, Leah—it should've never happened! Every choice I made was wrong! It was wrong from the *very* beginning!" He paused to pull himself together. "It was wrong, and because of it I've hurt *every single person* in my life! It should've never happened! I shoulda never asked you out."

Leah felt a snap of irritation at his last comment. "Geez—ouch, Jake! You make it sound like it all was because of *me*! That's a jerk thing to say!"

He sniffed. "You don't understand. You have no idea. No idea!"

"Well, explain it then! I'm not going anywhere."

He hesitated, letting out a long breath, as if grappling with how to proceed. "Do you remember when I first asked you out? Way back—at that restaurant on your birthday?"

"Yes, Jake. I remember it well."

"Well, I need to tell you something." He paused, struggling again. "The, um—the reason I asked you out was because—well, um, it wasn't because of *you*. I was—I was—"

Her shoulders were taut with anticipation. "Just *say* it!"

"Um, well, Danny stuck around that weekend for your birthday. I knew his plan. He'd been waiting for you to turn eighteen—to ask you out himself."

Leah lifted her head in surprise. "What?"

"So I, um—asked you first. To get at him."

She stared toward him in the darkness.

"I kinda had this thing with him—this competition, sort of."

Leah blinked, unable to speak.

"And then it was just fun. It didn't really change anything. We were friends, and I liked hanging out with you. But I always knew he liked you, so I kept it going. I knew it was wrong, Leah, but I've had this issue with my brother. He has everything together. He does everything right. I, um—I should've broken up with you."

The cold metal on her back gave her a chill. "So, you're saying you never—you never even *liked* me?"

"No! I'm not saying that! I mean, we were friends! It was fun and everything. I just didn't—you know—I never really—" He stopped.

Leah pressed her hands against her cheeks as a thousand memories zipped through her mind from a new perspective. With them came a thousand ways life could have been different, and it took every ounce of self-control not to completely blast him. "So why the heck didn't you break up with me, Jake? Why *didn't* you? You had four years to do it, for heaven's sake! Why'd you ask me to *marry* you? Holy cow—you could have simply broken up with me and started dating Rachel if you wanted her! Yeah, it would have been hard, but it wouldn't have destroyed me!"

"I know." He winced in pain as he shifted his body. "I guess—I guess I didn't want to hurt your feelings. I was too far into it."

Leah shook her head in disbelief. "Are you *kidding* me? Like everything else you did with Rachel wasn't going to hurt my feelings—?"

"And because of Danny," he broke in. "Mostly because of Danny."

"What about Danny?"

He hesitated. "Well—I guess it was my way of having power over him. You know, keeping him from what I knew he wanted. It was my way of assuring that he didn't have the totally perfect life."

Leah dropped her head into her hands with an incredulous groan. "Jake! Jake, you moron! Your stupidity is absolutely unfathomable! You—you have *issues*!" And to think she had wanted to *marry* him!

"I know that, Leah, I know that! It's been a full-time job working through them and repairing trust with Rachel. I—I—" His voice quavered. "She was devastated by what I did! I hurt her so badly! But I love her—I do!" He sniffed. "My dad—he's helped me a lot. I've had this thing where I always thought he preferred Danny over me. Danny was the perfect son, and I was the loser."

"Jake." She threw her head back. "The reason Danny's like he is, is because of his personality. You could never be like him if you tried!"

"I know."

474

"And the other reason Danny's like he is, is because he applies himself! He gets up early in the morning! He reads the Bible! He thinks about the choices he makes for himself so that they're the 'best' choices. He lives by his stinkin' principles—you know that! But that's why he has the life he has! Even *you* could be a better version of yourself, Jake, if you applied yourself!"

He sniffed again, and Leah felt him move to wipe his face. "We've had some hard talks, the two of us. He's hung in there with me. I don't deserve him, Leah. Honestly, you can't even know how much regret I live with on a daily basis."

Leah was silent, trying to take it all in.

"And now we're down here," he continued, "and if we don't get out, I'll never meet my new baby son—" His voice cracked as he broke down again. "Promise me, Leah—promise me—if you get out of here, and I don't—"

"Jake, don't!"

"No, I'm serious! I want you to tell my wife—tell Rachel that I love her with all my heart. I do—I love her!"

Leah swallowed. "I will, Jake."

"Thank you," he croaked. "I can't believe you even *talked* to me today! All these years I could only think of how much you must hate me! I've been terrified of running into you. I totally expected you to shred me—not that I don't deserve it. Thank you, Leah. Thank you for not killing me."

Leah gave a snort of irony. "I'm not sure how thankful you should be, considering you're currently *buried* with me!"

She sighed, reminded again of her vivid dream that morning. "Okay, Jake—I need to tell you something. First, you wouldn't be able to comprehend how much you hurt me. You can't. And now, finding out all this—I can't even—!" She shook her head, unable to express the tumble of emotions inside and needing several moments to contain herself. "Anyway, even after hearing all of that, Jake, I *still* forgive you. It's true—I *have* hated you! And bitterly! But I'm done with that. I'm choosing to let it go. I'm choosing to let *you* go."

"I don't deserve that," he said humbly.

"No, you *don't*—that's for sure. What you did was so wrong! I've wanted justice. I've wanted to pummel you with my anger, but Jesus took it instead. He was punished in your place."

"Yeah, I know all that, Leah—"

"—No, I don't think you do. It's more than churchy words, Jake. It's true. He took your punishment for everything you had coming—as he did for me and all I've deserved too." She paused. "Jesus freed me from my own sins. But he also freed me from your sins against me! I release you, Jake. I set you free. You don't owe me anything anymore, and I would highly recommend that you go to God yourself to be released from your guilt. It's not going to go away by itself. You need his forgiveness."

"I'm working on it, Leah! I'm trying to fix things."

"No, Jake. You can't *fix* what you've done! You can't make it right enough for me or anybody. It's beyond your ability to fix! You're going to have to ask God to do that job and give that burden to him."

. He sniffed. "Yeah, maybe."

"More than *maybe*, Jake. God forgives you. Danny certainly does, and so do I. Receive it, and let God fix it."

"Yeah. Thanks."

Then they fell silent and sat in the dark without talking for a long time.

"Your mom's too quiet," Jake murmured finally.

"I had the same thought," Leah replied. Indeed, she hadn't heard her mother say anything in quite a while, and worry was beginning to pluck at her. It was possible that she'd been listening to their conversation and didn't like it. Or she might have succumbed to the pain—fallen asleep or passed out. Leah wouldn't let her mind consider anything beyond that.

"You should check on her."

"I will, but first—"

"What?"

"I promise I'll do what you asked me earlier—give your message to Rachel. But if somehow *you* get out of here and something happens to *me*—"

He let out a breath. "Don't worry—I'll tell Danny. He deserves you. It figures—you were meant to be."

She nodded to herself in the dark. "Thanks. But I'm pretty sure he knows how I feel. I was thinking more about my dad."

"Your dad?" He sounded surprised.

"Yeah." She moved her arms, adjusting herself on her side. "It's a long story. But seriously, if it happens, I want you to tell him that I love him. Tell him that I'm thankful he's my dad and that I was looking forward to getting to know him. And tell him our time on my porch was one of the best days of my life. He'll know what I mean."

"All right—I will." He sighed. "Maybe you should pray again. You know, in case we—"

"God hears *your* prayers too, you know. *You* can pray. I get how you're feeling—like you're so far away you don't deserve to ask God for anything. But he's not like that. That's not how he sees you. He's for you and not against you. But don't worry about it now. I'll pray."

She did. She prayed for help, and this time Jake said, "Amen."

They sat quietly again.

"I suppose we'll eventually run out of air," he said tiredly. "Unless the rest of this caves in on us first. But then we won't be able to breath either, so either way we're gonna suffoca—"

Leah smacked him. "Jake, *please*! I'd rather listen to the worms crawl than that!"

He gave an uncomfortable grunt. "I can't feel my leg anymore. And my hip is aching something fierce from being stuck in the same position."

Leah slid back, pressing herself as tightly as possible against the safe. "Can you move now?"

With another grunt he shifted his body weight. "Okay, that helps a—"

A shower of dirt and debris suddenly rained down on them, and both of them began to cough.

"Don't move!" he choked.

Leah was stabbed with fear as she heard a sharp thud—more like *felt* it as the ground vibrated with some sort of blow. Was this it? Another thud. Then another. More dirt fell. Again, a sharp vibrating blow to the earth somewhere. And another. Something was giving way—the rest of the cellar finally caving in on them! As their little cavity shook and the ceiling continued to crumble, Jake found her hand and gripped it. She let her tears flow freely. Who would have thought her life would end like this?

Suddenly he burst out in a yell—"We're here!"—then immediately broke into a coughing fit.

Leah froze, utterly stunned. Someone was digging for them! It was a miracle!

"Hey! We're here!" Jake continued to shout hoarsely. With a surge of hope Leah joined him, yelling and coughing intermittently as the vibrating blows increased in intensity. Soon they could hear muted voices above them.

"Cover your head, Leah," Jake warned. "When they get closer, this is all going to loosen up. It'll probably all come down!"

He was right. It did. Without warning, their little cavity collapsed all at once, and the two were buried by a heavy rush of dirt. In the suffocating blackness, Leah heard Brother Warren's reminder in her head: *Jesus will never fail you. Your safest place is with him.*

"We've got two down here!"

Leah's eyes fluttered open at the urgent shout. Someone was leaning over her, and she was being strapped to something hard, her head stabilized. Then came the sensation of being lifted—of many strong arms jostling and passing her upwards in a rough climb to the brightness of day.

"Right here!" someone called. "Bring her over here!"

Her body bobbed up and down as a couple men carried her, until with a jolt, Leah was set onto the ground. Overcome with a fit of coughing, she fought to sit up until someone unstrapped her and she rolled to vomit on the grass. Then Jackie appeared, kneeling beside her and draping a blanket over her shoulders. She pulled it tight, hugging her over the top of it.

"Leah, thank God they found you! Thank God! We didn't know—we weren't sure—and then we thought—oh, thank God, thank God!"

Ahead of her a fire truck dominated her backyard—two fire trucks. A squad car with flashing lights was parked beside Peter's white truck, which in turn was parked at an odd angle, his driver's side door hanging open, as if he'd been in too much of a hurry to bother to close it. Behind her an ambulance arrived from the east side of the house, lumbering across the lawn toward the climbing tree and slowly backing toward her. Its doors popped open, and Jackie beckoned to the paramedics, who hastily approached Leah in their black pants and white uniform shirts, their arms laden with cases of equipment. Jackie moved to the side as they knelt to examine her.

"It's going to be all right, Leah," she cooed over and over, holding her hand. "They're working on getting Dan's brother out now. He's pinned, and they're cutting him out, but they're getting him! And don't worry—I called Dan to let him know what's happened. He's on his way."

Leah followed Jackie's anxious gaze toward the men crowded around the hole near the mangled mess of caved-in earth and equipment. Standing among the firemen were her cousin Marty and Professor Grant, both covered with dirt.

"My mom—" Leah said.

The paramedic was shining a light in her eyes, looking at her pupils.

"My mom—" she repeated.

He turned to Jackie. "Can you get her mother?"

"No—" Leah shook her head. "She's in there—down there—in front of the safe! She hurt her back!"

The paramedic met Jackie's eyes.

"Oh, God—help her!" Jackie said, rising to her feet. With a shout, she ran waving to the cluster of rescuers at the hole. Several men sprang into action.

"We're taking you in to get checked over," the paramedic was saying.

"I'm okay," Leah told him. "I'll wait for my mom." She moved to stand up, and he brought his hand under her arm to help her.

"That's right. Nice and easy. Come on, Miss," he encouraged. "Come with me. Nice and slow. We're going for a little ride in the ambulance. We'll have the ER look you over, just to be sure you're okay."

Leah shook her head. "My mom—"

There was an eruption of shouts and cheers as Jake was lifted out of the hole on a board and set on a waiting stretcher. Leah made a beeline to meet him at the ambulance, the paramedic hurrying along beside her.

"Jake!" she cried, reaching out for him.

He looked like a coal miner, caked with dirt, but he gave a weak smile, lifting a filthy hand to grasp hers.

"We made it!" he rasped, then coughed again. When he could speak, he added, "Your mom—I heard her. They're getting her out."

The ambulance doors were open and waiting. As they were sliding Jake in, Peter Watkins appeared around the back of the stretcher to give Leah a tight hug.

"This is all my fault," he told her. "I should have been here sooner! Dan called me at lunch to get my trailer off there. I had no idea—no idea! I should have called Marty to do it or something. I'm so sorry!"

Leah shook her head into his chest. "It's not your fault! I'm sorry you lost all your stuff—"

"No, no!" He squeezed her again. "No, that's all replaceable! I had no idea what was under there! When Marty called—" He shook his head. "Thank God it wasn't any worse!"

One of the paramedics touched Leah's arm, waving for her to join Jake in the ambulance.

"Go on, hon," Jackie encouraged from beside Peter. "Do what they say."

She shook her head. "I want to be with my mom. When they get her out I'll go with her."

"Your mom will go in the next one. Go now," the paramedic encouraged. "You're both heading to the same place. You can meet her there. Please!" He gestured.

"I'll take her!" Marty said, walking up behind them. "I'll drive her there myself."

Leah looked up in surprise.

"Your mom's going to need some help when they get her out of there," he said. "Come with me. We'll get you checked out, and then we'll find your mom at the hospital." He turned to the paramedic. "I'm her cousin."

"All right." He nodded, pointing a finger at his chest. "Make sure she gets there!" He shut the doors of the ambulance, tapped it twice, and raised his hand to the driver.

Peter laid his hand on Leah's shoulder. "Just so you know—I called Dan. He knows what's going on and says to tell you he's on his way."

"Okay, thanks," she said and turned to go with Marty.

Kyla suddenly appeared from around the side of the garage, running to meet her at the door of Marty's truck. She threw her arms around her and cried, and Leah cried with her. Finally she pulled back, wiping her cheeks. "Thank God you're okay! We were so scared, Leah!" She glanced questioningly at Marty holding the door.

"I'm taking her in," he said.

Kyla nodded. "Okay—I'll meet you at the hospital! I'm coming in! And Dan knows—I called him right away! He's already on his way back!"

Leah nodded. "Thank you."

Marty helped her in and buckled her up, and they started for town.

"You doing okay?" he asked, looking over.

Leah sniffed and nodded, suddenly noticing her black hands and dirt-caked clothes. She wondered what her face looked like. "Yeah, I'm okay. Thanks for the ride, Marty."

"Yeah," he said.

They were silent on Richmond Road, but when they exited onto the main highway, he looked over. "I need to ask you a question, Leah. Did that girl have anything to do with this?"

She met his eyes. Where did she begin?

He swore and turned back to watch the road. "What the heck were you doing down there? What reason would you have to open up that old storm cellar? Especially with all that equipment on there! I would have never let him park it there!"

Leah leaned her head back and sighed. "Oh, Marty, it's a long and complicated story!"

"Who is she?"

Leah opened her mouth to answer, but he swore again, continuing, "I got home early from work and let the dog out and was putzing with the stuff in the garage when I heard the racket of that trailer going in. I didn't know what it was, but the dang dog wouldn't stop barking, so I went to check it out and found him digging. That's the only reason I came over! The only reason! And that girl was standing at the back of the garage calling 911. She told me you were in there, and then she disappeared." He threw Leah a sharp look. "Tell me straight—did she have anything to do with this?"

"Sorta."

"Sorta? What the heck kinda answer is that? Who is she? She was in my garage trying to get into my house last night!"

Leah closed her eyes and let out a long breath. "I stumbled upon some family secrets. I found out that Mom had another child before me, and I hadn't a clue about it! No one's ever mentioned it—neither Mom nor Grandma. Maybe *you* already knew—there must have been rumors of some sort circulating in the family. Maybe your dad let on."

"I have no idea what you're talking about! And what the heck does this have to do with her?"

"Well, *that girl* just happens to be my half-sister and your cousin! Her name is Belinda Ann Taylor, but she was going by the name Brindle Baylor. I just found out today who she really is."

"What the heck?"

"I know! And she was sneaking into my house too, the rat!"

"Well, the police wanted to know what had happened, and I didn't know, and she was gone. If you ask me, I'd say she looked dang guilty by the way she disappeared! Did she make you go in there or something? 'Cause I need to know if this needs to go to the police! If it was an accident, that's one thing, but if it wasn't—!"

Leah shook her head. "It was Mom's idea to go in the cellar. She wanted to look for something down there, and it went south from there. But Brindle—Belinda—she has some serious issues with my mother, and she threw the bench platform down the stairs, and then the whole thing collapsed."

"Then you ought to report her. She should be held responsible."

"You're probably right."

He threw a hard look at her, then turned back to the road.

In the quiet Leah remembered that Brindle wasn't the only one who had issues with her mother. She turned to her cousin. "Marty, thank you. You saved my life! If you hadn't been there—"

He swore, shaking his head. "You were *dang* lucky! Dang lucky is all I can say! If it hadn't been for the dog!" He shook his head again. "And this guy just shows up out of the blue—one of the guys I played horseshoes with over the weekend! He said Peter's wife called him and told him to stop over at your house today after his class."

"Dr. Grant. The professor who Kyla works for."

He shrugged. "I didn't get his name. I just ran for shovels, and we started digging like heck where the dog was barking and pawing up the dirt. You were dang lucky. Dang lucky!"

Her mouth curled into a little smile. "I'd say it was a lot more than luck! It was definitely God watching over me. But thanks for *your* part in getting me out. And for this—" She gestured about the ride. "I'm truly grateful, Marty. And the stuff with my mom and your house—I wish I could make it all go away."

He lifted a few fingers on the steering wheel. "It's all right. It's not you."

"But I know it must be so disturbing and stressful for you. I'm sorry that everything is blowing up right now."

"It's not *you*, Leah. I'm dealing with a lot of other things in life right now. Personal stuff."

Leah nodded.

They rode in silence for a while.

As they neared the hospital, he turned to her. "Can I give you some advice?"

"What?"

"That Crawford weasel—stay away from him!"

"Phil Crawford?"

"Yeah. I caught him parked on the road next to your mailbox on my way to work this morning. If you're looking for your culprit, it's him."

Leah huffed. "Figures! I suppose it was obvious, given that Brindle, er, Belinda was living with him. Don't worry, I'm so done with him. But thanks for the heads-up."

"I don't think he'll be vandalizing your mailbox anymore. I pulled over and gave him a piece of my mind. Scared the livin' daylights out of him."

Leah smiled. "Thanks!"

He smiled back. Leah was glad. It was the first time she had seen him smile since they had reconnected.

"Can I give you some advice in return?"

He looked over.

"I've heard you can trust Peter Watkins—in case you ever need to talk to someone. I'm friends with his wife. Just letting you know." She shrugged.

He looked at her a moment, then jerked his chin in acknowledgment. "Okay, thanks."

Chapter Thirty-One

The blue curtain partition was flung aside as Kyla Watkins rushed into Leah's corner of the emergency room. Briefly acknowledging Marty on the chair where he sat, she dropped her purse onto the edge of the bed and came to hug Leah.

"Sorry I took forever," she gushed. "I was gonna come right in, but then I thought you'd need some time for everything, so I went and got you these." She plucked a cellophane-wrapped bouquet of flowers out of her purse. "Oops—they got a little crushed. And shoot—we don't have a vase either!" Her shoulders drooped. "Sorry—I was in a hurry. Are you doing okay?"

"I'm all right," Leah replied. She unwrapped the bundle and stared. Miniature roses. Pink ones, like the kind her grandmother had tended in her rose garden. Immediately she teared up, lifting them to her nose. It was like a hug from God and her grandmother all at the same time.

"Your yard's an absolute *mess*!" Kyla chattered on, wadding up the crinkly wrapper. "I can't even *believe* that all happened, and what a close call!" Drawing back, she added, "But *you* look a lot better than the last time I saw you! Holy cow—you looked like a chimney sweep!"

Leah smiled. "One of the nurses called me 'Pigpen'! They ruined a dozen washcloths on me!" She raised the flowers. "Thank you! These are *amazing*!" The plastic armband on her wrist snagged the sheet as she held them out for Kyla to sniff. She tugged it off. "Thanks for coming. Have you met my cousin Marty?"

Kyla nodded, turning toward him. "Yes, last night at your house. Hi, Marty. It was great of you to bring her in."

He unfolded his work boots as he sat up in the chair. "Hello. Appreciate your coming."

"And thank *God* you were there—right at the perfect time! Peter said you were one of the rescuers! So totally amazing!" She turned back to Leah, her eyes sweeping over the equipment around the bed. "So what's going on? Are you okay?"

"I'm still under observation, but I'm feeling all right. It's all the dust I breathed that's the biggest concern. I'm still waiting on the doctor to come back and tell me I can go. Hopefully it'll be soon. Mom's a couple doors down, but they want me to sit tight. They're running all kinds of tests on her, and when they're done with me, I can go sit with her. How'd you get in here? I thought they only let family in."

Kyla smiled sheepishly. "I told them you were my sister, which is true." She nudged her purse further over and sat on the bed. "So what happened? I want the full story please! I was outside playing with the kids when I got an urgent call from Peter to pray for you. He said Marty called saying the weight of his equipment had caved in the roof of an underground cellar in your yard—with *you* inside it! Did you know there was a cellar there before? What in the world were you doing in there? My word, Leah— we were so afraid you'd been killed!" She pressed a hand to her chest.

"It was crazy close! I can't say I've ever been more scared. But God rescued us!"

Kyla let out a breath. "You could have been crushed to death! And what's with Dan's brother showing up there? Why was *he* there? Isn't he the one that—?" Her brow rose in question.

"It's a long story, but yes—that's him. He was borrowing Danny's car for the weekend. And yes, thank God we weren't crushed! It's a miracle!"

"So what happened? Tell me the whole thing!" She cast a furtive glance at Marty, who had momentarily returned his attention to the television and lowered her voice, "You know—like with Brindle."

Leah moved her eyes to indicate she didn't want to talk about it with her cousin in the room. Instead, she listed out all the medical procedures she'd gone through since she'd arrived, including a chest scan and numerous blood draws.

After a short while, Marty rose to his feet. "If you don't mind, Leah, I'm going to head back—since you're not alone. There might be some way I could help out at your house."

Leah slid off the bed to hug him. "Thanks for the ride and the talk, Marty. Let's get together soon."

He gave a brisk nod. "That'd be good."

Once he was gone, Leah turned eagerly to Kyla and walked her through all the events of the afternoon, starting from their phone conversation in the bathroom. She gave a detailed account of meeting Brindle on the porch with her mother, then told of whisking her mom away for lunch and learning about the old storm cellar, which led up to her encounter with Jake at the Glendes'. Then she shared about her confrontation with Brindle and the horrific cave-in. Kyla shook her head over and over, repeating how thankful she was that they were all alive.

"So, were they there—those Krugerite coins or whatever they're called? Did you find them?"

Leah nodded. "Yep! Well, we didn't actually *see* them, but the safe is there. I'm betting they're all still inside!"

Kyla shook her head in awe. "And does *she* know that?"

"Yes, but she'd need an excavator to get to them. That safe's completely blocked by debris!"

Kyla gave a satisfied sigh. "Wow! Well, I called Dan right away, so hopefully he'll be here soon."

"Yeah, that's what you said. So did Peter. And Jackie too." She smiled, her cheeks warm.

Kyla dipped her chin. "I think it's a little obvious, my friend."

"Well, since my phone is buried in my backyard, can you text him that I'll be at the hospital with my mom? He can meet me here." She sighed. "He can't get here soon enough!"

"I'll do that."

And then Leah asked to use Kyla's phone to call her brother, Braydon, who was utterly confused at her news.

"Wait—what? Mom's in New Hampton? In the *hospital*? Since when? I didn't even know she was going there! She never said anything about it to me."

"It was likely a spur-of-the-moment thing," Leah told him and promised that she would call him with an update when she had more specifics of how their mother was doing.

It took another hour and a half for the doctor to finally release Leah, but then her shirt and jeans were so filthy that she convinced the nurse to let her stay in her hospital gown until someone could bring her clean clothes from home. Kyla texted Jackie about it right as Leah was being discharged. Then Leah walked Kyla to the ER door, where they said goodbye and parted.

Since Lenore was being admitted, Leah was directed to the elevators to find her mother's room upstairs. She was anxious to finally join her and find out how she was doing. Providentially, her mother's doctor was coming out of her room right as she arrived.

"Oh, she'll recover, but she'll be sore for a while," she told Leah grimly as they stood in the hallway. "Her left shoulder is pretty messed up. She's got a broken collarbone and a fractured rotator cuff. Plus, her hand—it was badly crushed, and her wrist is broken. She's scheduled for surgery in the morning for the shoulder. The first of many, I'm afraid. She's complained of back pain, but her MRI looked fine. Might just be pulled muscles from her arm being wrenched so hard. We're keeping an eye on things. If we can get some of that inflammation down it'll help. It'll take time, but she'll be okay."

Leah nodded in relief. "Okay—thanks."

"And how are you doing?" She glanced at Leah's robe.

"I'm good. They discharged me downstairs, but I'm waiting on some fresh clothes. I came to hang out here with Mom. It was a close call, and I'm thankful we still have each other."

The doctor slipped her pen into her pocket. "You're both pretty lucky, I'd say! I'm sure neither of you expected a trip to the ER today when you woke up this morning."

"Certainly not! But it wasn't luck that saved us—it was the hand of God."

Lenore was sleeping when Leah entered her room. Her shoulder and arm were wrapped, and she had a padded collar around her neck, which puffed out her thick hair even more. Leah spied a few clods of dirt in her part. She stood beside the bed with her hands on the rail looking at her mother's face, thinking about what the doctor had said and marveling at the brevity and fragility of life. Both of them were still there, having survived their freak accident, a luxury her grandparents had not had. She thought about the amazing timing of Belinda showing up in their lives and found herself vacillating between feelings of sympathy toward the girl and anger for her underhandedness. Even now she saw her sister in her mother's features. She regarded her for a little longer, then took the vinyl chair to wait.

After a while, a nurse came in to wake her mother for her next dose of pain medication, and afterward, when they had elevated the bed to a more comfortable position and had tucked several pillows all around her, Lenore spotted Leah for the first time.

"How long have you been here?" she asked.

"Not long."

Her eyes dropped to Leah's gown. "Are you hurt? Are they keeping you?"

Leah shook her head. "No. I couldn't bring myself to put my filthy clothes back on. Jackie, my next-door neighbor, is bringing me some clean stuff."

She gave a feeble nod.

Leah rose to stand beside the bed. "I love you, Mom! I came close to losing you."

Her mother met her eyes. "I'm sorry, Leah. I shouldn't have gone in there."

"But we're still here. Thank God for that!" She reached down to give her good hand a gentle squeeze. "I saw your doctor a bit ago. Your arm and shoulder sound pretty bad. Are you in a lot of pain?"

"I was, but not anymore. Whatever they gave me seems to be working—I'm feeling pretty dreamy." She stared ahead unseeing for a moment. "It was that blasted beam that saved me—the one pinning my hand. When everything caved in, it spun right off me and blocked the ceiling from landing on top of me. One of the young firemen that dug me out pointed it out."

"It was an act of God that we didn't die down there, Mom! Marty was the one who started digging for us—did you know that? He heard the crash, and his dog was barking, and"—she paused, wondering if she should tell her about Belinda calling 911—"and anyway, we didn't die. It was a miracle!"

Lenore looked away, murmuring softly, "There's some things that are worse than dying."

Leah blinked in surprise, then gave a deflated groan. How did her mother always find the bleak spot in every silver lining? "Oh, come on! What do you mean by that? Like what? What could be worse than *dying*?"

"Oh, nothing!"

"Nothing—*right*! Like having your long-lost daughter show up in your life again—is that what you meant? How is that worse than dying? I would think that's a *good* thing!"

She was silent.

"Is it because you were ashamed to be pregnant at sixteen? Goodness, Mom—who would judge you for that? Or did you mean that placing her for adoption was worse than death? I know it must have been terribly hard to do. My heart hurts even thinking about it! I get it, Mom—I get why it must be difficult to talk about."

Lenore shot her a hard look. "Oh, you get it, do you? Don't you start in on me, young lady! You don't know a single thing about it!"

"You're right! I know exactly nothing! But you're going to tell me!" She shook her head.

Leah slid her seat onto the edge of her bed. "Yep. You're going to tell me about it right now in fact!"

Lenore huffed. "No, I'm certainly not!"

Leah grabbed the cord and dragged the call button away from her. "Yes, you certainly *are*! I'm holding you hostage until you do! And if you don't, I'll twist your good arm first, then your broken one until you change your mind!"

Lenore's lip curled slightly at the humor.

Leah folded her hands, waiting.

She sighed heavily and looked away. After a long time, she spoke. "He was a coach. My cheerleading coach."

Leah straightened. "Belinda's father? Mom—that's illegal!"

"We loved each other."

Leah let out a breath. "That's still illegal! Was he prosecuted?"

She bit her lip and shook her head. "No one knew it was him."

Leah raised her brow. "Uh, I'm pretty sure Grandma Havi knew! His name was written in her journal—Todd something or other."

"I slept with Todd to have a scapegoat. It wasn't his."

Leah's head went back.

"You wanted to know! It's not so easy to understand now, is it?" Lenore brought her good hand up to move a strand of hair out of her face. "If I would've kept her, I would have had to share her with Todd and his parents. I couldn't do that." She sniffed.

Leah realized she was holding her breath. She exhaled and looked away, trying to process it all. "Wow! And all this went down right during the move—when Grandma got married."

She nodded. "Yes, and it *was* worse than death! Not only with the baby, but with *him*. I loved him!"

Leah rubbed her chin, trying to keep an even emotional response, trying to listen without judgment, but her heart was racing. "Thank you for telling me this, Mom," she said finally.

"You asked."

They were quiet, but all Leah could think of was burgundy-haired Brindle trying to find her mother for eight years and being refused in the end. Her deceptive and moody "friend" who'd reacted with repeated jabs any time Leah had brought up her own mother or grandmother in conversation.

Devious or not, it seemed that she should at least know her own mother.

"Did you know where she went when she was adopted?"

Lenore nodded. "Oh, yes. The Taylor family in Bridgewater."

"But Brindle—Belinda—told me she grew up in the foster system."

"I know nothing about that, and that's not my problem. That would be because of her parents—her adoptive parents."

"I know, Mom, but why don't you want to connect with her? Why not meet her? She said she's tried to contact you, and you've refused."

Her fingers twitched. "It's not an option. It brings up too many questions. There's no need to open that box."

Leah twisted on the bed, tossing the call button onto the sheet. "The box is *opened*! For heaven's sake, your daughter has been looking for you! She knows who you are and where you live! You had a conversation with her on my porch! It's time to open your life to her!"

"No! He was a good man and an upstanding citizen. There's no reason his name needs to be dragged down by this."

Leah frowned in surprise. "What are you talking about? This isn't about the jerk who got you pregnant! That was twenty-eight years ago! This is about connecting with your daughter *now*! And about me getting to know my half-sister—although I wanna smack that girl!"

Lenore scowled. "It's about a lot more than that! You just don't know."

Leah flayed her hands. "You keep saying that, Mom! If there's so much I don't know, then you should be the one filling me in!"

"Okay, then—you asked!" She raised her chin. "Belinda is not your step-sister, Leah."

"What do you mean?"

"Well, what the hell does it sound like? You're full-blooded sisters!"

"But how can that—" Leah blinked, then tipped her head in disbelief. "You went *back* to the guy?"

Lenore swallowed. "We never broke up."

"But—but what about Dad?"

Her mother didn't answer.

Leah stood and took a step backward. "*Don't tell me*—you did the same thing to Dad that you did to that Todd kid!"

She shook her head. "No. No, I didn't. It was different."

Leah folded her arms, leveling her eyes at her. "Mom, so help me—if you don't tell me the whole truth right now—"

"—The guy was married by then! But we still"—she dropped her eyes—"we still saw each other on the side. Then I met your dad. He liked me, and when I found out I was pregnant with you, I told him I'd been raped, and he was willing—" She glanced up at Leah and down again.

"Willing to marry you and be my dad." Leah stared at her dumbfounded. "Who is the guy? What's his name?"

She pressed her lips together and shook her head. "That I will not say. But he's dead now. He died five years ago."

Leah turned to pace at the foot of the bed, then dropped her arms and turned. "Dad never cheated on you, did he? Tell me the truth, Mom."

Her mouth opened and she looked away. "No. No, he didn't."

"And Braydon?"

"That's when your dad found out."

"Oh, my—" Leah put her face in her hands. She walked to the edge of the room and back, then took a deep breath, facing her. "Mom, I can't even tell you how disgusted and furious I am with you right now! You've lived a secret life! You broke up our family and pretended to be this poor, mistreated woman—"

"It always takes two, Leah!"

"Right—they *say* that, but sometimes it only takes one! One idiot doing something that's completely *wrong*! You know what bugs me? All my life you've thrown this 'Corolla Curse' thing in my face, stirring up this fear in me that I'm doomed to find anyone who will love me and be faithful to me, when all along *you* were the one—"

"—Well, you can't deny that the curse is true! Look what happened with Jake DeSoto!"

Leah shook her head. "No, Mom. No! What happened with Jake was a *good* thing. It was God saving me from greater pain. Marrying him would have been a nightmare! I'm not under the Corolla Curse. That was broken at the cross when I prayed in faith with Evelyn DeSoto!"

Lenore's face puckered. "Oh, stop with the churchy stuff, Leah! It's irrelevant to the conversation. You can't tell me that it isn't true! Maybe you can twist a happy ending out of that train wreck with Jake, but my life has been a perpetual cycle of bad luck!"

Leah set her hand on her hip. "Do you want to know why you're so 'unlucky'? I can tell you—it's called *sin*! It doesn't need a fancy label on it, like it's this special curse or something! You're not supposed to have an affair with a married man! He probably had a family!"

"Oh, now you sound just like my mother! Sin, sin, sin! My whole life she was self-righteous and judgmental toward me! She had a religious filter on *everything*!"

Leah made a little sound. "Did Grandma know about him?"

"Not at all."

Leah took a few breaths. "Mom, I could only count being like Grandma as a compliment! And as for being self-righteous—heck, I'm far from squeaky clean! I'll be the first to tell you what a loser I was to get myself in that relationship with Carlos. I totally used him. It was wrong, and I knew it the whole time, and it's only by the grace of God that I'm not still with him! I'm not being self-righteous or judgmental—I'm just telling you the truth!"

"You can talk all you want, Leah, but at the end of the day, all I can say is that I *loved* that man!" Her voice cracked with emotion.

Leah watched her mom weep, debating how far to go in the conversation. Her heart was pounding hard.

"Mom," she said quietly, "I love you very much, but here's the deal. You may have felt that you loved this guy, but that man—whoever he was—he did not love *you*. He was content to let you live with a heartache. He was content to let you be second or third or whatever you were to him. He didn't provide for you, he never took an interest in your life, and he never even bothered to get to know his own children! That is not a *real* man. In my eyes that's a very selfish man, and you, Mom, are a very *hurt* woman!"

Lenore sniffed, wiping her eyes with her good hand.

Behind Leah there was a sudden tap-tap-tap on the door.

"Hello?" Jackie Burke's voice came hesitantly from the hall. She peeked her head cautiously around the edge of the door, and spying Leah, smiled in relief. "Oh, good! I found you!"

"Jackie!" Leah exclaimed through her teeth.

"How're you doing, hon?" She spoke in hushed tones, entering timidly and casting a curious glance at Lenore, who had quickly pulled the sheet up to wipe her eyes. "Sorry to interrupt your special time with your mom, but Kyla said you needed some clothes." She held up a reusable bag. "I wasn't exactly sure what you needed, so I grabbed a few different things."

"Oh." Leah took the bag. "Thank you."

Jackie looked at her mother and smiled.

"Uh, Jackie, this is my mom—Lenore. And Mom, my neighbor, Jackie Burke."

Lenore gave a weak nod. "Hello."

"Hi. How unfortunate to meet like this!" Jackie clucked her tongue sympathetically. "How're you girls doing? So sorry about what happened! How absolutely traumatizing! Looks like you've got your arm all wrapped up—I hope it isn't broken!" Her eyes dropped to Leah's gown. "Leah, hon, how are you doing? Do you get to stay in the same room as your mom?"

Leah's hand went to her belly. "No, I'm free to go. I've just been waiting for my clothes." The plan to stay with her mom until Danny arrived was aborted. She only wanted to bolt. "Excuse me while I get dressed."

She changed quickly in the bathroom, kicking the stiff hospital gown and odd bootie socks under the sink. When she came out, she collected all her soiled belongings and shoved them into the empty bag.

"Okay—I'm ready."

"Oh!" Jackie's eyes widened in surprise. "I'm not in a hurry, dear, if you're still visiting with your mother!"

"Nope, I'm ready." She slid on her loafers, refusing to meet her mother's gaze.

"Well, all right." Jackie adjusted her purse on her shoulder and smiled, her eyes darting from one to the other.

Leah turned to her mother. "See you later, Mom. I'll probably stop in tomorrow after your surgery."

"There's no need to rush out of here! It's not like I'm too weak for conversation."

Her eyes were begging her to stay, but Leah couldn't right now. She offered a brisk nod, clutching her bag. "You should probably rest."

"Leah—"

"Bye, Mom! See you tomorrow." Without looking back, she stepped out into the hall.

Jackie hurried after, throwing her a look of concern. "Is everything all right?"

"Leah!" her mother called pathetically after her.

With a long breath, Leah lifted her eyes to Jackie's. "Jackie, do you mind meeting me at the elevators? There's a lounge there. I'll just be a second."

She patted Leah's arm. "Take your time, sweetie. Your mother needs you!"

Leah returned to her mom's bedside and stood there without speaking.

Lenore struggled for words. "I—I know you're right, Leah. I just can't turn it around. Sometimes I try, but I feel like—I feel like I'm locked into the way I am, and I can't change."

Leah folded her arms. "Are you asking me for help? You gotta do this yourself, Mom. But first you need to decide what kind of change you want. There are all kinds of books to coach you on being a nicer person, but that'd only slap a Band-Aid on an ugly wound. Your problem's a lot deeper than that. I think it's time to start facing some of the mistakes you've made in life, and to fix those, you need to turn to God."

She swallowed. "David—your dad—he came over to the house this morning to ask me to forgive him."

Leah was silent.

She sniffed. "He asked me to forgive him for all the ways he failed me as a husband."

"Do you? I'm sure he wasn't perfect. I know he drank a lot."

"He's not the one in need of forgiveness."

Leah studied her thoughtfully. "Mom, you've got some issues to deal with, but your starting point has to be with God. I know you bristle at the concept of 'sin,' but it explains a lot in life. It's reality. There *is* a standard of right and wrong, and *God* defines what that is. If you can't go there, nothing else is going to work out the way it should. But if you're willing, I'm confident that he'll walk you through everything else. He won't fail you—you can be sure of that."

Tears leaked out the corners of her eyes. "I don't know how to do that."

"Then be real about it! Start by asking him for help. He will. And if you want, I could probably find someone who would be willing to talk with you."

She nodded, sniffling. "Okay. Will you come back tomorrow? After my surgery?"

"Yes, Mom, I'll come back." She reached to take her mother's good hand in hers. "Listen—I want you to know that I forgive you for what you've done. Right now I'm having a really hard time taking it all in, but I forgive you. And I'm going to keep on forgiving you until I get over it."

Her voice quavered. "Thank you, Leah."

"But can we make one thing clear?"

Her eyes lifted questioningly.

Leah leaned down to look directly into her face. "My dad will never find out that I know he's not my father. Do you hear me?"

"He already knows he's not your father."

"No, Mom, listen to what I'm saying. You will never—and I mean *never*—tell him that I know all this! Do you understand?" After all the courage it had taken him to come to New Hampton and have that conversation with her on her porch, Leah didn't want to take *any* chance of deflating him or derailing his progress.

She nodded meekly.

"Say it!"

"I promise."

"It may come out some day. But never from *you*. Do you understand?"

"I understand."

Leah squeezed her hand and then kissed her on the forehead. "I love you, Mom."

"I love you too, Leah." She was crying freely now.

"See you tomorrow."

With another squeeze of her hand, Leah left the room. Ordinarily she wouldn't dream of walking away from someone who was crying, especially her mother, but in this case it seemed the right thing to do. If there was an opportune time for her mother to reach out to God, it was now, and Leah didn't want to muddy the waters.

As she started down the hall toward the elevators, she wondered how far Danny was from home, mentally calculating the soonest he could arrive, given that he had driven four hours to his destination and had to return the same distance. She needed him. She wanted to see him so badly it hurt.

Glancing ahead to locate a clock at the nurses' station, Leah suddenly stopped short in the middle of the hall at the sight of a pregnant woman rushing up to the counter from the elevators, her face distraught with worry. It was Rachel Steinburg, and she was gesturing animatedly with her hands, her dark, curly hair falling over her shoulder. No, Rachel *DeSoto*, Leah corrected herself. Jake's wife. And she was flanked by his parents, Rocke and Evelyn, as she earnestly inquired after her husband at the desk, then turned to hurry down the hallway in the direction she was pointed, opposite from where Leah stood, with Rocke and Evelyn closely at her heels.

Leah marveled. There was no sting in seeing her—Rachel. She couldn't exactly say that she felt *love* for her by any means, but the hatred was gone, and the hurt had melted away. Sometime soon she would have to have that awkward conversation with her—another hurdle to cross, for they were going to be in relationship for a long time—but tonight was not that night. Tonight was Rachel's night to rejoice that her husband was alive and that her daughter and unborn baby still had their father. When the time was right God would provide Leah an opportunity to talk with her, and he would be faithful to help her through it. Leah was learning that God was like that. He wouldn't fail her. And after that—maybe before, who knew?—

she would reconnect with Rocke and Evelyn too. The thought of it made her want to cry. What a good God she had—that he would restore to her what she had lost!

Jackie was seated in the corner of the elevator lounge playing a word game on her phone.

"Thanks for waiting," Leah said.

She popped her phone into her purse. "I'm not in a hurry, dear, not in a hurry! In all my years, one thing I've learned is that when you're given those tender moments with your family, you have to take them. They're precious gifts from God."

Leah gave a wisp of a smile and dropped her eyes. Tender moments. Tender moments were rare to nonexistent with her mother. Nevertheless, she *had* a mother. And as dysfunctional as their relationship was, she *did* love her.

"Well, I'm ready to go."

The sun was slipping below the horizon when they turned onto Richmond Road. Jackie turned into the convenience store at the corner to fill with gas and buy milk. Leah waited in the car.

"Would you like something from the drive-in next door, sweetie?" Jackie asked, leaning through the window. "A cone or slushy or anything? Hot dog?"

Leah shook her head. "No, thanks."

Jackie got in the car and buckled in. "You sure? Sometimes a little treat at the end of a hard day is refreshing."

She shrugged, relenting. "Well, all right. I guess I might be a little hungry."

The two zipped through the drive-through where Leah ordered herself a burger with a chocolate shake—the latter something she'd ordinarily never get, but as Jackie said, it had been quite a day, and it felt like a reward was in order. On a whim she ordered two.

"I'll put one in the freezer for Danny."

Jackie smiled approvingly and paid for it all. "That's a lovely idea. Now let's get you home."

The Glende house was quiet and dark when they drove up. Angel greeted them excitedly at the door and made his outdoor business quick to be near Jackie. Leah dropped the bag of dirty clothes in the corner of the living room while Jackie carried their food to the table. She rustled open the paper bag and handed Leah her sandwich. Leah thanked her again but couldn't sit down.

"I'm sorry Jackie. I hope you understand, but I think I need—it's been such a day—I think I need to be alone for a bit."

Jackie's face swung up. "Oh, my dear girl! I completely understand! Angel and I can go to our room—"

"No, no! No, please, Jackie! If you don't mind, I think I'll go over to my house for a while to sit alone on my porch."

She nodded. "That's a perfect idea! I'll be here if you need me."

"Thank you," Leah said, fetching her house keys.

By now only the faintest glow of light was left over the western hedge. Dozens of fireflies blinked in the dusk, and in wonder Leah paused in the middle of her lawn to observe them. Then with a giant breath of the sweet night air, she tipped her head back to watch the stars poke out one by one above her, each one held in place by a powerful God who knew them all by name.

Overcome, she set her food onto the grass and raised her hands, thanking God for sparing her life. Spreading her arms wide, she twirled, worshiping from her heart. God had saved her life on more levels than she could count, swooping in to rescue her like a hero, lavishing her with grace and mercy and enabling her to forgive even the unforgiveable. He had not given up on her in her dark valleys of kicking and screaming when she hadn't been able to handle her pain but had held on to her through it all— even redeeming those awful places to make things better than before. He had *loved* her, loved her so faithfully all those years, as he always would.

"Thank you," she said. "Thank you, thank you, *thank* you!"

Feeling she could burst with love and gratefulness, she dropped her arms, collected her food, and continued inside to put Danny's shake in the freezer. Then she returned to settle down on her porch to wait. She eyed the turn on her driveway. Without her phone she had no idea of what time it was, but surely he must be getting close to New Hampton by now. Stretching to click on the lantern on the end table, she settled down to enjoy her sandwich.

She had just taken her first draw on the heavenly shake when Midnight leaped up the steps, jutting his slobbery jowls onto her lap, panting excitedly and wagging his tail. She raised her half-eaten burger out of reach, scratching his ears and neck with her other hand.

"Midnight, you good dog!" she crooned, letting him lick her face. "You're a good, good dog! Yeah, buddy—you saved my life!"

His nose stretched upward, keen on her food, and Leah easily relented.

"All right—just this once, my friend." Gladly she broke up the entire remainder of her hamburger, portioning it out to him in small chunks. "Just this once, you good boy! You deserve it—every bite! You're a good, good dog!"

When the sandwich was gone Midnight continued to lick his chops expectantly, swinging his tail. Leah gave him a vigorous back scratch, then urged him to lie down, which he obediently did, dropping to the floor beside her chair, placing his paw affectionately over her foot.

She took another long sip of the shake, then rested the cold cup on her leg. It made her think of Brindle and all the fancy coffees she had brought almost every time she visited. The coffees, all the offers to help her—all had been a sham! She'd been buying her friendship to wiggle her way into her house, sneaking in while Leah wasn't around in search of her grandmother's journals—all to find the safe and the coins. What a master manipulator! Leah kicked herself for being so naive. Oh, how she'd like to get in that girl's face. She'd have a lot to say and oh, would she enjoy saying it!

And yet she was torn by the mind-boggling fact that they were sisters. *Sisters.* Who knew what Brindle's full story was? Glancing at the nearby pillar, Leah remembered the day that Brindle had spilled her coffee right there on the porch. She recalled that she had just asked Brindle about her family. In hindsight, it was obvious she hadn't wanted to talk about her family. As slippery-sly as she was, Leah had seen a glimpse of a heart in that conniving girl, one that had been wounded by who-knows-what-had-happened with her adoptive parents and apparent negative foster care experiences. And a heart that had painstakingly searched for her birth mother for eight long years. It was rather sad to think about.

Leah's eyes lingered on the porch pillar, her feelings a jumbled mess of wanting to hug Brindle and yell at her all at once. One thing was becoming clear: focusing on Brindle's deception appeared to have a multiplying effect. It not only stirred her up, but it also resurrected every old and ugly accusation toward Rachel, like a noxious weed springing up from the same root. Wasn't she trying to get past all that? It seemed those two women were a package deal: if she couldn't forgive Brindle, she knew she would never truly let Rachel go either. And vice versa. Guiltily Leah tapped the cup on her leg.

Out of the blue an idea popped into her head. She bit her lip, considering it for a moment; then decisively she rose and swiftly fetched the extra shake from the freezer. It was a crazy whim, she mused, either a God-idea or a really dumb one of her own. But she wouldn't know which until she stepped out in faith.

She whistled to Midnight. "Come on, boy! I need your help. And try to look mean."

Chapter Thirty-Two

With her car windows rolled down, Leah pulled quietly over onto the side of Reed Street and parked in front of Phil Crawford's town house. In the illumination of the streetlight, she saw Phil depositing a box in the trunk of Brindle's blue car. He straightened, slamming it shut with both hands, turning back for the house.

"Midnight, *stay!*" she commanded under her breath, leaving her canine partner in the front seat as she grabbed the shake and exited her car.

At the sound of the car door, Phil turned, looking dumbfounded as he recognized Leah in the dim light. His eyes lifted to the dog in the car behind her, where Midnight hung his head out the window panting.

She stepped onto the grassy boulevard. "Well, hey there, Phil! I was stopping by to see Brindle, but since you're here, I can let you know that Jackie's dog is okay." She took a few deliberate steps toward him. "You left her with a nice veterinary bill, but at least you didn't kill the poor thing!"

He gaped at her, then wordlessly swung on his heel, retreating jerkily toward the house. Brindle met him coming out the door with another box in her arms, murmuring that she had the last one. Her head rose, and seeing Leah on the sidewalk, she froze, her face blanched with fear.

"Leah!" she sputtered.

The screen door flopped shut as Phil disappeared inside, but Brindle stood petrified.

"Yep, it's me! Here—let me help you with that." She went to open the door to Brindle's back seat, noting it was tightly packed with her belongings. "I see you're moving!"

Brindle's eyes flicked to Midnight and back. "Wh-what do you want?"

Leah met her gaze directly. "A sister."

Brindle looked away, shaking her head. "Don't do this to me!"

Leah gestured to the car. "Come set that down."

The girl stared at her, then slowly approached to stuff the box onto the crowded seat. Leah held out the shake.

"What's this?" Brindle asked, regarding it suspiciously.

She held it out further. "A chocolate shake—take it! I finished mine already, but I got an extra. It's for you!"

Casting a quick glance up the street, Brindle stepped back and folded her arms. "Did you call the police on me?"

Leah shook her head. "Nope." She lowered the shake.

"Why not?"

She shrugged. "Marty said you called 911. It saved our lives. Thank you."

Brindle made a little sound and turned her face away. "What do you want, Leah? Don't mess with me! If you're going to turn me in, do it. If you want to ream me out, get it over with. But stop with the games!"

"I told you what I want."

Brindle shook her head. "That's not one of the options!"

"Why not?"

The girl narrowed her eyes. "What's *wrong* with you? Why are you here?" She threw a look over her shoulder, glancing down the street again.

"No one's on their way—don't worry," Leah told her. "And I'm not going to stop you from leaving." She switched the cup to her other hand. "I was just thinking—now that all the games are indeed over, I'm left with a sister I never knew I had, and I'd like to know her."

"Oh, no—I'm done with all that!" She shook her head. "I can't do it anymore! I've tried—believe me: I've tried! Your mother wants nothing to do with me."

Leah nodded. "I get that. But that's been *her* choice, and I'm not her. This is *my* choice!"

Brindle's chin lifted, regarding her thoughtfully.

Leah waited.

"How'd you find out?"

"Purely by chance. Just this morning I happened across it in one of the journals. Just this morning! And then it was confirmed when I found your birth certificate in the bin of Mom's stuff in the basement—the same one you discovered when we were down there together. But you already knew it before then."

Brindle closed her eyes and looked away. "We have nothing in common. I'm not religious. That stuff really irks me."

Leah shrugged. "Since when is that a requirement for sisters? And we *do* have a few things in common—we both share a liking for odd names and a poor taste in hair color. Did you do that two-tone pinky thing just for me?"

Brindle gave a hint of a smile. "Maybe. I'll admit I'm not crazy about it. Why'd you choose yours?"

"It was a desperate attempt to escape myself. But it's temporary." She held out the shake again. "Come on—here, take this! My hand's getting cold!"

Hesitantly, Brindle accepted it. She looked at it, then took a sip.

"I have a little brother that you should meet. His name's Braydon. He's seventeen."

Once again, the girl drew back, shaking her head.

"Why not? Why shouldn't he know he has another sister? And why shouldn't you know your own family?"

"*Step*-sister," Brindle corrected, pointing the shake at her, "code for 'outsider,' never to belong!"

"Baloney! You're only an outsider if you choose to stay outside. I'm asking you *not* to!"

"You don't know what you're asking! You don't even know me. You don't know anything about me."

"Yes, but that can change. I know you have a heart. I know you have feelings. I can see how crushed you've been from searching for your mother. It's *her* loss, Belinda. Her loss and my gain."

She winced. "Ah—you see, that's the problem! Your connection to her will always emphasize the fact that she despises me. Plus, you have a father. I have no one."

Leah paused, debating whether to share her recent family discovery with her. Yet it didn't feel like the appropriate time. "Then let's think about this logically," she said instead. "If you allow me into your life, then you'd have one person who's family. One's more than none. If you allow me *and* Braydon into your life, then that's two—it just doubled.

"And I'll let you in on a little secret," Leah continued. "Yeah, I have a dad, but he's been largely absent from my life until this week—truly, just this week! Something major went down in him—a turnaround in his life because of God—and it's only just now that I'm getting to really know him. I can't speak for him, but I think his heart would be large enough for another daughter."

Brindle's brow puckered. "Right—like he'd do that to someone who's not his own kid!"

503

A new appreciation for her dad washed through Leah. "You don't know my dad! He's got a really big heart. A really big heart."

"Just stop, Leah! I'm not some stray puppy looking for a home!"

Noting her anxiety, she nodded. "Okay. Okay—I'm sorry."

They stood in silence under the streetlight. Brindle had some more of the shake.

"So where are you going?" Leah asked.

"Back to Bridgewater."

"And Phil? Is he moving with you?"

Her head jerked back. "Him? No. No, we dated a couple years back, but we're not—no, he's not coming." She paused. "I made him do all those things, you know—the mailbox stuff. I know it was dumb."

"That was my guess. And you were at my house after the party, weren't you? On your way to find my cellar, right? Marty probably surprised you when he came to get the stuff from the garage."

Brindle met her eyes and looked down.

"If you let me be your sister, I'll let you read Grandma's journals— that is if you have any genuine interest in them."

"Now you're bribing me."

Leah nodded. "Yes, but she was a person worth knowing. They'd be worth your time. I'll warn you though—they're religious."

She laughed. "Figures!" Then growing sober, she looked at Leah with concern. "So are you all right? You weren't hurt from the cave-in—? I thought I killed you! When you walked up, I thought you were a *ghost*!"

"I'm all right."

"And the others?"

"Mom's got a broken shoulder and arm, but she'll recover. Jake injured his leg. We'd likely be dead if you hadn't called 911. It was pretty bad."

Brindle breathed out in relief and looked away, and the two stood without speaking for a long time. Finally she looked back. "Why? Why are you doing this? Why would you want a relationship with me after all I've done to you?"

"Do you want the nice answer or the honest answer?"

"Cut the crap."

"You're not going to like it then—it's religious!"

"Tell me anyway."

Leah paused. "Because I've been a complete jerk to God myself, and after all I've done, he still wants a relationship with me and sent Jesus to make it possible. He's forgiven me—that's why. And because he's forgiven *me*, I can forgive *you*. I want a sister, Belinda. I want to know you."

"I have a hard time believing that." She gave a defeated sigh. "That's part of it too—how do I even say I'm sorry? I don't even know how."

Leah shrugged. "Just say it!"

"Okay—I'm *sorry*, Leah!" She closed her eyes in shame. "I'm *really* sorry! I've been awful to you!"

"Thank you. I forgive you. I can truthfully say I've got the meanest sister in the world, but I *do* forgive you!" She grinned.

Belinda smiled faintly in return. Another silence passed.

"So those coins—how did that guy know? The old man. How did he know I was looking for them?"

"Brother Warren?" Leah asked.

"Yeah. At the Bible study. The way he looked at me—and he brought up that Bible story about the coins—it was like he *knew*. Did you tell him?"

Leah shook her head. "*I* didn't know at that point. But God knew, Belinda. And he knows a lot more about you! Brother Warren has said some things to me before that were a little scary too. But I've learned that it's God pursuing me—pursuing me because he loves me. And he loves you too."

"Yeah, whatever. I don't really believe all that." She cleared her throat. "Anyway, I should probably give you my correct phone number. You probably figured that out too."

"Yeah, I wondered about that. But my phone's buried in my backyard, so I'll give you mine instead. You can call me whenever you're ready. But I'll need a new phone, so give me enough time to get set up."

"Sorry about that too," she said guiltily, retrieving her phone from the console of her car.

Leah entered her number and handed it back. "Well, I should probably get going. I need to get the dog back before Marty realizes he's gone. Plus, I'm meeting someone."

Belinda glanced at Midnight with a look of amusement. "The guard dog thing was a clever move. It worked."

Leah smiled back. "He's actually a big baby." She reached to hug her and planted a kiss on her cheek. "Well, goodnight, my sister. Drive safely tonight."

Belinda pulled uncomfortably away. "Yeah, okay. Goodbye."

As Leah left, Belinda called after her, "Don't worry about me trying to take the house from you. I have no legal grounds to pursue that anyway."

Leah turned. "Thanks."

"And don't worry about"—she lifted a shoulder—"you know, the other stuff. I'll be leaving you alone. And so will Phil."

"Yeah, thanks. That was quite a show he put on with my mailbox and lawnmower. He's a brilliant actor for being such a jerk. You can tell him he owes me a new one of each. And let him know I won't need his help with my kitchen. My dad's gonna help with that."

"I'll tell him."

She continued to her car, then turned back once more. "Hey, Belinda—"

Belinda lowered the shake from her mouth with a questioning look.

"Don't wait too long to call me, okay? I'll drive up to Bridgewater to meet you."

"All right—we'll see. Good night, Leah."

Now back in her own driveway, Leah thanked Midnight again with another hearty neck scratch, and when she finished, the dog promptly trotted home, as if his business there was completed. With her hopes high, Leah hurried to the Glendes' in the dark to check if Brother Warren's vehicle was in their driveway yet—but it wasn't. She sighed. What was taking Danny so long?

Tired and starting to get impatient, Leah returned to her house for a quick shower. Her body begged for a good scouring from head to toe after that baptism in dirt, especially her hair. Funky or not, the water felt invigorating. Her old roots were starting to show, she noted as she dried off, but she wasn't too disappointed. She was more than ready to endure the awkward transition on her way back to her natural color. Then maybe she'd go blond again—or finally try the platinum—depending on Danny's preference. Anything but this horrible black!

Her arrival on the porch was in perfect time to see headlights pull off the road. With a surge of gladness, she flew to the driveway as Danny guided Brother Warren's car up beside her own. She met him at his door, and he caught her into a long embrace in which neither of them could speak. Finally he pulled back, searching her face by the light of the garage.

"Are you all right, Leah? Kyla said you weren't hurt, but you must be terribly shaken! It must have been awful!"

She nodded, not letting him go. "I'm okay. Better now that you're here. I've got a ton of bruises and a scratchy throat from hacking up buckets of dirt, but I'm all right. It'll probably be worse tomorrow. And shaken—?

Oh, yes!"

He bumped the car door shut with his foot and hugged her tightly again.

When their embrace finally loosened, Danny slid his phone out of his pocket and turned on the flashlight. "Please—if you don't mind, I'd like to see it. I don't have much battery left, but I'd like to go back to where it caved in. Peter said it's unbelievable. And tell me the whole story. I want to hear everything. Kyla said something about Brindle being involved, and then Jake showing up, and your mom too—goodness, all kinds of crazy!"

"Yeah. Yeah, it's going to take some time, but I'll tell you everything. We can go see it if you want. I haven't been back there yet." She shuddered.

"Come—we'll go together." He touched her arm, indicating for her to follow.

As they came around the side of the garage, Leah pointed out the gouges in the lawn from the firetrucks and other vehicles that had been back there, but when they got to the caved-in cellar, Danny was stunned.

"It's a miracle!" he exclaimed over and over, walking the perimeter, shining the light down onto the mangled mess of twisted machinery, examining it from different angles. "Nothing but a miracle that all of you weren't completely crushed!"

Leah led him around to an area next to a mound of dirt where they looked down at the side of the black metal safe glinting in the beam of light.

"That's where we were—Jake and I. Right there in that pocket beside the safe. Like a couple of rabbits in a little burrow. And down there—" She shone the light toward a cavity under a thick post wedged against the front of the safe. "Through that crack is where Mom was. I could barely touch her head from my spot. I guess when it happened the dog went nuts digging for us. Then Marty and Dr. Grant got shovels and went to it."

Danny stared soberly, shaking his head in amazement. Then suddenly he dropped to one knee, offering a prayer of thanks to God for preserving their lives. Leah's throat tightened. When he was finished, he rose and continued to survey the mess with the flashlight.

"How's your mom doing?" he asked.

"She's pretty beat up—shoulder, arm, hand. Surgery tomorrow. She's got a painful road ahead of her, but they say she'll be okay."

He nodded. "Same with Jake. His leg's pretty messed up, but he'll be okay too." He looked down at her. "I went directly to the hospital to meet you. I just got to your mom's room when Jackie texted that you were here."

"Oh, sorry. I changed my mind the last minute and had Jackie bring me home." She waved her hand. "My phone's down there somewhere."

"No, that's okay. I peeked in, but she was sleeping, and then since I was there, I stopped to check on Jake. Mom and Dad and Rachel were there with him."

"Yeah, I saw them arrive. But they didn't see me."

He turned to her in the dark. "I can't tell you how proud I am of you! Jake said the two of you talked—like, really talked."

"Oh, yes—we did! We talked!"

"Way to go, Leah!"

She blew out a breath. "You wouldn't even believe how crazy it was—that *he* of all people showed up here right when he did! Incredible timing! Absolutely crazy—but it was a God thing. God's done a miracle, Danny. That's all I can say. Getting out of there"—she waved at the hole— "*that* was more than amazing! A miracle, for sure! But what God's done in my heart—that's a miracle in its own right. I came out of a grave today— one much bigger than that!" She pointed.

"Praise God!" He wrapped his arm around her shoulder and gave her a squeeze.

Leah reached up to take his hand. "Come on—let's go sit on the porch. I have a lot to tell you. But first—how was your trip with Brother Warren?"

He laughed as they started back across the grass. "Well, it started out *miserable* because of the way I left you! That was so bad! I'm sorry, Leah!"

She smiled. "It's all okay now."

He shook his head. "I was such an idiot! And then when we were only a half hour from our destination, Peter called in a panic about this. Talk about a dilemma! Brother Warren was the first speaker up there tonight, so we had to quickly decide what to do—whether he was cancelling and coming home with me or staying. I urged him to stay—eight hours in a car is a long time for an eighty-two-year-old. Then I had to drop him off and quick find someone to care for him before I could get on the road again. My mind was going berserk! It's been a stressful day." He looked down at her. "Not quite as stressful as *yours,* of course!"

She nodded, squeezing his hand. "I am most definitely the winner!"

He chuckled as they paused in front of the cars on the driveway. "No question about that! All right—let's hear this! Give me the whole story!"

Leah started in by telling him of the surprise visit from her mother after he left and the phone call from Kyla in the middle of it. Then she shared the shock of Brindle showing up and the ensuing discovery of the storm cellar over lunch with her mom.

"Oh, man!" he said, shaking his head over and over. "Incredible! Just incredible! Who would have thought there'd be an underground cellar there? Hey—hold on one second—" He held his finger for Leah to wait as he retrieved his coffee from his front seat.

"Coffee at this hour?" she said. "Geez, Danny. It's kinda late!"

He tightened the lid and shrugged. "I've spent the whole day in a car!" He took a sip, then gestured to the porch. "Let's finish up there."

They sat side by side on the love seat as she continued to tell him about rushing next door only to find it was Jake.

"I thought you'd come back, and I was so relieved! I ran right over there. Oh, my gosh—when I saw his face—!"

"I should have told you he was coming."

"No, it was best the way it happened. So here's the thing. My worst fear has always been coming face to face with your brother, and today I would have totally freaked out if God hadn't already prepared my heart. I didn't tell you this earlier today, but I woke up to a powerful dream this morning, and let me tell you—I was severely humbled." She shared all the details with him as he attentively listened.

"So I guess if I believe Jesus was punished for what I deserved, then I'd be a fool to revel in the mercy of God for myself and still want God's anger poured out on Jake and Rachel."

Danny nodded. "Yes, I guess so."

She jabbed him playfully with her elbow. "You say that so nicely, like you're understanding this for the first time. I know you already get this, but it's new for me. Seriously, how could I want God to judge them harshly for their sins but show mercy on me for mine? I'd be such a hypocrite! If he died for all people, then he desires all people to be made right with him, and I should want that too. It's their choice to enter into it, but as far as it concerns me, I've decided to want the mercy of God for them. So I forgive them. I'm letting it all go and trusting God to deal with them." She looked down reflectively. "And I'm learning that he loves dealing with people kindly. Because he's good. And he loves mercy."

After a brief silence she looked up at him.

He nodded soberly. "Leah, that's very mature of you."

She let out a breath. "Honestly, Danny, it's about as basic as you can get! It's just that hurt can really cloud reality sometimes, and then it's like those hurts become a magnet for all kinds of lies. But guess what? He *loves* me—he does! He's a good father, and he's *just*. He knows how to make all things right. He's never going to leave me, and he won't fail me, even when it's hard." She heard Brother Warren's words in her head as she finished. "I can count on it."

Danny's head bobbed again. "Yes, you can."

And then she shared what had happened in the storm cellar from the beginning to the end. Danny tucked her hand under his as he quietly listened.

"There's some other crazy stuff too," Leah finished. "My mom and I had a talk at the hospital, which was, ah—a little life-altering, I'd say. But that's a long story that can wait until tomorrow. More family drama that I'd rather not go into now."

"Sure. But was it a good talk?"

"Um, I'd say it was a mix of good, bad, and ugly. Mostly ugly, but overall, I think it has the potential for good. I honestly can't talk about it now."

"Understandable."

Leah shifted excitedly. "But I do want to tell you about something else! After Jackie brought me home tonight, I did something pretty daring!"

"What's that?"

"I went to talk with Brindle—er, Belinda. I'm still not used to her name."

He leaned away in surprise. "You went over there? *Tonight?*"

"I know! It was a little risky—"

"*Risky*—I'd say!"

"—but it turned out to be a God thing." She shared the details with him and finished by saying, "I think I may have gotten a sister out of this thing. So that's another miracle to add to the mix. Can you believe it, Danny? Can you believe how wonderful God has been through all of this?"

"I'm blown away!" he agreed.

Then Leah giggled, telling him about the shake that she had bought for him and gave to Belinda instead, and how she had brought Midnight with her in the car for intimidation. He gave his trademark burst of laughter and reached to sip his coffee. Then he held it in his lap with both hands.

After a happy silence, Danny turned to look at her. "So. An interesting thing happened at the hospital."

Leah's brow went up. "Yeah?"

"My brother offered me his congratulations."

Leah looked at him in confusion for a second, then turned away with an embarrassed smile. "Oh, *that*! Yeah. Sorry. It was meant to be one of those 'eventually' things. A maybe-down-the-road thing, you know."

"Ah, I see." His chin lifted in a nod.

He continued to smile at her, and she squirmed awkwardly. "Sorry. I shouldn't have said anything."

He shook his head. "No, that's okay. I'm just enjoying watching you right now."

Blushing, she looked away.

He fingered the cup. "I was thinking . . . I was thinking that since it's all in the open now—how we feel about each other—that maybe we should just go ahead and make it official."

Leah turned back questioningly.

With a little smile Danny popped the top off his cup and dumped a little ring box out into his hand. Leah's jaw dropped in surprise.

"You faker!" she exclaimed and then laughed out loud. "Danny, you total faker!"

A grin spread across his face as he set the empty cup on the table and turned to her.

"Is that what I think it is?" Her hands went to her cheeks.

"I made a quick stop at my parents' house on our way to the conference."

She reached for the box, but he pulled it away. "Hey, now! Not so hasty! I have something to say to you first."

"Oh, gosh!" Leah folded her hands in her lap as he moved the coffee table away and slid out of his seat to face her on one knee.

"I'm not sure if you were aware of this, Leah, but ever since you were sixteen, I've had a terrible crush on you. I was counting the days until you turned eighteen to ask you out, and then I had to die a thousand deaths to see you fall in love with my brother. I've carried you in my heart all these years, and I've compared every other girl to you. The first week I came here, Brother Warren had a strong word for me to let you go and start praying for a wife. I was finally willing to do it, but in the wrestling, I asked God to bring me someone like you. I cannot believe the grace of God to bring you back into my life, and I ask you, Leah Labanora, to stay in it forever"—he opened the ring box—"as my wife."

Leah stared at the ring, suddenly lightheaded. Oh, she loved him! He was more than she could ever ask for, but in this moment beyond her wildest dreams came a stab of fear—although it was not even remotely related to the old family curse. No, her concern was questioning how an outstanding prize like Danny could want someone like her. He was a prince, and she was a spiritual infant. His life was marked by wisdom and integrity. Her judgements were immature and glaringly naïve.

She raised her eyes to his, speaking frankly, "Danny, are you sure about this? I've made some huge mistakes since I was that girl. I got myself messed up in more ways than I can count. My thinking's whacked, for one. I'm just now coming out of it. Plus, my family. You'd be marrying into all kinds of dysfunction, and do you really want to deal with all that? This image you've had of me all these years—I'm sorry, but you're probably going to be very disappointed in me, 'cause I'm far from perfect. I'm not sure you want this."

He looked at her, nodding thoughtfully, his forehead crinkled. "Okay. Yeah, you're probably right. Never mind." He snapped the box shut and moved to put it in his pocket.

Leah cried out in protest.

He smiled. "What—are you trying to sell me off or something? You think I haven't thought this through?"

"I'm—I'm just telling you I've got a few issues! I want to be up front with you!"

"Uh-huh. You're *afraid*. I get that. But listen—I'm not going anywhere. I'm asking you for keeps. For a lifetime. Not to just try it out to see if it works. I'm committing my life to you. I love you, Leah, and I know what I want. I want you as you are—warts and all. And if you say yes, then *you* get *me*, warts and all too. For life. Marry me, Leah!"

A smile spread across her face. "Well, then, it's a *yes*, and from a heart unmuddied by all the Jake stuff besides. I *do* want you, Danny, more than anything!"

He leaned forward to kiss her. "Thank you. I love you, Leah. I've loved you for a long time."

"I love you back. You've always been such a great brother and so kind to me. But today I realized I *loved* you—way more than a brother—and didn't want to be without you! Even before that kiss—which was awfully nice, I might add!"

He kissed her again.

Resting her forehead on his, she murmured, "Uh, Danny?"

"Yes?"

"I'm dying to see that ring!"

He laughed, handing it to her. "It's a family heirloom that my mom set aside for me. I hope you like it."

She slipped it onto her finger, examining it with awe. "It's absolutely perfect!" Happily, she sighed. "I'll put the house in a trust for Braydon. He can have it."

Danny looked at her in surprise. "Why?"

"Because I'm moving to St. Louis with you!"

"Ah, that." He got up and sat beside her again. "Yeah, so I talked with Brother Warren about the whole thing on the drive today. He suggested I stay on here and try to get a teaching job in the New Hampton area. I haven't actually signed my contract yet in St. Louis, so I could certainly give it a shot. If I needed to, I could go cover the position there until they find another teacher, but then come back here."

"I like that idea a lot!"

"Yes, I wasn't crazy about us being apart." He set the ring box on the table and took her hand. "Leah, I hope you're okay with all this. I know it's not the greatest timing for a proposal—after a day like today. It's probably been the surprise of your life!"

"Right! Well, I seem to be a magnet for surprises lately! In fact, I'd like to find a good counselor around here to help me deal with some of those surprises—but one with a godly perspective! Or at least someone like Jackie to help me get solid in walking with God. I'll talk to Brother Warren about that. And speaking of—I wonder if Brother Warren would marry us at his house."

"That'd be cool."

"I'd like Kyla to stand up for me, and I think you should ask Jake."

He flashed her a look.

"Well, you *should*—he's your brother."

"We'll have some time to figure that out."

Leah nodded, admiring the ring. "Right. We'll have to have a conversation with my dad."

Danny's eyes widened. "Oh—your dad! I should have asked for his blessing!"

"Well, that too, I suppose. You can take care of that tomorrow. I'm sure he'll give you his blessing freely—once we pick him up off the floor from the shock of it!"

He gave his hearty guffaw. "No doubt!"

"What I meant was that we need to ask my dad how soon we can get my house finished so we can live in it. Besides the kitchen, I'd like to build a deck off the dining room—Dad's idea." She paused, adding thoughtfully, "For that matter, we could probably do a whole new addition if those coins are still in the safe. A nice one! And now I can hire Peter to do some *real* landscaping! Oh, man—I'm ripping out those horrid arborvitaes first thing!"

Danny chuckled, dropping the ring box onto the table. "Whoa—I'm not in a rush or anything, but you *have* pointed out a number of times that I'm almost thirty! If we do all that, we might have to live in my cottage while it's under construction."

She reached to shake his hand. "Deal! I'd live in a tent with you, Danny DeSoto!"

He ignored her hand and muffled her hair. "I'll remember that! I might have to hold you to it someday! Come on—let's call it a night. I don't want Jackie waking up her dad with questions about where we are."

"You goofball!" she teased. "Brother Warren's not there, remember?"

"Oh, yeah!" He grinned, pulling her out of the love seat.

"But you *do* have your principles! Let's go tell Jackie our news! And Kyla. What time is it? Is it too late to call her?"

"Yes."

"Well, I might anyway. She wouldn't mind if I woke her up for this." She let out a long breath. "Boy, we are going to have one eventful day tomorrow—talking to my dad and telling my mom." She raised her brow. "*That* will be interesting!"

"Yes. And *my* family too. But we'll have all the grace we need for both."

Leah nodded. "Yes. Yes, we will."

He kissed her again, and they lingered, enjoying their newly kindled love. Eventually they turned out the lights and started back for their home next door. As they crossed the dewy grass, Leah linked her hand with Danny's, thinking how wonderful it was to know she was loved—loved by Danny, of course, and secretly for so many years, but more so loved by a very patient, kind, and faithful God who would never fail her as a father. She could count on that. Forever.

About the Author

The daughter of a cattle rancher, Joan Crombie grew up in a small town on the prairies of South Dakota. In 1985 she graduated from St. Olaf College with a B.A. in English Education. She and her husband Steven Crombie have been married for thirty-six adventurous years and have raised five children—one daughter and four sons. Currently they reside in beautiful southern Minnesota where they pastor a church.

Joan infuses her writing with wisdom gained from ministry and raising a family. She has always liked fiction where an ordinary girl unwittingly steps into a mystery, and in her stories, she seeks to couple that with helping her character identify lies she may have believed about God and combat those lies with biblical truth. Having experienced firsthand the freedom of a healed heart, her passion is to help women grow deeper in the love of God and knowledge of him as their very personal and caring Father.

Her hobbies include thrift shopping, reading, traveling, visiting historical museums, and spending time with her twelve delightful grandchildren.

To learn more about following God or about some of the concepts in this book, visit www.joancrombie.org.